THE BEFOR
FOUNDATION
FICTION ANTHOLOGY
Selections from the
American Book Awards
1980–1990

THE BEFORE COLUMBUS FOUNDATION FICTION ANTHOLOGY

Selections from the American Book Awards 1980 ◇ 1990

Edited by
ISHMAEL REED,
KATHRYN TRUEBLOOD, and
SHAWN WONG

W·W· Norton & Company
New York ◇ London

Library of Congress Cataloging-in-Publication Data
The Before Columbus Foundation fiction anthology: selections from the
American Book Awards, 1980–1990/edited by Ishmael Reed, Kate Trueblood,
and Shawn Wong.
  p.   cm.
  Includes index.
  1. Short stories, American.   I. Reed, Ishmael, 1938–   .
II. Trueblood, Kate.   III. Wong, Shawn, 1949–   .   IV. Before Columbus
Foundation.
PS648.S5B44   1992
813'.0108054—dc20   91–22503

ISBN 0-393-03055-5 (Cloth)
ISBN 0-393-30832-4 (Paper)

W.W. Norton & Company Inc., 500 Fifth Avenue, New York, N.Y. 10110
W.W. Norton & Company Ltd., 10 Coptic Street, London WC1A 1PU

1   2   3   4   5   6   7   8   9   0

For GUNDARS STRADS
for his unselfish and often unrewarded
sacrifice for the Before Columbus Foundation

*The editors of this anthology
would like to thank
the board of directors of the Before Columbus
Foundation*

ALTA
RUDOLFO ANAYA
MARIE ANDERSON
GEORGE BARLOW
JOHNNELLA BUTLER
BOB CALLAHAN
JEFF CHAN
LAWRENCE DI STASI
VICTOR HERNANDEZ CRUZ
ANDREW HOPE
YURI KAGEYAMA
DAVID MELTZER
SIMON ORTIZ
J. J. PHILLIPS
ISHMAEL REED
GUNDARS STRADS
JOYCE CAROL THOMAS
KATHRYN TRUEBLOOD
SHAWN WONG

Contents

Introduction:
Redefining the
Mainstream

W‌ITH the arrival of 1992, the five hundredth anniversary of the
"discovery of America" by Christopher Columbus, there may
never be a more appropriate moment in American literary history for the Before Columbus Foundation to restate its mission. The promotion of an American multicultural literary tradition has been the mission of the Before Columbus
Foundation for the past sixteen years. In 1990, cofounder Ishmael Reed said in a speech given in Seattle: "Our vision of the
future has room for the Asian, the African, as well as the Western [European]. We don't see these as dangerous times, as do
the paranoid monoculturalists. We see these as times fraught
with hope and change. As we approach the end of the century,
we have an opportunity to create a better world than the one
envisioned by those who lived to see the close of the nineteenth
century. But if we want to see that kind of world come about,
we have to work for it. Before Columbus has done some of the
groundbreaking, but other institutions have to begin to lay the
stones. We must go even farther—beyond Columbus."

Founded in 1976 by a group of writers, editors, educators,
and small press publishers, the Before Columbus Foundation
has promoted and disseminated contemporary American multicultural literature through its American Book Awards, literary
panels and seminars, and the quarterly *Before Columbus Review*, America's only multicultural book review. Through these
programs the Before Columbus Foundation has provided recognition and a wider audience for the wealth of cultural and
ethnic diversity that constitutes American writing. "Multicultural" is not a description of a category of American writing—it
is a *definition* of all American writing. The Before Columbus
Foundation believes that the ingredients of America's "melt-

ing pot" are not only distinct, but integral to the unique constitution of American culture—the whole comprises the parts. There are no outsiders.

The only accurate aspect of the melting-pot metaphor is heat—the heat of anger caused by ignorance and abuse. We can no more be melted into one alloy than we can expect the world to learn and speak Esperanto. The metaphor persists, however, and the Eurocentric point of view continues to be disseminated because it embodies a *come unto me* monopolistic attitude that obviates the effort to understand cultural difference—not merely racial difference.

Time magazine reported in an article entitled "Beyond the Melting Pot" (April 9, 1990): "By 2056, when someone born today will be 66 years old, the 'average' U.S. resident, as defined by Census statistics, will trace his or her descent to Africa, Asia, the Hispanic world, the Pacific Islands, Arabia—almost anywhere but white Europe."

Some organizations have coined the phrase "the majorification of America's minorities" to describe the cultural mission this fact seems to call for, and have started the movement. The mission is hidden behind a plea for public schools to return to a "basic skills" education—"basic skills" in this case meaning not only the three R's, but also the teaching of a monocultural standard. America's minorities, soon to be the majority, must be "majorified." Allan Bloom makes the plea in *The Closing of the American Mind* that "society has got to turn them into Americans." The monoculturalists always insist on a narrow place for minority cultures; an editor at a publishing house told the editors of an anthology of Asian-American literature that "the least ethnic pieces were the best." American dominant culture strains for cohesion to stabilize its channels of power and keep its mainstream flowing. Yet a narrow view of the mainstream ignores the tributaries that feed it. American culture is not one tradition, but all traditions.

The concept of a "mainstream" culture and "minority" cultures is the narrow view. Redefining the mainstream is the theme, the message, and the mission of the Before Columbus Foundation. We have purposely kept asking questions and listening to the answers. Something curious happens when one asks the same question over and over. We like to think the definition changes.

At a 1990 Before Columbus Foundation literary panel the question of how to go about "Redefining the Mainstream" of American literature was asked of writers Jessica Hagedorn, Jayne Cortez, J. J. Phillips, Oscar Hijuelos, N. Scott Momaday, John Barth, and Charles Johnson.

Jayne Cortez said the only "mainstream" she recognized was the Mississippi River, because it is in the middle of the country and has a Native American name. She also claimed that the American publishing establishment publishes what she considers "minority literature" and what remains unpublished is really, in fact, the "mainstream." N. Scott Momaday noted that American literature begins for him a thousand years ago and that somewhere in the more recent years of this enormous and rich history the "Puritan invasion" of America took place.

It takes fierce conviction to go on writing while your work eddies at the edges of the "mainstream," relegated to subculture status by a hyphen (African-American, Asian-American, Hispanic-American) despite demographic breakthroughs and democratic ideals. The luckier writers in this anthology have broken free and make a living at writing, but the majority do not, though they continue to publish with the small presses that keep them alive. Most large publishing houses still relegate multicultural literature to special-interest markets.

In 1978, the Before Columbus Foundation decided that one of its programs should be a book award that would, for the first time, recognize and honor excellence in American literature without discrimination or bias with regard to race, sex, creed, cultural origin, size of press or ad budget, or even genre. There would be no fees or forms. There would be no requirements, restrictions, or limitations. There would be no rankings, no first place, and no losers. There would be no categories ("best novel," "best black poet," or "best nonfiction work by an Asian American woman published by a West Coast small press," and so on); nor would "mainstream" white male Anglo-Saxon New York–based authors be excluded. Books could be submitted or nominated by anyone, including the author. Previously published books, neglected books, new editions—all would be eligible. The only criterion would be an outstanding contribution to American literature, in the opinion of the judges.

The winners of the American Book Awards are not selected by any quota or criteria for diversity. They simply come out that way. All winners are accorded equal standing and are recognized for the body of their work as well as for the particular work for which they receive the award. Their publishers are also honored for both their commitment to quality and their willingness to take the risks that accompany publishing outstanding books and authors that might not prove "cost-effective." There are special award designations (Lifetime Achievement, Editor/Publisher, Criticism, and Education) for contributions to American literature that go beyond single titles and for contributions that require distinction from strictly book-oriented consideration. However, these are descriptive rather than qualitative designations, and all winners remain on equal standing.

The first annual American Book Awards were held in New York City in the early spring of 1980, auspiciously, but also with a certain bewildered reticence on the part of the publishing industry. Many houses were unsure how to respond to what seemed on the surface an "ethnic" or "alternative" or even "literary vigilante" endeavor. The West Coast base of the Before Columbus Foundation also occasioned uncertainty. Then there was the distraction of a more amply financed, industry-sponsored award bearing the same name that appeared later that year—and that has since undergone several controversies and transformations, including a change of name. Nevertheless, many recognized the expansive "otherness" of the smaller but more inclusive upstart—an awards program that celebrated a multiplicity of small presses and emerging poets and numerous anti-mainstream tributaries. The awards ceremonies always featured subversive and uniquely American musical forms (jazz and blues from people such as Charles Brown, Allen Toussaint, John Handy, Bill Bell, and Steve Allen). People began to appreciate our difference, and began to wonder why we had to be called different at all. Over the years, support for these "other American" book awards grew slowly from a steady wellspring.

The second annual awards were again held in New York City, at Joseph Papp's Public Theater. Then the awards dared to defect back to the West Coast, to the Berkeley Repertory Theatre, to San Francisco's renowned Keystone Korner jazz club, and to the hallowed enclaves of the University of California at Berkeley. The awards then moved to the American Book-sellers Association conventions, the publishing industry's annual trade show, to provide better access for the award winners and their publishers to the media and the book trade. Sites for the awards ceremonies continued to span the nation: the Great American Music Hall in San Francisco, the Storyville Jazz Hall in New Orleans, the National Press Club in Washington, D.C., and on to Philadelphia, Anaheim, and Miami. There was even a USIA-sponsored trip to the Frankfurt Bookfair.

If the locations of the ceremonies were diverse, the award winners themselves also could not be pigeonholed. They could not be described as coming from a particular literary community, nor were they always "minority," "small press," or "nonmainstream" in origin. While sometimes radical, they were not radically distinct—just unique. And they came from all over America.

As the reputation of the American Book Awards spread, the public's impression matured. The industry and the media have come tentatively to accept and even embrace the perception of America as a multicultural literary community. The awards were never criticized for being too representative.

But is America ready to recognize the amazing cultural wealth it embodies? The signals are mixed, and most of the American Book Award winners are reserved optimists at best. We circulated a questionnaire asking American Book Award winners (fiction writers and poets) to tell us about their concerns, communities, and travails, and in their collective response we heard the chorus America must learn to sing, not someday soon, but now.

Duane Niatum noted, "Multiculturalism seems to be on the rise, but this is also paradoxical. Racism is also very much in vogue again." The hate crimes perpetrated in the last few years certainly support his view, and yet multiculturalism has finally become "news" and hit the front pages of national magazines and newspapers. Perhaps Carolyn Lau best explained the concurrent trends when she told us: "I think people feel that if I give up my prejudice, I lose my identity."

The American Book Award winners reacted strongly to the issue of naming and ethnicity. Not surprising. The vehemence of the opinions recorded by our questionnaire reveals real impatience with an entrenched point of view. Quincy Troupe felt that "we should *all* be called just plain American and fuck all this hyphenated bullshit." Gary Snyder suggested that "all whites" be called "Euro-Americans." In either case, the desire to claim and affirm equal validity for one's heritage is expressed, and such was the general sentiment among the American Book Award winners. As Juan Felipe Herrera said, "All communities are ethnic if they care to scratch themselves a bit."

Closely related to this issue of categorization was that of stereotypes in popular culture. When asked if he felt stereotypes persist and are being created in contemporary American culture, Amiri Baraka responded with an exclamatory "Recycled!" John Norton's reaction was subversive and insightful, along the lines of good advice for young writers: "I like to work the stereotypes and move them in unexpected directions. Play against the stereotypes and confound those who want to hold on to them." Clearly, old biases will not just go away and die; they must be disintegrated bit by bit.

In writing about their communities, these authors are a unique force in the revision of American culture and history. The work of the American Book Award winners is marked by a sense of indebtedness to the communities from which they came and the desire to give in return. It is a quality one rarely hears about when writers are interviewed. Linda Hogan told us: "I work frequently on reservations, which makes me feel rich and sustained, that my work is all that I want it to be, and returns love to the people I come from." The American Book Award winners don't balk at addressing the oppressive connotations that underlie the term "dominant culture." The New Mexico novelist Nash Candelaria sees his relationship to his community as essential to his work: "My goal is to place Hispanic North Americans in the context of U.S. history. Some of us have been here a long time, back before the Pilgrims, and deserve better than to be considered 'foreigners' in our own country and to be dealt with as stereotypes." Maurice Kenny stated simply and eloquently: "I have attempted in my poems and stories to clean the lies of history and the historian. I have attempted to bring my piece of kindling to the village fire." Milton Murayama was adamant about the writer's role in recording untold stories and the power of fiction to engage the reader's sensory imagination: "A writer is a historian. He can tell it in flesh and blood the way it was."

For women, the revision of history through literature is an ongoing claim to presence and power. Josephine Hendin explained the impetus for her novel: "I wanted to describe the relationship between an Italian-American father and daughter in a way that had not been done. So often the stories of immigrant life have been limited to the story of fathers and sons. . . . I tried to discuss the extent to which the conflict of generations may be shaped by the war between the sexes." Susan Howe sees her specialty as "North American history—specifically that of New England" and hopes in her work to "show that we have been told the wrong story . . . to continue to explore the gaps in the story of women and their role in early American culture and literature."

Overall, the questionnaires that came back to us revealed a high degree of political urgency and intensity about the need for social change. A number of writers reminded us of the power of literature to effect revolutionary change, and the writers they mentioned are a diverse lot: Thoreau, Brecht, Harriet Beecher Stowe, Whitman, Kerouac, Che Guevera, Malcolm X. William Oandasan noted the power of literature to "liberate, invade, and secure space in print through time."

American Book Award winners are keenly aware of their role as models for a generation of young who currently receive little recognition of their aspirations or cultural identity. Judy Grahn urged young writers to "believe in your own experience as true knowledge worthy of becoming literature." Cyn Zarco's advice was pragmatic, dispelling the destructive mystique: "Don't drink a lot and don't play with drugs. Your memory is a library and no one's in but you. Any writer who has to get high to write is no genius but one hungup dude. This romantic notion, poet manqué stuff is bunk. Feeling overwhelmed? Write it down and don't throw it away." Alma Luz Villanueva spoke in analogies relevant to feminist writers: "Have the receptivity of a pregnant woman and the tenacity of an Amazon warrior." Russell Banks addressed the conflict created by external success and internal isolation, the need to choose priorities: "Don't confuse your life's work with your career." The advice to young writers that we received is worthy of a book on its own, and any young writer would do well to tape, staple, or thumbtack such words of wisdom above the typewriter.

The writers who appear here are a diverse lot. Their past occupations include plumber, waiter, secretary, vegetable clerk, advertising copywriter, real estate salesman, foundry worker, social worker, newspaper stringer, editorial assistant, printer's assistant, technical writer, and railroad brakeman. Leslie Scalapino merely reported that she had worked at "odd" jobs. Jimmy Santiago Baca described his early years as "blind desperation" and himself as "a beggar on the fringe." John A. Williams gave us a list of jobs that read like a litany, after which he "freelanced and prayed." Salvatore La Puma described how he fed the creative flame while satisfying what exigencies required of him: "I wrote commercially for a dozen years to earn my living. Then wrote secretly, a sentence or a paragraph a day, to keep from being killed off. And waited until now for the quiet to arrive so I could hear my own voice. Waiting all these years hasn't wasted time. Along the way I've often been kicked in the ass, kicked a little myself, been down and out, risen from the dead, a little wild, a lot heartbroken, and witnessed friends and enemies living and dying, the bravery and idiocy in relatives, in my own children, and in myself. So I can write now, I hope, with a little understanding, if not forgiveness." Any young writer who feels trapped, deterred, isolated, weary, or just plain disillusioned should take heart in knowing that the lives behind the poems and stories in these volumes were as rich with struggle as his or her own.

There is affirmation to be found in the astounding variety of dictions, cadences, and forms that cover these pages, perhaps a range never made available before, one we hope is enabling, so that others may hear their own voices, distinct and clear at last. "Distinct" is the operative theme of this anthology. The challenge that America faces is to learn to celebrate difference rather than to fear and condemn it. This anthology is dedicated to that effort, and to writers like Jimmy Santiago Baca who see their role as "engagement at all levels, to intellectually confront, emotionally risk, and compassionately dream the vision of a better world into reality." We must begin by confronting the past so that the skeins with which we weave the future are strong and vibrant, and by contrast create a wondrous design. In the words of Victor Hernandez Cruz: "The works herein are defining not only our historical journey but also exposing an inner landscape taking shape today. Right here in Los Angeles. Right here in New York. Hello America. This is America."

The world is here in America, and English is a living language enriched by the legacy of immigrants, refugees, native peoples, and those brought by force. Alan Chong Lau shapes a language that reveals the pain of adaptation: "The day the language is sanitized to a uniformity devoid of nuance and personality, we are in trouble. At times, my work reflects the use of English by my ancestors. I can only hope I haven't lost it all." Hilton Obenzinger told us, "I write with my parents' Polish and Yiddish, plus some Hebrew and Arabic, along with my wife's Filipino, always jangling in my ears: these different languages chomp and coagulate into a pulp in my American mouth." Raymond Federman, a Jewish survivor of World War II, attributes an unusual liberation to the original estrangement: "As an incurable foreigner (I was born in France and learned my first word of English when I was nineteen), I use and abuse the English language because for me it is a borrowed language. I am free in it." Elizabeth Woody, a poet of Wasco/Navajo descent, keeps an ear finely tuned to the pressures that extend English beyond conventional usage: "The minds in my community on the reservation are quick and intelligent, and inventive with language. There are two or three languages wanting to live through English." The speech patterns of those not native to English make us hear the infinite possibilities of language, free us from the banal like the good cold shock of a dive into water. Clichés scatter; language is reimagined; an image suddenly brilliant emerges.

Gundars Strads
Kathryn Trueblood
Shawn Wong

Berkeley, Bellingham, and Seattle
January 1991

The Ocean of American Literature

ISHMAEL REED

In 1976, I applied for and received a modest grant from the Coordinating Council of Literary Magazines to begin a distribution outlet for "third world" magazines. The names of the magazines we distributed reflected the multicultural audience we were attempting to reach: *Roots, Ravens Bones Journal, Revista Chicano-Requena, Truck, Telephone, Tree, Black Scholar, Unmuzzled Ox, New World Journal, Carp, Sun Tracks, Tejidos, Obsidian, Puerto Del Sol, HooDoo, De Colores,* and *Tin Tan.*

The grant required that I have a partner, and so I chose poet Victor Hernandez Cruz, whom I'd met in New York in 1966. I was working in the Poetry in the Schools program then, and I remember going to Benjamin Franklin High School and announcing, during my reading there, that one of the best American poets was enrolled in the school. When I mentioned Victor's name, the students and teachers gasped. Victor Cruz, who has since that time gained a reputation as an international bilingual poet, was failing Spanish. He was eighteen at the time. By the early eighties, *Life* magazine would run a story in which Victor was featured as one of eleven of America's most distinguished poets.

The next member to join the distribution group—which I named Before Columbus, in order to acknowledge the existence of an American literature before the arrival of the Europeans—was Shawn Wong. Shawn had been introduced to me by playwright Frank Chin, whose work had appeared in a Doubleday anthology I edited entitled *Nineteen Necromancers from Now.* Shawn had also been one of the editors of the Asian-American issue of *Yardbird Reader,* which Al Young and I used to edit. He was also an editor of *Califia,* an anthology of multicultural writing that Al Young and I published.

We then added Rudolfo Anaya, who was beginning to build an international reputation with his novel *Bless Me Ultima.* Rudolfo had been my colleague on the board of the Coordinating Council of Literary Magazines and was one of those who was instrumental in changing the composition of the board from mostly white male to multicultural, not by demonizing white males but through dialogue.

With Shawn, Victor, Rudolfo, and me, Before Columbus included members of the main colored ethnic groups. Still, though our administrator, Mary Taylor, was of European ancestry, no one else from this important element was included on the board of Before Columbus, a group that defined multiculturalism inclusively. (When Mary left the organization, Gundars Strads took over her duties, and he has managed the foundation since then.) In 1977, then, we invited an Irish American writer and publisher, Bob Callahan, to join.

A few of the colored nationalists in the distribution group objected to our decision to add European American ethnics. One could understand their concerns. Many whites are educated to believe that it is their mission to lead and civilize those whom the educational system, whether consciously or not, treats as their inferiors. The Omniscient Boomers, whom we are so familiar with in California, pretend to know more about the cultures of other ethnic groups than the members of those groups, yet they fail to identify with their own ethnicity. They classify themselves simply as "white."

And the Omniscient Boomer is only the latest incarnation of the type that in American history has done so much to divide members of different ethnic groups. Before Omniscient Boomers, there were the sixties Liberals who believed that their role in the civil rights movement was to lead. The abolitionists of the nineteenth century made the same error. They didn't permit the Black antislavery lecturers in their employment to express independent judgment, and when their employees balked, as Frederick Douglass did, they were dismissed as being ungrateful. Such patronizing attitudes on the part of whites have made multiculturalism difficult to achieve and, unfortunately, such attitudes persist.

And so when some of the third world nationalists had reservations about the admission of European Americans into Before Columbus, they had a bitter history upon which to base those reservations. Not only do whites continue to stereotype the cultures of members of ethnic groups (including those of Irish and Italian American ethnics), but their judgments are usually based upon ignorance, since they've only read those tokens that have been presented to the public by the mass media. The American literary establishment seeks to set literary trends by retaining house hitpersons whose job seems to be to reward those who push an assimilationist patriotic literature—the literature of the mainstream—and chastise those whose literature might make the target audience of mostly white consumers uncomfortable. Haki Madabuti calls this "white nationalism," the tendency of some whites to give credit to other whites for supremacy in art forms that were created by members of colored ethnic groups. For Boomer-type cultural commentators on National Public Radio, for example, white musicians have "evolved" the blues or given sophistication to rock and roll lyrics. Some whites also have a tendency to divide and conquer when approaching the cultures of others, by, for example, congratulating different groups for not being like Blacks. A Chicano educator was recently praised on National Public Radio for not making demands upon the curriculum as "radical" as those of black educators.

We were lucky enough to enlist European-American writers whose intellects were restless enough to be willing to spend as much time on their cultures as we Hispanic, Native American, and African American writers have spent studying European culture. They were not running away from their own cultures into some homogeneous wasteland of whiteness, but were thoroughly steeped in Italian-, Irish-, and Jewish American cultures. Instead of practicing cultural imperialism upon us, they brought their own contributions to a cultural potluck. Not only have they learned from us, but we have learned about Irish

American, Italian American, and Jewish American cultures from them.

During a recent appearance in Washington, D.C., I was asked by an Italian American student for the names of books that would help her understand the Italian American tradition. Because of my contact with European-American ethnics in Before Columbus, I was able to provide some key titles. Through such experiences, we have found that the cultures of colored ethnics are not the only ones ignored by a school system devoted to luring students into the "mainstream," a code word for Eurocentrism. The Italian American, Irish American, and Jewish American cultures have also been lost.

The multicultural contacts within Before Columbus have added a dimension to our own creative work. It was because of my discussions with our Latvian American executive director, Gundars Strads, that I was able to include an Eastern European perspective in my novel *The Terrible Twos* (1982), which accurately predicted the ethnic uprisings that occurred behind the Iron Curtain in the late eighties and which was able to pinpoint the year when a Soviet American détente would happen— 1987, the year of Reykjavík. Our European American board members do not dismiss colored ethnic cultures as "arcane" or "exotic"; nor do they rely upon subsidized "third world" scouts to tell them what the natives are up to—the practice of some of our leading "intellectual journals," journals that embarrass themselves before the international community of scholars by accepting what amounts to often faulty and self-serving intelligence. Bob Callahan, Gundars Strads, Lawrence DiStasi, David Meltzer, and Kathryn Trueblood have gone beyond mere study of Asian American, Native American, African American, and Hispanic cultures. Alta, founder of Shameless Hussy Press, was the first to publish Ntozake Shange's *For Colored Girls Who Have Considered Suicide When the Rainbow Was Enuf*, and Bob Callahan was responsible for reprinting the works of Zora Neale Hurston well before the Hurston boom.

Clearly, by the end of the seventies, the Before Columbus Foundation's definition of multiculturalism was inclusive. We meant Italian Americans and Irish Americans, as well as Asian

Americans, African Americans, and Native Americans. We meant masculinists as well as feminists. In 1979, we enriched the provincial New York scene by sponsoring a huge reading of African American, Asian American, Hispanic, and European American writers at Columbia University, which was recorded on Folkways Records. Joe Knipscheer gave Before Columbus credit for inspiring Amsterdam's One World Poetry Festival of which he was codirector.

Also at the end of the seventies, we inaugurated the American Book Awards. They started humbly. I remember lugging the books by the winners to the West Side Community Center in 1978. About twenty people attended. Tisa Chang's Pan Asian Repertory Group provided a skit. The next year the awards were sponsored by the New York Shakespeare Festival. Among the presenters were Donald Barthelme, Toni Morrison, Stanley Crouch, and Ed Bullins, and the audience was enlightened and entertained by Hugh Masakela, Bill Cook, and Howard "Sandman" Sims. Since that time, the awards have been held in cities throughout the country. Except for the Oakland P.E.N./Josephine Miles awards, the judges for the other major awards are white males of similar tastes and backgrounds with, perhaps, a token "minority" guest judge who sits with the other panelists from time to time. A minority member who occasionally receives one of those awards doesn't know whether he or she is being recognized for talent or for race, or whether the award is based upon the mimicking of the literary establishment's political line at any given time. In the 1960s, the line was left-wing. During the late seventies and eighties, when feminists wielded some power, Black, Asian, and Latino male bashing was in. And as the decade of the nineties begins, there seems to be a preference for those who push blame-the-victim neoconservatism, or the notion that black talent is rare. This comforts the tastemakers in their essentially white settler mentality, afraid of being overrun by the "Other," as it is now fashionably called.

This is why I believe that the first recognition of the Before Columbus Foundation came from abroad. Those who decide the winners of the American Book Awards are drawn from backgrounds as diverse as our literatures. For this reason, we are often ahead of the other awards in recognizing literary talent. Jessica Hagedorn, for example, received an award from the American Book Awards in 1983. She wasn't recognized by the National Book Award until 1991. And since our judges and nominees are drawn from various ethnic groups, it is possible for more than one member of a particular ethnic group to win an award during a given year instead of every thirty years, like some of the other awards. In 1991, the National Book Award recognized one black writer. The 1990 American Book Awards recognized nine.

Those who oppose the multicultural curriculum say that such a curriculum would diffuse our common culture, by which they mean that the natives would stray from the true and correct European catechism. Oddly enough, many European intellectuals reject this notion. I have visited European universities, some of which were founded over seven hundred years ago, and have never found the sort of scornful criticism of multiculturalism that one finds written by American intellectuals for mass media publications. Indeed, on European campuses there seems to be an enormous interest in American culture, African American, Hispanic, and Asian American literatures included. I asked a European scholar the reason why, and he said it's because Europeans see the United States as a civilization, not merely a dominant mother culture with an array of little subcultures tagging along. Criticism of multiculturalism also reveals the lack of analysis that often underlies pronouncements issued by members of the humanities community, where offering proof for ideas doesn't seem necessary, despite the humanities' attempt to use the language of science.

The Before Columbus Foundation has discovered, through experimentation, that common ground does exist among the different cultures of the United States. Monocultural intellectuals and op-ed writers should have been present during the Before Columbus Institute, which was held at the University of California at Berkeley during the mid-eighties. Through team teaching, artists, scholars, and writers from different backgrounds were able to discover, by focusing upon themes found in their various literatures, that no group has a corner on universality. Such commonality was expressed by board member

Lawrence DiStasi, who, after watching Frank Chin's portrait of a Chinese American family in *The Year of the Dragon* (1974), said that this family could have been an Italian American family. We have plans under way to transform the Before Columbus Institute into an accredited college where scholars, artists, and students from throughout the United States and the world may assemble to discuss and study our common heritage, the heritage of the world.

Before Columbus does not believe that literature is like a laboratory frog, to be dissected so that its parts may be coldly examined. We believe that literature has a higher purpose. Margaret Atwood said of the late Northrop Frye, "He did not lock literature into an ivory tower; instead, he emphasized its centrality to the development of a civilized and humane society." We hope that Before Columbus has in its small way contributed to the development of such a society. We also hope that the reader of this anthology will discover that American literature in the last decade of this century is more than a mainstream.

American literature is an ocean.

THE BEFORE COLUMBUS FOUNDATION FICTION ANTHOLOGY

Selections from the
American Book Awards
1980 – 1990

James Welch

IN his four novels and one book of poetry, James Welch (1940–) captures the complexity of human struggle without succumbing to overcoded evocations of "the Indian" as poor welfare ward or once-noble savage. With an honesty sometimes brutal, other times wise, Welch tackles paradoxes in what it can mean to be American Indian. For people's identities as individuals and communities are never as static, fixed by a set of immutable social contracts and customs, as stereotypical thinking about "Indianness" would lead us to believe.

Few American Indian writers have dared present the varied and often harsh realities of Indian life as Welch does, and as he has said himself in interviews, few Indian role models existed for him when he began writing in the late 1960s. Through the encouragement of two writers at the University of Montana, John Herrmann and Richard Hugo, Welch says he began thinking of writing as a career. Herrmann made him realize that "writing . . . was something that a person could really do—an average person." Hugo, Welch claims, reinforced the idea that "if you could use language well enough, you could really create something that would be art." He also identifies luck as a key ingredient in his success, and luck figures as a motif in all his works.

Against the backdrop of countless portrayals of Indians by non-Indians throughout American literature, Welch's work stands in stark relief, perhaps because he writes out of a need to express and understand the experience himself as well as to interpret it for others. Most white writers who portray Indians, Welch says, "are either sentimental or outraged over the condition of the Indian. There are exceptions . . . [but] only an Indian knows who he is—an individual who just happens to be an Indian—and if he has grown up on a reservation he will naturally write about what he knows." What Welch knows of reservation life involves the despair of drinking, the loss of a sense of purpose in being, the mourning of a past that cannot be recovered or maybe even glimpsed—at least, not in a sustaining way. He employs humor in subtle and disconcerting ways; with poetic economy images leap and twist in surreal relation to one another, making bedfellows of great mystery and pathos.

Themes of hopelessness and despair begun in his poems (collected in *Riding the Earthboy 40*) receive full treatment in his first two novels, *Winter in the Blood* (1974) and *The Death of Jim Loney* (1979). But concerning *Fools Crow* (1986), his third novel and winner of the Before Columbus Foundation's American Book Award for fiction, Welch speaks of wanting to explore the source of what he calls a sense of "deep-seated defeat" in Indians today. Even though the novel is set in the nineteenth century, he looks for it to affect positively Indians of his time: "I think a book could make them understand, in a very simple way, events, so that . . . they could say, O.K., here I am standing on the street in 1982—how did I get here?" All three novels are centered around issues of self-worth in the face of overwhelming loss and grief, but in *Fools Crow* the author places the onus on non-Indians (Napikwans) who intentionally and mercilessly seek to destroy or subdue a people. For that Indian person "on the street" who wonders how he came to be who and where he is today, however, Welch provides more than another reason to blame "the white man"; he offers a vision of honor, a fragment of heritage to celebrate and extol, a reason for being. Whatever else Welch's writing may mean to readers throughout the test of time, it will certainly comprise a legacy for Indian people to draw upon.

I first encountered James Welch's writing, after years of working—getting by—as a secretary, as an outreach worker in a high school in Minneapolis (the city where Welch went to high school) for what they now call "at-risk" kids, and finally as a registered nurse. I had returned to college to pursue an undergraduate degree in English in hopes of fulfilling my lifelong dream of being a writer. And although I had read many novels—even identified with the dilemmas faced by characters like Dostoevsky's Raskolnikov and Hardy's Jude and Sue—it wasn't until I read *Winter in the Blood* that I realized my experience growing up on the Fort Peck Reservation could be told. I'm sure many other Indian writers could tell similar stories about first reading Welch, since he (along with N. Scott Momaday, Duane Niatum, Leslie Silko, and Simon Ortiz) were the first to carve out a place for Indian writing in the new wave of American ethnic literatures surfacing in the late 1960s. The novel's nameless protagonist could be someone I know, and the world he travels *is* beyond a doubt the world I had known as a mixed-blood Indian growing up in that part of the country (northeastern Montana) where *Winter* and Welch's second novel, *The Death of Jim Loney,* are set. Next time I see him, perhaps in Harlem, I'll have to thank him right—buy him a couple of crèmes de menthe. . .

—Kathryn Shanley

Chapters 7 and 8 from
FOOLS CROW

7

IT was late winter, that time when the willows turn color and begin to bud. All along the Two Medicine River the red and yellow spears lit up the days and made people think of the first-thunder moon and of breaking winter camp to follow the blackhorn herds. Men walked about and smoked and talked of their spring visit to the white trader's house on the Bear River. The hunting had been good, and within the lodges lay piles of soft-tanned robes. Some of the hunters would acquire the long-coveted repeating rifles. It was a time of anticipation and rest for the hunters, of feasts and games for all.

It was also a time of restlessness, and when the three young riders approached the village from the south, they could feel the intensity of the watchers' eyes. They drove twelve horses before them, and all the horses were big and strong. Even from a distance one could see that they were the kind the Napikwans used to pull their wagons.

Fast Horse recognized Owl Child's white horse with the red thunderbirds on each shoulder. Owl Child rode nonchalantly until they were close to the village. Then he dug his heels into the horse's flanks and galloped over. He carried across his lap a many-shots gun in a beaded and fringed scabbard. He also had a short-gun tucked in his belt. Many in the camp were afraid of him, for he had killed Bear Head, a great warrior, the previous summer in an argument over a Cutthroat scalp. Owl Child was a member of the Many Chiefs band led by Mountain Chief, one of the most powerful leaders of the Pikunis. Even at that Owl Child was something of an outcast, feared and hated by many bands of his own people. Fast Horse looked upon him with awe, for of all the Pikunis, Owl Child had made the Napikwans cry the most.

"Haiya!" Owl Child rode slowly through camp. "How is it you Lone Eaters stay in camp when the others are out hunting and raiding our enemies? Small wonder you Lone Eaters are so poor!" He rode up to the lodge of Three Bears, who had just emerged and stood wrapped in a three-point blanket. "Ah, Three Bears—we have just returned from the south. We come with horses we found on the other side of Pile-of-rocks River. We are on our way to the Many Chiefs camp on the Bear. But now we are hungry, for we have ridden far and fast."

"Did those horses belong to someone else?" said Three Bears.

"They were wandering by themselves and we thought to take care of them before they got lost and starved to death."

"Do those horses have the white man mark on them?"

Owl Child laughed. "We didn't notice any brand on them. Perhaps they are wild horses."

"Who is with you?" Three Bears' eyes were not good for distance.

"The brave warriors Black Weasel and Bear Chief."

"Then they are stolen from the Napikwans."

"What difference does that make?" said Fast Horse, who had walked over from his father's lodge. "The white ones steal our land, they give us trinkets, then they steal more. If Owl Child has taken a few of their horses, then he is to be honored."

"It is so, Fast Horse." Owl Child laughed. His eyes glittered. "It is the Napikwans who bring it on themselves. If they have their way they will push us into the Backbone and take all the ground and the blackhorns for themselves."

Three Bears turned to Fast Horse. "We do not want trouble with the whites. Now that the great war in that place where Sun Chief rises is over, the blue-coated seizers come out to our country. Their chiefs have warned us more than once that if we make life tough for their people, they will ride against us." He pointed his pipe in the direction of Owl Child. "If these foolish young men continue their raiding and killing of the Napik-

wans, we will all suffer. The seizers will kill us, and the Pikuni
people will be as the shadows on the land. This must not happen."

"Then you will not invite us to feast with you?" Owl Child's
face had turned hard with disappointment. "Mountain Chief
has great respect for you, Three Bears. He is not used to such
slights."

"It is not him I slight, Owl Child." He called into his lodge
for his women to make up a packet of meat. "He is a wise man
and he will know the truth of my words. If the Pikunis are to
survive we must learn to treat with the whites. There are too
many of them for your kind of actions."

"Someday, old man, a Napikwan will be standing right
where you are and all around him will be grazing thousands of
the whitehorns. You will be only a part of the dust they kick up.
If I have my way I will kill that white man and all his whitehorns before this happens." He looked at Fast Horse, his eyes
the gray of winter clouds. "It is the young who will lead the
Pikunis to drive these devils from our land."

Three Bears handed up the packet of boiled meat to Owl
Child. "It is done," he said, and turned and entered his lodge.

Owl Child laughed, a brittle laugh in the early afternoon
silence, and urged his horse into a trot. "Come visit, Fast
Horse," he called back. "We will show you what real Pikunis do
to these sonofabitch whites." Then he was galloping to rejoin
his comrades, who had continued to push the horses east toward the camp of Mountain Chief on the Bear River.

WHITE MAN'S DOG sat with Mik-api outside the old man's
lodge. They had been enjoying the warm sun and talking about
the properties of horses, how the long-ago people acquired
them from the Snakes and how the Indian ponies differed from
those of the whites.

White Man's Dog stirred the pot of berry soup he had
brought his old friend. It was beginning to steam. "Our horses
have smaller shoulders and their asses aren't so big. It's true
they do not have the endurance of those big old elk-dogs that
the white man runs." He laughed at his usage of the long-ago

term for horses. Then he sneaked a look at Mik-api. The many-faces man was slumped against his willow backrest, his mouth open, his snores almost sighs in the warm air. White Man's Dog brushed a fly away from his friend's hair and then thought, The first fly of spring, winter is truly over. Like the others, he was anxious to go to the trading fort on the Bear River. He and his father and brother had almost a hundred robes to trade, most of them unscarred prime cows. He had his mind on a many-shots, like the one Yellow Kidney carried on the raid.

He stopped stirring the soup. On the raid he had come to know Yellow Kidney, and it didn't seem possible that he was no longer among his people. Although the raid was successful—even now he could look out downriver and see his horses grazing among others—he felt that the loss outweighed any number of Crow horses. Something bad had happened on that raid, something White Man's Dog could not get out of his mind. But he didn't know what it was that had happened, and he didn't know how far-reaching the effects could be. Yellow Kidney was dead or captive or wandering. Fast Horse had not come near White Man's Dog since the morning of their talk. It was bad to lose trust in a friend like Fast Horse, but when young men got together and talked of raids, of war parties to gain honor, the name of Fast Horse never came up. The others had come to feel, like White Man's Dog, that Fast Horse had somehow been responsible for Yellow Kidney's fate.

But lately another concern had begun to agitate White Man's Dog—the Crow youth he had killed. When the news of this deed had gotten around camp, many of the men had honored him with scalp songs. His father had given him a war club he had taken from the Crows. And his brother and the other young men looked at him with respect. But White Man's Dog could not get out of his mind the look of fear on the youth's face as he rode down on him. He could not forget the feeling in his arm as his scalping knife struck bone in the youth's back. He should have stopped the attack then, but the youth would have warned the village. He had no choice but to kill. . . .

Then there was the dream. When he told the dream of the white-faced girls to Mik-api, the old man had grown silent. He smoked a long time. He smoked far into the night. Sometimes he dozed, other times he hummed, but always he would return to his smoking. Finally he tapped the pipe out and told White Man's Dog to go home and sleep, then prepare the sweat lodge in the morning.

After their purifying sweat, Mik-api led White Man's Dog into his lodge. He made the youth lie down and pretend to sleep. He took a root of tastes-dry and dropped it into the boiling water over the fire. After a while he dipped a bowlful and passed it under the nose of White Man's Dog, making his patient inhale the sharp steam. Mik-api then pounded some alum leaves and sticky-root in a wooden bowl. All the while he chanted and sang purifying songs. When the mixture had been pounded into a paste, he dipped his fingers into the pot of boiling water, then scooped the paste onto his fingertips and placed them on White Man's Dog's body. The young man flinched, but the steady pressure of Mik-api's hands against his chest made him relax. Four times Mik-api applied the compound. Then White Man's Dog slept, and while he was sleeping, Mik-api pulled an eagle wing from his medicine parfleche. He made motions of the eagle flying with his hands; then he struck the young man several times all over the body with the wing. As he burned some sweet grass and passed it over the body, he sang the purifying song, the gentle hooting, of the ears-far-apart. Finally he blew several shrill notes over his patient with his medicine whistle, and a yellow paint dripped from the end of it onto the forehead of White Man's Dog. Mik-api fell back on his haunches and said, "It is done."

When White Man's Dog awoke, he felt that he had been to another world and had returned. He propped himself up on his elbows and he felt light and free. He had dreamed of eagles and felt almost as though he had flown with them. He felt vaguely disappointed to be in this lodge lying on this robe. A voice nearby entered his ears.

"I have driven the bad spirit that caused your dream from your body. You will not be troubled anymore."

White Man's Dog looked across the fire and saw the dark eyes of the many-faces man. It was night.

"But I could not kill it. I could not see the dream clearly enough. I know it was a dream of death, but more than that I cannot say. I fear that the spirit is out there, floating, waiting to attach itself to another one of our people."

Now White Man's Dog stirred the berry soup and thought of that night many sleeps ago. He was relieved to be rid of the dream, the burden of it, but the fact that the spirit was still free troubled him. And, too, he felt that he had let Mik-api down in not telling the dream completely or correctly enough. He had not given enough to allow the many-faces man to work his magic.

He shook the memory out of his head and leaned forward to taste the soup. As he did so, he glanced between two lodges to the home of Yellow Kidney's family. The two boys were playing with a small animal, a gopher perhaps. Red Paint was on her knees, moving her arms and upper body back and forth. White Man's Dog could just see white hair on the edges of a skin. Red Paint was rubbing brains and grease into a deerskin to make it soft. As he watched her body arch back and forth over the skin, he forgot about the berry soup. He felt his penis begin to stiffen and he cast a quick glance in the direction of Mik-api, but the old man snored on. Red Paint was now back on her heels, wiping her hands on a calico rag. She was slender but the top of her loose buckskin dress had some shape. Her tight black braids just brushed the tips of her breasts as she worked the greasy mixture from her hands.

"She's getting to be a real woman," said Mik-api.

White Man's Dog grabbed the spoon and stirred the soup quickly. "Ah, you're awake. Good. It is time to eat this."

"It's a pity that one so young and handsome can find no one to hunt for her. What is she now, sixteen, seventeen? Her winters ride well on her. You can see how she has filled out."

White Man's Dog looked at her as though he had just noticed it.

"Yes, she is a woman and of the marrying age," continued Mik-api. "I suspect one of our fine young men will see that she gets everything she needs. Most of our young women this year are ugly. It seems to go in cycles. Some years all the young women are as beautiful as the doe. Other years they look like old magpies. Such a one as Red Paint would stand out in either case."

White Man's Dog looked at Mik-api, but the old man was looking into the distance, to the greening hills. He dished up two bowls of the hot soup and the men sipped it, watching a pair of white-headed eagles circling in the blue sky. They made White Man's Dog think of the dream in which he had joined them.

"How did you become a many-faces man, Mik-api?"

Mik-api didn't speak right away, but White Man's Dog had become used to waiting. He poured himself another bowl of soup, then sat back to watch the eagles.

"I am now of seventy-four winters but I wasn't always old. Once when I was a young man, not much older than you, I had my heart set on becoming a great warrior and a rich man. I learned the ways of the war trail and once went with a group into the country of the Parted Hairs. We were just out to enjoy ourselves, to look at new country and to take a few horses. We took two horses and then we fought all the way back to see who got to keep them."

Mik-api laughed softly. "There were fewer horses in those days. Each one was a precious possession. Some things were harder then, some things easier. There were very few of the Napikwans—it was when I was a youth that the first white men appeared in this country. They came up the Two Medicine River not far from here, and first they tried to treat with our people, then they tried to kill us. We grew frightened of their sticks-that-speak-from-afar and ran away, and then they ran away. I never saw these particular creatures, but you can imagine how different they looked to those who did. Our brothers, the Siksikas, had already seen these white people north of the Medicine Line. They were a little different and spoke a different tongue.

"Some winters later, more of these Napikwans came into our country, but they stayed in the mountains and they trapped the fine-furred animals—wood-biters, mink and otters. I remember seeing them sometimes, but they remained in the mountains and didn't bother us. Many of them were as furry as the animals they trapped. They always stunk like mink and so we avoided them. But a few of our less-fortunate girls went to live with them, and we didn't see much of the girls after that. I think these men hated each other, for you never saw two of them together, and our women who went with them became little more than slaves. I don't know what the trouble was, but you never saw children around their dwellings. At first we thought these Napikwans were animals and incapable of reproducing with human beings. But they were intelligent like human beings and they piled up many furs. Gradually they left the mountains and went away. They were not like these Napikwans today who live on the plains and raise their whitehorns. We could live with those first ones." Mik-api sipped his soup, lost in thought. Two yellow dogs walked tentatively up to the soup pot and sniffed. White Man's Dog shooed them away.

"Now I forget my story. Ah, yes, you ask me when I became one of the many-faces. It was in that season of the falling-leaves moon and I had been hunting in the mountains where the Shield-floated-away River begins. I had been lucky, and as I packed out one late morning I had a long-legs and a small sticky-mouth, gutted and cleaned, across my packhorses. I had killed these animals because my family wanted a change from the blackhorn meat. It was brushy all around and the riverbed was sandy, so I was riding down the middle of the river, singing my victory song. I was young then and somewhat foolish. I sang so loudly and the horse made so much noise sloshing through the water that I didn't hear anything else. But then I stopped to admire a grove of the small quaking-leaves. They had not yet lost their color and they were golden against the rock wall behind them.

"As I sat there in all that beauty I started to sing a song I had made up for my girlfriend, but I heard something else, a kind of wailing that reminded me of a puppy, but I knew no dogs lived around there so I guessed it must be a young coyote or a wolf. I dismounted there in the water, for I had always wanted one of these creatures for a pet. I took my lariat and crept into the bushes, but the wailing had stopped. I listened for a long time but it never started again. Just as I was about to leave, I saw some broken grass at my feet. Farther along I found the place where the thing had entered the brush. There was a trail of willows that did not stand straight. I took my knife in hand and followed the bent willows some way away from the river. Then

I saw something dark ahead, and as I crept closer I could see that it was a man. He lay on his back, his head propped against a rock, a knife in his right hand. I was off to one side and I thought to sneak up and lift the man's hair. But then the man flopped his head in my direction and I saw who it was. 'It is Head Carrier!' I cried out, for it was he who later became the great warrior of the ghost shirt now worn by Fast Horse. But he was a youth then, a year older than I. As I ran through the brush I saw him lift his head and knife at the same time. Then he recognized me. 'Oh, Spotted Weasel,' he cried—for that was my name then—'I am killed by the murderous Snakes.' With that he closed his eyes and rolled over.

"I ran to him, for I was sure he had passed to the Sand Hills. He had two broken-off arrows in him, one in his side and one in the guts. I pulled back his shirt and listened to his heart, and I could hear a faint murmuring. Then I rolled him onto his side. The arrow in his ribs had passed through his body and the arrowhead was sticky with blood. I managed to tie my lariat around the shaft and, with a great deal of effort, pull it through his body. But the arrow in his guts had not come through. I brought him water and made him drink but he couldn't take much. I bathed his wounds as best I could and I held him and cried. Along came dusk, and he opened his eyes and said in a weak voice, 'Go away, Spotted Weasel, let me die like a warrior.' I protested, telling him I would take him home so he could die with his people. 'No,' he said, 'I do not want my parents to watch me die. I want to die here, alone.'

"And so, still weeping, I left him there and wandered back into the brush. I could hear his death song getting fainter behind me. I found a slough and sat with my head in my hands. Oh, I was sad. All around me the green-singers were tuning up. I had never liked frogs, but as I cried I became aware of the beauty of their song. It filled me with so much sadness I thought my heart would fall down, never to rise, and I cried louder. Soon the biggest of the frog persons came up to me and said, 'Why do you weep when all we mean to do is cheer you up? Are you not grateful to us?' And so I told him about my friend, Head Carrier, who lay dying. Frog Chief said, 'I understand how it is with friends. But you people sometimes play with us and kill us for no reason. You are very cruel to your little brothers.' And I cried, 'Oh, underwater swimmer, if you will help me now I will tell my people to leave you alone. Never again will a Pikuni harm his little brothers.' So Frog Chief signaled me to be patient and dived into the slough.

He was gone for a long time. Seven Persons had begun to sink in the night sky when he came up again. He carried deep in his fat throat a ball of stinking green mud. He was exhausted, and I helped him crawl out on the bank. After a while he said, 'I had to go to the home of the chief of the Underwater People. He was reluctant to help, but after I told him your vow he gave this medicine to me. Now take it and smear it on the wounds of your friend.'

"I ran back to Head Carrier shouting and whooping, for I knew he would be glad to see me. But when I got there he was cold and stiff and his eyes stared up at the stars. Now I knew he had gone to the Shadowland. Without much hope I smeared the stinking mud on his wounds, then fell into a deep sleep. A small time later I felt something cold on my face, and when I woke up there stood Head Carrier, dripping wet. 'Wake up, you nothing-man,' he said to me, 'you have slept half the morning and I have already been swimming.' I sat up and looked at him, for I was sure he was a ghost who had come to torture me. But he said, 'When I woke up this morning I had the strangest feeling that I had gone to that place no man returns from. I dreamed that I had been killed off by the Snakes. And when I looked down I had some stinking stuff all over my body, so I went down to the river and washed it off.' I looked at his body and there was not a mark on it.

"Later, at a big ceremonial, I told this story to my mother's sister, who was a healing woman among the Never Laughs band. 'Foolish young man, why didn't you tell me of this sooner?' she said. 'Now I will teach you all the ways of healing, for you are truly chosen.' So I became a many-faces and so I am."

White Man's Dog sighed. The white-headed eagles were gone.

"Later still, I received some real medicine from the Black Paint People, but that is another story." Mik-api's voice trailed off.

White Man's Dog thought he saw a look of pain in the old man's eyes and it surprised him. He hadn't thought of Mik-api as having emotions anymore. He had thought many-faces men were beyond such frailties. The pained look had startled him but it pleased him as well. It pleased him to know that Mik-api still lived in the world of men.

8

ON the day before the Lone Eaters were to strike camp and journey to the trading house on the Bear River, Fast Horse sat alone behind his father's lodge, staring up at the Beaver Medicine bundle, which hung from a tripod. It was a large bundle, the size of a blackhorn calf, and its rawhide covering was yellowed and cracked. He had taken to sitting there by himself, day after day, looking at the bundle, trying to feel its power. His father, Boss Ribs, had kept the bundle for as long as he could remember, and both his father and he assumed that one day the bundle would be passed to him. His father had been waiting until Fast Horse was old enough, and patient enough, to learn all the songs and rituals associated with the objects in the bundle. All the living things in the country of the Pikunis had given their songs to the medicine bundle, and the power contained within was immense. But only if the ceremony was done right. And so Boss Ribs had been in no hurry to begin the teaching of his son. The time would come soon enough.

But all that had changed now because Fast Horse had changed. He had become an outsider within his own band. He no longer sought the company of the others, and they avoided him. The girls who had once looked so admiringly on him now averted their eyes when he passed. The young men considered him a source of bad medicine, and the older ones did not invite him for a smoke. Even his own father had begun to look upon him with doubt and regret. As for Fast Horse, the more he stared at the Beaver Medicine, the more it lost meaning for him. That would not be the way of his power. His power would be more tangible and more immediate.

Cold Maker—he scoffed at Cold Maker. One day, on one of his solitary, unsuccessful hunts, he had dismounted and challenged Cold Maker to do him in, to kill him on the spot; he had nothing to live for. At first, he had trembled, but when nothing happened, he grew louder, more angry. At the time, he wanted to die, he welcomed death, he wanted Cold Maker to clutch his heart in his icy fingers. He sang his death song and waited. Nothing. And then he grew bitter and he hated his people and all they believed in. They had no power. They were pitiful, afraid of everything, including the Napikwans, who were taking their land even as the Pikunis stood on it. Only Owl Child had power and courage. He took what he wanted; he defied the Napikwans and killed them. He laughed at their seizers and chiefs when they threatened revenge. And he laughed at his own people for their weak hearts.

As he stared at the scabby medicine bundle and thought these things, Fast Horse began to hear voices, shouts, and he saw some children running toward the east edge of camp. There was always a lot of commotion in camp, especially when visitors arrived, and Fast Horse thought they were probably hunters from one of the other bands. Out of mild curiosity, he stood and walked in that direction.

By the time he reached the edge of camp, there were already fifteen or twenty people standing there, talking among themselves. "I don't recognize the horse," said one. "Nor the strange blanket with which he hides his face," said another. "He is not from one of our camps," said a third.

The horse was small and white, with dark scars showing through the hair. It walked with a slow, awkward gait, as though it had been ridden into the ground at one time and had never recovered.

When the figure was a short distance from the camp, he slid his right leg over the horse's neck and jumped off. The horse lowered its head and began to eat the spring grass.

Fifty paces from the group the thin figure stopped and shook his head. The blanket fell away from his face, and the woman beside Fast Horse sucked in her breath. The face was gaunt, the skin stretched tight over the bones and deeply pocked. The man held his blanket over his arms in front of him. The people stared silently.

"Ha! Don't you recognize me, Lone Eaters? Have I been away so long, have I changed so much?" The man laughed. "You, Eagle Ribs, don't you know me?"

Suddenly Eagle Ribs, who had been at the front of the group, shouted and dropped his musket. He ran to the man, crying, "It is you! It is you!" He hugged the thin figure and called back to the people, "It is Yellow Kidney! He returns to his people!" In his excitement he had knocked the blanket from his friend. And now he saw the women put their hands to their mouths and cry out. The men stared. "What is this? Wretched Lone Eaters! Do you not recognize your brother?" He turned to his friend, and Yellow Kidney held up his hands. Where there had been fingers now there were none. Eagle Ribs started back. His mouth was open as though he had been caught in the middle of laughter, but no sound came out.

The people ran forward, past the dumb Eagle Ribs, to touch and embrace their brother. There was much crying. Two of the women ran toward camp to tell Heavy Shield Woman that her man had come home. A boy of ten winters picked up Eagle Rib's musket and tried to hold it to his cheek. Fast Horse was gone.

"THIS then is my story. You, Eagle Ribs, you, White Man's Dog, know the truth of what I am about to tell. But you don't know the all of it." Yellow Kidney looked at the men of the various groups of the All Friends society. They had smoked, and then they had eaten, and now many of them filled their short-pipes. The big lodge was heavy with the smell of meat and smoke. Three Bears burned some sage in the fire to sweeten it up. Then he too sat back. The women who had served the men were gone.

Yellow Kidney told of the journey to the Crow land, of the cold walking nights, of the lack of meat, and of the moment he sent White Man's Dog with the other young men to steal some

of the grazing horses. "Then I sent Eagle Ribs in one direction
and Fast Horse in another. There were fat buffalo-runners tied
up all through the camp. The camp itself was as large as the
valley, four hundred lodges at least. There were Napikwans
there too, traders or hide hunters. They were thick with the
Crows, many of them sitting at fires in the camp. But finally it
grew quiet. We had let the last of the drunken revelers wear
themselves out. I pulled my robe up over my head and walked
into the camp. Young Bear Chief and Double Runner have
seen me do this before. I walked boldly among the lodges until
at last I was standing in the middle of the camp, beside the
great lodge of their smoking societies. There I looked about,
and it did not take me long to find what I was looking for.
Night Red Light looked down from a hole in the clouds and I
saw clearly, not twenty-five paces away from where I stood, the
tipi of the blue buffalo. As you know, this is the lodge of our old
enemy, Bull Shield, who has made the Pikunis cry many times.
I approached his lodge with caution and there, tied to the
lodgepole, was the most beautiful black horse I had ever seen.
Now if I had been alone on this raid, I would have gone into the
lodge and cut Bull Shield's throat. Oh, how I wish I had! But I
was responsible for the young men who were with me, so I
decided to take the horse and leave. As I cut the lariat, I whispered in his ear. Then I began to lead him away. He was eager
to come with me. One could tell he was an intelligent animal.

"But we had not gone a hundred steps before I began to
hear a loud noise at the edge of the camp. I lowered the robe
from my head and turned my ears in that direction. The small
wind was behind me and so I could not hear distinctly. My ears
turned as big as the wags-his-tail's and soon I heard words, and
when I could make them out they were fierce words indeed—
"Oh, you Crows are puny, your horses are puny and your
women make me sick! If I had time I would ride among you
and cut off your puny woman heads, you cowardly Crows'—
said in the tongue of our people as clear that night as I tell you
now."

As if by magic, all the men quit smoking and swung their
heads in the direction of Eagle Ribs.

"No, no." Yellow Kidney laughed. "Eagle Ribs is a brave and wise horse-taker. He knows the consequences of such action. It was not his voice I heard that night."

"Fast Horse!" It was out of his mouth before White Man's Dog could think.

Yellow Kidney's dark eyes locked on his. After a moment he said, "It will be known. There is time."

"Where is Fast Horse?" said Three Bears. "He is a member of the Doves. He should be here." He nodded in the direction of the Doves, who sat the farthest away. Two of them stood and slipped out the entrance.

"I heard the first stirrings of excitement in a nearby lodge, and so I drew my knife. When a man emerged, carrying a short-gun, I stepped close to him and drove my knife into his heart. Then I began to hurry away, still leading the black horse, to the north edge of the camp. Three men ran past me, then another two, and I began to feel that my luck would hold, that I would be able to mount the black horse and ride off toward the Napikwans' wagons and there turn west to rejoin my comrades. But I saw a group of men beside a lodge, talking excitedly, and one pointed at me. I knew that I had been found out, so I dropped the horse and ran behind a tipi and ran some more. I heard shots being fired and more men yelling. Three men were running in my direction but they hadn't seen me yet, so I ducked into a lodge. I had my knife ready to strike the dwellers. As my eyes adjusted to the dim light of a night fire I saw several bodies along the walls, but none of them stirred. I began to think they were just piles of robes when on the far side I saw a figure rise up and throw the robe back. I had made up my mind to attack but I saw that it was a young girl. She just looked at me and her eyes were heavy with sleep. I thought it odd that the other figures had not been awakened by the gunshots. But this thought was erased quickly by the sounds of voices outside the lodge. I know enough of the Crow tongue to understand that they were saying I had come this way, that I had passed by. I had no choice but to try to hide so I crept over to the girl, put my hand over her mouth and crawled into the robe with her. I had just pulled it over our heads when I heard the flap being opened. There was a long silence as the observer passed his eyes over the robes. Than a couple of shots rang out a way off and I heard the flap drop shut.

"After a while I took my hand from the girl's mouth but she lay there with her eyes closed. I felt under the robe and she was naked and her skin was hot. I felt her breasts and her belly and they were hot and damp. I couldn't understand because the fire was hardly big enough to see by. It was cold in that lodge, but she was naked and sweating. The mind does funny things when it is confused, and I began to feel a stirring of excitement for this hot girl. By now all the commotion was at the other end of the camp. I found her there between the legs and entered her—not without some difficulty, for she was only on the verge of becoming a woman. When I had had my pleasure, I rolled away, and that's when it hit me that she hadn't moved, hadn't made a sound, only lay there with her eyes shut. I became afraid at these unusual circumstances, so I crept to the fire and took a burning stick. I pulled the robe back and looked at her. I had seen it before, some winters ago when our people were struck down, when half of the Lone Eaters perished. There on her face and chest were the dreaded signs. I had copulated with one who was dying of the white-scabs disease."

For the second time that night White Man's Dog spoke without thinking. "My dream! My dream!" He covered his mouth in horror, but the words were unmistakable in the silence of the lodge.

Rides-at-the-door looked sharply at his son. Several of the other men murmured their disapproval. It wasn't good for a young man to interrupt his elder, especially during such an important account.

White Man's Dog felt his face burn with shame; but more than that, he felt a heaviness come into his heart that made him weak, unable to speak even if he wanted to.

Yellow Kidney looked across the fire. "You heartless ones! Do not chide this young man. He acquitted himself bravely and wisely against the Crows. And now I hear from Heavy Shield Woman that he hunted for my family in my absence. He is a good young man, and I thank him before you members of the honor societies."

But White Man's Dog had not heard Yellow Kidney's

words. He knew too well what had happened in that lodge. He had been there in his dream and the girl, the white-faced girl, had lifted her arms, not for him but for Yellow Kidney. Why hadn't he told Yellow Kidney of his dream? Such a dream would have been a sign of bad medicine and they might have turned back. Yellow Kidney would still be a whole man, not this pitiful figure. . . .

It had grown quiet in the big lodge as the men watched Yellow Kidney fumble for his pipe and tobacco sack. The beading on the sack was of a different pattern from those used by the Pikunis. With his fists Yellow Kidney was able to dip his pipe into the sack and fill it. He held the pipe in the palm of his left hand and held a blunt twig in the crease of his other palm, tamping the mixture. One of the younger men picked a burning stick from the fire and came forward to light the pipe.

"Thank you, Calf Shirt. And now you, like the others, wonder what happened to my hands to make them thus." Yellow Kidney puffed on his pipe and looked around the lodge. He had the calmness of a man who has lived through the worst of it and questioned the worth of survival. He removed the pipe with a stubby scarred hand and continued. "As I said, my mind was very confused and I became frightened. I began to move around to the various robes and I threw them back and saw by the light of my fire stick that they were all young girls, dead, and covered with the white scabs. Oh, I was frightened. I dropped the burning stick and rushed out of there, not caring what I would encounter. Anything was better than that death lodge. As I stood outside, trying to keep my guts down, I noticed that it was snowing heavily. This end of camp was still quiet. I thought my luck would hold, in spite of what I had seen and done in that lodge. I thought the snow would add to the confusion and help me to escape. But then I saw two young men come toward me from a tipi off to my right. In my haste, I had left my robe inside the death lodge. It didn't take them long to recognize me as an enemy and one of them hurled a lance at me. I managed to duck out of the way, but the other had a musket, and as I turned to run I heard a blast and my right leg buckled. I had been shot in the thigh. And now they were upon me and one of them grabbed my hair and I felt cold steel against my forehead. They meant to scalp me.

"I must have fainted, for the next thing I knew I was surrounded by our enemies, and they were talking and laughing. But one of them was angry and argued with the others. Although I had only seen him twice before, I recognized this angry man. It was Bull Shield and I knew he wanted me for himself. I spit at him and called him a Crow dog-eater; then I began my death song, for I knew that they would now kill me. And I wanted to die a good quick death, scorning my enemies. How I wish it had been so! Several of them rushed at me with their knives and they would have killed me but for a strange thing—the angry Bull Shield bade them to stop. He had become calm and thoughtful. He spoke some words to the others. I could not understand them, for I sang loud in their faces. Four of them picked me up and carried me to a nearby big-leaf log. There they placed my hands against the rough bark. Bull Shield then unsheathed his heavy knife and began to saw my fingers off, one by one. At first I tried to be silent to show that it did not bother me. My hands were numb because of the cold. But then the pain hit the warm parts of me and coursed through my body like lightning. I nearly bit my tongue off. Then I screamed like a real-lion and fainted again.

"When I woke up I was sitting astride a scrawny white horse, my legs tied under its belly. They had looped the reins around my neck. I had gotten sick, for as my chin rested on my chest I saw the foul outpouring of my stomach frozen to my shirt. When I had the strength to lift my head, my eyes fell on Bull Shield. He was now wearing a full headdress and he had a repeating rifle propped in the snow at his feet. Then he signed to me: Go and tell the Squats-like-women this is what the mighty Crows do when they send their girls to steal our horses. One of them hit the bony horse on the rump, and they all set up a war cry as I left their camp in the driving snow."

There was a great outcry of sympathy for Yellow Kidney and a stronger berating of the Crows for this humiliation. Even Three Bears, who had long since left the hot words to the younger ones, expressed his anger. "Before this coming season of the high sun ends, we will make the miserable Crows to pay. Many of our brothers from the other camps will ride with us when they learn what has happened to Yellow Kidney. We will punish them severely." All in the lodge vowed they would join the war party. Some wanted to leave the next day, but it was agreed that they would go after the Sun Dance encampment. Three Bears wanted all the Pikunis to learn of Yellow Kidney's fate.

During the heated exchange, Riders-at-the-door had watched his son slip out of the lodge. He had been watching his son during Yellow Kidney's story, and he didn't know what to make of it. White Man's Dog had sat with his head down, apparently not even listening. Rides-at-the-door had seen this attitude before, and he didn't want to think he had seen it in his son; it was the attitude of one who has done a bad thing. And it had to do with Yellow Kidney's sad story. Now White Man's Dog had slipped out like a dog that had stolen meat.

"But go on, Yellow Kidney, tell us how you survived your misfortune," said Wipes-his-eyes, head of the Doves society. He was married to one of Yellow Kidney's sisters.

"It is difficult to remember what I did those first couple of sleeps, Wipes-his-eyes. The Crows had taken my capote—I remember seeing it on one of those who struck my horse—but they had tied one of the white men's blankets around my shoulders. All that day and the next I kept fainting. But my scabby little horse—the one you saw me arrive on—kept wandering. One night I awoke to find us standing in a grove of spear-leaf trees. My horse's head was down but he was not eating. I knew that he would soon collapse and then we would freeze to death. But the dawn came and I saw we were down in the valley of the Elk River. The snow had stopped, and the wind which had plagued us on the plains was no longer blowing. As I lifted my head to look around at my last day in Old Man's world, I saw on the other bank a small village. My head cleared and I saw smoke rising from the smoke holes of their lodges. I knew that it could be a party of Crow woodcutters or hunters, but I felt it would be better to die there than to live more hours of death. So I raised my horse's head and urged him forward. As we crossed the Elk River, I felt the cold water around my knees and twice the horse stumbled. Then I thought it would be better to drown. But we made it across and I rode right into the center of that small camp. I was too weak to cry out, and so I waited for them to come out of their lodges. Once again my head went black and this time I thought I saw my shadow slipping away. Ah, it was peaceful. I felt my body grow warm and cold at the same time. Then I was flying over the white plains, and ahead I saw the Sand Hills. I began to cry, for I saw the long-ago people standing before their lodges with their arms outstretched. But then they turned their faces away. I cried to Old Man to release me, for I wanted to join my father and my grandmother and my eldest son who died of the coughing sickness. They stood there with tears in their eyes. But then they too turned away and the Sand Hills hid themselves.

"I awoke in a darkened lodge with a strange man leaning over me. After a time I asked him if I was in the Shadowland, but he shook his head and signed to me that he did not understand my tongue. Then he made the sign for Spotted Horse People. I had been there for five sleeps. They had taken me in and were in the process of curing me. I didn't understand this last part and so I lifted my hands to sign to him my confusion. Then I saw my hands. They were wrapped in bundles of the white man's cloth and I remembered what had happened. Oh, I cried bitterly, for I had lost my ability to draw a bow, to fire a musket, to skin the blackhorns. I would be as useless as an old dog, and I not yet thirty-nine winters! I began to speak to the man again, to plead with him to retrieve my fingers, but again he made a sign that he didn't understand. Then he got up and went out of the lodge.

"It turned night and I lay there thinking of my Heavy Shield Woman, of my sons and daughter. I could never hunt for them, and I wanted to die right there rather than let them see me. I began to pity myself. I cried and cried and I asked Sun Chief why he didn't let his wretched Yellow Kidney die. What had I done to offend him so? Then I vowed that if he would let me die and give me back my fingers, I would hunt on behalf of all the old ones in the Sand Hills, since I could not hunt for my own family in this life.

"My crying and pleading were interrupted by the appearance of an old woman. She carried with her a medicine sack. She had a kind face and she wore her gray hair loose beneath a blackhorn-skin cap. She knelt beside me and gave the sign for medicine woman. There was a pot of boiling water behind her. She then unwrapped my hands and held them close to her face. They were very sensitive to air and I could even feel her breath on them. I drew them back and looked at them myself. They were black and puffed up like a bladder full of water. But beneath the black scabs I could see the pink new skin beginning to form. She made a paste of pounded-up bear grass and crow root and a leaf I didn't know. She sang a healing song and chewed some buffalo food and blew it on the wounds. Then she applied the paste and wrapped my hands in new cloths. One could tell by her presence that she was a practiced healer. She never smiled, but the kindly look did not leave her face. I fell asleep dreaming of my own dead grandmother.

"I continued to recover, drinking broth and eating of the wags-his-tail and prairie-runner meat they brought me. Then a few sleeps later I awoke in a sweat with a fearful pounding in my head. Then I began to get cold and my teeth chattered so I thought they would shatter. I tossed all night in such agony. When the medicine woman came to see me in the morning I had calmed down a little. But she looked at my face and her mouth fell open for I had begun to develop the little red sores. I saw them on my arms and I felt them around my mouth, and again I was besieged by the fever and chills. My body began to buck with such fury I was powerless to stop it. The old woman hurried out and returned with two older men. They had strips of rawhide in their hands. After they had tied me down, the woman signed that all of them had lived through the last plague of white scabs. They would not get it again. But by now I was tortured by red sores which were bursting all over my body and I was terrified of dying such a horrible death. This went on for how long I don't know because I was out of my head. I saw many things during my ordeal, things that would drive a healthy man out of his mind. Perhaps Old Man was being merciful in allowing me to die at last, but I had to question his method. Many times I returned to the Sand Hills only to be drawn back right on the edge. The only peace I knew was when my relatives smiled at me.

"Then one day I returned to the lodge. I was awakened by Sun Chief's warmth as he lit up the walls. Then I smelled a meat broth and I got a little hungry. I pulled myself up on my elbows and looked at my body. It was covered with a pale salve. Many of the white scabs had dropped off and I could see the angry scars. It was there, that day while looking at my scars and my hands, that I knew why I had been punished so severely. As you men of the warrior societies know, in all things, to the extent of my ability, I have tried to act honorably. But there in that Crow lodge, in that lodge of death, I had broken one of the simplest decencies by which people live. In fornicating with the dying girl, I had taken her honor, her opportunity to die virtuously. I had taken the path traveled only by the meanest of scavengers. And so Old Man, as he created me, took away my life many times and left me like this, worse than dead, to think of my transgression every day, to be reminded every time I attempt the smallest act that men take for granted." The energy had gone out of Yellow Kidney's voice and he sat motionless, looking down at the fire. The lodge was as quiet as death, except for the occasional *pop* of the pitchy wood. Outside, in the black night, a wind came down from the north and rattled the ear poles of the lodge. The tight skins around the lodgepoles flapped and the fire flickered, then blazed.

Three Bears spoke a prayer to all the Above Ones, thanking them for the return of their son, then said softly, "The spirits can be cruel, Yellow Kidney, but in their way there is a teaching." He looked at the younger men of the lodge. "Did you find Fast Horse?"

"No, his father has not seen him since midday," said one of the Doves.

"When he is found, tell him we would talk with him." Although it wasn't said, there was no doubt that it was Fast Horse's loud boasting that caused these bad things to happen to Yellow Kidney. But the men respected Fast Horse's father. The Beaver Medicine was the most powerful of the bundles and Boss Ribs had kept it well. Now his son would be punished.

Many of them hoped that Yellow Kidney would exercise his right to revenge his mutilation, to kill Fast Horse. If that didn't happen, they would probably banish the young man. That way, Boss Ribs could save some face.

Before they left, the men renewed their vow to make war on the Crows. It was decided they would do this in the moon of the yellow grass. They would make Bull Shield pay for his cruelty.

Three Bears called to Rides-at-the-door to stay when the men filed out. He lit his pipe and leaned back. His stiff back pained him badly and he needed to rest for a moment. Finally he said, "Why did White Man's Dog leave in the middle of Yellow Kidney's story?"

Rides-at-the-door looked at Three Bears, but the old man had closed his eyes. "I think he heard something that startled him. I don't know. It shamed me to see him leave."

"Perhaps he was just upset. Yellow Kidney is a pitiful man now. I don't know what he will do."

"I was afraid he would come back this way. As he said, he would be better off dead. It pains me to say it but I wish he had not come back. I fear more bad things will happen."

"Do you think he will attempt revenge—on Fast Horse?"

"Right now I don't think he knows. He pities himself and thinks only of his misfortune. Soon, though, he will begin to think of Fast Horse."

"It could set off something. Such bad blood in a small group like the Lone Eaters could go hard on everyone."

Rides-at-the-door thought for a while. He knew what should be done but he didn't like to say it. Boss Ribs was a friend of his and had already suffered much. Finally he did say it. "Fast Horse should be banished—tonight, if we can find him. The sooner he is gone, the sooner people will quit talking about him and Yellow Kidney. Perhaps we can prevent this revenge before Yellow Kidney has a chance to think of it."

"I feel as you do, Rides-at-the-door. Perhaps you can talk to Boss Ribs, persuade him to banish Fast Horse himself. If it can be done quietly, without commotion, our people will be able to forget this problem and get on with their affairs. There are some hotheads in this camp. We must cool them down."

"How I pity Boss Ribs! He has already lost two wives and three children to the Shadowland. To banish his own son—"

"Talk to him. Tell him it must be done for the good of his people—and for the safety of his son." Three Bears sat forward, and the pain made his eyes water. He knocked the ashes from his pipe. "One more thing. Heavy Shield Woman's man is back, thus fulfilling her prayers. I would like White Man's Dog to ride among the other bands and tell them of her vow to be Medicine Woman at the Sun Dance. He can start in the morning."

Rides-at-the-door had known Three Bears all his life and thought he knew the direction of the old man's mind, but Three Bears many times managed to catch him off balance. "Why White Man's Dog?"

Three Bears began the painful task of getting up. "I trust him," he said simply.

"What about our journey to the trading fort? The people expect to leave in the morning," said Rides-at-the-door, helping the old man to his feet.

"We can delay it a couple of sleeps. We must feast the return of our good relative, Yellow Kidney."

In spite of his concern for his son's action that night, Rides-at-the-door had to smile at his old friend's way of always trying to make things right for his people. That is why he is a chief, thought Rides-at-the-door.

Nash Candelaria

Nash CANDELARIA, born May 7, 1928, in Los Angeles, California, has often stated that he considers himself a Nuevo Mejicano (New Mexican) "by heritage and sympathy." He is a descendant of one of the pioneer families that founded Albuquerque in 1706, and his parents and sister were all born in the state. While he was growing up, he spent his summers with relatives in Los Candelarias, the Albuquerque neighborhood that carries his family name. Primarily known for his historical novels that interweave episodes of New Mexican history with the lives of the fictional Rafa family, he is also the author of short stories that deal with different aspects of the Hispanic experience in the United States, particularly the conflicts between the Anglo and Hispanic cultures.

Candelaria was brought up in English-speaking Catholic Anglo neighborhoods of Los Angeles. The juxtaposition of this environment with the family summers spent in New Mexico permitted him to feel part of both cultures, but it is clear from interviews he has given that racial prejudice and his mainstream language and customs also caused him to be rejected at times by both Anglos and Hispanics.

His educational background and career experiences have been quite different from those of most of the major Chicano writers. Others, such as Rudolfo Anaya, Aristeo Brito, Ana Castillo, Sandra Cisneros, Rolando Hinojosa, Tomás Rivera, and Alma Villanueva, have primarily received their training and continued to work in academic settings, often producing their works while teaching literature or creative writing in a college or university. In contrast, Candelaria's background is in science and he has always worked in a business environment. Encouraged to go to college by his secondary-school teachers, he graduated from the University of California, Los Angeles, in 1948 with a degree in chemistry. After graduation he worked as a scientist for a pharmaceutical company but found himself more and more attracted to writing. During this period he read extensively and took night courses in writing; then, after serving in the Air Force during the Korean War, he decided to make a career change and took a position as a science writer. Over the years he has continued to combine his academic training with his vocation as a writer. After he retires he plans to move to New Mexico and write full-time.

Candelaria has also stated that he was fascinated by his history courses in college, and this interest has manifested itself in his creative writing, particularly in his three historical novels. He feels that he is also following a family tradition, for one of his ancestors, Juan Candelaria, was the author of an early history of New Mexico in 1776, a history that contained some highly fictionalized episodes. His acclaimed "Rafa trilogy" of novels includes *Memories of the Alhambra* (1977), *Not by the Sword* (1982), and *Inheritance of Strangers* (1985). All three present a unique picture of New Mexico and its history preceding and since 1848, when the Southwest and California became part of the United States as a result of the Mexican War, for the story is told from the point of view of the conquered Spanish-speaking settlers who lived in the newly acquired territory.

Memories of the Alhambra deals with the present-day legacy of the subjugation of one culture (Mexican) by another (Anglo-American): the problem of identity. The main characters of the novel all grapple with their "Mexicanness" from different perspectives. José, the father, attempts to deny it, particularly its Indian component, through a futile search for pure-blooded Spanish ancestors; his wife, Theresa, attempts to escape it through upward mobility and an unending succession of moves to ever more "American" neighborhoods; and their son, Joe, learns to accept it and move onward. *Not by the Sword,* which in addition to its American Book Award (1983) was a finalist for the Western Writers of America's Best Western Historical Novel Award, moves back in time to the period of the Mexican War when the Rafas became Americans by conquest. It is a time of great change as twin brothers José Antonio and Carlos Rafa struggle to find their place in the new order and help their family survive defeat with grace and courage. *Inheritance of Strangers* is set in the 1890s, when the coming of the railroad and the opening of the West engulf the old cultures in their path. José Antonio Rafa, now an old man, recounts to his heirs the painful exploitation of the Nuevo Mejicano at the hands of a succession of unscrupulous Anglos; it is his attempt to pass on a sense of the family's history and traditions and its will to survive. The critics have noted that one of Candelaria's greatest strengths in these novels is his ability to blend the personal stories of his characters with the panoramic portrayal of the larger events of the time.

Candelaria's fourth novel, *Leonor Park,* will be published in mid-1991 by Bilingual Press. The author describes it as "a story about land and greed set in the 1920s in New Mexico," and he sees it as a continuation of his New Mexico trilogy. (There are Rafas among the main characters, and José and Theresa Rafa from *Memories of the Alhambra* appear in minor roles.) This time, however, the story is told more "from the personal point of view of family and sexual rivalry" rather than from the historical or mythological point of view.

The author has written that "what I am trying to do is to give Hispanics their proper place in U.S. history. As a group, many of us have been here a long time, longer than most Anglos, while the Native American part of us has been here longer than the Spanish Europeans. . . . What I want my writing to do is to help stake our Hispanic claim to North America and to write against stereotype in creating the characters whose stories I tell. In this competitive society, Chicanos have competed and succeeded and will continue to do so. That is part of the message I would want young people to get from my works."

—*Karen S. Van Hooft*

THERE had been a chance to observe this sick young man for several days now. He was, Tercero judged, barely past twenty years of age. Stocky and taller than the average New Mexican. His hair was black and his skin more ruddy than the tan of the local people. Startling, piercing blue eyes followed the movements of anyone in the hut. In his more lucid moments silence was his shield against their questions. Yet when he lapsed into a fitful sleep he spoke volubly in the strange language that many of the villagers referred to as the tongue of angels.

In the nights, after busy days directing the repair of the little chapel, of teaching prayers to children and adults alike, of counseling the sick or troubled, Tercero would often sit in the dark of the hut listening for a clue.

"Skihanach. Ballyshedy. Cork," he heard one night, mumbled repeatedly over and over again.

The word "cork" he recognized from his smattering of the American language. He listened carefully. "Cork." There it was again. Distinctly. Clearly. Was he thirsty, needing someone to remove the cork from a bottle of water?

"Skihanach. Ballyshedy." What did those words mean?

Two nights later, Tercero knelt in the flickering candlelight praying aloud because he felt the need to hear a human voice in the silent hut, even if only his own. His fingers had slipped over the beads of his rosary absentmindedly and his voice droned through his inattention, so that it might have been the murmur of the wind outside when he heard another voice in Spanish join him in an Ave.

"María santísima. Madre de Dios—"

In his surprise he almost stopped praying, but quickly he

forced himself to continue as if nothing had happened. He dared not look toward the pallet. It was a pleasant tenor voice that spoke Spanish with a lilt instead of the more typical syncopation of one whose native language it was. Yet it was passably decent pronunciation. Better than most of the Anglo traders one saw in New Mexico.

The two voices continued in unison through the cycle of beads. It was as if in common prayer they were coming to some agreement. When the rosary had been completed, Tercero crossed himself and stayed still in the silent room, waiting for the other one to speak. Finally it came.

"Are you praying because I'm going to die?"

Tercero rose and turned toward him. The piercing blue eyes followed him. Not hostile. Just wary. "No," he answered. "You're healing very well."

A deep sigh. Then a certain tightness around the chin and jaw. "You have taken my pistol."

"You will get it back when the time comes."

"When what time comes?"

"When we learn more about you. What you are doing here. A pistol is a dangerous weapon in the hands of someone who would do another harm."

The stranger looked around quietly in the dim interior. "Where am I?"

"In the hamlet of Los Bacas. Province of New Mexico. About a half day's ride from the Río Grande River along which is the trail to Santa Fe."

"Mexico."

"Yes. Mexico." The stranger looked once again into the sparsely lighted room, then sighed and closed his eyes. Tercero watched him drop quickly to sleep, then stood watching as if there might be some clue on his sleeping countenance. Now you know where you are, he thought. But we still know nothing about you.

Tercero thought about the stranger when he awakened during the night. There was no question that the man was a Catholic, but he was obviously no priest. His knowledge of Spanish was good, yet there was that strange tongue he spoke in his sleep. It was none of the common European languages—French, German, Italian; these he would recognize. There were few Catholics in Russia but some in Poland. As for Scandinavia, heathen Protestants there, while there were Catholics in southeastern Europe in Bohemia. "Skihanach. Ballyshedy. Cork," he thought. Portuguese? Could it be Portuguese? But why the American word "cork"?

The next morning they prayed together again, then exchanged a few words before Tercero went about his duties. "I am Father José Antonio Rafa," he said as he was about to leave. "Do you have a name?"

The stranger hesitated, perhaps deciding whether or not to tell his real name, though God knows what it would matter in this place. "Miguel," he finally answered.

"Do you have another name?"

"Not for now."

"Where do you come from, Miguel?"

"I would like my pistol back," was his answer.

"We will talk about that another time."

Two nights later, during another of his restless nights, Tercero felt a second attack of anxiety and his thoughts carried him far away. Carlos! he thought. What is it, Carlos? Drawn into himself, he did not hear the faint rustlings from the adjacent pallet. Even the opening and closing of the door made no impression on him, until suddenly his eyes popped open, and he knew that he was alone in the hut. Then the memory of the tiny noises came to him.

"Damn!" he thought. "What is that crazy fool trying to do?"

Quickly he slipped into his clothes. Unable to find his sandals, he ran barefoot into the night. The slightly waning moon was high and bright so that it was easy to see. Across the road and two houses away a dark figure moved stealthily toward the pasture, then stopped at the braying of a burro. What few horses there were, Tercero knew, were down the trail in Don Ignacio's pasture. A burro was not going to take anyone very far very fast.

Quickly he ran in the shadows, his bare feet padding softly in the dirt. The figure ahead leaned against a tree. Miguel had gone a long way in his weakened condition. Then he pushed off from the tree toward the burro who was now making a fearsome racket. A lighted candle shone in the window of the nearest hut. Tercero crossed the road in a rush and grasped Miguel, just as he had turned away from the burro to head further down the trail.

"Let go of me!" he snarled. Then the excitement and the fatigue overcame him and he sank slowly and softly to the ground.

"Crazy fool," Tercero said. "How far would you get before the Indians killed you? Or you died of thirst or hunger, not to mention fatigue?"

"Who is that?" came a shout from the candle-bearer who stood in the door of the hut.

"Father Rafa."

The man came forward, and the two of them lifted the fallen Miguel and carried him back to the hut. Tercero covered him and then lay in bed thinking. The stranger would soon be strong enough to leave. He did not have to run away. Although there was always the matter of a government passport, the man was free to go wherever he wished provided he did not steal a horse or mule or burro. Yet he did not seem to know that. His behavior was that of a fugitive. There had to be a way to get him to talk so that something could be done.

"We could turn him over to the authorities," Don Ignacio said the next morning.

"How long since you've seen an Army patrol here?" Tercero asked. Don Ignacio shrugged. "How long since anyone from here has gone to a villa where they have troops and government officials?"

"We could just let him run away."

"He would not last long on foot."

"That is his problem, Father. If he's fool enough, let him."

"I have to go back to Albuquerque soon," Tercero said. "I could take him with me." When he had said it, he realized the eminent sensibility of it. All he needed was Miguel's cooperation.

"YOU are a problem." Miguel sat up on his pallet and looked hard as Tercero spoke. "I have to return to the villa of Albuquerque. I should have left yesterday."

"Why tell me?"

"Do you have a passport?" Miguel shook his head. "It is my duty as a citizen of Mexico to turn you over to our government. You are in the country illegally."

"Not if I'm a Mexican citizen."

"You are no more Mexican than you are a priest." Sullen silence as Miguel turned his face to the wall. "You could stay with these poor people. Soldiers may not come here for months. Perhaps years. They took care of you here while you were injured. They would certainly welcome you when you are healed." Tercero could see only the back of his head. "You could go back to Albuquerque with me and there make your peace with representatives of the government. Then you would be free to do whatever you want."

"Where is my pistol?"

"What is a priest doing carrying a pistol? They tell me it is an American one. Are you a spy?" Silence. "But you are a Catholic."

"My brother is a priest."

"A Mexican priest?" A rueful smile and shake of the head. "How long is it since you have been to confession?"

Miguel turned his gaze back. His face was troubled but still set in that stubborn way of his.

"Would you like to make a confession?"

"I cannot, Father."

"You would have to say too much." No response. "Do you want to go with me to Albuquerque?" Again there was no answer. "I can wait one more week until you are stronger. But then I have to go."

Silence was Miguel's answer. But during the next week he did not try to run away, even though he went on daily walks to build his strength. Each night he joined Tercero for prayers, and the priest sensed a subtle shift in the praying. It was less the rote of duty and long habit and more as if they were urgent, spontaneous pleas for guidance. They were the same words but said for different reasons and so they sounded different. One night Miguel asked if he might accompany Tercero to Albuquerque. The next evening, after supper, he asked about confession.

"You are an honorable man, Father Rafa. You are bound to keep the secrets of confession."

"Yes."

"Before we go then, I want to confess. Bless me, Father, for I have sinned. My last confession was in March of this year—some four months ago."

"MY name is Michael Dalton," he began. "Miguel in Spanish. I was born in the townland of Skihanach, parish of Ballyshedy, County Cork, Ireland. I tell you this not because it has any relevance to the sins I have committed against God; for those sins I am just another nameless soul. I tell you this because I am a stranger in a strange land and must throw myself on the mercy of strangers who, thank God, share a common belief in Jesus Christ and the holy Catholic Church. Whatever the tongues we speak or the shades of our skin, we are truly brothers in the sight of the Almighty.

"I have lived in fear and trepidation over the past months. I will not delve too much into my origins. That is another world across the sea. I will only say that I come from a large and devout family. My father was an honest, hard-working man who farmed another man's land. My mother, God rest her soul, was a saint.

"Of my brothers and sisters there are four each. Nine children altogether. And I must mention my favorite uncle, Harry. He had served as a mercenary soldier for other armies in other lands. A world traveler. A man who has seen the Holy See in Rome and the bloody battlefields of Europe. It was from him that I learned the Spanish language since he served with the Spanish, among others. It was from him, too, that I learned that many Irish are descendants of Miletius, an ancient Spaniard from the Iberian peninsula. That the Irish and Spanish have more in common than their religion. But it was not the Spanish that brought me to this New World but another country. The United States of America."

The Irish Poor Law had pointed the way to salvation for many destitute farmers like the Daltons. As if the clouds had parted and a ray of sunshine had shown the way to heaven. The lord of their estate had shipped a goodly number of tenant farmers to America, including Miguel's father, who planned to send for the family as soon as he saved their passage money.

However, his mother had taken ill and died shortly thereafter. His brothers and sisters, all older, had reassessed that call to a far-off land in the light of their mother's death and all had decided to remain in Ireland: the brother who was a priest, the two sisters who were nuns, and the others who survived the best they could in a land of hopeless poverty.

Thus, when the first hard-earned funds for passage to America came, they all agreed that it should go to Miguel now that their mother was dead.

It had been a send-off, Miguel remembered, to rival the wake of the beloved patriarch of the largest, richest family in County Cork. America! My God, America! Friends would come up and shake his hand and slap his back and gaze at him in awe as if he were ascending body and soul into heaven the way the Blessed Virgin herself had been called.

The ship had sailed in early spring for Philadelphia where he was to join his father. He had not minded the crowded decks, the poor food, and brackish water. The misery was leavened by singing and dancing—even more intense when a fellow passenger died before reaching the promised land.

In Philadelphia another shock. There was no father to greet him. Bewildered, he wandered through the city searching for the last address he had, only to find that his father had died while he had been crossing the Atlantic Ocean. All that was left was a small bundle of worn-out work clothes, a pair of boots that needed resoling, and a packet of old letters from his dead mother, full of endearment and cheer and hope for their coming reunion in the brave new world. Neither had expected it to be the hereafter instead of Philadelphia. Miguel had sat on the steps of the boardinghouse in the poor section of the city and cried as if his heart would break.

But tears or no, loneliness or no, one must still eat. So he looked for work. Jobs were hard to find. There had been riots in Philadelphia the year before, protesting the influx of immigrants and the lack of work. The Catholic Church too had been the target of reactions.

Why did I leave Ireland? Miguel had thought in despair. I am just as unemployed here as there. I hear as much anti-Catholic raving as I would from an Irish Protestant. And if I want to fight my neighbor, I can fight the same Englishmen here. Though they may be masked by the faint veneer of having become new, free men—Americans—they carry the same old prejudices. For all of this, at least in Ireland I would be among family and friends. And yet, he thought, here there is still hope while in Ireland there is none.

If he had had the twenty-five dollars passage money or could have obtained a job on board ship, he would have sailed back to the Emerald Isle during those first few months. But somehow he survived. And when the Army sought recruits, there was none more eager than the hungry and homeless young Irishman who still hung on to a thread of hope.

"Oh, say were you ever in the Río Grande? Way, you Río." It was his destiny to be an American even if he had to fight for that right on the far shores of another alien country. "It's there that the river runs down golden sand. For we're bound to the Río Grande!"

WELL, where General Taylor's forces landed was nothing like the Emerald Isle. It was a place called Texas, which Miguel had never dreamed existed even in his most despairing nightmares.

They had camped on the river, on the Río Grande across from the Mexican town of Matamoros. "Mata moros," he had translated for his non-Spanish-speaking comrades: "Kill Moors." Who were the ancient enemy of the Spanish people and from whom King Ferdinand and Queen Isabella had freed their country even as Columbus was on his way across the ocean sea to discover a new world. Matamoros.

War had not been declared. The two armies were like lolling

giants observing each other from opposite banks of the river. The American army was a motley collection of regulars. Almost half were immigrants from other countries. Mostly Irish like Miguel. But German, English, Scottish, and others too. A polyglot of languages and temperaments.

"If we can make an Army of this sorry crew," his sergeant said over and over like a litany, "we can make a country out of this Godforsaken land!"

Then, as salve for the fleas and the dirt and the changeable weather that could be mild, hot, windy, or wet, came the enticements from the Mexicans across the river to the occupants of Fort Texas.

"The Commander-in-chief of the Mexican army, to the English and Irish under the orders of the American General Taylor: Know ye: That the government of the United States is committing repeated acts of barbarous aggression against the magnanimous Mexican Nation; that the government which exists under 'the flag of the stars' is unworthy of the designation of Christian. Recollect that you were born in Great Britain; that the American government looks with coldness upon the powerful flag of St. George, and is provoking to a rupture the warlike people to whom it belongs; President Polk boldly manifesting a desire to take possession of Oregon, as he has already done to Texas. Now, then, come with all confidence to the Mexican ranks; and I guaranty to you, upon my honour, good treatment, and that all your expenses shall be defrayed until your arrival in the beautiful capital of Mexico.

"Germans, French, Poles, and individuals of other nations! Separate yourselves from the Yankees, and do not contribute to defend a robbery and usurpation, which, be assured, the civilized nations of Europe look upon with the utmost indignation. Come, therefore, and array yourselves under the tri-colored flag, in the confidence that the God of armies protects it, and that it will protect you equally with the English.

> *Headquarters upon the road to Matamoros*
> *April 2, 1846*
> *Pedro de Ampudia"*

One was not certain exactly where these pieces of paper came from. There was all manner of opportunity. After the initial landing of the American forces, when most Mexican farmers on the Texas side of the Río Grande had fled across the river to Matamoros, there had been a settling into a tenuous but friendly tolerance. A few Mexican farmers came back across to their homes with their goats and fighting cocks and children. Others from Matamoros would cross daily by ferry to sell milk and cheese and fresh fruit, returning at the end of a busy day of commerce.

So there was ample opportunity for the notices to be surreptitiously left for a soldier to pick up. Other information came by word of mouth. That the Mexican government would pay the way of American soldiers to Mexico City where they could enlist in the Mexican army and form their own battalion.

There were other enticements. More meaningful ones to young men far from home. At times the army bands would serenade each other across the river, like lovers separated by the irreconcilable feuding of their families. It was like a summer picnic where one would speak loudly so as to be heard at a distance by the object of one's attention, yet one could not mingle intimately. Thus it was one morning, with the Mexican army band playing, that Miguel and his closest friend had meandered along the river north of the fort.

"I tell you, Mike," his friend had said. "If that sergeant of ours picks on me one more time, I'll—"

"Now, now. He's just one of those bigoted Ulster anti-Catholics. You should try to ignore him."

"We're supposed to be Americans. Every man jack of us. Catholic or no. Ulster or Dublin. Irish or German. Jesus! We're here to fight the Mexicans, and the man I hate most in the world is one of us."

"Just keep calm, Brennan. When the Mexicans start thumping that artillery across the river, there won't be time for privates to worry about sergeants or vice versa. Come on. Let's find a nice place and take a swim. That will cool you off. We can lie in the sun and listen to the band. Like a grand Sunday after mass with nothing to do but enjoy."

"I'll kill him!" Brennan hissed.

"After we take a swim."

As they walked silently along, Brennan brooded about his lot in life. It was true. Their sergeant was a bully who had already been shot at one dark night by an unknown assailant. Missed, worse luck. And Brennan had a penchant for arguing, for talking about his rights as a free American. He had never been hungry enough, Mike thought, nor lonely enough to let these things pass—like the night rumblings of one's stomach protesting a miserable meal, but a meal nonetheless.

From across the river drifted the faint sounds of laughter distorted by the distance. They were played with by the wind as if the sounds were a flock of birds moving this way and that on the currents of air. At once unified, yet separate and distinct, alternately coming into the focus to stay a moment, then disappearing.

Brennan looked up, eyes alert. "I think I hear the cooing of doves."

Mike smiled as they slowed their pace and kept under cover, moving along the bank. "Ahh," Mike sighed, holding Brennan back with an outstretched hand.

There across the river four brown-skinned young ladies were demurely bathing, laughing and splashing each other playfully. The two young soldiers squatted on their haunches and watched silently through a screen of brush. The girls had waded out waist deep, their long hair pulled and tied behind their heads, their breasts shiny from the reflection of sun on water.

"Those poor dears," Brennan whispered. "It must be colder than a sergeant's heart out there."

"And you have the remedy, I suppose."

Brennan smiled. "Look at that one. The little one on the right. Oh, I love you, darling," he whispered across the river. "I've only seen you once and more than modesty allows, but I love you anyway. Maybe more because I've seen more of you."

Mike had continued to look in silence, thinking his own private thoughts. There were no favorites. He watched them all in turn. Brown-skinned honeys whose complexions shaded from palest tan to deepest brown.

"Would you ever think," Mike finally said, "that there could be such variation in shape and color. And all girls from the same town in the same country."

"Let's go down there. Let's go take our swim before they go away."

Without responding, Mike crawled away from their vantage point and waved his companion to follow. He led the way back up the trail to that invisible point where they had first heard the laughter.

"What the hell are you doing?" Brennan asked.

"We've got to give them a warning," Mike answered softly. Then he started to whistle, and he let out a shout in sheer exuberance as he turned and walked noisily toward the river. The laughter seemed to be louder now, more shrill, faster.

When the young soldiers turned past the last cover of foliage onto the open riverbank, they slowed their pace, not knowing what to expect. It was silent now. Only the faint sounds of the Río Grande flowing toward the Gulf of Mexico. Even the Mexican army band was silent. Mike stopped on the slight rise and felt Brennan stop beside him. The four young ladies had all turned, still waist deep in the water, unashamed in their nudity, frozen like beautiful brown statues.

The two young men and four young women looked at each other for a moment in silence from opposite banks of the river. Then the girls turned, almost in slow motion, and in low voices that carried soft as a whisper, held an undecipherable conversation that no doubt centered about what they were to do.

"Halloo!" Brennan shouted, waving in what he hoped would be seen as a friendly gesture. "Don't be afraid! We won't harm you! For Christ's sake," he said in an undertone to Mike, "you know the language. Say something."

"¡No tengan miedo! ¡Somos amigos!"

They turned slowly toward each other again, like shy does ready to bolt if the young men came nearer. Mike and Brennan sensed this and stood still, hardly daring to even turn their heads.

"That little one," Brennan said. "Ask her her name. Tell her I'm crazy for her."

"¡No se espanten! ¡No más vamos a nadar!"

"They're not answering. What did you say to them? Ask her again."

"You just don't ask a girl's name so fast. We're enemy soldiers to them. I told them not to be afraid. We're just going for a swim."

"For God's sakes, ask her. Before they run away."

"¡Me llamo Miguel! ¡Mi amigo se llama Juan! ¿Cómo se llaman ustedes?"

The girls turned their heads toward each other slowly and once again exchanged words. Then their soft words became more distinct and bold. "¡Consuela! ¡Panchita! ¡Rosita! ¡María!" came across the water, followed by giggling.

"Is that just the name of one of them?" Brennan asked. "You know how these Mexican names are."

But Mike had watched closely as each girl had shouted the one name only. "The little one is Rosita."

Brennan waved his arms wildly. "¡Rosita!" he shouted. "¡Rosita! Beau-ti-ful! How do you say beautiful in Spanish?" he asked.

"Hermosa."

"¡Rosita! ¡Hermosa!"

Now she lifted her head alertly as if still listening, although the sound of the words had died away. Then, without haste, with a look of surprise on her face, she lifted her arms and folded them shyly across her breasts.

"Oh, God! Mike. Did you see that? Now I know I love her."

Not even removing his clothes, Brennan rushed to the river's edge, threw himself into the water, and thrashed out.

"Come back, you damn fool!" Mike shouted.

Now the girls were laughing at the crazy Americano. The sound of running footsteps grew louder and as Mike turned, a sentry burst through the brush, rifle in hand.

"Halt!" he shouted at the swimming figure. "Halt or I'll shoot!"

The thrashing stopped and Brennan paddled back to the bank of the river. Luckily the sentry was someone they knew. The girls, frightened, had waded from the water and were climbing up the opposite bank.

"¡Rosita!" Brennan shouted. "¡Mañana! How do you say 'here,' Mike?"

"Aquí."

"¡Rosita! ¡Mañana! ¡Aquí!"

"Come on out of there, Brennan," the sentry warned.

"He was just going for a swim," Mike said.

"I should turn you guys in. For all I know you were trying to swim across to join the Mexicans."

"Don't be silly." Brennan had walked out of the water and stood in the sunlight in his dripping uniform. He was ignoring the sentry, watching the girls disappear. Mike had started to walk back toward camp.

"Halt!" the sentry said. "Halt or I'll—"

"Oh, stow it, will you," Brennan said. "You take this all too seriously."

"If the sergeant should—"

"You know what the sergeant can do."

"You don't show the proper respect to a sentry of the United States Army who caught you consorting with the enemy." His face was red, and he held his rifle stiffly at port arms.

Mike walked back down the trail toward the sentry. "Aw, come on. We were only going for a swim like everybody else, and we saw those girls."

"They could have been decoys for Mexican soldiers waiting in ambush."

Mike looked at the sentry in surprise. He started to say "Don't be crazy," but thought better of it. What if the sentry decided to report them to their sergeant? "Yes," Mike said. "I hadn't thought of that."

"Be careful along the river," the sentry admonished.

Brennan was about to open his mouth, but Mike spoke before he could. "You're right. Thanks."

"Now you best get on back to camp."

They turned and picked their way along the trail, Brennan still dripping from his swim.

THE sentry had not needed to report them to their sergeant. They walked past him as they entered camp and Brennan's squishing boots and wet uniform were impossible to ignore. The sergeant took the bottle of Mexican brandy he had been bargaining for with a vendor and called them over. He checked with the sentries on duty along the river and had soon constructed his version of what had happened. Consorting with the Papists. Two days extra duty with restriction to camp and no more swimming. And if that wasn't enough, there would be more. Or hadn't one flogging taught Brennan anything?

Brennan brooded silently at supper. "It's only two days," Mike said.

"I'll kill him," Brennan said. "I'll kill the son-of-a-bitch."

Mike had stared at him. Brennan's complaint did not sound real. There was a tired, resigned quality to his words and tone. As if he had already decided upon something, but it was not to kill their sergeant. Just before taps Mike came upon him sitting alone on the outskirts of a campfire reading. Quickly he had folded the piece of paper and stuck it into his shirt pocket.

That night in their tent, Brennan lay on his back staring. "Tell me," he asked. "What did you dream about when you left Ireland?"

"Meat."

"Meat?"

"On the table. Any kind of meat. Lizard. Snake. Anything but potatoes. And a job. A permanent regular kind of a job that paid you enough that you could buy meat."

Brennan sighed. "You have the imagination of a peasant," he said. "I dreamed about my own place. My own home. With land around it. And trees. And my own little wife to greet me when I came in from the fields. With kids running alongside her shouting, 'Daddy! Daddy!' A family safe and happy in my own castle."

Mike turned on his side and looked at his friend. "You've decided already, haven't you?"

"Decided what?"

"You know."

"I don't know anything," Brennan said. "Except that I'm going to kill that bastard sergeant some day." But Mike could tell from his voice that he didn't mean it. He meant to do something else.

Mike had been asleep for some time when he heard the faint rustlings in the tent. He awoke with a fright, his heart pounding, to see his tentmate fully clothed and crawling out into the open campground.

"Brennan," he whispered. But Brennan had not heard him; he had disappeared. Hastily Mike dressed and stepped out, moving quietly so he would not be heard by the sentries. He ran quickly along the path that Brennan would probably follow to the river. The crazy fool! he thought. I have to bring him back.

At the site where they had seen the girls that previous morning, Mike saw the dark shape paddling strongly but quietly away from the bank. Mike ran even faster, kicking off his boots as he tried to get the swimmer's attention. "Brennan!" he called softly, afraid that a sentry might hear him. "Brennan, you damned fool!"

The swimmer did not seem to hear. Without thinking, Mike tossed his shoestring-tied boots around his neck and waded into the water. He swam strongly, turning so that the current added to the impetus of his efforts. When he caught Brennan he would persuade him to come back. Force him back if necessary. He was in midriver now, drifting south with the current so that he was below Brennan, who was closer to the Mexican side, swimming in an area made clear by moonlight.

"Deserter!" The shout rang clear through the quiet night air, even above the current of the river. A shot rang out, and Mike turned to look back upriver. Then another shot. "I think I got him!" the sentry shouted again. "Over there. He's getting close to the bank now." Then two more shots.

Frantic, Mike struggled even harder to reach the Mexican side, scrambling out of the water and keeping low as he ran toward cover. Christ! he thought. We're done for now. I'll never be able to get him back if he's been shot.

He headed upstream to look for Brennan. Some two hundred feet away he saw the dark shape struggling at the edge of the river, flopping like a fish on the end of a line. When he came up to him, he could see that Brennan was bleeding badly from two wounds. His struggle to get ashore ceased and when Mike pulled him from the water, the body was heavy as if it had settled into death.

From across the Río Grande the voices of the sentries still carried. "Hey! Charlie! I think there's another one." Then two shots in rapid succession.

Mike dragged Brennan away from the bank toward cover as two more shots sought him. Finally, out of breath and shaking with fear, he dropped onto the ground. He peered into Brennan's face, then felt for a pulse. There was none. He started to weep, placing his tired head on his arms as he lay on the ground. Minutes later the sounds of footsteps added to his terror. He looked up and there ahead under a tree was a squad of Mexican soldiers.

"Welcome to México, señores," one said in Spanish.

"MY friend was dead, Father," Miguel said to Tercero. "After they buried him they gave me what little he had. His pistol and ammunition which were in a waterproof pouch. His boots so that I had an extra pair. And this notice that, along with the thoughts of Rosita, sent him across the river."

Tercero took the folded and faded piece of paper:

"Soldiers! You have enlisted in time of peace to serve in that army for a specific term; but your obligation never implied that you were bound to violate the laws of God, and the most sacred rights of friends! The United States government, contrary to the wishes of a majority of all honest and honourable Americans, has ordered you to take forcible possession of the territory of a friendly neighbour, who has never given her consent to such occupation. In other words, while the treaty of peace and commerce between Mexico and the United States is in full force, the United States, presuming on her strength and prosperity, and on our supposed imbecility and cowardice, attempts to make you the blind instruments of her unholy and mad ambition, and force you to appear as the hateful robbers of our dear homes, and the unprovoked violators of our dearest feelings as men and patriots. Such villany and outrage, I know, is perfectly repugnant to the noble sentiments of any gentleman, and it is base and foul to rush you on to certain death, in order to aggrandize a few lawless individuals, in defiance of the laws of God and man!

"It is to no purpose if they tell you that the law for the annexa-

tion of Texas justifies your occupation of the Rio Bravo del Norte; for by this act they rob us of a great part of Tamaulipas, Coahuila, Chihuahua, and New Mexico; and it is barbarous to send a handful of men on such an errand against a powerful and warlike nation. Besides, the most of you are Europeans, and we are the declared friends of a majority of the nations of Europe. The North Americans are ambitious, overbearing, and insolent as a nation, and they will only make use of you as vile tools to carry out their abominable plans of pillage and rapine.

"I warn you in the name of justice, honour, and your own interests and self-respect, to abandon their desperate and unholy cause, and become peaceful Mexican citizens. I guarantee you in such case, a half section of land, or three hundred and twenty acres, to settle upon, gratis. Be wise, then, and just, and honourable, and take no part in murdering us who have no unkind feelings for you. Lands shall be given to officers, sergeants, and corporals, according to rank, privates receiving three hundred and twenty acres, as stated.

"If, in time of action, you wish to espouse our cause, throw away your arms and run to us, and we will embrace you as true friends and Christians. It is not decent nor prudent to say more. But should any of you render important service to Mexico you shall be accordingly considered and preferred.

> M. Arista
> Commander-in-chief of the
> Mexican Army
> Headquarters at Matamoros,
> April 20, 1846"

Tercero handed the sheet of paper back to Miguel. "So my friend was dead," Miguel said. "In the eyes of the army of the United States I was a deserter. In the eyes of the Mexican army I had come to join them. I should have gone to Mexico City to join other deserters who were to form their own battalion to be called San Patricio, Saint Patrick's Battalion. But that was not to be. The war began."

"Then the war has truly started?"

Miguel nodded. "At Matamoros. Just two days after I had swum the Río Grande. There were thirty other Americans there under the commander, Captain Riley. I . . . I acquiesced when they welcomed me. We fought in the battle with the artillery that laid waste to Fort Texas. A few days later, other troops of the Mexican army fought at Palo Alto and Resaca de la Palma."

The battle had lasted some two weeks after the artillery had begun the bombardment of the American fort across the river. At Matamoros they had been expecting a great victory. After all, was not right on their side? Ballrooms had been decorated for the celebration. There would be music and laughter. The women would dress in their finest. Happy day!

But the Battle of Matamoros went poorly. It became the Battle of Matamejicanos. The army retreated through the city in a rout. Halls were left half decorated. Citizens bolted their doors—as much from fear of Mexican troops as from the gringos. Inside the houses women wept and moaned. In some there was only fearful silence.

Outside the city the army panicked. General Arista ordered the troops to march toward Monterrey. Few seemed to hear the orders. In fear for their lives, they ran from the Americans, following blindly those who promised to lead the way to safety. Mike joined the mad stampede.

The Mexican cavalry overran the infantry, trampling their own comrades in their dash for safety. At the edge of the river a Catholic priest, Father Leary, held out his crucifix to hold back the panicked troops. They hesitated only for an instant, then rushed on, trampling him and others into the river, where those who were not already dead were drowned.

Out on the flat on the road from Matamoros, the battlefield was strewn with dead. One young girl—had it been Rosita?—wept piteously beside a fallen young soldier. When Mike looked back she was swishing flies from his bloodied head. Had it been her husband? Lover? Brother?

"I could no longer stand the madness of the war," Miguel said. "The ranks of the fleeing army dwindled each day. There was not enough leadership nor loyalty among the troops to enforce any kind of discipline. Desertions were the rule rather than the exception. Only fools continued on to Monterrey to be slaughtered."

At Camargo he had been assigned to a small party of messengers who were to carry the word to the outposts at Monterrey. He, the gringo who could speak Spanish, could give them the truth about American intentions and strength.

After Monterrey they were sent on to Chihuahua. Just before they had reached there and made their final report, they had been attacked by Apaches. He had been the only survivor. As he rode dazedly toward the town, he realized that he could ride on by. The information he had was old now and probably of little use. He would be just another of those many deserters from the Mexican army who had faded into the landscape. For most of all, he wanted to be out of the miserable war and alive.

Where did one go from Chihuahua? Certainly not toward Texas. Mike had seen enough of the Texas Rangers attached to the American army to know what awaited him there. Where the law was represented by cutthroats and bandits, there really was no law. And as a deserter to the hated Mexican side, he would be dealt with quickly and cruelly. So up the Chihuahua Trail, where with luck, he might take the Santa Fe Trail east toward Missouri, if he dared. Or perhaps he might find a place to settle and forget the past. So he joined a small group of traders on their way to El Paso del Norte.

It was in El Paso that he stole a priest's clothing. He felt badly about that. Guilty. In addition, he was taking the Lord's name in vain by wearing the clothes. It was from here that he set off alone, north along the Río Grande to places unknown. He would know when he found it. A place to stay put. To stop running. To forget his fears of the army—either army—and of the Apaches. He had traveled by night. Gone thirsty and hungry. That was nothing. Then his horse had died after they had crossed the Jornada del Muerto, Dead Man's March, and he had continued on foot until he had collapsed. The next thing he remembered was being in the hamlet of Los Bacas.

"As for my sins, Father. They have been many. Desertion. Twice. Stealing. A priest's clothing and more. Food. Water." He went on. No longer telling the story of how he came to be here, but of how he had offended God along the way. Tercero half closed his eyes and listened.

William Kennedy

BORN in 1928, William Kennedy made his living for most of his working life as a journalist while turning himself by dint of steady labor into a writer of fiction. His first novel, *The Ink Truck* (1969), appeared when he was over forty, and the books that followed had more than their share of rejections. However, in more recent times, solid publishing contracts, a MacArthur Foundation "genius grant," and work in the movies have changed his situation dramatically. Kennedy's extraordinary fiction now has a considerable audience, and he is famous in a literary way, with a secure reputation resting on his "Albany cycle" of novels. Three of these, *Legs* (1975), *Billy Phelan's Greatest Game* (1978), and *Ironweed* (1983), share a setting, New York's down-at-heels capital city; a time frame, roughly 1925 to 1938; and a vivid cast of characters both dead and alive, bums and bootlickers and honest workingmen, journalists, politicians, gamblers, and gangsters. A fourth, *Quinn's Book* (1988), is both a culmination and a new departure. Set in the middle of the nineteenth century, it involves ancestors of characters from the other novels and many curcial, shaping events of Irish American history.

What Kennedy's protagonists have in common is integrity (of sorts), and a resolute refusal of illusion or self-delusion. They include Legs Diamond (born John T. Nolan), underworld potentate and cold-blooded killer; Billy Phelan, small-time pool hustler of the Albany streets; and Daniel Quinn, Civil War correspondent and chronicler of his Irish American generation's ethnic experience. The least and greatest of these is Billy's father, Francis Phelan, an alcoholic vagrant, rail-riding Depression hobo, and twenty-year deserter of his family. And yet, in spite of all, Francis emerges as a plausibly heroic figure

holding to an austere set of values: "What he was was, yes, a
warrior, protecting a belief that no man could articulate, especially himself; but somehow it involved protecting saints from
sinners, protecting the living from the dead."

The Albany novels are strange, fascinating books, combin-
ing straightforward realism in the Irish American tradition of
James T. Farrell, blasé flights into the fantastic as in the "magic
realism" of South Americans such as Gabriel García Márquez,
and passages of compassionate lyricism—prose poetry, really—
reminiscent of the fictions of William Goyen and Faulkner.

Kennedy has acknowledged the legacy of his Irish American
forerunners, especially Farrell and Edwin O'Connor. Because
these earlier writers blazed certain trails through their shared
ethnic world, Kennedy has been free to strike out on his own.
He wanted to be surreal in a way that Farrell was not, and he
wanted to be harshly realistic in a way that O'Connor was not.
And so we have the Albany novels, which mix hard, gritty
realism with a surreal lyricism of great beauty in the depiction
of, among other things, an Irish American underclass of ruthless criminals, gamblers, and the homeless. Certainly, Kennedy
has his own full sense of his inheritance, and his own hard road
has given him a special appreciation for Farrell's example: "But
you think of Farrell. He never quit. It's an admirable thing,
because he was getting pleasure out of what he was doing. If
there are enough people who understand that, if there are other
writers getting some pleasure out of reading your twenty-eighth
novel, then maybe that's enough."

Kennedy begins *O, Albany!*, his nonfiction meditation on
his native city, by declaring himself "a person whose imagination has become fused with a single place." This "urban biography" combines the author's personal memories of the city and
its people with oral histories and historical documents. The
result is a bubbling pot of "memory and hearsay," a yeasty
sourcebook of the materials from which Kennedy's fiction continues to emerge.

—*Charles Fanning*

SINCE North Albany is and will remain a place of childhood, then it has no business changing or declining or metamorphosing. I will have none of that, and so you must look elsewhere for its modern particulars, bad cess to them. This is, arbitrarily, capriciously, the way it is with memory: a winter morning in the mid-1930s at 620 North Pearl Street, Eddie Carey's apartment house, and my mother is going down the front stoop on her way to work. She is about the sixth step from the bottom when her foot flies outward and she bumpity-bumps downward, coat twisted, hat knocked cockeyed. She is flummoxed and bruised and her glasses are broken, a newly arrived bundle on the sidewalk ice. Just then a young Greek on his way to work in a meat market up the street comes by and tips his hat to my mother, says, "Good morning, Mrs. Kennedy," carefully steps over her, and keeps walking. My mother accumulates herself, climbs back to our first-floor apartment to restructure her condition, and brings to the family a new understanding of Greek restraint. In the winter of another season we are living across the street at 607 in one of Eddie Carey's one-family houses and I am going out into the cold morning with freshly pressed cassock and surplice that I will wear to carry a candle at my first funeral mass. I will be let out of class at nine-fifteen at P.S. 20 (for this was the age when public schools cooperated with young boys who aspired to sainthood) to be on the altar when mass begins at nine-thirty. Father John J. O'Connor, pastor of Sacred Heart Church, celebrates the mass and then dons a special robe to fling holy water and incense at the dead man's coffin down there in the middle aisle. Back in the sacristy, I stand behind the priest as he starts to disrobe. He presents his back to me, disconnects his collar clasp. I am expected to take

the flowing robe from him and fold it, but I am so new at
funerals I am utterly unaware of this. "I knew you were dumb,
but I didn't think you were numb," the priest says to me and
hurls the robe at another boy. Heretofore Father O'Connor
mainly bored me. His sermons lacked verve. I didn't like him
much but I didn't think negatively about him because in the
second grade I had been quarantined with scarlet fever and he
came to the house and at our improvised altar gave me First
Communion. But as time went on and as I discovered he gave
harsh penances in confession (four rosaries, three stations of
the cross) and thought me numb and dumb, I reappraised him
and realized he was a mean-minded son of a bitch and I was
delighted when he was eventually transferred from Sacred
Heart to a rural parish for reasons never made public. Father
John J. Fearey, the assistant pastor, was the saintly priest you
went to for confession. You'd been sinning like a maniac all
week: robbing blind people, kicking cripples, coveting eight or
ten of your neighbors' wives and daughters, eating hamburgers
on Friday, going to movies that were listed Objectionable in
Part by the *Evangelist,* and you go in and tell your achievements to Father Fearey and he says, Ah, well, now, be a good
boy and say three Hail Marys and a good Act of Contrition.
Next? Joe Keefe might have been next but there he was, fighting Dixie Davis, a new kid, up on School 20's athletic field
across from my house, and it is one of the great fights of the
age. The combatants start at the north end of the two gravel
tennis courts where Charlie Bigley and his father are playing
singles, and they flail and thwack their way down the field to
the other end of the tennis courts, by the school. Joe's nose is
bleeding and I am of course rooting for him because he is my
buddy. But Dixie is getting in his licks. I think Joe might be
winning when his mother appears and says it is time he came
home and cut the hedges, which leaves it all unfinished. I
vaguely remember Joe and Dixie pledging to resume the combat but I'm not sure it ever happened. Nosebleeds were the
badge of victory because the bleeder usually quit. Only Joe
didn't. Buddy Salvador said he was not going to let anybody
know his nose was his weak spot or that he was a quick bleeder,
for they'd go for the nose right away. I never remember any-

body going for anything having to do with Buddy because he hit the long ball and was the guy you picked first in a choose-up game and had all the muscles a kid needed on Erie Street. That was the street where Dolly McAuley lived, a little dark-haired spinster (I think she colored her hair on into her seventies or even eighties) with a front room that had the sweet odor of antiquity to it. It probably dated to the 1860s, or earlier, with a huge ornate and always-shining silver stove in its center, great gilt-framed ancestors who overpowered what remained of the little room, and lace doilies and samplers and converted kerosene lamps and brocaded curtains with matching shawls on the horsehair chairs. I sat in this room with six dresses that had to be hemmed for my mother, and four white shirts with collars that had to be turned for my father, and Dolly would say, Yes, you can pick them all up Thursday, and on Thursday she would charge you thirty cents, or maybe sixty. Or maybe it was thirty cents to turn a collar, but how, you wondered, could she subsist on such earnings, unless she was still on the 1860 economy? Jim Yee, the Chinese laundryman on Broadway, charged fifteen cents to turn your shirt from a *sughan,* as my father would say, back into a garment suitable for dinner parties. Witty, toothless Chinaman (as everybody called anybody who looked Chinese, even if they came from Japan), Jim came to Albany after the First World War and survived into the Korean War (and beyond), when China was no longer an ally but the enemy, and so when you talked to him about China he smiled and pressed your shirt. Down the street from Dolly McAuley (she may have been related to Jimmy McAuley the ironworker, one of the toughest citizens the North End ever produced—he was in the Twenty-seventh Division in 1918, and on the ship going to France he fought the ship's champion and licked him) was where Eddie Carey had his North End Contracting Company and next door to him was where Father Francis Maguire established Sacred Heart Church in 1874: a pastor on horseback with a whip in his hand and a powerful fist that was called into use by neighbors in the age before they could ever, or would ever, think of calling in the police to stop a fight. Father Fearey, in a later age, confronted a husband just up the street from us in time to save the wife of the family from another uppercut, and then thrashed the husband to within an inch of the sod, advising him that the laying-on of hands was the province of thy God and my God, the Father. And I, as perhaps you have noticed, must be about my Father's business, so get up and leave the old girl alone. Father Maguire hated Erie Street because of the pigs and chickens that plagued his church during mass every time somebody left the church door ajar. But it was only temporary, for the funding of the real church was under way, and please, no donations over a hundred dollars (an exception being the Cassidy family—William Cassidy owned the *Albany Argus*—who donated the marble altar). Groundbreaking, with the help of mighty backs of the faithful themselves, began in 1876 and the church was finished in 1880, fourteen steps up now to the new sanctuary (at North Second and Walter streets) ensuring that only the most intrepid porkers could make it to mass. Out of that sanctuary in my time came six altar boys I knew well—Jackie Barnes, Red Robinson, Joe Girzone, and the three Kennedy brothers: Mike (I once saw him throw a football two and a half miles), John, and Tom. Jackie, Red, Joe, Mike, and John became priests, Tom a Christian Brother, for wasn't the cloth the grandest thing a young man could wear? I remember aspiring thus, but not beyond seventh grade, for even by then I intuited my embrace of the profane: I was drawing cartoons, printing my own newspaper, fixated on the world of print. I gave up drawing, perhaps in part intimidated by my betters: Billy Callagy, who could copy things and improve on the originals; and Bobby Burns, who invented complete comic strips, the hero of one unforgettably named Pimplepuss Perry. Bobby ran a clandestine dart game in his cellar that began to draw postprandial patrons about six-thirty. He was a double-twenty hustler with a spring in his arm and his knee that gave him a three-foot edge on the rest of us, and he financed most of his evenings at these games. Those evenings were usually spent at Mike DeTommasi's grocery store at Broadway and Bonheim Street, across from the Bond Bakery. On any given balmy night in 1940 or 1941 there might be thirty-five boys on the corner: Joe Sevrons (who worked for Mike), Ray Olcott, Jimsy Burns, Georgie Boley, Neil Gray, Billy Allen, Jack Dugan, Bob Linzey, the Blocksidge brothers, the Kennedy brothers, Ted Flint, Lou Pitnell (the younger), Danny Bobeck, Gordon Jalet with his miniature one-armed roulette wheel, accepting all bets. If it had been a hot summer day probably half the crowd would have been to Mid-City Park to swim. We sifted sand at Mid-City's beach in late May to earn a season pass to swim in Albany's best public pool, owned by Henry Gratton Finn, a bowlegged, curly-white-maned Irish macho who strutted around the pool in his ur-bikini like Charles Atlas. He had once ridden in a circus with Buffalo Bill, and had run off with the Upside-Down Man's wife from one such show, perhaps while the Upside-Down Man was sliding down the wire on his head. Finn also owned Mid-City's skating rink, for which Howard Pugh, whose singular sense of humor often involved a resonanat burp, had a predilection. Howard would, incomprehensibly to me, stare down from the rink's small balcony, enthralled by the skaters going round and round, a vision about as exciting to me as watching the weeds turn brown in October. There were girls down there, and I knew that as well as Howard and the rest of our crowd, but I was more enlivened when a carnival came to town—the O. C. Buck shows or the James Strates shows, among many. Gambling for useless gimcracks at these carnivals was very important, as was attendance at the sideshow to see the hydra-headed woman, the alligator-skinned hermaphrodite, and the human fetus kept alive by Spontaneous Electrolysis. The high dive, if they had one, was a high point, but far and away the most significant attraction was the kootch show, where you always watched the outdoor preview on the elevated platform in front of the tent, and sometimes even went inside, unless you were with a girl. I saw my first stripper at the O. C. Buck Show with Bobby Burns. After the first performance (thirty-five cents a ticket) they announced a second and special show for fifty cents extra in the back of the tent, and with some trepidation we paid and entered and saw a voluptuary named Carmen remove the ultimate garment before the eyes of a double dozen of us, I certainly the youngest. Carmen sat on the edge of a chair, then took the hat off a man at the rim of the stage in front of her, and passed the hat provocatively over her body. Some hooted and whistled at this sight, though I think my awe prevented such effusion. My thought was that the man would have to dispose of the hat immediately after the show but from the look of him in memory I wonder now if he perhaps did not take it home and have it bronzed. Walking home, Bob said to me that that was the closest I would ever get to a woman's anatomy until I was married and I thought that rather a pity: What a fate for such a sinner as I. Alas, Bob's prophecy proved incorrect but I will save that story for another day to give it its due. At this point my education in sensuality was largely restricted to party games, most notably at Patsy Selley's house, where Post Office was not only permitted but was the unstated reason that no one ever turned down an invitation, including the most significant and beautiful girls of our set. In what other province of North Albany society could a grammar-school undergraduate gain first-hand experience on how to behave when he found himself alone with a girl in a dark room? Patsy, a beautiful child with long curls like Shirley Temple's, danced on pointe in white toe shoes and tutu whenever our classes were called upon for performing artistry. I played banjo, but not while she danced. Or maybe I did. Maybe I played "The One Rose," and then Bob Burns would draw cartoons on an easel onstage and amaze us all. The vixens among us distinguished themselves offstage in a different style. Jean Pitnell went for older men, high-school freshmen, when she was still in seventh grade. Chloe Wood broke one of Bob Hancox's front teeth with a right cross and it was love in bloom for months thereafter. Ruth Hesser listed her order of preferences: Bill Callagy, then Bob Hancox, and me in the show position. She told us this while all three of us were climbing an apple tree to impress her. The girls of the North End were always a treasure to be zealously guarded—more so, perhaps, in my father's truculent time, and the time of Jack Murray, my next-door neighbor who became postmaster and president of Albany's Common Council. "If anybody came up from the South End and got out of line or started fooling around with the North End girls, then they got more than they were looking for," said Jack. But North Enders ran the same risk when they went to dances on South End turf, for neighborhoods were psychologically sovereign states where any intruder had to prove himself free of inimical design before he was given a visa. The North End lent itself to exclusion by its geography. Only Broadway—the Troy Road—ran through it on its way north. This was the main artery until 1925, when a bill sponsored in the Common Council by then-Alderman Jack Murray approved the cut-through for North Pearl Street, which until that time had dead-ended northbound at Pleasant Street. The cut-through opened Pearl to connect with its North End self, which began again at Emmett Street and ran into Menands. Eddie Carey built about thirty houses on Pearl between North First Street and Lawn Avenue, most of them one- and two-family homes, plus two apartment buildings (I lived in all three types), and created the style for the neighborhood: front and back yards, front and back porches, attic and full basement, garages attached to the one-families. Carey built about fifty houses in all, the first ten completed in 1925, and these, said a newspaper reporter, "wrought a miracle in the physical appearance of North Albany." The new School 20 was completed in 1923 on the site of the old North End School, fronting on North Pearl. And behind it, rising up to the ridge of Van Rensselaer Boulevard, were the hills that had been part of John Brady's farm. Before that the land had been a piece of the Patroon's feudal domain, called Rensselaerwyck, different from the Patroon's other domain, known as Beverwyck, the original part of the city. Jeremias Van Rensselaer, son of the first Patroon (Kiliaen Van Rensselaer), had established Rensselaerwyck with its center about at Tivoli Street. In time a manor house was built there on fertile flatland east of where Broadway runs, at the edge of what came to be called the Patroon Creek, once the main source of city water, and which still courses down to the river from the western highland. A colony of workers and servants grew around the Manor House and in time the settlement was called the Colonie, and annexed to Albany in 1815. This was the beginning of the North End. By the 1850s lumber was almost as important to the North Enders as Jesus and a good glass of ale, for the Lumber District had grown up between the river and the Erie Canal. The city was so proud of its leading enterprise that it called itself the White Pine Center of the World. On July 8, 1854, the District had forty-six firms, seven doing more than half a million dollars in business annually, twenty-nine over $100,000. The District ran northward from the sheltered harbor, known as the Basin, along the Erie Canal, to Lock Number 2 at North Street in North Albany. The logs came down the Canal, were turned into lumber in the District's sawmills (their boilers fired by wood shavings) and put on riverboats waiting at the slips that connected the Canal to the Hudson. My father remembered a social group called the Lumber Handlers. "All of Limerick was in that," he said, Limerick being the name of the North End. The Moulders was another such group he remembered, with many North Enders in it who worked at the foundries—Rathbone, Sard's, on Ferry Street, which employed 2,700 workers in 1885, making 220,000 stoves a year. The Lumber Handlers and the Moulders ran annual affairs in Union Hall, Downtown at Hudson Avenue and Eagle Street, until they put in roller polo and spoiled the dance floor's cork center with the skates. They put a new floor in, said my father, but it was never the same. My father and Bill Corbett, who worked for the post office, were almost the same age and both remembered learning to swim in the Canal (you were thrown in and swam or sank). They remembered Lagoon Island, an amusement park that ran down, and then P. J. Corbett, Bill's father, built it back up and called it Al-Tro (for Albany-Troy) Park on the Hudson, a grand place. Later still it was Dreamland, all of these near the foot of Garbrance Lane in Menands, and accessible by boat and foot. The last such place was not on the water but on the Troy Road. It was called Mid-City Park and it had a roller coaster and merry-go-round, pool and skating rink. It was fading seriously in the Depression years, though the pool and rink persisted. It stood next to Hawkins Stadium, the home of the Albany Senators in the Eastern League (Class A baseball). In an earlier age Albany had been in the International and State leagues, its games played at Chadwick Park, about where Hawkins was. Before that the Senators played at Riverside Park in Rensselaer, where Dewey Begley, a lifelong North Ender, remembers the players knocking the ball into the river. Dewey had a future as a pitcher, and was ready to go with the St. Louis Cardinals when he got such a pain in his back a doctor ordered him to stop playing. It turned out to be a kidney stone, and instead of going to the big leagues Dewey went on the police force for forty-two years, retiring as a captain. Professional ball was also played in Dewey's day at Island Park, where the Menands Bridge begins. The circus pitched its tent near the bridge in the 1930s and 1940s. In earlier eras the circus had come to Peacock Park in North Albany, where the Niagara Mohawk Power Company (the gasworks before it went straight) now stands. In my time the circus unloaded behind Union Station, Downtown, and every year at three in the morning on circus day Lou Pitnell and his father would be on the siding, watching it all happen. I made that scene only once, content generally to sit on the front porch at home and see the line of animals and wagons course through North Albany at a more civilized hour. The circus lions got loose in Menands once, and in the 1950s there was an elephant crisis. *Times-Union* city editor Barney Fowler put through some elephant photos that came from circus press agents and they appeared in print the next morning. Later that day when the circus itself arrived and some elephants broke loose and wandered around Downtown, an intrepid *Times-Union* photographer snapped them on their spree. Barney duly submitted the spectacular photos to Ed Nowinski, the news editor, who rejected them. We had elephants yesterday, said Ed. A vivid moment in my personal animal coverage was the obituary I wrote on Langford, widely known North Albany cat. He'd undergone surgery for a tumor and seemed to be recovering, but then, as his owner, Jerome Kiley, who cleaned beer coils for a living, told a gathering at Jack's Lunch, "Langford took a turn for the worse and they had to gas him." Mourners at Jack's chipped in six dollars for a floral wreath of pussy willows with a bird atop them and a card in the bird's beak with the message to the departed: "I don't have to worry about you anymore." Jim Dempsey, who was ninety-four when we talked, raffled off another cat during a fund-raiser for Sacred Heart Church in the early 1890s. A plaster-of-Paris cat was the presumed prize, but it was really a neighborhood cat Jim had stuffed into a box. Father Francis Toolan was pastor and a crowd gathered as Jim spun the raffle wheel. Professor O'Brien, principal of School 20, won and Jim handed over the box. When O'Brien took the cover off, the cat jumped out and ran away. "Father Toolan laughed till he cried," said Jim, "and Prof O'Brien didn't speak to me for a week." My father remembered another animal disaster: Hunky Bucher, who went hunting in Lamb's Lot with a shotgun taller than himself, shot a goat and had to pay a fine. Hunky stepped off his stoop one night, unaware that Dike Dollard, the paving contractor, had moved it to put in a sidewalk. "Hunky took one step," said my father, "and walked right off the edge. If he hadn't of been drunk he'd have died." More serious problems came in with the winter months. In mid-December in the nineteenth century when the Hudson froze solid and no lumber moved, the North End women smoked and salted meat and preserved vegetables, and men went to work cutting ice on the river, their teams of horses hauling huge blocks of ice up the frozen riverbanks. Jim Dempsey was around in 1890 when electric trolleys replaced the horsecars, but that didn't happen in the Lumber District, where the horsecar continued its run until about 1920; and its departure then meant the District was all through. Lumber supplies from the Adirondacks had already been dwindling in the 1890s, and by 1915 were all but exhausted. Lumber mills closed, the twenty-five-foot lumber piles vanished (Kibbee's was one of the last to go). And then the foundries left, the result of new Western ore sources and their owners' desire to situate their plants near coal mines. "The face of the neighborhood changed," Jack Murray said. The Eastern Tablet Company and the Albany Paper Works, both spin-offs from the lumber, opened up, and the Albany Felt Mill developed, providing new employment for North Enders. Skilled workers found jobs at Simmons Machine Tool, run by Charlie Simmons, a self-made millionaire who started as a machinist in the West Albany railroad shops; or they went with Ramsey Chain, founded by James H. Ramsey. Abetted by the money of millionaire Anthony Brady Farrell, Ramsey manufactured his own invention, the silent chain drive, next door to Simmons Machine in Menands, beginning in the 1920s. Everyone knew the Lumber District was gone for good when Dinny Ronan's Lumber District Saloon closed. His son Andrew kept on with the family grocery business, which had begun by serving canalboats and came to be the North End's largest grocery. Andy was also close to the O'Connells. "He could be very helpful if you were looking for something," said Jack Murray. "You couldn't make a move without him," said my father. Dan and Ed O'Connell came to the North End every Sunday for conferences with Ronan and other North End Democrats—Judge Brady, and Mike Conners (Dick's father), the insurance man, and Big Jim Carroll, my great-grandfather, and Will Cook, a noted orator who nominated Al Smith for governor during a Democratic convention at Saratoga and took a trolley to get there. The men met at the Phoenix Club, a small and pudgy brick building at Broadway and North First Street, a relic that had been the Patroon's land office, and to which the farmers of Rensselaer-wyck brought their rent in the form of tribute—corn, produce, hens, and chickens. Bill Corbett remembered the Phoenix Club's interior decor: "A pool table, a card table, and a lot of conversation." Some of the North End Democrats had been leaders before Dan's takeover, during the age when being a Democrat in this city was mostly a badge of honor. It got you little else, for the city was controlled by Billy Barnes, the Republican boss. Yet in the North End the Democrats always boasted that their ward, the Ninth, was the only one that never went Republican in the Barnes years. Homage to this solidarity was paid by the Republicans in the first decade of the century when they redistricted in order to move Gardner's boarding-house on Broadway, Downtown (near Orange Street), out of the Sixth Ward and into the Ninth, so its thirty-five Republican votes could perhaps tip a scale or two in the solidly Democratic North End—this desperate move recalled by Tim Lyden, a Sixth Ward Democratic alderman in a later age. Irish Democrats might have united against the enemy but they fought one another viciously, Big Jim Carroll once pulling Tom Martin off a trolley in order to knock him down for good and sufficient political reason. Rampant Democratic factionalism was encouraged by Barnes and was one of the secrets of his success. The O'Connells understood this and when they assumed power in the party they imposed a new harmony on it, centering control in their own ward leader, Joe Henchey, who would later become sheriff and remain leader of the Ninth Ward until his death in the 1950s. Henchey was a mystery to me as a child, merely a man with power I didn't understand. But I remember him vividly in a light-plaid, double-breasted suit with high collar, a very tight and carefully knotted tie, and rimless spectacles, walking up from the middle of our block, where he lived, and passing our house on a spring evening—no, it is early summer, but he is nevertheless wearing that tie, and he tips his sailor straw hat to my grandmother, who is sitting on our front porch after dinner, she having watered the geraniums and now waiting for Eddie Cantor to sing to her over the radio. Joe smiles from a face that is wrinkling badly and walks on to only God knows where, around the corner and down to Broadway, perhaps, to catch the Downtown bus. The trolleys were no longer running on Broadway and even the tracks had been taken up to be turned into shrapnel we assumed would be used against the Japanese. Some people were calling Jim Yee a Jap, which brought out the worst in his Chinese vocabulary. Bobby Burns was in the Navy by now, as was Bob Linzey. Charlie Bigley was a Marine, Ray Olcott was in the Navy Air Corps, Russ Blocksidge the Army Air Corps. We who were a shade too young to enlist or be drafted kept up with the progress of our friends through the picture gallery in the window of the elder Louie Pitnell's barbershop across from the carbarns. Snapshots, wallet photos, one or two eight-by-tens (I seem to remember Joe Murphy with a bomber and crew pictured on one of those—I think Joe was a pilot) were pinned up as families brought them along to Lou. Joe Keefe had an ear problem and the services wouldn't take him, so he enrolled in the Merchant Marine Academy and served that way and had the best-looking uniform of anybody in the war. Georgie Boley went into the Navy Air Corps and one day we heard he was dead. Then we heard Charlie Bigley, whose tennis serve I could never return, had caught it on the first wave at Saipan. Shadow Britt, a Marine, also caught it, and Joe Christian, who ran a pretzel business, lost two of his sons to the fighting. The score on all these matters was kept by both Sacred Heart Church and School 20, and for years after when you went to mass or into the school to vote, you saw the names and the gold stars on the Honor Roll. Those rolls are gone now, the war so very far away. Vinny Marzello went into the Navy Air Corps as a V-5 and came out of Quantico and transferred to the Marines as a fighter pilot, fought in the Pacific and survived. In the Korean War as a Marine pilot he destroyed a Communist MiG-15 in aerial combat, flew 142 missions, won eight Air Medals and two Distinguished Flying Crosses, and rose to the rank of captain. Then, in September 1954, on a routine flight as a test pilot, he failed to clear some trees at Atlantic City and never ejected. I liked Vinny a lot (he was a big kid, I was a little kid, and I'd look for him after mass to say hello) because he sold me his record player for fifteen dollars, the best acquisition of my life after my bicycle. I'd already bought a Tommy Dorsey record, "Not So Quiet Please," for the great drum solo by Buddy Rich, even before I owned a player. For two months before I got Vinny's machine I would take the record out and look at it and try to remember how the solo went, for the banjo was going out of style and I'd decided playing the traps was a nobler goal. I was wrong again, but children are supposed to be wrong, otherwise they would be as infallible as adults. This was the age of Glenn Miller and Artie Shaw and Harry James and Bing Crosby, who had a look-alike in my neighborhood: Ben Burns. Ben played golf, too, like Bing, and had Bing's smiling and genial personality. The difference was that Ben was for real and Bing turned out to be an authoritarian punk. The Andrews Sisters were very big and had a record, "Rum and Coca-Cola," that was so popular you couldn't buy a copy any place. Also you couldn't hear it on the radio because of the risqué lyrics about a mother and a daughter both working for the Yankee dollar you know how. When my uncle Pete McDonald got word of my deprivation, he convinced a Downtown bartender to take the record off the jukebox, and Pete brought it home to me, scratched all to hell, but invaluable, for playing the new records was a collective pastime as important as baseball or darts or hanging out at Mike's. It was what you did when it was raining or you were too exhausted to do anything else, though I don't remember much exhaustion in those days. The action seemed endless: tennis, ball games always, in all seasons, even playing with the older men, Andy and Jim and Red and Knockout Lawlor, all brothers, and Joe Murphy (not the pilot), who had played, I think, with Elmira, and Walt (Pansy) McGraw and Pete McDonald and Emerson Judge and John (Bandy) Edmunds, maybe the best baseball player the North End ever produced, a shortstop who went off to play in the big leagues but wouldn't put on a uniform, got homesick, came home a week later, and spent the rest of his life as a hoseman at the Engine Eight (Eightsies) Fire House at North First and Broadway, to which his sister Marie would walk five blocks down and five blocks back home carrying him a hot lunch in a picnic basket. These men gathered—not often enough—after dinner to chase flies and grounders and show us how it was done. Andy Kean would show up with a baseball doctor's kit full of thread and needles and thimbles and beeswax and scissors and tape to repair and do preventive maintenance on the assorted baseballs that those stalwarts were so anxious to knock the cover off of the way they used to. In the daylight hours when there was no game there was the wilderness of the old Brady farm, the Hills, which spread out between North Pearl at the bottom and Van Rensselaer Boulevard at the top, and this was a magical setting— open, grassy slopes that probably had been grazing land for decades and that abutted a gully (we called it the Gully) down which placidly coursed a creek (we called it the Creek) and up which you could walk like Natty Bumppo, beginning in the lowland swamp with its cattails and then into the apple-and-crabapple-tree zone that was all that remained of what I now assume was a Brady orchard, and then into the shallow beginnings of the Gully, where I took my first (and only) chew of tobacco and threw up, and up the rising gorge toward the Indian Ladder, rather steep on each side and across which someone, I think it was Jimmy Becker, felled an oak tree as a bridge, and up farther to the Cowboy Ladder—loose shale, down and up which you had to climb simply because it was there, and of course you slid and cut yourself and ruined your pants but that was what you were supposed to do. At night there was tennis and if the ball game hadn't started, or was over, you could take a seven iron and loft golf balls at the setting sun and the early moon. If no one was around to give you a game of anything you could take a rubber ball and go to one of two ledges at the side of School 20 and throw the ball against them, and if you caught either of the ledges just right the ball would not bounce back at you as usual but make a pop fly of itself, and so even in solitude the game was afoot. You were never solitary for very long, anyway, for it was an Irish neighborhood that believed in over-population. It was the same at the diner in a later year when you came home from the movies alone on the bus and stopped for a hamburger or a Danish or buttered toast. If there was no one there you just waited and they'd come, although you really didn't need them in the diner because there was always Rex, the English waiter, a witty magpie who showed off by carrying too many dishes at once, and Herbie Leahy, the night manager, who had great style. I remember him serving a cup of coffee with the panache of Humphrey Bogart, though he looked more like Richard Widmark. The diner was on Broadway, just north of North Third Street, next door to the Nehi bottling company. I seem to remember its arriving, all glistening chrome and red leatherette, one afternoon around 1937. It lasted into the 1960s but its real importance was in the war years, when you went there as ritual. Rex served my grandmother a French cruller with her tea one night and because it had vast, uninhabited space inside it she called it a Gone With The Wind and so did we all, ever after. Marge Keefe, a dark-haired beauty from Rensselaer, worked there as one of the first waitresses. She remembered Ralph Kiner coming in for coffee when he was playing for the Albany Senators and she remembered another player's refusing to sit next to a black man at the counter and bawling out the owner for letting blacks in. H. H. Monette, the owner, often had to provide transportation for his short-order cooks, who seemed to be occupationally drunk most of the time and not always sure what day it was. He would corral them at their fleabag hotel, then stop at King Brady's saloon, across the street from the diner, and get them a few shots to rev them up, at which point they would confront the grill and the frying pans with a smiling vigor, however artificially induced. Marge also remembered one man named Rummy who was cutting baloney with a butcher knife, his hand shaking so badly she feared for his thumb; and when she told Kenny Sharples, the day manager, the problem, Kenny bought Rummy another set of doubles at Brady's and that got him and his thumb safely through the lunch-hour rush. You couldn't always get into

Brady's, there being laws against serving alcohol on Sunday before one p.m. Brady's had a side door for customers in severe need but not everyone was let in, and some who weren't brought their own bottle to the diner and spiked their coffee with it after mass while waiting for the oasis to reappear on the corner. Marge remembered that her best tip, five bucks, came from one such anxious customer, whose bankroll matched his gratitude for small favors, like that essential cup of coffee. Marge's good looks and other endowments did not escape the eye of my uncle Peter, who brought his sisters to the diner to meet her, and when they approved he took my grandmother to lunch there to clinch the deal, and Pete and Marge were married fourteen or maybe it was sixteen years later, either figure a normal courting interlude for Irish aspirants to bonding. The diner ran out of food on V-J Night in 1945, not even a slice of bread left, and closed its doors for the first time because of the orgiastic all-night revel in peace. When you think of that peace settling in, and no war to seal the fate of your friends, then you look elsewhere for how people died strangely or prematurely. Alice Moffat, with a doll's face and pigtails, was killed sleigh riding: a car hit her. I think she was in fourth grade. A terrific neighbor, with a marvelous but sad smile, hanged himself one morning while the family was at church, and another neighbor I didn't know took the pipe in his garage. An elderly Irish woman who lived alone and was the best buddy and chief antagonist of my Aunt Libby, died and was buried without a wake: her son hated her and refused her the final farewell of the few friends she had left in the world. Russ Blocksidge died young in the Veterans Hospital. Ray Olcott came out of the service, went to college for a time and drove a cab but didn't like civilian life anymore. He was a cowboy at the wheel and claimed to have made it from downtown Albany to midtown Troy once in twelve minutes, which I think is physically impossible even on superhighways, but maybe not. Anyway, Ray wanted to fly, really, and reupped, in the Air Force this time, and wound up as a pilot in Korea. He was a Lutheran and wrote to Bobby Burns when he was into his fortieth or so mission that Bob should pray to J.C. for him. Bob wrote back that J.C. didn't listen to Lutherans and had an ear only for Catholics, but would pray anyway. The prayer didn't work. On his forty-ninth mission Ray's plane was shot down over North Korea. His two crewmen bailed out but Ray was wounded and went down with his plane. He was listed as missing, and still is, I think, but everybody agreed he was dead except his mother, who lived into the late 1970s insisting he was still alive in China. Bill Corbett's son Billy (called Snorko) was a classmate of mine in grammar school. He was a handsome, loose-limbed lefty who threw his bat after he hit a pitch, and so standing close to him at the plate was risky. He and I skipped school once when we were high-school sophomores and went to a dumb Claudette Colbert movie and got caught and reamed out by everybody. He fell ill with leukemia and lingered awhile in the hospital, but then at the age when the rest of us were heading for college, or a full-time job, Snorko died. The first death I saw close at hand was my mother's uncle, Johnny Carroll, who ran the North End Filtration Plant for the city, built in 1898 under the city's largest contract ever, $300,000, to filter Hudson River water when it was still filterable. But by the 1930s the plant was only standby equipment, a ghostly place where Johnny took me when I was looking for a sink to furnish my chemistry laboratory in the cellar of our house. He found one that probably dated to 1902 and had it trucked to my house and installed; and there the mad scientist of North Pearl Street learned how to use his Gilbert Chemistry Set to make green dye and fizzly gunpowder and to throw around terms like cobalt chloride without ever knowing what it was good for except turning itself purple if you left the top off. Hours and hours passed pleasantly by the sink and I thought only great thoughts of Johnny, who could make me laugh hysterically by shattering half a dozen saltine crackers while trying to butter them. He contracted bronchial pneumonia, coughing painfully and wasting away from the sliver of a man that he was all his life. When he died I cried because I thought I was supposed to cry. But what I didn't know was you can't really cry when you're supposed to if you don't mean it, unless you are an accomplished actor. And I can almost work up a tear now, forty years' distant, when I think what a loss to the family it was when that witty and wiry and wonderful fellow coughed his last. I feel con-

stricted when I think of ending this chapter, for every memory
stirs another one and I think of all the people I haven't mentioned. I haven't even mentioned the Paynes, Lottie the seam-
stress and her brother George, of Main Street, children of
slaves, the only black family in the neighborhood on into the
1940s. And Joseph K. (Fritz) Emmett, who was maybe North
Albany's most famous resident ever, a German dialect comedian and yodeler who was really an Irish tenor, an international
celebrity long before he retired in 1882 to build his castle-style
villa at the top of Van Rensselaer Boulevard. Governor David
B. Hill took it over after Emmett's tenure and eventually it
became the Wolfert's Roost Country Club, the social province
of the affluent Albany Irish. The villa burned in 1926 and a new
clubhouse was built on its site. And since we are on the Boulevard it is important to mention Bill Carey, son of Eddie, and
his story about the noontime rush at Gillespie's saloon at Genesee Street and Broadway during the free-lunch era that gives
insight into Irish pragmatism. Bill was five, sitting near the
food and twirling one of his gloves. The glove flew through the
air and landed in a kettle of Gillespie's famous soup. "Just then
the noon whistle blew and the men came in from the gasworks
for their lunch," said Bill. "I was crying to get my glove back
but they gave me a nickel to keep quiet about what happened
to the glove and they kept ladling out the soup." Gillespie's is
gone and the old Irish style is changed, but not rapidly enough
for some: Richard Shaw, for instance. He is an Irish-Catholic
priest who served in Sacred Heart parish during the 1960s,
when the Vatican was modernizing the mass and other Catholic rites, and he was pressing vigorously for the changes, following the Vatican lead. But the North Albany Irish refused to
change and viewed Shaw as a radical, a hippie. "I was the
obedient one, damn it," he said. "I was doing what the church
said to do. The old guy with the shock of white hair and jutting
Irish chin, and the old biddy saying her rosary, they were the
radicals. And the by-product of the battle everywhere was that
convents fell apart, the priesthood diminished, people were
leaving in droves." He was talking with bitterness, not only
about North Albany but of the change-resistant, conservative
Irish everywhere. This decline of Catholicism is well docu-

mented, and not all of it was the result of Irish knuckleheaded-
ness, though some of it surely was, often at high clerical levels.
One little-understood by-product of the controversy is the clarity of Irishness it brought to some Irish Catholics. Peggy Conners Harrigan, daughter of Richard J. Conners, granddaughter
of Michael Conners of Phoenix Club fame, remembered her
North Albany as being Irish, yes, but that was not all of it: "I
felt I had as much affinity with people whose names were Yanni
as I did with people with names like McNally. We were all
Catholics. I guess it's part of that melting-pot mystique fostered by the church so people growing up in an Irish area like
Albany would think of themselves as Catholic and then Irish,
rather than Irish and then Catholic." Her grandfather Michael, the first to make a major mark in the Conners family,
had been born in 1859 and was so conscious of the discrimination Irish Catholics faced he named his four sons Herrick,
Richard, James, and Edgar, "specifically non-Irish," said Peg,
"for he felt an Irish first name with the surname of Conners
would be a double handicap. It was hard to tell whether people
were having problems because they were Irish or Catholic or
both in the teens and 1920s. But people certainly weren't pushing Irish-bog values on their children." Quite true. We grew up
aware of our Irish connection but more aware of being North
End Democrats, really, more aware of being American and
Catholic, and eventually resistant to all of it, anxious to break
all such ties and assert a vigorous independence of mind and
spirit. I walked out of mass during narrowback sermons, refused
to sing "Too-ra-loo-ra-lo-ra," registered to vote as an independent, which raised eyebrows at the registration table in School
20, though my father, who was in line right behind me, never
blinked, and he always worked these polls as a Democratic
inspector. I believed the enemies in the world then were the
goddamn Irish-Catholic Albany Democrats, who were everywhere dominant, benighted, and pernicious. I thought myself
free, and found out that not only wasn't I free, I was fettered
forever to all of it, most surprisingly the Irishness, which was
the only element of my history that wasn't organized, the only
one I couldn't resign from, and, further, the only one that
hadn't been shoved down my throat. My family liked Bing

Crosby and Father Coughlin, sang a few Irish ditties when singing was in order, wore green on St. Patrick's Day, but knew nothing of Irish history, rarely spoke of the Irish Troubles then or now (my father sometimes mentioned the Black and Tans), had no more links to relatives there on either side of the family, and if they remembered the anti-Irishness that prevailed in nineteenth-century America, they repressed it. I vaguely remember my uncle's once calling somebody an "APA son of a bitch," those initials being a code word for the enemy, handed on from the 1890s, when the nativist American Protective Association, an anti-Irish, anti-Italian, anti-Catholic group that was more significant for its bigoted oratory than for any lasting changes it effected in law or culture, was active. I remember asking what the APA was, but got no satisfactory answer beyond "a bunch of Protestant bastards." In time such things seemed to fade, and yet with the passing years an Irish quality reemerged. Peggy Conners found herself and her family talking proudly of their Irish heritage, separate from their Catholicism. A pal of mine from Gloversville, Jerry Mahoney, said I got more Irish as I grew older. I think he was suspicious of it. I went to Ireland twice, and last year even started to write a book about the Irish, but that is a dead issue. I am not Irish but I am. I can't sing but I will. Some of my friends, a few years younger than I, reject their Irishness and believe they have made the leap into the great American puddle of ethnic meltedness. I know what they mean. I went to the St. Patrick's Night Dance at the Ancient Order of Hibernians in the mid-1970s and it was great sport, but very exhausting; and all that green made me colorblind for a week. Too much, too much. I am not *that* Irish. But I am not quite anything else, either. The North End made me and nothing exists powerful enough to unmake me without destroying the vessel. I try not to bear witness to the change in the neighborhood, try not to retrace old steps except in memory. It is sometimes true, as Proust said, that the only paradise is the paradise we've lost, and I have lost a bit of it. The loss began in the 1950s when the city housing project, Corning Homes, brought a thousand new people into the North End, right in the middle of the hills where the Gully and the Cowboy Ladder used to be. In their place came an island of strangers. Then Interstate 90 cut through, displacing seventy families, eliminating Genesee Street and Eightsies and the traction company's carbarns and Lou Pitnell's barbershop and Joe Whelan's saloon. The North End lived through this. In 1982 Ted Flint, a lieutenant on the police force and a lifelong pal of mine, was still living there; and so was Billy Blocksidge, who, like Ted, had put on some weight. Dick Conners is still a North Ender and commutes to the Assembly from Bonheim Street; and Bob Linzey's mother, Anne, still lives on Wolfert Avenue. My father lived on North Pearl until 1970, ten years after my mother died, and came with us for his last five years only after his willful solitude became not unbearable but unmanageable. When we moved him out I no longer had reason to go back. And so it ended there, and what is left to be stated is the synthesis of it all, which is not a bad story. It has politics in it, which North Albany certainly had in abundance, and it has some Kennedys, and it has significant song. It is really a story that goes to one of the mawkish essences of my life: the syrupy, sappy sentimentality that chokes in my gorge and makes me laugh and weep against my will, against all that is intelligent and genuinely holy. It is awful, it is certainly ridiculous, it is bathetic, and it is unpardonable. But there it is in the middle of me, and its epiphany took place at the Albany Institute of History and Art, where Dave Powers, the court jester from Jack Kennedy's administration, was telling funny stories about the long-gone Kennedy years. Just then a white-haired and handsomely attired man rose and asked a three-minute question, posing it in that muggled speech that sounds like George Plimpton speaking underwater. He cited a moment when Jack and Bobby, in their shirtsleeves, were standing on a table with drinks in their hands, arms locked with other friends, all singing "Heart of My Heart." And wasn't this behavior, inquired the man, beneath a president of the United States? Wasn't it little better than the lowbrow political antics that marked the Boston career of the Kennedys' ward-heeling grandfather, Honey-Fitz Fitzgerald? Dave Powers replied to the question before the man could sit down, asking the audience (a full house) how many knew "Heart of My Heart." Then, before the show of hands could be counted, he started to sing it and was joined by almost everybody, or so it sounded, in airing those unconscionable lyrics about being kids, being friends, harmonizing, parting. When the final line about a tear glistening was being sung by us all, Dave Powers shuffled off toward stage right. The man with muggled question, still standing—standing alone—intensified his protest in an ever-rising voice, his index finger raised and raised and raised again to vivify his inaudible point. And as Dave Powers descended the stairs to the auditorium, he, too, raised his index finger, and then rotated it, nail outward, to answer the man, thus resting his case to the thunderclap of applause that followed the final word of the song. I think of that thunderclap not as praise for the Kennedys or Powers or the song, though it was all of that, but as Albany's seal of approval on the mawkish corner of my soul; and bad cess to the critics. And on that note I, too, end my case for the North End, but not without a word for that young Greek fellow who is stepping over my mother on his way to work. On her behalf I forgive him his social delinquency, for it made a great story, which my mother told all her life. And telling stories, of course, was always a favorite pasttime in paradise.

Louise Erdrich

A REMARKABLE thing happens when an American Indian writer gains a national readership: the topography of Indian Country in the public's mind changes, albeit ever so slightly. That author's works begin to show up on college syllabi across the country; papers with the author's name in their titles appear on literary conference agendas and in reviews in major journals. Interviews with the author may even be featured in magazines like *People* or on television. Such has been the impact of Louise Erdrich's work, beginning with the publication of *Love Medicine,* a novel that won her the National Book Critics Circle Award for Best Work of Fiction for 1984 and has been translated into at least ten foreign languages.

Prior to Erdrich's rise to recognition, most Americans had never heard of the Turtle Mountain Chippewa—in fact, many Americans in the East, I'm sure, hardly know where North Dakota is or care. All of that is to say that Erdrich's "place" in American literature means very different things to different people, for in becoming well-known, she also becomes highly visible as an *Indian* writer. There's no escaping it. No matter how talented she may be, it is her "Indianness" that creates the distinctive context in which to reflect on Erdrich and her work. (An old story.) By way of example, quite by chance I met a woman who had served as a judge on a major award panel to which one of Erdrich's novels had been submitted. The woman told me that the committee decided against awarding Erdrich the prize because she collaborates with her husband, Michael Dorris, making it impossible for the judges to determine whether the novel was written by her. Since Erdrich speaks freely of her collaboration with Dorris, this attitude may seem understandable enough, but what of T. S. Eliot's collaboration with Ezra Pound? On a different occasion, I was told some-thing similar about the work of another highly visible Indian writer—that he could not write his books without help from his wife. In other words, Indians and writing do not go together in some people's mind. Add to that the pressure of being in the public eye—especially among Indians, who resent being "rep-resented" by a single person, experience, or text—and it is not difficult to guess why a long time elapsed before a second novel by writers like N. Scott Momaday (*House Made of Dawn,* 1968) and Leslie Silko (*Ceremony,* 1977). Against that back-drop, Erdrich's achievements seem nothing short of remark-able.

Love Medicine begins a quartet of novels (the others include *Beet Queen, Tracks,* and a fourth as yet unpublished) which depict the lives of three reservation extended families: the Kashpaws, the Lamartine/Nanapushes, and the Morriseys. Love medicine, a Chippewa potion ritualistically used to en-snare one's beloved, becomes a constituting metaphor for what binds these characters together—a little bit of magic and a whole lot of love. And unforgettable characters they all are: Lulu Lamartine, whose first "love affair" is an infatuation with a dead man she finds in the woods—an experience which ever after lends vitality to her love life, chiefly because she no longer fears death; Marie Kashpaw, who battles the devil in the form of a nun, Sister Leopolda (the episode included in this anthol-ogy), and is drawn into a marriage with Nector Kashpaw through the power embodied in the pair of geese he has just hunted and killed (geese hearts are a primary ingredient in love potions, because geese mate for life); and Nector himself, a onetime actor, who eventually becomes tribal chairman, pri-marily because of his wife Marie's prompting. Throughout the book he is in love with both Lulu and Marie. A constellation of other characters rotate around these three, in this text and as the narrative extends itself into the other two novels. The life stories grow and change as our understanding of the culture deepens and we begin to grasp what has gone before in the people's history, their struggle to retain a degree of cultural sovereignty.

Erdrich's novelistic technique involves building a center

through an accretion of stories, often presented in the first person. Those stories frequently appear in magazines before her novels and are anthologized as stories after the novels are published; in other words, they stand alone well. No doubt her talent for the discrete sketch originates in her poetry, as does her swift, intense command of metaphor. *Jacklight,* her first book of poetry, written before *Love Medicine,* snaps and flashes with magic and earthiness in rare combination, and suggests themes she later rendered in fiction. A second book of poems, *Baptism of Desire,* came out in 1990.

In addition to her achievements as a creative writer, Erdrich has proved her talents as an essayist, publishing pieces on a range of topics from a writer's sense of place to a survey of Holocaust literature (written with Dorris). Her contribution to American literary history will undoubtedly mean very different things to different people, but to my mind she gives us all what we want from a writer—daring imagination, vibrant language, and serious commitment.

—Kathryn Shanley

"Saint Marie" from
LOVE MEDICINE

Marie Lazarre

So when I went there, I knew the dark fish must rise. Plumes of radiance had soldered on me. No reservation girl had ever prayed so hard. There was no use in trying to ignore me any longer. I was going up there on the hill with the black robe women. They were not any lighter than me. I was going up there to pray as good as they could. Because I don't have that much Indian blood. And they never thought they'd have a girl from this reservation as a saint they'd have to kneel to. But they'd have me. And I'd be carved in pure gold. With ruby lips. And my toenails would be little pink ocean shells, which they would have to stoop down off their high horse to kiss.

I was ignorant. I was near age fourteen. The length of sky is just about the size of my ignorance. Pure and wide. And it was just that—the pure and wideness of my ignorance—that got me up the hill to Sacred Heart Convent and brought me back down alive. For maybe Jesus did not take my bait, but them Sisters tried to cram me right down whole.

You ever see a walleye strike so bad the lure is practically out its back end before you reel it in? That is what they done with me. I don't like to make that low comparison, but I have seen a walleye do that once. And it's the same attempt as Sister Leopolda made to get me in her clutch.

I had the mail-order Catholic soul you get in a girl raised out in the bush, whose only thought is getting into town. For Sunday Mass is the only time my father brought his children in except for school, when we were harnessed. Our soul went cheap. We were so anxious to get there we would have walked in on our hands and knees. We just craved going to the store, slinging bottle caps in the dust, making fool eyes at each other. And of course we went to church.

Where they have the convent is on top of the highest hill, so that from its windows the Sisters can be looking into the marrow of the town. Recently a windbreak was planted before the bar "for the purposes of tornado insurance." Don't tell me that. That poplar stand was put up to hide the drinkers as they get the transformation. As they are served into the beast of their burden. While they're drinking, that body comes upon them, and then they stagger or crawl out the bar door, pulling a weight they can't move past the poplars. They don't want no holy witness to their fall.

Anyway, I climbed. That was a long-ago day. There was a road then for wagons that wound in ruts to the top of the hill where they had their buildings of painted brick. Gleaming white. So white the sun glanced off in dazzling display to set forms whirling behind your eyelids. The face of God you could hardly look at. But that day it drizzled, so I could look all I wanted. I saw the homelier side. The cracked whitewash and swallows nesting in the busted ends of eaves. I saw the boards sawed the size of broken windowpanes and the fruit trees, stripped. Only the tough wild rhubarb flourished. Goldenrod rubbed up their walls. It was a poor convent. I didn't see that then but I know that now. Compared to others it was humble, ragtag, out in the middle of no place. It was the end of the world to some. Where the maps stopped. Where God had only half a hand in the creation. Where the Dark One had put in thick bush, liquor, wild dogs, and Indians.

I heard later that the Sacred Heart Convent was a catchall place for nuns that don't get along elsewhere. Nuns that complain too much or lose their mind. I'll always wonder now, after hearing that, where they picked up Sister Leopolda. Perhaps she had scarred someone else, the way she left a mark on me. Perhaps she was just sent around to test her Sisters' faith, here and there, like the spot-checker in a factory. For she was the definite most-hard trial to anyone's endurance, even when they started out with veils of wretched love upon their eyes.

I was that girl who thought the black hem of her garment would help me rise. Veils of love which was only hate petrified

by longing—that was me. I was like those bush Indians who
stole the holy black hat of a Jesuit and swallowed little scraps of
it to cure their fevers. But the hat itself carried smallpox and
was killing them with belief. Veils of faith! I had this confidence in Leopolda. She was different. The other Sisters had
long ago gone blank and given up on Satan. He slept for them.
They never noticed his comings and goings. But Leopolda kept
track of him and knew his habits, minds he burrowed in, deep
spaces where he hid. She knew as much about him as my
grandma, who called him by other names and was not afraid.

In her class, Sister Leopolda carried a long oak pole for opening high windows. It had a hook made of iron on one end that
could jerk a patch of your hair out or throttle you by the collar—all from a distance. She used this deadly hook-pole for
catching Satan by surprise. He could have entered without your
knowing it—through your lips or your nose or any one of your
seven openings—and gained your mind. But she would see
him. That pole would brain you from behind. And he would
gasp, dazzled, and take the first thing she offered, which was
pain.

She had a stringer of children who could only breathe if she
said the word. I was the worst of them. She always said the
Dark One wanted me most of all, and I believed this. I stood
out. Evil was a common thing I trusted. Before sleep sometimes he came and whispered conversation in the old language
of the bush. I listened. He told me things he never told anyone
but Indians. I was privy to both worlds of his knowledge. I
listened to him, but I had confidence in Leopolda. She was the
only one of the bunch he even noticed.

There came a day, though, when Leopolda turned the tide
with her hook-pole.

It was a quiet day with everyone working at their desks,
when I heard him. He had sneaked into the closets in the back
of the room. He was scratching around, tasting crumbs in our
pockets, stealing buttons, squirting his dark juice in the linings
and the boots. I was the only one who heard him, and I got
bold. I smiled. I glanced back and smiled and looked up at her
sly to see if she had noticed. My heart jumped. For she was
looking straight at me. And she sniffed. She had a big stark

bony nose stuck to the front of her face for smelling out brimstone and evil thoughts. She had smelled him on me. She stood up. Tall, pale, a blackness leading into the deeper blackness of the slate wall behind her. Her oak pole had flown into her grip. She had seen me glance at the closet. Oh, she knew. She knew just where he was. I watched her watch him in her mind's eye. The whole class was watching now. She was staring, sizing, following his scuffle. And all of a sudden she tensed down, posed on her bent kneesprings, cocked her arm back. She threw the oak pole singing over my head, through my braincloud. It cracked through the thin wood door of the back closet, and the heavy pointed hook drove through his heart. I turned. She'd speared her own black rubber overboot where he'd taken refuge in the tip of her darkest toe.

Something howled in my mind. Loss and darkness. I understood. I was to suffer for my smile.

He rose up hard in my heart. I didn't blink when the pole cracked. My skull was tough. I didn't flinch when she shrieked in my ear. I only shrugged at the flowers of hell. He wanted me. More than anything he craved me. But then she did the worst. She did what broke my mind to her. She grabbed me by the collar and dragged me, feet flying, through the room and threw me in the closet with her dead black overboot. And I was there. The only light was a crack beneath the door. I asked the Dark One to enter into me and boost my mind. I asked him to restrain my tears, for they were pushing behind my eyes. But he was afraid to come back there. He was afraid of her sharp pole. And I was afraid of Leopolda's pole for the first time, too. I felt the cold hook in my heart. How it could crack through the door at any minute and drag me out, like a dead fish on a gaff, drop me on the floor like a gutshot squirrel.

I was nothing. I edged back to the wall as far as I could. I breathed the chalk dust. The hem of her full black cloak cut against my cheek. He had left me. Her spear could find me any time. Her keen ears would aim the hook into the beat of my heart.

What was that sound?

It filled the closet, filled it up until it spilled over, but I did not recognize the crying wailing voice as mine until the door cracked open, brightness, and she hoisted me to her camphor-smelling lips.

"He *wants* you," she said. "That's the difference. I give you love."

Love. The black hook. The spear singing through the mind. I saw that she had tracked the Dark One to my heart and flushed him out into the open. So now my heart was an empty nest where she could lurk.

Well, I was weak. I was weak when I let her in, but she got a foothold there. Hard to dislodge as the year passed. Sometimes I felt him—the brush of dim wings—but only rarely did his voice compel. It was between Marie and Leopolda now, and the struggle changed. I began to realize I had been on the wrong track with the fruits of hell. The real way to overcome Leopolda was this: I'd get to heaven first. And then, when I saw her coming, I'd shut the gate. She'd be out! That is why, besides the bowing and the scraping I'd be dealt, I wanted to sit on the altar as a saint.

To this end, I went up on the hill. Sister Leopolda was the consecrated nun who had sponsored me to come there.

"You're not vain," she said. "You're too honest, looking into the mirror, for that. You're not smart. You don't have the ambition to get clear. You have two choices. One, you can marry a no-good Indian, bear his brats, die like a dog. Or two, you can give yourself to God."

"I'll come up there," I said, "but not because of what you think."

I could have had any damn man on the reservation at the time. And I could have made him treat me like his own life. I looked good. And I looked white. But I wanted Sister Leopolda's heart. And here was the thing: sometimes I wanted her heart in love and admiration. Sometimes. And sometimes I wanted her heart to roast on a black stick.

SHE answered the back door where they had instructed me to call. I stood there with my bundle. She looked me up and down.

"All right," she said finally. "Come in."

She took my hand. Her fingers were like a bundle of broom

straws, so thin and dry, but the strength of them was unnatural.
I couldn't have tugged loose if she was leading me into rooms of
white-hot coal. Her strength was a kind of perverse miracle, for
she got it from fasting herself thin. Because of this hunger
practice her lips were a wounded brown and her skin deadly
pale. Her eye sockets were two deep lashless hollows in a taut
skull. I told you about the nose already. It stuck out far and
made the place her eyes moved even deeper, as if she stared out
the wrong end of a gun barrel. She took the bundle from my
hands and threw it in the corner.

"You'll be sleeping behind the stove, child."

It was immense, like a great furnace. There was a small cot
close behind it.

"Looks like it could get warm there," I said.

"Hot. It does."

"Do I get a habit?"

I wanted something like the thing she wore. Flowing black
cotton. Her face was strapped in white bandages, and a sharp
crest of starched white cardboard hung over her forehead like a
glaring beak. If possible, I wanted a bigger, longer, white beak
than hers.

"No," she said, grinning her great skull grin. "You don't get
one yet. Who knows, you might not like us. Or we might not
like you."

But she had loved me, or offered me love. And she had tried
to hunt the Dark One down. So I had this confidence.

"I'll inherit your keys from you," I said.

She looked at me sharply, and her grin turned strange. She
hissed, taking in her breath. Then she turned to the door and
took a key from her belt. It was a giant key, and it unlocked the
larder where the food was stored.

Inside there was all kinds of good stuff. Things I'd tasted
only once or twice in my life. I saw sticks of dried fruit, jars of
orange peel, spice like cinnamon. I saw tins of crackers with
ships painted on the side. I saw pickles. Jars of herring and the
rind of pigs. There was cheese, a big brown block of it from the
thick milk of goats. And besides that there was the everyday
stuff, in great quanities, the flour and the coffee.

It was the cheese that got to me. When I saw it my stomach

hollowed. My tongue dripped. I loved that goat-milk cheese better than anything I'd ever ate. I stared at it. The rich curve in the buttery cloth.

"When you inherit my keys," she said sourly, slamming the door in my face, "you can eat all you want of the priest's cheese."

Then she seemed to consider what she'd done. She looked at me. She took the key from her belt and went back, sliced a hunk off, and put it in my hand.

"If you're good you'll taste this cheese again. When I'm dead and gone," she said.

Then she dragged out the big sack of flour. When I finished that heaven stuff she told me to roll my sleeves up and begin doing God's labor. For a while we worked in silence, mixing up the dough and pounding it out on stone slabs.

"God's work," I said after a while. "If this is God's work, then I've done it all my life."

"Well, you've done it with the Devil in your heart then," she said. "Not God."

"How do you know?" I asked. But I knew she did. And I wished I had not brought up the subject.

"I see right into you like a clear glass," she said. "I always did."

"You don't know it," she continued after a while, "but he's come around here sulking. He's come around here brooding. You brought him in. He knows the smell of me, and he's going to make a last ditch try to get you back. Don't let him." She glared over at me. Her eyes were cold and lighted. "Don't let him touch you. We'll be a long time getting rid of him."

So I was careful. I was careful not to give him an inch. I said a rosary, two rosaries, three, underneath my breath. I said the Creed. I said every scrap of Latin I knew while we punched the dough with our fists. And still, I dropped the cup. It rolled under that monstrous iron stove, which was getting fired up for baking.

And she was on me. She saw he'd entered my distraction.

"Our good cup," she said. "Get it out of there, Marie."

I reached for the poker to snag it out from beneath the stove. But I had a sinking feel in my stomach as I did this. Sure enough, her long arm darted past me like a whip. The poker lighted in her hand.

"Reach," she said. "Reach with your arm for that cup. And when your flesh is hot, remember that the flames you feel are only one fraction of the heat you will feel in his hellish embrace."

She always did things this way, to teach you lessons. So I wasn't surprised. It was playacting, anyway, because a stove isn't very hot underneath right along the floor. They aren't made that way. Otherwise a wood floor would burn. So I said yes and got down on my stomach and reached under. I meant to grab it quick and jump up again, before she could think up another lesson, but here it happened. Although I groped for the cup, my hand closed on nothing. That cup was nowhere to be found. I heard her step toward me, a slow step. I heard the creak of thick shoe leather, the little *plat* as the folds of her heavy skirts met, a trickle of fine sand sifting, somewhere, perhaps in the bowels of her, and I was afraid. I tried to scramble up, but her foot came down lightly behind my ear, and I was lowered. The foot came down more firmly at the base of my neck, and I was held.

"You're like I was," she said. "He wants you very much."

"He doesn't want me no more," I said. "He had his fill. I got the cup!"

I heard the valve opening, the hissed intake of breath, and knew that I should not have spoke.

"You lie," she said. "You're cold. There is a wicked ice forming in your blood. You don't have a shred of devotion for God. Only wild cold dark lust. I know it. I know how you feel. I see the beast . . . the beast watches me out of your eyes sometimes. Cold."

The urgent scrape of metal. It took a moment to know from where. Top of the stove. Kettle. Lessons. She was steadying herself with the iron poker. I could feel it like pure certainty, driving into the wood floor. I would not remind her of pokers. I heard the water as it came, tipped from the spout, cooling as it fell but still scalding as it struck. I must have twitched beneath her foot, because she steadied me, and then the poker nudged up beside my arm as if to guide. "To warm your cold ash heart," she said. I felt how patient she would be. The water came. My mind went dead blank. Again. I could only think the kettle would be cooling slowly in her hand. I could not stand it. I bit my lip so as not to satisfy her with a sound. She gave me more reason to keep still.

"I will boil him from your mind if you make a peep," she said, "by filling up your ear."

ANY sensible fool would have run back down the hill the minute Leopolda let them up from under her heel. But I was snared in her black intelligence by then. I could not think straight. I had prayed so hard I think I broke a cog in my mind. I prayed while her foot squeezed my throat. While my skin burst. I prayed even when I heard the wind come through, shrieking in the busted bird nests. I didn't stop when pure light fell, turning slowly behind my eyelids. God's face. Even that did not disrupt my continued praise. Words came. Words came from nowhere and flooded my mind.

Now I could pray much better than any one of them. Than all of them full force. This was proved. I turned to her in a daze when she let me up. My thoughts were gone, and yet I remember how surprised I was. Tears glittered in her eyes, deep down, like the sinking reflection in a well.

"It was so hard, Marie," she gasped. Her hands were shaking. The kettle clattered against the stove. "But I have used all the water up now. I think he is gone."

"I prayed," I said foolishly. "I prayed very hard."

"Yes," she said. "My dear one, I know."

WE sat together quietly because we had no more words. We let the dough rise and punched it down once. She gave me a bowl of mush, unlocked the sausage from a special cupboard, and took that in to the Sisters. They sat down the hall, chewing their sausage, and I could hear them. I could hear their teeth bite through their bread and meat. I couldn't move. My shirt was dry but the cloth stuck to my back, and I couldn't think straight. I was losing the sense to understand how her mind worked. She'd gotten past me with her poker and I would never be a saint. I despaired. I felt I had no inside voice, nothing to direct me, no darkness, no Marie. I was about to throw that cornmeal mush out to the birds and make a run for it, when the vision rose up blazing in my mind.

I was rippling gold. My breasts were bare and my nipples flashed and winked. Diamonds tipped them. I could walk through panes of glass. I could walk through windows. She was at my feet, swallowing the glass after each step I took. I broke through another and another. The glass she swallowed ground and cut until her starved insides were only a subtle dust. She coughed. She coughed a cloud of dust. And then she was only a black rag that flapped off, snagged in bob wire, hung there for an age, and finally rotted into the breeze.

I saw this, mouth hanging open, gazing off into the flagged boughs of trees.

"Get up!" she cried. "Stop dreaming. It is time to bake."

Two other Sisters had come in with her, wide women with hands like paddles. They were evening and smoothing out the firebox beneath the great jaws of the oven.

"Who is this one?" they asked Leopolda. "Is she yours?"

"She is mine," said Leopolda. "A very good girl."

"What is your name?" one asked me.

"Marie."

"Marie. Star of the Sea."

"She will shine," said Leopolda, "when we have burned off the dark corrosion."

The others laughed, but uncertainly. They were mild and sturdy French, who did not understand Leopolda's twisted jokes, although they muttered respectfully at things she said. I knew they wouldn't believe what she had done with the kettle. There was no question. So I kept quiet.

"Elle est docile," they said approvingly as they left to starch the linens.

"Does it pain?" Leopolda asked me as soon as they were out the door.

I did not answer. I felt sick with the hurt.

"Come along," she said.

The building was wholly quiet now. I followed her up the

narrow staircase into a hall of little rooms, many doors. Her cell was the quietest, at the very end. Inside, the air smelled stale, as if the door had not been opened for years. There was a crude straw mattress, a tiny bookcase with a picture of Saint Francis hanging over it, a ragged palm, a stool for sitting on, a crucifix. She told me to remove my blouse and sit on the stool. I did so. She took a pot of salve from the bookcase and began to smooth it upon my burns. Her hands made slow, wide circles, stopping the pain. I closed my eyes. I expected to see blackness. Peace. But instead the vision reared up again. My chest was still tipped with diamonds. I was walking through windows. She was chewing up the broken litter I left behind.

"I am going," I said. "Let me go."

But she held me down.

"Don't go," she said quickly. "Don't. We have just begun."

I was weakening. My thoughts were whirling pitifully. The pain had kept me strong, and as it left me I began to forget it; I couldn't hold on. I began to wonder if she'd really scalded me with the kettle. I could not remember. To remember this seemed the most important thing in the world. But I was losing the memory. The scalding. The pouring. It began to vanish. I felt like my mind was coming off its hinge, flapping in the breeze, hanging by the hair of my own pain. I wrenched out of her grip.

"He was always in you," I said. "Even more than in me. He wanted you even more. And now he's got you. Get thee behind me!"

I shouted that, grabbed my shirt, and ran through the door throwing it on my body. I got down the stairs and into the kitchen, even, but no matter what I told myself, I couldn't get out the door. It wasn't finished. And she knew I would not leave. Her quiet step was immediately behind me.

"We must take the bread from the oven now," she said.

She was pretending nothing happened. But for the first time I had gotten through some chink she'd left in her darkness. Touched some doubt. Her voice was so low and brittle it cracked off at the end of her sentence.

"Help me, Marie," she said slowly.

But I was not going to help her, even though she had calmly buttoned the back of my shirt up and put the big cloth mittens in my hands for taking out the loaves. I could have bolted for it then. But I didn't. I knew that something was nearing completion. Something was about to happen. My back was a wall of singing flame. I was turning. I watched her take the long fork in one hand, to tap the loaves. In the other hand she gripped the black poker to hook the pans.

"Help me," she said again, and I thought, yes, this is part of it. I put the mittens on my hands and swung the door open on its hinges. The oven gaped. She stood back a moment, letting the first blast of heat rush by. I moved behind her. I could feel the heat at my front and at my back. Before, behind. My skin was turning to beaten gold. It was coming quicker than I thought. The oven was like the gate of a personal hell. Just big enough and hot enough for one person, and that was her. One kick and Leopolda would fly in headfirst. And that would be one-millionth of the heat she would feel when she finally collapsed in his hellish embrace.

Saints know these numbers.

She bent forward with her fork held out. I kicked her with all my might. She flew in. But the outstretched poker hit the back wall first, so she rebounded. The oven was not so deep as I had thought.

There was a moment when I felt a sort of thin, hot disappointment, as when a fish slips off the line. Only I was the one going to be lost. She was fearfully silent. She whirled. Her veil had cutting edges. She had the poker in one hand. In the other she held that long sharp fork she used to tap the delicate crusts of loaves. Her face turned upside down on her shoulders. Her face turned blue. But saints are used to miracles. I felt no trace of fear.

If I was going to be lost, let the diamonds cut! Let her eat ground glass!

"Bitch of Jesus Christ!" I shouted. "Kneel and beg! Lick the floor!"

That was when she stabbed me through the hand with the fork, then took the poker up alongside my head, and knocked me out.

IT must have been a half an hour later when I came around.
Things were so strange. So strange I can hardly tell it for delight at the remembrance. For when I came around this was
actually taking place. I was being worshiped. I had somehow
gained the altar of a saint.

I was laying back on the stiff couch in the Mother Superior's
office. I looked around me. It was as though my deepest dream
had come to life. The Sisters of the convent were kneeling to
me. Sister Bonaventure. Sister Dympna. Sister Cecilia Saint-
Claire. The two French with hands like paddles. They were
down on their knees. Black capes were slung over some of their
heads. My name was buzzing up and down the room, like a fat
autumn fly lighting on the tips of their tongues between Latin,
humming up the heavy blood-dark curtains, circling their little
cosseted heads. Marie! Marie! A girl thrown in a closet. Who
was afraid of a rubber overboot. Who was half overcome. A girl
who came in the back door where they threw their garbage.
Marie! Who never found the cup. Who had to eat their cold
mush. Marie! Leopolda had her face buried in her knuckles.
Saint Marie of the Holy Slops! Saint Marie of the Bread Fork!
Saint Marie of the Burnt Back and Scalded Butt!

I broke out and laughed.

They looked up. All holy hell burst loose when they saw I'd
woke. I still did not understand what was happening. They
were watching, talking, but not to me.

"The marks . . ."

"She has her hand closed."

"*Je ne peux pas voir.*"

I was not stupid enough to ask what they were talking about.
I couldn't tell why I was laying in white sheets. I couldn't tell
why they were praying to me. But I'll tell you this: it seemed
entirely natural. It was me. I lifted up my hand as in my dream.
It was completely limp with sacredness.

"Peace be with you."

My arm was dried blood from the wrist down to the elbow.
And it hurt. Their faces turned like flat flowers of adoration to
follow that hand's movements. I let it swing through the air,
imparting a saint's blessing. I had practiced. I knew exactly how
to act.

They murmured. I heaved a sigh, and a golden beam of light suddenly broke through the clouded window and flooded down directly on my face. A stroke of perfect luck! They had to be convinced.

Leopolda still knelt in the back of the room. Her knuckles were crammed halfway down her throat. Let me tell you, a saint has senses honed keen as a wolf. I knew that she was over my barrel now. How it happened did not matter. The last thing I remembered was how she flew from the oven and stabbed me. That one thing was most certainly true.

"Come forward, Sister Leopolda." I gestured with my heavenly wound. Oh, it hurt. It bled when I reopened the slight heal. "Kneel beside me," I said.

She kneeled, but her voice box evidently did not work, for her mouth opened, shut, opened, but no sound came out. My throat clenched in noble delight I had read of as befitting a saint. She could not speak. But she was beaten. It was in her eyes. She stared at me now with all the deep hate of the wheel of devilish dust that rolled wild within her emptiness.

"What is it you want to tell me?" I asked. And at last she spoke.

"I have told my Sisters of your passion," she managed to choke out. "How the stigmata . . . the marks of the nails . . . appeared in your palm and you swooned at the holy vision. . . ."

"Yes," I said curiously.

And then, after a moment, I understood.

Leopolda had saved herself with her quick brain. She had witnessed a miracle. She had hid the fork and told this to the others. And of course they believed her, because they never knew how Satan came and went or where he took refuge.

"I saw it from the first," said the large one who put the bread in the oven. "Humility of the spirit. So rare in these girls."

"I saw it too," said the other one with great satisfaction. She sighed quietly. "If only it was me."

Leopolda was kneeling bolt upright, face blazing and twitching, a barely held fountain of blasting poison.

"Christ has marked me," I agreed.

I smiled the saint's smirk into her face. And then I looked at her. That was my mistake.

For I saw her kneeling there. Leopolda with her soul like a rubber overboot. With her face of a starved rat. With the desperate eyes drowning in the deep wells of her wrongness. There would be no one else after me. And I would leave. I saw Leopolda kneeling within the shambles of her love.

My heart had been about to surge from my chest with the blackness of my joyous heat. Now it dropped. I pitied her. I pitied her. Pity twisted in my stomach like that hook-pole was driven through me. I was caught. It was a feeling more terrible than any amount of boiling water and worse than being forked. Still, still, I could not help what I did. I had already smiled in a saint's mealy forgiveness. I heard myself speaking gently.

"Receive the dispensation of my sacred blood," I whispered.

But there was no heart in it. No joy when she bent to touch the floor. No dark leaping. I fell back into the white pillows. Blank dust was whirling through the light shafts. My skin was dust. Dust my lips. Dust the dirty spoons on the ends of my feet.

Rise up! I thought. Rise up and walk! There is no limit to this dust!

Toshio Mori

THE poet Lawson Fusao Inada, writing in the introduction to the 1985 University of Washington Press edition of Toshio Mori's collection of short stories, *Yokohama, California* (1949), claims, "This is more than a book. This is legacy, tradition. This is the enduring strength, the embodiment of a people. This is the spirit, the soul. This is the community, the identity. This is the pride, the joy, the love. . . . This is *Yokohama, California.* This *is* Japanese America." Inada credits this moving and sentimental collection of stories by Toshio Mori (1910–1980) as having "power" that comes from courage and conviction.

Although slated for publication in 1941 (World War II delayed its publication), *Yokohama, California* was finally published in 1949. It was the first collection of short stories published by a Japanese American. Almost as an apology for the years following the war, William Saroyan wrote in his introduction to the 1949 edition that Mori's characters "are Japanese only after you know they are men and women alive." Inada notes, "This is, of course, the old melting pot idea. In the guise of Americanization and universality, this was not so much acceptance but denial, domestication, and some folks were not about to melt down. A book like *Yokohama, California* is its best defense, its own integrity, and so be it if the characters are even *too* Japanese, this is its very strength."

In "Lil' Yokohama" the point is that this fictional town, Yokohama, California (somewhere in the East Bay area) is like any other town in America: ". . . we have twenty-four hours every day . . . just as in Boston, Cincinnati, Birmingham, Kansas City. . . ." Ah, but this town is Japanese America, and each of its facets is distinctly Japanese American from the nicknames of the baseball players, Slugger Hironaka, to the *sansei* (third-generation) baby born with the name Franklin Susumu Amano. They need no justification or rationale or explanation or apology for their existence.

In 1971, Inada, Frank Chin, Jeffery Chan, and I were just beginning to edit *Aiiieeeee! Anthology of Asian American Writers* (1974) when we found a copy of *Yokohama, California* in a used-book store for twenty-five cents. The notes inside the book said that Mori was born in Oakland, California, in 1910. Using our best researching tools we'd learned in college, we looked up his name in the phone book. He was listed with a San Leandro address.

Picture this: four young Asian American writers call Toshio Mori up out of the blue twenty-two years after the publication of his book—Inada, buzz-cut hairdo, black beret, and maybe an Army jacket; Chin, jeans, cowboy shirt, beads, long hair, and a mustache he once described as the kind of mustache that's as effective as a mustache as needles are at making a cactus look hairy; Chan, sandals, mountaineering-catalog look, going bald, smoking; and me, born in the year Mori's book came out, long hair, probably overdressed for the occasion. Three of us are pushing six feet tall and the other, well, he's wearing elevator sandals. We're eager and energetic, all of us born to edit and interview writers, all products of fine college English departments. We begin by saying to Mori that *Yokohama, California* is written and structured a lot like Sherwood Anderson's *Winesburg, Ohio.* Mori settles in and stares at the foursome with the phone-book research mentality and says quite calmly, "Sherwood Anderson writes like me, not the other way around." Inada writes, "What really distinguishes Mori from Anderson, or from any other writer for that matter, is the writing itself. No other writer writes like Mori. He achieved what few writers ever achieve—the *mezurashi*—'the highly unusual'—an individual style. He developed his own voice, his own way with words; he became a master craftsman; he is an authentic original."

—*Shawn Wong*

"Lil' Yokohama" from
YOKOHAMA, CALIFORNIA

IN Lil' Yokohama, as the youngsters call our community, we have twenty-four hours every day . . . and morning, noon, and night roll on regularly just as in Boston, Cincinnati, Birmingham, Kansas City, Minneapolis, and Emeryville.

When the sun is out, the housewives sit on the porch or walk around the yard, puttering with this and that, and the old men who are in the house when it is cloudy or raining come out on the porch or sit in the shade and read the newspaper. The day is hot. All right, they like it. The day is cold. All right, all right. The people of Lil' Yokohama are here. *Here, here,* they cry with their presence just as the youngsters when the teachers call the roll. And when the people among people are sometimes missing from Lil' Yokohama's roll, perhaps forever, it is another matter; but the news belongs here just as does the weather.

TODAY young and old are at the Alameda ball grounds to see the big game: Alameda Taiiku *vs.* San Jose Asahis. The great Northern California game is under way. Will Slugger Hironaka hit that southpaw from San Jose? Will the same southpaw make the Alameda sluggers stand on their heads? It's the great question.

The popcorn man is doing big business. The day is hot. Everything is all set for a perfect day at the ball park. Everything is here, no matter what the outcome may be. The outcome of the game and the outcome of the day do not matter. Like the outcome of all things, the game and the day in Lil' Yokohama have little to do with this business of outcome. That is left for moralists to work on years later.

Meanwhile, here is the third inning. Boy, oh boy! The southpaw from San Jose, Sets Mizutani, has his old soupbone working. In three innings Alameda hasn't touched him, not even Slugger Hironaka. Along with Mizutani's airtight pitching, San Jose has managed to put across a run in the second. The San Jose fans cackle and cheer. "Atta-boy! Atta-boy!" The stands are a bustle of life, never still, noisy from by-talk and cries and the shouts and jeers and cheers from across the diamond. "Come on, Hironaka! Do your stuff!" . . . "Wake up, Alameda! Blast the Asahis out of the park!" . . . "Keep it up, Mizutani! This is your day! Tell 'em to watch the smoke go by." . . . "Come on, Slugger! We want a homer! We want a homer!"

It was a splendid day to be out. The sun is warm, and in the stands the clerks, the grocers, the dentists, the doctors, the florists, the lawnmower-pushers, the housekeepers, the wives, the old men sun themselves and crack peanuts. Everybody in Lil' Yokohama is out. Papa Hatanaka, the father of baseball among California Japanese, is sitting in the stands behind the backstop, in the customary white shirt—coatless, hatless, brown as chocolate and perspiring: great voice, great physique, great lover of baseball. Mrs. Horita is here, the mother of Ted Horita, the star left fielder of Alameda. Mr. and Mrs. Matsuda of Lil' Yokohama; the Tatsunos; the families of Nodas, Uyedas, Abes, Kikuchi, Yamanotos, Sasakis; Bob Fukuyama; Mike Matoi; Mr. Tanaka, of Tanaka Hotel; Jane Miyazaki; Hideo Mitoma; the Iriki sisters; Yuriko Tsudama; Suda-san, Eto-san, Higuchi-san of our block, . . . the faces we know but not the names: the names we know and do not name.

In the seventh, Slugger Hironaka connects for a home run with two on! The Alameda fans go mad. They are still three runs behind, but what of that? The game is young; the game is theirs till the last man is out. But Mizutani is smoking them in today. Ten strike-outs to his credit already.

The big game ends, and the San Jose Asahis win. The score doesn't matter. Cheers and shouts and laughter still ring in the stands. Finally it all ends—the noise, the game, the life in the park; and the popcorn man starts his car and goes up Clement.

IT is Sunday evening in Lil' Yokohama, and the late dinners commence. Someone who did not go to the game asks, "Who won today?" "San Jose," we say. "Oh, gee," he says. "But Slugger knocked another home run," we say. "What again? He sure is good!" he says. "Big league scouts ought to size him up." "Sure," we say.

Tomorrow is a school day, tomorrow is a work day, tomorrow is another twenty-four hours. In Lil' Yokohama night is almost over. On Sunday nights the block is peaceful and quiet. At eleven thirty-six Mr. Komai dies of heart failure. For several days he has been in bed. For fourteen years he has lived on our block and done gardening work around Piedmont, Oakland, and San Leandro. His wife is left with five children. The neighbors go to the house to comfort the family and assist in the funeral preparations.

Today which is Monday the sun is bright again, but the sick cannot come out and enjoy it. Mrs. Koike is laid up with pneumonia and her friends are worried. She is well known in Lil' Yokohama.

Down the block a third-generation Japanese American is born. A boy. They name him Franklin Susumu Amano. The father does not know of the birth of his boy. He is out of town driving a truck for a grocer.

Sam Suda, who lives down the street with his mother, is opening a big fruit market in Oakland next week. For several years he has been in Los Angeles learning the ropes in the market business. Now he is ready to open one and hire a dozen or more men.

Upstairs in his little boarding room, the country boy has his paints and canvas ready before him. All his life Yukio Takaki has wanted to come to the city and become an artist. Now he is here; he lives on Seventh Street. He looks down from his window, and the vastness and complexity of life bewilder him. But he is happy. Why not? He may succeed or not in his ambition; that is not really important.

Sixteen days away, Satoru Ugaki and Tayeko Akagawa are to be married. Lil' Yokohama knows them well. Sam Suda is a good friend of Satoru Ugaki. The young Amanos know them. The Higuchis of our block are close friends of Tayeko Akagawa and her family.

Something is happening to the Etos of the block. All of a sudden they turn in their old '30 Chevrolet for a new Oldsmobile Eight! They follow this with a new living-room set and a radio and a new coat of paint for the house. On Sundays the whole family goes for an outing. Sometimes it is to Fleishhacker Pool or to Santa Cruz. It may be to Golden Gate Park or to the ocean or to their relatives in the country. . . . They did not strike oil or win the sweepstakes. Nothing of the kind happens in Lil' Yokohama, though it may any day. . . . What then?

Today which is Tuesday Lil' Yokohama is getting ready to see Ray Tatemoto off. He is leaving for New York, for the big city to study journalism at Columbia. Everybody says he is taking a chance going so far away from home and his folks. The air is a bit cool and cloudy. At the station Ray is nervous and grins foolishly. His friends bunch around him, shake hands, and wish him luck. This is his first trip out of the state. Now and then he looks at his watch and up and down the tracks to see if his train is coming.

When the train arrives and Ray Tatemoto is at last off for New York, we ride back on the cars to Lil' Yokohama. Well, Ray Tatemoto is gone, we say. The folks will not see him for four or six years. Perhaps never. Who can tell? We settle back in the seats and pretty soon we see the old buildings of Lil' Yokohama. We know we are home. . . . So it goes.

Today which is Wednesday we read in the *Mainichi News* about the big games scheduled this Sunday. The San Jose Asahis will travel to Stockton to face the Yamatos. The Stockton fans want to see the champs play once again. At Alameda, the Sacramento Mikados will cross bats with the Taiiku Kai boys.

And today which is every day the sun is out again. The housewives sit on the porch and the old men sit in the shade and read the papers. Across the yard a radio goes full blast with

Benny Goodman's band. The children come back from Lincoln Grammar School. In a little while the older ones will be returning from Tech High and McClymonds High. Young boys and young girls will go down the street together. The old folks from the porches and the windows will watch them go by and shake their heads and smile.

The day is here and is Lil' Yokohama's day.

J. California Cooper

J. CALIFORNIA COOPER'S first collection of short stories, *A Piece of Mine* (1984), was published by Robert Allen and Alice Walker, partners in Wild Trees Press. Her other works include *Homemade Love* (1986), *Some Soul to Keep* (1987), *Family* (1991), and seventeen plays for stage, radio, and television. Walker describes Cooper's storytelling voice in the introduction as "the voice of sister-witness that all of us, if we are lucky, and if we are loved, have in our lives. She is the woman you trust with your story *as it is happening to you;* she is the woman from whom you hide nothing. She is on your side. If you fall, she is the one to take the message to your mother and your children. It will be the right one."

The message, the story, the voice are one. Paule Marshall speaks of growing up in Brooklyn in the thirties and forties listening to the "kitchen talk" of her mother and her friends. Cooper's voice is as trustworthy, as honest, and as pure as someone you love sitting in the kitchen doing, as the Hawaiians would describe, "talk story":

> Life is really something too, cause you can stand stark raving still and life will still happen to you. It's gonna spill over and touch you no matter where you are! Always full of lessons. Everywhere! All you got to do is look around you if you got sense enough to see! I hear people say they so bored with life. Ain't nothing but a fool that ain't got nothing to do in this here world. My Aunt Ellen, who I'm going to tell you about, always said, "Life is like tryin to swim to the top of the rain sometime!"

Walker goes on to say that Cooper's "style is deceptively simple and direct, and the vale of tears in which some of her characters reside is never so deep that rich chuckle at a foolish person's foolishness cannot be heard. It is a delight to read her stories, to come upon a saying like 'There ain't so sense beatin round the bush with the fellow who planted it,' and to know it will be with you perhaps forever."

—Shawn Wong

"Swimming to the Top of the Rain" from HOMEMADE LOVE

MOTHERS are something ain't they? They mostly the one person you can count on! All your life . . . if they live. Most mothers be your friend and love you no matter what you do! I bet mine was that way. You ain't never known nobody didn't have one, so they must be something!

Life is really something too, cause you can stand stark raving still and life will still happen to you. It's gonna spill over and touch you no matter where you are! Always full of lessons. Everywhere! All you got to do is look around you if you got sense enough to see! I hear people say they so bored with life. Ain't nothing but a fool that ain't got nothing to do in this here world. My Aunt Ellen, who I'm going to tell you about, always said, "Life is like tryin to swim to the top of the rain sometime!"

One of the things I always put in my prayers is "Lord, please don't let me be no big fool in this life!" Cause you got to be thinking, and think hard, to make it to any kinda peace and happiness. And it seem like things start happening from the moment you are born!

My mama died from my being born the minute I was born! Now if you don't think that changed my whole life, you need to pray not to be a fool! She left three of us. My two sisters, I call them Oldest and Middle, and me. She had done been working hard to support herself for years, I learned, and finally for her two children after my daddy left. He came back, one more time, to make one more baby. I can look back now and understand, she was grieved and lonely and tired from holding up against hard times all by herself and wished this time he was back to stay and help, so she let him back in her bed. Probly to be held one more time by someone sides a child. Then I was made and she told him. He got drunk, again, but didn't beat her. There's some whippings people give you tho, without laying a hand on you, hurts just as bad, even worse sometime. He left, again. He musta broke somethin inside her besides her spirit and her heart cause when I took my first breath, she took her last breath. I wished I could of fixed it whilst I was inside her, so she could live . . . and I could get to have my own mama.

She had already told my sisters what my name was to be. I was called "Care." My first sister was "Angel" and the second "Better," four and five years old. But I call them Older and Middle.

We was alone, three babies.

Mama had two sisters we had never heard of. Somebody knew how to reach them cause one, Aunt Bell, who lived in a big city, came and got us and took us in. Had to, I guess. Cause wasn't nowhere else we could go at that time . . . three of us!? Musta been a shock for somebody wasn't expecting anything like that!

We think my Aunt Bell was a prostitute. Older say she was never in the little rooms she rented for us but once or twice a month. She would pay the rent, stock up the food, give us some little shiny toy or dress, lotsa warnings bout strangers, and leave us with a hug and kiss. If she had a husband we never met him. We were young and didn't understand a lot, but we loved that woman, least I did. Was somethin kin to me in her. She was so sad, even when she was smiling and laughing. I didn't see it, but I felt it. I'd cry for her when I thought of her and not know why I was crying! She took care of us for about five years, then she was dumped on our front porch, stabbed to death! We opened the door for sunlight and found her and darkness. That darkness moved right on into the house, into our lives, again.

I don't know if they even tried to find out who did it. Just another whore gone, I guess. Never mind the kind of person she was, trying to do for us and all. We had never really been full too steady, but we had always had something!

We was alone, again.

I found out early in life you going to find a lotta mean people everyplace, but sometime a few good ones somewhere. Someone came in and prepared for the tiny, short funeral. The

church donated the coffin and fed us. Somebody went through
Aunt Bell's few sad things she had there and that's when we
found out we had another aunt, Aunt Ellen. People should tell
the children where to look and who to look for, just in case! Do
we ever know what's goin to happen to us in this life? Or when?

Somehow they reached Aunt Ellen and she got there bout a
week after the funeral. We was all separated and could tell
people was getting tired of feeding and caring for us. Well,
after all, they was poor people or they never would have known
us anyway and they was already having a hard time before we
needed them!

Aunt Ellen was a husky-looking, mannish-looking woman
who wore pants, a straw hat and a red flowered blouse. I will
always remember that. I was crying when she came . . . scared. I
stared at her . . . our new mama . . . wondering what was she
going to be like. What would she do with us, to us, for us?
Would she want us? I was only five years old and already had to
worry bout my survival . . . our lives! I'm telling you, look at
your mama, if she be living, and be thankful to God!

She picked me up and held me close to her breast, under her
chin and she felt just like I knew my mama did. She took us all,
sat us down and just like we was grown, talked to us. "I ain't got
no home big enough for all us. Ain't got much money, done
saved a little only. But I got a little piece of land I been plannin
to build on someday and this must be the day! Now, I ain't got
chick or child, but now I got you . . . all of you. Ain't gonna be
no separation no more, you got me. I loved my sister and I love
you."

Three little hearts just musta exploded with love and peace.
I know mine did! I remember holding onto her pants, case she
disappeared, I could disappear with her!

She went on talking as she squeezed a cheek, smoothed a
hair, brushed a dress, wiped a nose. "I ain't no cookie-bakin
woman! But you learn to bake the cookies and I'll provide the
stove and the dough!" My sister, Older, could already cook
most everything, but we'd never had no stuff to cook cookies
with. "Now!" she went on as she stroked me, "You want to go
with me?" One nodded yes, one said "yes." I just peed I was so
happy! I kept putting her as my mama! "We'll try to swim to

the top of the rain together!" She smiled and I sensed that sadness again, but it went away quick and I forgot it.

When I hear people say "Homeland," I always know what they mean. There is *no place* like a home. She took us to that beautiful land on a bus, eating cold biscuits, bacon and pieces of chicken, even some cornbread. All fixed by our old neighbors. We stayed hither and yon while she mixed and poured the concrete and built that little cabin with four rooms. We lived in each room as it was finished. It was a beautiful little lopsided house . . . ours! Oh, other people came to help sometime, but we worked hardest on our own home! It took two more years to finally get a inside toilet and bath, but Aunt Ellen had to have one cause she blived in baths and teeth washing and things like that, tho I never saw her take one!

We lived there til we was grown. We tilled a little land, raised our own few pigs and chickens, and split one cow with another family for the milk. She raised us, or helped us raise ourselves.

Older sister quit the little schoolhouse when she was bout fifteen years old in the eighth or ninth grade and got married to a real light man. She just had to have that real light man! In a couple years she had two children, both girls. The light man left, or she left him and came home. Aunt Ellen said, "NO, no! I ain't holdin up no leaning poles! If you old enough to spread them knees and make babies, you old enough to take care yourself! You done stepped out into the rain, now you learn to swim!" Older cried a little cause I guess she was scared of the world, but Aunt Ellen took her round to find a job and a place to live. We baby-sat for her til she was steady. One day we looked up and she was on her own! And smiling! Not cause she was doing so good, but because she was taking care herself and her children and didn't have to answer to nobody! When her man came back, she musta remembered Mama, cause she didn't let him in to make no more babies!

Middle sister went on to the ninth grade, then went to nursing school. Just the kind teach you how to clean up round a patient. Aunt Ellen was proud. She was getting older, but not old yet, and said she would help anybody wanted to go to school long as they got a job and helped themselves too, and she did.

That left only me home with her, but I didn't want to go nowhere away from her!

We didn't have no lot of money, helping Middle go to school and taking care of ourselves. I couldn't even think of getting clothes and all those kind of things! I had me one good dress and a good pair of patent-leather shoes I wore to church every Sunday. So after I got out the ninth grade I asked a lady who sewed for a livin to teach me in exchange for housework and she did. That's why I know there's some nice white people who will help you. After I learned, she would pay me a little to do little things like collars, seams and things. Then I still watched her and learned more for free! I sewed for Aunt Ellen and me and Older's babies. We saved money that way. That's the same way I learned to play the piano . . . sewing for the piano teacher. I got to be pretty good. Got paid a little to play at weddings. Cause I won't charge for no funerals. Death already cost too much!

Middle graduated from that school, well, got out. Cause all they did was ask her was she all paid up and when she said yes, they handed her a paper said she was completed. She got married right soon after that to somebody working in a hospital and they moved to a city that had more hospitals to work in. Soon she had a baby girl. Another girl was good, but where was all our boy children? They necessary too!

One evening after a good dinner, me and Aunt Ellen sat out on the porch. I was swinging and she was rockin as she whittled some wood makin a stool for her leg what had started giving her trouble. She wanted something to prop it up on. Mosquitoes and firebugs was buzzing round us. She turned to me and said, "You know, I'm glad you all came along to my life. I did a lot of things I might never have got to, and now I'm glad they done! I got a family and a home too! I blive we gonna make that swim to the top of the rain! Things seem to be workin out alright! You all are fine girls and I'm proud of you. You gon be alright!"

Pleased, I laughed. "Aunty, you can't swim goin straight up! You can't swim the rain! You got to swim the river or the lake!"

She smiled. "Life is more like the rain. The river and the lake lay down for you. All you got to do is learn how to swim fore you go where they are and jump in. But life don't do that.

You always gets the test fore you learn the swimming lesson, unexpected, like rain. You don't go to the rain, the rain comes to you. Anywhere, anytime. You got to prepare for it! . . . protect yourself! And if it keeps coming down on you, you got to learn to swim to the top through the dark clouds, where the sun is shining on that silver lining."

She wasn't laughing, so I didn't either. I just thought about what she said till I went to sleep. I still ain't never forgot it.

The next day when dinner was ready, Aunt Ellen hadn't come in from the fields and it got to be dark. Finally the mule came home dragging the plow. I went out to look for her, crying as I walked over the plowed rows, screaming her name out, cause I was scared I had lost my Aunt Mama. I had.

I found her under a tree, like she was sleeping. Had a biscuit with a little ham in it, still in her hand. But she wasn't sleeping, she was dead. I couldn't carry her in and wouldn't leave her alone so just stayed out there holding her all night long. A kind neighbor found us the next day, cause he noticed the mule draggin the plow and nobody home.

I sewed Aunt Ellen's shroud to be buried in. I played the piano at her funeral too. Her favorite song, "My Buddy." I would have done anything for her. I loved her, my Aunt Mama, She taught me so much. All I knew to make my life with.

I was alone again.

Older and I buried her. Middle didn't come, but sent $10.00 I gave the preacher $5.00 and stuck the other $5.00 in Aunt Ellen's pocket, thinking, All your money passed out to us. . . . Take this with you. Later, I planted turnips and mustard greens all round her homemade grave, cause she liked them best. Then . . . that part of my life was over.

I was alone again, oh Lord. Trying to see through the rain. You ever been alone? Ain't had nobody? Didn't know what to do? Where to turn? I didn't. I was alone even with my sisters living. This was my life and what was I to do with it?

The house and land belonged to all of us. I tried to stay in that cabin, intended to, but it was too lonely out there. Specially when all the men started passing there late at night, stopping, setting. Rain coming to me just like Aunt Ellen said. I didn't want to be rained on, so I gave it out to a couple without a home and moved on down there where my middle sister was, in the city. I got a job living-in and was making a little extra and saving by doing sewing. I was hunting out a future.

I went to church a lot. I stick close to God cause when you need a friend, you need one you can count on! Not the preacher . . . but God! I steered clear of them men who try to get a working woman and live off her itty-bitty money. I ain't got to tell you about them! They dress and sit while she work! No! No! My aunt taught me how not to be scared without a man til the right one comes, and that's why I'll have something for him when he gets here!

I met that nice man, a very hard-working man at a church social. Was me and a real light woman liking him and I thought sure he would take to her, but he took to me. I waited for a long time, til after we were married to ask him why, cause he might think of something I didn't want him to think of. He told me, "I like her, I think she a fine woman, a good woman. But you can't like somebody just cause they light! Ain't no white man done me no favor by making no black woman a baby! What I care most bout skin is that it fits! Don't sag . . . or shrink when it gets wet!" He say, "I love your outsides and your insides, cause you a kind and lovin woman who needs a lotta love and don't mind lettin me know it! I need love too!" Then I knew I could love him with ease. And I did, through the years that passed.

My husband was a railroad-working man so we was pretty soon able to buy us a little home and I was able to stay in it and not go out to work. I made a little extra money with my sewing and teaching piano lessons. We was doing alright! We both wanted children but didn't seem to start up none, so I naturally came to take up more time with my nieces. That's when I came to know the meaning of the big importance of who raises you and who you raising!

I had urged Older to come to the city with her two girls, they were bout fourteen and fifteen years old round then. Middle didn't have no husband now, and her daughter was bout thirteen years old. I could see, tho they was all from one family, they had such different ways of doing things! With my husband gone two or three days a week, I had time to get to know them more.

Now, Older, she the one with the two daughters, she did everything for the oldest pretty, light one, leaving the other one out a lot. The oldest one had more and better clothes and was a kinda snotty girl. Demanding . . . always demanding! She was going to be a doctor, she said, and true enough she studied hard. She volunteered at the hospitals a lot. Getting ready, she said. She was picky bout her clothes and since her mama didn't make too much money and wouldn't let her work, she was always asking me to sew for her or do her hair. Her best friend was a white girl, live up the street, from a nice family.

I took to sewing, buying the material myself, for the youngest brownskin one. She was a little hard of hearing and didn't speak as prettily and clearly as her older sister, so they was always putting her off or back, or leaving her home when they go out. Now, she was not college-smart, but she was common-sense smart and a good decent girl, treated people right. That's what I like, so I helped her! She was never asking for nothing but was grateful for the smallest thing you did for her. That kind of person makes me remember my aunts and I will work my butt off for people like that! I was closest to her.

I spent time with Middle too. I love my family. Her daughter, thirteen or fourteen years old, was a nice quiet girl. At least I thought she was quiet. I found out later she was beaten under. She was scared to be herself. Her mother, Middle, had turned down her natural spirit! You know, some of them things people try to break in their children are things they may need when they get out in that world when Mama and Papa ain't there! The child was tryin to please her mama and was losing herself! And she wasn't bad to begin with! Now, it's good for a child to mind its mama, but then the mama got to be careful what she tells that child to do! She's messing with her child's life!

Middle was mad one day and told me she had whipped the child for walkin home holding hands with a boy! I told Middle, "Ain't nothing wrong with holding hands! Specially when you heading home where your mama is! Humans will be human! Some people wish their fourteen-year-old daughter was only holding hands!" I told her, "You was almost married when you was her age!" Middle told me I didn't have no kids so I didn't understand! I went home thinking children wasn't nothing but little people living in the same life we was, learning the same things we had to. You just got to understand bout life! I hear people say, "I ain't never been a mother before, how am I supposed to know what to do?" Well, let me tell you, that child ain't never been here before, been a child their age before either! How they always supposed to know what to do, less you teach em! How much do you know to teach em?

Several months later she whipped that girl, hard and long, for kissing a boy in the hallway. I told Middle, "She was in your hallway. What could she do out there and you in here?! If they was planning anything special, they got the whole world out there to hide in!" Middle said, "I wish she was just out there holdin hands walking home, stead of this stuff!" I looked at her trying to understand why she didn't understand when she was well off. "While you think you whipping something *out* of her, you may be whippin' something *in!* Talk to her more. Are you all friends? You know, everybody need a friend!"

She was so sad, my sister, I asked her, "Why don't you think about gettin married again? Get you some kissin stuff? Then maybe natural things won't look so dirty to you! You can be a mama and a wife, stead of a warden!" Middle just screwed up her face and say she know what she doing! Sadness all gone . . . madness too close. Things you feel sposed to make you think bout em! Think how you can help yourself. Hers didn't. She say, "The last thing I need is a man messing up my life again!" Well, it was her business, but it looked to me like she was gettin close to the last thing! I told my niece if she ever need a friend, come to me. I was her aunt and her friend, just like Aunt Ellen was to me! I left.

Life is something, chile! Sometime watching over other folks' life can make you more tired than just taking care your own!

Older's snotty oldest daughter had graduated with good grades from high school and was going out to find work to help send herself to college. Both she and her white girlfriend planned to go to college, but the white friend's family had

planned ahead and had insurance for education. They both
went out together to find work. They went to that hospital
where Oldest's daughter had volunteered steady, spending all
kinds of time and energy in most all the departments there.
Her friend hadn't. But when they had their interviews, her
friend got the job! Well, my niece was just done in or out,
either one or both! But her white friend told her, "I'm a minority, aren't I? I'm a female! At least one of us got it! That's
better than some man getting it!" Ms. Snotty just looked at her
and I don't think they're friends anymore, least not so close.
Anyway, my niece wrote a pack of letters and a month or so
later, she went on East and got a job. I can tell you now, she
didn't become no doctor, but she is a head nurse of a whole
hospital. Her mama surenuff scrimped and saved and made
herself and her other daughter go without to keep that girl in
school. I was giving my other niece all she had to keep her from
feeling too neglected. I loved that girl! I loved them both, but
people with certain kinda needs just get me!

Middle had told her daughter, "No company til you are
eighteen years old and through with school!" But she didn't
give her the hugs and kisses and touches we all need. So the girl
found her own. She was sixteen years old now, and she had
gotten pregnant. She and the boy wanted to get married but
Middle beat her and demanded on her to get an abortion. The
girl wouldn't have one, so Middle was going to show her how
her evil ways had cost her her mother, and how lost she would
be without her! She put her child out of her rented house! Her
own child! Seem like that was the time for Middle to act like
the mother she was always demanding respect for! That was
going to be her own grandchild! But . . . she put her out. I
didn't know it and that poor child didn't come to me. . . . What
had I missed doing or saying to show her I was her friend? Oh
Lord, I prayed for her safety. You know on the other side of
your door sits the whole world. The good people are mostly
home taking care of their family and business. It's the liars,
thieves, rapers, murderers, pimps, sadistics, dopers, crazy people who are out there . . . waiting . . . just for someone without
no experience. Thems who that child was out there with, the
minute her mama slammed that front door! And a belly full of

baby, no man and no mama. It's some things you don't have to live to understand. I wanted my grandniece. I would have taken care of it for her. And Middle would love her grandchile. It's a mighty dumb fool won't let their own heart be happy! If she was worrying bout feeding it . . . she got fed! And didn't have no mama! Trying to show what a fool her daughter was, she showed what a fool she was! Your chile is your heart, your flesh, your blood! And sometimes, your way! Anyway, life goes on. I couldn't find her til way later.

Older's daughter had done graduated and was a surgical or surgeon nurse, and had her own place and car and everything! Older was planning to go visit her and did, leaving the youngest daughter to stay home and watch the house with my help. When Older got back she was hurt and mad. She didn't want to tell it, but we finally got it out of her. Her snotty daughter had made her wear a maid's uniform, the one she had for her regular jobs. She had to cook and answer the door and stay out the way when company came! Not tell nobody that was her daughter! Can you believe . . . even can you imagine that?! Her mother!? Well, it's true, she did and she still does it! Then, shame of all shames possible to snotty sister, her young sister got a job as a maid in a whorehouse! Snotty and Middle hated that, but she made such good money, tips and all, and the girls giving her jewels and discarded furs and clothes and all. They wanted to use them, borrow her money but seem to hate her. Two ways. For having these things and for being low enough to work as a maid in a whorehouse! They made her sad. She was trying to swim to the top of the rain in her own way. I tried to love her enough, but there ain't nothin like your own mama's love!

Bout that time somebody told us about Middle's daughter. She was a prostitute trying to pay her own way, raising her daughter, living alone. She didn't have time to find a job before she started starving, so this was a way. She was trying to swim to the top of the rain, but was drowning. Middle took a gun down on that street and threatened to kill her! I talked to the young woman. She was still a good girl, just lost! But, loving her baby! That baby had everything! Was the fattest, cutest, sweetest, smiling baby I ever seen! Ohhh, how I wanted that baby! And I knew the pain, the great big pain I could see in her face she was going through. Who *wants* to sell their body? The *only* thing, no matter how long you live, that is truly yours, is your body. I don't care how much money you got!

Later, Middle told me, "Ohhhhh, I wish she was home just having one of them illegal babies! Oh, just to have her back home holding hands, or kissing in the hallway, even having that baby! I should a let her marry that boy when they wanted to! I'd rather kill her than see her be a prostitute!" She hurt and I could see it. It was the first time she had even blamed herself a little bit for her part in all this. I had a little hope for her.

The daughter brought the baby her mother had tried to make her get rid of and let her keep it sometime. Middle loved that grandchile so much, cause you see, she didn't have nothin else in her life. It was empty! I kept it whenever I could. That girl, her daughter, stayed sad . . . sad . . . sadder. She would look around her mama's house and make a deep sigh and go away looking hopeless. Her mama told her to come home, but she said it was too late.

I got involved round that time with Older's youngest daughter. She had fallen in love and was bout to marry a blind man. I thought that was good after I met him. He was so good-seeming, so kind to her, so sweet and gentle with her. My sister was going crazy cause he was blind! She didn't even think of his honesty and kindness and love for her daughter. She could only see he was blind. Oh Lord, deliver the innocent from some fools that be mothers, fathers and sisters. She married him anyway, bless her heart, and my sister had a heart attack . . . a real one! Her daughter she didn't love so much and her blind husband took care of her, better than she took care herself when she could. Her nurse daughter, said she couldn't! Didn't have time.

I was so busy being in my family's business I hadn't been in my own enough! My husband, have mercy, told me he was leavin me cause he had met someone he might could love and she was pregnant! I looked at him for bout a hour, it seemed, cause he was my life but I hadn't been actin like it! Been giving everybody else all my thoughts, time and life. But I had done learned bout happiness and I understood if he wasn't happy

here, he should be where he was happy! Ain't that what we all
live for? How could I get mad at a man who had give me
everything, including the chance to make him happy? I
washed, cleaned, packed his clothes, and let him go, clean
away. Then I went in the house, took the biggest bottle of
liquor I could find, sat down and drank for bout a week. Now, I
ain't crazy and a hangover ain't the best feeling in the world.
Life started again in me and bless my soul, even alone, I was
still alive!

I went out in my . . . *my* yard and saw one lone red flower,
dug it up and took it in the house. I told it, "You and me, we
alone. We can survive! I'm going to plant you and make you
grow. I'm going to plant me and make me grow. I'm going to
swim to the top of this rain!" I planted it, it wilted, it lay down
even. I let it alone cept for care. Let it grieve for its natural
place. I loved it, I talked to it. I went and put it back outside,
it's *my* yard too! It could be mine and still be free where it
wanted to be! In a day or two, it took hold again . . . it's still
livin! Me, I just kept carrying on with my swim.

I hadn't seen nobody, cause I didn't want to be bothered
with their problems, I had my own! Then Middle came to me.
My niece was in the hospital, dying from a overdose of dope in
her veins! Ohh Lord!

When I got to the hospital, I stood in the door and listened
to my sister talk to her daughter who could not hear her.
"Don't die, my little girl, *don't* die! Stay with me. You all I got.
What I'm gonna do . . . if you die? Stay with me, don't leave me
alone. Hold hands with anybody you wants to! I won't say
nothing! Kiss anybody you want to . . . I won't mind at all. Just
don't leave me, my baby! Have many babies as you want! I'll
love em all! Don't go. Child of mine, you can even be a prostitute. I don't care! Just live. I rather see you on dope than see
you dead! Cause if you got life, you got a chance to change.
Baby, I'm sorry. I'm *sorry!* Be anything you want . . . JUST
LIVE . . . don't die! Come home! *Don't die!*" She screamed
that out and I went in to help her grieve . . . cause the beautiful
young woman was dead.

After the funeral, the good thing Middle had left was the
baby she had tried to make her daughter get rid of. Her daugh-

ter had won that battle at the cost of her life, it seemed . . . so now, Middle was blessed to have someone to love and be with . . . in her empty life. I went on home to my empty life.

Things smoothed down. God is good. They always smooth down if you give life time.

One day, bout a year later, my doorbell rang and when I answered it, my husband was standing there with a baby in his arms who reached out for me the minute I opened the door. I reached back! I ain't no fool! He had got that young woman he thought he loved and she had got him, but after the baby was born, my husband wanted to rest and stay home when she wanted to play and go out. She left him with his baby. I tried to look sad for him, but my heart said, *"Good, Good, Good!"*

But he didn't look too sad. We talked and talked and talked and talked! I loved my husband and I knew he loved me, even better now. He wanted to come home and I wanted him home. And I wanted that baby. It was his and I musta not been able and she was. How lucky I felt that if I couldn't have one, he had give me one anyway. We didn't need to get married, we still was. Neither one of us had gone to the courts, thinkin the other one would. So I had a family.

Sometimes I hold my baby boy and look deep in his little bright, full of life eyes. I know something is coming in the coming years cause life ain't easy to live all the time. Even rich folks commit suicide. But I tell my boy, like my aunt told me, "Just come on, grow up, we gonna make it, little man, right through the storms! We gonna take our chances . . . and get on out there and take our turn . . . swimming to the top of the rain!"

Salvatore La Puma

SALVATORE LA PUMA might seem like an anomaly in contemporary American letters. Where most writers have tuned their literary chops in journalism, La Puma has spent most of his life selling real estate in California. Then at fifty-seven, an age when many writers coast on their youthful reputations, La Puma published a first collection of short stories, *The Boys of Bensonhurst*, that won him the Flannery O'Connor award for short fiction, the American Book Award, and a place in *Prize Stories 1988: The O. Henry Awards*. A subsequent novel, *A Time for Wedding Cake*, has earned La Puma a sizable movie option even before seeing print.

Anomaly, perhaps. But anyone at all familiar with Italian American artists knows that La Puma fits the Italianate tradition of late-blooming amateurs to a T. Sam Rodia started the Watts Towers in his forties, and worked on it for more than thirty years in his spare time. Ralph Fasanella began to paint almost by chance in midlife when a fellow union organizer suggested that the pain in his fingers might be due to a deep urge to draw—which it was, and which habit he had to feed working at his brother's gas station for years. Pascal D'Angelo learned to write evenings while living in a boxcar in New Jersey: he read newspapers to learn English, and then began writing his own stories, all the while working as a pick-and-shovel man whenever the railroads needed bodies. Pietro di Donato began his working life laying bricks—at the age of 13—and even at seventy-nine, as his *Christ in Concrete* is lauded as the undisputed classic of Italian American novels, calls himself not a writer, but a bricklayer.

To be sure, La Puma knew early on that writing was his calling. He loved to listen to stories his father, an opera buff and accomplished raconteur, would tell: "My father told stories in the oral tradition and kept listeners spellbound." Then a fortunate illness gave La Puma himself the storytelling bug: "Double pneumonia at age seven laid me out and was expected to kill me off. While lying in bed at home, I read the few children's books we had, then asked for more. But my parents were too paralyzed with fear and worry to go out and get them. Instead I was told to tell myself a story. So I did. And almost every day since then when I'm about to die from a physical ache, a big bill in the mail, a passionate love, I tell myself another story. Miraculously for the old times I got well. And once out of bed, announced that I would write stories when I grew up."

Heard stories. Overheard stories. A need for stories so powerful that one tells them to oneself to cure pneumonia. It is this immersion in an ancient oral mode that fixes La Puma in the center of the Italian-American literary tradition. Stories teach, stories cure, there's a story for every occasion, every problem, every mood. Lou D'Angelo called his book *What the Ancients Said,* because that's how his grandparents prefaced every proverb—the better to head off any new-worldly dispute about relevance. Pietro di Donato writes a prose that sounds like English thought out in Italian—oral prose, if such a thing can be said to exist, for the peasant tradition behind such writing is oral and orality retains, as Derrida points out, the presence and force of the father within it.

So, too, with Salvatore La Puma. His stories echo with the voice of an old "boy" of Bensonhurst sitting on the steps of New Utrecht High School, hearing in his mind's ear and feeling in his mind's gut the passionate goings-on of the days gone by that seem more real than yesterday. And they are. La Puma's Bensonhurst is a very specific time and place. All the stories in the collection take place in those now innocent-seeming years of 1939, '40, and '41 when an adolescent America was edging toward full commitment to world war. This is not to say that his Bensonhurst boys tramp barefoot through idyllic fields in never-ending summer. Far from it. These are street-bred Italian Americans who spend large hunks of time trying to seduce neighborhood girls in ornate basements, making fake olive oil for tough guys in their fedoras, and sometimes having to choose between the mob and the priesthood as the only safe haven from the consequences of murdering the landlord. Sometimes they win, and sometimes they lose, but always they live at full throttle in a world that is serious and sad and where the bizarre is commonplace: ghosts talk through mirrors, old men at death "know" that God plays the mandolin, dogs think in Sicilian and consider English "cat talk," priests fall for their parishioners and vice versa, and the neighborhood boys pay final tribute to their friend who has died too young by hiring a burlesque queen to strip for him in the funeral home the night before his burial—thus cheating death in the tradition of countless Sicilian folk tales.

These days Salvatore La Puma lives in California, where he is able to tell his stories full-time. A new short story collection is due in 1991, and a novel is in the works.

—Lawrence DiStasi

"Gravesend Bay" from
THE BOYS OF BENSONHURST:
STORIES

"YOU all know this one," said Carmine as the orchestra struck up "Do I Love You?" Applause rose in anticipiation. Melting girls were thinking that his singing, tainted with longing, could be the history of love.

"He's singing that for me," said Julia Albanesi, who sat with Tonino.

"I leave him in the dust," said Tonino, Carmine's rival on the track in 1940.

Carmine Carmellini, eighteen, hadn't studied voice as urged by his father, Mario, who slaved over his viola. Music had always come easily to Carmine; his voice served him well. He'd been pampered with applause since he was five.

From his mother, Carmine had inherited the looks of the eleventh-century Norman invaders of Sicily, Viking eyes and hair which made blue and yellow sparks in the bold Arab eyes of New Utrecht High's Sicilian girls. These girls were taught by their mothers to act like virgins with downcast glances, but whenever Carmine was singing or running or just passing by, they forgot.

"DID fifty laps," said Carmine, collapsing on the bench.

"Don't sit. Cool down slow," said Tonino, dragging Carmine to walk on the grass.

Both were about six feet tall. Carmine's legs, longer than Tonino's, knit yards together over cross-country distances, but before a finish line, his sap depleted, Carmine always unraveled and Tonino always won.

"I'm building up," said Carmine.

"Moving your arms is a waste. You ain't singing," said Tonino.

"I'll beat you next time," said Carmine.

"You're an old lady," said Tonino.

"EDWARD G. ROBINSON starts tonight," said Julia.

Julia's mother, Agnese Albanesi, sewed dresses in the storefront factory on 16th Avenue when orders came in. In the first year of her marriage to Rudy he claimed to have asthma in their tiny cavelike apartment downstairs in the rear of a four-family house. One day Rudy didn't stop his produce truck at the market at three in the morning, but kept going. In a pileup in Detroit he was killed the week before Julia was born.

"Robinson acts Sicilian," said Carmine.

Carmine liked Julia's heart-shaped face and bow mouth. She was one of the prettiest girls in school, didn't giggle, and looked sad, which got his sympathy.

"You can't tell between Jewish and us," said Julia, serving him her provolone sandwich. "We even look alike. Except *you're* different."

"I'm not inside," said Carmine. They were sitting on the grass oval inside the cinder track. "I get a kiss for dessert?"

"Mom's cookies," said Julia.

Julia made Carmine's lunch every school day, knitted his pullover, wrote him notes, and in her morning and evening prayers asked for Carmine's love.

"Let's go under the stairs," said Carmine.

Julia gave him her saucy red kisses, but he resisted the cookies under her clothes. He wanted to be in the chorus of angels eventually, and not a roasting chestnut, having gotten his religion, like his eyes and hair, from his mother.

Carmine and Julia went to the Hollywood once a week, held hands in the dark, then went for ice cream sundaes. If the weather was warm and the night late, he'd sing an Italian ballad in the school yard, and Julia would think his voice was the fallen angel's leading her into temptation. She would even put his picture on her dresser in place of the Sacred Heart, though over that blasphemous thought she chewed her nails.

Other boys jostled to sniff Julia's neck and rub against her hip, but she was so absorbed in Carmine she couldn't see anyone else. She kept his kisses in her diary, and some days lived only remembering them, especially as he was now running during lunch. Then she didn't eat lunch at all, and was soon swimming in her dress, and one day Carmine noticed her raw and bloody wrists. Skin from each wrist was missing like an absent watchband.

"Jesus. What happened?"

"I bite my wrists."

"That's crazy."

"The doctor says I'm nervous."

"About what?"

"It's a secret."

"Look, Julia. Everything works out. You don't have to be nervous."

"I'm really not," she said. "I'm biting them for a reason."

"Don't you have bandages?"

"I took them off."

"You have to stop."

"You can't make me."

"We won't go to the show."

"Then I'll kill myself."

"Quit it for me, Julia."

"That's the reason I'm doing it, Carmine."

"YOU could sing Verdi at the Met," said first violinist Patricia Schneck, her rosy face in the long vase of her neck.

Carmine and Patricia eyed each other like forbidden fruit. Sicilian students mixed agreeably with Jewish students who were in the majority at New Utrecht. The other's culture was approved of at home, but falling for it would bring their families' wrath, if not God's, down on their heads.

"I'd take voice if you taught it," said Carmine.

Patricia always seemed about to be captured by the crowd or another boy, so Carmine sought her out and he didn't let her get away. Sometimes he was in near panic, his lips drying and face flushing as if he'd run ten miles. He focused on no one else, phoning every night as if he didn't see her every day. That he was wild about her was infecting her with a wonderful illness of becoming wild about him, and they often laughed together like maniacs.

"You can't walk me home," she said as they left the April Festival.

Carmine stayed at her side in the crowd going up 79th Street. Ahead was the BMT elevated train and in the street below it the trolley car that she would take. Some of the guys stopped off at the candy store for "looseys," Camels and Chesterfields at a penny each, but Carmine was saving his breath for running and singing.

"Let's go down to the bay," he said. "They're making a new beach."

"I'm sorry," said Patricia. "I've French to read."

"Me too," he said.

"Gentiles should be with Gentiles. I'm not."

"Who cares?"

"Doesn't your father?"

"He doesn't."

"Your mother, then?"

"I'm not some kid does what his mother says."

The next afternoon and the next, Carmine asked her again to go to Gravesend Bay. Then Patricia stopped hearing the objection her father would make, and went. It was what she wanted to do all along. Steered by muscled men, the tractors coughed like old smokers as they pushed the bay back into the Atlantic by dumping in sand castles and boulders at the water's edge, turning on steel ribbon feet behind a fresh load. Tasting the salty air, Carmine carrying their books, they slogged through sand, holding hands. Midway on the new beach, laughing from exhaustion, they dropped, entertained by the whitecaps. Their kiss was small and fragile, as if breakable in two at any moment, but they were careful with it.

"Don't see anyone else," said Carmine.

"You have Julia."

"We stopped going out."

"We couldn't ever go to each other's house," said Patricia.

"It's not impossible," he said.

"You shouldn't break up with Julia. She's sick over you."

Patricia wanted to obey her father, Herbert Schneck, a decent man who gave all his work, play, and prayers to his family. But a woman was growing in Patricia, pink when she was with Carmine, absent of color when she wasn't. In the following weeks, if he didn't find her, she searched for him. They went often to Gravesend Bay, and stayed late after school.

DESPITE her husband's ridicule that God couldn't exist where stars were as plentiful as unanswered prayers, Anna Carmellini, believing the impossible sometimes comes true, went daily to the 8:00 A.M. Mass. On Sundays Mario kept her company at the high 11:15, where Anna always took communion, but Mario never did. Saturday evenings Anna also made her weekly confession at St. Finbar's, where afterward she said her penance.

"You have nothing to confess," said her husband when Anna returned late one Saturday night.

"You know my sins?" she said, almost as if she'd tell them, but then covered her mouth.

"True, you burn the pots, but I forgive you," he said, but Anna wasn't amused.

"Sin's in the heart," she said.

"Yours must be a lump of coal. I think you're never coming back from confession. Go to another priest."

"Father Hartigan's very pious," she said.

"What's an Irishman know about Sicilian sins?"

"I try to be a good wife, Mario."

"Tell me your sins, Anna. I forgive you better than the priest."

"Only God forgives. I want to offer my hair as a sacrifice."

"Your beautiful hair?" he said, shaking his head. "If there's a God, He'll cry like a baby."

"For the feast of Santa Lucia," she said. "And carry a candle and walk on my knees."

"That's for witches. Let's go to bed. I kiss your belly. Wherever you feel sin."

"We can't two more days. The cycle," she said. "But play your viola. I want to hear. While I say the rosary."

His viola, two violins, and a cello were in a string quartet. Their musica da camera made them famous on Manhattan's Upper East Side, but infrequent performances earned them little. Still, day and night, Mario crossed catgut with horsehair.

Haydn's Opus 33 rose from Mario's viola as from the bottom of the sea. He nodded to his instrument, caught in the ebb and flow of the music as Anna wished she could be caught up in religion.

Alone in their bedroom, Anna heard Mario's viola in the parlor, clever, graceful, and imaginative, but distant too, touching only her ears. Instead of his music, she preferred Carmine's singing, especially her favorite song at a family celebration, "La Donne è Mobile," which brought tears to her eyes.

Father Hartigan said God would give her peace, she should pray and make small sacrifices, though not her hair. "God forbid," he said.

After Mass one Thursday morning Anna met Father Hartigan in the school yard. Lined-up children were waiting to go in. Anna and the priest buttoned up jackets, tied shoelaces, dabbed away tears, and replaced lost or stolen lunch money as if the children were theirs. Anna's library opened at noon, and the priest was pleased she could substitute half a day for the sick nun. Her reading delighted the children.

It could be misunderstood why Anna and Father Hartigan were always together, but the nuns and other priests seemed not to notice. Anna noticed and so did he, but instead of their friendship ending, it grew. In his confessional Anna knelt for hours whispering with him about God and what He must be like, and of sinners to be forgiven, and in the code known only to themselves, they were talking about themselves.

One hot June Saturday night after confession the priest suggested they go for iced tea. Beside him in his Dodge, Anna was uneasy. Only rarely had she been alone with a man not her husband or a relative. Yet she wanted to be there. He was more than her priest, he was the man she should've had. The priest drove out of Bensonhurst and through strange streets, he and Anna wordless. When they returned to the neighborhood, he parked at Gravesend's dark and lonely beach, and still they didn't speak.

IN green shorts and a sleeveless white shirt, the school colors, Carmine ran before classes, breathing with his mouth open.

Marty Katz gave him lung and leg exercises, but his speed and endurance didn't improve. Running also took place in the mind, where Carmine fell down, thought Marty, but Marty didn't care that Carmine didn't win. Marty had Tonino for that. To sweat was reward enough. Those who had to win eventually did.

"Suppose your girl's waiting," said Marty. "She's a little fickle. Just might give it to any guy comes in first. Wouldn't you run harder?"

"If it was Patricia."

"She goes for you."

"Maybe I should convert to Jewish."

"You have to ask yourself. At your age, if you'd give up a piece of your dick."

"Would I have to?"

"Marry one of my daughters in six, seven years. I married an Italian."

A spring rain fell during the night. It wouldn't have mattered on the school track banked to drain and lift, but the cross-country was taking place at six in the morning on Prospect Park's pathways. Puddles like black glass had collected on the asphalt, and Carmine often didn't jump soon enough and splashed in the water. His wet feet slowed him down even more than usual.

Carmine began too fast, thinking he was inexhaustible. Singing, he was. But even with his desire for things out of reach, even believing, despite Tonino's jeering, that he could beat Tonino, Carmine was running out of gas.

Orange arrows on trees pointed to paths. Through the trees Carmine glimpsed the lake still and gray. The park was chosen for the absence of people going to the zoo or rowing at this early hour. By the boathouse were the few spectators from participating schools. Julia's red blouse caught his eye, then her blurred pretty face. Her wave boosted him on. His team had come on the school bus, but Julia had gotten up very early to take the BMT in the dark. Carmine wished he could give her the cup. She deserved it, but she also made him feel a little guilty.

Out of breath, dripping as if from a dozen faucets, bites itching, mouth cracking, Carmine was unable to live up to his standard and hated himself. Runner after runner was passing him by as he chugged on. Under the leafing maple, coaches in whites were clumped like toadstools on the damp earth. "Carmine, your girl's at the finish," called Marty. "Run like hell." Carmine couldn't believe in the illusion. Patricia was staying home this Saturday to practice Mozart.

JOBS were scarce that summer, and many girls who graduated with Julia had to stay at home crocheting tablecloths for their trousseaus. But Julia, then eighteen, was hired by Alfonso, the pastryman, for his 16th Avenue shop. With her triangular face, she was just too pretty to be sent away. Customers would be attracted by her for gelato and ices in the heat. Alfonso was right. Sad-eyed, naturally blushed, and figure ripe, she made boys whistle and want to draw her out. If she smiled they won something that showed they'd soon be men. Alfonso, near forty and married to a young woman, looked at Julia, yearning for a still younger bride.

Hiding her healing wrists in long-sleeved blouses, Julia seemed as happy or as unhappy as always, keeping her misery as she had her joy between the covers of her diary. She read newspapers and listened to the radio with her mother, and went to the movies with her friend Bianca whenever Bianca's Ernesto worked late or went downtown to study automotive mechanics.

When she came home from the movies one moonless night, time turning invisibly, her mother asleep in her room, Julia went into the kitchen and closed the door and windows. Turning on all the jets in the dark, she put her head in the oven. She despised heaven's mysterious design excluding men from her life. Her father had run away and died. Her mother's brother, their family adviser, had become senile and was taken away when she was fourteen. Now Carmine, at the show with Patricia, was also gone from her life. Julia knew all along he wanted Patricia, but she waited patiently, hoping their religions would clash like cymbals. It could still happen, but seeing them together tore Julia's heart out. To rid herself of heartache and the memory of Carmine, she breathed in the gas.

The heavy thud she made when she fell awakened her mother, and Agnese Albanesi rushed in and began screaming from her gut. Since they didn't own a phone, the landlord upstairs called the ambulance.

Old women in black, putting their heads together, whispered and stared as Carmine went by. Fearing him, they directed their pointer and pinkie devil-horns at him to ward off the evil he could bring into their lives. A week passed before he got up his nerve and went to the hospital. Julia was pale. Her ruffled nightgown was opaque in the second layer and sheer in the first. Seeing her he loved her, but not as he should. He never dreamed of Julia without her clothes.

Tonino, at Julia's bedside, had brought flowers, unlike Carmine. Awkward at the foot of the bed, his hands in and out of his pockets, Carmine knew he should kiss Julia, apologize, offer to kill himself instead, but he did none of that.

"That was dumb," said Carmine.

"Are you smart?" said Julia.

Getting up, Tonino said, "I'll come back," but was delayed by Julia's extended hand.

"You're sweet. The flowers," she said.

"Next time you get ice cream," said Tonino, and then went out.

"He steals things," said Carmine.

"He's taking the fireman's test," said Julia. "He's brave to be a fireman."

Still a little jealous, Carmine said, "Don't let him swipe your heart."

"You going to marry that girl?" asked Julia.

FOR a while after graduation Carmine didn't know what to do with himself. He'd discuss with his father summer jobs he should look for, but he'd do nothing about getting them. The one thing he knew how to do of course was sing, so finally he applied to The Glass Hat in Sheepshead Bay, and was hired after a fifteen-minute audition in which he sang "The Very Thought of You," "All the Things You Are," and "Wishing."

Carmine would be going to Brooklyn College, Patricia to Massachusetts, she wouldn't say where exactly. She came to The Glass Hat often, the headwaiter seating her close to the mike so Carmine could sing to her, and she and the patrons loved it. After two weeks a talent agent said, "You could be rich and famous, kid."

Carmine and Patricia were seeing each other a few times a day, made love at night on the new beach, and called each other hourly, often with nothing to say, as if their voices hid messages. They also made many promises. That midsummer their love was still perfectly whole, a china cup without the small chips that come after years of use. The passing season and the impossibility of their love made them cling to it as something precious about to slip through their fingers.

Neither family knew. Carmine and Patricia were protecting themselves from parents who would break them up, and protecting their parents from the misery of knowing. And besides, posting the news of a love about to end seemed pointless.

On a warm Monday night when the nightclub was closed Carmine and Patricia went to their place on the sand and uncovered something they tried to bury: they couldn't ever leave each other. A first love has no history of failure, no knowledge that a broken heart survives, and they thought if their love ended so too would their lives.

"I'll take morning classes. Sing at night," Carmine said.

"I'll take the same classes and work at night too."

"Your father will be sore."

"I might be miserable, Carmine. And your mother?"

"She'll say novenas."

"I'll never give up being Jewish."

"Marrying at city hall, I'll be excommunicated."

"Will you be hurt?"

"You can touch it where it hurts," he said.

ANNA and Father Hartigan grew comfortable riding around mornings, and in the afternoons she called in sick. They carelessly had egg creams in the Bay Parkway Cafeteria. They fumbled chopsticks over chow mein at Fat Choy's on 86th Street. Finally, Anna took the wheel, learning to drive within Bensonhurst, and sometimes the priest was recognized. One young woman shopping for shoes, a former nun, Cristina, saw them and phoned his pastor.

Like mannequins, they hadn't touched, kissed, or spoken a word about love. They yearned for something not even allowed into thought, were driven to be together as if they were whispered to by the same Holy Ghost who had visited Mary.

"You have to leave the parish," said Monsignor Kerry, bent and sprouting warts, avoiding the obvious questions, almost as if the same thing had happened to him once.

"It was nothing," said Father Hartigan. "But I'm ashamed."

"The nun will tell a hundred people, and each will tell another hundred," said the monsignor. "You don't stand a chance. You're one of them now. The sinners expect us to be their saints."

"Where will I be sent?"

"I'll recommend as far as possible. It's up to the bishop."

"How soon?"

"I'll call Monday. He'll need two, three days. Figure the end of next week. Next time, try the bottle, father. Won't get you in as much trouble."

Late Saturday night Mario called the church and the housekeeper fetched the monsignor. The monsignor couldn't remember having seen Anna at confession. She was at church so often she was almost another plaster statue. Surely he had seen her, but he was sleepy or drunk or feigning, and hung up on Mario before the conversation ended.

Wading fearfully into the early hours, Mario in his sleepless anguish thought of running to the church to tear down its doors. But Anna wouldn't be sleeping in a pew. Maybe she had been struck down by a careless driver. He called the police, but Anna hadn't been in an accident. They took her description and told him they would look for her in the morning.

They didn't have to. Someone found the priest's Dodge on the beach, a garden hose from the exhaust pipe run through an inch of rear-window space. The police told Mario and he woke Carmine. It was Carmine's last night in their apartment.

Carmine ran as never before, swift, at ease, without hungering for breath, without stretching for extra inches. He was the gazelle, running the miles to where police cars, ambulances, and people littered the sand.

The mask on Anna's face forced in oxygen.

"It's weak, but beating," said the man with the stethoscope.

The seat behind the wheel was vacant. Carmine heard the priest's name.

The priest had parked his car at night and they said the rosary until passing out. It was a miracle made by a mistake, as many of man's are: he'd neglected to fill his tank, and the engine had run out of gas before they could die. Father Hartigan was assigned to New Mexico's Pueblo Indians.

When Anna came home from the hospital, she shaved off her golden hair. As it grew back slowly, she seemed to be coming to her senses again and kissed Mario and took him between her legs, though she hardly said a word. Mario played his viola for her.

Forgiven by Mario, Anna then had to forgive Carmine for marrying a Jewish girl. They were invited for the first time two years later. After dinner Mario bounced their baby on his knee and asked Carmine to sing for his mother, but Carmine declined.

"He doesn't sing anymore. Not for a long time," said Patricia. "Now he runs fast. He's even faster than Tonino in their fireman's training."

Milton Murayama

A POWERFUL criticism of authoritarianism and tyranny in the Japanese American community from the nisei perspective is found in Milton Murayama's *All I Asking for Is My Body* (1975). The central character is the firstborn nisei son of sugar plantation workers in Hawaii. Toshio Oyama is seen through the eyes of another nisei—the narrator, his younger brother Kiyoshi. The two brothers represent two contrasting but also overlapping nisei responses to the problems of the Japanese family system before World War II.

The issei, "cut off from the world ever since they left their farming villages in Japan," have transplanted in Hawaii almost intact the feudal Japanese family, which constitutes a rigidly hierarchical pecking order that almost everyone in the Japanese American community supports. The Oyamas live on Pigpen Avenue next to an open sewage ditch, condemned to field labor to repay an enormous inherited debt. Just as the older Oyama sacrificed himself and his family, taking comfort in the belief that he was being filial, he expects his oldest son to accept responsibility for the as yet unpaid debt when his turn comes. Toshio is admonished that he must be a "good filial son"— patient, dutiful, hardworking, and mindful of his obligations to his parents. He is told stories of heroic young samurai in old Japan who sacrificed themselves for their parents, who suffered in silence even when falsely accused, and exhibited courage instead of selfishness by adhering to the traditional Japanese virtues of *gaman* (patience), *enryo* (restraint), and *yamato damashii* (Japanese spirit). Toshio, however, challenges the community's blind acceptance of these mores and values, which he contends serve only to justify the imprisonment of the individual within a self-perpetuating and exploitative hierarchy: "Hard work, patience, holding back, waiting your turn, all that crap, they all fit together to keep you down."

All I Asking for Is My Body is a rejection of the oppressive aspects of the Japanese family system and the plantation system that nurtured it, in favor of the freedom of the individual. Unquestioning adherence to inherited conventions is condemned as hypocritical self-service parading as virtue. There is little of value in the Japanese family or community in *All I Asking for Is My Body,* except perhaps for the relationship between the two nisei brothers, who complement each other and whose ideas and identities are developed during their dialogues. But even as an advocate of self-determination and human freedom, Toshio is not without his faults: at times he is stridently self-righteous and pigheaded. By contrast, his more conventional and sensitive younger brother's sympathy shifts across the generations between his parents and his brother.

As if in anticipation of being criticized for a negative depiction of the Japanese American family and community, Murayama has written:

> When you're dealing with two conflicting cultures, you face a problem. Are you going to be pro-one, pro-the-other, or impartial. If impartial, how? What I worked out was simple: I will use the same yardstick of honesty for both, I will criticize the Japanese family system with the same candor I criticize the plantation system. But what about the priority of values? What is number one? Here again the key was simple: Whatever promotes freedom is good, whatever suppresses it is not good. . . . Freedom was freeing oneself from group loyalties and collective myths and stereotypes. Freedom was finally freedom of mind.

Murayama has said that he wanted to "expose an authoritarian system from inside, from underneath," "to set the record straight" even if the picture presented was not attractive: "I want this history remembered, not lost—like it is, with love, with all the warts showing."

—Elaine Kim

"I'll Crack Your Head Kotsun" from
ALL I ASKING FOR IS MY BODY

THERE was something funny about Makot. He always played with guys younger than he and the big guys his own age always made fun of him. His family was the only Japanese family in Filipino Camp and his father didn't seem to do anything but ride around in his brand-new Ford Model T. But Makot always had money to spend and the young kids liked him.

During the summer in Pepelau, Hawaii, the whole town spends the whole day at the beach. We go there early in the morning, then walk home for lunch, often in our trunks, then go back for more spearing fish, surfing, or just plain swimming, depending on the tide, and stay there till sunset. At night there were the movies for those who had the money and the Buddhist Bon dances and dance practices. The only change in dress was that at night we wore Japanese zori and in the day bare feet. Nobody owned shoes in Pepelau.

In August Makot became our gang leader. We were all at the beach and it was on a Wednesday when there was a matinee, and Makot said, "Come on, I'll take you all to the movies," and Mit, Skats, and I became his gang in no time. Mit or Mitsunobu Kato and Skats or Nobuyuki Asakatsu and I were not exactly a gang. There were only three of us and we were all going to be in the fourth grade, so nobody was leader. But we were a kind of a poor gang. None of us were in the Boy Scouts or had bicycles, we played football with tennis balls, and during basketball season we hung around Baldwin Park till some gang showed up with a rubber ball or a real basketball.

After that day we followed Makot at the beach, and in spearing fish Skats and I followed him across the breakers. We didn't want to go at first, since no fourth-grader went across the breakers, but he teased us and called us yellow, so Skats and I followed. Mit didn't care if he was called yellow. Then at lunch-time, instead of all of us going home for lunch, Makot invited us all to his home in Filipino Camp. Nobody was home and he cooked us rice and canned corned beef and onions. The follow-ing day there was the new kind of Campbell soup in cans, which we got at home only when we were sick. So I began to look forward to lunchtime, when we'd go to Makot's home to eat. At home Father was a fisherman and so we ate fish and rice three times a day, and as my older brother Tosh who was a seventh-grader always said, "What! Fish and rice again! No wonder the Japanese get beriberi!" I was sick of fish and rice too.

Mother didn't seem too happy about my eating at Makot's. About the fourth day when I came home at sunset, she said in Japanese, "You must be famished, Kiyo-chan, shall I fix you something?"

"No, I had lunch at Makoto-san's home."

"Oh, again?"

Mother was sitting on a cushion on the floor, her legs hid under her, and she was bending over and sewing a kimono by hand. It was what she always did. I sat down cross-legged. "Uh huh. Makoto-san invited me. I ate a bellyful. Makoto-san is a very good cook. He fixed some corned beef and onions and it was delicious."

"Oh, are you playing with Makoto-san now? He's too old for you, isn't he? He's Toshio's age. What about Mitsunobu-san and Nobuyuki-san?"

"Oh, they still with me. We all play with Makoto-san. He invited all of us."

"Makoto-san's mother or father wasn't home?"

"No, they're usually not home."

"You know, Kiyo-chan, you shouldn't eat at Makoto-san's home too often."

"Why? But he invites us."

"But his parents didn't invite you. Do you understand, Kiyo-chan?"

"But why? Nobuyuki-san and Mitsunobu-san go."

"Kiyo-chan is a good boy so he'll obey what his mother says, won't he?"

"But why, Mother! I eat at Nobuyuki's and Mitsunobu's homes when their parents aren't home. And I always thank their parents when I see them. I haven't thanked Makoto's parents yet, but I will when I see them."

"But don't you see, Kiyoshi, you will bring shame to your father and me if you go there to eat. People will say, 'Ah, look at the Oyama's number two boy. He's a *hoitobo!* He's a *chorimbo!* That's because his parents are *hoitobo* and *chorimbo!*' "

Hoitobo means beggar in Japanese and *chorimbo* is something like a bum, but they're ten times worse than beggar and bum because you always make your face real ugly when you say them and they sound horrible!

"But Makoto invites us, Mother! Once Mitsunobu didn't want to go and Makoto dragged him. We can always have Makoto-san over to our home and repay him the way we do Mitsunobu-san and Nobuyuki-san."

"But can't you see, Kiyo-chan, people will laugh at you. 'Look at the Kiyoshi Oyama,' they'll say, 'he always eats at the Sasakis'. It's because his parents are poor and he doesn't have enough to eat at home.' You understand, don't you, Kiyo-chan? You're a good filial boy so you'll obey what your parents say, won't you? Your father and I would cry if we had two unfilial sons like Toshio . . ."

"But what about Nobuyuki and Mitsunobu? Won't people talk about them and their parents like that too?"

"But Kiyoshi, you're not a monkey. You don't have to copy others. Whatever Nobuyuki and Mitsunobu do is up to them. Besides, we're poor and poor families have to be more careful."

"But Mitsunobu's home is poor too! They have lots of children and he's always charging things at the stores and his home looks poor like ours!"

"Nemmind! You'll catch a sickness if you go there too often," she made a real ugly face.

"What kind of sickness? Won't Mitsunobu-san and Nobuyuki-san catch it too?"

She dropped her sewing on her lap and looked straight at me. "Kiyoshi, you will obey your parents, won't you?"

I stood up and hitched up my pants. I didn't say yes or no. I just grunted like Father and walked out.

But the next time I went to eat at Makot's I felt guilty and the corned beef and onions didn't taste so good. And when I came home that night the first thing Mother asked was, "Oh, did you have lunch, Kiyo-chan?" Then, "At Makoto-san's home?" and her face looked as if she was going to cry.

But I figured that that was the end of that so I was surprised when Father turned to me at the supper table and said, "Kiyoshi . . ." Whenever he called me by my full name instead of Kiyo or Kiyo-chan, that meant he meant business. He never punched my head once, but I'd seen him slap and punch Tosh's head all over the place till Tosh was black and blue in the head.

"Yes, Father." I was scared.

"Kiyoshi, you're not to eat anymore at Makoto-san's home. You understand?"

"But why, Father? Nobuyuki-san and Mitsunobu-san eat with me too!"

"Nemmind!" he said in English. Then he said in Japanese, "You're not a monkey. You're Kiyoshi Oyama."

"But why?" I said again. I wasn't being smart-alecky like Tosh. I really wanted to know why.

Father grew angry. You could tell by the way his eyes bulged and the way he twisted his mouth. He flew off the handle real easily, like Tosh. He said, "If you keep on asking 'Why? Why?' I'll crack your head *kotsun!*"

Kotsun doesn't mean anything in Japanese. It's just the sound of something hard hitting your head.

"Yeah, slap his head, slap his head!" Tosh said in pidgin Japanese and laughed.

"Shut up! Don't say uncalled-for things!" Father said to Tosh and Tosh shut up and grinned.

Whenever Father talked about this younger generation talking too much and talking out of turn and having no respect for anything, he didn't mean me, he meant Tosh.

"Kiyoshi, you understand, you're not to eat anymore at Makoto's home," Father said evenly, now his anger gone.

I was going to ask "Why?" again but I was afraid. "Yes," I said.

Then Tosh said across the table in pidgin English, which the old folks couldn't understand, "You know why, Kyo?" I never liked the guy, he couldn't even pronounce my name right. "Because his father no work and his mother do all the work, thass why! Ha-ha-ha-ha!"

Father told him to shut up and not to joke at the table and he shut up and grinned.

Then Tosh said again in pidgin English, his mouth full of food; he always talked with his mouth full, "Go tell that *kodomo taisho* to go play with guys his own age, not small shrimps like you. You know why he doan play with us? Because he scared, thass why. He too *wahine*. We bust um up!"

"*Wahine*" was the Hawaiian word for woman. When we called anybody *wahine* it meant she was a girl or he was a sissy. When Father said *wahine* it meant the old lady or Mother.

Then I made another mistake. I bragged to Tosh about going across the breakers. "You *pupule* ass! You wanna die or what? You want shark to eat you up? Next time you go outside the breakers I goin' slap your head!" he said.

"Not dangerous. Makot been take me go."

"Shaddup! You tell that *kodomo taisho* if I catch um taking you outside the breakers again, I going bust um up! Tell um that! Tell um I said go play with guys his own age!"

"He never been force me. I asked um to take me."

"Shaddup! The next time you go out there, I goin' slap your head!"

Tosh was three years older than me and when he slapped my head, I couldn't slap him back because he would slap me right back, and I couldn't cry like my kid sister because I was too big to cry. All I could do was to walk away mad and think of all the things I was going to do to get even when I grew up. When I slapped my sister's head she would grumble or sometimes cry but she would always talk back, "No slap my head, you! Thass where my brains stay, you know!" Me, I couldn't even talk back. Most big brothers were too cocky anyway and mine was more cocky than most.

Then at supper Tosh brought it up again. He spoke in pidgin Japanese (we spoke four languages: good English in school, pidgin English among ourselves, good or pidgin Japanese to our parents and the other old folks), "Mama, you better tell Kyo not to go outside the breakers. By-'n'-by he drown. By-'n'-by the shark eat um up."

"Oh, Kiyo-chan, did you go outside the breakers?" she said in Japanese.

"Yeah," Tosh answered for me, "Makoto Sasaki been take him go."

"Not dangerous," I said in pidgin Japanese; "Makoto-san was with me all the time."

"Why shouldn't Makoto-san play with people his own age, *ne?*" Mother said.

"He's a *kodomo taisho,* thass why!"

Kodomo taisho meant General of the kids.

"Well, you're not to go outside the breakers anymore. Do you understand, Kiyo-chan?" Mother said.

I turned to Father, who was eating silently. "Is that right, Father?"

"So," he grunted.

"BOY, your father and mother real strict," Makot said. I couldn't go outside the breakers, I couldn't go eat at his place. But Makot always saved some corned beef and onions and Campbell soup for me. He told me to go home and eat fast and just a little bit and come over to his place and eat with them and I kept on doing that without Mother catching on. And Makot was always buying us pie, ice cream, and chow fun, and he was always giving me the biggest share of the pie, ice cream, or chow fun. He also took us to the movies now and then and when he had money for only one treat or when he wanted to take only me and spend the rest of the money on candies, he would have me meet him in town at night, as he didn't want me to come to his place at night. "No tell Mit and Skats," he told me and I didn't tell them or the folks or Tosh anything about it, and when they asked where I was going on the movie nights, I told them I was going over to Mit's or Skats'.

Then near the end of summer the whole town got tired of going to the beach and we all took up slingshots and it got to be slingshot season. Everybody made slingshots and carried pocketsful of little rocks and shot linnets and myna birds and doves.

We would even go to the old wharf and shoot the black crabs which crawled on the rocks. Makot made each of us a dandy slingshot out of a guava branch, as he'd made each of us a big barbed spear out of a bedspring coil during spearing-fish season. Nobody our age had slingshots or spears like ours, and of the three he made, mine was always the best. I knew he liked me the best.

Then one day Makot said, "Slingshot waste time. We go buy a rifle. We go buy twenty-two."

"How?" we all said.

Makot said that he could get five dollars from his old folks and all we needed was five dollars more and we could go sell coconuts and mangoes to raise that.

"Sure!" we all said. A rifle was something we saw only in the movies and Sears Roebuck catalogues. Nobody in Pepelau owned a rifle.

So the next morning we got a barley bag, two picks, and a scooter wagon. We were going to try coconuts first because they were easier to sell. There were two bakeries in town and they needed them for coconut pies. The only trouble was that free coconut trees were hard to find. There were trees at the courthouse, the Catholic Church, and in Reverend Hastings' yard, but the only free trees were those deep in the cane fields and they were too tall and dangerous. Makot said, "We go ask Reverend Hastings." Reverend Hastings was a minister of some kind and he lived alone in a big old house in a big weedy yard next to the kindergarten. He had about a dozen trees in his yard and he always let you pick some coconuts if you asked him, but he always said, "Sure, boys, provided you don't sell them."

"Aw, what he doan know won't hurt um," Makot said. Makot said he was going to be the brains of the gang and Mit and Skats were going to climb the trees and I was going to ask Reverend Hastings. So we hid the wagon and picks and bags and I went up to the door of the big house and knocked.

Pretty soon there were footsteps and he opened the door. "Yes?" He smiled. He was a short, skinny man who looked very weak and who sort of wobbled when he walked, but he had a nice face and a small voice.

"Reverend Hastings, can we pick some coconuts?" I said.

Makot, Mit and Skats were behind me and he looked at them and said, "Why, sure, boys, provided you don't sell them."

"Thank you, Reverend Hastings," I said, and the others mumbled, "Thank you."

"You're welcome," he said and went back into the house. Mit and Skats climbed two trees and knocked them down as fast as they could and I stuck my pick in the ground and started peeling them as fast as I could. We were scared. What if he came out again? Maybe it was better if we all climbed and knocked down lots and took them somewhere else to peel them, we said. But Makot sat down on the wagon and laughed, "Naw, he not gonna come out no more. No be chicken!" As soon as he said that the door slammed and we all looked. Mit and Skats stayed on the trees but didn't knock down any more. Reverend Hastings jumped down the steps and came walking across the yard in big angry strides! It was plain we were going to sell the coconuts because we had more than half a bagful and all the husks were piled up like a mountain! He came up, his face red, and he shouted, "I thought you said you weren't going to sell these! Get down from those trees!"

I looked at my feet and Makot put his face in the crook of his arm and began crying, "Wah-wah . . ." though I knew he wasn't crying.

Reverend Hastings grabbed a half-peeled coconut from my hand and grabbing it by a loose husk, threw it with all his might over the fence and nearly fell down and shouted, "Get out! At once!" Then he turned right around and walked back and slammed the door after him.

"Ha-ha-ha!" Makot said as soon as he disappeared, "we got enough anyway."

We picked up the rest of the coconuts and took them to the kindergarten to peel them. We had three dozen and carted them to the two bakeries on Main Street. But they said that they had enough coconuts and that ours were too green and six cents apiece was too much. We pulled the wagon all over town and tried the fish markets and grocery stores for five cents. Finally we went back to the first bakery and sold them for four cents. It took us the whole day and we made only $1.44. By that time Mit, Skats and I wanted to forget about the rifle, but Makot said, "Twenty-two or bust."

The next day we went to the tall trees in the cane fields. We had to crawl through tall cane to get to them and once we climbed the trees and knocked down the coconuts we had to hunt for them in the tall cane again. After the first tree we wanted to quit but Makot wouldn't hear of it and when we didn't move he put on his *habut*. *Habut* is short for *habuteru*, which means to pout the way girls and children do. Makot would blow up his cheeks like a balloon fish and not talk to us. "I not goin' buy you no more chow fun, no more ice cream, no more pie," he'd sort of cry, and then we would do everything to please him and make him come out of his *habut*. When we finally agreed to do what he wanted he would protest and slap with his wrist like a girl, giggle with his hand over his mouth, talk in the kind of Japanese which only girls use, and in general make fun of the girls. And when he came out of his *habut* he usually bought us chow fun, ice cream, or pie.

So we crawled through more cane fields and climbed more coconut trees. I volunteered to climb too because Mit and Skats grumbled that I got all the easy jobs. By three o'clock we had only half a bag, but we brought them to town and again went all over Main Street trying to sell them. The next day we went to pick mangoes, first at the kindergarten, then at Mango Gulch, but they were harder to sell so we spent more time carting them around town.

"You guys think you so hot, eh" Tosh said one day. "Go sell mangoes and coconuts. He only catching you head. You know why he pick on you guys for a gang? Because you guys the last. That *kodomo tasiho* been leader of every shrimp gang and they all quit him one after another. You, Mit, and Skats stick with him because you too stupid!"

I shrugged and walked away. I didn't care. I liked Makot. Besides, all the guys his age were jealous because Makot had so much money to spend.

Then several days later Father called me. He was alone at the outside sink, cleaning some fish. He brought home the best fish for us to eat but it was always fish. He was still in his fisherman's clothes.

"Kiyoshi," he said and he was not angry, "you're not to play with Makoto Sasaki anymore. Do you understand?"

"But why, Father?"

"Because he is bad." He went on cleaning fish.

"But he's not bad. He treats us good! You mean about stealing mangoes from kindergarten? It's not really stealing. Everybody does it."

"But you never sold the mangoes you stole before?"

"No."

"There's a difference between a prank and a crime. Everybody in town is talking about you people. Not about stealing, but about your selling mangoes and coconuts you stole. It's all Makoto's fault. He's older and he should know better but he doesn't. That's why he plays with younger boys. He makes fools out of them. The whole town is talking about what fools he's making out of you and Nobuyuki and Mitsunobu."

"But he's not really making fools out of us, Father. We all agreed to make some money so that we could buy a rifle and own it together. As for the work, he doesn't really force us. He's always buying us things and making things for us and teaching us tricks he learns in Boy Scout, so it's one way we can repay him."

"But he's bad. You're not to play with him. Do you understand?"

"But he's not bad! He treats us real good and me better than Mitsunobu-san or Nobuyuki-san!"

"Kiyoshi, I'm telling you for the last time. Do not play with him."

"But why?"

"Because his home is bad. His father is bad. His mother is bad."

"Why are his father and mother bad?"

"Nemmind!" He was mad now.

"But what about Mitsunobu-san and Nobuyuki-san? I play with them too!"

"Shut up!" He turned to face me. His mouth was twisted. "You're not a monkey! Stop aping others! You are not to play with him! Do you understand! Or do I have to crack your head *kotsun!*"

"Yes," I said and walked away.

Then I went inside the house and asked Mother, "Why are they bad? Because he doesn't work?"

"You're too young to understand, Kiyo-chan. When you grow up you'll know that your parents were right."

"But whom am I going to play with then?"

"Can't you play with Toshi-chan?"

"Yeah, come play with me, Kyo. Any time you want me to bust up that *kodomo taisho* I'll bustum up for you," Tosh said.

That night I said I was going to see Mit and went over to Makot's home. On the way over I kept thinking about what Father and Mother said. There was something funny about Makot's folks. His father was a tall, skinny man and he didn't talk to us kids the way all the other old Japanese men did. He owned a Model T when only the *haoles* or whites had cars. His mother was funnier yet. She wore lipstick in broad daylight, which no other Japanese mother did.

I went into Filipino Camp and I was scared. It was a spooky place, not like Japanese Camp. The Filipinos were all men and there were no women or children and the same-looking houses were all bare, no curtains in the windows or potted plants on the porches. The only way you could tell them apart was by their numbers. But I knew where Makot's house was in the daytime, so I found it easily. It was the only one with curtains and ferns and flowers. There were five men standing in the dark to one side of the house. They wore shoes and bright aloha shirts and sharply pressed pants, and smelled of expensive pomade. They were talking in low voices and a couple of them were jiggling so hard you could hear the jingle of loose change.

I called from the front porch, "Makot! Makot!" I was scared he was going to give me hell for coming at night.

Pretty soon his mother came out. I had never spoken to her though I'd seen her around and knew who she was. She was a fat woman with a fat face, which made her eyes look very small.

"Oh, is Makoto-san home?" I asked in Japanese.

"Makotooooo!" she turned and yelled into the house. She was all dressed up in kimono. Mother made a lot of kimonos for other people but she never had one like hers. She had a lot of white powder on her face and two round red spots on her cheeks.

"Oh, Sasaki-san," I said, "I've had lunch at your home quite a few times. I wanted to thank you for it but I didn't have a chance to speak to you before. It was most delicious. Thank you very much."

She stared at me with her mouth open wide and suddenly burst out laughing, covering her mouth and shaking all over, her shoulders, her arms, her cheeks.

Makot came out. "Wha-at?" he pouted in Japanese. Then he saw me and his face lit up, "Hiya, Kiyo, old pal, old pal, what's cookin'?" he said in English.

His mother was still laughing and shaking and pointing at me.

"What happened?" Makot said angrily to his mother.

"That boy! That boy!" She still pointed at me. "Such a nice little boy! Do you know what he said? He said, "Sasaki-san . . .' " And she started to shake and cough again.

"Aw, shut up, Mother!" Makot said. "Please go inside!" and he practically shoved her to the door.

She turned around again, "But you're such a courteous boy, aren't you? 'It was most delicious. Thank you very much.' A-hahahaha. A-hahahaha . . .' "

"Shut up, Mother!" Makot shoved her into the doorway. I would never treat my mother like that but then my mother would never act like that. When somebody said, "Thank you for the feast," she always said, "But what was served you was really rubbish."

Makot turned to me, "Well, what you say, old Kiyo, old pal? Wanna go to the movies tonight?"

I shook my head and looked at my feet. "I no can play with you no more."

"Why?"

"My folks said not to."

"But why? We never been do anything bad, eh?"

"No."

"Then why? Because I doan treat you right? I treat you okay?"

"Yeah. I told them you treat me real good."

"Why then?"

"I doan know."

"Aw, hell, you can still play with me. They doan hafta know. What they doan know won't hurt them."

"Naw, I better not. This time it's my father and he means business."

"Aw, doan be chicken, Kiyo. Maybe you doan like to play with me."

"I like to play with you."

"Come, let's go see a movie."

"Naw."

"How about some chow fun. Yum-yum."

"Naw."

"Maybe you doan like me then?"

"I like you."

"You sure?"

"I sure."

"Why then?"

"I doan know. They said something about your father and mother."

"Oh," he said and his face fell and I thought he was going to cry.

"Well, so long, then, Kiyo," he said and went into the house.

"So long," I said and turned and ran out of the spooky camp.

Chester B. Himes

THE first thing that comes to mind when thinking about Chester Himes (1909–1984) is the directness of his prose and his overwhelming concern with truth. This is reflected in his prison writings, which first appeared in *Esquire* (c. 1935), and through all his novels, starting with three semi-autobiographical novels, *Cast the First Stone* (1952), *The Third Generation* (1954), and *The Primitive* (1955), up to and including *Blind Man with a Pistol* (1969), a novel which reflects the violence, the turbulence, the factionalism, the riots, and the assassinations of the sixties.

Himes's contribution to and expansion of American literature in style, content, and form is his ability to expose the contradictions inherent both in society and in the human condition. This exposure of the paradoxes and ambiguities of our existence is best observed when Himes is dramatizing the conflicts of race, class, or gender.

Perhaps Himes's style and demeanor as both a writer and a human being can be attributed to his having grown up in the Midwest as part of a middle-class family, his father being a professor and his mother a rather self-assured woman who stalked the streets in various southern towns with a handgun in her purse to protect her children from race-haters and baiters. His coming of age was grounded in the Roaring Twenties of free love, flappers, radio, telephone, phonograph, and jazz. He lived the "Great American Success Story" of rags to riches or riches to rags, have it either way. For pulling a Shaker Heights burglary Himes found himself behind bars at Ohio State Penitentiary doing a thirty-year stretch. It was while there that Himes, with time for reflection, put down the gun and picked up the pen.

An analysis of the plots of his novels prior to his departure from these shores in 1954, in the light of the principles which this society espouses, will reveal why he realized as a writer of color (a Black male who felt blackmailed, blackballed, and blacklisted by his own native country) he insisted in his works on telling the truth, exposing the contradictions of this society. Arthur P. Davis, in his book *From the Dark Tower: Afro-American Writers 1900–1960* (1981), states, "Himes's thesis says, in effect, that pressure on the Negro male makes him less than a man. This pressure, according to the author, often works through the Negro middle-class woman who fails to understand her mate and therefore rejects him. When the poor male runs to the white woman for solace, as he often does in Himes's works, he is again rejected, but for different reasons." This thesis left Himes with no future here in America unless he compromised his principles.

The novel that did the trick and forced him to leave the country was *Lonely Crusade* (1947). The Blacks detested it, and so did the whites. The Jews thought it was a piece of garbage, and the Communists wanted him burned at the stake or lynched. Arthur P. Davis goes on to note that in *Lonely Crusade* Himes "criticizes the Communists; he attacks white women who use black men to bolster their own feelings of insecurity; he strikes against the lack of understanding on the part of middle-class Negro women; and he spells out in great detail how hard, if not impossible, it is for the black Lee Gordons to be men."

One woman at his publishing house got so upset with the contents of *Lonely Crusade,* Himes, and his truth-telling that she stopped shipment of the new novel. Lost and alone, abandoned by his wife and his publisher and roasted by the critics, he booked ship to Paris to join the community of American expatriates who were for the most part down but not out. Echoes of Duke Ellington's rendition of "Am I Blue?" defined the age.

While in Paris, at the prodding of a French publisher, he began writing detective novels, commonly called Harlem Domestic Tales, such as *The Real Cool Killers* (1959), *The Crazy Kill* (1959), *All Shot Up* (1960), *The Big Gold Dream* (1960),

A Rage in Harlem (1965), *Cotton Comes to Harlem* (1965), *Run Man Run* (1967), and *Blind Man with a Pistol* (1969). These works demonstrate Himes's absolute "lightness of being"—his sharp eye and ear for satire and his coming to terms in the fifties and sixties with the utter meaninglessness and absurdity of human existence. Play it again, Sam, who gives a damn.

It took a young generation of writers who hit the streets in the sixties to set the stage and make America ready in its diversity to accept and celebrate the work of this master craftsman in all its gore as well as its glory. And here we have Chester B. Himes, bless his soul.

—Steve Cannon

Chapter 14 from
LONELY CRUSADE

LEE GORDON lay on the davenport, his head cushioned on the arm rest, reading "Lil Abner" in the Sunday comic section. Ruth sat across from him, curled in the deep armchair, musing over the pictures in the society section. Along with the faint perfume of freshly cut grass and flowers, a pleasant warmth stole in through the open windows and filled the room with the soft, wonderful glow of a lazy day. The serenity of a Sunday had enchanted them.

At her slight exclamation over something she had seen, he turned his head to look at her and thought how lovely she was in the pale-green robe with her hair down and her professional demeanor relaxed for a change. The impulse stirred in him to kiss her, but he was too lazy to move.

Just as his eyelids were about to close, the sharp sound of laughter from next door opened them. He raised himself on his elbows to watch the Morrows' teen-age daughter Yvonne, clad in printed shorts, scamper across the lawn with her Scotty, Zulu, at her heels. The muscles of her long brown legs rippled in the midday sunshine.

Sight of their well-trimmed lawn reminded Lee that his needed cutting but he put it quickly from his mind as a horrible thought and settled in complete relaxation. If life could be like this, just one long lazy day—he was thinking when the telephone rang.

"I'll answer it," he finally said.

"You're welcome," she smiled.

He struggled to his feet and went into the bedroom. During the few short minutes of conversation the pleasantness had gone from the day. For a long moment after cradling the receiver, he stood beside the night stand wondering what it was that Foster wanted of him as uneasiness settled in his mind. Then he went back into the living-room and announced to Ruth: "Foster wants us to come to dinner this afternoon. Would you like to go?"

She looked quickly up, frowning at the constraint now in his voice. "What's the matter, what's happened?"

"We have an invitation to Foster's for dinner this afternoon."

"Foster? Who are the Fosters?" She made it sound as distasteful as if she had spoken of filth.

"Foster," he said, "is vice-president of the board of directors of Comstock Aircraft Corporation, one of the major stockholders, and general manager in charge of production in the plant."

"Oh, Foster!" Her voice had a sudden singing quality. "Of course. For dinner?"

He gave her a sighing look as if torn between tears and laughter. She had gained her feet and was moving quickly toward the bath when suspicion overtook her. "What does he want, did he say?" she questioned sharply.

"It was his secretary who called. He only said that Foster wanted us for dinner."

But she would allow no stray doubts to dim her enthusiasm. "Oh, he probably has a job for you."

"I doubt it," he replied.

And then he recalled what Joe Ptak had said to him his first day on the job: "There is a man named Foster. If you want a job making twice as much as you do, go over and tell him you're working for me."

But if it was just concerning a job, why would Foster invite them both to dinner on a Sunday afternoon? his reason asked him. Was it to exert some kind of pressure on him, to put the fear of God in him, or have him slugged by goons? He thrust this from his thoughts as foolish. But then McKinley had said that Foster was "a bitter and ill-tempered man, given to violent rages," who "hated the union in a deadly manner." Afterward, at the meeting the week before last, McKinley had stated further that Foster had bought out one of the union leaders. Lee had thought it silly at the time but now it took the shape of credence. And then that "Beware!" McKinley had whispered just as he was leaving; had it been a warning that Foster would also try to buy him out? McKinley had been absent from the meeting the night before and only eight Negro workers had put in an appearance. Did that mean that something had already happened to him?

He checked his galloping imagination and took himself in hand. Just because Foster had asked them to dinner he was seeing goblins in the land. What harm could possibly come to them? As Rosie had said the other day, people had other things to think about besides dreaming up tortures for poor Negroes.

It was, no doubt, as Joe had stated and Ruth had guessed, that Foster wanted them out to dinner to offer him a job. After all, Jackie thought he was all right—swell, she had said—and she should know since she worked right in his office.

But his uneasiness would not relax and it kept him wondering just the same.

"What shall I wear, Lee?" Ruth called from the bathroom.

"Wear? Oh, just a dress. I don't suppose it's anything elaborate."

"You're a lot of help," she cried. "I mean what type of dress? Will there be sports, tennis or riding—"

"Oh, I don't know. He just said dinner."

"Do you think my black satin will be too flashy? It's for afternoon."

"Any dress. What difference does it make?"

"It makes a lot of difference if you're looking for a job. I don't want to appear too prosperous and still I want to make a nice appearance—"

"I'm not looking for a job," he growled.

"Oh, don't be so pessimistic, he might offer both of us a job."

Lee Gordon did not reply to that because he hoped it was not so. But it rooted in his uneasiness, and by the time he had combed and brushed his hair and changed his clothes he was of half a mind to call the whole thing off. Before he could reach a decision he looked out the window and saw the long green convertible pull up before the house.

"The car's here," he called, catching some of Ruth's excitement.

"I'm ready," she replied, and came dashing into the bedroom fresh from her bath.

Looking up again, Lee saw a short dark Negro in chauffeur's livery alight from the car and saunter toward the house, and he went to the door to meet him.

"You Lee Gordon?" the chauffeur asked.

"Yes, I am. We'll be right out."

"Mr. Foster wants you to come and see him. He sent me after you."

"Yes, I know. His secretary called."

The chauffeur gave a sheepish grin. "he been double-checking on me. He told me to call but I was going to surprise you."

"I can imagine." Lee started to withdraw but the chauffeur stopped him.

"This your house?"

"My wife's and mine," Lee replied.

"Partners, eh?"

"Well—yes."

"Nice place. Me and my old lady been thinking of buying a little place like this, but Mr. Foster says he's going to build us a house on his grounds and we just going to wait and let him do it."

Turning indoors, Lee called: "Ruth—"

She came quickly beside him, serene and svelte in a chic black ensemble, wearing the tiny professional smile she had developed for the working class.

But the chauffeur was not to be awed by people of his own race. "My name's Roy," he announced, letting them know that they were Negroes too. "This your wife?"

Lee felt a slight resentment at his familiarity. "Mrs. Gordon," he said.

But Roy mistook it for something else for he grinned engagingly at Ruth and said: "Lee's scared, but it ain't nothing bad. Mr. Foster ain't going to hurt him."

Now he permitted them to follow him to the expensive car. Climbing beneath the wheel, he left the front door open for them. "There's plenty room in front."

Ruth hesitated, but at Lee's nod she took the middle seat and he climbed in beside her. As the long low car moved into fluid motion, Roy asked as proudly as if it was his own: "How do you like it?"

"Oh, fine," Lee replied absently.

"Cost eight thousand dollars," Roy informed.

"Does Mr. Foster own many cars like this?" Ruth asked.

"Only seven," Roy grinned.

"How does he get along?" Lee murmured.

But Roy had given his attention to the traffic as they swept along Sunset out toward the Pasadena speedway and did not hear. On the wide, winding turnpike the long car flowed along at sixty, curving effortlessly past the green lush countryside. It was pleasant with the wind in their faces and the bright sun overhead. Life could be so simple, just floating along, Lee thought—no movement of the masses, no racial problems, no workers' unions, just relaxation and enjoyment.

But Lee could not relax. This crossing into the domain of wealthy white seclusion was never a casual thing, and to Lee Gordon it was something more. For now after seventeen years he was going back to the city where he had been born and he did not relish seeing it again. He had no pleasant memories of Pasadena; he had been born in the backyard and in his unhappiness had known only the back door. He and his parents had been driven away like thieves in the night.

Now he was going back to dine at the master's table, but without honor it seemed from their treatment by the chauffeur. He would be on his mettle, required to act a part that life had never given him a chance to rehearse, and now his thoughts concerned themselves with minor things. How should he act in Foster's presence?—like the timid Negro son of domestic servant parents; or the reserved and quiet Negro college graduate, picking his chances to speak, weighing his words for the impression they might make; or as the blustering unioneer, walking hard and talking loud and trying to give the appearance of being unafraid? He wondered how Ruth felt in this situation, how she would react, whether she would have any emotional advantage in being a woman. But Foster would expect more out of him, he knew.

And with this thought all of his senses tightened and panic overwhelmed him. It was as if the unseen gatekeepers of the white overlords demanded of him a toll to enter—an incredible toll in disquiet, anxiety, trepidation, and, greatest of all, in fear. He could not help his fear, he knew, and waited for it to strike. But from somewhere deep inside of him came the reassuring thought, he was not returning to Pasadena as a Negro begging opportunity or as a worker seeking a raise in pay, but as a representative of many people. And that made quite a difference, for when they turned into the private driveway and circled through the landscaped woods to draw to a stop before a huge colonial mansion and Lee looked up to see the tall, gangling man in a plaid woolen shirt and old corduroy trousers whom he knew immediately to be Foster, strangely he was not afraid. It was amazing what just the realization of the other people in the world could do for him, Lee Gordon thought, as he alighted from the car and helped Ruth to alight.

Foster came down the flagstone walk and met them by the two cast iron statuettes of pickaninnies that served as decorative hitching posts. His face was deeply seamed yet mobile with vitality, and his gray streaked hair still retained youthful cowlicks.

"Mrs. Gordon," he greeted first, touching her with a glance that was at once appraising and admiring from deep-set eyes of the youngest, brightest blue. Then turning to Lee he tapped him lightly on the chest in a friendly gesture. "Lee Gordon, I've seen you before."

"How do you do, sir," Lee mumbled stiffly, offering his hand.

Foster gave Lee's hand one quick, firm grasp and quickly let it go as his gaze raked Lee with bright penetration. And then to both he said with a sudden fascinating smile: "I'm delighted that you could come on such short notice." His voice was richly cordial without condescension or constraint, and in his slow enunciation was the hint of infinite patience.

"Oh, we think it grand of you to ask us," Ruth was the first to reply, looking up at him in feminine wonder and finding him completely charming.

"That rascal Roy didn't frighten you with his wild driving, did he?" he spoke again to Ruth.

"Oh, no, I enjoyed it," she replied.

"He must be lazy today; the sun's got him. He likes to rip and tear up and down the highways."

Roy stood to one side with a grin of ecstasy on his flat, black features. "Now you know I don't do that, Mr. Louie. You know I'm just like a lamb."

"A wolf, you rascal. You know you're a rascal." He turned his attention back to Lee and Ruth. "Roy's a great man with the ladies," adding dryly: "especially with my cars."

Roy turned to Lee and gave a companionable grin, different in both essence and execution from the one he had used on Foster. "Have a good time, Lee. Don't let Mr. Louie get you balled up in no argument. He likes to get people out there and then drop 'em."

"Lee is not like you," Foster said with a faint touch of sarcasm. "He's an arguer by profession."

"Well—by necessity more than by profession," Lee demurred.

Foster gave him another quick glance.

When they turned toward the house, Ruth exclaimed as if she had just noticed it: "Oh, what a magnificent place!—and so American."

She could have said nothing to please Foster more. He had erected this mansion of twenty-one rooms, each feature of which was an exact replica of features in the homes of early American patriots, upon his return from a war-crazy Europe in 1939, and had dedicated it in solemn thankfulness to the fact that he was an American. For Louis Foster considered being an American the greatest thing of all. He was an American-first-to-hell-with-all-others American. The difference between him and other American-Firsters being not that he loved his country less, but not so rhetorically.

"Would you like to see through it?" he asked.

"Oh, we'd love to," Ruth replied.

"We like it and we think everyone else should like it too," he smiled. "That's terribly presumptuous of us, isn't it?"

"Oh, not at all," Lee said.

Foster restrained from looking at him again, but the urge showed plainly in his gesture for them to walk ahead. From the outside the wide, rambling structure, with glass-enclosed verandas flanking the center section, seemed imposing, but inside the arrangement gave a sense of intimacy. They entered a tiny foyer, flanked by a powder room done in pale print and a tile-lined washroom, and then came into a wide, paneled hallway, at the end of which red-carpeted stairs, converging at a landing, led above. To the left, three steps led up to a small, book-lined living-room, beyond which were the bedrooms of Mr. and Mrs. Foster separated by a bathroom, hers furnished simply in a period style and his, in dark-toned, rugged, he-man fashion, smelling of horses and dogs. Returning through a flower room with a concrete floor and drain, they reentered the hall through a door beneath the landing, and crossed into the huge living-room that extended the depth of the house. An immense fire-place surrounded by mirrors occupied the center of the back wall. It was flanked by French doors looking out upon a patio, beyond which was the swimming pool. To the front, similar doors led to one of the enclosed verandas. Through an archway they entered the dining-room, which contained a mammoth banquet table, beyond each end of which grew an indoor hanging flower garden.

Until then they had met no other occupants of the house and Lee thought cynically: "Now we will go in and meet the servants," whose voices he could hear beyond the kitchen door. But with a curious realization of his misgivings, Foster did not take them through the kitchen as he did all other guests, and by not doing so earned Lee's eternal gratefulness.

"On Sundays the servants prepare a little buffet snack and take the remainder of the day off," he explained.

Neither Lee nor Ruth cared to comment on this, and Foster was afforded a faint amusement by their silence. All along he had been covertly appraising both of them, for although he prided himself on his knowledge of Negroes, these were of a type he had rarely seen, and he was curious to know all that went on behind the lean, dark features of this boy. That they were laboring under an emotional strain, he had no doubt, for he could fully comprehend the delicacy involved in any situation that put the three of them together on a social plane. He knew that he held in his power their peace of mind, and this brought forth a greater effort to put them at their ease than he would have made for any white persons, rich or poor.

Now he led them back through the living-room out into the patio. "We call this our 'WPA Project,' " he informed with a sweeping gesture toward the terraced landscape of which the swimming pool was but a tiny part.

"Oh, how beautiful!" Ruth involuntarily exclaimed, and Foster laughed delightedly.

"I think we must have built it just to startle people," he confessed with engaging candor.

"And named it after Roosevelt's relief program," Lee commented curiously.

Foster turned and looked at Lee until he drew his gaze, and then he smiled inclusively, "We discovered it to be a waste of time and money—also." But in his voice beyond control was the indication of his hatred.

For he abhorred Roosevelt with an intensity that he could not contain. Not only did he detest Roosevelt as a President, considering him a meddler, a socialist, and a stooge of Stalin, but he despised him as a man, a traitor to his heritage and profaner of tradition, "a cripple bastard with a cripple bastard's spitefulness and lack of honor," as he was wont to say.

So incensed had he become with the Roosevelt Administration that in 1934, at the age of forty-six, he had retired from active business, shut down the steel plant he had inherited, and spent the next five years abroad. For every subsequent event and occurrence detrimental to his personal prosperity and well-being and opposed to his personal convictions, he blamed Roosevelt; for Communism and unionism, as if Roosevelt had sired the one and given birth to the other; for the raise in taxes, which he considered more Marx than Morgenthau—as if one had a choice, he thought; for the entrance of the United States into the war. By God, with any other President under the sun the yellow-bellied Japs would have been afraid to breathe in America's direction! It took a war in Europe to send him back to a Rooseveltian America. And now just the thought of Roosevelt was riding him again.

But Lee did not know this and he was inclined to argue. "I

always thought that WPA saved the country from revolution," he contended.

"I have more faith in America than that," Foster quickly challenged.

But by now Lee had sensed the danger signs. "Well—yes," he said and let the matter be.

Seizing the opportunity, Ruth came quickly to his aid, bringing the conversation to safer matters. "Oh, there're the stables."

But Foster was also willing to let it pass, for he wanted no psychological barriers in between them when it came time to broach his proposition. So he became the charming squire again. "I imagine my daughters are down there. They're at the horsy age."

"Oh, do you have daughters?" Ruth asked.

"Three," Foster replied. "They're my pets"—which was an untrue statement, for of them, he liked only Hortense, slim, blond, and boy-crazy at sixteen. Martha, his oldest, who was nineteen and feeble-minded, he wished had never been born; and he resented Abigail, who at nine was the most serenely sensible of the lot, because Hortense did not have her mind. As an afterthought he asked: "Do you have children?"

It was Lee who answered: "No, we never could afford them."

Ruth wished he hadn't used the word "afford"; it sounded too much like a bid for sympathy, and now she sought to cover it. "Everything has been so—well—indefinite. The depression and now the war."

Foster did not want to dwell on it. "Would you like to take a dip? We keep the water tepid."

"Yes, we would!" they both replied in unison, and Lee thought: "Well at least we agree on one thing."

"But we don't have suits," Ruth added.

"I'm sure you'll find something here to fit," Foster said as he escorted them to the dressing-rooms in the tiny cottage called the "Dolly House" at the end of the pool. "I'll join you shortly."

The first to change, Lee came out alone, and suddenly was overwhelmed by the immensity of the place. For a moment it seemed that he stood naked in the windows of the house, and he walked quickly to the edge and dove beneath the water to escape the accusing eyes. When he came up for air a big bass laugh soared above him. Looking up he saw a grotesque woman with a bloated stomach, tall in the angle of his vision.

"I'm Mrs. Foster and you're Mr. Gordon," she said, laughing.

Thinking that she was laughing at him and hoping she was not, Lee became so painfully embarrassed he could not find his voice.

"No one introduced us; that's the way we do things around here," she said, dragging a canvas chair to the shade of a parasol. "Go right ahead and swim. I'll sit here and watch."

Lee mutely nodded and dove again to escape the sight of her.

What Foster had done to his wife, and why, no outsiders ever knew. At that time she was a fifty-year-old Ophelia, not so much an idiot as uncaring. Signs that once she had been beautiful were still visible in her full, florid face; but she had deliberately let her body go to seed as a defense against her husband's brutal passion. Now she wandered vacantly about the house, bemused with the cheap sherry she drank against reality, her deep pointless laughter echoing from room to room. Despised by Hortense, unknown to Martha, and ignored by Abigail—her daughters paid allegiance only to their father and obeyed only their nurse—she was not so much a mother as a stranger in the house. Denied voice in its management and forbidden the kitchen, on occasion, however, when Foster was absent and Charles his secretary elsewhere occupied, she would slip into the kitchen and ask the Negro cook: "If it's not too much trouble, if it doesn't upset your routine, if you don't mind, would you bake me a small chocolate cake? And just leave it in the pantry, I'll find it."

Now suddenly and without sound, Foster stood behind her, brown and muscular in blue swim trunks.

"I see you've met Mr. Gordon," he said blandly, and as Ruth came from the bathhouse, he added: "This is Mrs. Gordon. Mrs. Gordon, Mrs. Foster."

"Welcome to our swimming pool," Mrs. Foster greeted,

booming out her laugh. "I don't swim in there myself. Louis keeps his snakes in there and I let them have it."

"Snakes!" Ruth almost screamed, and Lee echoed: "In here!" swimming for the ladder.

"Dear, you know those little snakes have been gone for months," Foster said, giving his wife a slow imperturbable look.

"Well, they were there once and that's enough for me," she said, making herself more comfortable in the chair.

Foster turned to Ruth with an ingenuous smile. "They were just a pair of tiny water moccasins, pets of Martha's. They were perfectly harmless; she used to carry them around with her."

But the swimming pool had lost its attraction. Ruth went in for a few minutes out of courtesy but she did not enjoy it. Later, after they had showered, Foster mixed and served cocktails on the dining-room veranda. One by one the other members of the household—the three daughters, the secretary Charles Houston, a bachelor who had no other home and seemingly no other friends or relatives, and the middle-aged, motherly-appearing nursemaid Miss Martin, whom he had employed in London for the sole purpose, it sometimes seemed, to vent his spleen for the English, whom he loathed—drifted in and were introduced.

The conversation reverted to the house again, and Mrs. Foster commented that she did not like the automatic lights in all the closets. "Whenever I open one of those doors absentmindedly, the light pops on and frightens me to death."

"Oh, I think that's a good feature," Ruth said. "I mean when you get used to it," she added lamely.

To cover her embarrassment, Lee said politely that he enjoyed the swim. "The water was just right."

"Louis often invites Negro couples out to swim in his pool," Mrs. Foster informed them, and Lee wondered if the snakes had been there. "Our friends are horrified," she added frankly.

"Are you familiar with Pasadena?" Foster inquired.

"I was born here," Lee replied.

"Then you know of its narrow-minded traditions?"

"In a way."

"Are you a native also?" he inquired of Ruth.

"No, my home is in St. Louis. I came here on a visit with my mother eight years ago, and Lee and I were married."

"Oh, a real love match!" Mrs. Foster exclaimed.

Ruth smiled. "when I saw that guy I knew that he was mine."

"How wonderful!" Mrs. Foster said.

"Were your parents in business here, Lee?" Foster asked.

"No sir, they were domestic servants." Just the recollection of his background had compelled him to give the title of respect.

"And you completed college?"

"Yes sir—U.C.L.A. My mother helped and I worked also."

"There is no place like America," Foster said, and the emotion in his voice was genuine because the opportunity for betterment afforded by America was his special love. He was convinced that any American (except women, whom he did not consider men's equal; Negroes, whom he did not consider as men; Jews, whom he did not consider as Americans; and the foreign born, whom he did not consider at all), possessed of ingenuity, aggressiveness, and blessed with good fortune, could pull himself up by his bootstraps to become one of the most wealthy and influential men in the nation—even President. The fact that neither he nor any of his associates had been faced with this necessity had no bearing on his conviction. Like other fables of the American legend, the truth made little difference—as long as he believed, just as he now believed that there was no other place on earth where a Negro son of servant parents could achieve a college education. "No place like America," he repeated.

"No place!" Lee echoed, and he meant something else again.

"And this is the challenge which lies ahead," Foster continued as if Lee had not spoken, "whether we shall retain these principles of democracy or lose them to a handful of crackpots and Communists."

Now once again Lee Gordon felt the compulsion to agree, flatter, serve the vanity of this great white man, but he could not show such base servility in the eyes of his wife and expect her to still respect him. So he forced himself to offer a contradiction, "I don't believe that there are enough Communists in the United States to form any real danger."

"There is no danger in the Communists themselves," Foster said. "They're nothing but a bunch of malcontents, individual failures, and professional agitators. The danger lies in the people who are influenced by them."

"I doubt if many people are influenced by the Communists," Lee said. "Most people I've met are as opposed to Communism as I am."

This drew a smile of commendation from Foster and now his voice became inclusive again. "No, but they are influenced by the President who sanctions Communism, and they are influenced by the President's wife, who associates with Communists. Each time Mrs. Roosevelt attends a Communist demonstration it has a direct bearing on public opinion—and she knows this."

"Oh, but I don't think Mrs. Roosevelt is a Communist," Ruth protested.

Foster's face went completely still. "I've often wondered how colored people felt toward Mrs. Roosevelt," he slowly said. "I've always thought her patronizing friendliness toward colored people was a cheap political trick."

"I think she's a great woman," Mrs. Foster interposed with calm defiance.

Foster did not look at her, but when Ruth echoed: "Oh, I think so, too," he chose to answer.

"I know nothing of her greatness," he said, "but I doubt her sincerity. And I don't feel that the daredevil escapades in which she indulges are benefiting the colored people."

"I've never particularly been a fan of either of the Roosevelts," Lee ventured. "But I think we have to give Roosevelt credit for the way he's handling the war effort."

Foster appeared thoughtful. "Lee, I wonder if the war effort would not have gained impetus and cohesion without so much governmental interference."

"Well—big business has its own way of doing things—"

"But don't you think it's an effective way?"—this alchemy

of turning human effort into profit, which was always to Foster not only the zenith of a system, but the zenith of man—to become the maker of men, and with profit—"Look at what it's done for America."

"Well—yes. But I thought production was sort of slow getting under way after war was declared," Lee said.

"There has been so much governmental interference and red tape it is a miracle that production has reached its present peak," Foster insisted. "Take the President's fair employment directive, for instance. Before my retirement I employed colored workers in all of my plants on the same basis as others. Here at Comstock I have made no distinctions. Americans are inherently fair-minded, and many of us find such a dictatorial order unnecessary and offensive. I know of several instances where the results were actually adverse."

"You mean that it influenced firms against hiring Negroes?"

"Exactly. We Americans hate dictatorship. We are engaged in a war against it. And it appears as if that is what our President is endeavoring to establish."

"Oh, I don't think so," Ruth said. "The President must have extraordinary powers in time of war. Otherwise he could never get anything accomplished."

"But we have won quite a few wars and accomplished a great deal without the benefit of Franklin Roosevelt," Foster said, smiling at her.

Charles came in and interrupted the conversation with the announcement that it was time for dinner. They went into the dining-room and served themselves from the sliced rib roast and array of vegetables arranged on the buffet. During the meal the children dominated the conversation. Lee's experience with young white girls was a tragic memory and he felt stiff and ill at ease. With the unconscious cruelty of youth, the girls did nothing to allay his uneasiness. Hortense asked him if he had seen Roy's baby since she began to teethe, assuming that the two of them were old acquaintances, and Martha said witlessly: "She's the blackest little thing to be a baby," and blushed a moment afterwards.

And now that the sharp focus of his interest had become

diffused, Lee began to wonder again what it was that Foster wanted. A slow resentment against Foster, inspired by no particular incident, began building in his mind.

Dessert was a peach mousse which momentarily held the center of attraction, and afterward the grownups went into the living-room for Scotch-and-soda highballs.

Charles, acting as Foster's straight man, a role which was the major part of all his duties, said to Lee: "So you're the young man from the union? How do the workers react to being organized in time of war?"

"Well, we're making a little progress," Lee replied.

"Don't you think that during a war is a pretty bad time to be trying to organize workers in essential industry?" Charles asked bluntly.

"No, I don't," Lee replied. "I think it's the best time. We have full employment now and after the war there might be a great deal of unemployment. You know a union only organizes the employed; we can't organize the unemployed."

"That's what I mean," Charles said. "These people are working for the war and it's not fair to the boys at the front that they should be agitated by a union."

Foster had come up with a drink for Lee and he gave Charles an indulgent smile. "Charles is antiunion," he commented. "I can't do a thing with him."

"So I see," Lee said quietly.

"Yes, I am," Charles said. "I'm not blaming you, Gordon, but most of these fellows who run these unions are nothing but crooks. I know, I've been a member."

"All unions are not the same," Lee pointed out. "There are good unions and bad unions. Perhaps you belonged to a bad union. But our union is different. You can't condemn unionism itself because there are a few unions run by unscrupulous men." He turned to Foster. "What do you think, sir?"

The three of them were standing by the unlighted fireplace while across the room Ruth and Mrs. Foster were engaged in conversation. Outside, a soft golden twilight filled the patio with a burnished luminescence and turned the swimming pool to molten metal.

"The privilege of collective bargaining is the democratic right of all workers," Foster solemnly replied.

"I don't think they have the right to be carping at production in time of war," Charles said.

Foster made a slight gesture of annoyance. "I have never considered an honest union as an obstruction to management," he continued as if Charles had not spoken. "In fact, I think of it as an ally of management, both working together for the benefit of the employees and of the employers—"

"The trouble with the unions is their leaders," Charles interrupted. "Communists and opportunists have gained control of the unions and now they're only out to fleece the workers."

"There's not so much of that now," Lee said. "The way most unions—our union, for instance—are organized, the structure of the union, I mean, makes such corruption impossible."

"My boy, I have been dealing with unions and union men for thirty years," Charles said. "I know them pretty well, what they will do and what they will not do, those that are honest and those that are not. And I will tell you frankly there are very few, if any, top union men who are not thieves and liars by the clock. Your own union will not touch the problem of colored workers."

Caught off guard by the last remark, Lee could only stammer: "Well—but that's just during the war."

"But you just said that during a war was the best time to organize," Charles said insistently. "You know, as well as I, that colored people in industry pose a special problem that must be faced forthrightly by those who would claim to be their friends."

"Well—that's true," Lee had to admit, since not long before he had advanced the same argument to Smitty.

"No doubt your union leaders call Mr. Foster a dirty capitalist, but he has faced your people's problem squarely at Comstock. He has employed colored workers in all departments at the same rating and doing the same work as all others. Does that sound like a friend or an enemy?"

"Oh, I don't think Mr. Foster's an enemy." He appeared so

embarrassed that Foster gave him a reassuring smile. "But that's all the union wants. How would it interfere?"

"That's where I disagree with you," Charles said. "The union is controlled by Communists, and you must know where you colored people stand with the Communists by now."

"Well—"Cornered, Lee did not know what to say.

And there Charles left him. "I must run!" he exclaimed glancing at his watch. "It's been a pleasure talking with you, Gordon, but you're on the wrong team, boy."

"Glad to have met you too," Lee said.

Both he and Foster turned and watched Charles as he crossed the room and went from sight, and then Foster took the ball. "Of course, Charles' experience with unions has been pretty bitter. He is a highly qualified journalist, but because of political differences with the officials of the Newspaper Guild, he is not allowed to work."

"But he shouldn't condemn unionism as a whole," Lee said stubbornly.

"His bitterness impairs his judgment and gives rise to his silly bias," Foster commented dryly, and Lee looked up in sharp surprise, taking the bait as offered.

For this was the way it worked in all things concerning Negroes: Charles playing the perfect stooge, mouthing the maledictions while the master retained his dignity sacrosanct in the halo of impartiality and denounced Charles as the offensive ogre of the lot. This was the way it worked both on the Negroes whom Foster had to dinner and the Negro servants who served the dinner. For instance, the management of household affairs was ostensibly delegated to Charles but actually directed by Foster with picayunish attention to detail, even to the reprimanding of the servants and the more subtle punishment of arranging the meals so as to keep them late on their half-days off. While Foster, for himself, maintained a seemingly frank and good-humored relationship with the servants, kidding them, making humorous allusions to Charles's "choleric" disposition, and passing out the rewards, which were sometimes money and other times a day off. And though they were underpaid and overworked, the former to satisfy a vanity that they liked to work for him, and the latter because the work was there, they truly loved Foster and hated Charles. Foster appeared amused by this but actually it was a matter of great pride.

Now with this criterion, he went to work on Lee with complete confidence in its efficacy. "As for myself, I don't see the union in such awesome aspect. It has its faults, yes, but what large organization doesn't?"

"I am certainly glad to hear you say that, sir," Lee said, breathing a sigh of relief. "I thought perhaps the reason you had us to dinner today was something concerning the union."

"No, I am more concerned with people than with unions," Foster said with inspirational intensity, "with what affects them, their lives, and their futures, with the things that influence them, the courses they may take. It is always my most optimistic hope that I may be able to point out to them what will be beneficial and what may be detrimental. Only in this way may we preserve the spirit of our democracy—our American way of life. Are you proud to be an American, Lee?" he asked with sudden sharpness.

Taken aback by the suddenness of the question, Lee could only stammer: "Why—yes, sir."

"Your people have had a long hard struggle to attain their present position," Foster went on, "and it would grieve me to see you at this point alienate the good will of us who have your problem at heart and are not trying to use you to foster our own selfish ends."

"I'm sure we wouldn't want to do that," Lee Gordon said, and Foster smiled.

Now he would inject a little fun into this game the union played, Foster thought with a sense of secret satisfaction. For his object was not to break the union. He had not the slightest doubt but that he would squelch the union's campaign by simply continuing his present policy. The workers liked him; they were satisfied. He had them in his control and there was nothing to be feared. He wanted only to annoy the unionists by taking their favorite colored boy away from them. He could already see himself telling it as a joke at a board of directors meeting.

"I'm sure you wouldn't," Foster said, "and that is the reason, I must confess, that I am concerned with your people, with your thoughts and ambitions and political convictions—and with you, boy. I am concerned with you as a man."

Drawn by the quality of sincerity in Foster's voice, Ruth and Mrs. Foster had come over to join them and were there in time to hear Foster's last remark. Ruth looked sharply to see how Lee was taking it, whether he had kept his mind receptive to anything that Foster might have to offer.

But Lee experienced a slight withdrawing, a vague repudiation of the sincerity of this white millionaire who thought of him as a boy yet claimed to be concerned with him as a man. He knew that Foster was going to make him an offer and hoped that he would have the strength of will to refuse, because whatever Foster offered to a man whom he thought of as a boy would be a handout with condescension, like old clothes given to a servant.

Watching Lee's every expression with clinical appraisal, Foster was immediately aware of Lee's changed attitude, and he made a better offer than he had at first intended.

"For some time now," he said, "I've been considering employing a colored man in the personnel department at Comstock. I think you are the man for that job, Lee. I'll start you off at five thousand a year and you can report to work at eight o'clock tomorrow morning."

Foster could not bear to have a Negro, any Negro, dislike him. And before he would allow a Negro to really hate him, he would make the Negro rich.

Ruth gasped audibly at the offer, and Mrs. Foster's eyes went wide in amazement. Lee's breath turned rock-hard in his chest and his heart seemed caught in his throat. For he was not prepared to withstand such an offer as this—Lord God! Five thousand to start! He could have Ruth home—home! And he'd never have to be afraid anymore—

"You have a streak of stubborn integrity in you, boy, that I like," Foster said, smiling across at him, already gloating inwardly at putting this one over. "I'll see that you get the breaks."

And it was this that gave Lee Gordon the courage to refuse; because if he had integrity that could be bought, he had no integrity at all. And if one man held it in his power to make the breaks for him, he held it in his power to make the breaks against him. He would feel alone, lost in a white office, afraid, his destiny subject to the whims of this one man—better to be with the union where there would be others who were lost, lonely, and afraid. So he said: "Well—thank you, sir. I want you to know, sir, I certainly appreciate your considering me for the job. But I can't quit the union now. The union is depending on me."

Admiration was first in the eyes of both Ruth and Mrs. Foster, and it remained in the eyes of the older woman. But Ruth's next reaction was a sharp, deep hurt, because she thought that he had only been thinking of himself; if he had been thinking of her, or of them together, he could never have refused.

But it was shock that showed in Foster's face, stronger than his control. In the sudden fury that raced through his mind he thought with deadly venom: "You goddamn black bastard, you'll pay for this—" And then he composed his features to a stillness and kept his voice on an even keel: "I won't try to persuade you, boy, for I can understand your loyalty even though I know it to be misplaced."

It was the end of the afternoon and now Lee and Ruth awaited their dismissal. But Foster was not ready to dismiss them quite yet—This was the second colored boy, he was thinking. First a worker at the plant, the Lester McKinley boy, and now this boy. Either he was losing his touch or they were having too much war prosperity. But he would see, he would see. It goaded him to say: "I'd like to give you a bit of advice, boy, keep an eye on your fellow organizers. They're not as honest as you seem to think. Less than a week ago one of them came to me with an offer to break the back of the organizing campaign. I chased him from my office but there are other executives in the company who do not have my impartiality toward the union at this time."

But now that Lee had had the strength to refuse his offer, he could resist this scare of union treachery Foster sought to throw into him, and it was only out of politeness that he asked: "I don't suppose you want to tell me who it was?"

"I don't mind telling you; I would like to tell you. But it wouldn't do you any good; it would just get you into trouble. This man is too big for you to tackle; he is one of your big boys. I'm not telling you this to make you lose confidence in the union, or through any desire to undermine your loyalty. I am just advising you to watch your step."

"Well—thank you, sir," Lee Gordon said.

And now the silence dismissed them, and Ruth spoke the words of departure: "We've had such a wonderful time! I don't know how to express it, but I've enjoyed every minute."

"I have enjoyed it very much also," Lee echoed.

While waiting for the car to come and take them home, as at the beginning, they discussed for a moment the beautiful house. Foster was his charming self again, and when Roy sounded the horn, he gave Lee his quick, firm clasp and turned his devastating smile on Ruth.

But it was Mrs. Foster who walked to the door with them. She shook Lee's hand with added pressure and said with genuine emotion: "I wish you luck, both of you." And her parting smile to Ruth was completely wistful.

It was this memory they both carried as they walked down to the car unaccompanied, and now separated from each other by Ruth's reproachful silence.

Hisaye Yamamoto

IN 1986 the Before Columbus Foundation gave Hisaye Yamamoto (1921–   ) a lifetime achievement award in spite of the fact that she had not published a single book-length work. Her first collection of stories and essays, *Seventeen Syllables and Other Stories*, was not published until 1988. (A collection of five of her short stories was published in Japan in 1985 under the title *Seventeen Syllables*. The foundation noted that the significance of six major short stories, "Seventeen Syllables" (1949), "The Legend of Miss Sasagawara" (1950), "The Brown House" (1951), "Yoneko's Earthquake" (1951), "Epithalamium" (1960), and "Las Vegas Charley" (1961), qualified her for the award in terms of literary achievement in Asian American literature. She and Toshio Mori were the first Japanese Americans to gain recognition after the war. Four of her stories were listed in Martha Foley's annual *Best American Short Stories*, and "Yoneko's Earthquake" was included in *Best American Short Stories of 1952*. The others were published in *Kenyon Review, Arizona Quarterly, Carleton Miscellany, Partisan Review, Harper's Bazaar,* and *Furioso*.

The editors of *The Big Aiiieeeee! An Anthology of Chinese and Japanese American Literature* (1991) note: "Her modest body of fiction is remarkable for its range and gut understanding of Japanese America. The questions and themes of Asian-American life are fresh. Growing up with foreign-born parents, mixing with white and nonwhite races, racial discrimination, growing old, the question of dual personality—all were explored. . . . Technically and stylistically, hers is among the most highly developed of Asian American writing. . . . In her work we see how language adapts to new speakers, new experience, and becomes new language."

Although Yamamoto is best known for her stories of pre–World War II rural Japanese America in California's Central Valley, the story, "Eplithalamium," reprinted here concerns itself with post–World War II, post–concentration-camp years. Yuki Tsumagari, fresh out of the Topaz concentration camp in Utah, buries her too-Japanese identity, language, and sense of self in a Staten Island Catholic rehabilitation community for "alcoholics, the laicized priests, the mentally disturbed, the physically handicapped, the unwed mothers, the rejected Trappists, the senile, the offscouring of the world." Even readers who do not possess one iota of information regarding the Japanese American removal from the West Coast and incarceration can intuit it from Yuki Tsumagari's self-imposed exile after the war from mainstream America and mainstream Japanese America.

—Shawn Wong

"Epithalamium" from
SEVENTEEN SYLLABLES AND
OTHER STORIES

For Yuki Tsumagari, the Japanese girl from San Francisco, it was the next-to-the-last day at the Zualet Community on Staten Island. Tomorrow, Madame Marie would drive her to the village station and she would embark on the three-thousand-mile journey by bus which would take her back to her mother and father on Saturn Street, to her married younger brother and his wife (with the two little girls who looked just like Japanese dolls), to her friend Atsuko who had been her soul mate since they had first met during the war at the Utah concentration camp called Topaz.

Also, although she did not know it, today was her wedding day. Yet, she should have suspected something unusual. She had awakened in the morning with Hopkins running through her mind:

> The world is charged with the grandeur of God.
> It will flame out, like shining from shook foil;
> It gathers to a greatness, like the ooze of oil
> Crushed . . .

As bookish as she had been all her life, she had never come to consciousness before with poetry singing in her head. Perhaps this was to be the first and last time. In any case, the lines had sustained her all that strange day long; walking the wooded mile down Meadowvale Lane to meet Marco at the village trolley station (he had phoned and threatened, still drunk, to go away forever if she did not marry him that very day); riding with him on the trolley to St. George; standing before the city clerk in that little room with the podium, the American flag, and the potted palm, where a fellow civil servant had hastily been called in as a witness; promising to love, honor, and obey this inebriated man.

Afterwards, Marco was quite miffed because Yuki had refused to go to his hotel room with him. He went by himself to check out and return the key and must have found a bottle in his room because he came back to the rear stairway, where she had been waiting, drunker than ever. They rode the trolley only as far back as Princess Bay station, and because he was in no condition to take back to the Community, they remained there at the covered wooden waiting bench. He passed out with his head on her lap, and as she sometimes gazed down at that once perfect (many women had sought him), now battered face, flushed and swollen with drink, she thought, "This is my husband." For better or for worse, for richer for poorer, in sickness and in health, till death do us part.

The months since March, when he had first confessed his love, had been alternately lovely and sordid and terrible and sweet. She had got more than she bargained for, certainly. Once they had walked up Meadowvale Lane in the spring rain and stopped every few minutes to cling and kiss, careless of their sodden clothes and the few cars that slowly passed. There was scarcely a nook or cranny of the Community that they had not defiled, as well as the wooded stretch of beach belonging to a nearby monastery and seminary, and various parts of the woods. Against her will? Hardly (she had made no outcry; she could have firmly refused to go for those walks), but she had urgently sensed that it was against God's will, as though some supernatural agent had been sent to deter them from their immorality; each moment stolen for love had been unmistakably tainted.

On the beach belonging to the monastery, where Yuki had been so enchanted on Holy Wednesday and Thursday nights by the sweet, pure voices of the young seminarians as they took turns singing the psalms of the Tenebrae; where she had, amazed, felt the trickle of tears down her cheeks during a couple of the responsories when the black-gowned young men had clustered together (met together as though they might have been in some football huddle) and boomed out:

. . .Latro de cruce clamabat, dicens: Memento mei, Domine, dum veneris in regnum tuum. (The thief from the cross cried out: "Lord, remember me when Thou comest into Thy kingdom.")

. . . Quomodo conversa es in amaritudinem, ut me crucifigeres, et Barabbam dimitteres? (How art thou turned to bitterness, that thou shouldst crucify me, and release Barabbas?)

—it was there that she had learned for herself (pushed down with insistence onto the rocky ground amidst the trees) about man's desire. She had not known that it would be so painful the first time, or so quick. She thought, I am being killed! And she remembered that as a small child, it had taken the full strength of both her grandfather and father to hold her over the Japanese wooden tub of the bathroom for her mother to wash her hair, as she kicked and struggled and screamed, *"Shini-yoru! Shini-yoru!* I'm dying! I'm dying!"

Later (they had not been able to look at each other for awhile), as they sat on the huge damp rocks at low tide, some instinct, so positive that she had blushed for shame, informed her that they had been watched, in shocked silence, by some young seminarian who had come to pray by the ocean in solitude.

It was the same elsewhere. On another stretch of beach, semi-hidden by a semi-circle of rocks, they had either been nearly discovered or discovered by a couple of kids racing their horses up and down the edge of the water. In the woods, those enormous black mosquitoes (Staten Islanders claim that they come over in squadrons every summer from the marshes of New Jersey across the bay) had bitten every inch of her thighs. Near the creek, where she had been so delighted to find earlier that spring (it had been St. Joseph's Day) those first curious shells, striated maroon and pale green, of skunk cabbage, the back of her dress had been streaked with mud. And always there had been the anxiety of being suddenly come upon, of scandalizing the whole Community, and most of all, of giving grief to saintly, gentle Madame Marie.

Thus, she had become a physical, moral, and spiritual ruin. She had secretly endured a miscarriage towards the middle of

July, and hadn't been of much help to the Community since then, with general pains in the womb and kidney regions. She had bled for twenty days, and for a few days, she had barely been able to walk. She had hid in her room then, emerging only for meals. How relieved she was to remember that this was the only hard and fast Rule of the Zualet Community, that one show up for the three meals of the day.

Madame Marie, in her wisdom, had early suspected that something was amiss. "Are you having trouble with your period?" she stopped to ask one day when Yuki was making a halfhearted effort to straighten out the Clothes Room. The Clothes Room always needed straightening out—members of the Community were forever trying on this or that item of clothing contributed by its benefactors, and nothing was put back in order. "No," Yuki had lied. She had held up a large brassiere and tried to make a joke of it. "I've never needed one of these," she said. "Once I bought a couple, the smallest I could find, and they just kept hiking up on me and making me uncomfortable." Madame Marie had smiled. "Delusions of grandeur!" she commented. And the inquisition was over.

But the time Yuki had remained in her room for several days, Madame Marie had called her into her own cozy and book-lined room for a conference. Not a conference, exactly. She had glimpsed Marco and Yuki together in Yuki's room, too physically close to each other for mere conversation, and she had decided to tell Yuki a few of the love stories of the Zualet Community during its twenty years of existence.

Many alcoholics had come to the Community to recuperate, she said; a few had stayed on to help in the Work. And several of them had fallen in love with the idealistic young and not-so-young women who, like Yuki, had been drawn there ostensibly by God but probably more because of their own ambiguous reasons, to assist Madame Marie. One young woman had insisted on marrying one who also had the unfortunate compulsion of unbuttoning his fly in public. She had had several children by him before they had separated, and now she bitterly blamed the Community for the outcome. Another young woman had married one who had stopped drinking for two years. On their wedding night, he began drinking again and had not stopped since. That was seven children ago, and she still remained with him, although he had beaten her regularly and although she had had to work all these years as a waitress to support the family. "If I don't love him, who will?" Madame Marie quoted her as saying, and Yuki had been moved to tears. In contrast, there was the wise virgin who, immediately upon realizing that she was coming to regard an alcoholic with unseemly tenderness, had decided to leave the Zualet Community. Now she was leading a happy and useful life with a group of Catholic laywomen.

Madame Marie was trying to dissuade her from marrying Marco, Yuki knew. "But if I give him up, won't that be suffering, too?" she couldn't help asking. Suddenly, Madame Marie shook her head and looked away. "You'll never know how I suffered," she said. "You'll never know . . ." Then Yuki remembered Madame Marie's published autobiography, the book that had changed her whole life and brought her all the way across the country, in which she had told of the origins of the Zualet Community, of her meeting with René Zualet, the Basque scholar-farmer (now dead), who had eventually talked her into establishing this Catholic lay community where all would live together in Christian love and voluntary poverty, working on the land and studying together, accepting all who came because they had nowhere else to go—the alcoholics, the laicized priests, the mentally disturbed, the physically handicapped, the unwed mothers, the rejected Trappists, the senile, the offscouring of the world—as Ambassadors of Chirst. As a young woman, Madame Marie (then Marie Chavy, a carefree Greenwich Village refugee from a convent school) had lived with a man whom she loved very much. One day, while she was sitting alone on a bench in Central Park, eating a lunch of crackers and cheese, a pigeon (a dove sent from God?) had alighted on her shoulder, and she had experienced, over and above her earthly contentment, an illumination which had convinced her that man had been placed here upon this spinning globe to love and honor the Father, the Son, and the Holy Ghost. Her lover, a confirmed agnostic, had refused to marry her in the Church. So she had no choice but to leave him. And her autobiography had admitted that it had been many, many anguished nights before she had stopped yearning for the consolation of his arms.

So Yuki continued to bleed and confine herself to her room. Madame Marie sent in irrepressible Brigid McGinty, who, with her extravagant Brooklyn-Irish judgments of other members of the Community, could always make Yuki laugh, to cheer her up, but Yuki only succeeded in depressing Brigid McGinty. How could she possibly tell her? And she prayed and prayed, how she prayed, remembering how a woman had been healed of a discharge of years, merely by touching, in complete faith, the hem of Christ's robe. The bleeding stopped on August 5, on the Feast of Our Lady of Snows, which Madame Marie had appointed Yuki's feast day when she had learned that Yuki was the Japanese word for snow. Yuki presumptuously and gratefully accepted this miracle as a feast day gift from God.

She was able then to resume baking bread for the Community, eight loaves a day, but whether because Grace had totally deserted her (bread must be kneaded and backed with *caritas*, or it just won't come out right) or because Madame Marie or somebody had decided to try the heavier whole wheat flour from a nearby organic farm, Yuki removed from the oven batch after batch of wheaten bricks which could have been used for the new chapel Madame Marie had her heart set on building. Once she had been able to bring forth such loaves that someone had remarked, "Say, this is better than cake!"

And Marco became jealous of Chic, a new member of the Community, fresh from serving a term for forgery, who had enthusiastically taken over the cooking. His imagination and his rememberances of his own irregular life as a seaman had created a lively side romance, and his accusations had left Yuki miserable and helpless.

But some of the early weeks had been beautiful, before anyone had suspected that there was the least attachment between this tall Italian seaman from Worcester, Mass., this Marco Cimarusti, who had come to the Community to recover after a bender, and this plain-faced Japanese girl who had been such a serious and devout member of the Community for two years.

He was completely sober then, for almost a month, and there were stolen kisses in the morning, the joy of making piles of whole wheat toast for the breakfast table together, and the bittersweet of trying to say goodnight at curfew, loath to leave one another.

One day, when Marco was well and ready to leave the Community, he had gone out to the Battery to see if he could get a seasonal job as engineer on the *S.S. Hudson Belle,* one of the summer excursion boats which twice daily carries tourists and vacationers from such points as the Battery, Yonkers, Jersey City, Elizabeth, and Bayonne, to crowded Rockaway Beach and back, and which even schedules special moonlight dances and showboat cruises on certain nights. Madame Marie had given Yuki leave to go over to the Battery to wait with him till the boat got back in. His seaman friend Manuel, a Negro from Baltimore, who was a steward on the liner *America,* was with him, too, and the trio had sat there on a bench and talked about the warm weather. Meanwhile, a car crashed into a pole nearby and the police discovered it was driven by a couple of men from Seamen's House who had kidnapped a woman tourist, stolen her car, and kept her captive drunk in the rear seat. And in the playground, a little girl was hurt on the concrete, so the police were tending to that, too. Yuki was rather dazed by everything. She and Marco went over to get some coffee and doughnuts across the street, and they came back to sit there in the hot sun on a Battery Park bench, sipping from paper cups and watching the pigeons, waiting for the *S.S. Hudson Belle* to come in, waiting for the *Robert E. Lee.* Manuel was at the scene of the auto accident. When the boat came in, they gladly took Marco on; he waved goodbye from the gangplank, and Yuki noticed that he sure could have used a haircut.

Then Manuel and Yuki talked a bit. "I've knowed that man for five years," said Manuel. "He's my best friend, I guess. But the way he is, when he's drinking, you can't trust him with a quarter to go across the street and come back with a loaf of bread."

Well, to get back to Yuki's wedding day—several trolleys went by and curious passengers stared at this small Oriental girl wearing a blue-printed cotton dirndl and embroidered nylon blouse (the clothes that a generous visitor to the Community had taken off her back and given to Yuki, just because she had commented on how pretty they looked, had been her wedding dress), cradling on her lap the head of this mould of man, big-boned and hardy-handsome.

O bright unhappiness. O shining sorrow. Why this man? Yuki could not understand why she loved him. Because he represented all the courage, moral and physical, which she had always felt she lacked (she was afraid of elevators; she had never had the nerve to learn how to drive a car)? Because in spite of all he had been through (wounded three times in the recent war, he wore a good-sized crater just below his left rib), he retained an enormous vitality? "It's the physical attraction," Madame Marie had said. "He has a gift for work that not many are given. See how he spades the ground out there, with such ease, such grace. Oh, he is wonderfully made!"

Yuki remembered the bull sessions back in San Francisco. After Topaz, as soon as California had permitted the return of the Japanese, her father had resumed his former occupation as a gardener, and she had become chief cook and bottle-washer for a small Japanese daily which printed one page of English and three pages of Japanese. She was allowed a weekly column in which she was free to write as she pleased; this had attracted a bunch of somewhat younger companions who all dreamed of one day writing the Great Nisei Novel, and they had all talked of everything under the sun, mostly trying to analyze one another. Sometimes Yuki had been the one under the floodlight of their probing, and sometimes she had been made very uncomfortable, mostly because she was unmarried at 31 and did not appear particularly anxious to perpetuate an alliance with any male.

"What are you, anyway, a Lesbian?" someone had finally asked.

Yuki laughed. "No, I'd like to get married someday."

"Well, what kind of guy does it have to be? You sure must be particular."

"I read a poem by e.e. cummings once," said Yuki.

*". . . lady through whose profound and fragile lips the sweet
small clumsy feet of April came into the ragged meadow of
my soul.*

If someone would say such a thing to me, I'd melt. That would
be the end of my spinsterhood!"

"Do you know something? You're nothing but a shopgirl at
heart. 'Lady through whose profound and fragile lips. . .' Sheer
corn!"

(Then was this the why of her total response to Marco—
because she sensed that if he had been a poet, he would have
confirmed those gratifying lines? But there was no need for
poetry; the mere thought of Marco was enough to make her
bowels as molten wax. Not that he was exactly the inarticulate
man, when it came to recounting his sailing and drinking adventures. But then neither did Marco comprehend why he had
chosen her, after so many other women, some of them breath-
takingly beautiful, had indicated their willingness to marry him
at a moment's notice. As one member of the Community had
observed, Marco was the type of man who should have been
driving a Cadillac convertible, that expensive wristwatch glint-
ing in the sunlight as he impatiently drummed his left hand on
the outside of the door, waiting for the light to change—with
yes, some golden-haired goddess by his side. Yet, looking into
Yuki's plain brown face, he would say in puzzlement, "I can't
understand it. It's like you've got a rope tied around my neck
that won't let go." Or, "If I had a million dollars, I'd just sit
here all day long and just look at you!")

Yuki had shrugged. "You're a snob. What's so wrong about
being a shopgirl? Don't they come under human beings?"

But it was not only these friends that wondered about Yuki.
Her mother had sighed over her. *"Komaru-ne. . .* what a worry
you are. What's wrong with Michio-san? He's such a fine boy.
He would make a good husband. College education and everything, and a good job as a draftsman for the City." And she
would point up the model of her young brother Taro, a moder-
ately successful insurance salesman, who had early married a

suitable and sweet girl and had already presented her with two
splendid grandchildren.

"Mama, don't worry about me. It's just that I feel in my
heart that there are some things I have to do first, before I start
having children and settling down."

Her father would side with her. "Leave her alone, Mama.
She's happy, she's healthy. What more do you want?"

Usually, each time her mother got onto the subject, Yuki
could not help smiling. It always reminded her of the lyric of
the mother's fretting in a novel called *The Time of Man:*
"Where's the fellows that ought to be a-comen? . . . A big
brown girl, nigh to eighteen, and no fellows a-comen!" A couple of times, the echo in her mind of this singsong plaint,
"Where's the fellows that ought to be a-comen?" had made her
burst out giggling, and her mother, who saw not a whit of levity
concerning the matter at hand, had looked very much pained.

One day, however, Yuki had been feeling out of sorts when
her mother began on this perpetual theme.

"Maybe I'm a *katawa*, Mama," she had answered tartly.
"Nothing but a freak."

Her mother had fiercely denied such a possibility. "You're
not a *katawa!* How can you say such a thing? The midwife said
you were one of the most perfectly formed babies she'd ever
seen!"

Poor Mama. Now what would her mother say? She had been
distressed enough when Yuki had announced that she was
going to New York, and on such a bewildering mission. She had
been absolutely dismayed when Yuki had later written to say
that she had begun taking Catholic instruction. But Yuki had
for some reason never got around to being baptized. For one
thing, to reject Buddhism entirely and to accept the Catholic
theory that, as heathens, the most that good Buddhists could
hope for was not the Heaven where God, dazzling in all His
glory, would be met face-to-face, but merely a Natural Heaven
called Limbo, where only a profane serenity awaited—this
would be equivalent to rejecting her mother and father, and
Yuki could not bring herself to cause this irreparable cleavage.
For the time being, she consoled herself that she was in her

heart a Catholic, through what Fr. McGillicuddy had described as the "baptism of desire."

Sooner or later, her mother would have to learn that her
daughter had married an alcoholic, and a *hakujin* (white) alcoholic, at that. Suddenly, Yuki could not see ahead at all, because she did not care to contemplate either the suffering she
would have to inflict or that she herself would doubtless have to
undergo. She was leaving the Community tomorrow on the
advice of Madame Marie, who wanted her to consult her family before coming to any decision about Marco. She would, of
course, be unable to confess today's marriage to Madame
Marie (I will write later and explain, she promised herself).
Marco will join me in another week or so after he accumulates
enough bus fare. After another drinking bout, he had been
ousted from the engine room and was now, black bow tie and
all, a waiter on the *Hudson Belle*.

Finally, Marco came to enough so that the newlyweds could
catch the trolley to their own stop. He promptly bought a bottle at the village liquor store, and they had to take the taxi back
to the Community.

On the way, with Marco slumped heavily against her, Yuki
kept remembering Hopkins. Perhaps she wanted to believe
that this was a sign from God *(It is a wicked and unfaithful
generation that asks for a sign)* that this was the way He meant
it to be:

> *The world is charged with the grandeur of God.*
> *It will flame out, like shining from shook foil;*
> *It gathers to a greatness, like the ooze of oil*
> *Crushed . . .*
> *. . . And though the last lights of the black West went*
> *Oh, morning, at the brown brink eastward, springs—*
> *Because the Holy Ghost over the bent*
> *World broods with warm breast and with ah! bright wings.*

Anyway, she could not think of an epithalamium that she
would more prefer, Hopkins permitting. Incidentally, this
morning at Mass, Fr. McGillicuddy had worn red vestments. It

was the Feast Day of the Beheading of St. John the Baptist, and in this connection there always came to her mind that very last, that devastating line of Flaubert's *Herodias,* about Iaoka-nan's severed head: "As it was very heavy, they carried it alternately." The missal had also noted that it was the commemoration of St. Sabina, a Roman widow who had been converted by a maidservant, beheaded under the Emperor Hadrian, and secretly buried. A church had been built on the site of her home on the Aventine in 425. Considered a gem of basilical architecture, it was used as the station on Ash Wednesday. However, the missal had added, it was not certain whether such a woman had existed at all.

Hualing Nieh

HUALING NIEH (1925–   ) was born to Kuang and Kuo-yin (Sun) Nieh in Hupei, China. In 1964 she emigrated to the United States, and she became a naturalized citizen ten years later. She is married to the poet Paul Engle, with whom she has translated the poems of Mao Tse-tung. She has two children, Wei-Wei Wang Ruprecht and Lan-lan Wang King. Before moving to the United States she lived for many years in Taiwan and was the literary editor of the *Free China Fortnightly* from 1949 to 1960. She has written numerous collections of short stories and essays, as well as the novel *Mulberry and Peach: Two Women of China,* in Chinese. Nieh has also translated several pieces of American fiction into Chinese and written several critical works in English. Because of her work translating Western fiction, she has found herself influenced by F. Scott Fitzgerald, Hemingway, and particularly Ralph Ellison's *Invisible Man.* However, she says:

> From Chinese classical literature, Chinese classical poetry and modern literature I have learned a lot too. I am more and more Chinese in writing. Before, when I was in Taiwan, my way of writing was rather Western. Now, I think, in language, subject, content and maybe even in form the next book will be more Chinese.

She writes fiction only in Chinese despite her obvious control of English. She told Peter Nazareth in *World Literature Today,* "Fiction is my strong point. So when I write fiction, I cannot write in English. I have to write in Chinese." This may have kept her from being known in America and England, but she is "not forgotten by the Chinese"; and she is beginning to be discovered, in translation, in America.

Mulberry and Peach is a novel about a split personality, but this goes far beyond the split personality of Mulberry/Peach; for Nieh the split personality is a symbol of China and the Chinese in the twentieth century. Nieh says:

> In the twentieth century not just the Chinese but many people have a split personality. . . . I think this is especially true of the Chinese. This novel is also a kind of fable about the Chinese situation. It is not just about the Chinese, the people; it is also about the country.

She says she is "very obsessed with the . . . tragic situation of the Chinese" and that *Mulberry and Peach* "is about what it is to be Chinese in the twentieth century." Specifically, as a writer and a Chinese, Nieh herself feels a "split personality," because as a writer she had a duty to art, and as a Chinese she has a social responsibility to her country. In *Mulberry and Peach,* Nieh resolves this split in the form of Peach. She is a rebirth from Mulberry's past of a heroic figure, the Peach-Flower woman. In the end Peach emerges as a symbol of the author's "love of a China which is capable of change and capable of solving problems".

The question of revision of personal history is central to *Mulberry and Peach.* From the first sentence it is apparent that Peach was in fact Mulberry; her vehement denial " 'I'm not Mulberry. Mulberry is dead!' " to the immigration agent merely solidifies it. By the end we discover that in fact Peach is Mulberry's schizophrenic split personality. Peach has had to take over because Mulberry was not flexible enough to deal with the stress in her life. It is ironic that after all Mulberry has had to go through in China, life becomes too difficult for her to cope with in the relative freedom of America.

The most symbolic aspect of Mulberry and Peach, perhaps, is in the title itself. Hualing Nieh said to Peter Nazareth:

> Mulberry is a sacred tree for the Chinese because mulberry leaves fed the silkworms which made silk for China. Silk *was* China in

ancient times. So Mulberry Green is very Chinese. . . . Peach Pink, to the Chinese, is very symbolic. . . . to the Chinese the peach blossoms are exuberant, beautiful, brilliant, hopeful! So these two names represent meanings too, but in English translation, they are lost.

Even in the translation all is not lost. Nieh gives us several clear indications of the meanings of Mulberry and Peach. Mulberry's whole journey in China consists of running away and hiding. She does the same in the United States. To save herself, she even wants to abort her unborn child: this is the final symbol of Mulberry as the old, dead ways, and Peach as the future, full of hope. Even at a risk of deportation for immoral activities (the child is conceived in an adulterous affair), Peach in the end stands up for a chance at life, where Mulberry succumbs to fear. The fate of the child is the final conflict that brings Peach out permanently at the end of the novel as the dominant personality.

The novel ends with a folk tale about a bird who "wants to fill in the sea and turn it into solid ground." She attempts to do so by filling it with tiny pebbles she drops one at a time into the vast ocean. Despite ridicule and impossible odds she is determined in her task, and the story ends with her continuing to persevere. Nieh says that "the meaning is the human spirit will never die"; Peach is left, at the end of the novel, pregnant and full of life.

— *Wei Ming Dariotis*

Chapter 2 from
MULBERRY AND PEACH: TWO WOMEN OF CHINA

Mulberry's Notebook: Chü-t'ang
Gorge on the Yangtze River
(27 July 1945–10 August 1945)

CHARACTERS

MULBERRY (16 years old), during the Anti-Japanese War, Mulberry is running away from home with her lesbian friend, Lao-shih. Sometime after her parents' marriage, Mulberry's father became impotent as the result of a wound received in a battle between rival Chinese warlords. Later, the mother, who before her marriage had been a prostitute, began an affair with the family butler, and began to abuse her husband and children. As the story opens, Mulberry is running away to Chungking, the wartime capital of China.

LAO-SHIH (18), a dominating, mannish girl about Mulberry's age. Her father was suffocated in the huge tunnel in which people hid from the continuous Japanese bombing of Chungking in the summer of 1941.

THE OLD MAN (in his 60s), he represents the traditional type of Chinese. He has been in flight from the Japanese since they occupied Peiping, his home, in 1937.

REFUGEE STUDENT (in his 20s), he represents the generation growing up during World War II. He is patriotic, aware of his rootless condition. He is rebellious against the old system represented by his father, who had seven wives and forty-six children, and lived in a huge gloomy house in Nanking. His father works for the Japanese. The angry young man reveals the inevitability of the coming revolution.

PEACH-FLOWER WOMAN (in her 20s), she represents the natural life force, vital, exuberant, sensuous and enduring. It is this spontaneous life force that has enabled the Chinese to survive thousands of years of wars, revolutions and natural disasters. She became the wife of a boy seven years her junior when she herself was a child. She raised the baby husband, and worked hard on the farm. When the husband grew up, he left her and studied in Chungking. The rumour is that he lives with another woman in Chungking. Peach-flower Woman is going there with her baby to look for her husband.

THERE is no sun. There is no moon. There is no sky. The sky and the water are one, both murky. The river dragon stirs up the water. His hundred hairy legs and clumsy tail swish back and forth, churning the water.

From the window at the inn in Tai-hsi, I can see the mountains across the river, so tall I can't see the top, like a black sword piercing the sky. The sky dies without losing one drop of blood. The gorge suddenly darkens.

A torch flares up along the river. A paddlewheel steamboat, blasted in half by the Japanese, lies stranded in the dark water like a dead cow. Along the river several lamps light up. Near the shore are several old wooden boats. Our boat, crippled while rounding the sandbanks at New Landslide Rapids, is tied up there for repairs.

The village of Tai-hsi is like a delicate chain lying along the cliffs. There is no quay along the river. When you disembark you have to climb up steep narrow steps carved out of the cliff. When I crawled up those steps, I didn't dare look up at the peak, or I might have fallen back into the water, a snack for the dragon.

A torch bobs up the steps. After a while I can see that there is a man on horseback coming up the steps, carrying a torch. The torch flashes under my window and I glimpse a chestnut-coloured horse.

Lao-shih and I ran away together from En-shih to Pa-tung. I am sixteen and she is eighteen. We thought we could get a ship out of Pa-tung right away and be in Chungking in a flash.

When we get to Chungking, the war capital, we'll be all right, or at least that's what Lao-shih says. She patted her chest when she said that to show how certain she was. She wears a tight bra and tries to flatten her breasts, but they are as large as two hunks of steamed bread. She said, 'Chungking, it's huge city. The centre of the Resistance! What are you scared about? The hostel for refugee students will take care of our food, housing, school and a job. You can do whatever you want.' We are both from the remote mountains of En-shih and are students at the Provincial High School. Whatever I don't know, she does.

When we got to Pa-tung, we found out that all the steamships have been requisitioned to transport ammunition and troops. Germany has surrendered to the Allies and the Japanese are desperately fighting for their lives. A terrible battle has broken out again in northern Hupeh and western Hunan. There weren't any passenger ships leaving Pa-tung, only a freighter going to Wu-shan, so we took that. When we arrived in Wu-shan, we happened upon an old wooden boat which carried cotton to Feng-chieh, so we took that.

Towering mountains above us, the deep gorge below. Sailing past the Gorge in that old boat was really exciting, but it cracked up on the rocks of New Landslide Rapids and is now at Tai-hsi for repairs.

Lao-shih just went out to find out when the boat will be repaired and when we can sail. A unit of new recruits is camped out in the courtyard of the inn. Tomorrow they'll be sent to the front. I sit by the window and undress, leaving on only a bra and a pair of skimpy panties. The river fog rolls in and caresses me, like damp, cool feathers tickling my body. The river is black and I haven't lit the lamp. I can't see anything in front of me. The few lamps along the river go out one by one. Before me the night is an endless stretch of black cloth, a backdrop for the game I play with my griffin:

> Griffin, griffin, green as oil
> Two horns two wings
> One wing broken
> A beast, yet a bird
> Come creep over the black cloth

And the griffin comes alive in my hand, leaping in the darkness. The wings outstretched, flapping, flapping.

'HEY.'

I turn. Two eyes and a row of white teeth flash at me from the door. I scream.

'No, don't scream. Don't scream. I was just drafted and tomorrow I'm being sent to the front. Let me hide in your room just for tonight.'

I can't stop screaming. My voice is raw. When I finally stop, he is gone, but two eyes and that row of teeth still wink at me in the dark. A whip cracks in the courtyard.

'Sergeant, please, I won't do it again. I won't run away again . . .'

The shadows of the soldiers in the courtyard appear on the paper window. The man hangs upside down, head twitching. Beside him, a man snaps a whip and a crowd of heads looks up.

'LAO-SHIH,' I pause and stare at the jade griffin in my hand. One of its wings is cracked. 'I don't want to go to Chungking. I want to go home.'

'Chicken. You getting scared?'

'No, it's not that.'

'You can't turn back. You have to go, even if you have to climb the Mountain of Knives. That's all there is to it, you know what I mean. Anyway, you can't go back now. Everyone in En-shih knows you've run away by now. Your mother won't forgive you either. You know when she was drunk, she would beat you for no reason, until you bled. She will kill you if you go back.'

'No. She wouldn't do anything to me. As soon as I ran away, I stopped hating her. And I still have Father. He's always been good to me.'

'Little Berry, don't get mad, but what kind of a man is he, anyway? Can he manage his family? He can't even manage his own wife. He lets her get away with everything while he sits in his study, the old cuckold, meditating. You call that a man?

However you look at it, he's not a man.' She starts laughing. 'You said so yourself. Your father wounded his "vital part" during the campaign against the warlords . . .' She is laughing so hard she can't go on.

'Lao-shih, that's not funny.'

'So why can't a daughter talk about her father's genitals?'

'Well, I always felt . . .' I rub the jade griffin.

'You always felt guilty, right?'

"Mm . . . but not about his vital part!' I start laughing. 'I mean this griffin I'm holding. I stole it when I left. Father's probably really upset about it.'

'With all these wars and fighting, jewels aren't worth anything anyway. Besides, it's only a piece of broken jade.'

'This isn't an ordinary piece of jade, Lao-shih. This jade griffin was passed down from my ancestors. Originally jade griffins were placed in front of graves in ancient times to scare away devils. My great-grandfather was an only son, really sickly as a child, and he wore this piece of jade around his neck and lived to be eighty-eight. When he died he ordered that it be given to my grandfather and not used as a burial treasure. My grandfather was also an only son. He wore it his whole life and lived to be seventy-five. Then he gave it to my father who was also an only son. He wore the griffin as a pendant on his watch chain. I'll always remember him wearing a white silk jacket and pants, a gold German watch in one pocket and the jade griffin in the other pocket, and the gold chain in between, swishing against the silk. When he wasn't doing anything, he'd take it from his pocket and caress it and caress it and it would come alive. You know what I thought about when he did that?'

Lao-shih doesn't say anything.

'I would think about what my great-grandfather looked like when he died. Isn't that strange? I never even saw him. I would imagine him wearing a black satin gown, black satin cap, with a ruby red pendant dangling from the tip of the cap, black satin shoes. He would have a squarish head, big ears, long chin, and thick eyebrows, his eyes closed, lying in the ruby red coffin with the jade griffin clasped in his hands.'

'Now your younger brother is the only son. Your father will pass it along to him, and you won't get it.'

'Don't I know it. I wasn't even allowed to touch it. I used to get so upset, I would cry for hours. That was before the war when we still lived in Nanking. Mama took the jade griffin from my father's pocket. She said she should be the one to take care of the family heirloom and that father would only break it sooner or later by playing with it. She had it made into a brooch. I really liked to play with cute things like that when I was a kid, you know? I always wanted to wear the brooch. One day I saw it on Mother's dresser. I reached for it and she slapped me and by accident I knocked it to the floor. One of the wings was chipped and she shut me in the attic.

'It was pitchblack in the attic. I knelt on the floor crying. Then I heard a junk peddler's rattle outside. I stopped crying and got up. I crawled out the window and stood on the roof, looking to see where the rattle was coming from. The peddler passed by right outside our house. I took a broken pot from the windowsill and threw it at him, then went back to the attic. He cursed up and down the street. I knelt on the floor giggling hysterically. Then the door opened.

'Mother stood in the doorway, the dark narrow staircase looming behind her like a huge shadow. She stood motionless, her collar open, revealing a rough red imprint on her neck. She was wearing the jade griffin.

'In my head I recited a poem that my father had taught me. It was like a magic spell to me:

> Child, come back
> Child, come back
> Child, why don't you come back?
> Why do you come back as a bird?
> The bird's sad cries fill the mountains.

It's about a stepmother who is mean to her stepson. Her own son turns into a bird. I thought that Mother was my stepmother and that my little brother was her son. I thought if I said this poem, my little brother would turn into a bird. I decided that one day I would smash the griffin.'

'But now you want to give it back.'

'Mmm.'

'Little Berry, I think it's great you stole it. Your family loses twice: they lost their daughter and their jade. This time your mother might stop and think. Maybe she will change her ways.'
'Has the boat been repaired?'
'Not yet.'
'God. How long are we going to have to wait here?'

TAI-HSI has only one street, a stone-paved road that runs up the cliff. It's lined with tea houses, little restaurants, and shops for groceries, torches, lanterns, tow-lines. Lao-shih and I are eating noodles at one of the restaurants. The owner's wife clicks her tongue when she hears that our boat was crippled at New Landslide Rapids and will be heading for Feng-chieh once it's repaired.

'Just wait. New Landslide Rapids is nothing. Further on there's Yellow Dragon Rapids, Ghost Gate Pass, Hundred Cage Pass, Dragon Spine Rapids, Tiger Whisker Rapids, Black Rock Breakers and Whirlpool Heap. Some are shallow bars, some are flooded. A shallow bar is dangerous when the water is low, a flooded bar is dangerous when the water is high. If you make it past the shallow bar, you won't make it past the flooded one. If you get past the flooded one, you'll get stuck on the shallow one . . .'

Lao-shih drags me out of the restaurant.

'Little Berry, I know if you hear any more of that kind of talk, you won't want to go on to Chungking.'

'I really don't want to get back on that boat. I want to go home!'

Lao-shih sighs. 'Little Berry, if that's how you feel, why did you ever decide to come in the first place?'

'I didn't know it was going to be like this.'

'All right. Go on back. I'll go to Chungking all by myself.'

She turns away and takes off, climbing up the stone-paved path.

I have to follow. We get to the end of the path and stop. Before us is a suspension bridge. Beyond it are mountains piled on mountains, below, the valley. There's a stream in the valley and the waters are roaring. Even from this high on the cliff, we

can hear the sound of water breaking on the rocks. Six or seven
naked boys are playing in the stream below, hopping around on
the rocks, skipping stones in the water, swimming, fishing. One
of them sits on a rock, playing a folk song about the wanderer,
Su Wu, on his flute. There is a heavy fog. The mountains on
the other shore are wrapped in mist and all that is visible is a
black peak stabbing the sky.

'What do you say? Shall we cross the bridge?' Someone
comes up behind us.

It's the young man who boarded with us at Wu-shan. We
nicknamed him Refugee Student. He's just escaped from the
area occupied by the Japanese. When he gets to Chungking, he
wants to join the army and fight the Japanese. He is bare-
chested, showing off his sun-tanned muscular chest. This is the
first time we've ever spoken. But I dreamed about him. I
dreamed I had a baby and he was the father. When I woke up
my nipples itched. A baby sucking at my nipples would probably make them itch like that, itch so much that I'd want someone to bite them. I had another dream about him. It was by the
river. A torch was lit, lighting the way for a bridal sedan to be
carried up the narrow steps. The sedan stopped under my window. I ran out and lifted up the curtain and he was sitting
inside. I told that dream to Lao-shih. She burst out laughing
and then suddenly stopped. She said that if you dream of someone riding in a sedan chair, that person will die. A sedan chair
symbolises a coffin. I said, damn it, we shouldn't go on the ship
with him through the dangerous Chü-t'ang Gorge if he is going
to die!

'I WAS in the tea house drinking tea and I saw you two looking
at the bridge,' he says.

'So you've got your eye on us,' says Lao-shih, shoving her
hands in the pockets of her black pants and tossing her short
hair defiantly. 'Just what do you want, anyway?'

'Hey, I was just trying to be nice. I came over intending to
help you two young ladies across this rickety worn-out bridge.
Look at it, a few iron chains holding up some rotting planks. I

just crossed it myself a while ago. It's really dangerous. When you get to the middle, the planks creak and split apart. The waters roar below you and you're lost if you fall in.'

'That's if you're stupid enough to try it.'

'Miss Shih, may I ask what it is about me that offends you?' Refugee Student laughs.

'I'm sorry . . . and my name is Lao-shih.'

'OK, Lao-shih? Let's be friends.'

'How about me?' I say.

'Oh, you!' He smiles at me. 'But I still don't know your name. Lao-shih calls you Little Berry, kind of a weird name if you ask me . . .'

'I don't want you to call me that, either. She's the only person in the whole world who can call me that. Just call me Mulberry.'

'OK, Lao-shih and Mulberry. You've got to cross this bridge at least once. I just crossed it. It's a different experience for everyone. I wanted to see what it felt like to be dangling on a primitive bridge above dangerous water.'

'Well, what's it like?'

'You're suspended there, unable to touch the sky above you or the earth below you, pitch-black mountains all around you and crashing water underneath. You're completely cut off from the world, as if you've been dangling there since creation. And you ask yourself: Where am I? Who am I? You really want to know. And you'd be willing to die to find out.' He takes a stick and draws two mountain peaks in the dust and joins them with two long thin lines.

A burst of flames shoots up towards us from the valley.

'Bravo.' The boys in the valley clap their hands.

'Hey . . .' yells Refugee Student, 'if someone gets killed you'll pay.'

Lao-shih tugs at his arm telling him that the innkeeper told her never to provoke that bunch of kids. There are eleven of them altogether, thirteen or fourteen years old at the most. They live in the forest on the other side of the bridge. No one knows where they come from, only that they are all war or-phans and they live by begging along the Yangtze River. They travel awhile, then rest awhile before going on again. They want to go to Chungking to join the Resistance and save the country from the Japanese. They'll kill without batting an eye. They killed a man in Pa-tung. The ferry across the river wasn't running and there was no bridge, so the boys ferried people across. Someone on the boat offended them. They drugged him with some narcotic incense. They dragged him into the forest, cut open his stomach and hid opium inside it. Then they put him in a coffin and pretending they were a funeral procession, they smuggled opium to Wu-shan.

The boys are still laughing and cursing and yelling down the river. The one with the flute climbs up the mountain. His naked body is covered only with a piece of printed cloth frayed into strips. A whistle on a red string dangles on his chest. He leaps onto the bridge, but instead of walking across it, he grabs the iron chains and swings across from chain to chain with the flute clenched in his teeth. He swings to the middle of the bridge, one hand gripping the chain. With his other hand he takes the flute from between his teeth and trills a long signal to the kids in the valley below.

He shouts, 'Hey, you sons of bitches. How about a party tonight?'

'We'll be there in a minute. Let's catch some fish and have a feast.'

He grips the chain and swings on. The frayed cloth flutters as he moves.

The boys scramble up the mountain. One by one they leap onto the bridge and swing across to the other side. They're naked as well, except for the rags around their waists. It's almost dark. The fog is rolling in. They swing on and on, disappearing into the fog.

'Hey, you guys, swing across.' Their voices call to us through the fog.

'OK, here I come,' Refugee Student jumps onto the bridge and swings across.

'Come on!' says Lao-shih tossing her head and walking out onto the bridge. 'We can't let them think we're chicken.'

I go with her onto the bridge. The roar of the water gets louder. The bridge sways violently. I grip the railing and wait for it to stop swinging.

Dangling from the chain, Refugee Student turns and yells: 'Don't stop. Come on. There's no way to stop it. The faster it sways, the faster you have to walk. Try to walk in time to the swaying.' I grip the railing and move forward. I sway the bridge and the bridge sways me. I walk faster. The mountain, the water, the naked boys, Refugee Student, all fuse together in my vision. I want to stop but I can't and I start to run to the other side while the bridge sways and swings.

Finally our boat is repaired. Lao-shih and I climb aboard singing 'On the Sunghua River', a song about the lost home-land. Twelve oarsmen pull at the oars; the captain at the rudder. There are six passengers on board: an old man, a woman in a peach-flowered dress with her baby, Lao-shih, me, and that crazy refugee student.

We get through Tiger Whisker Rapids.

Rocks jut up from Whirlpool Heap. Black Rock Breakers is a sinking whirlpool. We get through it.

OUR old wooden boat is heading upstream in the gorge. To one side is White Salt Mountain. To the other, Red Promontory Peak. From both sides the mountains thrust upward towards the sky as if they were trying to meet, leaving only a narrow ribbon of blue sky above us. The noon sun dazzles an instant overhead, then disappears. The white light glistens on the cliffs. It's as if you could take a penknife and scrape off the salt. The river mist is white as salt. I stick out my tongue to lick it, but don't taste or touch anything. The water plunges down from heaven, the boat struggles up the water slope, climbing a hill of water. A mountain looms before us, blocking the way, but after a turn to the left and a turn to the right, the river suddenly widens.

The captain says that every June when the flood tides come you can't go upstream in this part of the river. Fortunately for us, the June tides haven't come yet. Clouds move south, water floods the ponds; clouds move north, good sun for wheat. Now the clouds are moving to the north. Rocks stick out from the river like bones.

WE reach the City of the White Emperor. From here it's only three miles to our destination, Feng-chieh.

The twelve oarsmen tug at the oars. Their gasps are almost chants, ai-ho, ai-ho. Black sweat streams down their bodies, soaking their skin, plastering their white trousers to their thighs. Their calves bulge like drumsticks.

The captain yells from the bow. 'Everyone, please be careful. Please stay inside the cabin. We're almost to Yellow Dragon Rapids. Don't stand up. Don't move around.'

Some men are struggling to tow our boat through the rapids, filing along the cliff and through the water near shore, the tow-line thrown over their shoulders padded with cloth, hands gripping the rope at their chest, their bodies bending lower and lower, grunting a singsong, hai-yo hai-yo as they pull. Their chant rises and falls with the ai-ho ai-ho of our crew. The whole mountain gorge echoes as if it were trying to help them pull the boat up the rapids. It's useless. Suddenly white foam sprays the rocks and a white wave crashes down on the boat. The tow-line pullers and the oarsmen stop singing. Everyone stares at the water. The men use all their strength to pull the tow-line, curving their bodies, bending their legs, heads looking up at the sky. Pulling and pulling, the men are pinned to the cliff, the boat is pinned to the rocks, twisting in the eddies. The rope lashed to the mast groans.

The captain starts beating a drum.

It's useless. The men are stooped over, legs bent, looking up at the sky. The boat whirls around on the rocks. One big wave passes by, another one rushes forward. The boat is stuck there, twisting and turning. The drum beats faster; it's as if the beating of the drum is turning the boat.

The tow-line snaps. The men on the cliff curse the water.

Our boat lurches along the crest of a wave, bobbing up and down, then lunges downstream like a wild horse set loose.

There's a crash. The boat stops.
The drum stops. The cursing stops.
We're stranded on the rocks.

FIRST DAY Aground.

Two rows of rocks rise out of the water, like a set of bared teeth, black and white. Our boat is aground in the gash between the two rows of teeth. Whirlpools surround the rocks. From the boat we toss a chopstick into the whirlpool and in a second the chopstick is swallowed up. Beyond the whirlpools, the river rushes by. One after another, boats glide by heading downstream, turn at the foot of the cliffs and disappear.

The tow-line pullers haul other boats up the rapids. They struggle through it. The tow-line pullers sit by a small shrine on the cliff and smoke their pipes.

'Fuck it! Why couldn't we get through the rocks? All the other boats made it.' Refugee Student stands at the bow waving at the men on the cliff. 'Hey . . .'

A wave billows between the boat and the cliff.

'Help.'

No response.

The oarsmen squatting in the bow stare at him.

'Hey. All you passengers in the hold, come out.' He yells to the cabin. 'We can't stay stranded here waiting to die! Come on out here and let's decide what to do.'

Peach-flower Woman comes out of the cabin holding her child. Lao-shih and I call her Peach-flower Woman because when she boarded the boat that day, she was wearing a flowered blouse, open at the collar, some buttons undone, as if she were about to take off her clothes at any moment.

The old man follows her out.

As Lao-shih and I scurry out of the cabin, Refugee Student claps his hands. 'Great. Everybody's here. We must shout together at the shore. The water is too loud.'

The old man coughs and spits out a thick wad of phlegm into the river. 'Please excuse me. I can only help by mouthing the words. I can't shout.'

'Something wrong with your lungs?' asks Refugee Student.

The old man's moustache twitches. 'Nonsense. I've been coughing and spitting like this for over twenty years. No one's ever dared suggest that I have TB.' He forces up another wad of phlegm and spits it into the river.

'If we're going to yell, let's yell,' I start shouting at the tow-line pullers on the bank. 'Hey!'

Lao-shih jumps up and yells along with me. 'Hey!'

There's no response. Lao-shih picks up a broken bowl from the deck and hurls it at the bank, shouting: 'You sons of bitches. Are you deaf?'

The bowl smashes on the rocks.

Peach-flower Woman sits on the deck, nursing her child. The baby sucks on one breast, patting the other with its hand in rhythm with its sucking, as if keeping time for itself, pressing the milk out. Drops of milk dribble onto the baby's plump arm. Peach-flower Woman lets her milk dribble out. With a laugh she says, 'Us country folk really know how to yell. That's what I'm best at. Hey—yo—'

The tow-line pullers on the bank turn around and stare at our boat.

'Go on singing. Sing. Don't stop now!' The old man waves to Peach-flower Woman. 'You sound like you're singing when you shout! If you don't sing, they'll ignore us.'

'Hey—yo—'

'Hey . . . Yo . . .' The mountains echo.

'Send—bamboo—raft—' shouts Refugee Student. Peach-flower Woman, the old man, Lao-shih and I all join in. 'Send—bamboo—raft—'

'Send . . . Bamboo . . . Raft.' The mountains mock our cry.

The tow-line pullers wave at us and shake their heads.

'Na—yi—na—ya—'

'Na . . . Yi . . . Na . . . Ya . . .'

We point to the bamboo on the mountains. 'Cut—bamboo—'

'Cut . . . Bamboo . . .'

They wave again and shake their heads.

'Na—yi—na—ya—'

'Na . . . Yi . . . Na . . . Ya . . .'

'Cut—bamboo—'

'Cut . . . Bamboo . . .'

They wave again and shake their heads.

'Na—yi—na—ya—'

'Na . . . Yi . . . Na . . . Ya . . .'

'Cut—bamboo—make—raft—'

'Cut . . . Bamboo . . . Make . . . Raft . . .'

The men on the cliff stop paying attention to us. The oarsmen squat on the deck, eating.

The captain finally speaks. 'What good will a raft do? There are rocks all around here. A raft can't cross.'

'How come our boat landed here?'

'We're lucky,' says the captain.

'If you're in a great disaster and you don't die, you're sure to have a good fortune later!' says the old man. 'Let's sing to the bank again!'

'Ho—hey—yo—'

'Ho . . . Hey . . . Yo . . .'

'Tell—the—authorities—'

'Tell . . . The . . . Authorities . . .'

Two of the tow-line pullers start climbing the mountain path.

'Good,' says the old man, 'those two will go tell somebody. Go on singing.'

'You sure know how to give orders! But you don't make a sound,' says Refugee Student.

'Forget it,' Lao-shih says, 'here we are fighting for our lives. Let's not fight among ourselves.'

'Hey—you—there—hey—'

'Hey . . . You . . . There . . . Hey . . .'

'Send —life—boots—'

'Send . . . Life . . . Boats . . .'

The two men on the path stop and turn to look at us.

'Good,' says the old man, 'they'll do it.'

'Na—na—hey—yo—'

'Na . . . Na . . . Hey . . . Yo . . .'

'Send—life—boats—'

'Send . . . Life . . . Boats . . .'

The two men on the path turn again and proceed up the mountain. Two others stand up.

'I've been steering boats in these gorges my whole life. I've only seen capsized boats, never life-boats.' The captain puffs away on his pipe.

A boat approaches us, riding the crest of a wave.

'Na—na—hey—yo—'

'Na . . . Na . . . Hey . . . Yo . . .'

'Help!—help!—'

'Help! . . . Help! . . .'

The boat ploughs over another large wave, wavers on the crest and glides down.

'There's an air raid alert at Feng-chieh,' someone shouts to us from the boat as it passes, turns a curve, and disappears.

A paddlewheel steamboat comes downstream.

'Hey, I have an idea!' says Refugee Student as he runs into the cabin.

He comes back out carrying the peach-flower blouse. He stands in the doorway of the cabin, the collar of the blouse tucked under his arm; he stretches out a sleeve and playfully tickles the arm hole as the blouse billows in the breeze.

'You imp,' laughs Peach-flower Woman. 'You're tickling me. You make me itch all over.'

Refugee Student waves the blouse in the air. 'I'm going to use this blouse as a flag. Come on, everyone, sing! The steamboat will see it in the distance and hear our song. Come on. Sing: "Rise up, you who will not be slaves." '

'No, no, not that Communist song. I don't know these new songs,' says the old man.

'Well, let's sing an old one, then. "Flower Drum Song",' I say.

'OK!' Lao-shih races over to pick up the drumsticks and pounds several times on the big drum.

We sing in unison.

'A gong in my left hand, a drum in my right
Sing to the drumbeat, chant to the gong.
I don't know other songs to sing
Only the flower drum song.
Sing now! Sing. Yi—hu—ya—ya—hey—'

Refugee Student waves the blouse. The old man taps chopsticks on a metal basin. I beat two chopsticks together. Laoshih beats the drum. Peach-flower Woman holds her child as she sings and sways back and forth.

The steamboat glides by.

We stop singing and begin shouting. 'We're stranded. Help! Save us! We're stranded! Help!'

The people on the boat lean against the railing and stare at us. Two or three people wave. The boat disappears.

The water gurgles on the rocks.

'It doesn't do any good to sing!' The captain is still puffing on his pipe. 'Even a paddlewheel wouldn't dare cross here. There's only one thing left to do. The oarsmen will divide into two shifts, and day and night take turns watching the level of the water. We have to be ready to push off at any moment. As soon as the water rises over the rocks and the boat floats up, the man at the rudder will hold it steady and the boat will float down with the current. If the water rises and there's no one at the rudder, the boat may be thrown against those big rocks and that'll be the end of us.'

Lumber planks, baskets, basins, and trunks drift down towards us with the current.

'There must be another ship capsized upstream on the rocks.' The captain looks at the black rock teeth jutting out of the water. 'If it rains, we'll make it. When it rains, the water will rise and when the water rises, we'll be saved.'

Someone has lit a bonfire onshore.

The sky is getting dark.

THE SECOND DAY Aground.

The sun glistens on the rock teeth. The water churns, boiling around the rocks.

'It's so dry, even the bamboo awning creaks,' an oarsman says.

OUR cabin is beneath the awning. It has a low, curved roof and two rows of hard wooden bunks, really planks, on each side.

The oarsmen occupy the half at the bow. That half is always empty; they are on deck day and night. The passengers occupy the half in the stern. Our days and nights are spent on these wooden planks. The old man and Refugee Student are on one side. Lao-shih, Peach-flower Woman and I are on the other side. 'The Boys' Dormitory' and 'The Girls' Dormitory' are separated by a narrow aisle. The old man has been complaining that we are brushing up against each other in the cabin and goes around complaining that 'men and women shouldn't mix.' So he has ordered that men can't go bare-chested and women can't wear clothing open at the neck or low in the back. His own coarse cotton jacket is always snugly buttoned. Refugee Student doesn't pay any attention to him and goes around naked from the waist up. Peach-flower Woman doesn't pay any attention either. She always has her lapels flung open, revealing the top of her smooth chest. The old man puffs hard on his water pipe, although there's no tobacco in it, and makes it gurgle. 'Young people nowadays!'

The old man sits in the cabin doorway all day long, holding his water pipe, looking up towards the small shrine on the shore and occasionally puffing a few empty mouthfuls on his pipe. Refugee Student paces up and down the aisle which is only large enough for one person to pass.

Lao-shih, Peach-flower Woman and I sit in the 'Girls' Dormitory' and stare at the water around us.

'Hey, you've been going back and forth a long time. Have you got to a hundred yet?' asks Lao-shih.

'Ninety-seven, ninety-eight, ninety-nine, one hundred. OK, Lao-shih, it's your turn.'

Lao-shih paces back and forth in the aisle.

Silence.

'. . . Ninety-five, ninety-six, ninety-seven, ninety-eight, ninety-nine, one hundred. OK, I'm done. Little Berry, your turn.'

I walk up and down the aisle.

Silence.

'Ninety-three, ninety-four, ninety-five, ninety-six, ninety-seven, ninety-eight, ninety-nine, one hundred. OK, Peach-flower Lady, your turn.'

She paces up and down with the baby in her arms.

Silence.

The old man begins murmuring, 'Rise, rise, rise, rise.'

'Is the water rising? Really?' Lao-shih and I leap down from the bunks and run to the doorway, jostling each other as we look.

'Who said it's rising?' The old man taps the bowl of his pipe.

'Didn't you just say it's rising?'

'What are you all excited about? Would I be here if the water was rising? I said rise, rise because it's not rising. This morning that little shrine was right next to the water, about to be flooded. But look, it's still safe and dry by the edge of the water. July is the month that waters rise in the Chü-t'ang Gorge. It's now mid-July and the waters haven't risen. So here we are stuck in this Hundred Cage Pass.'

'Hey, I've already counted to a hundred and five,' laughs Peach-flower Woman.

'You're done then. It's my turn again.' Refugee Student jumps down from his plank and starts pacing in the aisle again. 'Hundred Cage Pass! The name itself is enough to depress you! Hey, Captain,' he yells, 'how far is this Hundred Cage Pass from the City of the White Emperor?'

'What is Hundred Cage Pass?'

'What's this place called, then?'

'This place is near Yellow Dragon Rapids. It doesn't have a name. Call it whatever you like!'

'Call it Teeth Pass, then,' he mutters to himself. He calls out again. 'Captain, how far is this place from the City of the White Emperor?'

'Only a couple of miles. Beyond that are Iron Lock Pass, Dragon Spine Rapids, and Fish Belly Beach.'

'Captain, can we see the City of the White Emperor from here?' the old man asks.

'No, Red Promontory Peak is in the way.'

'If only we could see the City of the White Emperor, it would be all right.'

Refugee Student laughs. 'Old man, what good would it do to see it? We'd still be stranded here between these two rows of teeth.'

'If we could see it, we could see signs of human life.'

'We've seen people since we ran aground. The tow-line pullers, the people on the boats, the people on the paddlewheel, but none of them could save us.'

'I've been sitting here all day. I haven't even seen the shadow of a ghost on the bank.'

Lao-shih shouts from the door. 'There's another boat coming.'

The five of us rush to the bow.

The people on that boat wave at us and shout something, but the sound of the water breaking on the rocks is too loud and we can't understand what they're saying.

'A lot of . . .?'

'On the way?'

'It must be that a lot of rescue boats are on the way.'

'Yeah, a lot of rescue boats are coming!'

The boat glides away.

'A lot of rescue boats are coming?' says the captain. 'A lot of Japanese bombers are coming.'

We scurry back into the cabin.

In the distance we hear faint thunder.

'That's not aircraft, that's thunder.'

'Right, it's thunder. It's going to rain.'

'When it rains the water will rise.'

The thunder approaches. Then we hear the anti-aircraft guns and machine guns. Bullets pock the water spitting spray in all directions. The Japanese bombers are overhead. Lao-shih hides under her quilt on the bunk and calls out to me. 'Little Berry, Little Berry, hurry up and get under the covers.'

Suddenly Refugee Student shoves me to the floor and sprawls on top of me.

A minute ago, we were standing in the aisle. Now our bodies are pressing against each other. He is bare-chested and I can smell the odour of his armpits. Lao-shih's armpits smell the same way, that smell of flesh mixed with sweat, but smelling it on his body makes my heart pound. I can even feel the hair under his arms. No wonder Mother likes hairy men; I heard her say that once when I was walking by her door. The thick black hair (it must be black) under his arms tickles me. I'm not even scared of the Japanese bombers anymore.

The bombers pass into the distance.

We get up off the floor. Lao-shih sits on the bunk and glares at us.

'The boat that just passed us has capsized at the bend in the river,' shouts the captain from the bow.

'What about the people?' asks Refugee Student.

'They're all dead! Some drowned, some were killed by the Japanese machine gun fire.'

'I wish everybody in the world were dead,' says Lao-shih, still glaring at Refugee Student.

I go back to the 'Girls' Dormitory'. Lao-shih strains to scratch her back.

'I'll scratch it for you!' I stick my hand up under her blouse and scratch her back.

'That's good, just a little bit higher, near the armpit.' I scratch the part between her armpit and her back. She giggles. 'It tickles! Not so hard. It tickles.' She has only a wisp of hair under her arm.

Refugee Student is pacing up and down in the aisle. He raises his head. 'Bombers overhead, the Gorge below. So many boats capsized. So many people dead. Nobody cares if the boats capsize, or if people die. They are playing a game with human lives!'

'May I ask a question?' says the old man. 'Who's playing a game with human lives?'

Refugee Student, taken aback, says, 'Who? The government. Who else?'

'These gorges have been dangerous for thousands of years. What can the government do about it?'

'We're in the twentieth century now! Sir, have you heard of the invention of the helicopter? Just one helicopter could rescue the whole lot of us. A place like the Gorges should have a Gorges Rescue Station. As soon as we get to Chungking, we should all sign a petition of protest and put it in the newspapers. We have a right to protest. We're victims of the Gorges!'

The Peach-flower Woman laughs on her bunk. 'Sign our names to a petition? I can't even write my own name.'

'I'll write it for you!' Lao-shih eyes me. I take my hand out of her blouse.

The old man sits on his bunk, rocking back and forth. 'It's a great virtue for a woman to be without talent. A woman is . . .' he is seized with a coughing fit and gasps for breath.

Lao-shih mutters. 'Serves him right.'

Refugee Student looks at the old man and shakes his head. He turns to Peach-flower Woman. 'I'll write your name down on a piece of paper. If you copy it every day, by the time we get to Chungking, you'll have learned how to write it.'

'Forget it! Forget it! Too much trouble.' Peach-flower Woman waves her hand. 'I'll just make a fingerprint and when we get to Chungking, my man can write my name for me!'

'When we get to Chungking, I'm going to turn somersaults in the mud!' says Lao-shih.

'When we get there, I'm going to walk around the city for three days and three nights,' I say.

'When we get to Chungking, I'm going to go running in the mountains for three days and three nights!' says Refugee Student.

'When we get to Chungking, I'm going to play mahjong for three days and three nights!' says the old man.

'Hey, look at that big fish!' Peach-flower Woman points at a big fish which has just leapt out of the river onto the deck.

'A good omen! A white fish leaps into the boat!' The old man shouts, 'We'll get out of here OK.'

The five of us turn to look at the shrine on the bank.

The water still hasn't risen; the shrine is still dry.

'There's a shrine but nobody offers incense. It would be better if we tore it down,' says Refugee Student.

'You ought to be struck down by lightning for saying such a thing!' The old man's moustache twitches. 'And the fish, where's the fish?'

'The oarsmen just put it in a bucket. We can kill it tomorrow and have fresh fish to eat.'

'It must not be eaten. It must not be eaten. That fish must not be eaten.' The old man walks to the bow of the boat, scoops up the fish with hands, kneels at the side of the boat and spreads his hands open like a mussel shell.

The fish slides into the river with a splash, flicks its tail and disappears.

The old man is still kneeling by the side, his two hands spread open like a mussel shell; palms uplifted as if in prayer.

'Dinner time!' yells the captain. 'I'm sorry, but from now on, we're going to have to ration the rice. Each person gets one bowl of rice per meal!'

The two rows of teeth in the river open wider. Even the rocks are hungry!

'One bowl of rice will hardly fill the gaps between my teeth,' says Refugee Student, throwing down his chopsticks. 'I escaped from the Japanese-occupied area, didn't get killed by the Japanese, didn't get hit by bullets or shrapnel, and now I have to starve to death, stranded on this pile of rocks? This is the biggest farce in the world.'

'You can say that again,' I say to myself.

Lao-shih sits down beside me on the bunk. 'Little Berry, I should have let you go back home.'

'Even if I could go back now, I wouldn't do it. I want to go on to Chungking.'

'Why?'

'After going through all this, what is there to be afraid of? Now, I know what I did wrong. This disaster is my own doing. I've been thinking of all the bad things I did to people.'

'I have, too,' says Lao-shih. 'Once my father beat me. When he turned to leave, I clenched my teeth and said, I can't wait until you die.'

'I cursed my father, mother, and brother that way, too. I can't wait until you die,' I say.

'This is the biggest farce in the world,' says Refugee Student as he paces up and down the aisle. 'The first thing I'm going to do when we get to Chungking is call a press conference and expose the serious problems of the Gorges. All of you, please leave your addresses so I can contact you.'

'Leave it for whom?' asks the Peach-flower Woman. She is sitting on the bunk, one breast uncovered. The baby plays with her breast for a while, then grabs it to suck awhile.

We stare at each other. For the first time I ask myself: Will I make it alive to Chungking? If I live, I swear, I'll change my ways.

'Maybe we're all going to die,' says Lao-shih softly.

'Hah,' coughs the old man, turning his head aside, as if one cough could erase what Lao-shih has said. 'Children talk nonsense. All right. Let's do exchange addresses. When we get to Chungking, I invite you all to a banquet and we'll have the best shark fin money can buy.'

'If you want my address, then you've really got me there!' laughs Peach-flower Woman. 'When we get to Chungking, I won't have an address until I've found my man!'

'Don't you have his address?'

'No.'

'Didn't he write you?'

'He wrote his mother.'

'Are you married to him?'

'Yes, I'm his wife. When I went to his house, I was really young. He's seven years younger than I am. I raised him. He went to Chungking to study. I stayed at home taking care of his mother, raising his son, working in the fields, weaving, picking tea leaves, gathering firewood. I can take anything, even his mother's cursing, as long as he's around. But someone came back from Chungking and said he had another woman. I can't stand that. I told his mother I wanted to go to Chungking. She wouldn't allow me to go. She wouldn't even let me go out on the street. So I just picked up my baby, got together a few clothes, and took off. All I know is that he is studying at Chang-shou, Szechuan. When I get there I'm going to look for him. When I find him and if he's faithful, we're man and wife forever. But if he isn't, then he'll go his way, and I'll go mine.'

'Is the boy his?' asks the old man.

'Well, if he isn't my husband's, he certainly isn't yours, either.' She laughs, and lifts the baby up to the old man. 'Baby, say grandpa, say grandpa.'

'Grandpa!' The old man pulls at his greying beard with two fingers. 'I'm not that old yet!' He coughs and turns to Refugee Student. 'If it's an address you want, that's hard for me to produce as well. In June 1937, I left Peking, my home, and went to visit friends in Shanghai. July 7, 1937, the war broke out, and by the 28th, Peking had fallen. So these past few years, I've been fleeing east and west with my friends. When will this war end? I couldn't stay with my friends forever, so I left them.

I intend to do a little business between Chungking and Pa-
tung. I don't know where I'll live when I get to Chungking.'
    'My address is the air raid shelter in Chungking,' says Lao-
shih coldly.
    'You're kidding!' says Refugee Student.
    'She's not kidding,' I interrupt. 'Her mother died when she
was young. She escaped with her father from the Japanese-
occupied area. She went to En-shih to study at the National
High School; he went to Chungking on business. In 1941, the
Japanese bombed Chungking and more than ten thousand people suffocated in the air raid shelter. Her father was one of
them.'
    'That's right. The famous air raid shelter suffocation trag-
edy!' The old man talks as if Lao-shih's father became famous
because of that.
    Refugee Student looks at me.
    'I don't have an address either! My home is in En-shih. I ran
away.'
    'No place like home.' The old man takes a gold pocket watch
out of the pocket of his jacket and looks at the time. He re-
places it in his pocket, and suddenly I remember the jade griffin
on my father's watch chain and think of great-grandfather,
clutching the jade in his hands as he lay in the coffin. The old
man stares at me. 'I have a daughter about your age. After I left
Peking my wife died. Right now I don't even know if my own
daughter is dead or alive. Everyone has roots. The past is part of
your roots, and your family, and your parents. But in this war,
all our roots have been yanked out of the ground. You are lucky
you still have a home, and roots. You must go back! I'm going
to inform your father, tell him to come get you and take you
home.'
    'You don't know my family's address!' I sit on the bunk, one
hand propping up my chin and smile at him.
    The old man begins to cough again, and points his finger at
me. 'You young people nowadays. You young people.'
    'You sound like my father,' laughs Refugee Student. 'My
father had seven wives. My mother was his legal wife. Father
treated his seven wives equally: all under martial law. He calls
them Number Two, Number Three, Number Four, . . . accord-

ing to whoever entered the household first. Number Two was once one of our maids. She is five years younger than Number Seven. They got thirty dollars spending money per month and, every spring, summer, fall and winter, some new clothes. Once a month they all went to a hotel to have a bath and play mahjong. The seven women plus himself made exactly two tables. He took turns spending the night in their seven bedrooms, each woman one night, which made exactly one week. They had more than forty children; he himself can't keep straight which child belongs to which woman. The seven women called each other Sister, in such a friendly way, never squabbling among themselves, because they were all united against that man. Their seven bedrooms were all next to one another, dark and gloomy, shaded by tall trees on all sides. When the Japanese bombed Nanking, a bomb fell right in the middle of the house, and blasted out a crater as big as a courtyard. When the bomb hit, it was the first time those rooms were exposed to sunlight. My mother was killed in that bombing. The six women cried. My father didn't even shed a single tear. When the Japanese occupied the area my father collaborated. I called him a traitor and he cursed me as an ungrateful son. Actually, I don't have an address myself.'

We hear muffled thunder in the distance. It might rain. We look at each other, our faces brighten.

THIRD DAY Aground.

'There's thunder but no rain. The Dragon King has locked the Dragon Gate,' says the captain. 'From now on each person gets only one glass of fresh water a day. We only have two small pieces of alum left to purify the water.'

FOURTH DAY Aground.

Rain. Rain. Rain. We talk about rain, dream about rain, pray for rain. When it rains, the water will rise and the boat will float out from the gash between the teeth.

'I'm so thirsty.'

When people say they're thirsty it makes me even thirstier.

Here at the bottom of the gorge, the sun blazes overhead for a few minutes, yet we're still so thirsty. No wonder the legendary hunter tried to end the drought by shooting down nine of the ten suns.

The old man proposes to divine by the ancient method of sandwriting.

Refugee Student says he doesn't believe in that kind of nonsense.

Peach-flower Woman says divining is a lot of fun: a T-shaped frame is placed in a box of sand. Two people hold the ends of the frame. If you think about the spirit of some dead person, that spirit will come. The frame will write words all by itself in the sand, tell people's fortunes, write prescriptions, resolve grudges, reward favours, even write poems. When the spirit leaves, the frame stops moving.

Lao-shih and I are very excited about the sandwriting and fight over who gets to hold the frame and write for the ghost. The old man says he must be the one to hold the frame because only sincere people can summon spirits.

Instead of sand, we use ashes from the cooking fire and put them in a basin. Then we tie the two fire sticks together and make a T shape. The old man and I hold the ends of the stick. He closes his eyes and works his mouth up and down. The stick moves faster and faster. My hands move with the stick. These are the words written in the ashes:

DEEDS RENOWNED IN THREE-KINGDOMS FAME
ACHIEVED FOR EIGHTFOLD ARRAY

'That's his poem!' The old man slaps his thigh and shouts. 'It's the poet Tu Fu. I was silently reciting Tu Fu and he came. Tu Fu spent three years in this area and wrote three hundred and sixty-one poems here. Every plant and tree in this region became part of his poetry. I knew Tu Fu would come if I called him.' Then he addressed the ashes: 'Mr Tu, you were devoted to your emperor and cared about the fate of the country. You were talented, but had no opportunity to serve your country. You rushed here and there in your travels. Our fate is not unlike your own. Today all of us here on the boat wish to consult you.

Is it auspicious or inauspicious that we are stranded on these rocks?'

MORE INAUSPICIOUS THAN AUSPICIOUS

'Will we get out?'

CANNOT TELL

'Are we going to die?'

CANNOT TELL

'Whether we live or die, how much longer are we going to be stranded here?'

TENTH MONTH TENTH DAY

'Horrible, we'll be stranded here until the Double Tenth Festival. When will it rain?'

NO RAIN

The stick stops moving in the basin.
'Tu Fu has gone. Tu Fu was a poet. What does he know? This time let's summon a military man. We're stranded here in this historically famous strategic pass. We should only believe the words of a military man.' The old man shuts his eyes again and works his mouth up and down. We hold the stick and draw in the ashes.

DEVOTED SLAVE TO THE COUNTRY ONLY DEATH
STOPS MY DEVOTION

'Good. Chu-ko Liang has come. I knew his heroic spirit would be here in the Chü-t'ang region. Not too far from here, Chu-ko Liang demonstrated his military strategy, the Design of the Eightfold Array.' The old man concentrates on the ashes. 'Mr. Chu-ko, you were a hero. Your one desire was to recover the central part of China for the ruler of the Han people. Today China is also a country of three kingdoms: The National government in Chungking, the Communist government in Yenan, and the Japanese puppet government in Nanking. All of us here on the boat are going to Chungking; we are going there because we are concerned about the country. Now, instead, here we all are stranded in this rapids in a place not far from the Eightfold Array. Is it inauspicious or auspicious?'

VERY AUSPICIOUS

'Good, we won't die stranded here?'

NO

'Good! Can we reach Chungking?'

YES

'How long are we going to be stranded here?'

ONE DAY

'How will we get out of this place alive?'

HEAVEN HELPS THE LUCKY PERSON

'When will it rain?'

ONE DAY

'Mr. Chu-ko, when we get to Chungking, we will all go on foot to your temple and offer incense to you.'

The sticks stop moving.

The old man stares at the ashes. After a long time, he returns from his reverie. 'We're stranded in the midst of history! The City of the White Emperor, the Labyrinth of Stone called the Eightfold Array, Thundering Drum Terrace, Meng-liang

Ladder, Iron Lock Pass. All around us are landmarks left by the great heroes and geniuses of China. Do you know what Iron Lock Pass was? Iron Lock Pass had seven chains more than two thousand feet long crossing the river. Emperors and bandits in the past used those iron chains to close off the river and lock in the Szechuan Province. The Yangtze River has been flowing for thousands of years, and these things are still here. This country of ours is too old, too old.'

'Sir, this is not the time to become intoxicated by our thousands of years of history!' says Refugee Student. 'We want to get out of here alive.'

'I'm sure it will rain tomorrow. When it rains, the waters will rise.'

'Do you really believe in sandwriting?' I ask. 'Was it you writing with the sticks or was it really Tu Fu and Chu-ko?'

'You young people these days!' He strokes his beard. 'Here I am, an old man, would I try to deceive you?' He pauses. 'I really believe that heaven cares about us and answers prayers. Let me tell you a story from the *Chronicle of Devoted Sons*. There was a man called Yü Tzu-yü who was accompanying his father's coffin through the Chü-t'ang Gorge. In June the waters rose and the boat which was supposed to carry the coffin couldn't sail. Yü Tzu-yü burned incense and prayed to the Dragon King to make the waters recede. And the waters receded. After Yü Tzu-yü escorted the coffin through Chü-t'ang Gorge, the waters rose again.'

'Who's the devoted son aboard this boat?' asks Peach-flower Woman with a laugh.

No one answers.

'HOW long have we been stranded here?'

'Has it been five days?'

'No, seven.'

'Six days.'

'Well, anyway, it's been a long, long time.'

'The moon has risen.'

'Ummm.'

'What time is it?'

'If the moon is overhead, it must be midnight. Do you have a watch?'

'Yes. It's stopped. I forgot to wind it. Who else has a watch?'

'I do, but I can't see what time it is. It's too dark.'

'It's so quiet. Only the sound of water on the rocks.'

'Is everyone asleep?'

'No.'

'No.'

'Then why don't you say something?'

'I'm so hungry and thirsty.'

'There went a big wave.'

'How can you tell? You can't see them from here.'

'I can hear them. It's very quiet, then suddenly there's a loud splash and then everything's quiet again.'

'Can you hear anything else?'

'No.'

'Are they still fighting?'

'Who?'

'Those people on the bank.'

'Oh, they won't come down here to fight. Mountains on both sides, water below, sky above.'

'Hey, everyone, say something. OK? If nobody speaks, it's like you're all dead.'

'What shall we say?'

'Anything.'

'When it's quiet like this and nobody is speaking, it's really scary. But when you talk it's also scary, like a ghost talking.'

'Well, I'll play my flute, then.'

'Good idea. I'll tell a story while you play the flute.'

'I'm going to play "The Woman and the Great Wall".'

'It was a moonlit night. Quiet like this. He woke up smelling gunpowder . . .'

'Who is "he".'

'The "he" in the story. He woke up smelling gunpowder. There were ashes everywhere. Even the moon was the colour of ash. When he woke up, he was lying under a large tree on a mountainside. The slope faced the Chialing River. Thick black columns of smoke arose from Chungking on the opposite bank.

Reflected in the waters of the river, the black pillars of smoke looked like they were propping up the sky. Between the columns of smoke everything was grey as lead, as if all the ashes in Chungking had been stirred up.

'He stood up, shaking ashes and dust off his clothes. He had just woken up. He had been hiding in the air raid shelter dug into the mountain for seven days and nights. The Japanese bombers had come squadron after squadron, bombing Chungking for more than one hundred fifty hours. More than two hundred people had hid in the shelter. Eating, drinking, defecating, urinating, all inside the shelter. He couldn't stand it anymore and had gone outside. Another squadron of bombers appeared, and he didn't have time to run back to the shelter. He heard an ear-splitting crash and sand scattered in all directions. When he awoke, he saw someone digging at the entrance of the shelter. A bomb had destroyed the shelter. He took to his heels, afraid he might be dragged back by the dead inside the shelter. He ran and ran. He didn't know where he was running to. Only by running could he be safe. Suddenly he heard a voice calling out, "Let me go, let me go!" '

'Hey, keep on playing the flute, don't stop.'

'You want me to keep on playing the same song over and over?'

'Yeah. Go on with the story.'

'All right. The voice kept repeating. "Let me go. Let me go." He stopped, looked all around. There was no one in sight, only some graves. There weren't even any tombstones. He walked to the right. The voice came from the left. He walked to the left. Then the voice came from the right. He walked straight ahead. The voice was behind him. He turned and walked back. The voice was silent. He couldn't keep walking in the opposite direction. That direction would take him back to the shelter that was full of dead bodies. He had to keep going forwards. He heard the voice again. "Let me go, let me go." The voice seemed to come from under his feet. He stopped. It was coming from the right. He walked to the right and the voice got louder. He saw an empty grave. The coffin had probably been removed recently. A woman was lying in the grave, her head sticking out of the grave, her eyes closed, repeatedly

mumbling, "Let me go." He dragged her out of the pit. Then
he recognised that she had been among the people hiding in
the shelter. He couldn't tell if she was the ghost of someone
killed in an explosion, or a living person who had escaped the
bombing. He had a canteen with him. He poured some water
down her throat. She regained consciousness. He asked her
how she got out of the shelter and into the grave. She stared at
him, as if she hadn't heard. She said, "Tzu-jao, can't you run
faster than that?" He told her his name was Po-fu. The woman
said, "Don't try to fool me. Has the soldier gone?" He said,
"The bombers have gone." She became impatient and repeated over and over, "I mean the Japanese soldier who tried to
rape me. Has he gone?" The man said, "There are no Japanese
soldiers in Chungking." '

'The flute sounds especially nice tonight. That poor lonely
woman looking for her husband and crying at the Great Wall.
What about the woman?'

'Which woman? The woman at the Great Wall or the
woman in the grave?'

'The one in the grave. Hurry up and tell us the rest of the
story. It's like a modern-day Gothic.'

'OK. The woman sat down, beating the ground with her fist
over and over. "This isn't Chungking. This is Nanking. We've
just gotten married. The Japanese have just invaded the city."
The man groped for his watch in his pocket, struck a match,
and showed her the name Po-fu engraved on the watch. The
woman said, "Don't try to fool me, Tzu-jao! This is a matter of
life and death. Run quick. The Japanese are combing Nanking
for Chinese soldiers. They think that anyone with calluses on
his hands is a soldier: rickshaw pullers, carpenters, coolies. Yesterday in one day they took away one thousand three hundred
people. The dogs in Nanking are getting fat, there are so many
corpses to feed on." The woman looked around and asked,
"Has the soldier gone?" He could only reply, "Yes, he's gone."
The woman pointed to the river. "It was on that road through
the bamboo thicket. I was walking in front. He was walking
behind me. You know, Tzu-jao, we have been married more
than a week and you still haven't been able to touch me. You
called me a stone girl." '

'What do you mean, "stone girl"?'

'Stone girl. It means a girl who can't have sex.'

'Go on, you're just getting to the best part.'

'The woman kept on talking like that. She said, "It happened on that road through the bamboo thicket. I was walking in front. He was walking behind me. In full daylight, he stripped off his clothes as he followed me, throwing his uniform, boots, pants, underwear down at the side of the road. He stripped naked, leaving only his bayonet hanging by his side. When he was wearing his uniform, he seemed so much taller. Naked he looked shorter, even shorter than I am. He ripped off my clothes. He tossed me about like a doll. He threw down his bayonet. Just then, Tzu-jao, you came running up. Don't you remember? You ran out of Nanking, but you came back into the city. That Japanese was a head shorter than you. When he saw you, he jumped on your back, two hands gripping your neck. He was biting the back of your neck with his teeth. You reached back and grabbed his penis. You couldn't hold onto it. It was too small. As last you got it. You pulled it back and forth with all your strength. He screamed. Some people from the International Relief Committee came running up. The head of the committee was a German. He ordered the Japanese soldier to leave. But the soldier kept biting your neck. You wouldn't let go of his penis. Finally the German put out his arm and the Japanese saw his Nazi insignia. He slipped off your back and ran. He didn't even pick up his clothes or his bayonet." '

'What a good story. Then what happened to her?'

'When? After the rape incident in Nanking? Or after the bombing in Chungking?'

'After the bombing.'

'Her husband and son were looking for her. Just before the bombers hit, her two-year-old son started crying in the shelter. The people in the shelter cursed him and wanted to beat him to death. The father had to take the child outside. The mother was too anxious to stay in the shelter. She went outside to look for her husband and son. Then the bombers hit and bombed the shelter. After the bombing was over, she didn't know how she got into the grave. She didn't remember anything. She thought she was in Nanking and was reliving the past. Her husband had gone with their child to the police station to look at the list of the dead. I took her to the police station. She was still suffering from shell-shock and didn't recognise her husband and child. She said she had just gotten married and didn't have any children. She still believed she was in Nanking and was reliving the slaughter. When I saw that she was reunited with her husband and child, I left.'

'You? Are you telling us a story, or is that something that really happened to you?'

'It really happened to me. We've been stranded here so long that it seems like a story from a former life,' says the old man.

Refugee Student is still playing 'The Great Wall' on his flute.

> With the New Year comes the spring
> Every house lights red lanterns
> Other husbands go home to their families
> My husband builds the Great Wall

A big wave passes with a crash. Then it's quiet. Another crash, then it's quiet. Human heads are bobbing in the water, their eyes wide open and staring at the sky. Everything is silent.

A large eagle flies overhead. It circles the heads and flaps its huge black wings. It is beautiful. It is dancing.

Suddenly the old man and Lao-shih are sitting on the eagle's wings, each sitting on one side, like on a seesaw. The eagle wheels in the air. They wave at me.

Refugee Student suddenly appears, riding on the eagle's back. He begins to play his flute to the rhythm of the eagle's dance.

The eagle carries them off down the river.

The human heads float downstream.

I call to the eagle, begging them to stop. I want to fly away on the eagle, too.

Peach-flower Woman, her breasts exposed, appears, riding the crest of a wave. She waves at me. She wants me to join her on the waves.

The sound of the flute gets louder.

I wake up. The flute is coming from the stern. Lao-shih, the old man, and Peach-flower Woman are all asleep. Peach-flower Woman hugs her child to her bare breasts.

I sit up.

The sound of the flute suddenly stops.

I go out of the cabin and walk around the bales of cotton which are piled in the stern.

Refugee Student, bare-chested, is lying on the deck.

The gorge is black. He reaches up to me. I lie down on top of him. We don't say anything.

My virgin blood trickles down his legs. He wipes it off with spit.

THE SIXTH DAY Aground.

There is shouting on the river.

We run out. A ship tilts down over the crest of a wave. It spins around in the whirlpool. The people on the ship scream, women and children cry as it spins faster and faster, like a top.

White foam bubbles around the lip of the whirlpool. The foam churns up into a wall of water, separating us from the spinning ship. Then the wall collapses with a roar. The ship splits open like a watermelon. Everyone on board is tossed into the water.

Another huge wave rolls by. Everyone in the water has disappeared.

Silence.

The river rushes on. The sun dazzles overhead.

The beating of the drum begins.

Refugee Student, his shirt off, thick black hair bristling in his armpits and above his lip, is pounding on the drum, every muscle straining, teeth clenched. He raises the drumsticks over his head and pounds on the drum with all his strength. He isn't beating the drum. He is beating the mountains, the heavens, the waters.

The mountains, the heavens, the waters explode with each beat.

'Don't stop, don't stop. A victory song,' shouts the old man.

A crow flies toward our boat.

Refugee Student throws down the drumsticks and glares at the crow.

'Black crow overhead, that means if disaster doesn't strike misfortune will,' Peach-flower Woman says as she holds her child.

I pick up an empty bottle and throw it at the crow. 'I'll kill you, you stupid bird.' The bottle shatters on a rock.

Lao-shih picks up a bowl and hurls it at the crow. 'You bastard. Get out of here!' The bowl shatters on a rock.

The crow circles overhead.

The old man shakes his fist at the crow. His face turns purple. 'You think you can scare us, don't you? You think I'll just die stranded here, do you? When the warlords were fighting, I didn't die. When the Japanese were fighting, I didn't die. Do you think I'm going to die now, on this pile of rocks? Hah!' He spits at the crow.

'Goddam motherfucker,' shouts Refugee Student, leaping at the crow. 'You can't scare me. Just wait and see. I won't die. I'll survive and I'll raise hell, that'll show you. Mountains, waters, animals, crows. Can you destroy the human race? You can destroy a man's body, but you can't destroy his spirit. Ships capsize, people drown, mountains are still mountains and water is still water. Millions of people are being born, millions of people have survived these rapids. The world belongs to the young. Don't you know that, you bastard? People won't die out. Don't you know that? They won't die out.'

The old man claps his hands. 'Attention, please. Everybody. This is a matter of life and death. I have something to say that I can't hold back any longer. I think the captain has been playing a game with our lives. This gorge is even more dangerous than Hundred Cage Pass. Of course he knows this danger. He's been sailing these gorges all his life. This boat should only carry freight; they shouldn't allow passengers. He certainly shouldn't take our money before we arrive safely at our destination. The ticket for this old wooden boat costs as much as a paddlewheel. But since he has taken passengers and taken our money, he is responsible. First, he ought to ensure our safety; next, he ought to take care of feeding us. When we cracked up on New Landslide Rapids, we were delayed four days in Tai-hsi. We trusted the captain. We didn't ask him to return our money. We got back on the boat. Then the tow-line broke at Yellow Dragon Rapids. We've been stranded here since then. The Yangtze River, several thousand miles long, is the greatest river in Asia, and we have to ration drinking water. What a joke. From that day on, he took no emergency measures. Not only that, but when we were screaming for help at the top of our lungs, he made sarcastic remarks. The captain and the crew know how to handle boats. In case anything happens, they'll know what to do and how to escape. We don't know what to do. The passengers and the crew make thirteen people, but there are only six of us, and we are all either too old or women and children. We're outnumbered and we can't fight them. And so, I want to stand up and be counted and speak out for justice. I represent the six passengers, including the baby, and I demand that the captain do something.'

The oarsmen and the passengers are silent.

The captain, squatting on deck, blank expression, sucks the empty pipe in his mouth. 'You people just don't understand the difficulties in sailing these Gorges. We boatmen make our living by relying on the water and the sky. If it doesn't rain, the water won't rise and there's nothing we can do about it. Whether it's sailing the river or riding a horse, there's always danger involved. There's a slippery stone slab in front of everyone's door. No one can guarantee you won't slip on it and crack your skull. For human beings there is life and death, for things there is damage and destruction. It all depends on the will of Heaven. If you want someone to die, the person won't die. But if Heaven commands it, he will die. All I can do now is ask that you passengers calm down and wait patiently a while longer.'

'God, wait for how long?'

'If we have to wait, we at least ought to have food to eat and water to drink!'

'There's plenty of water in the river, and plenty of fish.' says the captain. 'If there's no more firewood, then eat raw fish. If there's no more alum, then drink muddy water. We boatmen can live like that. Can't you?' He sucks hard on his pipe. 'When our tobacco is gone, we smoke the dregs; when that's gone, we smoke the residue.' He reaches down and strikes the drum. 'Those who can't eat raw fish can chew the leather on this drum.'

Refugee Student spits at the captain. 'I'll chew on you.'

The captain throws his head back and laughs. 'Go ahead and chew. Go ahead and slice me up. Kill me. What good will that do? When the water rises and the ship floats up, you will need someone at the rudder.'

'DICE!' I yell as I cross the aisle into the 'Boys' Dormitory'. The old man is sitting on his bunk, rolling three cubes of dice around in his hand. I snatch them away and cast them on the bunk. 'Come on, let's gamble. Everybody, come here.'

'Just what I was thinking!' As soon as the old man gets excited, he starts coughing. 'You should live each day as it comes. I still have four bottles of liquor in my suitcase. I was going to give it to friends in Chungking. To hell with them, let's drink now.' He opens a bottle, gulps down a few swallows and strips off his coarse cotton jacket. He bares his chest. A few hairs stick out of his armpits.

The five of us crowd together in a circle. Lao-shih has ignored me all day. I want to sit next to her on the bunk, but I also want to sit beside Refugee Student. In the end I squeeze in between them. We pass the bottle around the circle. I've never drunk liquor before. I gulp down several swallows in one breath. My face burns. My heart pounds. My left hand rests on Lao-shih's shoulder and my right on Refugee Student's shoulder.

We put the dice in a porcelain bowl in the middle of the circle.

I raise my hand and shout, 'I'll be the dealer!'

'I'll be the dealer.'

'I'll be the dealer.'

'I'll be the dealer.'

'I'll be the dealer.'

'Let's decide by the finger-guessing game. Two people play; the winner gets a drink; then plays the next person. The last one to win gets to be dealer!'

'Let's begin. Two sweethearts!'

'Four season's wealth!'
'Six in a row!'
'Lucky seven!'
'Pair of treasures!'
'Four season's wealth!'
'Three sworn brothers.'
'Pair of treasures!'
'Eight immortals!'
'Six in a row!'
'One tall peak!'
'Four season's wealth!'
'Lucky seven!'
'All accounted for!'
'Three sworn brothers!'
'Six in a row!'
'Pair of treasures!'
'Eight immortals!'
'Lucky seven!'
'I win, I win,' yells Peach-flower Woman. 'I'm the dealer. Place your bets.'
'OK. Fifty dollars!'
'Sixty!'
'Seventy!'
'Eighty!'
'Another seventy!'
'Another eighty!'
Peach-flower Woman laughs. 'You just bet more and more. I haven't got that kind of money. If I win, I get to be the dealer again. If I lose, I'll give up. I get first crack at this!' She grabs the dice and throws them into the bowl with a flourish.

They spin in the bowl.

I take a drink. I see several dice spinning crazily in the bowl.

'Five points! The dealer has got five points!'

'I only want six points, not a single point more!' The old man cups the dice in his hands, blows on them, and then his hands open slowly like a mussel shell opening.

The dice spin in the bowl.

He bends over, glaring at the dice and yelling, 'Six points, six points! Six points! Six points . . . oh, three points.' He lifts

Peach-flower Woman's hand and sticks the bottle in it. She takes a drink. She's still holding the bottle and he lifts her hand and puts the bottle in his mouth. He pulls her toward him with his free arm and presses her face against his naked chest. He strokes her face. He finishes off the liquor with one gulp and sucks on the empty bottle like a baby.

'Sir, men and women should not mix. The booze is all gone. I don't have anything for you either. You are supposed to be respectable. You shouldn't touch a woman's body like this,' laughs Peach-flower Woman as she struggles out of his embrace and straightens up. Her chignon comes undone and hair straggles across her chest. The buttons of her blouse pop open, exposing most of her breasts.

The dice click as they spin.

'Six points! Six points! Six points! I only want six points!' Lao-shih yells, rolling on the bunk.

I roll next to her, turn over and climb on her back, as if riding a horse, bumping up and down as if keeping time. I yell with her: 'Six points! Six points! Six points! Six points! Six points! If you keep on ignoring me, I won't let you go. Six points! Six points!'

She suddenly stops yelling, yanks me off and rolls over on the bunk and grabs me. Our faces press together, legs curl round each other, rolling this way and that. She mumbles. 'If you ignore me, I won't let you go. If you ignore me, I won't let you go.'

'Four points,' yells Peach-flower Woman. 'You got four points, Lao-shih! OK, Mulberry, it's your turn.'

I struggle out of Lao-shih's embrace, roll over to the circle and stuff the dice in my mouth. I spit them out into the bowl. 'Six points, come on, six points! Six points! Six points!' Refugee Student is sprawled beside me on the bunk. I pound on his hip with my fist. 'Six points! Six, six, six, six points. How many? How many did I get?'

'Five points. The dealer also got five. The dealer wins!' Another bottle of liquor is passed around.

Refugee Student sits up, grasps the dice with his toes and tosses them into the bowl. He looks at me and begins singing in a flirtatious way. The dice, as if minding their own business, clatter in the bowl.

> Wind blows through the window
> My body is cool
> The willow tree whistles in the wind
> Lovers behind the gauze curtain
> I have a husband, but we're not in love
> Ai-ya-ya-erh-oh!
> Ai-ya-ya-erh-oh!

'Too bad, you lose. You only got three points.' Peach-flower Woman smiles at Refugee Student. With one sweep she rakes in the money.

She beat all of us.

We place larger and larger bets. In the end, we take out all our money and valuables and place them down. Lao-shih and I share our money. We have only two hundred dollars left in our purse. I put down the two hundred dollars. She puts down the purse. The old man bets his gold watch. Refugee Student bets his flute.

We lose again. Refugee Student wins twenty dollars, the price of the flute. He proposes that we change dealers. The three losers all agree. Of course, he gets to be the dealer. In any case, since he's won once already, he's probably the only one who can beat Peach-flower Woman. But the three of us losers don't have anything else to bet.

'I have an idea,' says Refugee Student. 'We play only one more game. This time it will be a game of life or death. Everyone take out his most prized possession. If you don't have anything, then bet yourself. I'm the dealer. If I win, I'll take things, if there are any. If not, I'll take people!'

'And what if you lose?'

'All I've got is myself, you can do what you want with my body, cut it in two, chop it up, lick it, kiss it, fuck it.'

'Good Heavens!' laughs Peach-flower Woman, as she looks at her baby asleep on the bunk. 'My most valuable possession is my son.'

Refugee Student leans over to her and says in a low voice, which everyone can overhear: 'Your most valuable possession is your body.'

The old man chuckles. 'What you say sounds reasonable. I'll bet my house in Peking. If you win, you can go back and take possession. I hope to retire there once the war is over.'

'I'll bet my family heirloom!' I yell as I step over to the 'Girls' Dormitory' and fish out the jade griffin from the little leather case by my pillow and return to the 'Boys' Dormitory'. 'Hey, everybody, this is my family heirloom.'

The old man's eyes suddenly light up. He tries to take it out of my hand. Refugee Student snatches it first and holds out his hand, staring at me. 'Are you going to bet this piece of junk?'

'Yeah.'

'I'd rather have you! A sixteen-year-old virgin!'

Lao-shih jerks me behind her and thrusts out her chest. 'Hey, Refugee Student, I'll make a deal with you. I'll bet this person here! If I win, you get out of my way! If you win, I'll get out of your way. You know what you did.'

'What did I do?'

'Mulberry, did you hear what he just said.'

'I heard. So what did *I* do?'

'Did you hear what she said, Miss Shih?' Refugee Student says. 'Two negatives make a positive. They cancel each other out. OK, everybody, back to your places. I won't steal your precious treasure. So what are you going to bet? Speak up!'

'I don't have anything. I have only myself.'

'OK, if I win, I'll know what to do to you,' Refugee Student leans over to Lao-shih and stares greedily into her eyes.

'Drink up! Come on and drink. It's the last half bottle.' The old man raises the bottle to his lips.

We pass the bottle around. The liquor is gone. The dice click.

We shout.

'One, two, three.'

'One, two, three.'

'Four, five, six.'

'Four, five, six.'

'One, two, three.'

'One point!'

'OK, it's one point.'

'Come on, be good, be good, another one!'

'Be good, be good, don't listen to him. Let's have a two.'

'OK, four points, great, the dealer got only four points.'

The dice click again.

'Five points! Five points! Five points. Hey, you little beauties, did you hear me, I only want one more point than that bastard. Keep my house in Peking for myself. Five points. Five points, please, five points . . . Ah! You fuckin' dice, you did it, you did it! Five points!'

The dice click again.

'Five points, five points, five points, I don't want any more, don't want any less, just give me five points. Good Heavens, let me win just this once in my life. Just this once. Only five points, only five points. Have they stopped? How many did I get? Six points, six points, thank Heavens.'

Everything is floating in front of my eyes. I feel the boat floating underfoot, everyone, everything is floating. The jade griffin is floating. It's my turn, they tell me. I grab the dice and throw them in the bowl. I get a six. They tell me I only picked up two dice and want me to throw again. Lao-shih stuffs the cubes in my hand. I can't hold on to them, they slip from my hand into the bowl. I hear Lao-shih moaning, 'It's over, it's over.'

Dealer, Refugee Student:	Four points
Old man:	Five points
Lao-shih:	Six points
Mulberry:	Three points
Peach-flower Woman:	Four points

'Dealer, I beat you by one point!' says the old man. 'You little punk, I want you to kneel before me and bow three times and kowtow nine times. Nine loud thumps of your head.'

Refugee Student kneels down on the bunk.

'No, no,' says the old man, crossing his legs on the bunk like a bodhisattva statuette. 'Haven't you ever seen your old man pray to his ancestor? Did he ever kneel on a bunk and kowtow

to his ancestors that way? Humph. You have to kneel properly
on the floor. Knock your head against the floor so I can hear it!'
    Refugee Student jumps down from the bunk into the aisle
and bends down.
    'Hey, you punk, just slow down a little. Have you ever seen
anyone kowtowing half-naked? Go put your clothes on!'
    Refugee Student grinds his teeth.
    Lao-shih, Peach-flower Woman and I burst into laughter.
    He puts on his shirt, squeezes down in the narrow aisle be-
tween the two rows of bunks.
    The old man sits erect on the bunk, strokes his beard and
raises his voice like a master of ceremonies, 'First kowtow, second kowtow, third kowtow.'
    Refugee Student stands up, bends and bows with uplifted
hands, then kneels back down. 'Fourth kowtow, fifth kowtow,
sixth kowtow!' He gets up again and bows and kneels back
down. 'Seventh kowtow, eighth kowtow, ninth kowtow. Ceremony finished.'
    Refugee Student scrambles to his feet and points at me. 'I
beat you by one point. It's time to settle with you.'
    'That's easy. You won, take the jade griffin.' I pick it up and
give it to him.
    He doesn't take it and just looks at me. 'What would I do
with that? I'm a wanderer. All I want is a pair of grass sandals, a
bag of dried food, and a flute. This jade griffin is nothing but a
burden. Anyway,' his voice becomes oddly tender, 'I owe you
something. I'll repay you by giving back your jade griffin.'
    'You don't owe me anything. You said yourself, "two nega-
tives make a positive." I don't owe you anything either.' As I'm
talking, I try to put the jade griffin in his hand. I'm sure I'm
holding it securely, but when I raise my hand, it slips through
my fingers and falls. I let out a cry.
    The griffin breaks in two on the floor.
    The old man picks up the two halves and fits them together.
It looks as if they're still one piece.
    'All right, we'll do it this way. You take one half, I'll take the
other,' Refugee Student says and stuffs one half into my hand.
    'OK, problem solved,' Lao-shih rubs her palms together and
noisily grinds her teeth. 'Now, I get to settle with the dealer.

I'm the real winner; I beat the dealer by two points. I only wanted the satisfaction of beating you. I won't cut you in two or chop you up. I won't chew on you. I only want you to dress up like a girl and sing the Flower Drum Song.'
'Good idea.' I also want to get even with him. I toss my half of the jade griffin into the opposite bunk.

The three of us, Lao-shih, Peach-flower Woman and myself, strip off his clothes, leaving only his underpants. I remember when he lay naked on the deck, his weight on my body, head hanging over my shoulder, my thighs wet and sticky. I'm still a little sore there. I couldn't stop caressing his body, like a rock in the sun, so smooth, warm, hard. So a man's body was that nice. I wished I could stroke him forever, but when he used all his strength to push into my body, it hurt. How could Peach-flower Woman sleep with her man every night? And even have a baby? I don't see how she could bear the pain.

We dress him in Peach-flower Woman's clothes. He wears the peach flower blouse, blue print pants, a turban of a blue-flowered print wound around his head, two red spots painted on his cheeks, his masculine eyebrows thick and black.

He daintily folds his muscular hands and curtsies. He picks up Peach-flower Woman's red handkerchief and dances with it like a woman, twisting, turning and singing.

> "You say life is hard
> My life is hard
> Looking for a good husband all my life
> Other girls marry rich men
> My husband can only play the flower drum."

The old man, sitting on the bunk, laughs until he has a coughing fit. Lao-shih, Peach-flower Woman and I roll with laughter on the bunk.

Suddenly Refugee Student leaps on the bunk and jumps on Lao-shih. 'If you ignore me, I won't let you go! I'm your girl. You have to give me a kiss!' He presses his mouth to hers and strokes all over her body. Lao-shih begins choking and can't speak.

I tackle him to save Lao-shih. 'Good, I've got you both!' He turns over and grabs us both, one on each side, arms locked around our necks, holding us down. 'You come here, too,' he says to Peach-flower Woman. 'I can put you on my chest.' Lao-shih and I beat on his chest with our fists.

He suddenly lets go and rolls over to Peach-flower Woman. He stretches up his hands to her, fingers curled like claws and moves closer and closer to her, saying, 'Now, I am going to settle with you!'

She laughs, her blouse still unbuttoned, straggling hair on her breasts. 'What do you want? Take all the money I've won?'

'Me? I want you!'

She points a finger at him. 'Let me ask you, are you man enough to deal with me?'

'If he isn't, I am,' chuckles the old man.

Refugee Student doesn't say anything. He rips open her blouse and jumps on her, grabs one of her breasts and begins to suck on it. The old man jumps over and grabs her other breast.

She laughs, her full breasts shaking. 'Do anything you want with my poor old body. Just don't take away my baby's food. My milk is almost gone!'

The baby on the bunk starts to cry.

She shoves them aside and goes to pick up the baby.

'I have an idea. I still have two cigarettes. Be my guest.' Refugee Student gropes in his pocket and pulls out two cigarettes—The Dog with a Human Head brand—and steps over to Peach-flower Woman.

She is lying on the bunk nursing her child. Refugee Student lights a cigarette, grabs Peach-flower Woman's right foot and sticks it between her toes. He presses his face against her sole and smokes, his two hands holding her foot.

The old man does the same with her left foot.

She lies flat on her back, her limbs flung out as the child clutches her breast and sucks loudly and the two men hold her feet and suck on the cigarettes.

She laughs and jerks back and forth. 'You devils, you're tickling me. You sex fiends. When you die, you'll get what's coming to you.'

'Listen, listen. The bombers are coming back.' I hear the droning of aircraft.

WE sit up stiffly in our bunks.

The roar comes toward us.

It's twilight in the Gorge, the time when day can't be distinguished from night, or clear dusk from a cloudy day.

The captain and the crew are in the bow.

'Hey, the bombers are coming. Come and hide in the cabin. Don't endanger everybody's lives!' shouts the old man.

No response.

'Look at that,' says the captain, 'three planes in each formation. Nine altogether.'

'Motherfuckers, those traitors. Only traitors aren't scared of bombers.' Refugee Student gnashes his teeth.

A boat comes downstream. People on board are yelling. Gongs are crashing.

The bombers are overhead. We sprawl on the bunks. I cover my head with the quilt, the rest of my body exposed.

The yelling, the gong, the roar of the planes get louder.

'I can't hear you,' the captain is shouting to the people on the other boat, 'say it again.'

Shouting, gongs, bombers.

'The Japanese have surrendered!' the captain finally yells.

We rush to the bow. A flame shoots up in the sky, bursting into colourful fireworks. A huge lotus flower opens above the Gorge.

The airplane sprinkles coloured confetti and flies off down the river.

The boat, separated from us by the churning rapids, glides downstream to the sound of cheering and gongs.

'Victory, victory, vic . . . tory . . . tory . . .'

The echoes of their cheers, the confetti swirl around us and disappear into the river.

'There are thunderheads on those mountains,' shouts the captain. 'It's going to rain. We'll float away.'

Dark clouds appear overhead.

Refugee Student, still dressed as the flower drum girl, snatches up a drumstick and pounds on the drum. The drum is thundering.

Leslie Marmon Silko

"I THINK I am trying to say that my very life means more to me than it would have meant if you hadn't written *Ceremony.*" Thus pronounces James Wright, in his first letter to Leslie Silko (1948–), dated August 28, 1978. What followed was a profoundly moving exchange of letters between the two writers, continuing until Wright's death from cancer in 1980. The title of their published correspondence, collected in *The Delicacy and Strength of Lace* and edited by Wright's widow (Anne Wright), suggests Silko's powerful and abiding influence as a writer. Not coincidentally, the Spider Woman myths of the Laguna tradition provide the delicate structure of the book.

Through an intricate weaving together of American Indian stories, myths, and poems, she presents in *Ceremony* (1977) the struggles of both a young Laguna soldier, traumatized by his World War II experiences in the Philippines, and a people, wracked by their experiences in their homeland, to pull fragmented selves together into a functional whole. Tayo's pain and confusion over the loss of his brother and his mistaking the Japanese soldiers for the people back home—in particular, his Uncle Josiah—leave him sorely in need of healing, a healing which Anglo medicine or values cannot provide. Tayo's story, while involved with American Indian tradition and history, also speaks to the dilemmas postmodern humans face in this nuclear age, in that the dropping of the atomic bomb forever changed our concept of dis-ease and mortality.

Silko began publishing in the early 1970s, most notably appearing in Kenneth Rosen's celebrated anthology of American Indian writing, *The Man to Send Rainclouds* (1974), titled after Silko's lead story in the volume. Her short fiction has also been published in *Best American Short Stories of 1975* and *200*

Years of Great American Short Stories, as well as numerous journals and magazines. In describing her heritage, Silko says, "I grew up at Laguna Pueblo. I am of mixed-breed ancestry, but what I know is Laguna. This place I am from is everything I am as a writer and human being." Silko's rootedness in the Southwest is reflected in the setting for virtually all of her work, with the notable exception of "Storyteller," which is set in Alaska and which provides the title for her second book. Her prose resonates with "the beauty ways," the harmony so valued by Navajo and other Southwest tribal traditions, even when disharmony and injustice are her themes.

Family photographs of pueblos, Southwest landscapes, and people lie interspersed with stories, anecdotes, and poems in *Storyteller* (1981), a collection of new and previously published writings which followed *Ceremony* into print. Widely acclaimed, the book rightly explodes all expectations we may have of formal literary categories and, indeed, of language experience itself. More than words on a page, the work is as close to the multi-media event of storytelling as can be. In 1981, Silko was awarded the prestigious MacArthur Fellowship, enabling her to take five years off from academic teaching to engage in writing full-time. *Almanac of the Dead* is the as yet unpublished fruit of that labor; it will reflect her research into ancient Mexican cultures.

As more and more American Indian writers begin taking up the pen to recover and recreate their histories, to exorcise the hurt and devastation caused by Euro-American efforts to inflict cultural genocide on Indian people and to destroy or usurp their environment, Silko will continue to stand as a visionary, who fought to move us all toward a more compassionate view of the interrelatedness of all things. As she writes in "Storyteller": "It will take a long time, but the story must be told. There must not be any lies."

—Kathryn Shanley

Excerpts from
CEREMONY

Sunrise.

TAYO didn't sleep well that night. He tossed in the old iron bed, and the coiled springs kept squeaking even after he lay still again, calling up humid dreams of black night and loud voices rolling him over and over again like debris caught in a flood. Tonight the singing had come first, squeaking out of the iron bed, a man singing in Spanish, the melody of a familiar love song, two words again and again, *"Y volveré."* Sometimes the Japanese voices came first, angry and loud, pushing the song far away, and then he could hear the shift in his dreaming, like a slight afternoon wind changing its direction, coming less and less from the south, moving into the west, and the voices would become Laguna voices, and he could hear Uncle Josiah calling to him, Josiah bringing him the fever medicine when he had been sick a long time ago. But before Josiah could come, the fever voices would drift and whirl and emerge again—Japanese soldiers shouting orders to him, suffocating damp voices that drifted out in the jungle steam, and he heard the women's voices then; they faded in and out until he was frantic because he thought the Laguna words were his mother's, but when he was about to make out the meaning of the words, the voice suddenly broke into a language he could not understand; and it was then that all the voices were drowned by the music—loud, loud music from a big juke box, its flashing red and blue lights pulling the darkness closer.

He lay there early in the morning and watched the high small window above the bed; dark gray gradually became lighter until it cast a white square on the opposite wall at dawn. He watched the room grow brighter then, as the square of light grew steadily warmer, more yellow with the climbing sun. He had not been able to sleep for a long time—for as long as all things had become tied together like colts in single file when he and Josiah had taken them to the mountain, with the halter rope of one colt tied to the tail of the colt ahead of it, and the lead colt's rope tied to the wide horn on Josiah's Mexican saddle. He could still see them now—the creamy sorrel, the bright red bay, and the gray roan—their slick summer coats reflecting the sunlight as it came up from behind the yellow mesas, shining on them, strung out behind Josiah's horse like an old-time pack train. He could get no rest as long as the memories were tangled with the present, tangled up like colored threads from old Grandma's wicker sewing basket when he was a child, and he had carried them outside to play and they had spilled out of his arms into the summer weeds and rolled away in all directions, and then he had hurried to pick them up before Auntie found him. He could feel it inside his skull—the tension of little threads being pulled and how it was with tangled things, things tied together, and as he tried to pull them apart and rewind them into their places, they snagged and tangled even more. So Tayo had to sweat through those nights when thoughts became entangled; he had to sweat to think of something that wasn't unraveled or tied in knots to the past—something that existed by itself, standing alone like a deer. And if he could hold that image of the deer in his mind long enough, his stomach might shiver less and let him sleep for a while. It worked as long as the deer was alone, as long as he could keep it a gray buck on an unrecognized hill; but if he did not hold it tight, it would spin away from him and become the deer he and Rocky had hunted. That memory would unwind into the last day when they had sat together, oiling their rifles in the jungle of some nameless Pacific island. While they used up the last of the oil in Rocky's pack, they talked about the deer that Rocky had hunted, and the corporal next to them shook his head, and kept saying he had dreamed the Japs would get them that day.

The humid air turned into sweat that had run down the corporal's face while he repeated his dream to them. That was the first time Tayo had realized that the man's skin was not much different from his own. The skin. He saw the skin of the corpses again and again, in ditches on either side of the long muddy road—skin that was stretched shiny and dark over bloated hands; even white men were darker after death. There was no difference when they were swollen and covered with flies. That had become the worst thing for Tayo: they looked too familiar even when they were alive. When the sergeant told them to kill all the Japanese soldiers lined up in front of the cave with their hands on their heads, Tayo could not pull the trigger. The fever made him shiver, and the sweat was stinging his eyes and he couldn't see clearly; in that instant he saw Josiah standing there; the face was dark from the sun, and the eyes were squinting as though he were about to smile at Tayo. So Tayo stood there, stiff with nausea, while they fired at the soldiers, and he watched his uncle fall, and he *knew* it was Josiah; and even after Rocky started shaking him by the shoulders and telling him to stop crying, it was *still* Josiah lying there. They forced medicine into Tayo's mouth, and Rocky pushed him toward the corpses and told him to look, look past the blood that was already dark like the jungle mud, with only flecks of bright red still shimmering in it. Rocky made him look at the corpse and said, "Tayo, this is a *Jap!* This is a *Jap* uniform!" And then he rolled the body over with his boot and said, "Look, Tayo, look at the face," and that was when Tayo started screaming because it wasn't a Jap, it was Josiah, eyes shrinking back into the skull and all their shining black light glazed over by death.

The sergeant had called for a medic and somebody rolled up Tayo's sleeve; they told him to sleep, and the next day they all acted as though nothing had happened. They called it battle fatigue, and they said hallucinations were common with malarial fever.

Rocky had reasoned it out with him; it was impossible for the dead man to be Josiah, because Josiah was an old Laguna man, thousands of miles from the Philippine jungles and Japanese armies. "He's probably up on some mesa right now, chopping wood," Rocky said. He smiled and shook Tayo's shoulders. "Hey, I know you're homesick. But, Tayo, we're *supposed* to be here. This is what we're supposed to do."

Tayo nodded, slapped at the insects mechanically and staring straight ahead, past the smothering dampness of the green jungle leaves. He examined the facts and logic again and again, the way Rocky had explained it to him; the facts made what he had seen an impossibility. He felt the shivering then; it began at the tips of his fingers and pulsed into his arms. He shivered because all the facts, all the reasons made no difference any more; he could hear Rocky's words, and he could follow the logic of what Rocky said, but he could not feel anything except a swelling in his belly, a great swollen grief that was pushing into his throat.

He had to keep busy; he had to keep moving so that the sinews connected behind his eyes did not slip loose and spin his eyes to the interior of his skull where the scenes waited for him. He got out of the bed quickly while he could still see the square of yellow sunshine on the wall opposite the bed, and he pulled on his jeans and the scuffed brown boots he had worn before the war, and the red plaid western shirt old Grandma gave him the day he had come home after the war.

The air outside was still cool; it smelled like night dampness, faintly of rain. He washed his face in the steel-cold water of the iron trough by the windmill. The yellow striped cat purred and wrapped herself around his legs while he combed his hair. She ran ahead of him to the goat pen and shoved her head under his left arm when he knelt down to milk the black goat. He poured milk for her in the lid of an old enamel coffeepot, and then he opened the pen and let them run, greedy for the tender green shoots of tumbleweeds pushing through the sand. The kid was almost too big to nurse any more, and it knelt by the doe and hunched down to reach the tits, butting her to make the milk come faster, wiggling its tail violently until the nanny jumped away and turned on the kid, butting it away from her. The process of weaning had gone on like this for weeks, but the nanny was more intent on weeds than the lesson, and when Tayo left them, the kid goat was back at the tits, a little more careful this time.

The sun was climbing then, and it looked small in that empty morning sky. He knew he should eat, but he wasn't hungry any more. He sat down in the kitchen, at the small square table with the remains of a white candle melted to a nub on the lid of a coffee can; he wondered how long the candle had been there, he wondered if Josiah had been the one to light it last. He thought he would cry then, thinking of Josiah and how he had been here and touched all these things, sat in this chair. So he jerked his head away from the candle, and looked at the soot around the base of the coffeepot. He wouldn't waste firewood to heat up yesterday's coffee or maybe it was day-before-yesterday's coffee. He had lost track of the days there.

The drought years had returned again, as they had after the First World War and in the twenties, when he was a child and they had to haul water to the sheep in big wooden barrels in the old wagon. The windmill near the sheep camp had gone dry, so the gray mules pulled the wagon from the springs, moving slowly so that the water would not splash over the rims. He sat close to his uncle then, on the wagon seat, above the bony gray rumps of the mules. After they had dumped water for the sheep, they went to burn the spines from the cholla and prickly pear. They stood back by the wagon and watched the cows walk up to the cactus cautiously, sneezing at the smoldering ashes. The cows were patient while the scorched green pulp cooled, and then they brought out their wide spotted tongues and ate those strange remains because the hills were barren those years and only the cactus could grow.

Now there was no wagon or wooden barrels. One of the gray mules had eaten a poison weed near Acoma, and the other one was blind; it stayed close to the windmill at the ranch, grazing on the yellow rice grass that grew in the blow sand. It walked a skinny trail, winding in blind circles from the grass to the water trough, where it dipped its mouth in the water and let the water dribble out again, rinsing its mouth four or five times a day to make sure the water was still there. The dry air shrank the wooden staves of the barrels; they pulled loose, and now the rusty steel hoops were scattered on the ground behind the corral in the crazy patterns of some flashy Kiowa hoop dancer at the Gallup Ceremonials, throwing his hoops along the ground where he would hook and flip them into the air again and they would skim over his head and shoulders down to his dancing feet, like magic. Tayo stepped inside one that was half buried in the reddish blow sand; he hooked an edge with the toe of his boot, and then he let it slip into the sand again.

The wind had blown since late February and it did not stop after April. They said it had been that way for the past six years while he was gone. And all this time they had watched the sky expectantly for the rainclouds to come. Now it was late May, and when Tayo went to the outhouse he left the door open wide, facing the dry empty hills and the light blue sky. He watched the sky over the distant Black Mountains the way Josiah had many years before, because sometimes when the rain finally came, it was from the southwest.

Jungle rain had no begining or end; it grew like foliage from the sky, branching and arching to the earth, sometimes in solid thickets entangling the islands, and, other times, in tendrils of blue mist curling out of coastal clouds. The jungle breathed an eternal green that fevered men until they dripped sweat the way rubbery jungle leaves dripped the monsoon rain. It was there that Tayo began to understand what Josiah had said. Nothing was all good or all bad either; it all depended. Jungle rain lay suspended in the air, choking their lungs as they marched; it soaked into their boots until the skin on their toes peeled away dead and wounds turned green. This was not the rain he and Josiah had prayed for, this was not the green foliage they sought out in sandy canyons as a sign of a spring. When Tayo prayed on the long muddy road to the prison camp, it was for dry air, dry as a hundred years squeezed out of yellow sand, air to dry out the oozing wounds of Rocky's leg, to let the torn flesh and broken bones breathe, to clear the sweat that filled Rocky's eyes. It was that rain which filled the tire ruts and made the mud so deep that the corporal began to slip and fall with his end of the muddy blanket that held Rocky. Tayo hated this unending rain as if it were the jungle green rain and not the miles of marching or the Japanese grenade that was killing Rocky. He would blame the rain if the Japs saw how the corporal staggered; if they saw how weak Rocky had become, and came to crush his head with the butt of a rifle, then it would be the rain and the green all around that killed him.

Tayo talked to the corporal almost incessantly, walking behind him with his end of the blanket stretcher, telling him that it wasn't much farther now, and all down hill from there. He made a story for all of them, a story to give them strength. The words of the story poured out of his mouth as if they had substance, pebbles and stone extending to hold the corporal up, to keep his knees from buckling, to keep his hands from letting go of the blanket.

The sound of the rain got louder, pounding on the leaves, splashing into the ruts; it splattered on his head, and the sound echoed inside his skull. It streamed down his face and neck like jungle flies with crawling feet. He wanted to turn loose the blanket to wipe the rain away; he wanted to let go for only a moment. But as long as the corporal was still standing, still moving, they had to keep going. Then from somewhere, within the sound of the rain falling, he could hear it approaching like a summer flash flood, the rumble still faint and distant, floodwater boiling down a narrow canyon. He could smell the foaming floodwater, stagnant and ripe with the rotting debris it carried past each village, sucking up their sewage, their waste, the dead animals. He tried to hold it back, but the wind swept down from the green coastal mountains, whipping the rain into gray waves that blinded him. The corporal fell, jerking the ends of the blanket from his hands, and he felt Rocky's foot brush past his own leg. He slid to his knees, trying to find the ends of the blanket again, and he started repeating "Goddamn, goddamn!"; it flooded out of the last warm core in his chest and echoed inside his head. He damned the rain until the words were a chant, and he sang it while he crawled through the mud to find the corporal and get him up before the Japanese saw them. He wanted the words to make a cloudless blue sky, pale with a summer sun pressing across wide and empty horizons. The words gathered inside him and gave him strength. He pulled on the corporal's arm; he lifted him to his knees and all the time he could hear his own voice praying against the rain.

It was summertime
and Iktoa'ak'o'ya-Reed Woman
was always taking a bath.
She spent all day long

sitting in the river
splashing down
the summer rain.

But her sister
Corn Woman
worked hard all day
sweating in the sun
getting sore hands
in the corn field.
Corn Woman got tired of that
she got angry
she scolded
her sister
for bathing all day long.

Iktoa'ak'o'ya-Reed Woman
went away then
she went back
to the original place
down below.

And there was no more rain then.
Everything dried up
all the plants
the corn
the beans
they all dried up
and started blowing away
in the wind.

The people and the animals
were thirsty.
They were starving.

So he had prayed the rain away, and for the sixth year it was
dry; the grass turned yellow and it did not grow. Wherever he
looked, Tayo could see the consequences of his praying; the
gray mule grew gaunt, and the goat and kid had to wander
farther each day to find weeds or dry shrubs to eat. In the
evenings they waited for him, chewing their cuds by the shed
door, and the mule stood by the gate with blind marble eyes.
He threw them a little dusty hay and sprinkled some cracked

corn over it. The nanny crowded the kid away from the corn. The mule whinnied and leaned against the sagging gates; Tayo reached into the coffee can and he held some corn under the quivering lips. When the corn was gone, the mule licked for the salt taste on his hand; the tongue was rough and wet, but it was also warm and precise across his fingers. Tayo looked at the long white hairs growing out of the lips like antennas, and he got the choking in his throat again, and he cried for all of them, and for what he had done.

FOR a long time he had been white smoke. He did not realize that until he left the hospital, because white smoke had no consciousness of itself. It faded into the white world of their bed sheets and walls; it was sucked away by the words of doctors who tried to talk to the invisible scattered smoke. He had seen outlines of gray steel tables, outlines of the food they pushed into his mouth, which was only an outline too, like all the outlines he saw. They saw his outline but they did not realize it was hollow inside. He walked down floors that smelled of old wax and disinfectant, watching the outlines of his feet; as he walked, the days and seasons disappeared into a twilight at the corner of his eyes, a twilight he could catch only with a sudden motion, jerking his head to one side for a glimpse of green leaves pressed against the bars on the window. He inhabited a gray winter fog on a distant elk mountain where hunters are lost indefinitely and their own bones mark the boundaries.

He stood outside the train depot in Los Angeles and felt the sunshine; he saw palm trees, the edges of their branches turning yellow, dead gray fronds scaling off, scattered over the ground, and at that moment his body had density again and the world was visible and he realized why he was there and he remembered Rocky and he started to cry. The red Spanish tile on the depot roof got blurry, but he did not move or wipe away the tears, because it had been a long time since he had cried for anyone. The smoke had been dense; visions and memories of the past did not penetrate there, and he had drifted in colors of smoke, where there was no pain, only pale, pale gray of the north wall by his bed. Their medicine drained memory out of his thin arms and replaced it with a twilight cloud behind his eyes. It was not possible to cry on the remote and foggy mountain. If they had not dressed him and led him to the car, he would still be there, drifting along the north wall, invisible in the gray twilight.

The new doctor asked him if he had ever been visible, and Tayo spoke to him softly and said that he was sorry but nobody was allowed to speak to an invisible one. But the new doctor persisted; he came each day, and his questions dissolved the edges of the fog, and his voice sounded louder every time he came. The sun was dissolving the fog, and one day Tayo heard a voice answering the doctor. The voice was saying, "He can't talk to you. He is invisible. His words are formed with an invisible tongue, they have no sound."

He reached into his mouth and felt his own tongue; it was dry and dead, the carcass of a tiny rodent.

"It is easy to remain invisible here, isn't it, Tayo?"

"It was, until you came. It was all white, all the color of the smoke, the fog."

"I am sending you home, Tayo; tomorrow you'll go on the train."

"He can't go. He cries all the time. Sometimes he vomits when he cries."

"Why does he cry, Tayo?"

"He cries because they are dead and everything is dying."

He could see the doctor clearly then, the dark thick hair growing on the backs of the doctor's hands as they reached out at him.

"Go ahead, Tayo, you can cry."

He wanted to scream at the doctor then, but the words choked him and he coughed up his own tears and tasted their salt in his mouth. He smelled the disinfectant then, the urine and the vomit, and he gagged. He raised his head from the sink in the corner of the room; he gripped both sides and he looked up at the doctor.

"Goddamn you," he said softly, "look what you have done."

There was a cardboard name tag on the handle of the suitcase he carried; he could feel it with the tips of his fingers. His name was on the tag and his serial number too. It had been a long time since he had thought about having a name.

The man at the ticket window told him it would be twenty-five minutes before the train left on track four; he pointed out the big doors to the tracks and told Tayo he could wait out there. Tayo felt weak, and the longer he walked the more his legs felt as though they might become invisible again; then the top part of his body would topple, and when his head was level with the ground he would be lost in smoke again, in the fog again. He breathed the air outside the doors and it smelled like trains, diesel oil, and creosote ties under the steel track. He leaned against the depot wall then; he was sweating, and sounds were becoming outlines again, vague and hollow in his ears, and he knew he was going to become invisible right there. It was too late to ask for help, and he waited to die the way smoke dies, drifting away in currents of air, twisting in thin swirls, fading until it exists no more. His last thought was how generous they had become, sending him to the L.A. depot alone, finally allowing him to die.

He lay on the concrete listening to the voices that surrounded him, voices that were either soft or distant. They spoke to him in English, and when he did not answer, there was a discussion and he heard the Japanese words vividly. He wasn't sure where he was any more, maybe back in the jungles again; he felt a sick sweat shiver over him like the shadow of the angel Auntie talked about. He fought to come to the surface, and he expected a rifle barrel to be shoved into his face when he opened his eyes. It was all worse than he had ever dreamed: to have drifted all those months in white smoke, only to wake up again in the prison camp. But he did not want to be invisible when he died, so he pulled himself loose, one last time.

The Japanese women were holding small children by the hands, and they were surrounded by bundles and suitcases. One of them was standing over him.

"Are you sick?" she asked.

He tried to answer her, but his throat made a coughing, gagging sound. He looked at her and tried to focus in on the others.

"We called for help," she said, bending over slightly, the hem of her flower-print dress swaying below her knees. A white man in a train uniform came. He looked at Tayo, and then he looked at the women and children.

"What happened to him?"

They shook their heads, and the woman said, "We saw him fall down as we were coming from our train." She moved away then, back to the group. She reached down and picked up a shopping bag in each hand; she looked at Tayo one more time. He raised himself up on one arm and watched them go; he felt a current of air from the movement of their skirts and feet and shopping bags. A child stared back at him, holding a hand but walking twisted around so that he could see Tayo. The little boy was wearing an Army hat that was too big for him, and when he saw Tayo looking he smiled; then the child disappeared through the wide depot doors.

The depot man helped him get up; he checked the tag on the suitcase.

"Should I call the Veterans' Hospital?"

Tayo shook his head; he was beginning to shiver all over.

"Those people," he said, pointing in the direction the women and children had gone, "I thought they locked them up."

"Oh, that was some years back. Right after Pearl Harbor. But now they've turned them all loose again. Sent them home. I don't guess you could keep up with news very well in the hospital."

"No." His voice sounded faint to him.

"You going to be all right now?"

He nodded and looked down the tracks. The depot man glanced at a gold pocket watch and walked away.

The swelling was pushing against his throat, and he leaned against the brick wall and vomited into the big garbage can. The smell of his own vomit and the rotting garbage filled his head, and he retched until his stomach heaved in frantic dry spasms. He could still see the face of the little boy, looking back at him, smiling, and he tried to vomit that image from his head because it was Rocky's smiling face from a long time before, when they were little kids together. He couldn't vomit any more, and the little face was still there, so he cried at how the world had come undone, how thousands of miles, high ocean waves and green jungles could not hold people in their place. Years and months had become weak, and people could push against them and wander back and forth in time. Maybe it had always been this way and he was only seeing it for the first time.

THE Army recruiter had taped posters of tanks and marching soldiers around the edge of a folding table. The Government car was parked next to the post office under the flagpole, and he had set up the table next to the car, trying to find shelter from the wind. But the posters were flapping and twisting around, and the brittle edges of the paper were beginning to split and tear. There was a chill in the wind during the last days the sun occupied a summer place in the sky—and something relentless in the way the wind drove the sand and dust ahead of it. The recruiter was sitting on his folding chair, but he had to keep both hands on his pamphlets to keep them from scattering. He had been waiting for more people to show up before he began his speech, but Rocky and Tayo and old man Jeff were the only people out in the wind that afternoon.

"Anyone can fight for America," he began, giving special emphasis to "America," "even you boys. In a time of need, anyone can fight for her." A big gust of sand swirled around them; Rocky turned his back to it and Tayo covered his face with his hands; old man Jeff went inside the post office. The recruiter paused to rearrange the pamphlets and check the damage the wind had done to the posters. He looked disgusted then, as though he were almost ready to leave. But he went on with his speech.

"Now I know you boys love America as much as we do, but this is your big chance to *show* it!" He stood up then, as he had rehearsed, and looked them in the eye sincerely. He handed them color pamphlets with a man in a khaki uniform and gold braid on the cover; in the background, behind the figure in the uniform, there was a gold eagle with its wings spread across an American flag.

Rocky read each page of the pamphlet carefully. He looked up at Tayo and his face was serious and proud. Tayo knew right then what Rocky wanted to do. The wind blew harder; a gust caught the pamphlets and swirled them off the card table. They scattered like dry leaves across the ground. The recruiter ran after them with his arms out in front of him as if he were chasing turkeys. Rocky helped him pick them up, and he nodded sharply for Tayo to help too. Rocky talked to the recruiter about the training programs while they shook sand out of the brochures and folded them up again.

"I want to be a pilot." He paused and looked at the recruiter. "You can fly all over the world that way, can't you?"

The recruiter was packing the leaflets into a cardboard box; he didn't look up. "Sure, sure," he said, "you enlist now and you'll be eligible for everything—pilot training—everything." He folded the legs under the little table and slammed down the lid of the car's trunk. He glanced at his big chrome wristwatch.

"You men want to sign up?"

Rocky looked at Tayo as if he wanted to ask him something. It was strange to see that expression on his face, because Rocky had always known what he was doing, without asking anyone.

"And my brother," Rocky said, nodding at Tayo. "If we both sign up, can we stay together?"

It was the first time in all the years that Tayo had lived with him that Rocky ever called him "brother." Auntie had always been careful that Rocky didn't call Tayo "brother," and when other people mistakenly called them brothers, she was quick to correct the error.

"They're not brothers," she'd say, "that's Laura's boy. You know the one." She had a way of saying it, a tone of voice which bitterly told the story, and the disgrace she and the family had suffered. The things Laura had done weren't easily forgotten by the people, but she could maintain a distance between Rocky, who was her pride, and this other, unwanted child. If nobody else ever knew about this distance, she and Tayo did.

HE was four years old the night his mother left him there. He didn't remember much: only that she had come after dark and wrapped him in a man's coat—it smelled like a man—and that there were men in the car with them: and she held him all the way, kept him bundled tight and close to her, and he had dozed and listened, half dreaming their laughter and the sound of a cork squeaking in and out of a bottle. He could not remember if she had fed him, but when they got to Laguna that night, he wasn't hungry and he refused the bread Uncle Josiah offered him. He clung to her because when she left him, he knew she would be gone for a long time. She kissed him on the forehead with whiskey breath, and then pushed him gently into Josiah's arms as she backed out the door. He cried and fought Josiah, trying to follow her, but his uncle held him firmly and told him not to cry because he had a brother now: Rocky would be his brother, and he could stay with them until Christmas. Rocky had been staring at him, but with the mention of Christmas he started crying and kicking the leg of the table. There were tears all over his face and his nose was running.

"Go away," he screamed, "you're not my brother. I don't want no brother!" Tayo covered his ears with his hands and buried his face against Josiah's leg, crying because he knew: this time she wasn't coming back for him. Josiah pulled out his red bandanna handkerchief and wiped Tayo's nose and eyes. He looked at Rocky sternly and then took both of the little boys by the hand. They walked into the back room together, and Josiah showed him the bed that he and Rocky would share for so many years.

When old Grandma and Auntie came home that night from the bingo game at church, Tayo and Rocky were already in bed. Tayo could tell by the sound of his breathing that Rocky was already asleep. But he lay there in the dark and listened to voices in the kitchen, voices of Josiah and Auntie and the faint voice of old Grandma. He never knew what they said that night, because the voices merged into a hum, like night insects around a lamp; but he thought he could hear Auntie raise her voice and the sound of pots and pans slamming together on the stove. And years later he learned she did that whenever she was angry.

It was a private understanding between the two of them. When Josiah or old Grandma or Robert was there, the agreement was suspended, and she pretended to treat him the same as she treated Rocky, but they both knew it was only temporary. When she was alone with the boys, she kept Rocky close to her; while she kneaded the bread, she gave Rocky little pieces of dough to play with; while she darned socks, she gave him scraps of cloth and a needle and thread to play with. She was careful that Rocky did not share these things with Tayo, that they kept a distance between themselves and him. But she would not let Tayo go outside or play in another room alone. She wanted him close enough to feel excuded, to be aware of the distance between them. The two little boys accepted the distance, but Rocky was never cruel to Tayo. He seemed to know that the narrow silence was reserved only for times when the three of them were alone together. They sensed the difference in her when old Grandma or Josiah was present, and they adjusted without hesitation, keeping their secret.

But after they started school, the edges of the distance softened, and Auntie seldom had the boys to herself any more. They were gone most of the day, and old Grandma was totally blind by then and always there, sitting close to her stove. Rocky was more anxious than Tayo to stay away from the house, to stay after school for sports or to play with friends. It was Rocky who withdrew from her, although only she and Tayo realized it. He did it naturally, like a rabbit leaping away from a shadow suddenly above him.

Tayo and Auntie understood each other very well. Years later Tayo wondered if anyone, even old Grandma or Josiah, ever understood her as well as he did. He learned to listen to the undertones of her voice. Robert and Josiah evaded her; they were deaf to those undertones. In her blindness and old age, old Grandma stubbornly ignored her and heard only what she wanted to hear. Rocky had his own way, with his after-school sports and his girl friends. Only Tayo could hear it, like fingernails scratching against bare rock, her terror at being trapped in one of the oldest ways.

An old sensitivity had descended in her, surviving thousands of years from the oldest times, when the people shared a single clan name and they told each other who they were; they recounted the actions and words each of their clan had taken, and would take; from before they were born and long after they died, the people shared the same consciousness. The people had known, with the simple certainty of the world they saw, how everything should be.

But the fifth world had become entangled with European names: the names of the rivers, the hills, the names of the animals and plants—all of creation suddenly had two names: an Indian name and a white name. Christianity separated the people from themselves; it tried to crush the single clan name, encouraging each person to stand alone, because Jesus Christ would save only the individual soul; Jesus Christ was not like the Mother who loved and cared for them as her children, as her family.

The sensitivity remained: the ability to feel what the others were feeling in the belly and chest; words were not necessary, but the messages the people felt were confused now. When Little Sister had started drinking wine and riding in cars with white men and Mexicans, the people could not define their feeling about her. The Catholic priest shook his finger at the drunkenness and lust, but the people felt something deeper: they were losing her, they were losing part of themselves. The older sister had to act; she had to act for the people, to get this young girl back.

It might have been possible if the girl had not been ashamed of herself. Shamed by what they taught her in school about the deplorable ways of the Indian people; holy missionary white people who wanted only good for the Indians, white people who dedicated their lives to helping the Indians, these people urged her to break away from her home. She was excited to see that despite the fact she was an Indian, the white men smiled at her from their cars as she walked from the bus stop in Albuquerque back to the Indian School. She smiled and waved; she looked at her own reflection in windows of houses she passed; her dress, her lipstick, her hair—it was all done perfectly, the way the home-ec teacher taught them, exactly like the white girls.

But after she had been with them, she could feel the truth in their fists and in their greedy feeble love-making; but it was a truth which she had no English words for. She hated the people at home when white people talked about their peculiarities; but she always hated herself more because she still thought about them, because she knew their pain at what she was doing with her life. The feelings of shame, at her own people and at the white people, grew inside her, side by side like monstrous twins that would have to be left in the hills to die. The people wanted her back. Her older sister must bring her back. For the people, it was that simple, and when they failed, the humiliation fell on all of them; what happened to the girl did not happen to her alone, it happened to all of them.

They focused the anger on the girl and her family, knowing from many years of this conflict that the anger could not be contained by a single person or family, but that it must leak out and soak into the ground under the entire village.

So Auntie had tried desperately to reconcile the family with the people; the old instinct had always been to gather the feelings and opinions that were scattered through the village, to gather them like willow twigs and tie them into a single prayer bundle that would bring peace to all of them. But now the feelings were twisted, tangled roots, and all the names for the source of this growth were buried under English words, out of reach. And there would be no peace and the people would have no rest until the entanglement had been unwound to the source.

HE could anticipate her mood by watching her face. She had a special look she gave him when she wanted to talk to him alone. He never forgot the strange excitement he felt when she looked at him that way, and called him aside.

"Nobody will ever tell you this," she said, "but you must hear it so you will understand why things are this way." She was referring to the distance she kept between him and herself. "Your uncle and grandma don't know this story. I couldn't tell them because it would hurt them so much." She swallowed hard to clear the pain from her throat, and his own throat hurt too, because without him there would have not been so much shame and disgrace for the family.

"Poor old Grandma. It would hurt her so much if she ever heard this story." She looked at Tayo and picked a thread off the bottom of her apron. Her mouth was small and tight when she talked to him alone. He sat on a gunny sack full of the corn that Robert and Josiah had dried last year, and when he shifted his weight even slightly, he could hear the hard kernels move. The room was always cool, even in the summertime, and it smelled like the dried apples in flour sacks hanging above them from the rafters. That day he could smell the pale, almost blue clay the old women used for plastering the walls.

"One morning," she said, "before you were born, I got up to go outside, right before sunrise. I knew she had been out all night because I never heard her come in. Anyway, I thought I would walk down toward the river. I just had a feeling, you know. I stood on that sandrock, above the big curve in the river, and there she was, coming down the trail on the other side." She looked at him closely. "I am only telling you this because she was your mother, and you have to understand." She cleared her throat. "Right as the sun came up, she walked under that big cottonwood tree, and I could see her clearly: she had no clothes on. Nothing. She was completely naked except for her high-heel shoes. She dropped her purse under that tree. Later on some kids found it there and brought it back. It was empty except for a lipstick." Tayo swallowed and took a breath.

"Auntie," he said softly, "what did she look like before I was born?"

She reached behind the pantry curtains and began to rearrange the jars of peaches and apricots on the shelves, and he knew she was finished talking to him. He closed the storeroom door behind him and went to the back room and sat on the bed. He sat for a long time and thought about his mother. There had been a picture of her once, and he had carried the tin frame to bed with him at night, and whispered to it. But one evening, when he carried it with him, there were visitors in the kitchen, and she grabbed it away from him. He cried for it and Josiah came to comfort him; he asked Tayo why he was crying, but just as he was ashamed to tell Josiah about the understanding between him and Auntie, he also could not tell him about the picture; he loved Josiah too much to admit the shame. So he held onto Josiah tightly, and pressed his face into the flannel shirt and smelled woodsmoke and sheep's wool and sweat. He even forgot about the picture except sometimes when he tried to remember how she looked. Then he wished Auntie would give it back to him to keep on top of Josiah's dresser. But he could never bring himself to ask her. The day in the storeroom, when he asked how his mother had looked before he was born, was the closest he'd ever come to mentioning the picture.

"So that's where our mother went.
How can we get down there?"

Hummingbird looked at all the
skinny people.
He felt sorry for them.
He said, "You need a messenger.
Listen, I'll tell you
what to do":

Bring a beautiful pottery jar
painted with parrots and big
flowers.
Mix black mountain dirt
some sweet corn flour
and a little water.

Cover the jar with a
new buckskin
and say this over the jar
and sing this softly
above the jar:
After four days
you will be alive
After four days
you will be alive
After four days
you will be alive
After four days
you will be alive

THE Army recruiter looked closely at Tayo's light brown skin and his hazel eyes.

"You guys are brothers?"

Rocky nodded coolly.

"If you say so," the recruiter said. It was beginning to get dark and he wanted to get back to Albuquerque.

Tayo signed his name after Rocky. He felt light on his feet, happy that he would be with Rocky, traveling the world in the Army, together, as brothers. Rocky patted him on the back, smiling too.

"We can do real good, Tayo. Go all over the world. See different places and different people. Look at that guy, the recruiter. He's got his own Government car to drive, too."

But when he saw the house and Josiah's pickup parked in the yard, he remembered. The understanding had always been that Rocky would be the one to leave home, go to college or join the Army. But someone had to stay and help out with the garden and sheep camp. He had made a promise to Josiah to help with the Mexican cattle. He stopped. Rocky asked him what was wrong.

"I can't go," he said. "I told Josiah I'd stay and help him."

"Him and Robert can get along."

"No," Tayo said, feeling the hollow spread from his stomach to his chest, his heart echoing in his ears. "No."

Rocky walked on without him; Tayo stood there watching the darkness descend. He was familiar with that hollow feeling. He remembered it from the nights after they had buried his mother, when he stuffed the bed covers around his stomach and close to his heart, hugging the blankets into the empty space of loss, regret for things which could not be changed.

"Let him go," Josiah said, "you can't keep him forever."

Auntie let the lid on the frying pan clatter on top of the stove.

"Rocky is different," she kept saying, "but this one, he's supposed to stay here."

"Let him go," old Grandma said. "They can look after each other, and bring each other home again."

Rocky dunked his tortilla in the chili beans and kept chewing; he didn't care what they said. He was already thinking of the years ahead and the new places and people that were wait-ing for him in the future he had lived for since he first began to believe in the word "someday" the way white people do.

"I'll bring him back safe," Tayo said softly to her the night before they left. "You don't have to worry." She looked up from her Bible, and he could see that she was waiting for some-thing to happen; but he knew that she always hoped, that she always expected it to happen to him, not to Rocky.

Paule Marshall

PAULE MARSHALL (1929–   ) is the author of several major
works of fiction, *Brown Girl, Brownstones* (1959), *Soul Clap
Hands and Sing* (1961), *The Chosen Place, the Timeless People* (1969), *Praisesong for the Widow* (1983), and *Reena and
Other Stories* (1983).

In a 1982 interview, "Talk as a Form of Action" with Sabine
Brock, published in *History and Tradition in Afro-American
Culture* (1984), Marshall notes that

> there was nowhere in the literature where I could turn where I saw
> not myself so much reflected but young women like myself re-
> flected. Gradually, I mean these things were not conscious, in
> some deep inner place I began wanting to attempt . . . to get
> something of the reality and texture and meaning of their life
> down on paper. . . . I was very much taken with [Gwendolyn
> Brooks's] *Maud Martha* because I think she in a sense was a truly
> vanguardal breaththrough character in American literature in the
> sense that Brooks took the life of a terribly ordinary young woman
> and made it something of art. . . . I sensed that this was the kind of
> thing I would attempt when I started writing: to say that there was
> something of worth, something to celebrate, that there was some-
> thing to acknowledge about the life of women who had been sim-
> ply dismissed by society.

Paule Marshall's *Praisesong for the Widow* (1983) is a heroic journey of rediscovery, reexamination, recovery, and ultimately redefinition of place and self. Avey Johnson, a Black
middle-aged, middle-class suburban widow, sets out on a Caribbean cruise following the death of her husband, Jay. Instead of
relaxation and healing, Avey Johnson undergoes a self-examina-

tion in dreams and at the hands of a spiritual father who asks her, "And what you is? What's your nation?"

In the process of her answering, she understands the price paid for acceptance was a loss of history, place, identity:

> Something vivid and affirming and charged with feeling had been present in the small rituals that had once shaped their lives. . . . something in those small rites, and ethos they held in common, had reached back beyond her life and beyond Jay's to join them to the vast unknown lineage that had made their being possible.

For any widow left alone to define her life alone, the cliché is that the future is unknown and undefined. What Avey Johnson finds is that the past is unknown and forgotten, and even actively relinquished, as was her Harlem childhood. Before she can define her future and herself, she must define her past. Her journey to the past is inheritance—an inheritance of the heroic African praisesong, her West Indian African American roots, perhaps simply the naming of names:

> All that was left were a few names of what they called nations which they could no longer even pronounce properly, the fragments of a dozen or so songs, the shadowy forms of long-ago dances and rum kegs for drums. The bare bones. The burnt-out ends. And they clung to them with a tenacity she suddenly loved in them and longed for in herself. Thoughts—new thoughts—vague and half-formed slowly beginning to fill the emptiness.

In her own name she is reminded that her great-aunt insisted that she call herself not Avey, but Avatara. The name itself is answer for the "half-formed" emptiness, and it identifies the familiar, the well-defined, and above all, the rooted.

—Shawn Wong

Chapters 1 and 2 from
PRAISESONG FOR THE WIDOW

1

"WHAT the devil's gotten into you, woman?"

He stood breathing his annoyance down on her from the foot of the recliner, his figure in the dark three-piece business suit blocking out the afternoon sun and causing a premature dusk to fall on the balcony.

Avey Johnson could not see his face—she had no wish to; it was enough to imagine the deep scowl there—but the white lambskin apron and the white gloves he had been buried in as a Master Mason stood out sharply in the false dusk. He seemed taller than she remembered him and more severe.

"Do you know what you're playing around with?"

He meant the money: the fifteen hundred dollars she had just forfeited by walking off the ship; the air fare she would have to turn around and spend tomorrow; the cost of the hotel room tonight. From the anxiety in his voice, she could tell he was including other, more important things. "Do you know what you're playing around with?" said in that tone also meant the house in North White Plains and the large corner lot on which it stood, and the insurance policies, annuities, trusts and bank accounts that had been left her, as well as the small sheaf of government bonds and other securities which were now also hers, and most of all the part interest guaranteed her for life in the modest accounting firm on Fulton Street in Brooklyn which bore his name. The whole of his transubstantiated body and blood. All of it he seemed to feel had been thrown into jeopardy by her reckless act.

"You must want to wind up back where we started."

He meant Halsey Street. Whenever there had been a discussion between them about money, whenever they had argued, in fact, he had never failed, no matter what the argument was about, to bring up the subject of Halsey Street, holding it like the Sword of Damocles over everything they had accomplished.

He never referred to it by name. It was always "back where we started" or "back you know where," refusing to let the name so much as cross his lips—although his refusal only served ironically to bring the street and the fifth floor walkup where they had lived for twenty years more painfully to mind.

Like someone unable to recover from a childhood trauma— hunger, injury, abuse, a parent suddenly and inexplicably gone—Jerome Johnson never got over Halsey Street. When she had long purged her thoughts and feelings of the place, and had come to regard the years there as having been lived by someone other than herself, it continued to haunt him, and to figure in some way in nearly everything he did.

It was Halsey Street, for example, which prompted him— over her objections—to build an additional pantry in the house in North White Plains, which he kept stocked with enough canned goods to last out a war. That street in Brooklyn accounted for the raft of insurance policies he took out to cover everything—fire, theft, life, loss of limb—that might happen to them or the house. It was also Halsey Street, and specifically the block they had lived on, with its noisy trolley and the knot of old tenements down the street from their apartment house, which kept him going at the same unrelenting pace long after his business was firmly established, both mortgages on the house had been paid up and Marion, their youngest, was out of college, teaching, on her own.

And it was Halsey Street finally which caused him the night before his last stroke to cry out, appalled, in his sleep as he lay in the bed next to hers, "Do you know who you sound like, who you even look like . . . ?" He was repeating for the last time the question which had plagued his sleep for years, which he had first asked her all the way back on a Tuesday evening in the winter of '47. That was the night when it appeared that the ruin and defeat steadily overtaking the block had reached their walkup and was about to lay claim to them also.

She had been eight months pregnant with Marion at the time. Far too soon for it to have happened again. Annawilda wasn't even two yet, and Sis, who had been born the year after Jay came out of the army, would only be five her next birthday. Too soon. Moreover, she had only just started back to work a few months ago. As she had done before with Sis, the moment Annawilda was weaned she began leaving the two of them with the middle-aged West Indian widow down the block who minded children by the day and had returned to her job as a Grade II clerk with the State.

She tried everything in the beginning: the scalding hot baths, castor oil, the strong cups of fennel root tea she had learned about from her mother. She bought the unmarked packet of small brown pills in the drugstore and swallowed them all at one time. She douched one day until it seemed her entire insides had been flushed down the bathtub drain. And as she lay there exhausted with no sign of the hoped-for blood, she actually considered for a moment going back on the promise she had made to herself at the death of her friend, Grace, with whom she had graduated from high school. (Grace had found somebody somewhere and had had it done, and her death from a massive hemorrhage afterwards had made Avey promise herself "never that.") Another day, while Jay was at work and the children asleep, she raced up and down the five flights of stairs between their apartment on the top floor and the vestibule. For close to a half-hour she practically took and hurled her body down the steep steps and then up again, down and up repeatedly until she finally collapsed on the landing outside their door. All to no avail.

Jay's face when she told him had mirrored everything she felt. After a long despairing silence he had started to say something, to ask a question which she easily read in his eyes, and then he had quickly checked himself, also remembering Grace, who had been part of the crowd they went around with when they first married and still lived in Harlem. The question remained unasked, but as the months went by and she started to show, his eyes began to shy helplessly away from her stomach. She also avoided the sight of it in the mirror. By her sixth month she was so large she was forced to give up her job again.

Jay by then had started putting in longer hours at the small department store in downtown Brooklyn where he worked in the shipping room, as the assistant to the man in charge. Long after the store had closed he would still not be home. A backlog of orders had kept him. A truckload of merchandise had arrived just at closing time and he had stayed to check it in. They were doing inventory. The boss had asked him to work late again. There had been a large shipment to prepare for the next morning.

There was no reason to doubt him. The shipping room often remained in operation after the store itself had closed. And he had worked overtime before. Yet, as his lateness grew to be a regular thing and his look when he was home became more evasive and closed, as she was reduced to spending her evenings after the children were asleep wandering about the cramped apartment, staring at the place in front of the kitchen sink where the linoleum had worn through to the floorboards or at the clothes in the bedroom closet she could no longer fit into, something shattered in her mind. It seemed the china bowl which held her sanity and trust fell from its shelf in her mind and broke, and another reason for his lateness began to take shape in her thoughts with the same slow and inevitable accretion of detail as the child in her womb.

She began seeing them: the white salesgirls at the store (it would be years before they started hiring colored), the younger ones with their flat stomachs and unswollen breasts and their hair swept up on a rat into a pompadour or combed so it hung over one side of the face *à la* Veronica Lake. They were behind every counter in the stores downtown. Girls from Flatbush and Bensonhurst and Bay Ridge, who had to paint the lipstick above the natural line of their lips to give them the fullness they lacked, whose loose, flat-cheeked behinds suggested Jell-O that had not yet set.

No, it was probably someone closer to her age, in her mid-twenties or older even, a woman whose husband might have been killed in the war. Someone like that would be more likely to appeal to him.

Pacing the small rooms each evening, her mind a pile of angry shards, she began blaming them. They had long been intrigued by him. There was the reputation he had acquired around the store of being hard-working, efficient, dependable. His was the kind of highly organized mind and photographic memory which permitted him to keep track of practically every piece of merchandise that came and went on the trucks for the day. It was Jay, the salesgirls secretly knew, as did everyone else in the store, who actually ran shipping and receiving and not the Irishman in charge, although he had to be careful not to make it appear so.

"Two jobs for the salary of one," he would say at home, trying sometimes to laugh it off. "They really got themselves a good thing in me."

At work he would be so absorbed in what he was doing he would scarcely notice the salesgirls when they came into the shipping room on one pretext or another. The bolder ones would stop to chat, insisting that he take heed of them, and he would be friendly enough, exchanging the usual light banter with them, gracing them with his smile, but his mind they could tell would all the while be on the sheaf of orders and invoices in his hand.

He wasn't at all the way a colored guy was supposed to be! (She could almost hear them thinking it.) Where were his jokes and his loud talk? Where his thrilling, deep-throated nigger laugh to send the terror and delight rippling like arpeggios over their flesh? Why didn't he play the clown, act the fool, do a buck-and-wing in appreciation of their interest? Or at least roll his eyes until only the whites showed like Mantan Moreland in the movies?

"And what's wit' the mustache a'ready?"—saying it to themselves in the hopeless Brooklynese they spoke. That, more than anything else about him she was certain, puzzled, irritated and at the same time held them in thrall. Now there was nothing unusual about a colored man having a mustache. But Jay had not been satisfied to copy the somewhat modest style of the day. Instead, he had gone to the sepia-colored photograph of his father in the family album they had started compiling, and as a kind of tribute perhaps had taken as his model the full, broad-winged mustache the older man had sported around World War I.

Jay didn't wear his quite as full. The shape was the same, with the thickness that more than filled the space above his lip tapering off into a pair of wings that curled down at the tips to embrace the corners of his mouth. And there was the same distinctive, slightly rakish look to it.

To care for the mustache he kept on a shelf in the medicine cabinet a small tortoiseshell rake, a diminutive pair of surgical scissors, a tiny brush and a vial of light, delicately scented oil, a drop of which he would apply when finished to give it a faint gloss. Most of his time in the bathroom each morning was spent fussing with it. And once a month he took the subway back to his old neighborhood in Harlem to have it properly trimmed and groomed by his favorite barber.

The mustache was his one show of vanity, his sole indulgence. It was also, Avey sensed, a shield as well, because planted in a thick bush above his mouth, it subtly drew attention away from the intelligence of his gaze and the assertive, even somewhat arrogant arch to his nostrils, thus protecting him. And it also served to screen his private self: the man he was away from the job.

If the salesgirls only knew what he was like at home! (Or had been like before this latest blow.) The change that came over him from the moment he stepped in the door! His first act after greeting her was to turn up the volume on the phonograph which would already be playing their favorite records. Then, as if it was something apart from him, the sore spent body of a friend perhaps, he would lower his tall frame into the armchair, lean his head back, close his eyes, and let Coleman Hawkins, The Count, Lester Young (old Prez himself), The Duke— along with the singers he loved: Mr. B., Lady Day, Lil Green, Ella—work their magic, their special mojo on him. Until gradually, under their ministrations, the fatigue and strain of the long day spent doing the two jobs—his and his boss's—would ease from his face, and his body as he sat up in the chair and stretched would look as if it belonged to him again.

Some days called for the blues. Those evenings coming in he didn't even stop to take off his coat or hat before going to the closet in their bedroom, where at the back of the top shelf he kept the old blues records in an album that was almost falling apart. The records, all collector's items, had been left him by his father, who had been a scout for Okeh Records in the twenties. The names on the yellowed labels read Ida Cox, Ma Rainey, Big Bill Broonzy, Mamie Smith . . .

In his hands the worn-out album with its many leaves became a sacred object, and each record inside an icon. So as not to risk harming them he never stacked them together on the machine, but played them individually, using the short spindle. A careful ritual went into dusting each one off, then gently lowering it onto the turntable, sliding the lever to "on" and finally, delicately, setting the needle in place.

And he never, no matter how exhausted he was, sat down when listening to the blues records. As the voices rose one after the other out of the primitive recordings to fill the apartment, he would remain standing, head bowed, in front of the phonograph.

"You can't keep a good man down," Mamie Smith sang on the oldest and most priceless of the 78s. He always saved this one for the last. By the time it ended and he carefully replaced it in the album with the others, his head would have come up and the tension could almost be seen slipping from him like the coat or jacket he would still have on falling from his shoulders to the floor. He would be ready then, once the album was back on its shelf in the bedroom closet, to sit and listen to the other records.

The Jay who emerged from the music of an evening, the self that would never be seen down at the store, was open, witty, playful, even outrageous at times: he might suddenly stage an impromptu dance just for the two of them in the living room, declaring it to be Rockland Palace or the Renny. And affectionate: his arms folding around her from behind when she least expected them, the needful way he spoke her name even when they quarreled—"Avey . . . Avey, would you just shut up a minute!" And passionate: a lover who knew how to talk to a woman in bed.

If the salesgirls only knew his passion at times! But they weren't stupid. They had sensed something of the other Jay behind that carefully protected public self. The little veiled knowing smile he treated them to when they stopped to chat,

the mustache with its dramatic air, the arch to his nostrils—
these things alerted them. They had spied the lover in him, and
in their fantasies would draw his lips under the shapely bush of
hair down to theirs and wrap their pallid flesh in the rich seal-
skin brown of his body.

They had long made up their minds to have him! And finally
one day, the day perhaps when she first started to show and his
eyes began avoiding her stomach, he had turned from his work
when the one favored came over (the somewhat older woman,
surely), and the look he had given her, his smile, had spoken
quietly of what he could be like at other times, in a more private
place.

The first time she accused him he stared at her for an in-
credulous moment and then burst out laughing. "I've got
enough women for the moment, thank you," he said. "There's
you first of all, and you're easily a dozen women in one. Then
the two ladies inside"—he waved toward the bedroom at the
back of the apartment where the children were asleep. "And
what's probably another young lady on her way . . ." The wave
took in her swollen middle, although his eyes didn't follow it
there. "That's more than enough women for one poor colored
man—at least," he added with a wink, "for the time being."

That was the first and last time he joked about it. On subsequent evenings when, incensed by his lateness, she brought it
up again, he tried reasoning with her; tried calming her. Would
he be so foolish as to risk losing the job over one of those silly
white girls down at the store? Or worse, risk finding himself
down at the bottom of the East River tied to a ton of concrete
when her father or older brother found out? Brooklyn might be
the North but it wasn't all that different from Kansas (he had
been born and raised there) when it came to such matters and
there were more ways to lynch a colored man other than from a
tree. Besides, with all the worries he had the furthest thing
from his mind was the thought of some other woman.

Or where, he argued at other times, did she think he was
getting the money to pay all the bills on his own now that they
were missing her salary, if he wasn't actually putting in the
extra hours? Did he suddenly have to start bringing home his
pay envelope unopened as proof? Didn't she realize he needed

all the overtime he could get if they were to keep afloat? "I mean, be reasonable, Avey, it's rough on me too."

Part of her saw the logic of this. That part also knew, perhaps better than he did, that it wasn't really a question of some woman, real or imagined. Even if she did exist, she was merely the stand-in for the real villain whom they couldn't talk about, who stood cooly waiting for them amid the spreading blight of Halsey Street below. And there didn't seem to be any escaping him. It was as if the five flights of stairs from their apartment to the street had become the giant sliding pond inside Steeplechase Park at Coney Island which she remembered from her childhood, and that she and Jay had already begun the inevitable long slide down.

All this she understood, but her understanding did nothing to contain her rage. She continued over the weeks to accuse him, helpless to stop herself as her ballooning stomach and the oncoming winter and the increasingly treacherous climb down the stairs kept her confined all day with the children to the four small rooms on the top floor.

Finally, an exasperated Jay ceased trying to reason with her, and took to answering her outbursts when he came in with a stubborn silence and the usual averted gaze.

Until that fateful Tuesday night during her eighth month.

It had snowed all day, the first heavy snowfall of the winter. A strong wind had accompanied the snow, piling it in great drifts up the high stoops of the brownstone houses on the block and plastering it over the ravaged fronts of the tenements. By the time evening came Halsey Street looked as though a huge dust cover had been flung over it to hide the evidence of its decay.

The snow also muffled the clang of the trolley which continued to run despite the storm and the rattle of the chains on the tires of the occasional passing car. The silence outdoors only served to magnify the sounds inside the apartment as Avey, the children in bed, took up her angry vigil on a chair at the living room window.

The ticking of the clock, whose every stroke added to his lateness, seemed louder. The knocking in the pipes as the meager heat struggled to reach the top floor was more maddening than ever. (The radiators had been only lukewarm since morning, so that in addition to the kerosene burner they used to supplement the heat, she had had to keep the oven of the gas stove lighted all day.) Loudest of all in the silence the snow had brought was the coughing of Sis and Annawilda in the back bedroom. It was a sound heard all winter. One night, she feared, one of them would quietly choke to death on the phlegm trapped in her throat while she and Jay slept.

The child inside her would fall heir to the same winter-long cold. All the cod liver oil, orange juice, Scott's Emulsion and the like she fed it, all the sweaters she piled on its small body even at night, would not prevent the rattling cough and the clogged asthmatic breathing once winter settled into the porous brick of the aging building like "the misery" into the bones of the old.

In the room they went to after work the radiator threw off the heat in visible waves, creating a summer of warm shimmering light and air for them behind the drawn shades. It was so warm in the room there was never a need for a blanket. They would even fling off the top sheet, and laugh as it snapped and billowed like a sail above their nakedness before falling to the floor.

Suddenly she was struggling to her feet, and the restless pacing that was a nightly ritual began. Even though her ankles had been swollen for some weeks now, she still spent the better part of each evening wandering from one room to the other.

She usually followed a set path. From the living room overlooking Halsey Street her lumbering steps would take her through the short passageway that led past the kitchen and bathroom crowded together in the middle of the apartment to the door of the children's room, which she always left half open. After listening in despair to their breathing she would return to the front of the house, and drift into the narrow hallway bedroom off the living room where she and Jay slept. (They had given the children the larger room to the back, away from the noise of the trolley.)

Some nights she was scarcely conscious of being on her feet or of the endless trudging back and forth, until she would feel the child inside her begin to twist and tumble against the wall of her belly, as if made nervous by her seething thoughts. Or she would be brought to herself by a sudden racket under her feet, as the old man downstairs, who complained constantly about the noise the children made over his head, would start banging with a broom handle—or perhaps it was the cane he used—on his ceiling.

That Tuesday night, more agitated than usual, she suddenly broke off the pacing once she reached the hallway bedroom, and first yanking on the ceiling light and then pulling open the door to the closet, she planted herself in front of the full-length mirror on the inside of the door, and for the first time in months actually looked at herself.

The beige chenille robe she had had to wear all day over her clothes to keep warm could no longer be buttoned beyond the third one down. And there was an orange stain on the collar where Annawilda, tiring of the mashed carrots she was feeding her for lunch, had sprayed her with a mouthful. (Forgetting herself, she had slapped her sharply on the leg, and then had had to walk her in her arms for a half-hour before she quieted down.) On her water-logged feet was a pair of Jay's old slippers, the only things she could fit into now. And had she remembered to comb her hair that morning? She stole a furtive glance upward. It didn't appear so.

Who—*who*—was this untidy swollen woman with the murderous look? What man wouldn't avert his gaze or try to shut out the sight of her in someone else's flesh? Even the clothes hanging next to her in the closet, which she could see at an angle in the mirror, appeared to have turned aside from her image. The dark green pleated skirt she glimpsed at the end of the rack had been bought during the one brief year she had gone to college—the first year they were married, while Jay was in the army—taking classes in general studies at Long Island University in the evenings after work. She had thought of herself as a coed and had bought the skirt, and kept it although it was over six years old. The brown tailored suit there she had worn the day she had attended her first union meeting as an organizer of the clerical workers in her section of the Motor Vehicle Bureau. Tuesday, she suddenly remembered with an enraged pang, was the day the meetings were usually held. And the teal blue dress hanging beside it she had worn to work along

with her high-heeled shoes and her hair done in a flawless page-
boy no more than four months ago . . .

In the warm pool of light from the lamp beside the bed, the
woman's stomach was flat, smooth, a snow-white plain, with the
navel like a tiny signpost pointing to the silken forest below. Jay
could not get over the flatness. Stroking it, he would tell her—
his mouth against her ear, her lips—what it did to him, how it
moved him. Talking as his hand slowly and with the lightest
touch moved down. Until, under his caress and the quiet power
of his voice, the woman would cry out and pull him down be-
tween her arched, widespread legs.

Her own legs in the next three or four weeks would find
themselves in the same position: raised, bent, open wide. But it
would not be that lovely flowering gesture of arousal and invitation. Nor would her cries be those of ecstasy. Moreover, on the
other side of the sheet they would have flung over her knees,
her feet would be strapped into the stirrups at the bottom of
the table. And although she would beg them not to do it, her
hands would be tied as usual to the long bars on either side.

There was the sound of glass on the verge of falling and
shattering as she slammed the closet door and left the room.
Out in the living room, her mind inflamed, she resumed her
heavy-footed prowling.

What if she had a difficult time with this one, as had been
true with Sis. Then, her arms already bound at her sides, she
had been left to lie for hours screaming up into the antiseptic
lights of the labor room. From time to time the nurse had
appeared to feel the high mound of her stomach and to chide
her about the noise. And the doctor the few times he came
simply repeated after examining her that she wasn't ready yet.
It had taken ten hours in all.

And how would she make it down those stairs? The thought
brought her to a standstill on the cold floorboards. The last
time, with Annawilda, it had taken three people—Jay, the doctor and the ambulance driver—to maneuver her unwieldy body
down the five flights. It had been like lowering a stricken
climber, his bulky clothes frozen solid on him, down a snow-
covered mountain.

This time she might not even make it down to the street and

the waiting ambulance. This time when her water broke, Jay might be at work or—and she trembled with rage at the thought—lying somewhere with the woman's legs locked around him. She would have to send Sis to ask a neighbor to go to the candy store up on Broadway and call the ambulance. But by the time all this was done and the ambulance arrived it might be too late. The head might present itself even as they were bringing her down the stairs. She would find herself giving birth on one of the dim landings, with her screams and curses echoing from the top floor to the street, terrifying the children.

2

THAT Tuesday night she met him in a fury at the door.

As he had done so often over the past four or five months, Jay simply stood and heard her out in silence for a time, the windblown snow on his hat and overcoat and flecked on his mustache, and on his haggard face, in his evasive eyes the look of someone who carried a weight on his spirit that was as heavy in its way as the child in her womb.

She bet it was nice and warm where he'd just come from. Their little hideaway. That wasn't some dump where you had to keep the stove on all day so's not to freeze to death. No, the love nest had heat all the time. Why didn't he just stay there? Why bother coming home at all? Shouting it at him. Brooklyn. She hated it! Why couldn't he have found a job in the City? She was somebody who was used to the City. Everybody she knew was there. She couldn't even get to see or talk to her mother. She should never have moved with him to this godforsaken place. Should never have let him stick her up on some freezing top floor having a baby every time she looked around. Should never have married him . . .

Normally he would have turned from her by then and gone to hang up his damp coat in the bathroom or to sit in a chair, his head bowed, till she was done. And he did start to move away, but as if the knife edge in her voice tonight had finally succeeded in cutting away whatever it was that had kept his own anger in check over the months, he stopped and, suddenly hurling the newspaper in his hand to the floor, began shouting also.

No sooner did his voice erupt than a small figure appeared at the head of the passageway. On all the other evenings when only her mother was to be heard in the living room, Sis had not stirred. But the sound of Jay answering back at last, and with the same if not greater fury in his voice, had brought her at a run from the back bedroom.

Wearing a sweater over her pajamas and woolen socks, she hung for a moment in the opening, fear written on the face which everyone said had taken the best from them both. Then, cautiously, she started across the living room, and coming to a halt just outside their raging circle, she quietly asked them to stop. Like a mediator seeking to introduce a note of reasonableness and calm, Sis pleaded with them to be still, not realizing that she couldn't be heard in the hailstorm of recriminations filling the room. The two quarreling weren't even aware of her presence. Abandoning the quiet tone after a time, she tried ordering them: "Stop shouting, do you hear me! Stop it!"— growing angry herself now. Until finally, in tears, she started hitting them. Rushing wildly back and forth between them—a referee who had become part of the fight—she pummeled first one and then the other with her fists.

Sis dealt her ineffectual little blows, and from her crib in the bedroom, a terrified Annawilda sent up the ear-splitting shriek, which she could sustain for what seemed hours without taking a breath. Even the unborn child was in an agitated state. Dimly, in the hysteria overtaking her, Avey felt it pounding away with its little watery limbs on the wall of her stomach like an outraged neighbor in a next-door apartment protesting the noise.

". . . cooped up all day looking at the beat-up linoleum in that closet of a kitchen . . ." She was scarcely conscious anymore of what she was saying.

"Okay," he cried, "you go take my job at the store then! Go on. Go on down there and see how you like working for some red-faced Irishman who sits on his can all day laughing to himself at the colored boy he's got doing everything . . ." His anger was such his nostrils were arched high and quivering and the muscles along his jawline were as hard and prominent as bone under his dark skin. He was fed up with her complaints and criticism and suspicions. She didn't appreciate when someone was trying their best. It was her attitude more than anything else that was making them so miserable. A year of college and she thought she was somebody. A prima donna from Seventh Avenue in Harlem. He should have left her right there. Should have turned and run the other way when he saw her coming.

Finally, with their voices stranded on a peak from which they would never, it seemed, find the way down, an inflamed and trembling Avey stepped to within inches of him. One hand was raised to strike him. The other hand had grabbed the distraught Sis and was holding her fiercely to her side. The huge belly thrust forward defiantly, and she was screaming in his face, *"Goddamn you, nigger, I'll take my babies and go!"*

It took some time in the silence that fell for Jay to find his voice again, and when he did it was scarcely audible. "Do you know who you sound like," he whispered, choked, appalled, "who you even look like?"

There was no need for him to elaborate. She knew who he meant. They had both watched any number of times the woman he was referring to as she opened the drama that took place nearly every Saturday morning on the sidewalk below their bedroom window.

Sometime between midnight and dawn, when Halsey Street stood empty and the trolley had all but ceased to run, the woman, who was not much older than herself, would be seen leaving the cluster of three or four tenements which had already given way to the ruin slowly overtaking the rest of the block.

Out of the wide-open front door with its broken lock, past the overflowing garbage cans at the gate, she would come, a housedress thrown over her nightgown in the summer, a rag of a coat on in winter, the headtie she slept in still on, railing loudly to herself, waking the street, the dialogue already under way. Up past the one- and two-family brownstones and their still presentable-looking walkup she would charge, headed for Broadway and the string of beer gardens which peeped out from the darkness under the El like the eyes of the Gold Dust twins on the boxes of soap powder.

By the time she found him, the rotgut in the false-bottom glass would have already eaten into his Friday's pay. And his buddies whom he had set up repeatedly at the bar would have drunk their share of it. The same for the fly young thing perched on the stool next to his, with her powder and store-bought hair and paste diamond rings. She too would have had hers by then.

". . . Spending your money on some stinking 'ho . . . !" *whose brains are red jelly stuck between 'lizabeth Taylor's toes . . .*

("Oh-oh, here come your folks again, Jay." "*My folks?* Who told you I was colored, woman? I'm just passing to see what it feels like." Vaudeville-like jokes which they sprinkled like juju powders around the bed to protect them. Jokes with the power of the Five Finger Grass Avey's great-aunt Cuney used to hang above the door of the house in Tatem to keep trouble away.)

Down the five stories from their bedroom the woman's voice—loud, aggrieved, unsparing—did violence to the stillness as she herded the man, stumbling along in surly compliance just ahead of her, back down Halsey Street. He was a tall, solidly built man perhaps a few years Jay's senior. Occasionally, in the light of the streetlamps, his shoulders could be seen to flicker under the whiplash of her voice. Sometimes when her abuse became too much he would start around menacingly in his tracks: "Look, don't mess with me this morning . . ."

But she never left off telling him about himself—his no-'count, shiftless ways, his selfishness, his neglect of his own. ". . . Spending damn near your whole paycheck on some barfly and a bunch of good-timing niggers and your children's feet at the door . . ." She sent her grievances echoing up and down the deserted street, and strumming along the power line to the trolley, telegraphing them from one end of Brooklyn to the other. She acquainted the sleeping houses with her sorrow.

Her rage those dark mornings spoke not only for herself but for the thousands like her for blocks around, lying sleepless in the cold-water flats and one-room kitchenettes, the railroad apartments you could run a rat through and the firetraps above the stores on busy Fulton Street and Broadway; waiting, all of them, for some fool to come home with his sodden breath and half his pay envelope gone. Lying there enraged and vengeful, planning to put the chain on the door, change the lock first thing in the morning, have his clothes waiting out in the hall for him when he came lurching in at dawn. Or she'd be gone, her and the kids. She'd just take her babies and go! The place stripped of all sign of them when he got there. Vowing as she lay there straining to hear his unfocused step on the stairs and the key scratching blindly around the eye of the lock, that there would be no making up this time, no forgiving. This was one time he wasn't going to get around her with his pleas and apologies and talk, with his hands seeking out her breasts in the darkness. Not this morning! "Nigger, you so much as put a finger on me this morning and you'll draw back a nub!" Praying (Lord, please!) that he wouldn't turn on the light and simply stand there looking at her with his shamefaced self, his pain, until her love—or whatever it was she still felt for him—came down.

Some Saturdays the woman even made the five-story leap to the hallway bedroom to stand over Avey—or so she felt at times. Lying there next to Jay, listening to the voices from below, she would sense the woman's enraged presence on her side of the bed; would feel her accusing eyes in the darkness. Yeah, they saw, the eyes said, the way she always quickened her step when passing the house. They had seen her many a time from the upstairs window hurrying by with her nose in the air and her gaze trained straight ahead. She thought she was better. She didn't want anything to do with her kind. She couldn't wait till she could move from around them.

Standing over her, the woman also envied her for having found a Jay—steady, dependable, hard-working Jay—who didn't throw his money away in bars. With a man like that she had a chance to make it from Halsey Street. Where did they make his kind? How had she landed him? She wasn't anything all that much to speak of with her dark self and that rare lip of hers. Her hair didn't even cover her neck and it was far from what you'd call good. Lashing out at her for her luck.

Then, abruptly, her manner would change, her anger would vanish and, bending close to Avey, tears in her eyes, she would quietly beg her not to turn her back on them, not to forget those like herself stranded out there with the men who just wouldn't do right.

". . . What kinda man is you anyway, spending all your money on . . ."

"Goddamit, din' I tell ya don' mess with me this mornin'!"

He swung around, a hard palm raised, but the woman long anticipating his move leaned easily out of its way. And when he righted himself, after being thrown off balance by the missed blow, she gave him a light contemptuous shove forward, setting him on course again but also, at the same time, dismissing his threat. Because she knew his would be a different tune once she had him home, in bed, with her back turned to him like the Great Wall of China. He'd be sounding a whole lot different then: "Now, baby, why you wanna act like that? Gotcha back all turn to me and everything. I was only having a little taste with the fellas, that's all. A man works all week taking Charlie's shit he gots to relax hisself a little come the weekend. You know what it's like out there . . . Whore? What whore? You not gon' believe this, baby, but I don't even know that girl. She just somebody be 'round the bar. Come on, sugar. How'm I suppose to sleep with your sweet butt lyin' up here next to me? Lemme just res' a hand on it. You know you my weakness. Baby . . ."

> *Love in the garbage-strewn dawn,*
> *Above the jimmied mailboxes*
> *And the gaping front door; its aphrodisiac*
> *The smell of cat piss*
> > *on the cellar landing.*

"Goddamn you, nigger, I'll take my babies and go!"

Her cry that Tuesday made the scene they witnessed almost every weekend so vivid, it seemed that they had changed places with the two down in the street; had even become them. She was suddenly the half-crazed woman, her children left alone in the apartment, scouring the bars and beer gardens in her night-gown, and Jay was the derelict husband taking the wild swings at her under the streetlamps, the delinquent husband whom she would inevitably search the bars in vain for one night and never see again.

As if that inevitable night had already caught up with them, she thought she saw Jay take a slight step backwards. Without his actually moving, he appeared to be slowly backing toward the door to the hall which stood just a few feet behind him. Moving away from her and the tearful Sis, whom she still held pinned to her side, away from the huge melon of a stomach. And although he continued to stare appalled at her, his eyes gave the impression as he crept backwards of being tightly closed against the sight of his slippers on her feet and the chenille robe with the stain on the collar. His hands, the gloves still on them, appeared to be clapped over his ears to shut out Annawilda's prolonged shriek from the bedroom.

Any second and he would be at the door. A swift turn and he would have snatched it open. Before either she or Sis could think to run after him or find the voice to call him back, he would be racing down the stairs, taking them three and four at a time in his haste to be gone. The loud slam of the front door would reach them up the five flights. And the last they would see of him ever as they rushed to the window would be his dark figure in the overcoat fleeing up Halsey Street through the high snow.

As he stood there straining to make his escape, another force equally strong held him in place and even seemed to be trying to nudge him toward them. His anguished face, his eyes under the hat with the melted snow on the crown and brim reflected the struggle. He was like an embattled swimmer caught in the eye of two currents moving powerfully in opposite directions. That Tuesday night it was impossible to tell which one would ultimately claim him.

It appeared finally that the street had won. All of a sudden, in the interminable silence, there could be heard the faint scraping of his shoe on the floor, and one foot could actually now be seen moving back. One foot and then the other and he would have taken the first (and she was convinced) irreversible step toward the door.

Before the step could be completed, he stopped short with a kind of violence, the other current asserting its hold on him.

He drew himself up, tensing every muscle of his body to the point where it was clearly painful and he was trembling. Having steeled both his body and his will, he stepped forward, Jay stepped forward, and the sound of his tears as he held her and Sis, the strangeness of it in the small rooms, brought Annawilda's shrill cry to a startled halt for a moment.

John A. Williams

"I BECAME a writer by accident," John A. Williams has said. "I became a writer because I couldn't find a job. When I began the process of becoming a writer, it wasn't for the money and it wasn't for fame; it was to keep my sanity and to find some purpose in my life." Despite the various assaults on his sensibilities as a Black man and the vagaries of American publishers, editors, and academics, Williams has managed to realize both goals through his career as a prolific writer of both fiction and nonfiction.

In a personal essay he included in *Flashbacks: A Twenty-Year Diary of Article Writing* (1974), he began with this observation: "To be a writer who is Negro in America today is to be variously a figure of tragedy, satire and comedy. The situation hurts, it is bittersweet and is funny as hell, for writing after all is a very stupid compulsion." Williams exposes the machinations of this "bittersweet" situation—the gap between talent and recognition in Black artists—in a number of his works. His tone of critical political assessment typifies his best work in fiction and nonfiction. As critic Gilbert H. Mullen has noted, Williams personal and artistic worlds can never be apolitical; throughout his career Williams has artfully fleshed out "those points on the literary and historical map that have always been central to his vision: racism, exploitation, and oppression; characters on a collision course with history who seek nevertheless personal and political affirmations."

Born the oldest of four children on December 5, 1925, in Hinds County, Mississippi, John Alfred Williams grew up in Syracuse, New York, in the Fifteenth Ward, then a community composed of blacks, Jews, Italians, Irish, Poles, Indians, and others. "The people shared conversation and other small joys," Williams recalled in his autobiographical odyssey *This Is My Country Too* (1966), and "the religious holidays of all were greatly respected." For him the ward was home and the rest of Syracuse radiated outward from it. "It was a city within a city and at dusk the year around, you could see men in all sizes, shapes and colors returning to it from their jobs, such as they were." World War II interrupted Williams's high school education; in 1943 he joined the Navy and served in the Pacific, where he was disillusioned by racism in the military. He would later write about his experience in his sixth novel, *Captain Blackman* (1972). After receiving an honorable discharge in 1946, he returned to Syracuse to get married, and in that same year he graduated from high school and enrolled at Syracuse University. He received a B.A. in journalism and English in June 1950 and started graduate school (also at Syracuse, in English) right away. To support his family (he and his wife had two sons by now), he left graduate school in January 1951 and went to work in a foundry where he had worked earlier. A back injury forced him out of the foundry, so he took other jobs: supermarket clerk, caseworker at the Onondaga County Welfare Department, life insurance agent, staff member (publicity special events) for CBS and NBC TV, fund-raiser for the National Committee for a Sane Nuclear Policy.

Williams has said that his writing career began with the poetry he wrote when he was in the Pacific. As an exercise in imagery, rhythm, and sparseness, he liked poetry. But his professional career began with his writing for monthlies, dailies, and weeklies. He was a reporter (underpaid and without byline, he remembers) for the *Chicago Defender* and the *Syracuse Progressive Herald.* In 1958 he was a correspondent in Europe for *Ebony* and *Jet* magazines and the National Negro Press Association. He wrote print and radio advertising copy, publicity copy, and speeches, and once even put out his own weekly newsletter. In 1963 he traveled across the United States on a two-article assignment for *Holiday,* and the following year he traveled extensively in Europe, Africa, and the United States for *Newsweek.* These journeys and others greatly strengthened his fiction and his journalism. *This Is My Country Too* is an expansion of the *Holiday* assignment, and his personal experiences as a civil rights activist and a journalist for *Newsweek* inform other books, such as *Africa: Her History, Lands and People* (1963), an overview for young readers; and *The King God Didn't Save* (1970), both a comprehensive indictment of historical distortions of the life and death of Martin Luther King, Jr., and a philosophical inquiry into the making of American heroes.

All of John A. Williams's novels are, to some extent, autobiographical. *The Angry Ones* (1960), *Night Song* (1961), *Sissie* (1963), *The Man Who Cried I Am* (1967), *Sons of Darkness, Sons of Light* (1969), *Mothersill and the Foxes* (1975), *The Junior Bachelor Society* (1976), *!Click Song* (1982), *The Berhama Account* (1985), and *Jacob's Ladder* (1987) all articulate the vision of a writer who has embraced the challenge of integrating the public self and the private self, the public voice and the private voice in an effort to achieve wholeness in a modern world that can confuse, fragment, and destroy its inhabitants. The author never wanders far from actual facts and experiences with which he is closely familiar, and in *John A. Williams: The Evolution of a Black Writer* (1975), Earl A. Cash argues that Williams remains close to his immediate experiences because they are tragic enough that there is little need to turn elsewhere: "The admixture of fiction and fact (particularly well-known facts) by Williams furnishes his novels with an historical realism which adds more authenticity to nonfactual elements."

In further efforts to correct American history—which he feels has been "poorly illustrated for too long"—Williams has written a biography of Richard Wright for young readers, *The Most Native of Sons* (1970), and has edited several anthologies of Black writing, *The Angry Black* (1962), *Beyond the Angry Black* (1967), and *Amistad*, Volumes I and II, with Charles F. Harris (1970 and 1971). Williams has also held visiting professorships at City College of New York, the College of the Virgin Islands, and Boston University. He was Distinguished Professor at City University of New York from 1973 to 1977, and is currently Professor of English at Rutgers University, Newark.

—George Barlow

Chapter 1 from
!CLICK SONG

Hᴵˢ blue eyes twinkled slightly, and he extended his hand. "Paul Cummings."

"Cato Douglass." (Cato *Caldwell* Douglass. At home and in the marines they called me C.C.)

He was tall, tending toward gaunt, in his rumpled Eisenhower jacket, and his face was sharp with angles. He studied me; for a fraction of a second he seemed anxious and the next vaguely arrogant. I had met people like him before, the other, white marines, who chatted with you (seemingly secure in the knowledge that, even though you were a marine too, you were not *quite* like them) when their northbound ships stopped at our atoll, and then went away, leaving us to man our antiaircraft guns against Zeros that no longer came that far south. We had had our combat and had been written up in the magazines back home; we'd disgrace no one.

He rocked slightly and ran his hand through light brown hair that was longer than most men were wearing it.

He did not remember me, but I'd seen him in my Survey of Western Literature class. The hall teemed with people. Students answered the roll for friends who were cutting, and the instructor peering out over the mob, composed mainly of veterans, accepted any voice as proof of presence. I couldn't cut; I was the only black person in the class.

We talked of the branches we'd served in, our wives, the university—tentative touchings to see which kind of a relationship, if any, would work.

"This Professor Bark's supposed to be a pretty good writer."

"Oh, yeah?" I said. "Poetry?"

"Short stories. Mostly for *A.M.*"

"Ummm," I said. I didn't know what *A.M.* was.

He sensed that and said, *"Atlantic Monthly,"* without making me feel like a fool. "Are you a poet?"

"I write some but—"

"I do a lot of it myself," he said, treading confidently over my words. "But I think I'm ready for fiction."

A coed with honey-colored hair, and skin the complexion of unfrothed cream, walked briskly by, her buns rolling and swelling in fetching movements.

Paul's eyes followed her with a nonchalant lust. "We dreamed of women like that, right? I never saw anything like that in two years in Europe."

I wondered what his wife looked like and I wondered about him. I'd never known a white man who even implicitly was willing to share with a black man both women and career.

After that first class—in which Bark spattered the awkward silence with the question "Why do you want to be writers?" an asking that made us turn to the windows and look past each other until he, eyes filmed over with amusement, his tone barely hopeful, then asked, "Would Some One Care To Read?" while Paul, to my surprise, looked straight past him in those large, almost unbearable silences, and then, as if pushing upward against wet snow (pushing, I now know, against the historicity of the situation), I raised my hand and read—Paul and I began our afterclass beer routine.

I read the long poem about Gittens of our regiment, who, under those lean, breeze-blown palm trees and glaring white sand beaches lapped by blue-green tongues of the sea, went madder in that incongruous paradise, under which three thousand Japanese bodies were buried, earlier and more quietly than the rest of us. Not wanting him to be sectioned-eight in a fleet hospital back on Guadalcanal, we did not turn him in. He was not violent. About once a week he said plaintively, "I'm going home," and loped to the beach and dove into the sea to begin his ten-thousand-mile swim to Philadelphia. We would coax him out. Once he did not say anything, so we did not see him go, and never saw him again.

"Good story in that poem," Paul said. A sneer, I thought, lurked on the edges of his smile. "Probably a better story than a poem."

But I was still bathed by Bark's glance (Heyyyy, who's this nigger?) and nod, still elated that after I'd read, broken the ice, the class had come clamoring after, hands raised like the spears of a medieval mob.

Paul did not volunteer to read, though he had material.

My wife, Catherine, did not really share my elation. Her smiles were filled with pride, and she embraced me as if performing a ritual. Great, I thought. Paul's jealous and Cat yet doesn't know what it's all about.

When she met Paul and Janice (who looked like the coed who had passed us in the hall the day of Bark's first class) she expressed reservations about them. And that is what she called them, Them, or Those People. She seemed to think that they were leading me somewhere or interfering with our life.

It was very late in the semester when Paul read, and I was impressed by his vocabulary and by the very force so filled with assurance with which he read. He had talked a lot about this story. But I was made uncomfortable by it. It was a tale of a tough soldier and a tender whore. Hemingway lurked behind every adjectiveless sentence. I winced when the class, one by one, implacable as a giant amoeba, began to devour him whole. Paul had held forth throughout the semester, offering extensive and exuberant criticism of everyone's work (some of it quite good), buttressed by the statements or works of a multitude of writers whose names hovered always at the ready on his lips. Now he was forced to defend every image, metaphor, period and comma—even concept—like a trapped dog. When the class was at last finished with him, and Paul, slumped low in his chair, rapping his teeth with a pencil, his ears a bright red, gave a loud sigh, Bark offered his comments, sewed Paul back up and wiped away the blood.

I had been promised by Paul's attitude that he was always, at all times, producing nothing short of literary dynamite. It had been, in fact, a small, damp firecracker. Over our beer several times I caught his eye just as it had finished some secret peremptory glance at me. What had I perceived about him, his work, was what the glance asked.

I *had* discovered something; *re* discovered something; and as we sat there, he rather subdued and I patient and, yes, patroniz-

ing, I thought back to my boyhood in my home town, specifically of *mornings, springing from Tim Hannon's milk wagon
into the daybreaking cool, a metal six-bottle carrier gripped in
my hand, the smell of fresh milk, Tim's fat-man sweat and
warming horseflesh in my nostrils, when I entered buildings with
contempt that once I had held in awe because of their sturdy
brick façades and cream-colored trim; they were in the white
section of town. For years passing them along a proscribed trail I
had a souring resentment of the residents. That had passed when
I first went inside. The carpets were dirty and spotted and they
stank; the walls needed plastering where they were not already
stained beyond repainting back to a respectable color, and there
was always a strangely lackluster commingling of cooking smells
and the odors of fat old dogs and cats. Invariably I set the bottles
upon swollen roaches and beads of ratshit, holding my breath
until I got back outside, where, at least, the buildings* looked
good.

Even so, the year I met Paul the world cracked open for me,
revealing endless possibilities to be achieved with words. Something began to click within me. I could write! I choked on
words, drowned in them, constructed them into ideas; I wal-
lowed in their shapes and sounds, their power to stroke or stun,
sing or sorrow, accuse or acclaim. Living meant suddenly more
than having a college education and being a husband and father. My life, then close to mounting twenty-two years, seemed
presented to me once again. I exulted in the gift in quiet ways
that I hoped would attract no one's attention.

I had not had much of a life until the war, to which I'd fled
with dreams of screaming down on the dirty Japs or dirty Huns
in my silver, bullet-spewing fighter plane, or leading a charge
against them on the ground, knee-deep in their bodies. Fled
from rat's-ass-end jobs that generations of my family, bitter
resignation etched upon their faces, had settled in. The war got
me away. It whetted my appetites; its horrors expanded my
mind; and what men did to other men in it, underlining the
whimsy of the species, brought me at last before Words as the
keys to understanding.

We, Paul and I, shared a love of words and writing, and we
understood, in that way people often have with each other, that

he was the tutor and I the pupil. It was a role he enjoyed; he found it natural. We moved that year and the next, as seniors, from poetry to fiction and back to poetry, the Queen, once more, meeting her demands of precision and grace with the energy of the young, if not the skill of masters-to-be. We spent hours over beer gone stale talking of writing; missed dinners or were late for work talking of writing and writers; shouted writing above the din of small-time bop-playing student bands. But Paul hated bop anyway.

He preferred Dixieland and folk songs and the ballads that came out of the Spanish Civil War, and there were times when I visited Janice and Paul in New York and went to the Stuyvesant Casino to listen to Dixieland over pitchers of beer, and to be near the writers talking of J. D. Salinger and e. e. cummings. And how many nights back on campus did we end the evening with great, mournful choruses of "Irene Good Night"? A hundred, a thousand, and Catherine liked not one of them. She looked at those times the way a smooth, brown doe would look if does could show anger or disgust.

Looking at her then I would think, It's going.

And I would be afraid.

We had had a thing of long standing, through the gray last days of the Depression, through mutual embarrassments endured in homes where the lights had been turned off because our parents hadn't been able to pay the bill; we shared the youthful shame of being seen in clothes worn too often to school and to parties, of lunch periods in high school during which we ate no lunches because we didn't have them—while we pretended that we simply weren't hungry. After I fled to the marines when they finally allowed us in, she was my girl back home, her letters, tenderly scented, recalling spring proms, following me across the Pacific. She was waiting when I returned. We married and I took her away to school with me.

Won't you come along with me . . .

Catherine was not enrolled. We had not the money for her to do so, even part time. But we had planned, yes, planned. We would do my assignments together; she would use my textbooks. What I learned, she would learn. She, too, would be studying Bacon and Johnson and Burton and Brown and Her-

rick, Cleveland, Lovelace, Marvell, Donne, Suckling and Cra-
shaw; she would come to read Anglo-Saxon. Catherine would
know an incline from a syncline, a fold, a fault, geological time
from pre-Cambrian to Neolithic, the shapes of oceans millions
of years ago. She would study the palatals, sibilants and glottals;
she would get to know it all. She wouldn't have the diploma,
but that was all bullshit anyway.

We went on one or two field trips and hoarded our money to
see road company productions of Broadway hits, often with
Paul and Janice. The months passed. I would return from my
copyman job in an advertising agency (sometimes, for small
things, they let me write copy) to find the books untouched, the
assignments undone, and when I started to talk about the lessons, a look of fright raced across her face, to be replaced by a
grin, a grin with curling bottom lip. "Honey, I don't want to be
bothered with that stuff."

To not want to know. There was, of course, nothing special
about wanting to know *that* stuff, but all knowing is like climbing steps: one bit of knowledge lifts you to the next step, or
should.

So I would look at Catherine and think, *It's going.*

She talked of the days when, finished with school, we would
find ourselves respected citizens of a community where I
taught literature. Teaching she understood. The writing was
frightening her. First, she told me I was working too hard,
staying up half the night writing those poems and stories which
were, she said when she glanced at them too quickly to have
read them, "nice." Then she called me crazy, after which,
months later, she tangled the ribbon of the typewriter, that
tough little L. C. Smith-Corona portable, so much that it took
me a day and a half to straighten it. She stopped giving it up; I
had to take it; and after a while I stopped taking it.

We lay in bed listening to each other's breathing, I waiting
for her touch, she waiting for mine. Too much drinking at
parties gave us our release; the mornings found us distant but
polite as ever. It was still going. I didn't want it to go. I felt I
owed it more than I'd given it, our marriage, and what of the
kids we'd wanted to have? Who else did I know well enough,
had known long enough, to want to have kids with?

On one of those nights when we lay in bed I said, "Catherine, I know it's not going okay with us. I don't really know why. I want it to be okay."

I felt her turning toward me. She sighed. "I guess it isn't going so hot."

"Then let's have a baby," I said. "We'll be able to manage through graduate school."

"Cate, do you *really* want to? Really?"

I thought I would hesitate, but I didn't. I said, "Yes, yes, I want to."

We giggled and embraced and fondled each other until I whispered, "We might as well begin right now."

She kissed me and got up and went to the bathroom. She slid back into the bed, murmuring, "All clear."

Paul and I finished college high as soldiers made ready for combat. We did not attend our graduation, and in the quiet summer hiatus, when Catherine went home to visit her father with the news that she was pregnant, I labored in the agency full time or worked at home, taking only a couple of weekends to visit Paul and Janice and to make the pilgrimage to Birdland.

In the fall, Catherine's belly swelling, I joined Paul in Bark's advanced writing course. Last year his look had been like a sad, slow sigh: *Quo vadis, Africanus?* The nigger in his look was gone. It would take me a long time to understand his new one.

Paul and I regularly submitted our work, mostly poems, to the "little" magazines. Once, to what I suspect was Paul's chagrin, Karl Shapiro of *Poetry* returned a poem with a note penciled in about the lines he liked.

Recklessly confident, I took to sending my poems to Elder Poets for their comments. William Carlos Williams had sent them back with an angry note—didn't I know that when I wrote to Elder Poets I should enclose a stamped, self-addressed envelope? He did not say marvelous things about my poems. I told Paul.

"Say," he said, "what made you send your poems to WCW and not to someone like Langston Hughes?"

I said, "I went to see Hughes the last time I was in New York."

He sat upright in the booth where we were drinking beer. A distance seemed to grow in his eyes. "What'd he say?"

I told him what Mr. Hughes had told me about my work— exaggerating ever so slightly. (I didn't tell him what else Mr. Hughes said because I didn't want to believe it and I wouldn't forget it either: I would have to be ten times the writer a white man was and then it would be hell, which was not exactly an unusual experience. Agents would return manuscripts with rust marks from paper clips because they hadn't bothered to read the material. Agents and editors would tell you to forget race— but they rarely published anything by a Negro that wasn't about race. Still, they didn't want you to be too serious about anything, even if you were able. But if I just *had* to be a writer, all this and more wouldn't stop me, and that was good. And I certainly had to read Llewellyn Dodge Johnson's works if I hadn't already.)

Paul leaned back in a posture of muted arrogance, his eyes sparkling with a paternal kindness served up with a smile. "Hughes is good for what he does," he said. "I never liked his collection *Fine Clothes to the Jew.*"

I didn't know it. I said, "What do you mean he's good for what he does?" I was rising to Hughes's defense.

"Well! He's not a William Carlos Williams, is he now?"

WCW was assigned; Hughes was not. And Mr. Hughes was not one of those writers who came every Thursday afternoon to read or to regale us with tales of writers and writing—Edel, Bowen, Auden, Ciardi.

And Paul's credentials got in my way. That liberal background in a liberal New York City neighborhood. That union father who fought through the labor wars and was now with Harry Bridges on the Coast. Paul's position in the Students for Democratic Action, which paralleled mine as president of the university chapter of the NAACP. But even with these things between me and my reality, I was beginning to sense machinations, like tiptoeing actors moving behind a set. I suppose that was why, in spite of our drinking days and nights, I had withheld confidences he on the other hand shared with me, perhaps, I sometimes thought, too openly, too eagerly. (I do not know why so many white men seem to do that, as if too heavily burdened.)

However, like entering boot camp or even changing schools, this writing, and its attendant fevers, was new to me and I must have carried my naïveté like a badge. That I had killed three men for sure (I think of them), and perhaps another two, during the war was not preparation for this or what lay ahead. Like most combat veterans, I felt that nothing in civilian life could ever match those encounters with that kind of death.

I did not know that there was another, more cancerous and far less glorious dying; it attacked in tandem, head and soul.

SIX months into her pregnancy Catherine accused me of not trying to save the marriage. I was doing the same old things, spending most of my spare time writing or talking with Paul about writing. I laughed and tried to comfort her. If I was spending too much time writing, it was because I was trying to build a future for us; if I spent too much time talking with Paul, it was only so that I could learn from him. The rest of the time, I reminded her, I had to work at the agency to help stretch out the GI Bill and, naturally, I had to go to my classes.

The explanations did no good. She turned inward, and when the baby was born on a bitter March day, the old sense of impending loss and fear assailed me once again. I felt it twice over now.

At the end of the first year Cat and Glenn—for so we named him—went home to visit her father. I think she enjoyed being away from me. I had suggested that we all go, but she insisted that all of us couldn't afford the trip. She was right; there would have been sacrificing later, which I was willing to do. That summer, however, I didn't visit Paul and Janice. I worked and painted the house and thought from time to time of the war in Korea. I was glad I had dependents and relieved that Glenn was a baby. No more war for us, I thought.

Catherine's return did not give our marriage the boost that it needed. Instead, as the year progressed, she and I became one of those habits, limping along, our lives leaking apart.

When I was alone with Glenn, I would talk to him. He took his pacifier from his drooling mouth as if trying to respond. He made this sound: !Click !Click, and then, surprised, he would begin to cry until I went !Click !Click. Then he smiled, as if understanding.

At the same time, a certain wan quality came upon Paul, and, strangely, a sheen of gaiety to Janice. Winter came, blustering down from the Laurentians, piling foot upon foot of snow upon the campus. Milk froze. Icicles formed. Cold seemed to have penetrated not only the world but souls as well.

On such a morning, leaving for a class in Anglo-Saxon, I stuck my hand in the mailbox and came up with a letter of acceptance of a story by *Neurotica.* I reopened the door and told Catherine. "Is that good?" she said. I closed the door and hiked down to the bus stop, itching to tell Paul. I felt sharply triumphant when I told him that afternoon over beer. I had read the letter 151 times, knew it by heart. It was my first acceptance.

Shock burst in his eyes like puffs of ack-ack. He tried to smile, then laugh. He hadn't sold anything, and there was again distance in his eyes. Finally, he laughed. *"Neurotica?* What's that, a disease?"

"It's published in New Orleans. Editor's G. Legman."

"A Jew," he said, curling his bottom lip.

Sometimes Paul puzzled me: Was he for or against Jews? There was much news about the death camps in Europe.

"Does it make a difference, and anyway, how do you know?"

"The name."

"C'mon," I said. I was remembering something Richard Wright said: something like a Jew-hater being but three letters removed from being a Negro-hater. And that was something else about white men: they tended to think that they could share the garbage of their psyches with black people, who would lap it up and rise on tiptoes, singing brotherhood. "I don't give a fuck what he is, man," I said. "He's got good taste, better than yours. You didn't like the story—"

"Which one was it?"

" 'The Age of Bop.' I read it last year. Did some more work on it."

"Bach?"

"Bop, man, bop. B-O-P. Bird. Monk. Diz. Max. Fats. Miles—"

"Oh! *Be*-bop!"

"Yeah," I said. "Some Jewish guys play it, too."

He ignored that. He wanted to talk about the story.

"I'd like to look at it," he said.

"Why? It's being published. I don't need any criticism—"

"No, no—"

I lied. "I don't have a copy." I was learning. Paul never passed his work around, but freely criticized whatever work of others that came into his hand. "You wouldn't be jealous?"

His smile was genuine, disarming. "No. I mean, who ever heard of *Neurotica?*"

"You're holding out for *A.M.* or *Harper's* or *Esquire*, right?"

Still smiling, in a parody of the filmic tough guy, he turned up a corner of his mouth. At that moment he reminded me of a marine hero who, after Guadalcanal and Henderson Field, was sent back home to go on tour. His second hitch took him to Iwo. At home he must have begun to believe the stories of his invincibility; through the corps, island to island, the story went that he leaped atop a rock on Iwo, shouting that the Japs couldn't kill him, he was Johnny Barone. The Japanese did not understand English; they buried Barone on Iwo.

But *I* understood English, or was beginning to. Nevertheless, it was later that I would come to understand. Paul had been so sure of himself, of what he *was* because it had been there all the time, under a veneer of acceptable, right things; there all the time the way it must have been for boxers before Jack Johnson and baseball players before Jackie Robinson.

Sitting there, both of us raking feelings we'd not dared to touch before, I thought of the past summer and my visit to the city while Catherine and Glenn were away again. Paul and Janice loved Leadbelly and Blind Willie Lemon and Pops Foster. I could say that they patronized their pained music. They were warm to the old, black, white-haired fugitives from the Deep South. Yet when I managed to get them to the Royal Roost or Birdland, Paul and Janice were stiff and strange, even antagonistic, toward the music of Fats Navarro and Bird. They didn't understand it.

Paul ordered another round, lit a cigarette and said, "Yeah, I guess I am jealous, and yeah, I suppose I still have some of the white chauvinist in me." (That term was big on campus. The lefty students were all using it, and it crept into general usage. White chauvinist.)

I said, "Yeah."

Our studies eased to their appointed ends, both of us publishing a lot of poetry in third- or fourth-rank publications.

In the spring, walking slowly back home through the panty-raids and clots of weary athletes trudging to their dorms after hours of practice, Catherine said, "When we go home this summer, we're not coming back." She didn't stop, didn't break stride. Neither did I. But I summoned words to give me time to think: "What do you mean?"

"You know what I mean, Cato."

I sighed. We kept moving, our feet making soft sounds in the roadway.

"Leave Glenn," I said.

She turned to me, still not breaking stride, and arched her brows. Women do not think men capable of caring for children; neither do the courts. I thought I could. I also knew that Catherine would refuse, because Glenn was the trophy of our marriage. He made her a woman, a wife and a mother, titles the Western woman and perhaps even the world woman cherish.

Catherine said, "Shit," and kept on walking.

"What happened to it?" I asked.

She kept walking and shrugged her shoulders.

"Was it all me?"

"I want to say yes, but it wasn't all you, Cato."

"Look, we can—"

Laughter echoed down the block from a fraternity party. I wondered if she felt as much an alien in that place at that moment as I did.

Her hand, long and slim, fell gently upon my wrist. "Let's let it go," she said almost pleadingly. I could not meet her gaze. I saw, I thought, an endless string of commitments broken, underlining my life. She read me.

"Don't feel guilty, Cato. It's just something we were never trained up to handle."

"*What* something?"

"What you want to be and do."

We walked through a stretch of gravel.

"But Glenn—" I finally said.

"You can see him any time you want to, and of course one day he'll be big enough to travel by himself."

We were back on pavement now. "Why are we so much nicer now?"

She smiled in the dusk. "Because it's over, and we're both relieved. Never thought it would be this easy, did you?"

"I didn't want it."

"I think you did."

I wondered what my father would have said. He had stumbled through his time, filled, I felt, with remorse for having deserted us. Once while on leave from Camp Lejeune I met him in Washington between his convoys in the merchant marine. The last one had seen half the convoy destroyed by German submarines. He did not look too well—nervous, more gray than black of skin. He was doing it, he said, to make some money so I could get a start after the war; he'd never done anything for me before.

"When you get married, son, make it work. It's a lot of trouble, but it ain't no good the other way." We had a couple of drinks and he took me to meet his woman. I returned to camp and he returned to the convoys.

My mother died while I was overseas and they wouldn't let me go home. My father's ship was torpedoed and he froze to death six hundred miles from Murmansk and sank in the Barents Sea. I was not surprised to find that he had left nothing for me after all. But now I wondered if he had felt, when he went away, the same low-moaning emptiness I was already beginning to feel.

As soon as the baby sitter left, we undressed slowly, got into bed and made love half the night.

And when summer came, they went. It hurt.

Paul and Janice returned to New York, where he thought he might take some more writing courses. I worked at the agency and at home. I learned during that time that loners are people to be feared. They make good commandos and shit like that; also good wide receivers. They are small, often warped planets around whom the universe revolves. We admire them, but secretly we fear them. In a scheme where things are paired, night and day, man and woman, boy and girl, the two sides of the DNA ladder, where Yin and Yang and the double placing of the acupuncturist's needles exist, who wants to be a loner? Until God made Eve, Adam in his incredible loneliness must have fornicated with anything and everything he could get a grip on, creating for later generations the heritage of bestiality.

August was my deadline. To get out. To move to New York. To carry my recommendations, crisply enveloped, to the job markets of the Big Apple. Paul and Janice said nothing about the end of my marriage, but then we were the new breed; we did not waste words over such happenings. I had told them before they returned to New York.

Two weeks before I was to leave, a note from Paul informed me that they were looking forward to my staying with them, even though things were a little rocky. My presence might help. I wondered what was going on.

Bienvenido N. Santos

IN Bienvenido Santos's collection of short stories, *Scent of Apples* (University of Washington Press, 1979), the theme of exile and separation is at the center of each of the post–World War II stories. In his preface to the collection Santos writes:

> All exiles want to go home. Many of the old Filipinos in the United States, as in these stories, never return, but in their imagination they make the journey a thousand times, taking the slowest boats because in their dreamworld time is not as urgent as actual time passing, quicker than arrows, kneading the flesh, crying on their bones. Some fool themselves into thinking that theirs is a voluntary exile, but it is not. The ones who stay here to die know this best. Their last thoughts are of childhood friends, of parents long dead, old loves, of familiar songs and dances, odors of home like sweet sun on brown skin or scent of calamondin fruit and fresh papaya blossoms.

For Alipio Palma, in "Immigration Blues," the sweat smell of the Philippines and the memory of those left at home have all faded. At the end of his life he is alone, living in a house in San Francisco, where he proclaims that "across that ocean is the Philippines." Irony is the measure of his existence in America. As long as he remains in America he is the living embodiment to Filipinos of the American dream of success, but in America he is the "outsider." He is exiled both from his homeland and from real acceptance and inclusion in the American dream.

S. E. Solberg, writing about Santos's short stories in "An Introduction to Filipino American Literature" (*Aiiieeeee! Anthology of Asian American Literature*, 1974), notes:

Whether it be in the hurt and recrimination of one interracial marriage, or in the warmth and mutual support of another, these pinoys wore their pain with honor. By way of contrast, the educated, the wealthy, scrambling opportunistically for what they might gain out of the carnage that was the postwar Philippines, serve both as prologue and epilogue to Santos's vision of corruption on high and the strength and persistence of traditional ideals in the little man.

Santos himself spent much of his career traveling back and forth between the Philippines and the United States. Through a variety of circumstances the exile he wrote about invaded his own life; as he says, "Each time I left the United States for the Philippines, I thought I was going for good. In 1946, after an enforced stay of five wartime years, I returned to my family at the foot of Mount Mayon, vowing in my heart I would never leave home again." In 1958, after the publication of a collection of short stories (*You Lovely People*, 1955), he left again. Over the next thirty years he wrote and traveled back and forth between the Philippines and Iowa, San Francisco, and Wichita, where, in 1973, he was appointed Distinguished Writer in Residence at Wichita State University.

His other works include several collections of short stories, *You Lovely People* (1955), *The Day the Dancers Came* (1979), *Dwell in the Wilderness: Selected Short Stories 1931–1941* (1985); and the novels *Villa Magdalena* (1965), *Volcano* (1965), *The Praying Man* (1982), *The Man Who Thought He Looked Like Robert Taylor* (1983), and *What the Hell for You Left Your Heart in San Francisco* (1987).

—Shawn Wong

"*Immigration Blues*" *from*
SCENT OF APPLES:
A COLLECTION
OF STORIES

THROUGH the window curtain, Alipio saw two women, one seemed twice as large as the other. In their summer dresses, they looked like the country girls he knew back home in the Philippines, who went around peddling rice cakes. The slim one could have passed for his late wife Seniang's sister whom he remembered only in pictures because she never made it to the United States. Before Seniang's death, the couple had arranged for her coming to San Francisco, filing all the required petition papers to facilitate the approval of her visa. The sister was always "almost ready, all the papers have been signed," but she never showed up. His wife had been ailing and when she died, he thought that hearing of her death would hasten her coming, but the wire he had sent her was neither returned nor acknowledged.

The knocking on the door was gentle. A little hard of hearing, Alipio was not sure it was indeed a knocking on the door, but it sounded different from the little noises that sometimes hummed in his ears in the daytime. It was not yet noon, but it must be warm outside in all that sunshine, otherwise those two women would be wearing spring dresses at the least. There were summer days in San Francisco that were cold like winter in the Midwest.

He limped painfully to the door. Until last month, he wore crutches. The entire year before that, he was bed-ridden, but he had to force himself to walk about in the house after coming from the hospital. After Seniang's death, everything had gone to pieces. It was one bust after another, he complained to the few friends who came to visit him.

"Seniang was my good luck. When God decided to take her, I had nothing but bad luck," he said.

Not long after Seniang's death, he was in a car accident. For almost a year he was in the hospital. The doctors were not sure he was going to walk again. He told them it was God's wish. As it was he was thankful he was still alive. It had been a horrible accident.

The case dragged on in court. His lawyer didn't seem too good about car accidents. He was an expert immigration lawyer, but he was a friend. As it turned out, Alipio lost the full privileges and benefits coming to him in another two years if he had not been hospitalized and had continued working until his official retirement.

However, he was well provided. He didn't spend a cent for doctor and medicine and hospital bills. Now there was the prospect of a few thousand dollars compensation. After deducting his lawyer's fees it would still be something to live on. He had social security benefits and a partial retirement pension. Not too bad, really. Besides, now he could walk a little although he still limped and had to move about with extreme care.

When he opened the door, the fat woman said, "Mr. Palma? Alipio Palma?" Her intonation sounded like the beginning of a familiar song.

"Yes," he said. "Come in, come on in." He had not talked to anyone the whole week. His telephone had not rung all that time, not even a wrong number, and there was nobody he wanted to talk to. The little noises in his ears had somehow kept him company. Radio and television sounds lulled him to sleep.

The thin one was completely out of sight as she stood behind the big one who was doing the talking. "I'm sorry, I should have phoned you first, but we were in a hurry."

"The house is a mess," Alipio said truthfully. Had he been imagining things? He remembered seeing two women on the porch. There was another one, who looked like Seniang's sister. The woman said "we," and just then the other one materialized, close behind the big one, who walked in with the assurance of a social worker, about to do him a favor.

"Sit down. Sit down. Anywhere," Alipio said as he led the two women through the dining room, past a huge rectangular table in the center. It was bare except for a vase of plastic flowers as centerpiece. He passed his hand over his face, a mannerism which Seniang hated. Like you have a hangover, she chided him, and you can't see straight.

A TV set stood close to a wall in the small living room crowded with an assortment of chairs and tables. An aquarium crowded the mantelpiece of a fake fireplace. A lighted bulb inside the tank showed many colored fish swimming about in a haze of fish food. Some of it lay scattered on the edge of the shelf. The carpet underneath was sodden black. Old magazines and tabloids lay just about everywhere.

"Sorry to bother you like this," the fat one said as she plunked herself down on the nearest chair, which sagged to the floor under her weight. The thin one chose the end of the sofa away from the TV set.

"I was just preparing my lunch. I know it's quite early, but I had nothing to do," Alipio said, pushing down with both hands the seat of the cushioned chair near a moveable partition, which separated the living room from the dining room. "It's painful just trying to sit down. I'm not too well yet," he added as he finally made it.

"I hope we're not really bothering you," the fat one said. The other had not said a word. She looked pale and sick. Maybe she was hungry or cold.

"How's it outside?" Alipio asked. "I've not been out all day." Whenever he felt like it, he dragged a chair to the porch and sat there, watching the construction going on across the street and smiling at the people passing by who happened to look his way. Some smiled back and mumbled something like a greeting or a comment on the beauty of the day. He stayed on until he got bored or it became colder than he could stand.

"It's fine. It's fine outside. Just like Baguio," the fat one said.

"You know Baguio? I was born near there."

"We're sisters."

Alipio was thinking, won't the other one speak at all?

"I'm Mrs. Antonieta Zafra, the wife of Carlito. I believe you know him. He says you're friends. In Salinas back in the thirties. He used to be a cook at the Marina."

"Carlito, yes, yes, Carlito Zafra. We bummed together. We come from Ilocos. Where you from?"

"Aklan. My sister and I speak Cebuano."

"Oh, she speak? You, you don't speak Ilocano?"

"Not much. Carlito and I talk in English. Except when he's real mad, like when his cock don't fight or when he lose, then he speaks Ilocano. Cuss words. I've learned them myself. Some, anyway."

"Yes. Carlito. He love cockfighting. How's he?"

"Retired like you. We're now in Fresno. On a farm. He raises chickens and hogs. I do some sewing in town when I can. My sister here is Monica. She's older than me. Never been married."

Monica smiled at the old man, her face in anguish, as if near to tears.

"Carlito. He got some fighting cocks, I bet."

"Not anymore. But he talks a lot about cockfighting. But nobody, not even the pinoys and the Chicanos are interested in it." Mrs. Zafra appeared pleased at the state of things on her home front.

"I remember. Carlito once promoted a cockfight. Everything was ready, but the roosters won't fight. Poor man, he did everything to make them fight like having them peck on each other's necks and so forth. They were so tame, so friendly with each other. Only thing they didn't do is embrace." Alipio laughed, showing a set of perfectly white and even teeth, obviously dentures.

"He hasn't told me about that, I'll remind him."

"Do that. Where's he? Why isn't he with you?"

"We didn't know we'd find you. While visiting some friends this morning, we learned you live here." Mrs. Zafra was beaming on him.

"I've always lived here, but I got few friends now. So you're Mrs. Carlito. I thought he's dead already. I never hear from him. We're old now. We're old already when we got our citizenship papers right after Japanese surrender. So you and him. Good for Carlito."

"I heard about your accident."

"After Seniang died. She was not yet sixty, but she had this heart trouble. I took care of her." Alipio seemed to have forgotten his visitors. He sat there staring at the fish in the aquarium, his ears perked as though waiting for some sound, like the breaking of the surf not far away, or the TV set suddenly turned on.

The sisters looked at each other. Monica was fidgeting, her eyes seemed to say, let's go, let's get out of here.

"Did you hear that?" the old man said.

Monica turned to her sister, her eyes wild with panic. Mrs. Zafra leaned forward, her hand touching the edge of the chair where Alipio sat, and asked gently, "Hear what?"

"The waves. Listen. They're just outside, you know. The breakers have a nice sound like at home in the Philippines. We lived in a coastal town. Like here, I always tell Seniang, across that ocean is the Philippines, we're not far from home."

"But you're alone now. It's not good to be alone," Mrs. Zafra said.

"At night I hear better. I can see the Pacific Ocean from my bedroom. It sends me to sleep. I sleep soundly like I got no debts. I can sleep all day, too, but that's bad. So I walk. I walk much before. I go out there. I let the breakers touch me. It's nice the touch. Seniang always scold me, she says I'll be catching cold, but I don't catch cold, she catch the cold all the time."

"You must miss her," Mrs. Zafra said. Monica was staring at her hands on her lap while the sister talked. Monica's skin was transparent and the veins showed on the back of her hands like trapped eels.

"I take care of Seniang. I work all day and leave her here alone. When I come home, she's smiling. She's wearing my jacket and my slippers. You look funny, I says, why do you wear my things, you're lost inside them. She chuckles, you keep me warm all day, she says, like you're here, I smell you. Oh, that Seniang. You see, we have no baby. If we have a baby . . ."

"I think you and Carlito have the same fate. We have no baby also."

"God dictates," Alipio said, making an effort to stand. In a miraculous surge of power, Monica rushed to him and helped him up. She seemed astonished and embarrassed at what she had done.

"Thank you," said Alipio. "I have crutches, but I don't want no crutches. They tickle me, they hurt me, too." He watched Monica go back to her seat.

"You need help better than crutches," Mrs. Zafra said.

"God helps," Alipio said, walking towards the kitchen as if expecting to find the Almighty there.

Mrs. Zafra followed him. "What are you preparing?" she asked.

"Let's have lunch," he said, "I'm hungry. I hope you are also."

"We'll help you," Mrs. Zafra said, turning back to where Monica sat staring at her hands again and listening perhaps for the sound of the sea. She had not noticed nor heard her sister when she called, "Monica!"

The second time she heard her. Monica stood up and went to the kitchen.

"There's nothing to prepare," Alipio was saying, as he opened the refrigerator. "What you want to eat? Me, I don't eat bread so I got no bread. I eat rice. I was just opening a can of sardines when you come. I like sardines with lotsa tomato juice, it's great with hot rice."

"Don't you cook the sardines?" Mrs. Zafra asked. "Monica will cook it for you if you want."

"No! If you cook sardines, it taste bad. Better uncooked. Besides it gets cooked on top of the hot rice. Mix with onions, chopped nice. Raw not cooked. You like it?"

"Monica loves raw onions, don't you, Sis?"

"Yes," Monica said in a low voice.

"Your sister, she is well?" Alipio said, glancing towards Monica.

Mrs. Zafra gave her sister an angry look.

"I'm okay," Monica said, a bit louder this time.

"She's not sick," Mrs. Zafra said, "But she's shy. Her own shadow frightens her. I tell you, this sister of mine, she got problems."

"Oh?" Alipio exclaimed. He had been listening quite attentively.

"I eat onions, raw," Monica said. "Sardines, too, I like uncooked."

Her sister smiled. "What do you say, I run out for some

groceries," she said, going back to the living room to get her bag.

"Thanks. But no need for you to do that. I got lotsa food, canned food. Only thing I haven't got is bread," Alipio said.

"I eat rice, too," Monica said.

Alipio reached up to open the cabinet. It was stacked full of canned food: corn beef, pork and beans, vienna sausage, tuna, crab meat, shrimp, chow mein, imitation noodles, and, of course, sardines, in green and yellow labels.

"The yellow ones with mustard sauce, not tomato," he explained.

"All I need is a cup of coffee," Mrs. Zafra said, throwing her handbag back on the chair in the living room.

Alipio opened two drawers near the refrigerator. "Look," he said as Mrs. Zafra came running back to the kitchen. "I got more food to last me . . . a long time."

The sisters gaped at the bags of rice, macaroni, spaghetti sticks, sugar, dried shrimps wrapped in cellophane, bottles of soy sauce and fish sauce, vinegar, ketchup, instant coffee, and more cans of sardines.

The sight of all that foodstuff seemed to have enlivened the old man. After all, food meant life, continuing sustenance, source of energy and health. "Now look here," he said, turning briskly now to the refrigerator, which he opened, the sudden light touching his face with a glow that erased years from his eyes. With a jerk he pulled open the large freezer, cramped full of meats. "Mostly lamb chops," he said, adding, "I like lamb chops."

"Carlito, he hates lamb chops," Mrs. Zafra said.

"I like lamb chops," Monica said, still wild eyed, but now a bit of color tinted her cheeks. "Why do you have so much food?" she asked.

Alipio looked at her before answering. He thought she looked younger than Mrs. Zafra. "You see," he said, closing the refrigerator. He was beginning to chill. "I watch the papers for bargain sales. I can still drive the car when I feel right. It's only now my legs bothering me. So. I buy all I can. Save me many trips. Money, too."

Later they sat around the enormous table in the dining

room. Monica shared half a plate of boiling rice topped with a sardine with Alipio. He showed her how to place the sardine on top, pressing it a little and pouring spoonfuls of tomato juice over it.

Mrs. Zafra had coffee and settled for a small can of vienna sausage and a little rice. She sipped her coffee meditatively.

"This is good coffee," she said. "I remember how we used to hoard Hills Bros. coffee at . . . at the convent. The sisters were quite selfish about it."

"Antonieta was a nun, a sister of mercy," Monica said.

"What?" Alipio exclaimed, pointing a finger at her for no apparent reason, an involuntary gesture of surprise.

"Yes, I was," Mrs. Zafra admitted. "When I married, I had been out of the order for more than a year, yes, in California, at St. Mary's."

"You didn't . . ." Alipio began.

"Of course not," she interrupted him. "If you mean did I leave the order to marry Carlito. Oh, no. He was already an old man when I met him."

"I see. We used to joke him because he didn't like the girls too much. He prefer the cocks." The memory delighted him so much, he reared his head up as he laughed, covering his mouth hastily, but too late. Some of the tomato soaked grains had already spilled out on his plate and on the table in front of him.

Monica looked pleased as she gathered carefully some of the grains on the table.

"He hasn't changed," Mrs. Zafra said vaguely. "It was me who wanted to marry him."

"You? After being a nun, you wanted to marry . . . Carlito? But why Carlito?" Alipio seemed to have forgotten for the moment that he was still eating. The steam from the rice touched his face till it glistened darkly. He was staring at Mrs. Zafra as he breathed in the aroma without savoring it.

"It's a long story," Mrs. Zafra said. She stabbed a chunky sausage and brought it to her mouth. She looked pensive as she chewed on it.

"When did this happen?"

"Five, six years ago. Six years ago, almost."

"That long?"

"She had to marry him," Monica said blandly.

"What?" Alipio shouted, visibly disturbed. There was the sound of dentures grating in his mouth. He passed a hand over his face. "Carlito done that to you?"

The coffee spilled a little as Mrs. Zafra put the cup down. "Why no," she said. "What are you thinking of?"

Before he could answer, Monica spoke in the same tone of voice, low, unexcited, saying, "He thinks Carlito got you pregnant, that's what."

"Carlito?" She turned to Monica in disbelief. "Why, Alipio knows Carlito," she said.

Monica shrugged her shoulders. "Why don't you tell him why?" she suggested.

"As I said, it's a long story, but I shall make it short," Mrs. Zafra began. She took a sip from her cup and continued, "After leaving the order, I couldn't find a job. I was interested in social work, but I didn't know anybody who could help me."

As she paused, Alipio said, "What the heck does Carlito know about social work?"

"Let me continue," Mrs. Zafra said.

She still had a little money, from home, and she was not too worried about being jobless. But there was the question of her status as an alien. Once out of the community, she was no longer entitled to stay in the United States, let alone secure employment. The immigration office began to hound her, as it did other Filipinos in similar predicaments. They were a pitiful lot. Some hid in the apartments of friends like criminals running away from the law. Of course, they were law breakers. Those with transportation money returned home, which they hated to do. At home they would be forced to invent stories, tell lies to explain away why they returned so soon. All their lives they had to learn how to cope with the stigma of failure in a foreign land. They were losers and no longer fit for anything useful. The more sensitive and weak lost their minds and had to be committed to insane asylums. Others became neurotic, antisocial, depressed in mind and spirit. Some turned to crime. Or just folded up, in a manner of speaking. It was a nightmare. Antonieta didn't want to go back to the Philippines under those circumstances. She would have had to be very convincing to prove that she was not thrown out of the order for immoral reasons. Just when she seemed to have reached the breaking point, she recalled incidents in which women in her situation married American citizens and, automatically, became entitled to permanent residency with an option to become U.S. citizens after five years. At first, she thought the idea of such a marriage was hideous, unspeakable. Perhaps other foreign women in similar situations could do it—and have done it—but not Philippine girls. But what was so special about Philippine girls? Nothing really, but their upbringing was such that to place themselves in a situation where they had to tell a man that all they wanted was a marriage for convenience was degrading, an unbearable shame. A form of self-destruction. Mortal sin. Better repatriation. A thousand times better.

When an immigration officer finally caught up with her, he proved to be very understanding and quite a gentleman. Yet he was firm. He was young, maybe of Italian descent, and looked like a salesman for a well-known company in the islands that dealt in farm equipment.

"I'm giving you one week," he said. "You have already overstayed by several months. If in one week's time, you haven't left yet, you might have to wait in jail for deportation proceedings."

She cried, oh, how she cried. She wished she had not left the order, no, not really. She had no regrets about leaving up to this point. Life in the convent had turned sour on her. She despised the sisters and the system, which she found tyrannical, inhuman. In her own way, she had a long series of talks with God and God had approved of the step she had taken. She was not going back to the order. Anyhow, even if she did, she would not be taken back. To jail then?

But why not marry an American citizen? In one week's time? How? Accost the first likely man and say, "You look like an American citizen. If you are, indeed, and you have the necessary papers to prove it, will you marry me? I want to remain in this country."

All week she talked to God. It was the same God she had worshipped and feared all her life. Now they were *palsy walsy*, on the best of terms. As she brooded over her misfortune, He brooded with her, sympathized with her, and finally advised her to go look for an elderly Filipino who was an American citizen, and tell him the truth of the matter. Tell him that if he wished, it could be a marriage in name only. For his trouble, she would be willing to pay. How much? If it's a bit too much, could she pay on the installment plan? If he wished . . . otherwise . . . Meanwhile He would look the other way.

How she found Carlito Zafra was another story, a much longer story, more confused and confusing. It was like a miracle, though. Her friend God could not have sent her to a better instrument to satisfy her need. That was not expressed well, but it amounted to that, a need. Carlito was an instrument necessary for her good. And, as it turned out, a not too unwilling instrument.

"We were married the day before the week was over," Mrs. Zafra said. "And I've been in this country ever since. And no regrets."

They lived well and simply, a country life. True, they were childless, but both of them were helping relatives in the Philippines, sending them money and goods marked Made in U.S.A.

"Lately, however, some of the goods we've been sending do not arrive intact. Do you know that some of the good quality material we send never reach our relatives? It's frustrating."

"We got lotsa thieves between here and there," Alipio said, but his mind seemed to be on something else.

"And I was able to send for Monica. From the snapshots she sent us she seemed to be getting thinner and more sickly, teaching in the barrio. And she wanted so much to come here."

"Seniang was like you also, hiding from immigration. I thank God for her," Alipio told Mrs. Zafra in such a low voice he could hardly be heard.

The sisters pretended they didn't know, but they knew practically everything about him. Alipio appeared tired, pensive, and eager to talk so they listened.

"She went to my apartment and said, without any hesitation, marry me and I'll take care of you. She was thin then and I thought what she said was funny, the others had been matching us, you know, but I was not really interested. I believe marriage mean children. And if you cannot produce children, why get married? Besides, I had ugly experiences, bad moments. When I first arrived in the States, here in Frisco, I was young and there were lotsa blondies hanging around on Kearny Street. It was easy. But I wanted a family and they didn't. None of 'em. So what the heck, I said."

Alipio realized that Seniang was not joking. She had to get married to an American citizen, otherwise she would be deported. At that time, Alipio was beginning to feel the disadvantages of living alone. There was too much time in his hands. How he hated himself for some of the things he did. He believed that if he was married, he would be more sensible with his time and his money. He would be happier and live long. So when Seniang showed that she was serious, he agreed to marry her. It was not to be in name only. He wanted a woman. He liked her so much he would have proposed himself had he suspected that he had a chance. She was hardworking, decent, and in those days, rather slim.

"Like Monica," he said.

"Oh, I'm thin," Monica protested, blushing deeply, "I'm all bones."

"Monica is my only sister. We have no brother," Mrs. Zafra said, adding more items to her sister's vita.

"Look," Monica said, "I finished everything on my plate. I've never tasted sardines this good. Especially the way you eat them. I'm afraid I've eaten up your lunch. This is my first full meal. And I thought I've lost my appetite already."

The words came out in a rush. It seemed she didn't want to stop and she paused only because she didn't know what else to say. She moved about, gaily and at ease, perfectly at home. Alipio watched her with a bemused look in his face as she gathered the dishes and brought them to the kitchen sink. When Alipio heard the water running, he stood up, without much effort this time, and walked to her saying, "Don't bother. I got all the time to do that. You got to leave me something to do. Come, perhaps your sister wants another cup of coffee."

Mrs. Zafra had not moved from her seat. She was watching the two argue about the dishes. When she heard Alipio mention coffee, she said, "No, no more, thanks. I've drunk enough to keep me awake all week."

"Well, I'm going to wash them myself later," Monica was

saying as she walked back to the table, Alipio close behind her.

"You're an excellent host, Alipio." Mrs. Zafra spoke in a tone like a reading from a citation on a certificate of merit or something. "And to two complete strangers at that. You're a good man."

"But you're not strangers. Carlito is my friend. We were young together in this country. And that's something, you know. There are lotsa guys like us here. Old-timers, o.t.'s, they call us. Permanent residents. U.S. Citizens. We all gonna be buried here." He appeared to be thinking deeply as he added, "But what's wrong about that?"

The sisters ignored the question. The old man was talking to himself.

"What's wrong is to be dishonest. Earn a living with both hands, not afraid of any kind of work, that's the best good. No other way. Yes, everything for convenience, why not? That's frankly honest. No pretend. Love comes in the afterwards. When it comes. If it comes."

Mrs. Zafra chuckled, saying, "Ah, you're a romantic, Alipio. I must ask Carlito about you. You seem to know so much about him. I bet you were quite a . . ." she paused because what she wanted to say was "rooster," but she might give the impression of over-familiarity.

Alipio interrupted her, saying, "Ask him, he will say yes, I'm a romantic." His voice held a vibrance that was a surprise and a revelation to the visitors. He gestured as he talked, puckering his mouth every now and then, obviously to keep his dentures from slipping out. "What do you think? We were young, why not? We wowed 'em with our gallantry, with our cooking. Boy those dames never seen anything like us. Also, we were fools, most of us, anyway. Fools on fire."

Mrs. Zafra clapped her hands. Monica was smiling.

"Ah, but that fire's gone. Only the fool's left now," Alipio said, weakly. His voice was low and he looked tired as he passed both hands across his face. Then he raised his head. The listening look came back to his face. When he spoke, his voice shook a little.

"Many times I wonder where are the others. Where are you? Speak to me. And I think they're wondering the same, asking the same, so I say, I'm here, your friend Alipio Palma, my leg is broken, the wife she's dead, but I'm okay. Are you okay also? The dead they can hear even if they don't answer. The alive don't answer. But I know. I feel. Some okay, some not. They old now, all of us, who were very young. All over the United States of America. All over the world . . ."

Abruptly, he turned to Mrs. Zafra, saying, "So. You and Carlito. But Carlito, he never had fire."

"How true, how very very true," Mrs. Zafra laughed. "It would burn him. Can't stand it. Not Carlito. But he's a good man, I can tell you that."

"No question. Dabest," Alipio conceded.

Monica remained silent, but her eyes followed every move Alipio made, straying no further than the reach of his arms as he gestured to help make clear the intensity of his feeling.

"I'm sure you still got some of that fire," Mrs. Zafra said.

Monica gasped, but she recovered quickly. Again a rush of words came from her lips as if they had been there all the time waiting for what her sister had said that touched off the torrent of words. Her eyes shone as in a fever as she talked.

"I don't know Carlito very well. I've not been with them very long, but from what you say, from the way you talk, from what I see, the two of you are very different."

"Oh, maybe not," Alipio said, trying to protest, but Monica went on.

"You have strength, Mr. Palma. Strength of character. Strength in your belief in God. I admire that in a man, in a human being. Look at you. Alone. This huge table. Don't you find it too big sometimes?" Monica paused perhaps to allow her meaning to sink into Alipio's consciousness, as she fixed her eyes on him.

"No, not really. I don't eat at this table. I eat in the kitchen," Alipio said.

Mrs. Zafra was going to say something, but she held back. Monica was talking again.

"But it must be hard, that you cannot deny. Living from day to day. Alone. On what? Memories? Cabinets and a refrigerator full of food? I repeat, I admire you, sir. You've found your place. You're home safe. And at peace." She paused again this time to sweep back the strand of hair that had fallen on her brow.

Alipio had a drugged look. He seemed to have lost the drift of her speech. What was she talking about? Groceries? Baseball? He was going to say, you like baseball also? You like tuna? I have all kinds of fish. Get them at bargain price. But, obviously, it was not the proper thing to say.

"Well, I guess, one gets used to anything. Even loneliness," Monica said in a listless, dispirited tone, all the fever in her voice gone.

"God dictates," Alipio said, feeling he had found his way again and he was now on the right track. What a girl. If she had only a little more flesh. And color.

Monica leaned back on her chair, exhausted. Mrs. Zafra was staring at her in disbelief, in grievous disappointment. Her eyes seemed to say, what happened, you were going great, what suddenly hit you that you had to stop, give up, defeated? Monica shook her head in a gesture that quite clearly said, no, I can't do it, I can't anymore, I give up.

Their eyes kept up a show, a deaf-mute dialogue. Mrs. Zafra: Just when everything was going on fine, you quit. We've reached this far and you quit. I could have done it my way, directly, honestly. Not that what you were doing was dishonest, you were great, and now look at that dumb expression in your eyes. Monica: I can't. I can't anymore. But I tried. It's too much.

"How long have you been in the States?" Alipio asked Monica.

"For almost a year now!" Mrs. Zafra screamed and Alipio was visibly shaken, but she didn't care. This was the right moment. She would take it from here whether Monica went along with her or not. She was going to do it her way. "How long exactly, let's see. Moni, when did you get your last extension?"

"Extension?" Alipio repeated the word. It had such a familiar ring like "visa" or "social security," it broke into his consciousness like a touch from Seniang's fingers. It was quite intimate. "You mean . . ."

"That's right. She's here as a temporary visitor. As a matter of fact, she came on a tourist visa. Carlito and I sponsored her

coming, filed all the necessary papers, and everything would
have been fine, but she couldn't wait. She had to come here as a
tourist. Now she's in trouble."

"What trouble?" Alipio asked.

"She has to go back to the Philippines. She can't stay here
any longer."

"I have only two days left," Monica said, her head in her
hands. "And I don't want to go back."

Alipio glanced at the wall clock. It was past three. They had
been talking for hours. It was visas right from the start. Marriages. The long years and the o.t.'s. Now it was visas again.
Were his ears playing a game? They might as well as they did
sometimes, but his eyes surely were not. He could see this
woman very plainly, sobbing on the table. Boy, she was in big
trouble. Visas. Immigration. Boy, oh, boy! He knew all about
that. His gleaming dentures showed a crooked smile. He turned
to Mrs. Zafra.

"Did you come here," he began, but Mrs. Zafra interrupted
him.

"Yes, Alipio. Forgive us. As soon as we arrived, I wanted to
tell you without much talk, I wanted to say, 'I must tell you why
we're here. I've heard about you. Not only from Carlito, but
from other Filipinos who know you, how you're living here in
San Francisco alone, a widower, and we heard of the accident,
your stay in the hospital, when you were released, everything.
Here's my sister, a teacher in the Philippines, never married,
worried to death because she's being deported unless something turned up like she could marry a U.S. citizen, like I did,
like your late wife Seniang, like many others have done, are
doing in this exact moment, who can say? Now she'd accept it.'
But I didn't have a chance to say it. You welcomed us like old
friends, relatives. Later every time I began to say something
about why we came, she interrupted me. I was afraid she had
changed her mind and then she began to talk, then stopped
without finishing what she really wanted to say, that is, why we
came to see you, and so forth."

"No, no!" Monica cried, raising her head, her eyes red from
weeping, her face damp with tears. "You're such a good man.
We couldn't do this to you. We're wrong. We started wrong.

We should've been more honest, but I was ashamed. I was afraid. Let's go! let's go!"

"Where you going?" Alipio asked.

"Anywhere," Monica answered. "Forgive us. Forgive me, Mister. Alipio, please."

"What's to forgive? Don't go. We have dinner. But first, let's have *merienda*. I take *merienda*. You do also, don't you? And I don't mean snacks like the Americans."

The sisters exchanged glances, their eyes chattering away.

Alipio chuckled. He wanted to say, talk of lightning striking same fellow twice, but thought better of it. A bad thing to say. Seniang was not lightning. At times only. Mostly his fault. And this girl Monica . . . Moni? Nice name also. How can this one be lightning?

Mrs. Zafra picked up her purse and before anyone could stop her, she was opening the door. "Where's the nearest grocery store around here?" she asked, but she didn't wait for an answer.

"Come back, come back here, we got lotsa food," Alipio called after her, but he might just as well have been calling the Pacific Ocean.

Mrs. Zafra took time although a supermarket was only a few blocks away. When she returned, her arms were full of groceries in paper bags. Alipio and Monica met her on the porch.

"*Comusta?*" she asked, speaking in the dialect for the first time as Monica relieved her of her load. The one word question seemed to mean much more than "How are you?" or "How has it been?"

Alipio replied in English. "God dictates," he said, his dentures sounding faintly as he smacked his lips, but he was not looking at the foodstuff in the paper bags Monica was carrying. His eyes were on her legs, in the direction she was taking. She knew where the kitchen was, of course. He just wanted to be sure she won't lose her way. Like him. On his way to the kitchen, sometimes he found himself in the bedroom. Lotsa things happened to men his age.

Raymond Federman

WE had just driven out to one of the suburbs of Berlin, Raymond Federman and I, and were admiring the lovely wooded scenery of the neighborhood, the majestic vista rolling down to the lake from the old chateau where we were so warmly received by the German literary functionaries in this setting at once distinguished and so Old World, with its ample if not overbearing furniture, its splendid staircase, its imposing decoration, and in fact we might have been a little put out by the scene had it not been for that warm welcome. As it was we had a feeling of benign superciliousness—yes it was a scene a bit too aristocratic for our plebeian blood, but was it not a setting which by our age and accomplishments we after all deserved? The German functionaries did nothing to disabuse us of this attitude, quite the contrary.

It was only later, much later and back in the States, that we remembered that Wansee was where it all began, and very likely in that same chateau: the Wansee conference where the idea of the final solution was endorsed as the right one for their Jewish problem and set in motion by the Nazi elite.

Reflecting on this now it becomes impossible to maintain that Jews are European, even European Jews like Federman. Yes, many Jews have European reflexes, those Jews with long histories of European evolution. But then Europeans by now have profoundly Jewish reflexes: relativity, consciousness of self, collective social responsibility, via Reb Karl, Reb Albert, Reb Sigmund, to name just a few from the merely recent past.

But Europe is just one part of a long story. And the story Federman tells is the end of the chapter, or rather, what happens after the chapter has ended. The characters have disappeared, the tragedy is over, the stage is bare. Even Samuel

Beckett, Federman's friend and great model, has finally effaced himself for the last time. Twenty or thirty million people have been slaughtered in the Old Country within six years. The great tradition of humanism wasn't worth shit in a chateau, a foxhole, a death camp, a stately state palace. Never mind post-modern, we're all post-humous as Europeans, including the Europeans themselves. Post-human.

And never mind human. How could one even assume the arrogance of individual identity after all those identities were exxed off the surface of the planet? How could one even presume to be a person after all that, much less a human? And how much less so Federman, whose family were among those abruptly exxed?

What kind of dunce could still claim to know the plot now that the continuity has been shattered? The narrative continues, to be sure, but provisionally, unpredictably, you never know what's going to happen next.

One day, Federman, who must be twelve or thirteen at the time, is in the apartment with his family, poor, relatively recent immigrants to France, when the Germans come, he's pushed into a closet by his mother, and suddenly he's an orphan, a fugitive jumping from freight train to freight train, a farm laborer in the south of France, a factory worker in Detroit, a white named Frenchy in a black ghetto, a swim champ, a jazz musician, a paratrooper in Korea, a student in New York, a poet, a jock, a Ph.D., a gambler, a Casanova of note, a professor in California, a novelist in Buffalo, an honored literary guest in Germany. A great story, but what's the plot? and which one of the above is the hero? and where's the verisimilitude? and when is the beginning, the middle, the end? and why should this irrational discontinuity be related in sequential sentences from left to right, left to right to the bottom of the printed page? and how in the name of probability can it be called real?

No, the book of life cannot be paraphrased, it cannot be prescribed, it cannot be predicted, it cannot be dictated, it cannot be imitated, it cannot resemble some other book, it cannot begin, it cannot end, it cannot be made up, it cannot be about major characters or minor characters or any characters other than those of the alphabet, it cannot be about the right ideas, it cannot be controlled, it cannot be about reality, because life is not about reality. It is it. If it weren't, what would be? There is only one thing you can do with the book of life: add to it. Federman writes books that add to it, that's why they don't seem to be like other books, why they're sometimes strange, because life is sometimes strange. Stranger than fiction, as they say.

It's December 18, 1990, today. Two oh eight in the afternoon. The stage, as usual, is bare. Fiction is always after the fact. After the last fact. The last fact is that I'm thinking about Federman and myself in Berlin and how that's part of his story and how he writes his story. The next fact will be Federman's fiction becoming part of your story. As you read it. Date and time as yet unknown.

—Ronald Sukenick

Excerpt from

SMILES ON WASHINGTON SQUARE

(A LOVE STORY OF SORTS)

At first Moinous doesn't understand why Sucette wants him to meet her family. Why she insists on this trip up to Boston. By train. There is no talk of marriage, or anything like that, between them, even though they are now living together in Sucette's apartment, on 105th Street. Certainly not. That would be so incongruous, in spite of the ruses of desire. They are so ill-matched. And there is the difference in age between them. Almost ten years. But Moinous goes and meets The Clique, as Sucette calls her family.

Sucette's father. A tall, angular man with thin lips, a strong chin, sleek white hair that clings close to his high-vaulted skull. Chairman of the board of some corporation or other, Sucette explains later on. A standoffish man, not very affable, who speaks only in monosyllables. What did you say your last name is, young man? he asks Moinous after a brusque handshake upon their first man-to-man meeting in the library of the huge old house where Sucette was raised. It is not easy for Moinous to react correctly with such a person. Being there, being present in front of this man, in front of what appears to be a monument of righteousness, he feels compromised and doesn't know if he should drop to the floor and crawl in silence, or if he should leap on the antique desk in the library and become a brawling superman of arrogance.

Sucette's mother. Still quite attractive for her age. Late fifties. Very blond and charming, but stern and waspish to the tips of her fingernails. Extremely inquisitive. She keeps asking Moinous about his life, his work, his parents, his plans, his ambitions. Moinous tries to avoid her squinting eyes as he mumbles vague answers. To his surprise, he notices how terribly flat-chested she is, even though Sucette is rather buxom.

And her sister too. Yes, that weekend Moinous also meets Sucette's sister, who lives with husband and children in the family house.

Two years younger than Sucette, the sister is stunningly beautiful. Savagely seductive with her sandy-blond hair. But fidgety and insecure. Everyone in the family keeps mentioning her nervousness and insecurity, and that makes her even more nervous and insecure. She seems quite taken with Moinous, who senses that something interesting could unfold between them if they were left to themselves. Moinous, who has remained very French in his attitude toward women, finds *les femmes américaines* to be too self-explanatory. The trouble, however, is that the explanation keeps changing. And what makes it even more troublesome, in the case of the sister, is that the provocation of her body is tempered by the elegance of her clothes and the savoir-faire of her gestures. This confuses him, as everything else does in America.

Indeed, Moinous often wonders about his failure to adapt to a world which is so out of step with its ideals. Often wonders, in spite of his pernicious and incurable optimism, why he abandoned the rationality of Europe, however unreal and obsolete it may be, for the temptation of trying to achieve comfort, and perhaps even success, in such a disjointed reality.

Moinous tells Sucette, when they are alone for a moment during the weekend, that her sister is making big eyes at him. And Sucette retorts, Oh I'm not surprised, my sister is always ready to jump into bed with the first guy who smiles at her. Go ahead, if that's what you want. I don't care.

No no, that's not what I mean. I was just. And Moinous blushes.

And besides, Sucette tells him, one does not say Making big eyes in English. It's not correct. One says Making eyes. Sucette often corrects the little mistakes Moinous makes in his adopted tongue, even though he argues in his defense that the English language is totally irrational.

Okay, Moinous tries to explain, but in France we say *Faire les gros yeux* when somebody makes a pass at you.

Well, maybe in France, but now you're in America. You better get used to that. Sucette does not always correct Moinous with such a sarcastic tone of voice, but this time she is irritated. The whole weekend is turning into a disaster. Especially with the sister's husband.

A self-impressed braggard with no feeling for others, Sucette's brother-in-law is a big loud bully of a man in search of a destination, but who pretends to have reached it. The only son of one of the best families in Boston, Sucette whispers to Moinous when she sees his puzzled look upon being introduced to the brother-in-law. He knocked up my sister when she was in college, Bennington, and they had to get married. They've been living here in this house ever since. Almost ten years now. He used to play football. For Army or Navy, I forget which.

The brother-in-law, freckled and puffy, constantly teases people, including his own three lovely daughters. But especially his wife, whom he treats with unabashed vulgarity. How do you like my gorgeous wife? he asks Moinous as he pats her on the rump. Wouldn't you want to play with that if you had a chance? Hey man, look at those boobs.

Matthew, please, stop that, you're embarrassing me, the sister whines as she pushes him away, tossing her head aside so that her blond mane flies sensuously across her face. Moinous is horrified by this scene, and consequently fails to recognize the voluptuous look Sucette's sister throws his way from behind the screen of her hair.

Somehow, the brother-in-law and Moinous manage to become buddies during the weekend because of their army experiences, even though there is a difference in age, and evidently they were not of the same rank. Moinous made only corporal, in the paratroopers, and even then he got busted to Pfc because of a dumb mistake in Tokyo. The brother-in-law was a captain in the Marines, he explains. No, he does not explain, he asserts in a commanding voice while laughing at his own embarrassing Marine Corps stories.

Nonetheless, he is impressed that Moinous was with the tough 82nd Airborne Division, and that he made forty-seven jumps out of a plane. Three in combat, Moinous specifies. In Korea. Not the most ideal type of terrain for parachuting with all those crummy rice paddies. I tell you, I'm lucky I didn't get hurt, or even killed over there. The brother-in-law never went overseas. He trained the dumb recruits somewhere in Texas, he giggles. But now he's in the reserves.

Much of the conversation, when the whole family is gathered, especially during the sumptuous meals served by the two maids, Margie and Molly, centers around Matthew's and Moinous's adventures in the service. Matthew during the Second World War, Moinous in the Korean War. These army reminiscences make it somewhat easier for Moinous to endure the weekend. It also gives him a chance to boast about how he served America even though he was not yet a citizen. But now I am an American, he declares emphatically. I became a citizen in Tokyo, a year ago.

Oh my goodness, how could that happen? Sucette's mother inquires with a supercilious smile which Moinous interprets as a sign of curiosity and a signal for him to tell the story of how he became a citizen in such unusual circumstances. The whole family is sitting around the dinner table, the first evening of Moinous & Sucette's visit to Boston.

You see, Moinous begins after clearing his throat and half rising from his chair to better tell his story, during the Korean War a new law was passed by the Congress of the United States. Before that you had to wait five years, and you could become a citizen only on American soil. But this new law made it possible for people who were overseas to become citizens on foreign land, and after only a few months in the service. I think three months, or something like that. So they gathered all the foreigners, I mean all the foreign soldiers who were serving in the U.S. Army in the Far East, and brought them to Tokyo. I was in a foxhole then, near Inchon, and let me tell you, it was rough. I mean cold as hell. And those little guys kept coming at us from all sides. Anyway, the captain of my outfit called me and said, Corporal, get your gear together and your ass moving, eh, you're on your way to Tokyo. That's exactly what he said to me. I was a corporal at the time in charge of a sixty-millimeter-mortar squad. What's going on? I asked. Don't know, the captain answered. The order just came in for you to report immediately to General Headquarters in Tokyo. Not the foggiest idea what it's all about, but dammit must be important, just when I need every goddamn man I've got.

You see, Moinous explains, we were getting ready for this new offensive. A big spring offensive. It was in March. Or perhaps April. Moinous takes a sip of wine from the finely etched half-filled crystal goblet in front of him, and continues.

What the hell do they want with me? I said to myself. But of course, I didn't argue. An order is an order when you're in the army. Right. Moinous pauses as he looks at the brother-in-law, who gives him an approving nod. And besides, Moinous goes on, I was so glad to get out of that mud pile. So I packed my stuff in my duffel bag and got on this Air Force plane which flew me to Tokyo. I was excited about going to Tokyo, as you can well imagine. You know, the nightlife and all that. Especially after more than six months in a foxhole on the front line. Wow was I horny. And nervous too because I had no idea what this was all about. In Tokyo they gathered all of us foreigners. Hungarians, Poles, Italians, Rumanians, you know, all kinds of foreigners, even two Arabs. I was the only Frenchman in the group. Then they explained to us that we were going to be naturalized. They even issued new uniforms for everybody, and we had a full dress rehearsal before the big day.

Moinous is getting so excited by his story that he is now standing up and gesticulating like a puppet. When the day came, he goes on, we all assembled in this huge auditorium at the Ernie Pyle Center. It's like a recreation center in Tokyo where they have billiards, bowling alleys, Ping-Pong tables, movies, and all sorts of things like that for the soldiers to relax. It's really a great place. You can even meet girls there, nice American girls, I mean, when they have dances. Anyway, we were sitting in the auditorium, very sharp and spit-shined in our new uniforms, and they had all these officers in full parade dress, and even two generals for the occasion. One of them a three-star general, because you see it was an important historic event. First time, you understand, first time in the history of this country that foreigners were being naturalized overseas. The generals made speeches about America, about freedom, and duty, and responsibility, you know, junk like that. Then an orchestra played music. A military band. They played all these bombastic tunes like *The Star Spangled Banner. America the Beautiful. God Bless America.* It was very nice. After the music our names were called alphabetically. The colonel who called the names had difficulties pronouncing some of them. When he came to my name he got it all wrong and everybody laughed, including the two generals. And I did too.

Moinous stops a moment to smile and clear his throat while the whole family waits for the rest of the story, forks and knives neatly resting on the plates. When my turn came I went up on the stage, from the right side. Shook hands with the officers who formed a line up there, and with the two generals in the middle who congratulated me. It was not easy, you see, because first you had to salute and then shake hands, with the same hand, while grabbing your diploma with the other hand. But we had rehearsed, so nobody really goofed too much. After that you walked across the stage, saluting and shaking hands with all the other officers. At the end of the line there was a guy who took your picture. I still have it. Someday, Sucette, remind me to show it to you. I really look great in my paratrooper uniform. On the left side of the stage there was a sergeant. I still remember his face well. All red and puffy. A big fat sonofa, oops, excuse me, who gave each of us a little American flag. There was a box full of them because there must have been more than a hundred of us foreigners becoming citizens that day. You know, those little flags you put on cakes.

Moinous stops talking and draws in the air, in front of his face, with his index finger, a little imaginary rectangle. Then we went back to our seats holding the diploma in one hand and the flag in the other. It felt stupid.

When I was back in my seat, I looked at this little flag, and you won't believe what was written on the side. Like this, up and down, on the side: MADE IN JAPAN. No I'm not kidding. That's what it said. MADE IN JAPAN. I mean, the flag, the flag was made in Japan. Can you believe that?

Moinous stops and sits down, expecting a reaction to his story. As he pulls his chair closer to the table he knocks his fork to the floor. His head under the table, he waits for the reaction. Perhaps even some laughter. A touch of polite laughter. After all it is a funny story. But no one around the table says anything. Except finally, Sucette's father, after a long silence and a little cough. Well, I guess that was the best way for them to take care of this matter since it is the law. It would have been too much trouble for them to bring all these people back to the States. Or to ship American-made flags to Japan.

As he emerges from under the table holding his fork, Moinous looks at Sucette imploringly, sort of asking if he goofed in telling this story. She gives him an almost imperceptible reassuring nod, which he interprets as meaning, It's okay, it's okay. But he knows, he knows, it's not okay.

The conversation drifts to something else. The brother-in-law is now telling one of his Marine Corps stories. Half-listening while chewing a piece of meat, a rather delicious piece of roast beef au jus, Moinous reflects on how remarkable it is that such an ordinary consciousness as the brother-in-law somehow always manages to entertain a human dialogue even in the midst of the most uncongenial situation. If only Moinous could be like that. But unfortunately for him, when talking with people like these he has a feeling that he must constantly account for the embarrassing circumstances of his being. He may have escaped the big-scale xenophobic pomposity of Europe, but now he must confront and endure the Disneyland mentality of America.

Fuck them, Moinous thinks, now chewing the baked potatoes. I yam what I yam and that's all that I yam, he says to himself in piteous self-justification. Not aware, of course, that he has mentally echoed Popeye the sailorman. But that's how this toot toot American gets under your skin and into your bones if you don't watch out. In this land of comic-book mentality, the self will dash its hopes without any help from the outside if given time to prey on itself. Moinous is no exception. He is quickly learning that the attainment of hope and success in America creates an equal aching void to take the place of unfulfilled hope and desire. It will take Moinous a long time, and many more disastrous encounters with people such as these, to realize that hope never ceases to be a torture.

Later, he will tell Sucette. You know something, I don't think I'll ever understand your family.

And Sucette will tell him. Maybe that's because here in America people are not what they say they are, whereas in Europe they are what they say they are.

Well, I don't know. I'm not sure you've got it right, Moinous answers. I think it's the reverse. Sometimes I have the feeling it's easier to know the people you're talking to when they lie about themselves rather than when they tell the truth. But that's not the case with your family. They confuse me with their looks of integrity. They make me feel insignificant and poor.

That's exactly what I mean, Sucette replies. My family is inscrutable. The order and sanctity of their Puritanism screen the ontological weaknesses of their lives. You see, they always identify poverty less with evil than with unimportance. That's why they are so unintelligible to an outsider like you. Or at least, think they are. And why you are so insignificant to them.

Then why the hell did you bring me here? Moinous cries out. To humiliate me?

No, darling, not to humiliate you, but to confirm our love, Sucette answers as her face softens with tenderness.

Suddenly Moinous realizes that from being a lover in Sucette's comfortable New York apartment, here, in this stuffy Boston house he has become a mere situation. He is about to burst into rage when he notices how Sucette's mouth is now set in a bitter grimace and her eyes full of pain like those of a martyr whose body bristles with arrows. Moinous reaches for Sucette's hand and squeezes it. Oh but I do love you, I do, I swear, in spite of them. However, for the first time in his life Moinous understands what quicksand love is.

Nevertheless, Moinous has never met people like these. How could he have? Not in the kind of sordid life he's led up to now in America. First two years working in a Detroit factory, then the next two years in the army, as a draftee, and now jobless in New York. Consequently, with the little experience he has, he cannot recognize how typical, how stereotypical these people are. And that's even true of the three lovely blond daughters of Sucette's sister.

Nine, seven, and six. Immaculately scrubbed and groomed, always dressed in matching jumpsuits or sailor dresses, they too act as if they have been programmed by some ultramoral superpolite mechanism. However, the presence of Moinous in the house seems to have disrupted their behavior. During the entire weekend they look at him with flirty adoring blue eyes. And since Moinous loves little girls, always has, and even knows by instinct how to deal with them on their own level, he keeps smiling at Sucette's nieces or making funny faces at them whenever he has a chance and no one is looking. The three little dolls cannot refrain from giggling and from wiggling their charming derrières as they chase up and down the stairs to hide in the secret nooks and crannies of this enormous house, even though their grandmother constantly reprimands and reminds them to behave.

That weekend, Moinous also meets Sucette's great-grandmother on her father's side, whose ninety-fifth birthday is being celebrated. All my other grandparents are dead, Sucette explains, but this one is like Plymouth Rock. She believes she's historically immortal, and so far seems to have proved it. Totally senile, but remarkably sprightly, she scoots around the house in an electric wheelchair, bumping into the furniture, knocking over the plants as she mumbles under her breath. At the dining table she presides at one end, but usually falls asleep by the second course. Sucette is very fond of her great-grandmother, even though the old lady does not recognize her and keeps asking who that is whenever Sucette enters the room.

Yes, Moinous meets all of them in Boston, during that extraordinary weekend. Including Thomas, the butler, who's been with the family for over thirty-five years, and the two maids, Margie and Molly, both rather plump and imperious, but friendly with Moinous, within the limits of their domestic capacity. Perhaps they sense that he would be more comfortable talking or even flirting with them in the kitchen than making conversation with the family at the dining table.

Moinous feels miserably out of place in this environment. Perhaps that is Sucette's intent. She wants him to know where she comes from. What her background is. And so on. Just in case. But it's not easy for Moinous to understand this milieu, and to fit in. And it gets more and more unbearable as the weekend progresses. It's one of those long three-day weekends.

By the second evening at dinner, Moinous is totally ignored. No one is talking to him anymore. The conversation is all about the family. How Sucette's poor aunt Beth still hasn't recovered from her husband's sudden death, you remember Uncle George of course, who had that fatal seizure last spring, what a pity, such a fine, gentle man, and how Aunt Beth is still perturbed that Sucette could not make it to the funeral, it's really a shame, and how the whole family, yes Aunt Beth too, is planning to spend the month of July in the New Hampshire cottage, and will Sucette be able to join them, it would be so wonderful to have everybody together for once, and how Father has been working so hard lately, you know, with the way the economy is going, those goddamn commies are ruining the country, and how Matthew is seriously considering running for office in the next election, as Lieutenant-Governor of Massachusetts, yes he's been approached, and how Mother is seeing a specialist for her anxieties, oh nothing really serious, and how the three darling girls are doing so well in school, and how Sucette's sister is hoping to get away to Europe with a friend in a couple of months, it will be so much fun and so relaxing, if only Sucette could come along, but she's so busy in New York, on and on and on.

Blahblahblah, blahblahblah, Moinous grumbles to himself as he is getting more and more annoyed. And embarrassed too, because the men have to wear jackets for dinner, and the sleeves of his sport coat are worn through at the elbows and he tries to keep them tucked below the table while eating, which is not very comfortable, and on top of that he doesn't know which of the three forks he's supposed to use for the fish, and Sucette is hardly paying attention to him now, and he feels like getting up from the table to go and hide in the bathroom for a while, and perhaps even cry.

As Moinous sits there, crushed by his own superfluous presence and the lurking insecurities of his being, he has a sudden urge to scream, to jump up and down and scream in the middle of all that politely hushed clank of the serving dishes and that sweet buzzing of conversation. He feels like shouting vile obscenities. Something like, Fuck you all and your fucking lovely family life. Perhaps even in French. *Allez tous vous faire enculer dans les miches.* Moinous often regresses into the safety of his native tongue whenever he is troubled. Of course, that would not be very civilized. But then Moinous could explain, paraphrasing Freud, that the first man who hurled a foul word at his adversary was the true founder of civilization.

Instead, as the voice of the brother-in-law gets louder and louder since he's now explaining his political views, and his gestures more and more uncontrolled, and he loses all human attributes as he turns into a wild beast, his voice becoming a groan and his hands gigantic paws, Moinous begins to undress the people around the table. Except Sucette, who seems to have fallen asleep in the middle of the brother-in-law's vocifera-tions, her head resting on her folded arms on the table.

Moinous sees Sucette's mother sitting upright across from him with bare breasts bursting out of her blouse which she has unbuttoned with quick nervous fingers. She is holding her breasts with her hands and thrusting them at Moinous. They are small and wrinkled, but with large brown nipples that stare at Moinous like tired eyes. Without abandoning her supercil-ious expression, she strokes her breasts and leans over the table to offer them, and the thick milk now dripping from the swol-len nipples, to the guest of honor, as her mouth splits open and Moinous notices, for the first time, the huge gap between her two front teeth.

Sucette's father, meanwhile, is standing naked at the head of the table. His skin is pale, pale bluish like that of a corpse, and hairless. He has an enormous erection protruding out of his foreskin above his deflated cullions, and the old penis is all red, crimson red, and he too leans forward, his skinny thighs pressed hard against the edge of the table, and he places his raw burn-ing member in his stemmed crystal glass and shakes it with two fingers as the iced water splashes over, and his thin lips break into a painful grimace.

Sucette's sister is on her knees, her dress pulled up to her furry golden crotch, and she is fondling Moinous's fly while panting and drooling from the mouth, and with trembling but expert fingers she extricates his phallus which brusquely swells in her hand, and she slides it in her mouth and sucks it with wet abandon.

On the other side of the table, Sucette's three lovely nieces have taken off their sailor dresses and discarded their lace pan-ties. They are giggling and rolling on the carpeted floor while fingering each other's rosy twats. And even the great-grand-mother is involved. She has removed her false teeth from her mouth and is playing with them on the table, making the complete set of yellowish dentures, upper and lower, walk and talk like some miniature monster among the silver, the crystal and the porcelain, knocking over the glasses, as she goes quack-quack, click-click, with her empty mouth all sucked in.

While all this is going on, Margie and Molly, quite unconcerned, continue to circulate around the table, picking up the glasses, refilling them with wine, removing dishes. The whole scene unwinds like the reel of a silent movie, except for the quackquacks and clickclicks of the great-grandmother.

Slouched in his chair, legs wide apart, Moinous is ready to explode and abuse the inside of the sister's mouth when, all of a sudden, the brother-in-law, who all the while has been going on with his political ranting, knocks over his glass of wine with a sweeping gesture. The red liquid slowly spreads on the white damask tablecloth. The bloodlike stain brings everyone back to the formality of the moment, and at once they are all properly seated and dressed. Sucette is awake, rubbing her eyes with the back of her hand. The others are staring at the clumsy brother-in-law with sanctimonious eyes. Then the conversation buzzes again in its normal flow. Margie and Molly have rushed to wipe the spilt wine and refill the glasses.

Moinous murmurs an excuse, to no one in particular, gets up, and goes to the bathroom. He locks the door. Drops his pants to his feet, and with angry frustration masturbates violently in front of the mirror until he ejaculates in the sink. He turns the water on and watches his sperm go down the drain.

Later, at the end of the weekend, on the express train back to New York City, Moinous tells Sucette about his fantastic vision of her family at the dinner table.

Don't you think, Sucette asks, not even trying to hide her irritation, that such puerile fantasies show a twisted imagination and a lack of emotional unity?

We all live like cockroaches in the crevices of our twisted imagination, Moinous retorts. We fluctuate between glandular activity and pure sensuality, between loneliness and mental discomfort. Somewhere in there our emotions float like wrecks, and there never is any emotional unity. Besides, such unity is impossible since we don't know whether emotions are based in the body or if they originate in the mind. So don't give me all that stuff about twisted imagination and lack of emotional unity.

What's gotten into you? Sucette's face is all flushed now as she continues the argument. That's not what I was asking. Who is talking about the split between mind and body. You always misunderstand everything I say. I was merely expressing an opinion about fantasy. And anyway, I warned you about my family.

Well, keep your opinions to yourself, Moinous replies, obviously disturbed. And next time don't ask me to go with you to Boston. Their first fight. First inevitable lovers' quarrel. And for the rest of the train ride back to New York they hardly talk to each other. Sucette seemingly engrossed in the novel she is reading. *Lie Down in Darkness,* by William Styron. Moinous staring out of the train window at the rainy New England landscape. Yes, it is raining again.

Of course, all this happens several months after the exchange of smiles on Washington Square. Smiles which will lead to nothing unless Moinous & Sucette meet again, by chance.

Between this second chance encounter, at the Librairie Française, and the disastrous weekend in Boston, Moinous will become better acquainted with Sucette. He will learn all about her life and background during their intimate conversations. Except that it will be a slow, gradual revelation. For unlike Moinous, who gladly squanders his inner life without any restraint, Sucette does not reveal herself easily. She is prudent with spoken words. She has been forced into prudence of language and manners early in her youth, and only as she grows older does she learn romance and the gestures of passion. The natural sequel of an unnatural beginning. Consequently, Sucette operates out of the grating dissimilarity of extremes, in the imaginary void where they merge. So it takes time for her to reveal to Moinous the details of her two abortions, her one miscarriage, her nervous breakdown, and her two divorces. All this and more she gradually tells Moinous in the long hours they spend together talking. Talking and loving each other, of course. During the long hours of night especially. Sitting close to each other, or lying in bed, bodies entwined. Most love stories are nocturnal. That's what makes them fascinating.

But as she stands on Washington Square, that rainy afternoon, time must seem endless to Sucette in the prospect of her future involvement with Moinous. And vice versa. Since they are both in a state of emotional availability within the confines of their loneliness, anything can happen. Except that neither of them can anticipate the consequences of their love story. That's always the case. The quick smiles they exchange may be enough to engender that story, but not enough to reveal the intensity of its hope, nor the fury of its conditional disappointment.

That day, however, unlike Moinous, who has nothing better to do but wander aimlessly in the city, Sucette has a reason for being on Washington Square. A political reason. Besides, she doesn't have a steady job. Doesn't need one. She has private means. That's why she can be in the Village on a regular workday. She too is unemployed, in a manner of speaking, but not because she was fired, or laid off, or anything like that. No, Sucette has never really had to work. Except during the period when she ran away from home, at the age of twenty-seven, and no one knew where she had gone. For two years she worked in a factory in Brooklyn. Completely cut off from family support, she had to work, or she would have starved. Though at the time there was another reason, an idealistic reason, for her to take this factory job. When she arrived in New York from Boston, Sucette joined a Communist cell as a gesture of rebellion against her family and her background, and it is as a Fellow Traveler that she was assigned a job in a Brooklyn factory to try and indoctrinate her fellow workers.

This was five years ago. Almost five years. At about the same time Moinous arrived in America from France. And now Moinous is starving. Well, almost. But that's nothing new for him. Most of his life he's been suffering the humiliation of poverty and deprivation. This is why Sucette's smile on Washington Square means so much to him, even though she does not speak to him on that occasion. That smile represents a touch of human contact, full of compassion, inadvertent as it may be, in the bleak solitude of his present situation. Moinous is not very good at reading signs, especially Anglo-Saxon signs. Or rather, he often misreads the signs others send him. He quickly gets carried away. For no sooner does Moinous put his body in order than his mind trips him.

Even though Sucette has now drifted away from her involvement with her Fellow Travelers, it is for political reasons that she is on Washington Square that day, in spite of the rain. She came by taxi from her cozy apartment on 105th Street. She has a purpose that afternoon. Yes, a political purpose. She is participating in an anti-McCarthy demonstration. This is the period when the Senator from Wisconsin is doing his red-baiting. Like millions of other outraged Americans who have finally caught on to his demagogical tactics, Sucette is very disturbed by The Senator's reckless accusations, and on that day has decided to do something about it. Whereas Moinous has no specific purpose for being here, except perhaps to look at the arch, or talk to the pigeons. In English or in French, depending on his mood, or in both simultaneously. Especially to the one-legged pigeon with whom Moinous has established a friendly relationship.

Moinous notices that crippled bird one day when he sits dejectedly on a bench in the Square, pitying himself because he's just lost his job. This seems to happen to him with some regularity. He takes out his sandwich from his coat pocket, unwraps it, and slowly chews on the two dry slices of white bread with a piece of domestic Swiss cheese in between. The bird hops over on one leg. At first Moinous thinks the other leg is folded under into the bird's feathery belly. Nothing unusual about that. Moinous has seen pictures of birds standing on one leg. Pink flamingos. Storks. But on closer inspection, and particularly since the bird keeps tumbling over onto its side like a drunkard, Moinous realizes that indeed this bird has only one leg. What are you, my poor little fellow, some kind of handicapped war veteran? Moinous asks, attempting a smile of compassion in the midst of his self-pitying mood. He throws a piece of bread on the ground. The pigeon pecks at it while balancing himself precariously on one leg, then looks up and gives a little squeak. An almost human squeak which nearly brings tears to

Moinous's eyes. From that day on, Moinous and the one-legged pigeon become fast friends. They see each other regularly by the same bench, whenever Moinous comes down to Washington Square.

However, the day Moinous & Sucette smile at each other, the pigeons are not there on the Square. Not because of the rain. Pigeons are well-known for being rainproof. But because of the demonstration. Or rather they are not hopping on the ground carefree as usual, but gloomily perched high up on the arch, away from the crowd. Therefore, Moinous cannot talk to his one-legged friend, even though he thinks he sees him, way at the top of the arch, dripping with rain. Moinous doesn't know about the demonstration. He just stumbles into it, and indeed is very surprised to see so many people assembled on the Square in such bad weather. Maybe two hundred or three hundred of them, he estimates as he mingles with the demonstrators.

Moinous likes to walk in the streets of New York when he has nothing else to do. Alone. For hours. Even five years after first seeing this city, he is still astonished by the beauty, by the grandoise magnificence of this amazing city. Its incredible shape, and the way the streets and the avenues crisscross in neat patterns to form blocks, as they are called here. The spectacular buildings. Those immense towers that reach into the sky. Those skyscrapers. And the wind, ah the relentless wind that blows through these corridors of glass walls and brings tears to your eyes, especially late at night when you're walking all alone. This is how Moinous described New York City in a letter to a friend back in France, soon after he arrived in America, trying to be as poetic as he could to give his friend a real sense of how fantastic this city is, though the friend never answered. Unless the reply got lost in the mail, Moinous speculated. For at the time he still thought, as most foreigners do, that letters from Europe often get lost in the mail. In any event, this was the end of his correspondence with his friend in France. Nevertheless, five years later, Moinous still finds New York fascinating.

And especially the people. Ah the mass of people in the streets. All of them rushing from one part of the city to another with such intensity, and always carrying packages or boxes or briefcases or suitcases. Moinous never carries anything like that. Except, of course, when he stops at the grocery store on his way home to his furnished room in the Bronx to buy a loaf of bread or some cheese or a box of noodles or other essentials like these for survival. So many interesting people one can meet in New York, by chance. If only Moinous knew how to take advantage of chance encounters, he could talk to some of these people as he wanders in the streets, and these fortuitous encounters could lead to unusual situations. Perhaps even result in love affairs.

Yes, Moinous likes to walk in the city in search of the unexpected. Walking alone gives him a chance to contemplate his problems and sort out his confused inner life. Not without a touch of self-pity. But that's justifiable. Two weeks already without a job, and at most three dollars left to survive, and nothing in sight. Nothing. No need to whine about it, Moinous says to himself. These are hard times. Lots of other guys in the same lousy situation.

Sucette doesn't have to worry about such problems of daily survival. She has her income. But she cares about humanity, and about injustice and civil rights. She does indeed. That's why she is on Washington Square that afternoon, and why she is demonstrating, with hundreds of other concerned citizens, against Senator McCarthy's abuse of human rights.

She is carrying a sign, as many other demonstrators on the Square are too. Holding it high above her head. A large rectangular piece of cardboard nailed to what looks like a broomstick. It proclaims, in handwritten letters, freedom of speech and freedom of political action. Moinous cannot read exactly what it says because the ink of the words is being washed away by the heavy downpour.

After they eventually meet, Moinous will question Sucette about her political activities, because he cannot understand why someone like her, someone so well off and so secure in her life-style, would want to get involved with other people's miseries, and Sucette will explain that it's because she is very concerned about what's happening in America. Dear love, you must understand that we live in a strange period of history, and in a very sick world. Behind our outrageous optimism and our glorified self-righteousness lurks a dreadful absurdity. America may think it is the guardian angel of the world right now, but thirty years from now we, and I mean you and I darling, will have to account for the stupidities of our time. The anxious, confused years we are now living will lead us into tragic moments.

And Sucette will go on explaining, though Moinous will ultimately discover all that for himself, years after he & Sucette have parted and he has learned to understand and even question his adopted country, that America is a chronically ailing society, but which believes, every decade or so, to have found a cure for its illness. The sicker it gets, you see, the more it believes in its power of recuperation and recovery. At the moments of high fever, pseudophysicians appear everywhere and make history. They become the doctors of the incurable. Frantic politicians, demented military strategists, obsessed ideologists, immunizing leaders, philosophical chiropractors, utopian anaesthetists, they all examine the illness demagogically, and the more incurable it is, the more they make believe they have found a cure. They convulse in front of the patient, and the convulsions become contagious.

Sounds serious, Moinous says, shaking his head concernedly. Yes, it is serious, Sucette continues, her face glowing with excitement. In order for America to believe in its national good health, it must be made to believe in the existence of a germ which can be isolated and against which it is possible to be inoculated for protection. And so, periodically, America exposes such a germ, and quickly offers a cure.

How do they do that? Moinous interrupts to show that he's still with Sucette.

Well, it's simple. Get rid of the spades, the spics, the spooks, the chinks, the coons, the colored, the niggers, the schwartzes. Burn the commies, the pinkos, the pansies, the jigs, the reds, the commie crapola, the liberals, the atheists. Lock up the gooks, the japs, the redskins, the weirdos, the black beauties, the bleeding hearts, the jungle bunnies, the dopies. Exterminate the freaks, the beatniks, the yids, the kikes, the hebes, the chosen people, the evolutionists. Oppress the meatheads, the dingbats, the dumbells, the hillbillies, the dumb polacks. Suppress the queers, the fairies, the lesbs, the fags, the queens, the fruits, the abnormals. Execute the four-eyes, the sheenies, the yanks, the rebs. Deport the dagos, the mics, the frogs, the krauts, the macaronis, the chicanos, and America will be healthy again.

Wow, that's incredible. Incredible. Moinous is so impressed with Sucette's diatribe, but especially with her amazing vocabulary, that he keeps repeating, Wow, that's incredible. And then he asks, Will you teach me all these American words?

Oh don't worry, Sucette replies, you'll learn them all soon enough. Especially how they are used to abuse one's fellowman. But now you understand why I have to get involved. Why I was demonstrating on Washington Square against that lunatic.

Indeed Moinous will understand and even witness, in the many years he will live in America, that all it takes is to create a scare, a red scare, a black scare, a youth scare, a yellow scare. All it takes is to fabricate a crisis. Any crisis. Economic, social, spiritual, ethnic, pathetic, anti-intellectual. And immediately America is on her way to a speedy recovery.

Strange paradox which Moinous cannot comprehend at first. But then Moinous is rather ignorant of the political situation in America at the time when he meets Sucette. He is too busy with his own survival to be involved in other people's misery. He simply lives out the consequences of politics as best he can. For if there is one question Moinous dreads and to which he has never been able to invent a satisfactory reply, it is the question, What the fuck am I doing here in the middle of all this?

And Moinous often asks this question of himself. Which means that he is not often happy with what he is doing and where he is doing it. Naturally, that question implies that Moinous would prefer to be doing something else, somewhere else. But even that something else, somewhere else, would probably elicit the same question from him. What the fuck am I doing here?

Therefore, on this dull, irksome afternoon, when Moinous wanders in the midst of all these shouting people gathered on Washington Square, he doesn't know about the demonstration, and is surprised to see this crowd. And especially all these policemen, some on foot, others on horseback, surround the place. What the hell is going on? Moinous wonders.

He came all the way down to the village to talk to his friend Charlie. The one-legged pigeon. That's what he calls him now. Charlie. Or Charlot, when he speaks French to him. For it seems that the one-legged pigeon, Charlie-Charlot, is a bilingual bird who responds just as well to French as to English.

In any case, Moinous comes all the way to Washington Square to see his friend Charlie because he has nothing better to do that afternoon since he's been fired from his last job. Not that it was the ideal job. Deliveryman for a dry cleaners on the East Side. Of course, that's not his profession. Just another job until something better and more permanent comes along. Moinous takes what he can get these days, since, according to the latest economic reports, there is a recession in America, and things will get worse, the newspapers are saying, before they get better.

Yet, in spite of all, there is a brighter and richer future ahead of him. And of course, there is also the eventual encounter with Sucette, which may perhaps lead to emotional involvement. For as Moinous will someday discover, in America the struggle for survival does not exist within the individual psyche alone, but within the collective unconsciousness of Capitalism. This discovery will not only help Moinous overcome and even forget the misery and loneliness of his early years in America, but also help him recuperate and perpetuate the dominant illusions of his youth. That's why America is called the land of opportunity.

And so, not only is there a more prosperous and happy future ahead of Moinous, but also a more intellectual, and perhaps even an artistic one. After all, he is not a dumb guy, even though he's been pushed around by fate, and by all sorts of unfortunate circumstances which are the cause of his present existential fiasco. No, Moinous is not dumb. On the contrary, bright, sensitive, full of energy, determined almost to the point of stubbornness, ambitious within the confines of reason, talented in many ways, even kind and generous on occasions.

The fundamental problem with Moinous is that he has

never been able to function within the traditional rules of social behavior and decorum, and even if he were to become sufficiently confident to propose his own rules, he would soon be disobeying them as well. As a foreigner, Moinous is culturally and socially deprived.

As a matter of fact, that's exactly what one of his army buddies tells him one day when they are playing basketball. Shooting baskets for fun and relaxation in the gym at Fort Bragg where Moinous is stationed before being shipped overseas, and he keeps missing the hoop.

The problem with you, my man, the buddy says, a fast kid from New Jersey, is that you don't have the moves. As a frog who didn't get raised in this country, you are definitely deprived, culturally and socially, if you know what I mean.

Well it's because in France we don't play this fucking game, Moinous replies while piteously attempting another hook shot. You give me a soccer ball and I'll show you some moves.

And certainly, Moinous will have to go a long way before he learns the moves of the American-way-of-life. But what he needs right now is more class. More polish. Sophistication, in other words. And especially more education. Not experience. He's had plenty of that, even though he's only twenty-three years old. What Moinous needs is good solid intellectual and social education. And who knows, perhaps when Sucette begins to care for him after they come together, this will become possible.

For eventually, Moinous & Sucette may indeed come together, and that will have to be told, one way or another. However, to describe now how their rapture gushes out when finally they come together would be an impropriety. It would probably sentimentalize that precious moment and as a result vulgarize it. Too many love stories degenerate into cheap romances by being prematurely and superficially described. It would be unfair to Moinous & Sucette to turn their love affair into a mockery of itself.

Besides, right now, neither of them is concerned with this question. Right now Sucette is demonstrating against McCarthy with some measure of intensity and integrity, while Moinous, jobless and depressed, stumbles into the political gathering on Washington Square totally unaware of what is going on. And of course, neither of them can anticipate what will unfold. For without expecting it, they find themselves decoyed into a gratuitous exchange of smiles which may not lead to anything, unless they talk to each other.

Sucette will perhaps forget this brief incident when she returns to her apartment and settles in for a quiet evening with a good book. Probably the second volume of Franz Kafka's *Diaries* which she has just received as a gift from her friend Richard. Or else she will work on her short-story assignment for the creative writing workshop she is taking at Columbia University. The story is due in a couple of weeks, and right now the plot is not going anywhere. Perhaps she will make Moinous a character in that story. Yes, a chance encounter for her heroine. That might make something happen.

And by the time Moinous gets back to his furnished room in the Bronx, just off the Grand Concourse, he too will forget the charming blonde who smiled at him so compassionately down in the Village, when he discovers that he's been evicted from his room for not having paid the rent in more than three weeks. The landlady threatened him several times these past few days.

Or else, even more depressed than earlier because of this new unfortunate turn of events, Moinous will build this chance encounter all out of proportion in his mind, and imagine himself already in love with this mysterious, beautiful woman. Yes, he will project into that smile the entire scenario of his love story. For indeed, one cannot write off the inequality between imagination and emotion in the mind of a lonely person.

Therefore, in spite of its rather problematic beginning, the love story of Moinous & Sucette will have to unfold, one way or another.

And if Moinous were familiar with Kafka's work, which regrettably he is not at this time, he would perhaps remember this marvelous passage from *The Diaries,* and quote it to himself to justify his present confusion. *The beginning of every story,* writes Kafka, *is ridiculous at first. There seems no hope that this newborn thing, still incomplete and tender in every joint, will be able to keep alive in the completed organizations of the world, which, like every completed organization, strives to close itself off. However, one should not forget that the story, if it has any justification to exist, bears its complete organization within itself even before it has been fully formed. For this reason despair over the beginning of a story is unwarranted.*

Frank Chin

Wʜᴇɴ Frank Chin's first novel, *Donald Duk,* was published in 1991 (Coffee House Press), I was surprised that reviewers referred to the book as his "first novel." I first met Frank Chin (1940–   ) in 1969, and ever since then I've thought of him as a novelist first and a playwright and essayist second. In the sixties, his unpublished novel *A Chinese Lady Dies* won the Jackson Award from the San Francisco Foundation. It was the first Chinese American novel I had ever read. I was a nineteen-year-old undergraduate at the University of California at Berkeley and an aspiring writer.

Reading *A Chinese Lady Dies* nearly destroyed my ambition to be a writer. It was all of Chinese America, everything real, significant, and substantial about the place we come from, inhabit, and occupy. What else was there left to say? In one stroke, Chin's novel defined the tradition and history of Chinese American writing and its future. It was dense and complex and bopped along in a kind of word jazz that conveyed the first real and accurate sense of the Chinese American self, one that didn't depend on the stereotypes of our being foreign and alien in American pop culture. The Chinatown he described didn't hum to the neon and local color critics say should have been in our writing to give it "place." His writing in *A Chinese Lady Dies* left everyone else on the "outside" foreign and alien, as in this description of Chinese New Year's celebration in San Francisco's Chinatown:

> The air was very black for all the lights of the celebration. The rain was heavy. The rain was thorough. The shattered water came glistening fishscales, down, gigantic noisy tin and silver dandruff

crashing out of nowhere in a constant, hypnotic, illogical noise people ceased to hear, ceased to realize was working on their nerves like termites in the woodwork, he knew. Dirigible knew the rain was working on him. He knew the rain was working on everyone. The people were stupid. They were numbed stupid. One by one, he saw people glazed and glistening from the rain, like madmen spit in the face asking why in delirium. The tapping of the rain, the shrill flutelike cleanliness of the rain, the wet, worked in all the nerves, in every organ, in every globule of fat, every ounce of hearing. It confused him he realized, as no one else realized they were confused by the rain working on them, making them grope and blink to perceive the grand spectacle of the New Year's celebration through faulty senses, through encumbrances, picking bits of the lion dancers, the string of fifty thousand fat firecrackers through the static over shortwave radios.

In the sixties and seventies, Asian American writers called Chin both the conscience of Asian American writing and the "godfather," they critized him as well for being a relic of the sixties in his emulation of black rhetoric. The poet Wing Tek Lum once compared Chin's absence at an Asian American writers' conference to "a meal without rice."

Without a doubt he is an essential ingredient and a pioneer. Chin's play *The Chickencoop Chinaman* was the first Asian American play on the New York legitimate stage when it was produced at the American Place Theatre in 1972. His second play, *The Year of the Dragon,* was not only staged at the American Place Theatre in 1974 but also filmed for television on the PBS *Theater in America* series in 1975. The plays were published in one volume by the University of Washington Press. A collection of eight short stories, *The Chinaman Pacific & Frisco R.R. Co.,* was published by Coffee House Press in 1988. He is also the coeditor with Jeffery Chan, Lawson Fusao Inada, and myself of two anthologies of Asian American writing, *Aiiieeeee!* (1974, Mentor) and *The Big Aiiieeeee!* (1991, Meridian).

In his essay "Come All Ye Asian American Writers of the Real and Fake," he states, "It matters that all the Chinese and Japanese American writers in this book, no matter what they believe or what literary form they favor, make the difference between the real and the fake." What he offers us here in his story, "The Only Real Day," is the real.

—Shawn Wong

"The Only Real Day" from
THE CHINAMAN PACIFIC &
FRISCO R.R. CO.

THE men played mah-jong or passed the waterpipe, their voices low under the sound of the fish pumps thudding into the room from the tropical fish store. Voices became louder over other voices in the thickening heat. Yuen was with his friends now, where he was always happy and loud every Tuesday night. All the faces shone of skin oily from the heat and laughter, the same as last week, the same men and room and waterpipe. Yuen knew them. Here it was comfortable after another week of that crippled would-be Hollywood Oriental-for-a-friend in Oakland. He hated the sight of cripples on his night and day off, and one had spoken to him as stepped off the A-train into the tinny breath of the Key System Bay Bridge Terminal. Off the train in San Francisco into the voice of a cripple. "Count your blessings!" The old white people left to die at the Eclipse Hotel, and the old waitresses who worked there often said "Count your blessings" over sneezes and little ouches and bad news. Christian resignation. Yuen was older than many of the white guests of the Eclipse. He washed dishes there without ever once counting his blessings.

"That's impossible," Huie said to Yuen.

Yuen grinned at his friend and said, "Whaddaya mean? It's true! You don't know because you were born here."

"Whaddaya mean 'born here'? Who was born here?"

"Every morning, I woke up with my father and my son, and we walked out of our house to the field, and stood in a circle around a young peach tree and lowered our trousers and pissed on the tree, made bubbles in the dirt, got the bark wet, splattered on the roots and watched our piss sink in. That's how we fertilized the big one the day I said I was going to Hong Kong tomorrow with my wife and son, and told them I was leaving my father and mother, and I did. I left. Then I left Hong Kong and left my family there, and came to America to make money," Yuen said. "Then after so much money, bring them over."

"Nobody gets over these days, so don't bang your head about not getting people over. What I want to know is did you make money?"

"Make money?"

"Yes, did you make money?"

"I'm still here, my wife is dead . . . but my son is still in Hong Kong, and I send him what I can."

"You're too good a father! He's a big boy now. Has to be a full-grown man. You don't want to spoil him."

Yuen looked up at the lightbulb and blinked. "It's good to get away from those *lo fan* women always around the restaurant. Waitresses, hotel guests crying for Rose. Ha ha." He didn't want to talk about his son or China. Talk of white women he'd seen changing in the corridor outside his room over the kitchen, and sex acts of the past, would cloud out what he didn't want to talk about. Already the men in the room full of fish tanks were speaking loudly, shouting when they laughed, throwing the sound of their voices loud against the spongy atmosphere of fish pumps and warm-water aquariums. Yuen enjoyed the room when it was loud and blunt. The fishtanks and gulping and chortling pumps sopped up the sound of the clickety clickety of the games and kept their voices, no matter how loud, inside. The louder the closer, thicker, fleshier, as the night wore on. This was the life after a week of privacy with the only real Chinese speaker being paralyzed speechless in a wheelchair. No wonder the boy doesn't speak Chinese, he thought, not making sense. The boy should come here sometime. He might like the fish.

"Perhaps you could," Huie said, laughing, "Perhaps you could make love to them, Ah-Yuen gaw." The men laughed, showing gold and aged yellow teeth. "Love!" Yuen snorted against the friendly laugh.

"That's what they call it if you do it for free," Huie said.

"Not me," Yuen said taking the bucket and waterpipe from Huie. "Free or money. No love. No fuck. Not me." He lifted the punk from the tobacco, then shot off the ash with a blast of air into the pipe that sent a squirt of water up the stem. "I don't even like talking to them. Why should I speak their language? They don't think I'm anything anyway. They change their clothes and smoke in their slips right outside my door in the hallway, and don't care I live there. So what?" His head lifted to face his friends, and his nostrils opened, one larger than the other as he spoke faster. "And anyway, they don't care if I come out of my room and see them standing half-naked in the hall. They must know they're ugly. They all have wrinkles and you can see all the dirt on their skins and they shave their armpits badly, and their powder turns brown in the folds of their skin. They're not like Chinese women at all." Yuen made it a joke for his friends.

"I have always wanted to see a real naked American woman for free. There's something about not paying money to see what you see," Huie said. "Ahhh and what I want to see is bigger breasts. Do these free peeks have bigger breasts than Chinese women? Do they have nipples as pink as calendar girls' sweet suckies?" Huie grunted and put his hands inside his jacket and hefted invisible breasts, "Do they have . . .?"

"I don't know. I don't look. All the ones at my place are old, and who wants to look inside the clothes of the old for their parts? And you can't tell about calendar pictures . . ." Yuen pulled at the deep smoke of the waterpipe. The water inside gurgled loudly, and singed tobacco ash jumped when Yuen blew back into the tube. He lifted his head and licked the edges of his teeth. He always licked the edges of his teeth before speaking. He did not think it a sign of old age. Before he broke the first word over his licked teeth, Huie raised his hand. "Jimmy Chan goes out with *lo fan* women . . . blonde ones with blue eyelids too. And he smokes cigars," Huie said.

"He smokes cigars. So what? What's that?"

"They light his cigars for him."

"That's because he has money. If Chinese have money here, everybody likes them," Yuen said. "Blue nipples, pink eyelids, everybody likes them."

"Not the Jews."

"Not the Jews." Yuen said. "I saw a cripple. Screamed

'Count your blessings!' Could have been a Jew, huh? I should have looked . . . Who cares? So what?"

"The Jews don't like anybody," Huie said. "They call us, you and me, the Tang people 'Jews of the Orient.' Ever hear that?"

"Because the Jews don't like anybody?"

"Because nobody likes the Jews!" Huie said. He pulled the tip of his nose down with his fingers. "Do I look like a Jew of the Orient, for fuckin out loud? What a life!" The men at the mah-jong table laughed and shook the table with the pounding of their hands. Over their laughter, Yuen spoke loudly, licking the edges of his teeth and smiling, "What do you want to be Jew for? You're Chinese! That's bad enough!" And the room full of close men was loud with the sound of tables slapped with night-pale hands and belly laughter shrinking into wheezes and silent empty mouths breathless and drooling. "We have a Jew at the Eclipse Hotel. They look white like the other *lo fan gwai* to me," Yuen said, and touched the glowing punk to the tobacco and inhaled through his mouth, gurgling the water. He let the smoke drop from his nostrils and laughed smoke out between his teeth, and leaned back into the small spaces of smoke between the men and enjoyed the whole room.

Yuen was a man of neat habits, but always seemed disheveled with his dry mouth, open with the lower lip shining, dry and dangling below yellow teeth. Even today, dressed in his day-off suit that he kept hung in his closet with butcher paper over it and a hat he kept in a box, he had seen people watching him and laughing behind their hands at his pulling at the shoulders of the jacket and lifting the brim of his hat from his eyes. He had gathered himself into his own arms and leaned back into his seat to think about the room in San Francisco; then he slept and was ignorant of the people, the conductor, and all the people he had seen before, watching him and snickering, and who might have been, he thought, jealous of him for being tall for a Chinese, or his long fingers, exactly what he did not know or worry about in his half-stupor between wakefulness and sleep with his body against the side of the train, the sounds of the steel wheels, and the train pitching side to side, all amazingly loud and echoing in his ears, through his body before sleep.

Tuesday evening Yuen took the A-train from Oakland to San

Francisco. He walked to the train stop right after work at the restaurant and stood, always watching to the end of the street for the train's coming, dim out of the darkness from San Francisco. The train came, its cars swaying side to side and looked like a short snake with a lit stripe of lights squirming past him, or like the long dragon that stretched and jumped over the feet of the boys carrying it. He hated the dragon here, but saw it when it ran, for the boy's sake. The train looked like that, the glittering dragon that moved quickly like the sound of drum rolls and dangled its staring eyes out of its head with a flurry of beard; the screaming bird's voice of the train excited in him his idea of a child's impulse to run, to grab, to destroy.

Then he stood and listened to the sound of the train's steel wheels, the sound of an invisible cheering crowd being sucked after the lights of the train toward the end of the line, leaving the quiet street more quiet and Yuen almost superstitiously anxious. Almost. The distance from superstitious feeling a loss or an achievement, he wasn't sure.

He was always grateful for the Tuesdays Dirigible walked him to the train stop. They left early on these nights and walked past drugstores, bought comic books, looked into the windows of closed shops and dimly lit used bookstores, and looked at shoes or suits on dummies. "How much is that?" Yuen would ask.

"I don't know what you're talking," Dirigible, the boy of the unpronounceable name, would say. "I don't know what you're talking" seemed the only complete phrase he commanded in Cantonese.

"What a stupid boy you are; can't even talk Chinese," Yuen would say, and "Too moochie shi-yet," adding his only American phrase. "Come on, I have a train to catch." They would laugh at each other and walk slowly, the old man lifting his shoulders and leaning his head far back on his neck, walking straighter, when he remembered. The boy. "Fay Gay" in Cantonese, Flying Ship, made him remember.

A glance back to Dirigible as he boarded the train, a smile, a wave, the boy through the window a silent thing in the noise of the engines. Yuen would shrug and settle himself against the back, against the seat, and still watch Dirigible, who would be walking now, back toward the restaurant. Tonight he realized again how young the Flying Ship was to be walking home alone at night through the city back to the kitchen entrance of the hotel. He saw Dirigible not walking the usual way home, but running next to the moving train, then turning the corner to walk up a street with more lights and people. Yuen turned, thinking he might shout out the door for the boy to go home the way they had come, but the train was moving, the moment gone. Almost. Yuen had forgotten something. The train was moving. And he had no right. Dirigible had heard his mother say that Yuen had no right so many times that Dirigible was saying it too. In Chinese. Badly spoken and bungled, but Chinese. That he was not Yuen's son. That this was not China. Knowing the boy was allowed to say such things by his only speaking parent made Yuen's need to scold and shout more urgent, his silence in front of the spoiled punk more humiliating. Yuen was still and worked himself out of his confusion. The beginning of his day off was bad; nothing about it right or usual; all of it bad, no good, wrong. Yuen chewed it out of his mind until the memory was fond and funny, then relaxed.

"Jimmy Chan has a small Mexican dog too, that he keeps in his pocket," Huie said. "It's lined with rubber."

"The little dog?" Yuen asked. And the men laughed.

"The dog . . ." Huie said and chuckled out of his chinless face, "No, his pocket, so if the dog urinates . . ." He shrugged, "You know."

"Then how can he make love to his blonde *fangwai* woman with blue breasts if his pocket is full of dogpiss?"

"He takes off his coat!" The men laughed with their faces up into the falling smoke. The men seemed very close to Yuen, as if with the heat and smoke they swelled to crowding against the walls, and Yuen swelled and was hot with them, feeling tropically close and friendly, friendlier, until he was dizzy with friendship and forgot names. No, don't forget names. "A Chinese can do anything with *fan gwai* if he has money," Yuen said.

"Like too moochie shi-yet, he can," Huie shouted, almost falling off his seat. "He can't make himself white!" Huie jabbed his finger at Yuen and glared. The men at the table stopped.

The noise of the mah-jong and voices stopped to the sound of
rumps shifting over chairs and creaks of table legs. Heavy arms
were leaned onto the tabletops. Yuen was not sure whether he
was arguing with his friend or not. He did not want to argue on
his day off, yet he was constrained to say something. He knew
that whatever he said would sound more important than he
meant it. He licked his teeth and said, "Who want to be white
when they can have money?" He grinned. The man nodded
and sat quiet a moment, listening to the sound of boys shouting
at cars to come and park in their lots. "Older brother, you
always know the right thing to say in a little pinch, don't you."

"Your mother's twat! Play!" And the men laughed and in a
burst of noise returned to their game.

The back room was separated from the tropical fish store by
a long window shade drawn over the doorway. Calendars with
pictures of Chinese women holding peaches the size of basket-
balls, calendars with pictures of nude white women with large
breasts of all shapes, and a picture someone thought was funny,
showing a man with the breasts of a woman, were tacked to the
walls above the stacked glass tanks of warm-water fish. The
men sat on boxes, in chairs, at counters with a wall of drawers
full of stuff for tropical fish, and leaned inside the doorway and
bits of wall not occupied by a gurgling tank of colorful little
swimming things. They sat and passed the waterpipe and tea
and played mah-jong or talked. Every night the waterpipe, the
tea, the mah-jong, the talk.

"Wuhay! Hey, Yuen, older brother," a familiar nameless
voice shouted through the smoke and thumping pumps.
"Why're you so quiet tonight?"

"I thought I was being loud and obnoxious," Yuen said.
"Perhaps it's my boss's son looking sick again."

"The boy?" Huie said.

"Yuen stood and removed his jacket, brushed it and hung it
on a nail. "He has this trouble with his stomach . . . makes him
bend up and he cries and won't move. It comes and goes,"
Yuen said.

"Bring him over to me, and I'll give him some herbs, make
him well in a hurry."

"His mother, my boss, is one of these new-fashioned people

giving up the old ways. She speaks nothing but American if she can help it, and has *lo fan* women working for her at her restaurant. She laughs at me when I tell her about herbs making her son well, but she knows . . ."

"Herbs make me well when I'm sick."

"They can call you 'mass hysteria' crazy in the head. People like her mean well, but don't know what's real and what's phony."

"Herbs made my brother well, but he died anyway," Huie said. He took off his glasses and licked the lenses.

"Because he wanted to," Yuen said.

"He shot himself."

"Yes, I remember," Yuen said. He scratched his Adam's apple noisily a moment. "He used to come into the restaurant in the mornings. I'd fix him scrambled eggs. He always use to talk with bits of egg on his lips and shake his fork and tell me that I could learn English good enough to be cook at some good restaurant. I could too, but the cook where I wash dishes is Chinese already, and buys good meat, so I have a good life."

Huie sighed and said, "Good meat is important I suppose." Then put his mouth to the mouth of the waterpipe.

"What?" Yuen asked absently at Huie's sigh. He allowed his eyes to unfocus on the room now, tried to remember Huie's brother's face with bits of egg on the lips and was angry. Suddenly an angry old man wanting to be alone screamed. He wiped his own lips with his knuckles and looked back to Huie the herbalist. Yuen did not want to talk about Huie's brother. He wanted to listen to music, or jokes, or breaking bones, something happy or terrible.

"His fine American talk," Huie said. "He used to go to the Oakland High School at night to learn."

"My boss wants me to go there too," Yuen said. "You should only talk English if you have money to talk to them with . . . I mean, only fools talk buddy buddy with the *lo fan* when they don't have money. If you talk to them without money, all you'll hear is what they say behind your back, and you don't want to listen to that."

"I don't."

"No."

He received a letter one day, did he tell you that? He got a letter from the American Immigration, and he took the letter to Jimmy Chan, who reads government stuff well . . . and Jimmy said that the Immigration wanted to know how he came into the country and wanted to know if he was sending money to Communists or not." Huie smiled wanly and stared between his legs. Yuen watched Huie sitting on the box; he had passed the pipe and now sat with his short legs spread slightly apart. He was down now, his eyes just visible to Yuen. Huie's slumped body looked relaxed, only the muscles of his hands and wrists were tight and working. To Yuen, Huie right now looked as calm as if he were sitting on a padded crapper. Yuen smiled and tried to save the pleasures of his day-off visit that was being lost in morbid talk. "Did he have his dog with him?" he asked.

"His dog? My brother never had a dog."

"I mean Jimmy Chan with his rubber pocket."

"How can you talk about Jimmy Chan's stupid dog when I'm talking about my brother's death."

"Perhaps I'm worried about the boy," Yuen said. "I shouldn't have let him wait for the train tonight."

"Was he sick?"

"That too maybe. Who can tell?" Yuen said without a hint, not a word more of the cripple shouting "Count your blessings!" at the end of the A-train's line in Frisco. It wouldn't be funny, and Yuen wanted a laugh.

"Bring the boy to me next week, and I'll fix him up," Huie said quickly, and put on his glasses again. Yuen, out of his day-off, loud, cheerful mood, angry and ashamed of his anger, listened to Huie. "My brother was very old, you remember? He was here during the fire and earthquake, and he told this to Jimmy Chan." Huie stopped speaking and patted Yuen's knee. "Yes, he did have his little dog in his pocket . . ." The men looked across to each other, and Yuen nodded. They were friends, had always been friends. They were friends now. "And my brother told Jimmy that all his papers had been burned in the fire and told about how he came across the bay in a sailboat that was so full that his elbows, just over the side of the boat,

were in the water, and about the women crying and then shouting, and that no one thought about papers, and some not even
of their gold."

"Yes. I know."

"And Jimmy Chan laughed at my brother and told him
that there was nothing he could do, and that my brother
would have to wait and see if he would be sent back to China
or not. So . . ." Huie put his hands on his knees and rocked
himself forward, lifting and setting his thin rump onto the
wooden box, sighed and swallowed, "my brother shot himself." Huie looked up to Yuen; they licked their lips at the
same moment, watching each other's tongues. "He died very
messy," Huie said, and Yuen heard it through again for his
friend, as he had a hundred times before. But tonight it
made him sick.

The talk about death and the insides of a head spread wet all
over the floor, the head of someone he knew, the talk was not
relaxing; it was incongruous to the room of undershirted men
playing mah-jong and pai-gow. And the men, quieter since the
shout, were out of place in their undershirts. Yuen wanted to
relax, but everything was frantic that should not be; perhaps he
was too sensitive. Yuen thought, and wanted to be numb. "You
don't have to talk about it if it bothers," Yuen said.

"He looked messy, for me that was enough . . . and enough
of Jimmy Chan for me too. He could've written and said my
brother was a good citizen or something . . ." Huie stopped and
flicked at his ear with his fingertips. "You don't want to talk
anymore about it?"

"No," Yuen said.

"How did we come to talk about my brother's death anyhow?"

"Jimmy Chan and his Mexican dog."

"I don't want to talk about that anymore, either."

"How soon is Chinese New Year's?"

"I don't think I want to talk about anything anymore," Huie
said, "New Year's is a long ways off. Next year."

"Yes, I know that."

I don't want to talk about it," Huie said. Each man sat now,
staring toward and past each other without moving their eyes,

as if moving their eyes would break their friendship. He knew that whatever had happened had been his fault; perhaps to-night would have been more congenial if he had not taken Dirigible to the used bookstore where he found a pile of sun-shine and nudist magazines, or if the cripple had fallen on his face, or not been there. Yuen could still feel the presence of the cripple, how he wanted still to push him over, crashing to the cement. The joy it would have given him was embarrassing, new, unaccountable, like being in love.

"Would you like a cigar, ah-dai low?" Huie asked, with a friendly Cantonese "Older Brother."

"No, I like the waterpipe." Yuen watched Huie spit the end of the cigar out onto the floor.

"You remind me of my brother, Yuen."

"How so?"

"Shaking your head, biting your lips, always shaking your head . . . you do too much thinking about nothing. You have to shake the thinking out to stop, eh?"

"And I rattle my eyes, too." Yuen laughed, knowing he had no way with a joke, but the friendliness botched in expression was genuine, and winning. "So what can I do without getting arrested?"

"I don't know," Huie said and looked around, "Mah-jong?"

"No."

"Are you unhappy?"

"What kind of question is that? I have my friends, right? But sometimes I feel . . . Aww, everybody does . . ."

"Just like my brother . . . too much thinking, and thinking becomes worry. You should smoke cigars and get drunk and go help one of your *lo fan* waitresses shave her armpits properly and put your head inside and tickle her with your tongue until she's silly. I'd like to put my face into the armpit of some big *fangwai* American woman . . . with a big armpit!"

"But I'm not like your brother." Yuen said. "I don't shoot myself in the mouth and blow the back of my head out with a gun."

"You only have to try once."

Yuen waited a moment, then stood. "I should be leaving now," he said. Tonight had been very slow, but over quickly.

He did not like being compared to an old man who had shot himself.

Huie stood and shook Yuen's hand, held Yuen's elbow and squeezed Yuen's hand hard. "I didn't mean to shout at you, dailow."

Yuen smiled his wet smile. Huie held onto Yuen's hand and stood as if he was about to sit again. He had an embarrassingly sad smile. Yuen did not mean to twist his friend's face into this muscular contortion; he had marred Huie's happy evening of gambling, hoarse laughter, and alcoholic wheezings. "I shouted too," Yuen said finally.

"You always know the right things to say, older brother." Huie squeezed Yuen's hand and said, "Goodnight, dailow." And Yuen was walking, was out of the back room and into the tropical fish store. He opened the door to the alley and removed his glasses, blew on them in the sudden cold air to fog them, then wiped them clean.

For a long time he walked the always-damp alleys, between glittering streets of Chinatown. Women with black coats walked with young children. This Chinatown was taller than Oakland's, had more fire escapes and lights, more music coming from the street vents. He usually enjoyed walking at this hour every Wednesday of every week. But this was Tuesday evening, and already he had left his friends, yet it looked like Wednesday with the same paper vendors coming up the hills, carrying bundles of freshly printed Chinese papers. He walked down the hill to Portsmouth Square on Kearney Street to sit in the park and read the paper. He sat on a wooden bench and looked up the trunk of a palm tree, looking toward the sounds of pigeons. He could hear the fat birds cooing over the sound of the streets, and the grass snap when their droppings dropped fresh. Some splattered on the bronze plaque marking the location of the birth of the first white child in San Francisco, a few feet away. He looked up and down the park once, then moved to the other side of the tree out of the wind and sat to read the paper by the streetlight before walking. Tonight he was glad to be tired; to Yuen tiredness was the only explanation for his nervousness. Almost anger. Almost. He would go home early;

there was nothing else to do here, and he would sleep through his day off, or at least, late into the morning.

HE entered the kitchen and snorted a breath through his nose. He was home to the smell of cooking and the greasy sweat of waitresses. His boss wiped her forehead with the back of her arm and asked him why he had come back so early; she did not expect him back until dinnertime tomorrow and was he sick? He answered, "Yes," lying to avoid conversation. All warfare is based on deception, he thought, quoting the strategist Sun Tzu, the grandson. He asked the young woman where her son the Flying Ship was, and she said he was upstairs in his room sleeping, where he belonged. Yuen nodded, "Of course, it's late isn't it," he said, avoiding the stare of her greasy eyes, and went upstairs to his room across the hall from the waitresses' wardrobe. He looked once around the kitchen before turning the first landing. He saw the large refrigerators and the steam table, and realized he was truly tired, and sighed the atmosphere of his day off out of his body. "You're trying to walk too straight, anyway, Ah-bok," his boss, Rose, said, calling him uncle from the bottom of stairs. He did not understand her joke or criticism or what she meant and went on up the stairs.

At the top of the stairs he turned and walked down the hall, past the room of his boss and her paralyzed husband, and past Dirigible's room, toward his own room across the hall from the wardrobe and next to the bathroom. Facing the door was the standup wardrobe, a fancy store-bought box with two doors, a mirror on the inside, and a rack for clothes, where the waitresses kept their white-and-black uniforms and changed. A red-headed waitress was sitting inside the wardrobe smoking a cigarette. She sat between hanging clothes with her back against the back of the wardrobe, her legs crossed and stretched out of the box. One naked heel turned on the floor, back and forth, making her legs wobble and jump to the rhythm of her nervous breathing.

Yuen walked slowly down the hall, his head down, like a car full of gunmen down a dark street, his fingers feeling the edges of his long hair that tickled the tops of his ears. He looked down to the floor but could no longer see the bare legs jutting from out of the box, the long muscles under the thighs hanging limp and shaking slowly to the turning heel. He knew she was ugly. He snorted and walked close to the far wall; he would walk past her and not at her. She did not move her legs. He stopped and leaned against the wall and lifted one foot after the other and gingerly swung them over the waitress's legs. As his second foot went over her ankles, he glanced into the box and saw her pull a strap over her shoulder and giggle. Dry rock and unnatural white teeth in there. He hopped to keep his balance. She kicked. "Hiya, Yuen," she said to him stumbling down. He felt his shoe scrape the waitress's leg, skin it a little, heard her yelp, and fell on her. "Oh, my God!" she growled and went crazy, tangling her legs and arms with his, jumping into the box to stamp out the cigarette she had let fall from her mouth laughing. The smell was sweet, dusty, and flowery inside the box, like a stale funeral. Huie wanted to stuff his head into a *fangwai* woman's armpit, did he? Yuen looked, as he stumbled to his feet out of the sweet choking smell, and could not make out any distinct armpits in the flurry of flesh and shiny nylon slip and uniforms, and flying shoes, shouting and pounding after her cigarette. He couldn't find his hat. He looked under the waitress.

The waitress stood from out of the wardrobe up to her skinny and flabby self and pulled her slip straight around her belly. She looked down to Yuen, his head nodding and dangling on his neck. He looked like a large bird feeding on something dead, and the waitress laughed. "Come on there, Yuen," the waitress said. "I was just playing." She bent to help the man up. She took his shoulders with her hands and began pulling gently. The door to the bathroom was open and the light through the doorway shone white on the front of her powdered face. Yuen saw her face looking very white with flecks of powder falling from light hairs over her grin, a very white face on a grey wrinkled neck and a chest warped with skin veined like blue cheese. He did not like her smiling and chuckling her breathing into his face or her being so comfortably undressed in front of him.

"Are you all right now, Yuen?" she asked. He did not understand. He felt her holding him and saw her smiling and saw her old breasts quiver and dangle against her slip and the skin stretch across her ribs, not at all like the women in the calendars and magazines, Yuen thought. He took his shoulders closer to his body and she still held him, squeezing the muscle of his arm with strong hands, and pulled him toward her and muttered something in her rotten-throated voice. He leaned away from her and patted his head to show her he was looking for his hat. He chanced a grin.

She looked at his head and moved her fingers through his hair. "I don't see a bump, honey. Where does it hurt?"

Her body was too close to his face for him to see. The smell of her strong soap, stale perfume, layers of powder hung into his breathing. He was angry. "My hat! My hat!" he shouted in Chinese. He took an invisible hat and put it on his head and tapped the brim with his hands.

The waitress, also on her knees now, moved after him and felt his head. "Where does it hurt?" she said. "I don't feel anything but your head."

He stood quickly and leaned against the wall and glared stupidly at her.

"I was just trying to see if you're hurt, Yuen," the waitress said. "Did I touch your sore or something?" She held her arms out and stood. A strap fell from her shoulder; she ignored it and stretched her neck and reached toward him with her fingers. "I was just joking when I kicked you, honey. I thought it was funny, the way you were stepping over me, see?" All Yuen heard were whines and giggles in her voice. He shook his head. He held his coat closed with his hands and shoved at her with his head. *"Chiyeah!* Go away! *Hooey la!"*

A door opened and Dirigible stepped into the hall in his underwear. "What's wrong?" he asked. The waitress turned then, fixed her slip, and brushed her dry hair out of her face. "Make him understand, will you?" she said pointing at Yuen. She jabbed her arm at Yuen again. "Him. He's . . ." She crossed her eyes and pointed at her head.

"She's drunk!" Yuen said. "Tell her to go away."

"I was joking! Tell him I didn't mean to hurt his old head."

"Don't let her touch you, she's crazy tonight. Ask her why she here so late. What's she been doing here all night?"

"Do something! I can't."

"What? What?" Dirigible said. "What? I don't know what you're talking," sounding as if he were being accused of something.

The waitress was in front of the boy now and trying to explain. Yuen stepped quickly down the hall and pushed the boy into his room and closed the door. "Go to sleep . . . you'll get a stomach ache," he said.

"What'd you push me for?" the boy asked in English. He kicked the door and tried to open it, but Yuen held the knob. The boy shouted. His anger burst into tears.

"Coffee," Yuen said to the waitress and pointed at her, meaning that she should go have coffee. The waitress nodded quickly, took a robe from the wardrobe, and went downstairs.

Yuen went to his room without looking for his hat. The boy opened his door and followed the old man. He stood in the doorway and watched Yuen hang his overcoat in his closet. Yuen did not notice the boy and locked the door in his face.

The old man put a hand under his shirt and rubbed the sweat under his armpit. He loosened his belt and flapped the waist of his underwear before lying on top of his bed. He felt under the pillow for his revolver; it was big in his hand. Then he swallowed to slow his breath and sat up to take off his shoes and socks.

He saw the dark stain of blood on the heel of his right shoe, and dropped it onto the floor. 'I guess, I can't tell,' he thought. 'She'll say I kicked her.' He rapped the wall to speak to Dirigible. "*Wuhay! Ah-Fay Shurn ahh,* don't tell nutting, okay?"

"I don't know what you're talking. You . . ." Yuen heard nothing through the wall. He wished that Dirigible spoke Chinese better than he did. What the hell was he learning at that Chinese school if not Chinese?

"You hit me in the face," Dirigible said.

"I did not."

"You did, and it hurt," the boy said. Dirigible. The flying ship that doesn't fly anymore. The body had the name of an extinct species. He was playing himself more hurt and younger than he was. "Don't be a baby," Yuen said.

"You hit me in the face."

"Uhhh," Yuen groaned, and rolled away from the wall. He would buy the little Dirigible a funnybook in the morning. He would buy Dirigible a dozen funnybooks and a candy bar in the morning. He leaned back into bed and began unbuttoning his shirt.

He stopped and blinked. Someone knocked at his door again. He'd almost heard it the first time. He almost felt for his revolver. He heard, "Ah Yuen bok, ahhh! I got some coffee, uncle. Are you all right? Anna says you hurt your head?" Rose, his boss, Dirigible's mother.

"Go away, I'm sleeping."

"But Anna says you asked for coffee. Have you been drinking?"

"I don't want any coffee."

"Since you're here, I told the colored boy not to come in tomorrow morning . . . What's your hat doing in the bathroom?"

"Leave it," Yuen said. "Just leave it. I'll get it in the morning." He coughed and rolled over on the bed and coughed once into the pillow.

"By the way, you got a letter today. Your American name on it. Nelson Yuen Fong . . . Your name looks nice," the voice outside said.

"What?"

"Nothing. I'll keep it until tomorrow for you."

He coughed phlegm up from his chest, held it in his mouth, then swallowed it. His face was warm in his own breath against the pillow. He relaxed the grip of his lids on his eyes for sleep. The hat was probably all dirty if it was in the bathroom, he thought and did not get up to urinate, get his hat, or shut off the light.

The hallway outside was quiet now. He felt his eyes smarting and felt stale and sour. He was not sure whether or not he was asleep. It was late; the night was wider, higher without lights on the horizon or lengths of sound stretching down the streets.

The air was not silent but excited, jittery without noise. Yuen heard sounds on the edge of hearing, and listened for them, the small sounds of almost voices and cars somewhere. He occasionally heard nothing. Perhaps he was sleeping when he heard nothing. If he opened his eyes now, he would know . . . but he could not open his eyes now. He decided he was asleep, and was sleeping, finally.

What had the waitress been doing up here all this time? Entertaining the man who would never play a Japanese general or Chinese sissy sidekick who dies in the movies ever again, if he ever did, by inflicting her flesh on his mute, immobile, trapped, paralyzed self? Or perhaps a show, a long striptease for the boy to watch from his room through his keyhole. Or had she been inside his room? He had no right. How had they met? Come up the stairs one day from a smoke of the waterpipe in the cold dry room where the potatoes and onions were kept and peeled, looking forward to an hour on his bed with one or two picture magazines full of strippers showing their breasts. The sight of the boy, nine or ten years old, holding his revolver stopped the man from stepping into his own room. The unexpected boy caught Yuen dirty-minded, his mental pecker hanging out. He had a loaded gun in his hand, between Yuen and his girlie magazines. His son. The knees. The boy's knees. That was funny. That was laughable now.

Tomorrow he would buy Dirigible a dozen funnybooks and a big candy bar, even if he was not angry or scared anymore.

And now truly asleep, he was sitting at a table with this boy, but the boy was his son, then Huie's dead brother with bits of scrambled eggs drying on his lips. The flesh all over the skull looked as if it had been boiled in soup to fall off the bone. Yuen wiped the boy's lip but more egg came up where he had wiped the egg off. Then the lips were gone. The lipless boy laughed, took Yuen's hand, and pulled him up. They walked from the table and were in a field with not a bird in the sky above them, smooth as skin, blue as veins. The boy pointed, and there, on the edge of the world was the peach tree. They dropped their trousers, aimed their peckers to the horizon, and pissed the long distance to the tree and watched the streams of their yellow liquid gleam and flash under the bright sky before it arched into the shadow of the mountains. They pissed a very long time without beginning to run out. Yuen was surprised he was still pissing. He squinted to see if he was reaching the tree. The boy was laughing and pissing on Yuen's feet. Yuen was standing in a mud of piss. "What are you doing?"

"Coffee," the boy answered in the waitress's voice and laughed. Birds. They were in the sky out of nowhere and dove on him, silent except for their wings breaking the dive. I'm going to die. Too moochie shi-yet. I'm going to die. And continued fertilizing the peach tree on the horizon. He had not shouted. "It's true!" He woke up to the sound of his voice, he was sure, and heard only the curtains shuffling in front of his open window. He felt under the sheets around his ankles to see if there was any wet. There was not. He hadn't wet the bed. He got up and spat into the wash basin in the corner. He didn't curse the spring handles on the taps. He turned out the light, sat on the edge of his bed, and listened for a hint of waitresses lurking in the silence outside his door, then returned to sleep.

He bathed with his underwear on this morning and plugged the keyhole with toilet paper. He combed his hair and returned to his room. He had found his hat on the lid of the toilet. He did not like the hat any longer; it was too big and the band was dirty. The dream had left him by the time he went downstairs for breakfast, but he knew he had dreamed.

He sat down at a table at the end of the long steam table. He could hear a waitress laughing shrilly outside in the dining room, not the same waitress as last night, he knew, for the breakfast waitresses were different from the ones at dinner. He took a toothpick from a tin can nailed to the end of the steam table and put it in his mouth and sucked the taste of wood and read his Chinese paper. He did not goodmorning his boss. She was younger and should be the first to give greetings, out of respect. But she was his boss. So what. He was reading about Chiang Kai-shek making a speech to his army again. He liked Chiang Kai-shek. He decided he liked Chiang Kai-shek. Chiang Kai-shek was familiar and pleasant in his life, and he enjoyed it. "He made another speech to his army," Yuen said.

Dirigible said, "He made one last week to the army."

He's forgotten last night, Yuen thought, and answered, "That was to the farmers. This time it's to the army. Next week to everybody." This was part of every morning also.

Rose wiped her hands on her apron and sat down next to Yuen. She took an envelope from her pocket and unfolded it. Before removing the letter, she turned to Dirigible and said, "Go upstairs, change your pants. And comb your hair for a change."

"I'll be late for school. I gotta eat breakfast."

"Go upstairs, huh? I don't have time to argue!" Rose said.

"Can I use your comb, ah-bok?"

"You have your own comb. Don't bother people. I wanta talk to ah-bok."

Yuen gave Dirigible his comb, which he kept in a case. Rose watched the boy go past the first landing and out of sight and then took the letter out of the envelope. "I read this letter of yours," she said. She looked straight at Yuen as she spoke, and Yuen resented her look and the way she held his letter. "Who said you could?" he asked, "It might have been from my son. What do you want to read my mail for, when you don't care what else I do?"

"Now, you know that's not so!" Rose said. "Anyway, it's addressed to your American name, and it's from the U.S. Immigration."

"Well . . . What did Anna tell you about last night? You know what she was really trying to do, don't you? I'll tell you I don't believe a word that woman says. She eats scraps too. Right off the dirty dishes.

"Oh, Yuen bok, you're so old, your brain's busting loose. She was just trying to see if you had a cut or a hurt on your head was all."

"Aww, I don't like her no matter what," Yuen said. He went to the steam table and ladled cream of wheat into a bowl and sat down to eat it. "What are you looking at? You never seen me eat before?"

"Don't you use milk?" Rose asked.

"No, you should know that."

"But your letter, Yuen bok. You're in trouble."

"What for?"

"It's from the immigrators, I told you. They want to know if you came into this country legally."

Yuen looked up from his cereal to the powder and rouge of her face. The oil from her Chinese skin had soaked through and messed it all up. She smiled with her lips shut and cheeks pulled in as if sucking something in her mouth. He did not like Rose because she treated him with disdain and made bad jokes, and thought she was beautiful, a real femme fatale behind the steam table with an apron and earrings. And now she did not seem natural to Yuen, being so kind and trying so to soften the harshness in her voice. "That's a bad joke," Yuen said.

"I'm not joking. Do I look like I'm joking, ah-bok? Here, you can read it for yourself if you don't believe me." She shoved the letter to him. He pushed his cereal bowl aside and flattened the letter on the table. He put his glasses on, then without touching the letter, bent over it and stared. He saw a printed seal with an eagle. The paper was very white, and had a watermark that made another eagle. He removed his glasses and licked his teeth. "You know I don't read English."

"I know," Rose said. "So why don't you eat your breakfast and I'll tell you what the letter says. Then you can get the dishes done."

Yuen nodded and did as she said. She wiped her hands on her apron and told him that the letter said the immigrators wanted to know if he had any criminal record with the police in the City of Oakland and that he was to go to the Oakland Police and have his fingerprints taken and get a letter from them about his criminal record yes or no. "I will talk to Mrs. Walker who was a legal secretary and she can help me write a watchacall, a character reference for you."

"Why tell people?"

"They ask for letters making good references about you, don't they? You want to stay in this country, don't you?" She folded the letter and ran her thumb along the creases, leaving grey marks where her fingers had touched. Yuen took the letter and unfolded it again and put on his glasses again and stared down at the piece of paper. He took a pencil and copied something he saw in the letter on a napkin. "What's this?" he asked, pointing at the napkin.

"That's a T," Rose said.

"What's it mean?"

"It doesn't mean anything. It's just a T."

"Did I make it right?"

"You are not going to learn to read and write English before this afternoon, ah-bok."

Yuen lost interest in his T and wiped his face with his napkin. "T Zone wahh. Camel cigarette!" he mumbled. He remembered cigarette ads with the pictures of actors' heads with a T over their mouths and down their throats. Rose didn't know everything. She was not his friend. He sighed and straightened in his seat. He was sure Rose heard all the little gurgles and slopping sounds inside him. It ached to sit straight. He had to sit straight to feel any strength in his muscles now. The ache gave a certain bite to the fright. He thought about aching and wanting to ache, like nobody else. Every white muscle in his body felt raw and tender, from the base of his spine, and the muscles from his neck down to his shoulder, and the hard muscles behind his armpit. He was conscious of every corner and bend in his body, and all this was inside him, private, the only form of reliable relaxation he had. He wanted to sit back and enjoy himself, ignore the letter and travel the countries of his aches. He looked to Rose. She looked away. He saw she knew he was frightened. He did not want her pity, her face to smile some simpering kindly smile for his sake, for he had always pitied her, with her reasonable good looks, her youth, and a husband she keeps in a room like a bug in a jar, who won't be going to Hollywood after all. He didn't want to need her English, her letter full of nice things about him, her help.

Rose patted Yuen's shoulder and stood up and went to the foot of the stairs and called for Dirigible to come down. "You'll be late for school!" Then to the old man, "I'm going to have to tell him, you know."

"Dritchable?" Yuen said, botching the name.

"Everyone will know sooner or later. They come and ask

people questions. The immigrators do that," Rose said. They could hear Dirigible stamping on the floor above them.

Yuen put the letter in his shirt pocket and removed his glasses and put them and the case in the tin can with the toothpicks. His place. He went around the steam table to the dishwashing area, lit the fires under the three sinks full of water, and started the electric dishwashing machine slung like an outboard motor in the well of the washing sink.

He put a teaspoonful of disinfectant into the washwater, then a cup of soap powder. He watched the yellow soap turn the water green and raise a cloud of green to the top of the water. He turned and saw Dirigible sitting at the table again. "*Wuhay!* Good morning, kid," he shouted over the noise of the dishwashing machine. Dirigible looked up and waved back, then looked back at the breakfast his mother had set in front of him. "Come here, Dritch'ble, I got money for funnybooks!" Yuen switched off the machine and repeated what he'd said in a lower voice.

"Dirigible's late for school. He has to eat and run," Rose said. She turned to Dirigible and said, "Be sure you come right home from school. Don't go to Chinese school today, hear?"

"It's not my day to read to Pa."

"Just come home from school, like I told you, hear me? She leaned through a space between a shelf and the steam table to see the boy, and steam bloomed up her face and looked like a beard.

"Oh, boy!" Dirigible said, and Yuen saw that the boy was happy.

"What did you tell him?" he asked Rose.

"That he didn't have to go to Chinese school today."

"Why? Don't you want him to be able to talk Chinese?"

"I want him to take you to the city hall this afternoon and do what the letter says," Rose said. She lifted her head back on her neck to face Yuen, and Yuen looking at her without his glasses on saw her face sitting atop the rising steam.

"I don't want a little boy to help me," he said. "You think I'm a fool? I'll call Jimmy Chan and ask him to help me. Dritch'ble too young to do anything for me."

Rose flickered a smile then twisted herself out from between the shelf and the steam table. "You've been watching too much television, ah-bok. Chinatown's not like that anymore. You can't hide there like you used to. Everything's orderly and businesslike now."

"How do you know Chinatown? You watch television, not me. I know Chinatown. Not everybody talks about the Chinese like the *lo fan* and you. You should know what you're talking about before talking sometimes. Chie!"

"Ham and!" a waitress shouted through the door.

"Ham and!" Rose repeated. "I'm just as much Chinese as you, ah-bok, but this is America!"

"The truth is still the truth, in China, America, on Mars . . . Two and two don't make four in America, just because you're Chinese."

"What?" the waitress said, jutting her head through the kitchen door, in the rhythm of its swing.

"Eggs how?" Margie asked.

"Oh, basted."

"Basted," Margie said, and reached for the eggs. "Listen, ah-bok. I don't want to get in trouble because of you. I worked hard to get this restaurant, and I gave you a job. Who else do you think would give you a job, and a room? You're too old to work anywhere else, and you'd have to join the union and learn English. You don't want to learn English. That's your business, but if you get in trouble here, I'm in trouble too. Now just do what the letter says. And just don't argue with me about it. No one is trying to hurt you." She brought three cooking strips of bacon from the back of grill toward the center where she kept the iron hot.

"Me make trouble for you? You said I am in trouble already."

"I am trying to help you the best way I can. Now let me alone to cook, and you get back to the dishes. Can't you see I'm nervous? Listen, take the day off. I'll call the colored boy. I shouldn't have told him not to come in. I don't know what I was thinking . . . Now, please, ah-bok, leave me finish breakfast, will you?"

"I'm sorry, I'll get the dishes . . ." Yuen said.

"I said take the day off." Rose said. "Please." She quickly

slid the spatula under another egg order on the griddle and flopped them onto a plate. She forgot the bacon.

"The bacon," Yuen said.

She ignored him and said, "Dirigible, you don't have time to finish your breakfast. Take that little pie in the icebox for your teacher and go to school now."

Dirigible looked to Yuen. "I'll walk you to school," Yuen said. Rose snapped, "Be back in time for the dinner dishes . . . Oh, what . . . Forget I said that, but both of you be back after school."

Looking down the street, they could see the morning sun shattered in the greasy shimmer of Lake Merritt. The grass on the shore was covered with black coots and staggering seagulls. Yuen had his glasses on and could see the trees on the other side of the lake and sailors walking with girls, and he could smell the stagnant water as he walked the other way with Dirigible.

The boy watched the ground and stayed inside Yuen's shadow as they walked. Yuen glanced at the boy and saw him playing his game with his shadow and knew the boy had forgotten last night, the waitress. They were beyond the smell of the lake now and inside the smell of water drying off the sides of washed brick buildings, and Yuen's morning was complete and almost gone. "What're you carrying there?" Yuen asked.

"A pie for teacher," Dirigible said.

Yuen smiled his wet smile. They stopped at the street that had the train tracks in the center. "Mommy said your hat was in the toilet."

"Do you want to go to San Francisco with me?"

"I can't. I have to go home right after school. You too."

"I mean right now. Would you like to go to San Francisco on the train, right now?"

"I have to go to school."

"I'll take you to my friend's and he'll give you some herbs that will make your stomach stop hurting again." Yuen put a hand on the boy's shoulder and stood in front of him. What happens to boys born here? Are they all little bureaucrats by ten years old? They no longer dreamed of the Marvelous Traveler from the outlaws of Leongsahn Marsh come to deliver an invi-

tation to adventure? "I'll buy you five funnybooks and a candy
bar."

"But it doesn't hurt."

"For when your stomach does hurt. These herbs and it
won't hurt again." Then inspiration in his instinct had the
words out of his mouth before they'd come to mind. "How
about I buy you special Chinese funnybooks? Chinese fighters
with swords and bows and arrows, spears, big wars, heads cut
off. And the head cut off spits blood in the face of its killer.
You'll like them."

There were more people on the train now than at night. The
train was dirtier in the day. They caught the A-train at the end
of the line near Dirigible's school. As the train started to pull, it
rang its electric bell, screeching like a thousand trapped birds.
They hummed and rattled across Oakland, onto the lower level
of the Bay Bridge toward San Francisco. Dirigible ate the little
pie and Yuen put his arm over the boy's shoulders when people
boarded, and let go on the bridge. He was glad to have the boy
with him. Good company. He was young and didn't have to
know what Yuen was doing to have a little adventure. Yuen
enjoyed being with the boy. That was something he could still
enjoy.

The train moved quickly, swaying its cars side to side over
the tracks. Yuen looked only once out of the window to the
street full of people. He had been in Oakland for twenty years
now, and he still felt uncomfortable, without allies in the
streets. On the train he could sit and did not have to walk
among people with hands out of their pockets all around him.
The train moved him quickly out of the moldy shadows between tall buildings, and was moving down a street lined with
low wooden houses now. He could see Negro women with
scarves around their large heads. Elephant-hipped women with
fat legs walking old and slow down the street. The feelings he
had for them were vague and nothing personal, but haunted
him. The train passed them, and now there were no more
houses. They whirred into the train yards, and the A screamed
its crazed electric birds toward the bridge.

They passed broken streetcars and empty trains in the yards,
and saw bits of grass growing up between the crossties. Beyond

the yards they saw the flat bay and the thick brown carpet of dung floating next to the shore. And they could smell the bay, the cooking sewage, the oily steel. Last night he slept past this part of the trip. "Shi-yet," he said sniffing. The boy smiled. Yuen realized now what he was doing. He was trying to be brave, and knew he would fail. He felt the letter in his coat pocket without touching the letter and thought of how he would take the letter from his pocket to show Jimmy Chan.

The sounds of the wheels on the rails changed in pitch and they were on the bridge now, with shadows of steelwork skipping over their faces. They were above the bay and could see the backs of seagulls gliding and soaring parallel to them, their beaks split in answer to the electric bell. Yuen could see the birds stop and hang on the air with their wings stiff, then fall and keep falling until the bridge blocked his vision, and in his mind he counted the splashes on the bay the seagulls made. He looked down to Dirigible again and saw pie on the boy's lips. Dirigible took his hand out of the paper bag and grinned. "That's bad for your stomach," Yuen said. Too nervous to smile. No, not nervous, he thought, angry. Calm, numbly angry. It wasn't unpleasant or aggravating or lonely, but moving very fast, train or no train, he without a move felt himself hurtling home. The electric birds screamed and they were moving in a slow curve toward the terminal at the San Francisco end of the line.

Chinatown was very warm and the streets smelled of vegetables and snails set out in front of the shops. Among the shopping Chinese women, Yuen saw small groups of lo fan white tourists with bright neckties and cameras pointing into windows and playing with bamboo flutes or toy dragons inside the curio shops. Yuen stopped in front of a bookstore with several different poster portraits of a redfaced potbellied, longbearded soldier in green robes. "Know him?" Yuen asked. The boy glanced, "Sure, I've seen him around."

"Who is he?"

"He's you," the boy said, looking caught again. Yuen took him inside and bought an expensive set of paperbound Chinese funny books that looked like little books and came in a box. Yuen opened up one of the books to the pictures and chuckled, delighted. "See, here?" He snatched at the tale of the 108 outlaw heroes of legendary Leongsahn Marsh in curt, chugging Cantonese babytalk the boy might understand. "Heh heh, look like a Buddhist monk fella, huh? Very bad temper this guy . . . Now this guy, look. He catch cold, get drunk on knock out 'Mickey Finn' kind of booze, not knock out, and gotta cross the mountain. *Don't cross that mountain alone!* they say. *Fuck you!* he says. *Oooh, big tiger eat you up there. Better not go!* they say him. *Don't try to fool me!* he says and he goes and they can't stop him go. Up the mountain at night. The tiger jump him! Whoo! He gotta sniffle and sneeze. Runny eyes and cough. And he drunk too much wine suppose to knock people out. And he thinks maybe he should not have come up to the mountaintop after all, but gotta fight anyway, and *kawk kawk kawk kawk!* punch and kick and push the tiger's face in the dirt and punch and kick 'em and kill that tiger. They call that one Tiger Jung. He's my favorite of the 108 heroes," Yuen said and sighed, smiling. "One by one, you know, all the heroes are accused of crimes by the government. They say he commit a crime he didn't and they make him run, see? And one by one, all the good guys made outlaw by the bad government come to Leongsahn Marsh and join the good guy, Soong Gong. Yeah, sure. *Sam Gawk Yun Yee, Sir Woo Jun,* I memorize 'em all. All the boys like to see who know more. Then you see them in the opera, and . . ." Yuen signed again and wouldn't finish that thought. "Soong Gong. They call him the Timely Rain, Gup Sir Yur. Every boy like you in the world for awhile is like these guys. Before you lie, before you betray, before you steal. You know if you stay honest, don't sell out, don't betray, don't give up even if it means you run all alone, someday, someone will tap you on the shoulder and, *You!* the Marvelous Traveler will say. *Our leader, the Timely Rain, has long admired your gallantry. Soong Gong says he is a man of no talent, but asks you to join us and our rebel band and do great things.* But you grow up. You sell out, you betray, you kill . . . just a little bit. But too much to expect the Marvelous Traveler to come with any message from the Timely Rain."

The dining room of Jimmy Chan's restaurant was dark with the shadows of chairs stacked and tangled on the tabletops. A white-jacketed busboy led Yuen and the boy between the tables sprouting trees of chairs to the office. Yuen left Dirigible outside to read his funnybooks, then went inside after removing his hat. Rose's lessons in American servility got to him at the oddest times.

Jimmy Chan's bow tie was very small against his fat bellying throat. The tie wriggled like the wings of a tropical moth when he spoke. Jimmy Chan's dog walked all over his desk and Jimmy laughed at it when Yuen came in. Instead of greeting Yuen, he said, "It's a chee-wah-wah. How about that? Please, have a seat."

"How are you?" Yuen asked. "I've been trying to catch you to ask you out for coffee and see how you are. But a busy man about town, like Jimmy Chan . . ." Yuen said, opening with a courtesy, he hoped. The knack for saying the right thing. Huie said Yuen had it. Or had Huie just been saying the right thing himself?

I'm busy all right. Busy going bankrupt to hell and damn."

Yuen nodded, then too quickly put his hand into his coat pocket, as if he'd been bitten there. Then, "I got a letter from the United States of America," Yuen said.

"I can't help with letters from the government. I can't tamper with the government. I'm going to be naturalized next year, but I know people who think I'm a communist. Why? Because I have a big restaurant. What kind of communist owns a restaurant with a floor show and a fan dancer? I'm going bust, I tell you the truth. People say Jimmy Chan is a smuggler. I'm not a goddamn-all-to-hell smuggler any more than you are. But what the hellfuck are my problems compared to yours? Where's a crooked cop when you need one, huh? You need money for a lawyer? What you need is a lawyer to tamper with the government, you know that?"

"Maybe you could read the letter?" Yuen held the letter out. Jimmy Chan put a cigar into his mouth and took the letter. The dog walked over to sniff Jimmy's hands and sniffed at the letter. "Don't let the dog dirty the letter," Yuen said.

"You should let him piss on it. Ha ha. It's a chee-wah-wah. You think I'd let my chee-wah-wah walk on my desk if it was going to dirty things up? You think these papers I have on my desk mean nothing? . . . I'm sorry if I seemed short-tempered just then, uncle, you asked with such force. You see, men with letters like this have come in before, and never, ever, have they ordered me or asked me anything straight out. I was surprised. You should be in business. You should be a general!" Jimmy turned and held the letter up to the light and stared at the watermark. "Fine paper they use," he said, and patted the dog.

"I thought you could give me some advice."

"You don't want advice," Jimmy Chan said. "You want me to help you. Perform a miracle. But you said advice. I'll take you on your word and give you advice. If you have no criminal record, you have nothing to worry about. There is no advice to give you. Just do what the letter says. Want me to translate it? It says go to the police. Get your fingerprints made and sent to Washington. Get your record of arrests and have the police send a copy to the government. It says it's only routine. Right here, just like this. I am routine."

"They might send me back to China."

"Not if you're all legal."

"Well, still . . ."

"Uncle, my sympathy is free. My advice too. I sympathize with you. You can't hide from them. They even have Chinese working for them, so you can't hide. I sympathize with you, but the only Chinese that get ahead are those who are professional Christian Chinese, or, you know, cater to that palate, right? You didn't know that when you came here, and now you're just another Chinaman that's all Chinese and in trouble. I can't help you."

"You could write a letter for me telling them I'm all right," Yuen said. He leaned back as Jimmy Chan pushed papers to both sides with his hands and elbows.

"Uncle, I don't know you're all right. And I don't want to know. I can help when I can help because I don't ask for secrets, I don't ask questions, and I don't trust anybody. I'd like to help you. I'm grateful to your generation, but your day is over. You could have avoided all your trouble if you had realized that the *lo fan* like the Chinese as novelties. Toys. Look at me. I eat, dress, act, and talk like a fool. I smell like rotten flower shop. And the *lo fan* can't get into my restaurant fast enough. They all call me Jimmy. I'm becoming an American citizen, not because I want to be like them, but because it's good business. It makes me wealthy enough to go bankrupt in style, to make the *lo fan* think I belong to them. Look! They like the Chinese better than Negroes because we're not many and we're not black. They don't like us as much as Germans or Norwegians because we're not white. They like us better than Jews because we can't be white like the Jews and disappear among the *lo fan.* But! They don't like a Chinaman being Chinese about life because they remind them of the Indians who, thirty-five thousand years ago, were Chinese themselves, see? So . . . .!" Jimmy Chan clapped his hands together and spread them with the effect of climaxing a magic trick and looked about his office. He adjusted his bow tie and grinned. "This is being a professional Christian Chinese!"

"Indians?" was all Yuen could say that made sense.

"But helping you would be bad for me. So I write a letter for you. I get investigated, and then I get a letter. I don't want to be investigated. I want to become a citizen next year. Nobody likes me. Your people don't like me anymore because I'm really nobody, and you'll say I stepped on you to become a citizen and a professional Chinese. I have no friends, you see? I'm in more trouble than you."

"I'm going then. Thanks," Yuen said, and stood.

"Listen, uncle," Jimmy said from his seat, "don't do anything goddamn silly. If I can help with anything else, I'll be happy to do it. Want a loan? A job?"

"No," Yuen said and started to leave.

"Uncle, I trust you. You know what I mean. I know you have a job and keep your word and all that." Jimmy stood and took a long time to walk around his desk to Yuen's side. He put an arm around his shoulders. "You are a wise man . . . If you die, die of old age. I feel bad when I can't help, and I feel real bad when men die." He grinned and opened the door for the old man. "But you are a wise man."

"Didn't even offer a drink," Yuen said outside with the boy.

Pigeons dropped from the sky to walk between the feet of people and peck at feed dropped from the cages of squabs and chickens in front of the poultry shops. "Stupid birds," Yuen said. "Someone will catch one and eat it." He laughed and the boy laughed.

"I'm hungry," Dirigible said.

As they left the restaurant, Yuen walked quickly. He held Dirigible's hand and pulled him down the streets and pointed at fire escapes and told him what Tongs were there and what he had seen when he had been at parties there, and he walked over iron gratings in the sidewalk and pointed down inside and told Dirigible that at night music could be heard down there. They passed men sitting next to magazine stands and shook hands. Then Yuen went to the bank and withdrew all his money in a money order and borrowed a sheet of paper and an envelope, and in Chinese wrote his song: "This is all the money I have. You will not get anymore. I'm dead. Your father," and signed it. He put the letter and the money order in the envelope, addressed it, then went to the post office branch and mailed it. San Francisco was nothing to him now. He had said goodbye to his friends and seen the places he used to visit. They were all dirty in this daylight. The value of his death, to himself, was that nothing in his life was important; he had finished with his son that he hadn't seen in twenty years or more, and his friends, and San Francisco. Now he was going home. The tops of the buildings sparkled with their white tile and flags, Yuen saw. Jimmy Chan was wrong, he thought. But he helped me start the finish. The Grandson, Sun Tzu, the strategist says, "In death ground, fight." I am. I'm a very lucky man to know when all I am to do in life is done and my day is over. Jimmy Chan is too professional to know that. He doesn't see the difference between me and Huie's dead brother. Too bad. No cringing. No excuses. He walked quickly down the hill, believing himself to the bus stop. Dirigible had to run to keep up with him.

"What did you take him to San Francisco for? And why go to San Francisco, anyway? Do you know I had to wash all the dishes and cook, too? That colored boy wasn't home, you know," Rose said. "Criminey sakes, you think I'm a machine or something?"

"I'm sorry," Yuen said. Rose wouldn't understand anything he said right now. Better she not know what good shape he was in. No explanations.

"Well, you have to hurry, if you're going to get back in time to help me with the dinner dishes. I'm sorry, I didn't mean that, ah-bok, I'm just worried. All right?" She put a hand on his shoulder.

"All right."

Rose took the letter from Yuen's pocket and sat down at the kitchen table and read it over. Yuen sat down next to her and put a toothpick in his mouth. Rose stared down at the letter and began scratching a slow noisy circle around her breast. She talked to Dirigible without looking at the boy. "Uncle's in trouble, dear, I mean ah-bok has to go to the police and get his pictures taken. And you have to take him there and help him answer the questions the police will ask in this letter."

"I've been walking all day, Mommy. I don't wanta walk no more," Dirigible said. "Why don't you go?"

"You got a car," Dirigible said, stepping backward.

"Listen," Rose said. "You take this letter." She lifted the letter and pinned it with a safety pin inside Dirigible's coat. "And you go to where the fingerprint place is and you tell them to read the letter, that the United States Immigrators want them to read it, and that everybody, everybody, likes Yuen-bok, okay? And you take him." She gave the boy some crackers to eat on the way and helped Yuen to his feet.

"Do you know how to get there?" Yuen asked at every corner. They walked streets full of rush-hour traffic, walked past parking meters and a bodybuilding gymnasium. Yuen put an arm about Dirigible and held him. "Where are we in all this?" Yuen asked and pushed Dirigible toward the edge of the sidewalk with each word.

"We have to go fast now, ah-bok, or the police will close," the boy said.

The streets were not crowded, but everywhere on the sidewalks along the sides of the buildings Yuen saw people walking, all of their eyes staring somewhere beyond him, the pads of fat next to their stiff mouths trembling with their steps. They all moved past him easily, without actually avoiding him. Yuen held the boy's hand and walked, numbing himself to the people.

The long corridor of the city hall was full of the sound of feet

and shaking keys against leather-belted hips, and waxed reflections of the outside light through the door at the corridor's end,
shrunk and twisted on the floor, as they walked further down,
past men with hats on and briefcases, policemen picking their
noses, newspaper vendors with aprons. "Where do we go?"
Yuen asked.

"I don't know," Dirigible said. "I can't read all the doors."

In a low voice, almost as smooth as an old woman's, Yuen
said, "Do you see any Chinese around? Ask one, he'll help us."
His hand rested on the back of the boy's neck, and was very still
there as they walked.

"Excuse me . . ." a large man said, walking into them. They
all tried to walk through each other a moment, then fell with
the large man holding Dirigible's head and shouting a grunted
"excuse me." Their legs all tangled, and they fell together in a
soft crash. The man stood and brushed himself off. "I'm terribly sorry. Just barged out of my office, not thinking. Or thinking when I should have been watching my step. Are you all
right? Your father looks a little sick."

"I have a letter," Dirigible said, and opened his jacket to
show the letter pinned to the inside of his lapel.

"What's this?" the man asked, bending again. "A safety pin.
All you people are safety pinning each other, my god!" he
muttered. He took the letter and took a long grunt to stand up.
Dirigible turned and helped Yuen, who was still on the floor,
waiting, and staring with drool over his lip up at the strange *lo
fan.* Yuen lifted himself to a crouch, rested, then stood and
held himself steady, leaning on the boy.

"Immigration people want him fingerprinted," the man
said. "You poor kid." He brushed his hair under his hat as he
spoke. "I'll take you there. It's upstairs. Don't worry, if things
go badly, you can call me, Councilman Papagannis." He adjusted his hat with his fat fingertips and walked quickly upstairs,
swinging his arms with each step. They walked into a narrow
hall with benches. At a desk, sitting on a high stool, in front of a
typewriter, his sleeves rolled sloppily over his elbows, was a
police sergeant, typing. "You can wash that ink stuff off your
fingers in there, through that office, you see?" he was saying as
they walked up to his desk. "What do you want? You'll have to

wait in line. All these men here are in a hurry to get finger-printed too."

"But I got a letter and supposed to tell you how people like Yuen-bok. Him." Dirigible pulled Yuen to the desk.

"What?" the police sergeant asked.

"Immigration people want him fingerprinted, photo-graphed, and a copy of his record," Councilman Papagannis said. "Here's the letter. I'm Councilman Papagannis. I'd like to see them out of here in a hurry, you know, for the boy's sake." The councilman shook the sergeant's hand, then removed his tight-fitting hat.

"It says here, they want a copy of his record, too," the ser-geant said.

"Well, do it!" the councilman said, stuffing himself between Yuen and the boy. The police sergeant took out a form and put it in the typewriter; then he picked up the telephone and asked for the city's record on Nelson Yuen Fong. He put the tele-phone down and looked up to the councilman. "Never heard of him," he said.

"Surely you have a form for that contingency, sergeant."

"Surely."

"Who said, 'The mills of the gods grind slow, but they grind exceedingly fine'? or something like that. The mills of the sys-tem are a-grinding, young man," the councilman said, marvel-ing at the sergeant's checking boxes on a form. The police sergeant removed Yuen's hat with a short motion of his arm, "Hair color, grey," he said and began typing. He dropped the hat onto Yuen's head.

Yuen took the hat from his head and looked inside the brim. "What for?" he asked.

"Nothing," Dirigible said and took the hat and held it. Yuen watched now, his eyes wide with the lids almost folding over backwards. This was a fine joke for Yuen now. They were all so somber for his sake, and he had finished already. He could say anything and they would not understand, but Dirigible might understand a little, and Dirigible was too young to see the humor of the situation. Dirigible shouldn't be here, Yuen thought. I'll buy him a funnybook on the way home. He'll like that and won't feel so bad.

Dirigible yanked Yuen up to the edge of the police sergeant's desk and held his sleeve tightly. "How much do you weigh?" the police sergeant asked.

"He don't talk American," Dirigible said.

"What is he?"

"He's alien," Dirigible said.

"I mean, is he Filipino, Japanese, Hawaiian?"

"He's Chinese."

"Fine people, the Chinese," the councilman said.

"Fine," the police sergeant said and typed. "Now ask him how much he weighs."

Dirigible pulled at Yuen's coat until the man half-knelt. Dirigible's first word was in English and jittery. Yuen frowned, then smiled to relax the boy. The boy stamped his foot and snapped his glare burning from the police sergeant to Yuen. Yuen should have known the boy would hate him for not being able to speak English Longtime Californ'.

"You how heavy?" Dirigible said, blushing, sounding stupid to everybody, and cracked the accent on the *choong* word for "heavy" in a flat accent, but meaning "onion" when high-toned. Both the boy and Yuen heard "heavy" waver into "onion" and blushed. "What do you mean?" Yuen asked instead of laughing. "Take it easy, kid."

"You are how many pounds?"

"What's your old man say, boy?"

"We don't talk good together yet," Dirigible said, crunching his tongue into English, while still lugging his tongue in gutless Chinese, "You are HOW MANY POUNDS?" The boy stood straight and shouted, "How heavy the pounds?" as if shouting made it more Chinese.

"Oh, how many pounds do I weigh?" Yuen grinned and nodded to the police sergeant and the councilman. The police sergeant nodded and pointed at Yuen's stomach then patted his own belly. "Hundred and thirty pounds heavy," Yuen said.

"One hundred and thirty pounds," Dirigible said. The police sergeant typed.

After the questions, the police sergeant stepped down from his high stool and held Yuen's arms. "Tell him we're going to take his picture now, boy." Dirigible told Yuen what he'd heard old Chinese say to children all the time, and Yuen asked Dirigible to ask the police sergeant if he could comb his hair before being photographed. The men laughed when Dirigible asked.

Dirigible stepped away from Yuen and snuck a pinch of the blue stripe of the police sergeant's trousers, to see if what looked like shiny wire was metallic to the fingertips and wasn't sure. Yuen turned his head and combed his hair with his pocketcomb.

The police sergeant kicked a lever that turned Yuen's seat around. He snapped a picture. Yuen yelled once as the chair spun ninety degrees with the snap and stunned humm of a huge spring in the floor. "Atta boy, Nelson!" the police sergeant cheered. "Now for the fingerprints." He took the frames from the camera and tapped Dirigible next to the ear. "Tell your father to get down now."

"Ah-bok ahhh, get down now."

They walked home with the first blue of the dark night coming. Yuen patted the boy's shoulder and kept asking him to stop and buy some funnybooks, but the boy pulled Yuen's sleeve and walked on quickly, saying he was hungry and wanted to get back to the hotel kitchen. "Come on, ah-bok. I'm hungry," Dirigible said whenever the old man stopped to sit on a garbage can and nod his head at every streetcorner with a city trashcan. He sat as if he would sit forever, without moving his body or fixing the odd hairs the wind had loosened, his head nodding slowly like a sleeping pigeon's. "Are you mad at me?"

"No," the boy said in a hurry.

"Your mother's waiting for us, isn't she?" Yuen said. He stood and walked a little and said, "You're a funny son . . ." He muttered to himself louder as they neared the Eclipse Hotel. All his old age shook and fattened up the veins in his hands as he tried to touch Dirigible's nose or his ears or poke the soft of the boy's cheeks. "You're almost as tall as me . . . Did you see the policeman's face when he saw me?" In his slouching walk Yuen and the boy were very close to the same height. Yuen took a breath and tried to straighten up a thousand years, then sighed. He was too tired. Not important. "And that chair . . ."

He walked slower as they came to the back door of the

restaurant. He looked up to the light over the door with pigeon droppings painting the hood. That light had gone out only once while he lived here, and he had changed the bulb himself. He had polished the hood and wiped the bulb. It was his favorite light in the whole restaurant, perhaps because it was the light that helped him open the door when he returned tipsy from San Francisco, or perhaps because it was the only light outside, back of the building. Thinking about a light bulb is stupid, he thought. He could enjoy stupidity now, after all this time of trying to be smart, trying to be tall, stupidity was inevitably on the way to rounding out the circle and resting it in silence.

Yuen could hear Margie shouting the names of foods back to the waitresses as if cussing them out and didn't seem to hear a thing. He could hear the little screech of ice-cold meat slapped flat onto a hot steel griddle before the grease cackles, running water, the insulated door of the walk-in refrigerator stomping shut, and didn't hear a thing. He held Dirigible's wrists. He could see from the ease with which the boy moved his arms that his considerable strength was nothing. "Help me upstairs," he said. "I don't feel well."

He leaned heavily on the boy, pushed himself upright against the wall as they climbed. Dirigible was very strong, Yuen felt, very strong. And very angry. The boy pushed at Yuen, upping the old man onto the next step up, up the stairs to his room.

In his room, Yuen did nothing but sigh and sigh and fall backward onto his bed. He stared a moment at the ceiling. The boy did not leave the room. Yuen closed his eyes and pulled at his nose and wiped it with his fingers and stared at the boy. He saw the boy clearly now, and the smile on his face closed shut, then the mouth opened to breathe. It no longer felt like his face he was feeling, no part of him. The old man's fingers, nothing felt like anything of his now. It all felt like old books in old stores. "I have an idea," he said slowly, and took the gun from under his pillow. "We used to try to swallow our tongues to choke ourselves when we were scared, but we always spit them out, or couldn't get them down. I want you to watch so you can tell them I wanted to."

"I don't know what you're talking." Dirigible eyed the gun.
"I'm going to die by myself," Yuen attempted in Chinese
for dummies.

The boy stared, eyes big as black olives, "Who? You . . .
what are you doing?"

"Your mother can find another dishwasher. She's a good
businesswoman."

"Who'll buy me books?"

Yuen pointed the gun at one ear, then switched hands, and
pointed the gun at the other ear. He looked at the gun and held
it with both hands and pointed it at his mouth, aiming it into
his mouth, toward the bulge at the back of his head. He could
be angry at the boy, even knowing the boy knew nothing else to
say, he could be angry, but wasn't. Dirigible hit himself with a
fist and shouted, "Ah-bok!" Dirigible leaned and fell backward,
stepped once toward the old man before stopping against the
towel rack. The boy was weeping and groaning, holding an
imaginary pain in his shoulder.

Yuen looked over the gun and watched the boy's rhythmless
stumblings in the close room. He eased the hammer to safe and
sighed a longer sigh than he had breath. He went to the boy
and pulled him to the bed and sat him and wiped his face with
his hand. "It's all right, Dritch'ble." Yuen worked for enough
breath to speak. "Get up. Go downstairs, now." He bent to
untie his shoelaces, dropping the gun to the floor when his
fingers could not work them. "Wait. Will you help me bathe? I
feel very weak." He'd failed. But he had known he would. He'd
expected it.

"Yes."

"I have soap. All kinds. You can have some . . ."

"I have soap too."

He patted the boy's shoulders with his hands and clutched
into them with his fingers as he pulled himself to standing.
"You're an odd son," Yuen said, before turning to undress.
"Help me with this."

Dirigible held a towel about Yuen's pale waist as he took
him out of his room to the bathroom and helped him into the
tub. Dirigible plugged the tub and turned on the water, with
Yuen curled up on the bottom, waiting. He didn't complain

about the temperature. He leaned forward and asked the boy to scrub his back. His body was loose over his bones, and the same color as his colorless wrists with fat spongy veins piping through the skin. He took the boy's hand and looked into his face with eyes covered with raw eggwhite. "You didn't write me," he said clearly and, his body quivering, rippling water away from his waist, Yuen died. He closed his eyes with his mouth opening to breathe or sigh, and at the end, his chest was low, his ribs showed, and he was dead. There was no more for him. He had finished it.

Dirigible lifted his hands from the water and put his cheek on the edge of the tub. Yuen's death had seemed nothing special, nothing personal. He had given up the boy also. The boy tried to work a tear loose. He felt he should. Tears not all for Yuen, but for himself, because Yuen had been *his*.

Rose came up the stairs and walked down the hall noisily, saying, "Well, how did it go, you two?" before she leaned her head into the bathroom.

John Oliver Killens

I F you tell enough good stories, then your life becomes one. That is exactly what happened to John Oliver Killens of Macon, Georgia.

His written tales include short stories, plays, and scripts, but he probably will remain best known for the novels *Youngblood* (1954), *And Then We Heard the Thunder* (1962), *'Sippi* (1967), *The Cotillion* (1971), and the posthumously published *Great Black Russian* (1989). Good stories all.

Youngblood depicts the struggle of an African-American family in Georgia during the first half of the twentieth century. There are echoes of Richard Wright's work as Killens mines the terrain of the segregated South. The precedent of Wright's prose to some extent diminished the impact of Killens's novel, but Killens's South is perhaps a richer template and holds forth greater possibility for black unity and redemption. That "Youngblood," a surname, serves as the book's title underscores the author's concern with clan and community.

And Then We Heard the Thunder traces the social ripening of Solly Saunders, an African-American GI serving the United States during World War II. Saunders is torn between accepting token progress for himself and casting his lot with other black soldiers who, to varying degrees, rebel against Jim Crowism in the U.S. Army. Most significantly, Saunders risks all by siding with blacks during a race riot involving Black and white troops stationed in Australia. Much of the material for the book is drawn from Killens's own World War II experiences.

'Sippi chronicles activities surrounding the civil rights and Black Power movements. The selection chosen for this anthology illustrates several themes pervasive in the Killens canon, such as white paternalism, emasculation of Blacks, problems of

Black male–white female attraction, and Black courage. The action occurs approximately two-thirds of the way through the novel, during the summer of 1965, as Chuck Othello and Carrie return to Wakefield County after their first year at their respective colleges.

The Cotillion, set in 1960s Harlem, lampoons the pretensions of the Black middle class. The Czar and Russian aristocracy are rebuked in *Great Black Russian,* which dramatizes the life of Alexander Pushkin, the brilliant nineteenth-century Russian writer of African descent.

Killens continually sought to ennoble people of African ancestry in particular and the working class overall. He ridiculed the notion of art for art's sake, viewing his writing as a vehicle of social protest and change. His detractors have typically claimed that his fiction is overly sentimental in spots, too journalistic in general, needlessly repetitious, and peopled with an excess of insufficiently realized characters who serve as little more than mouthpieces. And it does appear that psychologically, despite the diversity of setting, Solly Saunders, Chuck Othello, and Pushkin are pretty much the same character. However, the fictional whole is much greater than the sum of the parts in this case. And at its center is an uncompromising and invaluable central intelligence that keeps the volume pumped up about racial injustice and economic exploitation.

Along with Wright, Langston Hughes and Margaret Walker are the literary influences Killens always acknowledged. The resultant blend yields a considerable talent and confidence in rendering Black speech and rhetorical forms, and Killens's fiction is a vast storehouse of African-American folk expression, especially humor. As Ben Ali Lumumba tells us in the foreword to *The Cotillion,* Killens said, "I decided to write my book in Afro-Americanese. . . . And I meant to do myself some signifying. I meant to let it all hang out."

In *'Sippi,* Reverend Purdy preaches perhaps *the* classic African-American sermon, Black English all the way. For example:

> Douglass and Tubman and Turner was they brother's keeper. Yes they was. When they theyselfs got free, they didn't stop fighting

like you woulda done. They dedicated they lives to the freedom of they black brothers and sisters!

Purdy's oratory opens yet another window onto Killens and his achievement. He was a tireless teacher and promoter of other literary careers. He taught in creative writing programs at Fisk, Howard, and Columbia universities and Medgar Evers College, served as the first chairman of the Harlem Writers Guild, and organized several black writers' conferences, the last when he was nearly seventy years old.

And he left us with memories of rich oral narratives. One about the discipline involved in cutting two hundred pages, at the publisher's request, from the manuscript of *Youngblood*, which originally ran one thousand pages. Another about that trimmed text turning up in *'Sippi* and other pieces. Recounting how a branch of the military purchased five thousand (or was it ten thousand?) copies of *And Then We Heard the Thunder* to dump into the ocean. One more about looking out from a hotel room in Tashkent in the Soviet Union, a place he had heard about from Hughes, and watching native Blacks slap each other five in greeting.

Killens died in 1987 at the age of seventy-one in New York City. During his final week or so, the Dow Jones Industrial Average plunged 508 points in one day. Was it eerie affirmation of his long-held belief that a nation that emphasizes free enterprise over free people will forever be on shaky ground and a reminder, at the time of his own death, for writers remaining and those yet to arrive?

John Oliver Killens was a good storyteller, a *very* good story himself, and a great man.

—*Keith Gilyard*

2

THE Man must have had spies around the place. The next morning after Othello's return home for the summer, Charlie Wakefield sent for him.

It was Saturday, and at first he went to Wakefield's office in the city, but they told him Jimmy Dick was working in his office at his new house that particular morning, as he sometimes did on Saturdays. So the young man from the University walked out to the new house.

Manicured hedges, ten to twelve feet high, fenced off the new house from the highway. Beyond the hedges, for two hundred yards, giant oak trees stood in staggered formation, exactly one hundred in number. They were formidable and awe-inspiring like soldiers on guard duty. Beyond the great trees was the manor house, a low-slung rambling ranch-type mansion sprawling awesomely and arrogantly all over the bright-green countryside. Othello stood now facing the front of the mansion. God only knew how many rooms there were, or even how many wings, since they seemed to go off in fifty-odd directions. He stood for a moment making up his mind. The thing was this. All his life till last September, he had always gone around the back, and even this time, he started automatically in the backward direction, but pulled himself up short. He thought of Ron, he thought of the interminable discussions he had had with Ron about black manhood, about Malcolm, about Martin Luther King and John Lewis and Whitney Young and Wilkins and all the rest, James Farmer, James Foreman, but especially John Lewis and Malcolm, because Malcolm was Ron's patron saint. And John Lewis was the shining prince. He thought of

Naomi Hester. Beautiful, glorious, wonderful Naomi Hester. After all, he *was* a man. He looked around him, as if he thought Lewis or Naomi or Ron were watching him. He was different, wasn't he? He was different from the boy who'd left Wakefield County in the autumn time. Why go to the University if you didn't change? He was different because he had been away somewhere, he himself had seen new places, talked to different kinds of people. He had been to college and it had spoiled him for the back-door entrance. It was his Great White Father's fault for sending him to college.

He wiped his face with a white handkerchief and started for the front entrance and pushed his finger on the thing that made the chimes go off inside the house. He swallowed hard and dug in like Willie Mays at home plate.

He waited in a nervous sweat and thought the door would never open, hoped the door would never open. Maybe no one was at home. Hopefully. Come again some other day. But he learned that doors do open finally. The butler was a small black man, a family retainer from way back.

"Boy, ain'tchoo Jess and Carrie's young 'un?"

"I'd like to see, I mean, I have an appointment with Mister Wakefield."

Old man Ross Baker said, "Boy, I know your mama and papa taught you better manners than that. You go around the back now, and I'll tell Mister Charlie you looking for him."

"I am not going around the back." He felt sweat pouring from all over his body now. He had taken a good bath in the big tin tub before leaving home, but it was all washed away in sweat now. "I am not here looking for a handout. Mister Wakefield wishes to see me. If you'll—"

"College sure do turn some people into a educated fool!" Ross Baker offered his opinion. Gratuitously.

They stood there staring one another down, young black face versus old black face. Baker would guard the sweet white sanctuary with his very life, and Chuck would guard his young black manhood. A good-natured, tolerantly amused voice broke into the hateful standoff. "All right, Uncle Ross, show the gentleman in. I'm expecting him."

"But he—I mean—"

"Show Mister Chaney in, Uncle Ross. Is your hearing good?" Even though Othello felt relieved, he didn't like the amusement he heard in Wakefield's voice. Mister Charlie was having himself a ball at the expense of his two favorite "niggers."

He walked past the grumbling butler and followed Wakefield down a long corridor and turned left down another corridor and finally reached the Great Man's office, which was an inch deep in carpeting. Chuck thought his feet would disappear from sight. The Great Man went behind his desk and sank back into a swivel chair, sighing deeply. "Sit down," he said. "Sit down—sit down and make yourself at home."

Othello sat down and his whole body almost sank out of sight, this time for real among the goose-feathered couch. It was as if somebody had pulled a chair out from under him. The Great Man knew what had happened and was smiling, actually laughing at him beneath his composed face. Which did not help Othello's frame of mind or disposition.

"Don't let Uncle Toms like Ross get you upset. They'll never change," the Great Man chuckled. "But they don't really mean any harm."

Othello's voice almost trembled with his anger. "Sir, I believe you sent for me."

Mister Charlie said, "I certainly did. I certainly did." Then he looked up at the ceiling for a moment, then back at Othello. "Oh yes. What are your plans for the summer, son?"

I am not your son. "I don't have any definite plans. I'm going to get some kind of job." But not in your cotton field, old buddy. Wakefield's hair was as white as balls of cotton now and ebbing at the hairline. He looked ten years older than Othello remembered him looking when he'd left for the University. He was still an impressive-looking bastard, but time was suddenly and swiftly etching the story of his life in deep lines upon his face. He was aging in a hurry, although he carried himself like a man fifteen or twenty years his junior. He got up and walked around the desk and rested his backside on its edge. "What are you majoring in at the University?"

"I haven't decided yet—I—"

"Business Administration. That's the main problem—your

race don't know anything about administration. It's not you all's fault. You never had the opportunity for experience."

Othello stared at Wakefield. Before he'd gone to the University, he had never thought of Wakefield as talking with a Southern accent, but now he sounded as if he were coming on strong with a caricature of a Mississippi peckerwood. It was fantastic how the man had changed, Othello thought. Or maybe the change was in Othello's hearing. In his perspective and perception.

"Business Administration would be just the thing. And this summer you can work for me and I'll teach you something about business from actual experience." The Great Man had developed a twitch at his left cheekbone. "Do you have a driver's license?"

"No, sir."

"We'll take care of that on Monday. You take the weekend off, get yourself together. And report to me here on Monday morning bright and early. You'll be working some of the time right here in this wing of the house. So you don't need to come through the front door and give Uncle Ross an ulcer at his age. He's got enough complaints already. There's a—" He stopped. He stared at Othello who was staring at him blank-faced now. "It has nothing to do with your color. I'm above those kind of considerations. It's just more convenient. I had this wing built to function as an office away from the office. I use this entrance sometimes my own self, when I come from town and I want to come straight to my work. You understand?"

Othello said he understood.

ALL through the long hot summer, he kept cool. And saw very little of Jake and Bessie Mae and Cora Mae, who were in the heat of things. He reported at the side entrance to the mansion every weekday morning at eight o'clock, and Wakefield was usually there and explained to him some aspect of his forty-million-dollar empire. Some mornings, Wakefield would take him on a tour of the Wakefield complex which stretched out all over the county and for miles and miles. Wakefield Textile was in Yazoo City, Wakefield's Department Store in Jackson.

"Keep your eyes open, boy." It wasn't long before Othello figured what his job really was to be that summer. He was a glorified chauffeur. After all the Wakefield "horse-manure-à-la-Business Administration" was cleared away, he was a chauffeur pure and simple. "Learn everything about the Wakefield operation, boy. The day is coming when colored men going to be managers of things. And I want you to be ready. The Negro race needs experienced, intelligent, educated leadership, instead of all this violence and hotheadedness."

It was all right with Othello, the chauffeur's job. And it was a whole lot better than other jobs, or no job at all. And at least once a week, he drove the Great Man somewhere outside the county. And he liked to drive and he liked going places, seeing other faces. He saw very little of Carrie Louise that summer, just fleeting glimpses, here and there, because he always used the side entrance, and she was almost never in that wing of the house. Which was fine with Chuck Othello. The only other place he saw her was in church. She still went to worship at Mount Moriah Baptist Church at least twice a month.

He arrived for work one Monday morning in the middle of July, and Carrie Louise was seated behind her father's desk.

She said, "Good morning, Othello. How was college?"

He said, "Where is Mister Wakefield?"

She looked him up and down. She was as fresh-faced as she'd ever been. When she smiled her entire face smiled with her; her eyes, cheeks, teeth, lips. "I asked you a question first," she said, "Didn't they teach you any manners up at your college?"

He did not like to be laughed at, especially by a rich, empty-headed white bitch like this one. His face grew warm now, and he tasted his great anger on his lips and in his mouth and throat. "College was just fine. Is your father coming to the office today?" Wakefield was ever punctual.

"My father is a little bit under the weather this morning."

"Anything serious?" If she wanted to play the game of smiling stares, he certainly was not going to let her stare him down. He was not going to let her castrate him. So he stared back at her and through her, blank-facedly, as if she were invisible, or better still, nonexistent. She got the message.

"Nothing serious," she said. "He'll be at his post tomorrow. Generally speaking, he's as healthy as a horse. I expect it was a case of one Scotch and branch water too many." She laughed. "Sit down, Othello Chaney."

"Did he send me a message or something? Is there anything special this morning?"

Her whole face smiled at him. "I'm afraid your colleague was in no shape to send messages this morning. Will you please sit down for a moment? You certainly are a fidgety boy."

He sat, wondering now and curious too, as to what this white girl thought there was for the two of them to talk about in 'Sippi. He sat and waited.

She said, "You sure have grown. I remember you almost as long as I remember my own self."

He thought to himself, "What is this? Reminiscence Week?" He stared across the desk at the yellow-haired white girl. He wasn't exactly smiling at the moment, but during his sojourn at the University he had developed an expression which made it seem as if a smile were always lurking just out of sight beneath the surface of his face.

She said, "Do you remember how we used to romp and tear together over in the other house?"

He said, "I remember." What in the hell did she want from him?

She said, "We were such good friends in those days. Then one day we grew up and I don't know you anymore."

He said, *"C'est la vie."* What else is new?

But he remembered all right. He remembered the romping and the tearing, but there were other memories he remembered. He had been about five years old when he learned the difference between black and white, and he had learned his lesson painfully. His mother had whipped it into him. And this girl across the desk had been the instigator with her Mama-and-Papa business. The two of them naked and belly to belly in the guest room in the Big House. He never would forget the incident. After his mother whipped him, later in the day, he'd seen the white girl weeping in his mother's arms. It was a long time afterward that he was able to understand the terror which must have struck his mother's heart. A black boy and Miss Rich White Bitch belly-to-belly in Big House, Mississippi. But the white girl in his mother's arms was something else again.

Carrie Lou's face turned red like a beet, as she remembered now the time when she lay on this black boy naked as she came into the world and mouth to mouth out in the woods that day when he had nearly drowned. She felt a strange heat move all over her body, and she could no longer look him in the face. She had never related the incident to a living soul. How could she? Even now as he sat there, she was so embarrassed, she thought she would go right through the floor. Or was it really embarrassment? But it had been completely innocent. Hadn't it?

She told him, speaking quickly now, about her college roommate who was a Negro. He said, "Oh." Cool as dry ice. The girl's name was Sherry Kingsley and her father was a famous lawyer in New York and a state senator, and wealthy, and she and Sherry had become good friends. Othello's comment was "That's good," a bored expression on his face. Sherry Kingsley was into everything, she knew everybody. "David Woodson, John Lewis, Martin King, all the leaders. Foreman, Farmer, Malcolm X." The girl was almost out of breath. "I met some of them my own self." Othello thought, Big deal. But he was entirely unimpressed. It was strange, he thought, to hear this 'Sippi white girl name-dropping colored VIP's as if she herself were basking in the sunlight of their celebrity.

She looked him in the face again now. "Were you active in the Movement at the college?"

He had almost relaxed, but with this question, all his danger signals started flashing again. "What movement?"

"The Movement," she said, almost impatiently. "The civil rights movement—the black revolution."

He stared, wordless, at the girl. What the hell did she know about the Movement? "I'm afraid I spent most of my time with my head in the books."

She said, "And what about the Movement around here? Is anything happening?"

He said, "Happening?" So that was what she was all about.

She wanted information about the Movement here in Wakefield County. She just wanted to do a little old espionage for the cause of white supremacy. Just a little old harmless espionage by getting this stupid colored boy to spill his chitterlings. She probably had made up that wild story about having a Negro roommate, Sherry Whatchamacallit.

She said, "You know what I mean. Is anybody into anything?"

He was glad he could say truthfully he knew nothing about anything, he had been too busy. At the same time he was somehow ashamed that he had kept himself aloof, aloft. He said, "You know as much about it as I do."

She said impatiently, "Oh I know all about the voter registration drive, and I think it's simply marvelous, but I want to know the inside of everything. I want to be a part of it. I know they've put hundreds of good colored folks off the land for exercising their constitutional rights. I know they've set up tents for some of them to live in on a couple of acres of land owned by the Mount Moriah Baptist Church. And I think it's a sin and a shame, and I think it's just marvelous how the colored stick together, and live in tents."

She knew more than he did already.

She said, "You've been over to Tent City, haven't you?"

Othello had not been over to Tent City. He had heard his parents mention it, in passing. He had read what David Woodson had said about it in *Democracy* magazine. He thought, Well, my little spy, you will not get anything from this interview, for the simple reason that the man is ignorant of what is going on. He don't know nothing and don't say nothing, he just keep rolling along.

He stood up and told her, "I can't help you at all. And I have to be running along. Tell your father I'll see him tomorrow morning."

He went over to Tent City that afternoon, where about forty-five families were living in Army surplus supply tents. Some had been there since the middle of winter. Othello asked one elderly lady how they made it, especially in the wintertime. She said, "Indeed, darling, in some ways it's better than them shacks they moved us out of. It was like living outdoors in them doggone things whenever the weather got bad. It rained inside them devilish shacks and leaked outdoors."

Tent City was four rows of olive-drab pyramidal tents. The men had built an outhouse at the edge of one end of the row of tents and a common kitchen at the other end. Children ran around all over the place and especially underfoot.

David Woodson had interviewed every family in Tent City for his article in *Democracy* magazine.

"My name is George Booker. I'm fifty-five years old. I've cropped shares for Mister Billy Watson since I was eleven years old. I've always lived on the Watson plantation. And likewise my wife, Sojourner. I and her has five children. Cropping shares is the only work I ever known. What is we going to do?"

"My name is Matthew Jackson. I'm seventy-five years old. Mister Johnson told me, me and my family had a place to stay as long the Johnson plantation existed. I done worked for Mister Johnson all my life. He always told me I and mine was like one of the family. And that ain't too much of a big lie, cause some of mine sure do favor some of his mighty much. I has five children and eight grand. Six of the grand lives with me and Queen Esther who is my first and only wife."

Othello stopped at the end of the second row of tents. An old withered black woman sat in front of the tent in an ancient cane-back chair. She was mumbling something to herself. Her face seemed to wear a thousand wrinkles. He seemed to be drawn to her as if by an invisible magnet. What was she mumbling to herself about? Was she trying to say something to him? He stood above her now and saw her old lips barely moving.

He said, "Yes, m'am, what is it you're saying?"

It was her eyes that held him, fascinated him, mesmerized him. Large and wide and luminous were her youngish eyes, filled with the pain and anguish of the ancient ages. "I don't understand you, Mama."

Her eyes appeared to him to be all-knowing and all-seeing. He thought she said, "Ain't this a damn shame? Come almost a hundred years down this long and lonesome road to go on to Glory in a doggone tent. Worked in the Master's vineyud all my life. Always sowing, never reaping, and come to the end of the row to die in a damn tent!" She laughed and shook her head from side to side. "Jesus darling, you sure got a funny sense of humor. I'm tellin' you the natural truth." She laughed some more. Bitter laughter. "Niggers sowing—white man reaping. He got the whole world in his hand. Splain it to me, Jesus. Don let your servant stop believin! It's too late, Master! Too late! Too late!" She was laughing and crying simultaneously. Laughing, crying, mumbling. "You is mysterious, Jesus darling. You is really somethin!"

He felt his own eyes filling up, and he moved away from her, stumbling over a tent stave. He somehow managed not to fall. He'd wanted to plead with her, tell her not to stop believing. A hundred years of walking down that long and lonesome road to sit and die outside a tent at the journey's end. As he walked away from the camp ground he ran into Carrie Louise, who was just driving up in a Jaguar. She bounced out of the car with her arms full of packages.

"Give me a hand," she told him.

He took some of the packages. "These are for the campers!" she told him, almost gaily. "Thought you told me you'd never been to Tent City."

"This is my first trip," he said weakly, angrily, as he followed Lady Bountiful, which was how he thought of her now, as she strode up the row of tents toward the outdoor kitchen. "This is Luke Gibson," Lady Bountiful told Othello, as they gave the tall black man the packages. He seemed to be in charge of the kitchen force.

She didn't need to introduce him to Luke Gibson. He had known the sad-faced man all of his life. She was bubbling over with enthusiasm. "Luke doesn't live here. He's a volunteer worker like you ought to be. He still lives on Rab Johnson's plantation. He refused to move. Isn't he heroic? Everybody loves him. Every time I bring something, I tell him to take some of it home to his own family, wife, mother-in-law, and seven children. And he always says, 'Yessum,' but he never takes a thing. He is as true a Christian as any white man in all of Mississippi."

Chuck Othello slipped away as she went from tent to tent asking the campers how they were doing this beautiful summer afternoon. She wanted them to love her, even as they all loved old stubborn old Luke Gibson.

And they really did love old Luke Gibson, and the stand he was taking against one of the "baddest" Mister Charlies the state had ever known. Everybody talked about it everywhere Othello went among his kind of people. He heard his own mother, Mama Carrie, pray for old Luke every night. Luke and his wife and his mother-in-law and his poor little innocent children. Especially his children. Everybody admired Luke for his stand against the Man, even as they feared for him, because the Man he'd picked to stand against had a fearsome reputation when it came to colored people. Almost overnight, soft-spoken, churchgoing, God-fearing Luke Gibson had become a folk legend and a hero. Before now, folk had thought of him as the gentlest kind of a man. Wouldn't harm a gnat if it were sipping in his buttermilk. And suddenly—strength. John Henry. "Should've been named John Henry steada Luke Clarence Booker Gibson."

ONE night Othello ran into Uncle Bish. He was stoned, drunk as a cooter, and was finding it almost impossible to navigate. He emerged from Douglass Alley and stumbled along Walnut Street, half-walking, half-running. "Hey there. Chuck Othello." He looked like an accident going somewhere to happen. He had put on weight around the middle and lost weight in his face and shoulders, and was just as Othello's father had described him: ". . . as raggedy as jaybird in whistling time." Othello never found out when "whistling time" was. But he had heard the expression all his life. And it seemed to fit Uncle Bish at the moment.

Uncle Bish walked now rocking and reeling with his shoulders thrust forward as if he were bucking a tornado, but there was no wind stirring in the air at all. He was so high a good strong wind would have put him into orbit. He walked a little ahead of Othello about half of a step. "Let's go git us a little old taste, Othello. Don't worry 'bout nothing. I got the money. I'm a working man. I'm the establishment soup-pen-tendant. That's what my bossman said I am. I got a good job. Don't pay no tention to these niggers round here." Othello's father had told him about Uncle Bish's job as porter at the *Wakefield Daily Chronicle*, which was edited and published by Congressman Rogers Jefferson Davis Johnson.

"No thank you, Uncle Bish. I got to—"

Uncle Bish stopped and turned toward Othello and his feet got tangled with each other and he went down in a heap. "Somebody tripped me," he mumbled. Othello went to pick him up. "I don't need no help," he said, using his body to keep Othello from picking him up. "I can git up by my own self!"

Othello released him and he tried to get up through his own efforts and fell flat on his face. He rolled over and looked up at Othello. "Goddamn!" he said, laughing masochistically. "I'm like Dusty Fletcher—I ain't never seen no whiskey that wouldn't let you go *no*-where!" He stared up at Othello through bloodshot eyes. His red eyes looked like lighted lanterns. "Whatchoo standing up there looking like two dogs on a knot's dick? Ain'tchoo gon help the old man git to his feets?"

Othello helped Bish to his feet and Bish draped his arm around Othello's shoulders and they made it up the dimly lit street. "Come on, Othello, let's go git us a little taste. I got plenty money. Don't worry about a thing. Open the door, Richard. The man's out here. Wheee-eee! I would holla but the town too small!"

"You don't need no more whiskey, Uncle Bish. I'm going to take you home."

"Whoa—there," Uncle Bish sang out, and imitated a donkey, as he became suddenly immobile and balled up into a knot and used all his strength to keep himself immobile, in very much the manner of a stubborn jackass, which is what Othello was just ready to call his childhood hero. A damn jackass!

"Come on, Uncle Bish, doggone your time!"

"I liked to heard you then, boy! You watch your langwich! I'll rap your platter till your head git flatter. I'll wash your mouth out with lye soap, you don't mind." They were underway again. "You doin the right thing, Othello. Tell em your name is West and stay away from all that nigger mess. A nigger ain't shit no way you take him. I oughta know, cause I been a nigger all my days. I tol' Mister Congusman Johnson, I'm a xpert on niggers. Been one all my natural life—been one all my life."

Othello closed his eyes momentarily as they stumbled up the streets. A single tear spilled down his face, as his mind conjured a memory of Uncle Bish when he was his childhood hero. He was almost every black child's hero. He'd had the biggest heart in Wakefield County. Generous to embarrassment. And the children loved him. And he loved the children. "The black man's future," he would say, "is our childrence." Speaking proper, putting on airs. "They our treasure, more valuable than gold. Can't take it with you nohow. Some of these white folks think they gon pay their way through them Pearly Gates. Gon bribe Saint Peter." He used to be hard on Mister Charlie Peckerwood. He didn't even sound like Uncle Bish anymore.

"This ain't the way to Bennie's," he said, pulling himself up short again, rearing and bucking.

They were going through Crackerville now, where the really poor white peckerwoods lived. They got underway again. "Even a poor white trash is better'n a nigger. A nigger ain't shit! I sure am glad you one nigger boy got sense enough not to git mixed up in that nigger mess with silver rights and all that shit. Silver rights! Silver rights! Voter reddistrayshon! Ain' nothing to it. How it's gon be anythin to it when it's niggers running it? Stands to reason."

They were at the edge of Crackerville now where it ran smack into Black Tybee. Ragged-assed white kids were playing ring games beneath a lamp post.

> *Little Sally Walker*
> *Sitting in a saucer*
> *Cryin and a-weepin'*
> *For all she has done—*

When they saw Bish coming, the game broke up and they ran toward Bish and Chuck Othello with their hands held out. "Uncle Bish! Uncle Bish!"

Before Othello knew what was happening, Bish was emptying his pockets of coins and throwing them to the children, who scrambled for them on the ground in front of them. A dark-brown-skinned little girl ran from across the road toward the crowd with her hands out. "Git back, black bitch!" Bish shouted at her. "Don't you put your black hands on my money!" He reached in his pockets and started to hand out dollar bills to the happy peckerwood children. "Here, pretty children! Here! Here! Git back, black bitch!" He kicked at her. "Git back, black bitch!" The little black girl's eyes filled and tears spilled down her cheeks; she turned and ran back into the darkness from whence she had come.

"Uncle Bish!" Othello cried out. "What's the matter with you? Are you losing your mind, or something?" Othello snatched some bills from Bish's hand and shooed the white children away. "All right! All right! That's enough of that! Give Uncle Bish his money back." The children scampered.

And they got underway again going up a dusty road of a street that was entirely blacked-out. No street lights anywhere at all. They were truly in Black Tybee. "What in the devil you want to give your money away like that, Uncle Bish?"

"Don' worry bout nothin! Donchoo worry bout a thing."

"If you're going to give a little money away, why to white children? Why'd you chase the colored girl?"

"Cause she was black. That's how come."

"What's that got to do with it? That's how come she should get a preference, if anything."

"Cause she black and her foots stink and she don't love Jesus and God don't love ugly and a nigger ain't shit!"

They were in front of his house and started into the yard, and Othello felt a wetness fall upon his sock. He held out his free hand palm upward to see if it were raining. It wasn't raining. And then it reached his nostrils, and he knew that Uncle Bish was pissing his pants. Then Bish broke wind protractedly, like rifle fire, and another kind of stench assaulted Othello's nostrils, turned his stomach over. "Uncle Bish!" He knew somehow that Uncle Bish had shitted in his pants. They had reached the steps by now, and Bish stood still as death, but his pants did not keep quiet, as he lost control of all his functions. Crying, breaking wind, urinating, defecating. He sank down upon the steps and wept like a lonely child without a loved one in the entire world.

Miss Easter Lillie, a stout, tall, high-yaller woman, came to the door. "Lord Savior, do pray!" she murmured. And she and Othello struggled with him to get him into the house. Uncle Bish mumbling all the while, "A nigger ain't shit, Chuck Othello. A nigger ain't shit! You stick with Charlie Wakefield like you got some sense. Stay way from that fool boy of mine in the Bottom. Stick with Charlie Wakefield. A nigger ain't shit! I oughta know. I'm a xpert on niggers. Been one all my life!"

And all the way home that night Othello's eyes were never dry. He wept for Uncle Bish, for the man he remembered Bish once was and for the thing he had become. He woke up off and on all night long, and each time it was thoughts and dreams of Uncle Bish that waked him. How had it happened? How in God's name had it happened?

The next night he went to see Little Jake and Bessie Mae Moocho and talked to them about the Movement. They were up to their ears, committed and active. They moved him with their dedication, but he could not be involved, he really could not. He was just too doggone busy. He held hands one night and swapped spit with Cora Mae Rakestraw, and she talked on and on about the Movement. It was unbelievable. Maybe it's a fad, he tried to rationalize it. For hundreds of years, black folk had laughed or wept only on command, only with permission from their kindly masters. "If Cap'n Charlie shouted 'Shit!' you squatted and strained lustily," in the words of Othello's roommate, Ron. No back lip. Just hang your head when Cap'n speaks to you. Don't fret your head about such things as citizenship and ownership. Only men can vote and have possession. There are no such things as black men. The only men are white men. So you must govern yourselves accordingly. But suddenly black men appeared as if from nowhere, appeared in all their blackness. Black men stood straight, and white men scratched their heads in consternation. Some even panicked.

His mother and father, humble, God-fearing people had begun to talk about Charlie like a dog. Reverend Purdy and Luke Gibson were on every black lip in the county. To the city fathers they were wanted men, public enemies. One and Two, in the order named. One evening after work, Othello stopped by the church to see his pastor, who invited him to dinner at the parsonage. He drove an ancient Packard and was probably the world's very worst driver, as he sped along at ten and fifteen miles an hour. Othello felt naked and exposed as they drove nonchalantly through the downtown area. He could feel the stabs of hatred from the angry looks of white folk, as he drove around with Public Enemy Number One. It seemed to Othello that his pastor had to make a million stops before heading home. It was nerve-racking. One of the last stops was at a bakery shop, and he had to park the car on an incline. Purdy got out of the car unconcernedly and took a brick out from under his seat and put it behind a back wheel to keep the car from rolling back downhill, and he ambled into the bakery. Othello thought his pastor would never return, as cracker after cracker drove alongside and stared at the car, and threw angry white looks at Othello, or so he imagined. Reverend Purdy stopped by his combination barber shop and shoe shop. He stopped at this place and that. It was a long time after dark by the time he headed home for real. He lived out in a brand-new settlement for Negroes, where the teachers and the preachers and the mail carriers and Pullman porters lived; people E. Franklin Frazier called "black bourgeoisie," but whom ordinary folk called "nigger rich."

There was no moon out that night as they sailed down the main highway at thirty miles an hour. Then they turned off the main highway and onto a dirt road which led to the new development. They had gone about two hundred yards, when a blast of siren broke the silence of the peaceful countryside. Out of nowhere a squad car flew past them for about fifty yards and threw a roadblock across the narrow road; two cops emerged from the car and came running toward the old Packard which had chugged down to a halt.

One of the policemen threw the beams of his flashlight onto the windshield, temporarily blinding them. The cops came up to the car, one on Reverend Purdy's side, the other on Othello's. They dipped the beams of their flashlights into their faces again, and then into the back of the car.

Reverend Purdy asked politely, "What's your problem, Officers?"

"We ain't got no problem. You the one got a problem, boy."

"It's been a long time since I was a boy, Mister Officer."

"Never mind. What you mean tearing up the highway a while ago at eighty miles an hour?"

Reverend Purdy laughed a dry laugh. "You must be got the wrong party, Officer. This old buggy ain't done eighty miles an hour in so long, it wouldn't know what it was all about."

The other cop said, "That's that nigger preacher been raising all that hell round here, ain't it?"

The first cop said, "You must been drunk or something, driving that fast like you done lost your mind or something."

"No, sir. You got the wrong party again. Cause I'm a man of the cloth, and I don't never imbibe, although I don't hold it against a man who do."

The other cop said, "You know how to drive, boy? You, boy, you, you sitting next to the preacher."

"I know how to drive," Othello said. "And I have my driver's license."

The first cop said, "Well, we gon take you down to the lockup, preacher, and you can tell that lie to the shaff, and see if he believes you like your flock do evey Sunday." The other cop had come and joined the first one on Reverend Purdy's side.

Reverend Purdy said, quietly, "No, sir. I have to be getting along home. I got company for supper. And being as how I ain't broke the law, I don't see what business I could possibly have with the shaff."

All during this time Chuck had a feeling of profound ambivalence. He was indignant, because he knew the cops were deliberately gunning for his pastor. In his anger he sympathized with his pastor all the way. And he hated these peckerwoods as much as anybody. At the same time, he could have kicked himself for being caught out on this lonely and deserted road. These cops could do anything they wanted with them. He and his pastor were completely helpless. The night came suddenly alive with all the sounds of night in Mississippi. Frogs croaking, crickets giggling; he even thought he heard some owls hooting. And whippoorwills. He was with the Movement all the way, but he wanted to pick his own arena for the fight, and he damn sure wouldn't pick a dark and lonely spot like this, where the only lighting was from the blinking lightning bugs.

His belly flip-flopped as he heard the first cop say, "All right, preacher, you gon come peacefully, or do I got to pull you out the car? You want us to start some rough stuff? We damn sure can accommodate you." He put his hand on his gun which rested snugly in its holster.

Reverend Purdy reached over Othello into his glove compartment and took a gun out and placed it on his thigh. There was a slight tremor in his voice now. "You gentlemen might try to take me outa this car, and one of y'all might get me, but one of y'all ain't going to feel so good about it, cause he going to meet his Maker, 'bout the same time I do. And that's my promise. I might board the train for Glory in the next few minutes, but this is one train gon be integrated." They both had their hands on their guns now, and he had his hand on his gun, and there was that moment when the whole world hung in balance for these four men. Sweat rained from all over Chuck Othello. The policemen looked at Reverend Purdy, then at each other. Which of them would make the first move and which would live to tell the story? And be a county hero. And get a fat promotion. They looked back at Reverend Purdy. The first cop said, "All right, boy. We gon let you go this time beingst it's your first offense and seeing as you a man of God. But you better watch your step from now on in."

His pastor said simply, dryly, "Thank you, kindly."

The lawmen backed away and walked back to their car and got in and drove past them back down the road from whence they came. Reverend Purdy gazed into his rear-view mirror, then took a large colored handkerchief out of his back pocket and wiped his face. "Whew!"

Othello said, in open boyish admiration, "Reverend Purdy, you sure did stand up to them. You sure got a lot of courage! I mean to tell you. Man! You shook them to their natural chittlings!"

Reverend Purdy said, "I figured it this way. I done lived up off my knees all this time, I ain't gon do no different this late in the game. I don't git on my knees to nobody but the Good Lord up on High, and He sure don't look like none of them peckerwood policemen. Leastways I sure God hope He don't."

Othello said, "Yeah, but I mean, they had you where they

wanted you way out here in the middle of nowhere. They had both of us where they wanted us."

"Well, you right about that, son. But the way I figured it, to go or not to go, the percentages was in my favor. If I had gotten out the car they could've whipped both of our heads till their arms got weary and shot us in the back and locked our dead bodies up for resisting arrest. That's how come I figured I had nothing to lose by not gitting out the car. On the other hand, I figured that they loved their little white lives just as much as I loved my black one. I figured they might even love they lives more than they love they white supremacy or whatever you call it. And it looks like Reverend Purdy gambled rightly."

He laughed a short and angry laugh and wiped his heavy brow again and started up the car and took off slowly down the lonesome road.

Josephine Gattuso Hendin

LIKE many ethnic writers of her generation, Josephine Gattuso Hendin's first impulse with respect to her Italian American background was escape. Born in a Little Italy in Astoria, Queens, she spent much of her adolescence "reading my way through the public library. . . . I think that I was motivated to read in large part because I was looking for an escape from the very limited world in which I lived." Immersion in books in a more formal way in college and graduate school continued this movement out: a Woodrow Wilson Fellowship to Columbia University led to a teaching career at Yale and then a professorship in American literature at New York University. Two critical studies, one on Flannery O'Connor, the other *Vulnerable People*, a study of American fiction since 1945, completed her drive to "find other worlds through reading."

Then in 1985, Hendin began a reverse movement, a move toward the dream of her childhood to be a writer, a move toward the internalized but never forgotten landscape of Italian American life in Queens. A novel, *The Right Thing to Do*, resulted and was published in 1988. Its title refers to two of Hendin's chief themes as an Italian American writer: first, what she calls the "abiding moral concerns of Italian life," which find expression in Italian-Americans' punctiliousness in "fulfilling their moral obligations, keeping their word, behaving properly toward others"; second, what she sees as the cultural orientation of Italian Americans toward behavior—toward *doing* the right thing rather than figuring out how that "doing" might feel.

The Right Thing to Do embodies these themes in both the father figure, Nino—the preserver of the cultural demand to "do the right thing" no matter who gets hurt—and his daughter, Gina—who does worry about feeling, and about achieving the kind of free self-expression in her academic lair in New York City that her father finds both foolish and frightening, i.e., American. An irremediable conflict between father and daughter results. The clash of their apparently incompatible worlds girds the novel with images of obsession (his) and refusal (hers) and change in a world where the constantly reiterated wisdom is: "What is in our hearts has nothing to do with it. Our duty is to follow what has been ordained for us. The right thing to do is to do what has always been done. *All change is for the worse.*"

The torment of Hendin's young heroine in both rejecting and accepting that notion—which is Hendin herself, and all of us, at once accepting and rejecting a heritage we can neither tolerate nor forget—gives the story its power. Hendin finds room not only to depict a Gina who fights her way out of the patriarchal straitjacket designed for her—finding, as she does so, allies in the other women of her family—but also to write what she has called a "love letter" to her old neighborhood. The result is a story whose triumph is elegaic, a story that Irving Howe calls "funny, touching and shrewd."

Josephine Gattuso Hendin continues to divide her time between scholarly writing and fiction—with a new novel in the early stages. As she said in a recent interview: "With fiction, as with so many other things in life, once is never enough."

—*Lawrence DiStasi*

Chapter 3 from

THE RIGHT THING TO DO

SHE could see him in the distance, trying to hide behind a newspaper as he sat on the bench in front of the ruins of P.S. 5. For days she had caught glimpses of him reflected in store windows. Turning suddenly she had caught sight of him limping into a doorway or stepping back deeper into a subway car. He was unmistakably there now, waiting to see where she would go. He was still at it. Once or twice you could meet Nino by chance. But this was something else. I haven't fooled him at all, she realized. How long had he been doing this, watching her drop off a weekly supply of unread books before, dressed demurely as a Catholic schoolgirl, she went to meet Alex and strip?

Gina stepped back into the library, unable to decide what to do. Should she meet Alex anyway? Should she try to lose Nino on the train? Should she call his shot and just confront him? Should she spend the evening in the library and make Nino wait for nothing? What was the right thing to do?

If he wants to follow me, I'll give him a chase he won't forget, Gina thought grimly. It came to her, the determination to make him run, run, run in the sunlight that was still hotter than kisses. It came like a fire itself, freeing and fueling her rage. Who was he not to believe what she said? He wouldn't stand for the truth; he wouldn't stand for her lying. So let him not stand at all, let him exhaust himself until he couldn't tell the difference between truths and lies. A war was a war. Once he realized he wasn't going to win, he would give up.

Gina moved out onto the library steps, walking slowly so that he would be sure to see her. What if he didn't get up? What if he were only reading the paper? Geared for war, the possibility of a missed fight wasn't what she wanted. But she could tell now for sure, seeing him gathering himself together, that he was following. She moved toward the station, deliberately crossing the street so that he could climb the long staircase of the El without fear that she would see him. The shaded stairway seemed cool; out on the subway platform the sun shone down on the hot, splintering wood. She loved this platform. From the end, looking over the dome of Saint Demetrios's Church, she could see the New York skyline, suspended in the shimmering heat.

On the street below were the private houses, the six-story apartments, the little yards overpacked with rosebushes and fig trees—the vestigial village beyond which the city stood like a mirage. Were you thirsty? The city was water. Were you low? It was all height and promise. Were you lonely? There was Alex. She could hardly keep her mind on Nino. That was the trouble with Nino. When he was around, he focused everything. When he was gone, it seemed as though he didn't exist at all. I'm not, she realized, purposeful enough for a good vendetta. I don't want revenge, I want out. But there he was, committed to pursuit to the last drop of blood. She looked away, into the rosebushes pinned and pruned on their trellises.

It was the month they call in Sicily the time of the lion sun. There the heat ruled without rivals. Here in Astoria the rose-packed gardens hurled sweetness into the dust-laden air, the smells of cooking bubbled from open kitchen windows into streets pungent with car exhausts, the El rained soot on the street below; all seemed fused into a seething life that was fair match for the ravenous sun. The BMT went crashing around the curve from Hoyt Avenue, its wheels grinding to an ear-splitting stop on the hot rails. Gina got on the train. Peering through the filmy car window she saw Nino limping into the next car. She settled nervously into a seat facing the Manhattan skyline, still visible through the streaked windows as the train screeched on.

There it was. At work, every day, in the city, typing pastdue bills, or letters politely requesting payment, the beauty of it receded before the familiar routine of drudge-work. But even the bills she typed sometimes seemed launched into that other world where people lived gracefully, lightly, never paying their dues. Not my lot, she thought wistfully. With Nino your bills were always due. You could meet them on the infinite installment plan. Pay-as-you-go-to-the-grave in regular portions of work, marriage, christenings, funerals. Spellbound you paid and paid. What made it all work for so long? What was the magic? The sense of fear? Just fear of Nino's rages, the wreckage he made with his words and his cane? It was part of it. You couldn't shortchange his menacing voice and punishing ways. But it wasn't that alone that made it seem impossible to default on Nino. He had an air of being right. Nino! she wanted to scream. You can't collect from me! But his air of certainty made her feel doubtful, confused. How could you set your confusion against all his conviction? And so she felt only a sense of faint dread, a sudden exhaustion that paralyzed the will to cross him. Her weariness came before the fight, making it all seem hopeless before it had begun.

The train plunged into the tunnel that brought not a darkness but only a harsher light. The fluorescent rods, exposed through the broken shields, showed the ragged papers and soot swirling slowly as the train lumbered under the river. The thought of the river overhead, the oily surface stained by chaotically moving tides, pressing its weight year after year against the concrete and steel, never failed to bring the question to mind: When would it give? When would it break, when would the barricade yield passage beneath the surface, finally giving way to the tides? It was a kid's thought. It should have passed long ago. But it didn't. In Sicily, near Amerina, there was a lake, Perguas, where Hades was supposed to have risen to go foraging for a woman. When he kidnapped Persephone, he took her back through the milky water to the underground place, the hell that was his to rule. Her trip through the water—suspended, airless in alien hands—must have been terrifying. It was just a story, a story without a place in a subway car inscribed with graffiti. Yet it stayed in her mind like the image of Nino in the next car.

The train was really speeding now, rocking into the bright blue bulbs that lit the tunnel's sides. She could see herself moving toward the door that led to his car, forcing it open, feeling the hot wind between the cars, standing before him, screaming hello over the noise. Maybe that would be the best. The train lurched violently to one side, hurling her against the seat. It hadn't been much of an idea, anyway. Whatever she said, he would refuse to acknowledge; he wouldn't seem even slightly surprised. That would end the ride, but he'd take it as her capitulation, her recognition that he had found her out.

By now, Nino had read the sports news so many times he remembered it even better than usual, and he usually remembered it all. After the train had passed Bloomingdale's, his curiosity and suspicion rose. He hadn't thought she was going shopping, but still, he nodded, fanning himself with the *News*, you never know. She was, he could see, leaning forward and stretching by the window, arching back in her seat, staring at the lights in the tunnel. When Union Square came and went, he saw her rise.

Eighth Street, he thought. She could catch him on that stop easily, if she hesitated after getting out. He would have to move quickly to avoid getting caught in the door. The absence of a crowd, the midday silence of the station, all gave him pause. He was so easy to spot, a crippled old man. But she moved very quickly, without looking back when she left the station. Heading west, she stopped at the corner, waiting for the light to change. She walked slowly, glancing in store windows. She stopped near University Place, studying the display carefully. He ducked into the doorway of a butcher shop, watching her through a rack of prime rib roasts until she finished window-shopping and went on, turning down University Place. Hobbling quickly, he glanced into the window to see what had made her stop so long. Red lace bras with feathers sprouting from the top, transparent bikini underpants with little red lips embroidered on them, black see-through camisoles, some with cutouts where the nipples would be—Nino clenched his teeth, dug his cane into the sidewalk, and marched on.

She was heading into Washington Square Park. In the heat, only the elegant mansions on the north side seemed to remain intact. Everything else seethed, bubbled. Once, Nino thought, peering at her from behind a tree, this was a potter's field, just a burying ground for the poor. Now, he thought disgustedly, looking at the addicts, winos, and stoned drifters lying on the grass, it looks as though the bodies have surfaced again. There she was in the middle of it all, buying a soda from a vendor, drinking on a bench in the blistering sun. You could barely see south to Judson Church, the fog of marijuana was so dense. The noise of conga drums, rude and numbing, thudded through the heat. She sipped her diet soda, taking it all in. He edged behind her, moving behind a tree so that even if she turned she couldn't spot him.

Glancing up, Nino met Garibaldi's eye. There the statue was, newly whitewashed in its frozen stride. Garibaldi stood balanced on his right foot, his left leg about to move forward; his right hand was poised on the sword strapped to his left side. Was he taking it out of the sheath, or putting it in? Politics aside, that was the kind of man you could see would use his sword to defend the right things. But the question came back. Was he drawing his sword against some tyrant, or was he putting it away because he had already won? The face, whitewashed of its lines, smoothed by rains and snows, couldn't tell you much anymore. But the stance was proud, a gentleman's stance without being showy. There he was, after all these years, a warrior with a paunch, not too proud when he had to leave Italy to help out Meucci, the inventor, in his candle factory in Staten Island. And then even after going back to Italy to lead victorious armies, to keep writing to Meucci as "Dear Boss"!

Nino shook his head. There was a man for you. And people say Italians are lousy fighters, never able to go the distance.

Gina's hands held the can of soda like a chalice. She had the mentality of a three-year-old, Nino thought, shaking his head. He had taken her here through the park so many times on the way to Aunt Tonetta's. They had even sat on the bench where she sat now. In those days he didn't have to hide behind her! He had bought the ice cream pop, the soda, the lemon ice she had held so solemnly. He had sat with her, telling her stories, or rushing her along so they wouldn't be late. The new playground on the south side, with its fancy swings and fake hills, hadn't been there.

Rising, turning, Gina glimpsed Nino's face, darkened with sentiment, still turned toward the statute. Garibaldi again, she thought disgustedly. The whitewashed statue was already flecked and pitted with soot, chips had fallen from the pedestal where skateboards had crashed into it. Yet the sight of him had always made Nino gab. What hypocrisy, a petty tyrant like him talking about a liberator. She stuffed the straw into the soda can with her right fist. Striding toward a garbage basket, she hurled the soda into it through a mass of bees hunting for sugar. She had to walk slowly, she realized, or he would lose her, fall too far behind in the winding streets that he used to take her through on the way to visit relatives whose hearts and mouths were always open. By now, each had had his appointed funeral and gone on.

Nino moved after her as she walked south, ambling across West Third, he only dimly realizing they were on their way past Aunt Tonetta's on Thompson Street. How he remembered the wine she used to make, thick as chocolate and half as sweet, bubbling in soda glasses a third full of Seven-Up. Past the lemon ice stand, past the old playground, she crossed Houston, pausing by Saint Anthony's Church. She was moving south. Where was she going? But the question faded as memories hit, as his shirt dampened and ran with sweat in the heat, his neatly knotted tie under the starched collar wet as a marathon runner's sweatband. No more village now. No hotpants, no serapes. The little boys of six and seven in shorts, squatting to draw circles for games of war on the sidewalk, older boys wrapping tape on a broomstick, kids playing boxball, seemed like new versions of old snapshots of himself. His glasses steamed. His rage faded; he kept on, propelled as much by his past as by her. So many mirrors in so many strange faces. Now she was moving east, backtracking, weaving between Spring Street and Houston.

Suddenly she was gone. On the right an empty lot studded with refuse, wild grass, old bottles. On the left an almost unbroken row of tenements. He knew she hadn't reached the corner. He covered the block again. There it was, a narrow alley. Jersey Street? Maybe through here. As he went in, it widened to almost six feet, cutting through the center of the block, virtually paved with broken glass. Green beer-bottle glass, brown glass from other beers, and clear long shards lay shining on the cobblestones in patches where the sun knifed through the alley, all gleaming, even in the shadows. He dragged his left foot gingerly, afraid of falling into the shimmering, cutting edges. Halfway through he realized where he was. He was moving toward the old cathedral on Prince and Mott. He could see ahead of him the chin-high wall of rust-colored brick, the sagging wooden door painted shut to the rectory's back entrance. In the old country the priests could confuse you. There was an old saying: The hand raised in benediction was also the hand that took bread from your mouth. Here in the old days the Irish priests just drenched you with contempt. He grasped the cool, shaded brick wall of the alley. The alley, he remembered, had always been here. Once it had a street sign—Jersey Street? Maybe not. Anyway, it was long gone. He was losing his balance, leaning against the wall as his bad leg, numbed, came to rest. Without going farther, he could picture what was outside. The sagging wooden door would blend into the old brick wall continuing the length of Prince Street, turning the corner at Mott and circling the block, enclosing the old garden cemetery of Saint Patrick's. He forced himself onward, spotting Gina as she slowly reached the corner, letting her hand drift along the hot brick wall. Her dark hair, brushed back by the hot breeze, her white skirt flaring over curving hips, her bare brown legs, sandaled feet—she looked achingly familiar, one of the girls he would have watched forty years ago, leaning against the hot brick wall with his friends. Teasing, cajoling, from the safety of the gang they would call, entice, never getting a response.

He was never very good at it. He was much too shy for even the most promiscuous to pay any attention to him. Yet, in the end, it had paid off. Meeting Mariana, the baker's daughter, on the subway, she had trusted him. For days and evenings after that, they met out of the neighborhood, touched in alleys they didn't know. He could almost feel her soft cotton blouse, smell her rosewatered body, feel the beads of wetness on her arms in the summer heat, in the sun that was hotter than caresses. He grasped the rough brick wall. Mariana that night, that last night when they had gone to Coney Island and stayed, walking under the boardwalk at nightfall. He swallowed painfully. How silky her breasts, her belly had been against the cooling, grainy sand.

This was ridiculous. He forced himself to move against the dizziness, the blinding dizziness of the yellow sun, the rods of light forcing their way between the tenements across the street into his eyes. They were tearing now. Suddenly the air seemed to be thickening. To move was to move against a vapor-wall filled with ghosts, ghost smells, ghost memories rising from the cemetery like the scent of dreams and nightmares. The Del-Monte funeral home, still there—a good business, death!—the grocer with his cheeses and salamis—the store that had sold espresso pots and china had given way to dry goods. But nowhere was Gina to be seen.

Nino circled the block, moving toward the main entrance of Saint Patrick's. How many years since he had been inside! His eyes raked the cemetery. She wasn't there, browsing among the tombstones or the ill-kept grass. How nice it had once been, with sprinklers going all the time and Father Montale planting herbs to border the path. He had a regular collection: thyme, sweet basil, dill; and even, hidden away from view, so nobody would get the wrong idea, a grape arbor concealed behind a ramshackle fence at the corner.

Nino fell back quickly against the wall as he opened the door. So there she was. She was reading the names of people who had donated stained-glass windows to the church. The yellow light, pouring through the brilliant blue and red glass, lit the interior in an odd, garish way. How dusty it seemed inside. The cream-colored walls and painted spindle fences around the altar somehow looked out of place. There was not enough marble in this country to make a proper show when they built this, Nino thought. He edged back out the door, hiding behind it, waiting for her to leave.

In the chapel in back of the church he had married Laura. He swallowed; his throat felt painfully parched. How different his life might have been if he had married Mariana. He had been young and a great dancer. And she was luscious, sweet, voluptuous. It was the summer. The New York summer sweated sex even out of a dead man. He sighed, looking up when the church door slammed. Gina was striding down the walk leading to Mott Street. He rose, limping after her. In the old days he could have outsprinted her for miles, miles, miles. If he had married Mariana, she wouldn't be here at all, he mused. Mariana. It was better not to wonder what had happened to her. How could he have married her, after all? She had let him have his way with her without being married. If she was willing to do that, she could have done it with someone else while married to him. Once you cross a line, you keep crossing. That was human nature.

Nino limped forward. The air was almost unbreathable. All the exhausts of the city, the basements exhaling roach poisons, the fumes of cars, the light pollen of surviving grasses, the rolling dust and soot flurries, were crashing in his lungs. And look at her, that bitch. His suit jacket too was drenched now, sopping and stuck to his body on the shadeless street. And she, running on, gliding over the sidewalks in bare legs and sandals, her white dress still white.

He began to cough, a slow wracking cough, spewing out the city vapors, the memories that stuck like tar in his throat. She moved down Mott past the pork butcher's store on Spring Street, where hams and sausages hung from rope over the white porcelain display; on she went past Kenmare Street, past the liquor shop on Broome with a window full of Mondavi reds, *Zinfandel* in blackish letters on a paper banner. There, she was slowing, finally slowing, standing in front of the Villa Pensa, looking across the street. His tired eyes followed her glance. Ferrara's. How large it had become. She crossed in the middle of the street, not bothering about the desultory traffic, and strolled under the Pasticceria sign into the store.

Nino waited for the light to change and dragged himself across the street. How flashy Ferrara's had gotten. The window was full of packaged boxed candies with fancy Ferrara labels; coffee cans in red and green blared the name again. Sleek display cases showed the pastries. Shiny black-lacquer ice cream parlor chairs; yellow formica tables. Where were the little wooden chairs, the chipped Carrara marble tables, the cozy friendliness of the old place with its trays of pastries? The young waiters, each trying to look like Valentino, had waltzed them around when they felt like it. He leaned against the window and felt its coolness. Now there was even air conditioning. He could see her at a table near the door, ordering. Dizziness and exhaustion rolled over him in waves. His good leg was throbbing horribly, pain working itself up from his toes, through his arch, past the ankle ringed with popping blue veins.

"Come and have some iced coffee," Gina said, reaching uncertainly for his arm. How could she have done it, she thought, looking at his thin hair matted with sweat, the lines deepening in his face, the heightened color in cheeks that seemed to burn with fever. She began to feel remorse. No, she couldn't be drawn that way into regret. If she didn't harden herself against him, she would always be bound to him. She had had her revenge. It wasn't sweet; but it had made the point, all the same.

Nino, sunk in his dizziness, looked at her without recognition, or even, for a moment, surprise. Leaning on her arm, he moved with her into the coolness, the dry frigid air sending a shiver through his body, shocking him into humiliation and sorrow.

"What's this?" he asked, sitting at the chair she held out for him.

"Iced expresso. Better than amphetamines," she joked, adding cream to her huge goblet filled with coffee. "All you have to do is sip, and it sends"—she groped—"a rush of energy into your veins."

She was looking at him steadily, her clear dark eyes probing his. When had she seen him? he wondered. How long had she known he was following her? It was incredible.

"I'm always willing to try something new," he said, aiming for a casual tone. He took a long drink. The black coffee, slightly bitter, smoothed the lump in his throat. The coolness of the place was steadying. To be cool! That it should seem like such a luxury to sit down, to rest, to drink. He should throw it in her face for humiliating him like this. She knew he had nearly killed himself for her; because of her he was dizzy, weak. The waiter was putting another iced coffee in front of him. She must have signaled for it. How self-possessed she was, the little bitch. He watched her, adding sugar and cream to the coffee.

"Why don't you save yourself the trouble and just order coffee ice cream?" he asked her mildly.

"This way it comes out just the way I want," Gina said. The waiter brought them two sfogliatelli. She was really doing it up, he thought. He should crack her across the face with his cane. It would serve her right! But you only did that to a girl her age for one reason, and he wasn't about to do that in public. Not in this neighborhood, where everyone would know what it meant.

I've got him now, Gina thought. He looked awful. It ought to teach him a lesson, not to try to follow me. It was one thing to demand you acted a certain way at home. It was his, after all, rotten as it was. But quite another to think you could dictate everything else. It was a question of freedom. She hated him when he was dictatorial; but now she realized she found him more troublesome when he was pathetic. Since she felt she had won, she was prepared to be kind. Up to a point.

"What a coincidence that we decided to go for a walk in the same place at the same time," Gina said, smiling sweetly and touching his hand.

"Not really," Nino said smoothly. "You've already made it clear it was no coincidence at all."

He was turning it all around; never say die, Nino, right? Her resolve against him was so saturated with shame and wariness it was rapidly retreating to diplomacy. "I was looking for Columbus Park," she lied.

"But you didn't find it," he pointed out.

"No," she agreed. "I didn't."

"You didn't find it because it isn't here," he pointed out. "It's been west and south of here—between Baxter and Mulberry—since the 1890s, when they leveled the ragpicker settlement to build it." My God, would she have been willing to walk all the way past Canal?

"Amazing how many slums and cemeteries have been turned into parks," she choked out.

"Amazing how many parks are turning into slums and cemeteries," he countered.

"Oh, sure. It's one big burial ground." So he wasn't willing to give up. What a dope she had been to think he might.

"Not really," he said. "Not really. What makes you say that?

Do you feel ready to go? Is this your idea of putting your life in order?"

She ignored him and sipped her coffee.

"Where were you going?" he demanded softly, gripping her arm.

Gina tightened her face into a smile. "It's just what you said, Nino. I was just going out with you, in my own way." She looked him in the eye.

He looked at her coldly. The enormity of her gall was hard to take in. To think that she could do this to him—drag him around by the nose, and then, when he was exhausted, humiliate him with kindness! She was forcing his hand. He shook his head. If she could do this, she could do anything. He would have to assume that she had. He had no choice.

"Finish your pastry," he ordered. "It's time to go."

"Go where? You're not going to run my life."

"Home," Nino said. "I've had enough walking." He signaled for the check and paid it. "Thanks for your hospitality." He grinned.

He held the door open, ushering her into the street. The thickening evening air, rising from the hot street in steamy fumes, enfolded them.

IT had been a perfect morning, Alex thought, running his nails through Gina's hair as he stretched beside her under the light sheet. In his mind he could see the cables of the bridge, the walkway rising out of the steaming traffic, the wind coming up, blowing the noise away. On the Brooklyn Bridge, the wooden walkway climbed above the traffic, suspended, separate, hanging. If you looked down, you could see the water shimmering between the slats of wood. The moving cars were a blur of color. In the distance the ferries to Staten Island came and went, looking like the round-bottomed ships of a hundred years before. Governor's Island faced them; beyond it, to the right, stood the Statue of Liberty. The sunlight glinted and shone on the river. The hot wind whipped the whitecaps, and blew through the cables crisscrossing toward the arches.

She had been restless all the while. He had motioned her to a bench, but she wouldn't sit down; she kept reaching in all directions, her tense hands curling around the cables as if she were ready to climb. She probably believes she can fly. The truth was, her energy often irritated him. She could fly over his moods as though they didn't exist. She always seemed to have an unswervable, hidden purpose of her own. They had been lovers for weeks now, and she had never asked him anything much about himself. Not that she talked about herself. It wasn't that she was selfish; she wasn't. But there were things you could say to her and things you couldn't. She doesn't think about herself, but she doesn't think about me, either, he concluded. She reminded him of one of these mafiosi who takes you to lunch, tells you sincerely that he holds you in the highest regard, and apologizes that there's nothing personal in it when he shoots you before dessert. She loved him, he could see that, but there didn't seem to be anything personal in it.

On the bridge she hadn't seemed to know he was there. She was revved up on the heat and light, on whatever it was that made her reach so steadily outside herself. Then, in bed, touching him, she would be so filled with everything, she would confuse him with her exaltation. She was so loving it was hard to be annoyed. Maybe I'm better off that she doesn't ask what I feel. She doesn't know my problems, my lows. She has no idea who I am. Hades one-upped because Persephone mistakes him for a fellow flower picker.

Gina turned toward him, and smiled, as she rolled up on top of him. She began to kiss his chest, nuzzling softly into him as she caressed his body. In the distance, he could see the luminous clock hands showing a yellow-green 8:00 P.M. as they brightened in the darkening room.

WHEN Gina didn't get home by seven, Nino and Laura decided to get on the BMT. They got off at Union Square and walked for a block; then, convinced they would never make it on foot to Avenue D, Laura hailed a cab. The whole neighborhood had changed.

"You don't want to go there," said the old cab driver. "It's not the same neighborhood."

"I have to go there," Nino said, consulting the note he had made of Alex's address. At the Motor Vehicle Bureau they had records you could trust. Now he even knew his age: twenty-six. He gnashed his teeth.

"You better be careful," the driver said, watching him limp out of the cab with Laura behind him. "Old people are a big target here."

"That's right," Nino said. "The old and the young get it first."

They got lost in two alleys before they found his apartment.

"It's not even a tenement," Nino said.

"It's the worst place I've ever seen," said Laura. "Is that the door?"

Nino hesitated, trying to decide whether he should knock with his cane or his fist. He pounded the door with his fist.

"Don't answer it," Gina whispered to Alex.

"Why not?" asked Alex. "It's probably Kevin. I want you to meet him."

"I just have a bad feeling," she insisted. "Would Kevin bang on the door like that?"

Alex shrugged.

"Let me get dressed first," Gina said, reaching for her skirt.

"Here, take this," said Alex, throwing her the silky orange kimono he had bought her.

She tied it as he pulled on his pants and called, "Just a minute."

When he opened the door, Nino and Laura ignored him. "I thought you'd be here," Nino said. Gina clutched the kimono around her as his cane whacked across her shoulders. "Get your clothes on," he said. Alex took a step toward her, but stopped. She turned to him, humiliation sweeping over her like a sandstorm.

"These are your parents?" Alex said to her. "You'd better get dressed."

It was all collapsing, the sense of privacy, safety, freedom, all falling in. She squeezed into the tiny bathroom with her clothes.

"You've taken advantage of my daughter," Laura sobbed.

"I'm not taking advantage of anyone," he said. "I haven't forced her to come here. She wants to be here."

"Watch what you say," Nino said. "Remember, you're in trouble enough as it is."

"What would your parents say if they knew? Do you think your parents would approve of this?"

"Why don't you ask them?" he said, dialing a number. He handed the telephone to Laura, who became totally disconcerted.

His father answered.

"My name," Laura said uncertainly, "is Laura. Your son . . . I'm in your son's apartment and I discovered him here with my daughter. He's taken advantage of her—she's very young . . ." Laura began to cry. "No, I don't think he's used physical force. But he's taken advantage of her all the same. . . . If she wants to be here, it's because he's made her want to be here. . . . What do you mean, what do I expect you to do? I expect you to stop him. . . . You have no business telling me that. Don't you know right from wrong? Haven't you got any morals?"

She turned, still holding the phone. "He says if she wants to be here, there's nothing any of us can do about it and then he hung up."

"Like father, like son," Nino agreed.

"You," he said to Gina as she came out, dressed, "you get out in the hallway. It would serve you right if you got bitten by the rats. And you," he said, poking Alex with his cane, "I'm not finished with you. In fact, I haven't even started." He nodded to Laura to leave and began to walk out. Gina came back into the room to see Alex. He turned away from her. "You'd better go," he said. "All of you."

They walked through the dark alleyway and turned on Avenue D toward Fourteenth Street. In the darkness, the slight movements of cats through garbage cans, the breeze ruffling newspapers, the crackle of wrappers tumbling down the street seemed like explosions. They were going off like grenades in Gina's brain. She couldn't stop seeing Alex turn from her; the angle of his head, his dismissal. The scene kept playing before her eyes. He had been glad to get rid of all of them.

"So this was the point of taking me to lunch," she said to Nino. "This was why you came to the office."

"So you can still talk," Nino said. "I found out his name."

"Why didn't you just ask me? If you had just asked me, I would have told you."

"Why should I think you would tell me if you hadn't before? Why did you hide him?" he hissed. "Are you ashamed of him? You ought to be. What's he hiding behind that beard? Why didn't you bring him to the house?"

"Because I know how you hate everyone who isn't exactly like you. I didn't want you to spoil it for me, the way you have now."

"I spoil it for *you!* You're the one who spoiled your life. You have the judgment of an idiot! You expect me to approve of my own daughter becoming a whore?"

"Nino, be quiet," Laura said. "Wait until we get home."

"If you gave him a chance, you would have liked him. He's very decent."

"Decent!"

"He may not be like you," she said, "but he . . . has been good to me. People do things differently now. This isn't Sicily."

"Don't mention Sicily to me. In Sicily you wouldn't be alive."

"If his not coming to the house is an issue, he will come to the house."

"The fact that he didn't insist on meeting your family shows he doesn't take you seriously. The fact that you didn't insist shows you're a fool. I could have looked him over and told you he was no good. You don't have to ask someone like that his intentions," Nino concluded, "because you already know what they are."

Gina groaned. She couldn't say what her own intentions were, much less his. Nino was great at ruining things by pushing them to a crisis, forcing you to make choices. It was like running a race in which the hurdles were raised and raised until you finally tripped. No matter how much you practiced and trained, you could never win because the hurdles would always loom higher and higher. It taught you your limitations, gave you a sense of the boundaries of your feelings. Would you marry him? Would you spend the rest of your life with him? The questions, raising the prospect of eternity with Alex, were making her realize how little she wanted anyone "forever." What about Alex's intentions? He wants to "improve" me, she thought wryly. To play Svengali to my Trilby, Pygmalion to my Galatea. He wants to free me from the burden of my working-class practicality. He wants to show me that the only thing that matters is having a good time, now. Nino had certainly loused that up for tonight.

She could see how wounded Nino was by the sight of her in Alex's place. Well, he brought it on himself by going there.

"You don't know what his intentions are," she said. "You don't know him at all. Give him a chance. He never came to the house because I wouldn't let him. Despite what you think, nothing happened between us."

Nino stared at her. "Because I don't have a good leg, it doesn't mean I don't have one to stand on. If you're lucky, nothing irreversible happened. If it did, I warn you," he said, lifting his cane and resting it against the right side of her face, "you'll have to keep it, raise it. You won't get a dime from me to do it. Then maybe you'll learn your lesson."

"You have nothing to worry about," she said, pushing his cane away, but actually it was the first time it had occurred to her that she did.

"You have no shame," he said. "Look at you." Her face was dead white. "You're pretty calm. You don't feel affected. You talk, but you forget what to say, how to apologize, how to repent for sneaking around."

"It's an open question which one of us is more of a sneak," she said evenly.

"I'm your father," he said. "It's my job."

When they reached Union Square she hesitated at the edge of the subway stairs. If she turned and ran, she could go back. He would want her back, alone.

"Hurry up," said Nino, banging his cane on the sidewalk. "Do you think I'm going to take a cab? I've already spent more than you're worth tonight."

She stiffened. It was easier to hate him than to feel humiliated by him. Nino had hurt her, but not as badly as Alex. He had been upset by her parents' barging in. How could he not be? But she had been shocked by his look of pettish disgust. He had behaved as though she and Nino and Laura were droning insects who had started him out of a sound sleep and driven him to retreat under his covers. There was something cowardly in his air of being too fastidious to deal with them. Dialing his father, getting rid of her along with them—he had taken the easy way out.

She had never put into words what she saw in Alex. Initially she had been attracted to him because he seemed so polished and yet so relaxed and amused. He had a kind of self-assurance she hadn't seen in anyone before. He was older than she, but that wasn't it. He had an aloof superiority that wasn't connected with anything real, like money or possessions or achievements. It was an air of knowingness, of being part of an elect who knew it all and never had to get upset. Nino was always upset about something.

Alex never sweated for anything. Yet he could work meticulously at his Chinese. He had majored in mathematics, but had never gotten his degree. He didn't need to know Chinese to be a mathematician. The difficulty of the language seemed to make it all the more important to him. She loved to watch him work on his ideographs. Yet she noticed that with all his apparent interest, he was still working on the same chapter, perhaps even the same page. A lot of what he did seemed to have become an end in itself, a diversionary tactic to ward off the finality of a decision about what to do with his life.

I'm being hard on him because he hurt me, Gina thought. I care for him because he is always interesting to me. He made me realize how lonely I was. She had always had friends, but never anyone who could unleash such intense feelings of joy and intimacy. Sometimes, with other girls, she could talk about going to school. Her friend, Nancy, was brilliant, but even worse off than she. Her father worked hard, but there were nine kids in the family and all the boys would get to go to college before she would. She had wanted to be a doctor, but had won a scholarship to nursing school and had taken it, just to get away.

Gina had always felt like something of a misfit among the

other girls. They could talk about makeup and clothes or even books or people, but then would come the moments when they would make quick and easy confessions to each other that seemed to be the cement between them. She had lots of weaknesses to confess, but she could never talk, could never make a show of her helplessness. When her friends came up to commiserate with her after Nino had brought that rejection letter to school, she had politely rebuffed them. Was it pride or fear? She had too much of both. She had seen them confide only to regret it when their confidantes talked, talked, talked. She was too much like Nino—imposing absurd standards of conduct nobody met, digging in behind them and finding nothing but isolation.

They had reached the subway platform. The sight of it made her want to turn and run back to Alex. She couldn't. Not tonight. The idea of escaping from Nino began to flicker in the back of her mind. What could she say to him now? Should there be an open confrontation, no lying, just a statement that Alex was what she wanted? If she were a man, it would have been easier. Nino respected physical power. He would have condemned a man for fooling around with a "nice" girl, but he would have understood. Her being a woman triggered emotions of protectiveness and honor that sprang out of a dim Sicilian past. That was it, she thought. For Nino the loss of honor had less to do with her than with a judgment on him. It was his vanity that was at stake. He needed to be so respected that nobody would mess with his daughter.

She and Alex had not paid him the respect he thought he deserved. He had sent out his bill of obligations due. And now he wanted it paid in the coin of sentiment and right behavior: apologies, marriage, everlasting repentance. She would never be able to meet his price. He had come to foreclose on her freedom. Father, daughter, lover—they all seemed cast into the roles of an Italian opera. She was determined that no one should die in the last act. Especially she herself.

Nino was bent on getting what was due him. Maybe she could meet his demands, up to a point.

"Let me ask if we could compromise," Gina said to Nino in a conciliatory tone.

"You aren't in a position to bargain for anything," he answered. But she could see his curiosity was piqued.

"I'll have him come to the house and you can talk to him. Until then, in return, you do nothing."

"And you?" Nino demanded. "What do you do?"

Gina shrugged noncommittally.

"That's reasonable," Laura said quickly. "Until we find out what the situation is, it pays to do that. We may," she said softly, "need him to . . . you . . . if she . . ." her voice trailed off. When the train reached their stop, none of them had a word to say. They walked home slowly, keeping pace with Nino's limp. When they got home, all his rage seemed to have drained into exhaustion. Nino sat down.

"I can't think anymore tonight," he said. "Get out of my sight," he said to Gina. "I'll tell you what I intend to do with you in the morning."

She walked into her room. Laura came in behind her. Sitting numbly on the bed, she looked at her mother. Her eyes began to burn.

"How could you do this?" Laura said. "Didn't I always give you the best advice?"

"I took it. You always said, 'Never marry a Sicilian.' So I didn't. I haven't." Gina looked at her mother. Her eyes filled with tears. I know why he does this. But not you. Not you.

"This time," Laura said, looking at the floor, "he's right. This is the right thing to do." She reached out to smooth Gina's hair, but Gina moved out of reach.

Gina sat, waiting for her to leave. When she did, Gina pressed her face into the pillow, trying to bury her revulsion and pain. But it was there waiting for her when Nino banged on her door the next morning. "You," he said, knocking open the door, "invite him to dinner. We'll see what he is."

She looked at him. She felt embalmed, but picked up the telephone and did what he asked. Alex was curt but agreed to come for coffee. "Dinner," he explained, "will be too long. I'll speak to your father, then maybe we can take a walk."

It was only eight o'clock in the morning, but it was already 91 in the shade. She stayed in her room, so that Nino would have to come in and ask her if Alex was coming. When she said yes, he nodded and locked her in her room. It was when she heard the lock turn that she made up her mind to get away. I can climb out the window, she thought at first. It was just a few feet from the ground. But then there was too much still unplanned. Tomorrow she would register for school at Hunter College. She would need a place to stay. Fear welled up around the thoughts of escape, but somehow making plans forced it back until even the fear was a kind of encouragement. Outside, the wet heat seemed to whiten as the day went on. In the dim, shaded room where the sun never reached, she figured and slept. When she woke, her sheets were wet with blood. Rolling them into a ball, she smiled. Her mood seemed to lighten; her freedom seemed to surge with the streaming blood.

Forgetting Nino had locked the door, she tried it. It was open and he had gone. She ran a bath and rinsed the sheets in the sink before throwing them in the washing machine. It was all coming together, she thought. Her luck! Had it been waiting for her there, someplace unknown, before now? She would never leave anything to chance again. But she had touched it, her luck, at last. Her belly felt flat and warm. Everything was working. Maybe it would always work, maybe she could always feel this sense of possessing and repossessing herself, of retrieving herself. The thought of leaving home made her feel better and better. She thought of discussing it with Alex, but he would assume she was leaving for him. He'd probably be afraid she wanted to live with him. She didn't. She would plan her escape herself.

Her desk was still cluttered with last term's reading. She began to arrange things for her big move. She picked up her books and sorted them into stacks. *Hero with a Thousand Faces; The Myth of the Eternal Return; Into Eden: American Puritanism.* That book had led to her first conversation with Alex. She had read it for a course and decided to finish it over the summer. Alex had seen it on her desk and told her his father had written it. She had been even more impressed when she learned that his father had come from a down-and-out Ohio family and, after his success as a historian, had become cultural advisor to the American embassy in Paris. Not bad for a poor farm boy.

There was a kind of redemption in escaping the place where you were born, the limits of the world around you. Even just reading multiplied environments because you could, at least for a while, live in the world of the book. What she loved about anthropology was the mass of possible worlds it offered. The concrete problems of life were deadeningly repetitive, but the immense variety of cultural solutions was dazzling. Why did she have to live the way Nino lived or think the way Nino thought? She began to hum. She was tired of thinking about her own feelings. Anthropology and history took your mind off emotions. She was anxious to get back to school.

ALEX arrived with bouquets of lilac and mimosa. He gave one to Laura, who took it into the kitchen and started to cry. The mimosa was for Gina, who just held it and looked at him. He was very elegant in a heavy woolen suit with a vest, a pale blue shirt, and a silk tie. From the sofa where he sat with his bad leg elevated, Nino watched him too.

"It's interesting that you can wear a suit like that this time of year without sweating," Nino said. He was enjoying this more than he had expected.

"It seemed appropriate to wear a suit, Mr. Giardello, and this is the only one I have," Alex said, and smiled.

"Sit down, sit down. Have some coffee," Nino said as Laura returned with a pot of espresso. "Take off your jacket. After all, we're practically related."

Alex sat down, slightly disconcerted. He did not remove his jacket. Gina stood in the doorway, watching.

"You know," Nino continued, "we're an interesting family. Gina's cousin—she must have told you about him. He is an excellent marksman. He's in the Army now, but still active in the National Rifle Association."

"I'm not much for violence," said Alex.

"Among friends, violence is never necessary," Nino agreed. "Of course, none of us is for violence. However, sometimes," he shrugged, "there is no other way."

Laura had begun to pray to Saint Anthony. Gina could tell by the angle of her eyes.

"Where are you from?" Nino asked, beginning in earnest.

"Amsterdam, I was born in Amsterdam," Alex said. "Then I lived in Paris. I came here when I was six."

"Ah," Nino said. "An immigrant."

Alex looked at him. "You might say. My father was working in Europe."

"What do you do besides working as a stamp perforator?"

"I have a leave of absence from Brown. After three years, I wanted some time off."

"Backed out just before the end? If you wanted to get away, why did you hang around a school?"

Alex shrugged.

"What were you studying?"

"Mathematics and chemistry."

"Chemistry," Nino said. "Now that's a good subject. Well, did you flunk out? Were you about to flunk out?"

"No," said Alex. "I did very well. I went to Stuyvesant. I did all right," he said lamely.

"So the reason you quit was something else."

"I was uncertain what I wanted to do, or whether I wanted to stay there. I heard the opportunities might be better out west and thought I might finish there."

"So you are confused. You thought to better yourself and in the process you did nothing. Confusion," Nino said, "is a bad business. Perhaps I can help you. You don't have to be confused anymore." Nino tapped him on the chest. "When you're in trouble, you know exactly where you are."

Alex stared at him. Finally he recovered himself enough to say, "There is no reason for me to think I'm in trouble. I wouldn't be troubled by marrying your daughter, if that's what you're concerned about. I'll marry her."

There was an audible intake of breath from Laura which Nino ignored. Gina felt as though she were watching an ancient ritual of sacrifice. She and Alex were the offerings, but also the reasons for each other's victimization. Each of them was being used to trap the other. Nino was in his element. She could see that he was pleased at how it was going and had sensed that Alex could be made to do whatever he wanted.

"Have some of this," Nino said, almost smiling as he poured

anisette into an empty water glass and handed it to Alex. He waited for Alex to taste it before he poured some into his own black coffee and took a long drink.

"One month should be enough time to make all the arrangements," Nino said genially. "We don't have to settle the details tonight."

"What do you know about baseball?" Nino asked.

"Nothing," Alex answered.

"I thought so," Nino said. "I've been a Yankee fan since 1935."

"It's getting late," Alex said. "May I take Gina for a walk?"

Nino looked at Laura. Everyone in the neighborhood would know. But if they were going to get married, they would know anyway. Finally Nino said, "A short walk is OK. Turn left immediately as you leave the house."

"Why?" Alex said.

"Because that's the right way to walk," Nino said.

Alex nodded and rose from his chair. "It was nice to have met you," he said, extending his hand. Nino shook it. "Thank you for the coffee, Mrs. Giardello," he said to Laura.

"You're very welcome," Laura said.

Alex began walking down the long hall. Its uneven floor, lumpy walls cluttered with yellowed pictures, and lack of natural light suggested catacombs for the living dead. Her father's questioning was bad enough, but the cramped ugliness of the place was repulsive. How could they stand it?

Gina could see how Alex had taken it in. She had never liked the living room, but she had been able to shut it out except as a too-crowded alcove on the way to her room. Now she saw that the gray-beige paint Nino had chosen was so grim it must have looked aged even while it was being applied. The paltriness of the room came down on her. The new fluted silk lamp shades had plastic shrouds, the green sofa lay under its vinyl-backed throw, the heavy wooden table with its linen cloth was covered by clear plastic—even the furniture was suffocating. The huge table filled the center of the room, leaving barely enough space to edge around it to the chairs. After dinner it could be pushed into place against the wall, baring the honey-colored floors Laura carefully scrubbed and waxed, scarred despite all her care by chairs being pushed back from the table. She knew Alex had seen it that way. It was best to say nothing.

Gina followed Alex quickly out of the apartment, leaving without a word. On the street, he turned to her and asked, "I think I did OK, don't you?"

"You were great," she said. How could he know that nothing he did or didn't do would have made a difference? "You look terrific in a suit."

"It's too hot, but I thought it would impress them," he said simply. The sound of thunder rumbled through the thick, hot air.

"I'm sure it did," she said, wanting to take his hand. But she wouldn't until they made their way past the neighbors her mother always called "the brigade." There they were—Mrs. Di Costa in black twenty years after the death of her husband, Mrs. Cerisi mourning the son lost in World War II. Her daughter, Mrs. Picci, was there in black for the husband shot in Korea. They were the mothers and grandmothers of the kids who played in the yard. Every time she saw them, they seemed to spell out the succession of weddings, births, funerals, visits to the sick and dying, appearances at wakes. One wake after the other until finally you yourself were the main attraction, the guest of honor. To the right they stretched on, more neighbors looking for a breeze in the heat. To the left there were private houses where no one sat outside. They turned left, avoiding the gossipy super's wife Laura called "the radio."

Alex took off his jacket and threw it over one shoulder. "Your father is a riot," he said, shaking his head. " 'When you're in trouble, you know exactly where you are.' Too much! and 'What do you know about baseball?' " Alex laughed.

Gina gave him a hard look.

"Well, I mean they're old-fashioned and worried about you. It'll be all right now. I think they'll leave us alone."

"Nino won't leave us alone," Gina said.

"Why not? Did he mean that about getting married?" Alex asked.

"Do you mean *you* didn't mean it?" Gina asked him pointedly.

"I don't know. I never thought about it."

"You just agreed to marry me in a month," Gina said.
"Aren't you aware of that."

"We were just talking. In a way, it was funny being looked
over. Nobody ever did that to me before. Do you want to get
married?" Alex asked, wondering if she had put the old man up
to this.

"Do you think I do?" Gina asked.

"I don't know. I haven't figured you out yet. If it's that
important to you, I guess we could do it," Alex said.

He probably would marry her if she pressed him, but that
didn't mean he would behave any differently than if he were
single. She suspected that, either way, he would turn Nino into
the stuff of anecdotes. He didn't take anything seriously, she
realized.

"I could never accept a deal Nino had made," Gina said
softly.

"Don't look at it that way," Alex said. "We only agreed in
principle. We never got to the details." He started to laugh. He
put his arms around her, and pulled her toward him. "Now that
we're engaged, we can do it solemnly." He laughed, kissing her.

"I have to get back," she said, laughing despite her turmoil.

"I'll take you home," he offered.

"No, I'd rather you didn't," she answered. She could see the
two of them running the gauntlet of staring women in perpetual black. They parted without touching at the station. The
thunder sounded closer now.

When she came back she found her mother stuffing lilacs
into a garbage bag.

"How could you do it?" Laura asked. "I still can't understand it."

"Do what? Look, it's not as though I'm pregnant. I haven't
done anything. He was very polite to you." She retrieved a
branch from the garbage bag. "I'm hot and I have my period,"
she said. "Just leave me alone about it. I can't go through life
doing only what you tell me."

"If you would only listen to me. Arthur would make such a
good husband. He's loyal, hard-working, and he isn't Sicilian,"
Laura whispered.

"Neither is Alex."

"He's too peculiar. You'll never know what he thinks. Besides, just listening to him, you can see he has no future. Not to mention that he's strange."

Gina went into her room, but Laura was determined to continue and followed her in.

"He thought you might accept him because he was so polite despite what Dad did."

"What did your father do? He just told the truth. If he thinks we would accept him, that proves he has no sense of reality. Listen to me. You're not pregnant. Thank God! This isn't Sicily. No one has to know this. Just forget about him. I promise that I won't let your father make you marry him. I swear it," Laura pleaded.

Gina said nothing. Laura waited until it was clear there was no reason to think waiting would do any good.

Alone, Gina undressed for bed. She could hear Laura and Nino talking in the living room, but could not make out what they were saying. The evening had been a disaster. Not a run-of-the-mill disaster, but a debacle. Still, the thought of Alex made her smile. She was tired of heavy feelings and grim moods.

She was in a deep sleep when Nino pounded at her door and barged in. He stood over her, enraged. "You're never to see or talk to him again," he said. "Understand?" he demanded. He raised his cane as if to hit her, but caught himself and, instead, swept it across the surface of her desk, knocking her neat piles of books and papers to the floor. "It's finished. This time you're getting off easy, but I intend to make sure there is no next time. This is the end. Just accept that, and don't try to talk your way out of it."

She stared at him in silence.

"Just remember, you go to school, you cut him out of your mind. He's an idiot."

"He was willing to marry me. Wasn't that what you wanted?"

"You think I wanted you to marry the kind of man who would marry a woman he already knew was a whore?" Nino said. His words roused him to look for something else to knock over and he waved his cane.

"Don't do that!" Gina cried, catching the end of the cane and holding it fast.

Nino looked at her, startled.

"You made your point. You got what you said you wanted. Isn't that enough for one night? Do you have to stage a terrorist raid, too?"

The quiet, even fury in her voice chilled him.

"You've humiliated me, pushed me around, destroyed something that meant a lot to me. Isn't that enough?"

"Someday you'll thank me for destroying it," Nino said quietly.

Gina let go of his cane. "Don't bet on it."

Nino leaned toward her. "Someday *he'll* thank me for destroying it. You have no heart. You're all ice and steel."

"My heart be—longs to Dad—dy, Da—da—da, Da—da—dad—dy," Gina sang with a malicious smile.

"That'll be the day," Nino said, his face darkening with sorrow. He turned to leave the room, pausing to knock the stacked papers from the top of her bookcase. "Just remember, this is the end of it." He slammed the door behind him.

She felt trapped in the shambles he had made of her room. The walls seemed to move in; even the alley outside the narrow window seemed part of a prison. Always the sense of suffocation that felt like an emptying out of life, a loss of will as well as air. It was too narcotizing to be painful; too terrible, too dreary too familiar to tolerate anymore. Why not simply leave? It wasn't only for Alex. There were lots of times when even he got on her nerves, when his humor seemed only deceptive or just too precious for her. What drew her to him, in a way, was Nino.

Nino made everthing so rough, so bleak, so guarded, that the craving for color, for softness, was overpowering. She would give anything to be out of here, and—why not?—in Alex's whitewashed room, feeling his touch and the light hair on his back, the sun gleaming on his body. . . . Should she live with him? Just move in? That would be one way. And even that would be better than staying here. This was the place of old humiliations and failures. How many nightmares had there been of planes crashing, of sleek, fast-moving trains suddenly derailing, falling into space and flames. Here she would always have nightmares that narrowed everything to death or mutilation or worse: the fear, coming again and again in dreams, of being paralyzed from the neck down, unable either to die or live. It was these that frightened her more than anything, more than Nino. They say you make your own nightmares; you can have them turn out any way at all. But these fearful dreams flourished only here. They grew in Nino's house like living plaster, sealing everything into grim stability.

Yet something was giving way. Even the heat seemed to be breaking. She could hear thunder cracking high overhead; lightning flashed sharply on the wall outside. The rain would come, finishing off the heat that had lingered into September. She scooped papers from the floor, crumpled them into a ball, and threw it against the wall. She had to find a place where she could breathe.

Toni Morrison

IN an interview with Gloria Naylor in the July 1985 *Southern Review,* Toni Morrison recalled that the idea for the novel *Beloved* came when she "became obsessed by two or three little fragments of stories that [she] heard from different places." One was the newspaper clipping about a fugitive slave woman, Margaret Garner, who, as historian Herbert Aptheker recounts,

> when trapped near Cincinnati, killed her own daughter and tried to kill herself. She rejoiced that the girl was dead—"now she would never know what a woman suffers as a slave"—and pleaded to be tried for murder. "I will go singing to the gallows rather than be returned to slavery." [Quoted in Angela Davis, *Women, Race and Class,* p. 21]

Garner struck two of her other children with a shovel, but only wounded them. Morrison was particularly taken by Garner's interviews:

> She was a young woman. In the inked pictures of her she seemed a very quiet, very serene-looking woman and everyone who interviewed her remarked about her serenity and tranquility. She said, "I will not let those children live how I have lived." . . . And her mother-in-law was in the house at the same time and she said, "I watched her and I neither encouraged her nor discouraged her." They put her in jail for a little while and I'm not even sure what the dénouement is of her story. But at that moment, that decision was a piece, a tail of something that was always around." [*SR,* pp. 583–84]

That "something that was always around" became clear to Morrison when she thought of another story she had read in the collection of pictures by the late photographer James Van der Zee, *The Harlem Book of the Dead,* published by Camille Billops. She continued, explaining that in the fashion of the day, Van der Zee photographed "beloved, departed people in full dress or in your arms. . . . they were affectionate photographs taken for affectionate reasons." Van der Zee recounted the story of an eighteen-year-old girl who suddenly slumped while dancing at a party. There was blood on her, and when asked, "What happened to you?" all she would say was "I'll tell you tomorrow. I'll tell you tomorrow." It seems that a jealous boyfriend had shot her with a silencer, but she wanted him to get away. She died and he most likely got away. "What made those stories connect, I can't explain," says Morrison,

> but I do know that in both instances, something seemed clear to me. A woman loved something other than herself so much. She had placed all of the value of her life in something outside herself. That the woman who killed her children loved her children so much; they were the best part of her and she would not see them sullied. She would not see them hurt. She would rather kill them, have them die. . . . And that this woman . . . had such affection for a man that she would postpone her own medical care . . . and die to give him time to get away so that, more valuable than her life, was not just his life but something else connected with his life. Now both of these incidents seem to me, at least on the surface, very noble, you know, in that old-fashioned sense, noble things, generous, wide-spirited, love beyond the call of . . .
> GN: . . . of a very traditional kind of female . . .
> TM: That's right. Always. It's peculiar to women. . . . it's interesting because the best thing that is in us is also the thing that makes us sabotage ourselves, sabotage in the sense that our life is not as worthy as our perception of the best part of ourselves.

I decided to share the quote from Aptheker and this lengthy segment from Morrison's interview because *Beloved* is more than a ghost story about the return to Sethe of her murdered child. It is a story about love and how it must be redeemed from bondage, when it is contorted by the brutalities humans visit upon one another. It is the story of how Sethe keeps alive the "memory" of the slave life on "Sweet Home" plantation. It is the story of how Paul D, Sethe's soulmate and alter ego of sorts, while forced to serve on a Georgia chain gang, had "killed the flirt whom folks called Life for leading them on." "Life was dead. Paul D beat her butt all day every day till there was not a whimper in her." *Beloved* is the story of how Sethe, Denver, and Paul D must remember so that the past can be embraced, understood, and simultaneously released in order to live as fully as possible in the present. And this is only part of what *Beloved* is about.

Beloved helps us to remember and thereby make greater sense and use of today.

—Johnnella E. Butler

Editor's Note: Because Toni Morrison does not wish to have her novel *Beloved* excerpted, she has graciously consented to allow us to reprint her story "Recitatif" instead.

"Recitatif"

MY mother danced all night and Roberta's was sick. That's why we were taken to St. Bonny's. People want to put their arms around you when you tell them you were in a shelter, but it really wasn't bad. No big long room with one hundred beds like Bellevue. There were four to a room, and when Roberta and me came, there was a shortage of state kids, so we were the only ones assigned to 406 and could go from bed to bed if we wanted to. And we wanted to, too. We changed beds every night and for the whole four months we were there we never picked one out as our own permanent bed.

It didn't start out that way. The minute I walked in and the Big Bozo introduced us, I got sick to my stomach. It was one thing to be taken out of your own bed early in the morning—it was something else to be stuck in a strange place with a girl from a whole other race. And Mary, that's my mother, she was right. Every now and then she would stop dancing long enough to tell me something important and one of the things she said was that they never washed their hair and they smelled funny. Roberta sure did. Smell funny, I mean. So when the Big Bozo (nobody ever called her Mrs. Itkin, just like nobody every said St. Bonaventure)—when she said, "Twyla, this is Roberta. Roberta, this is Twyla. Make each other welcome." I said, "My mother won't like you putting me in here."

"Good," said Bozo. "Maybe then she'll come and take you home."

How's that for mean? If Roberta had laughed I would have killed her, but she didn't. She just walked over to the window and stood with her back to us.

"Turn around," said the Bozo. "Don't be rude. Now Twyla. Roberta. When you hear a loud buzzer, that's the call for din-

ner. Come down to the first floor. Any fights and no movie."
And then, just to make sure we knew what we would be missing, *"The Wizard of Oz."*

Roberta must have thought I meant that my mother would
be mad about my being put in the shelter. Not about rooming
with her, because as soon as Bozo left she came over to me and
said, "Is your mother sick too?"

"No," I said. "She just likes to dance all night."

"Oh," she nodded her head and I liked the way she understood things so fast. So for the moment it didn't matter that we
looked like salt and pepper standing there and that's what the
other kids called us sometimes. We were eight years old and got
F's all the time. Me because I couldn't remember what I read
or what the teacher said. And Roberta because she couldn't
read at all and didn't even listen to the teacher. She wasn't
good at anything except jacks, at which she was a killer: pow
scoop pow scoop pow scoop.

We didn't like each other all that much at first, but nobody
else wanted to play with us because we weren't real orphans
with beautiful dead parents in the sky. We were dumped. Even
the New York City Puerto Ricans and the upstate Indians
ignored us. All kinds of kids were in there, black ones, white
ones, even two Koreans. The food was good, though. At least I
thought so. Roberta hated it and left whole pieces of things on
her plate: Spam, Salisbury steak—even jello with fruit cocktail
in it, and she didn't care if I ate what she wouldn't. Mary's idea
of supper was popcorn and a can of Yoo-Hoo. Hot mashed
potatoes and two weenies was like Thanksgiving for me.

It really wasn't bad, St. Bonny's. The big girls on the second
floor pushed us around now and then. But that was all. They
wore lipstick and eyebrow pencil and wobbled their knees while
they watched TV. Fifteen, sixteen, even, some of them were.
They were put-out girls, scared runaways most of them. Poor
little girls who fought their uncles off but looked tough to us,
and mean. God did they look mean. The staff tried to keep
them separate from the younger children, but sometimes they
caught us watching them in the orchard where they played
radios and danced with each other. They'd light out after us
and pull our hair or twist our arms. We were scared of them,

Roberta and me, but neither of us wanted the other one to know it. So we got a good list of dirty names we could shout back when we ran from them through the orchard. I used to dream a lot and almost always the orchard was there. Two acres, four maybe, of these little apple trees. Hundreds of them. Empty and crooked like beggar women when I first came to St. Bonny's but fat with flowers when I left. I don't know why I dreamt about that orchard so much. Nothing really happened there. Nothing all that important, I mean. Just the big girls dancing and playing the radio. Roberta and me watching. Maggie fell down there once. The kitchen woman with legs like parentheses. And the big girls laughed at her. We should have helped her up, I know, but we were scared of those girls with lipstick and eyebrow pencil. Maggie couldn't talk. The kids said she had her tongue cut out, but I think she was just born that way: mute. She was old and sandy-colored and she worked in the kitchen. I don't know if she was nice or not. I just remember her legs like parentheses and how she rocked when she walked. She worked from early in the morning till two o'clock, and if she was late, if she had too much cleaning and didn't get out till two-fifteen or so, she'd cut through the orchard so she wouldn't miss her bus and have to wait another hour. She wore this really stupid little hat—a kid's hat with ear flaps—and she wasn't much taller than we were. A really awful little hat. Even for a mute, it was dumb—dressing like a kid and never saying anything at all.

"But what about if somebody tries to kill her?" I used to wonder about that. "Or what if she wants to cry? Can she cry?"

"Sure," Roberta said. "But just tears. No sounds come out."

"She can't scream?"

"Nope. Nothing."

"Can she hear?"

"I guess."

"Let's call her," I said. And we did.

"Dummy! Dummy!" She never turned her head.

"Bow legs! Bow legs!" Nothing. She just rocked on, the chin straps of her baby-boy hat swaying from side to side. I think we were wrong. I think she could hear and didn't let on. And it shames me even now to think there was somebody in there after all who heard us call her those names and couldn't tell on us.

We got along all right, Roberta and me. Changed beds every night, got F's in civics and communication skills and gym. The Bozo was disappointed in us, she said. Out of 130 of us state cases, 90 were under twelve. Almost all were real orphans with beautiful dead parents in the sky. We were the only ones dumped and the only ones with F's in three classes including gym. So we got along—what with her leaving whole pieces of things on her plate and being nice about not asking questions.

I think it was the day before Maggie fell down that we found out our mothers were coming to visit us on the same Sunday. We had been at the shelter twenty-eight days (Roberta twenty-eight and a half) and this was their first visit with us. Our mothers would come at ten o'clock in time for chapel, then lunch with us in the teachers' lounge. I thought if my dancing mother met her sick mother it might be good for her. And Roberta thought her sick mother would get a big bang out of a dancing one. We got excited about it and curled each other's hair. After breakfast we sat on the bed watching the road from the window. Roberta's socks were still wet. She washed them the night before and put them on the radiator to dry. They hadn't, but she put them on anyway because their tops were so pretty—scalloped in pink. Each of us had a purple construction-paper basket that we had made in craft class. Mine had a yellow crayon rabbit on it. Roberta's had eggs with wiggly lines of color. Inside were cellophane grass and just the jelly beans because I'd eaten the two marshmallow eggs they gave us. The Big Bozo came herself to get us. Smiling she told us we looked very nice and to come downstairs. We were so surprised by the smile we'd never seen before, neither of us moved.

"Don't you want to see your mommies?"

I stood up first and spilled the jelly beans all over the floor. Bozo's smile disappeared while we scrambled to get the candy up off the floor and put it back in the grass.

She escorted us downstairs to the first floor, where the other girls were lining up to file into the chapel. A bunch of grownups stood to one side. Viewers mostly. The old biddies who wanted servants and the fags who wanted company looking for children they might want to adopt. Once in a while a grandmother. Almost never anybody young or anybody whose face wouldn't scare you in the night. Because if any of the real orphans had young relatives they wouldn't be real orphans. I saw Mary right away. She had on those green slacks I hated and hated even more now because didn't she know we were going to chapel? And that fur jacket with the pocket linings so ripped she had to pull to get her hands out of them. But her face was pretty—like always, and she smiled and waved like she was the little girl looking for her mother—not me.

I walked slowly, trying not to drop the jelly beans and hoping the paper handle would hold. I had to use my last Chiclet because by the time I finished cutting everything out, all the Elmer's was gone. I am left-handed and the scissors never worked for me. It didn't matter, though; I might just as well have chewed the gum. Mary dropped to her knees and grabbed me, mashing the basket, the jelly beans, and the grass into her ratty fur jacket.

"Twyla, baby. Twyla, baby!"

I could have killed her. Already I heard the big girls in the orchard the next time saying, "Twyyyyyla, baby!" But I couldn't stay mad at Mary while she was smiling and hugging me and smelling of Lady Esther dusting powder. I wanted to stay buried in her fur all day.

To tell the truth I forgot about Roberta. Mary and I got in line for the traipse into chapel and I was feeling proud because she looked so beautiful even in those ugly green slacks that made her behind stick out. A pretty mother on earth is better than a beautiful dead one in the sky even if she did leave you all alone to go dancing.

I felt a tap on my shoulder, turned, and saw Roberta smiling. I smiled back, but not too much lest somebody think this visit was the biggest thing that ever happened in my life. Then Roberta said, "Mother, I want you to meet my roommate, Twyla. And that's Twyla's mother."

I looked up it seemed for miles. She was big. Bigger than any man and on her chest was the biggest cross I'd ever seen. I swear it was six inches long each way. And in the crook of her arm was the biggest Bible ever made.

Mary, simple-minded as ever, grinned and tried to yank her hand out of the pocket with the raggedy lining—to shake hands, I guess. Roberta's mother looked down at me and then looked down at Mary too. She didn't say anything, just grabbed Roberta with her Bible-free hand and stepped out of line, walking quickly to the rear of it. Mary was still grinning because she's not too swift when it comes to what's really going on. Then this light bulb goes off in her head and she says "That bitch!" really loud and us almost in the chapel now. Organ music whining; the Bonny Angels singing sweetly. Everybody in the world turned around to look. And Mary would have kept it up—kept calling names if I hadn't squeezed her hand as hard as I could. That helped a little, but she still twitched and crossed and uncrossed her legs all through service. Even groaned a couple of times. Why did I think she would come there and act right? Slacks. No hat like the grandmothers and viewers, and groaning all the while. When we stood for hymns she kept her mouth shut. Wouldn't even look at the words on the page. She actually reached in her purse for a mirror to check her lipstick. All I could think of was that she really needed to be killed. The sermon lasted a year, and I knew the real orphans were looking smug again.

We were supposed to have lunch in the teachers' lounge, but Mary didn't bring anything, so we picked fur and cellophane grass off the mashed jelly beans and ate them. I could have killed her. I sneaked a look at Roberta. Her mother had brought chicken legs and ham sandwiches and oranges and a whole box of chocolate-covered grahams. Roberta drank milk from a thermos while her mother read the Bible to her.

Things are not right. The wrong food is always with the wrong people. Maybe that's why I got into waitress work later—to match up the right people with the right food. Roberta just let those chicken legs sit there, but she did bring a stack of grahams up to me later when the visit was over. I think she was sorry that her mother would not shake my mother's hand. And I liked that and I liked the fact that she didn't say a word about Mary groaning all the way through the service and not bringing any lunch.

Roberta left in May when the apple trees were heavy and

white. On her last day we went to the orchard to watch the big
girls smoke and dance by the radio. It didn't matter that they
said, "Twyyyyyla, baby." We sat on the ground and breathed.
Lady Esther. Apple blossoms. I still go soft when I smell one or
the other. Roberta was going home. The big cross and the big
Bible was coming to get her and she seemed sort of glad and
sort of not. I thought I would die in that room of four beds
without her and I knew Bozo had plans to move some other
dumped kid in there with me. Roberta promised to write every
day, which was really sweet of her because she couldn't read a
lick so how could she write anybody. I would have drawn pictures and sent them to her but she never gave me her address.
Little by little she faded. Her wet socks with the pink scalloped
tops and her big serious-looking eyes—that's all I could catch
when I tried to bring her to mind.

I was working behind the counter at the Howard Johnson's
on the Thruway just before the Kingston exit. Not a bad job.
Kind of a long ride from Newburgh, but okay once I got there.
Mine was the second night shift—eleven to seven. Very light
until a Greyhound checked in for breakfast around six-thirty.
At that hour the sun was all the way clear of the hills behind the
restaurant. The place looked better at night—more like shelter—but I loved it when the sun broke in, even if it did show all
the cracks in the vinyl and the speckled floor looked dirty no
matter what the mop boy did.

It was August and a bus crowd was just unloading. They
would stand around a long while: going to the john, and looking
at gifts and junk-for-sale machines, reluctant to sit down so
soon. Even to eat. I was trying to fill the coffee pots and get
them all situated on the electric burners when I saw her. She
was sitting in a booth smoking a cigarette with two guys smothered in head and facial hair. Her own hair was so big and wild I
could hardly see her face. But the eyes. I would know them
anywhere. She had on a powder-blue halter and shorts outfit
and earrings the size of bracelets. Talk about lipstick and eyebrow pencil. She made the big girls look like nuns. I couldn't
get off the counter until seven o'clock, but I kept watching the
booth in case they got up to leave before that. My replacement
was on time for a change, so I counted and stacked my receipts

as fast as I could and signed off. I walked over to the booth, smiling and wondering if she would remember me. Or even if she wanted to remember me. Maybe she didn't want to be reminded of St. Bonny's or to have anybody know she was ever there. I know I never talked about it to anybody.

I put my hands in my apron pockets and leaned against the back of the booth facing them.

"Roberta? Roberta Fisk?"

She looked up. "Yeah?"

"Twyla."

She squinted for a second and then said, "Wow."

"Remember me?"

"Sure. Hey. Wow."

"It's been a while," I said, and gave a smile to the two hairy guys.

"Yeah. Wow. You work here?"

"Yeah," I said. "I live in Newburgh."

"Newburgh? No kidding?" She laughed then a private laugh that included the guys but only the guys, and they laughed with her. What could I do but laugh too and wonder why I was standing there with my knees showing out from under that uniform. Without looking I could see the blue and white triangle on my head, my hair shapeless in a net, my ankles thick in white oxfords. Nothing could have been less sheer than my stockings. There was this silence that came down right after I laughed. A silence it was her turn to fill up. With introductions, maybe, to her boyfriends or an invitation to sit down and have a Coke. Instead she lit a cigarette off the one she'd just finished and said, "We're on our way to the Coast. He's got an appointment with Hendrix." She gestured casually toward the boy next to her.

"Hendrix? Fantastic," I said. "Really fantastic. What's she doing now?"

Roberta coughed on her cigarette and the two guys rolled their eyes up at the ceiling.

"Hendrix. Jimi Hendrix, asshole. He's only the biggest— Oh, wow. Forget it."

I was dismissed without anyone saying goodbye, so I thought I would do it for her.

"How's your mother?" I asked. Her grin cracked her whole face. She swallowed. "Fine," she said. "How's yours?"

"Pretty as a picture," I said and turned away. The backs of my knees were damp. Howard Johnson's really was a dump in the sunlight.

JAMES is as comfortable as a house slipper. He liked my cooking and I liked his big loud family. They have lived in Newburgh all of their lives and talk about it the way people do who have always known a home. His grandmother is a porch swing older than his father and when they talk about streets and avenues and buildings they call them names they no longer have. They still call the A & P Rico's because it stands on property once a mom and pop store owned by Mr. Rico. And they call the new community college Town Hall because it once was. My mother-in-law puts up jelly and cucumbers and buys butter wrapped in cloth from a dairy. James and his father talk about fishing and baseball and I can see them all together on the Hudson in a raggedy skiff. Half the population of Newburgh is on welfare now, but to my husband's family it was still some upstate paradise of a time long past. A time of ice houses and vegetable wagons, coal furnaces and children weeding gardens. When our son was born my mother-in-law gave me the crib blanket that had been hers.

But the town they remembered had changed. Something quick was in the air. Magnificent old houses, so ruined they had become shelter for squatters and rent risks, were bought and renovated. Smart IBM people moved out of their suburbs back into the city and put shutters up and herb gardens in their backyards. A brochure came in the mail announcing the opening of a Food Emporium. Gourmet food it said—and listed items the rich IBM crowd would want. It was located in a new mall at the edge of town and I drove out to shop there one day—just to see. It was late in June. After the tulips were gone and the Queen Elizabeth roses were open everywhere. I trailed my cart along the aisle tossing in smoked oysters and Robert's sauce and things I knew would sit in my cupboard for years. Only when I found some Klondike ice cream bars did I

feel less guilty about spending James's fireman's salary so foolishly. My father-in-law ate them with the same gusto little
Joseph did.

Waiting in the check-out line I heard a voice say, "Twyla!"

The classical music piped over the aisles had affected me and
the woman leaning toward me was dressed to kill. Diamonds on
her hand, a smart white summer dress. "I'm Mrs. Benson," I
said.

"Ho. Ho. The Big Bozo," she sang.

For a split second I didn't know what she was talking about.
She had a bunch of asparagus and two cartons of fancy water.

"Roberta!"

"Right."

"For heaven's sake. Roberta."

"You look great," she said.

"So do you. Where are you? Here? In Newburgh?"

"Yes. Over in Annandale."

I was opening my mouth to say more when the cashier called
my attention to her empty counter.

"Meet you outside." Roberta pointed her finger and went
into the express line.

I placed the groceries and kept myself from glancing around
to check Roberta's progress. I remembered Howard Johnson's
and looking for a chance to speak only to be greeted with a
stingy "wow." But she was waiting for me and her huge hair
was sleek now, smooth around a small, nicely shaped head.
Shoes, dress, everything lovely and summery and rich. I was
dying to know what happened to her, how she got from Jimi
Hendrix to Annandale, a neighborhood full of doctors and
IBM executives. Easy, I thought. Everything is so easy for
them. They think they own the world.

"How long," I asked her. "How long have you been here?"

"A year. I got married to a man who lives here. And you,
you're married too, right? Benson, you said."

"Yeah. James Benson."

"And is he nice?"

"Oh, is he nice?"

"Well, is he?" Roberta's eyes were steady as though she
really meant the question and wanted an answer.

"He's wonderful, Roberta. Wonderful."

"So you're happy."

"Very."

"That's good," she said and nodded her head. "I always hoped you'd be happy. Any kids? I know you have kids."

"One. A boy. How about you?"

"Four."

"Four?"

She laughed. "Step kids. He's a widower."

"Oh."

"Got a minute? Let's have a coffee."

I thought about the Klondikes melting and the inconvenience of going all the way to my car and putting the bags in the trunk. Served me right for buying all that stuff I didn't need. Roberta was ahead of me.

"Put them in my car. It's right here."

And then I saw the dark blue limousine.

"You married a Chinaman?"

"No," she laughed. "He's the driver."

"Oh, my. If the Big Bozo could see you now."

We both giggled. Really giggled. Suddenly, in just a pulse beat, twenty years disappeared and all of it came rushing back. The big girls (whom we called gar girls—Roberta's misheard word for the evil stone faces described in a civics class) there dancing in the orchard, the ploppy mashed potatoes, the double weenies, the Spam with pineapple. We went into the coffee shop holding on to one another and I tried to think why we were glad to see each other this time and not before. Once, twelve years ago, we passed like strangers. A black girl and a white girl meeting in a Howard Johnson's on the road and having nothing to say. One in a blue and white triangle waitress hat—the other on her way to see Hendrix. Now we were behaving like sisters separated for much too long. Those four short months were nothing in time. Maybe it was the thing itself. Just being there, together. Two little girls who knew what nobody else in the world knew—how not to ask questions. How to believe what had to be believed. There was politeness in that reluctance and generosity as well. Is your mother sick too? No, she dances all night. Oh—and an understanding nod.

We sat in a booth by the window and fell into recollection like veterans.

"Did you ever learn to read?"

"Watch." She picked up the menu. "Special of the day. Cream of corn soup. Entrées. Two dots and a wriggly line. Quiche. Chef salad, scallops . . ."

I was laughing and applauding when the waitress came up.

"Remember the Easter baskets?"

"And how we tried to *introduce* them?"

"Your mother with that cross like two telephone poles."

"And yours with those tight slacks."

We laughed so loudly heads turned and made the laughter hard to suppress.

"What happened to the Jimi Hendrix date?"

Roberta made a blow-out sound with her lips.

"When he died I thought about you."

"Oh, you heard about him finally?"

"Finally. Come on, I was a small-town country waitress."

"And I was a small-town country dropout. God, were we wild. I still don't know how I got out of there alive."

"But you did."

"I did. I really did. Now I'm Mrs. Kenneth Norton."

"Sounds like a mouthful."

"It is."

"Servants and all?"

Roberta held up two fingers.

"Ow! What does he do?"

"Computers and stuff. What do I know?"

"I don't remember a hell of a lot from those days, but Lord, St. Bonny's is as clear as daylight. Remember Maggie? The day she fell down and those gar girls laughed at her?"

Roberta looked up from her salad and stared at me. "Maggie didn't fall," she said.

"Yes, she did. You remember."

"No, Twyla. They knocked her down. Those girls pushed her down and tore her clothes. In the orchard."

"I don't—that's not what happened."

"Sure it is. In the orchard. Remember how scared we were?"

"Wait a minute. I don't remember any of that."

"And Bozo was fired."

"You're crazy. She was there when I left. You left before me."

"I went back. You weren't there when they fired Bozo."

"What?"

"Twice. Once for a year when I was about ten, another for two months when I was fourteen. That's when I ran away."

"You ran away from St. Bonny's?"

"I had to. What do you want? Me dancing in that orchard?"

"Are you sure about Maggie?"

"Of course I'm sure. You've blocked it, Twyla. It happened. Those girls had behavior problems, you know."

"Didn't they, though. But why can't I remember the Maggie thing?"

"Believe me. It happened. And we were there."

"Who did you room with when you went back?" I asked her as if I would know her. The Maggie thing was troubling me.

"Creeps. They tickled themselves in the night."

My ears were itching and I wanted to go home suddenly. This was all very well but she couldn't just comb her hair, wash her face and pretend everything was hunky-dory. After the Howard Johnson's snub. And no apology. Nothing.

"Were you on dope or what that time at Howard Johnson's?" I tried to make my voice sound friendlier than I felt.

"Maybe, a little. I never did drugs much. Why?"

"I don't know, you acted sort of like you didn't want to know me then."

"Oh, Twyla, you know how it was in those days: black—white. You know how everything was."

But I didn't know. I thought it was just the opposite. Busloads of blacks and whites came into Howard Johnson's together. They roamed together then: students, musicians, lovers, protesters. You got to see everything at Howard Johnson's and blacks were very friendly with whites in those days. But sitting there with nothing on my plate but two hard tomato wedges wondering about the melting Klondikes it seemed childish remembering the slight. We went to her car, and with the help of the driver, got my stuff into my station wagon.

"We'll keep in touch this time," she said.

"Sure," I said. "Sure. Give me a call."

"I will," she said, and then just as I was sliding behind the wheel, she leaned into the window. "By the way. Your mother. Did she ever stop dancing?"

I shook my head. "No. Never."

Roberta nodded.

"And yours? Did she ever get well?"

She smiled a tiny sad smile. "No. She never did. Look, call me, okay?"

"Okay," I said, but I knew I wouldn't. Roberta had messed up my past somehow with that business about Maggie. I wouldn't forget a thing like that. Would I?

STRIFE came to us that fall. At least that's what the paper called it. Strife. Racial strife. The word made me think of a bird—a big shrieking bird out of 1,000,000,000 B.C. Flapping its wings and cawing. Its eye with no lid always bearing down on you. All day it screeched and at night it slept on the rooftops. It woke you in the morning and from the *Today* show to the eleven o'clock news it kept you an awful company. I couldn't figure it out from one day to the next. I knew I was supposed to feel something strong, but I didn't know what, and James wasn't any help. Joseph was on the list of kids to be transferred from the junior high school to another one at some far-out-of-the-way place and I thought it was a good thing until I heard it was a bad thing. I mean I didn't know. All the schools seemed dumps to me, and the fact that one was nicer looking didn't hold much weight. But the papers were full of it and then the kids began to get jumpy. In August, mind you. Schools weren't even open yet. I thought Joseph might be frightened to go over there, but he didn't seem scared so I forgot about it, until I found myself driving along Hudson Street out there by the school they were trying to integrate and saw a line of women marching. And who do you suppose was in line, big as life, holding a sign in front of her bigger than her mother's cross? MOTHERS HAVE RIGHTS TOO! it said.

I drove on, and then changed my mind. I circled the block, slowed down, and honked my horn.

Roberta looked over and when she saw me she waved. I didn't wave back, but I didn't move either. She handed her sign to another woman and came over to where I was parked.

"Hi."

"What are you doing?"

"Picketing. What's it look like?"

"What for?"

"What do you mean, 'What for?' They want to take my kids and send them out of the neighborhood. They don't want to go."

"So what if they go to another school? My boy's being bussed too, and I don't mind. Why should you?"

"It's not about us, Twyla. Me and you. It's about our kids."

"What's more *us* than that?"

"Well, it is a free country."

"Not yet, but it will be."

"What the hell does that mean? I'm not doing anything to you."

"You really think that?"

"I know it."

"I wonder what made me think you were different."

"I wonder what made me think you were different."

"Look at them," I said. "Just look. Who do they think they are? Swarming all over the place like they own it. And now they think they can decide where my child goes to school. Look at them, Roberta. They're Bozos."

Roberta turned around and looked at the women. Almost all of them were standing still now, waiting. Some were even edging toward us. Roberta looked at me out of some refrigerator behind her eyes. "No, they're not. They're just mothers."

"And what am I? Swiss cheese?"

"I used to curl your hair."

"I hated your hands in my hair."

The women were moving. Our faces looked mean to them of course and they looked as though they could not wait to throw themselves in front of a police car, or better yet, into my car and drag me away by my ankles. Now they surrounded my car and gently, gently began to rock it. I swayed back and forth like a sideways yo-yo. Automatically I reached for Roberta, like the old days in the orchard when they saw us watching them and we had to get out of there, and if one of us fell the other pulled her up and if one of us was caught the other stayed to kick and scratch, and neither would leave the other behind. My arm shot out of the car window but no receiving hand was there. Roberta was looking at me sway from side to side in the car and her face was still. My purse slid from the car seat down under the dashboard. The four policemen who had been drinking Tab in their car finally got the message and strolled over, forcing their way through the women. Quietly, firmly they spoke. "Okay, ladies. Back in line or off the streets."

Some of them went away willingly; others had to be urged away from the car doors and the hood. Roberta didn't move. She was looking steadily at me. I was fumbling to turn on the ignition, which wouldn't catch because the gear shift was still in drive. The seats of the car were a mess because the swaying had thrown my grocery coupons all over it and my purse was sprawled on the floor.

"Maybe I am different now, Twyla. But you're not. You're the same little state kid who kicked a poor old black lady when she was down on the ground. You kicked a black lady and you have the nerve to call me a bigot."

The coupons were everywhere and the guts of my purse were bunched under the dashboard. What was she saying? Black? Maggie wasn't black.

"She wasn't black," I said.

"Like hell she wasn't, and you kicked her. We both did. You kicked a black lady who couldn't even scream."

"Liar!"

"You're the liar! Why don't you just go on home and leave us alone, huh?"

She turned away and I skidded away from the curb.

The next morning I went into the garage and cut the side out of the carton our portable TV had come in. It wasn't nearly big enough, but after a while I had a decent sign: red spray-painted letters on a white background—AND SO DO CHIL-DREN****. I meant just to go down to the school and tack it up somewhere so those cows on the picket line across the street could see it, but when I got there, some ten or so others had already assembled—protesting the cows across the street. Police permits and everything. I got in line and we strutted in time on our side while Roberta's group strutted on theirs. That first day we were all dignified, pretending the other side didn't exist. The second day there was name calling and finger gestures. But that was about all. People changed signs from time to time, but Roberta never did and neither did I. Actually my sign didn't make sense without Roberta's. "And so do children what?" one of the women on my side asked me. Have rights, I said, as though it was obvious.

Roberta didn't acknowledge my presence in any way and I got to thinking maybe she didn't know I was there. I began to pace myself in the line, jostling people one minute and lagging behind the next, so Roberta and I could reach the end of our respective lines at the same time and there would be a moment in our turn when we would face each other. Still, I couldn't tell whether she saw me and knew my sign was for her. The next day I went early before we were scheduled to assemble. I waited until she got there before I exposed my new creation. As soon as she hoisted her MOTHERS HAVE RIGHTS TOO I began to wave my new one, which said, HOW WOULD YOU KNOW? I know she saw that one, but I had gotten addicted now. My signs got crazier each day, and the women on my side decided that I was a kook. They couldn't make heads or tails out of my brilliant screaming posters.

I brought a painted sign in queenly red with huge black letters that said, IS YOUR MOTHER WELL? Roberta took her lunch break and didn't come back for the rest of the day or any day after. Two days later I stopped going too and couldn't have been missed because nobody understood my signs anyway.

It was a nasty six weeks. Classes were suspended and Joseph didn't go to anybody's school until October. The children—everybody's children—soon got bored with that extended vacation they thought was going to be so great. They looked at TV until their eyes flattened. I spent a couple of mornings tutoring my son, as the other mothers said we should. Twice I opened a text from last year that he had never turned in. Twice he yawned in my face. Other mothers organized living room sessions so the kids would keep up. None of the kids could concentrate so they drifted back to *The Price Is Right* and *The Brady Bunch*. When the school finally opened there were fights once or twice and some sirens roared through the streets every once in a while. There were a lot of photographers from Albany. And just when ABC was about to send up a news crew, the kids settled down like nothing in the world had happened. Joseph hung my HOW WOULD YOU KNOW? sign in his bedroom. I don't know what became of AND SO DO CHILDREN****. I think my father-in-law cleaned some fish on it. He was always puttering around in our garage. Each of his five children lived in Newburgh and he acted as though he had five extra homes.

I couldn't help looking for Roberta when Joseph graduated from high school, but I didn't see her. It didn't trouble me much what she had said to me in the car. I mean the kicking part. I know I didn't do that, I couldn't do that. But I was puzzled by her telling me Maggie was black. When I thought about it I actually couldn't be certain. She wasn't pitch-black, I knew, or I would have remembered that. What I remember was the kiddie hat, and the semicircle legs. I tried to reassure myself about the race thing for a long time until it dawned on me that the truth was already there, and Roberta knew it. I didn't kick her; I didn't join in with the gar girls and kick that lady, but I sure did want to. We watched and never tried to help her and never called for help. Maggie was my dancing mother. Deaf, I thought, and dumb. Nobody inside. Nobody who would hear you if you cried in the night. Nobody who could tell you anything important that you could use. Rocking, dancing, swaying as she walked. And when the gar girls pushed her down, and started roughhousing, I knew she wouldn't scream, couldn't—just like me—and I was glad about that.

WE decided not to have a tree, because Christmas would be at my mother-in-law's house, so why have a tree at both places? Joseph was at SUNY New Paltz and we had to economize, we said. But at the last minute, I changed my mind. Nothing could be that bad. So I rushed around town looking for a tree, something small but wide. By the time I found a place, it was snowing and very late. I dawdled like it was the most important purchase in the world and the tree man was fed up with me. Finally I chose one and had it tied onto the trunk of the car. I drove away slowly because the sand trucks were not out yet and the streets could be murder at the beginning of a snowfall. Downtown the streets were wide and rather empty except for a cluster of people coming out of the Newburgh Hotel. The one hotel in town that wasn't built out of cardboard and Plexiglas. A party, probably. The men huddled in the snow were dressed in tails and the women had on furs. Shiny things glittered from underneath their coats. It made me tired to look at them. Tired, tired, tired. On the next corner was a small diner with loops and loops of paper bells in the window. I stopped the car and went in. Just for a cup of coffee and twenty minutes of peace before I went home and tried to finish everything before Christmas Eve.

"Twyla?"

There she was. In a silvery evening gown and dark fur coat. A man and another woman were with her, the man fumbling for change to put in the cigarette machine. The woman was humming and tapping on the counter with her fingernails. They all looked a little bit drunk.

"Well. It's you."

"How are you?"

I shrugged. "Pretty good. Frazzled. Christmas and all."

"Regular?" called the woman from the counter.

"Fine," Roberta called back and then, "Wait for me in the car."

She slipped into the booth beside me. "I have to tell you something, Twyla. I made up my mind if I ever saw you again, I'd tell you."

"I'd just as soon not hear anything, Roberta. It doesn't matter now, anyway."

"No," she said. "Not about that."

"Don't be long," said the woman. She carried two regulars to go and the man peeled his cigarette pack as they left.

"It's about St. Bonny's and Maggie."

"Oh, please."

"Listen to me. I really did think she was black. I didn't make that up. I really thought so. But now I can't be sure. I just remember her as old, so old. And because she couldn't talk—well, you know, I thought she was crazy. She'd been brought up in an institution like my mother was and like I thought I would be too. And you were right. We didn't kick her. It was the gar girls. Only them. But, well, I wanted to. I really wanted them to hurt her. I said we did it, too. You and me, but that's not true. And I don't want you to carry that around. It was just that I wanted to do it so bad that day—wanting to is doing it."

Her eyes were watery from the drinks she'd had, I guess. I know it's that way with me. One glass of wine and I start bawling over the littlest thing.

"We were kids, Roberta."

"Yeah. Yeah. I know, just kids."

"Eight."

"Eight."

"And lonely."

"Scared, too."

She wiped her cheeks with the heel of her hand and smiled. "Well, that's all I wanted to say."

I nodded and couldn't think of any way to fill the silence that went from the diner past the paper bells on out into the snow. It was heavy now. I thought I'd better wait for the sand trucks before starting home.

"Thanks, Roberta."

"Sure."

"Did I tell you? My mother, she never did stop dancing."

"Yes. You told me. And mine, she never got well." Roberta lifted her hands from the tabletop and covered her face with her palms. When she took them away she really was crying. "Oh shit, Twyla. Shit, shit, shit. What the hell happened to Maggie?"

Lionel Mitchell

As he lay in a coma at Bellevue, Lionel Hampton Mitchell died last week at forty-two of pneumonia propelled by AIDS. For something under a year, his three-hundred-pound bulk had been shrinking. At first, I thought he was giving his heart and his system a break, since Lionel was a diabetic prone to ruthless consumption of sweets. But now and then he would abstractedly say, as though to himself, "I hope it isn't AIDS." As he got smaller, I began to worry about him. An odd sort of stoicism had come into his demeanor and the once wonderful voice, capable of filling city blocks with the width of his anger, had begun to lose its power. The clever eyes so rich with ideas and worlds, wit and information, seemed to cast less light. He appeared forever tired, and a bewildered sadness I had never seen in him replaced the pugnacious spirit that could be as compelling as it was overwhelming when the barbs in his bloodstream took to the air for a vituperative attack. Then I would ask him if he was ill and Lionel would answer that he was losing weight at the advice of his doctor after a mild stroke. I now think that Lionel knew what was happening to him and, as some have suggested, chose to face his end in secret.

I had first met Lionel at the Bini Bon, a cheap Lower East Side restaurant where struggling artists of one kind or another came for the heavy-duty breakfasts. I was talking with David Murray when this rotund Negro in a nappy sweater started expounding on the nature of New York, sometimes sniffing and barely sneering as he explained the interwoven corruption of Manhattan. As I got to know him better I found out that he was a writer working on a book about lower Manhattan called *Traveling Light.* I saw a hilarious essay he wrote and began to encounter him on Second Avenue. When he was in a public place, Lionel would usually find someone to make the butt of a joke or the object, if not the subject, of a long lecture about some point in military history, literature, social origins, or whatever. Once, he stood up as he argued with someone, saying, "You don't know anything about black culture. Have you ever been in the Baptist church? Can you preach, you understand what I mean? *Preach!*" Lionel then summoned an enormous baritone and commenced to chant about the camel going through the eye of the needle, using "you got to bend down" as a kick phrase. All the while he was moving for the exit, and a jaunty step came into his hulking stride as he reached for the doorknob, still preaching, his words now hot with biblical references and that combination of flower and sweat so basic to the near-song of the Negro pulpit style. Lionel knew all heads had turned in his direction and he made a theatrical dip as he raised one finger in the air, reiterated his kick phrase—"Whoa, you got to bend down, you got to *bend* down!"—and went into the street.

But Lionel Mitchell wasn't only a character. He was a man of the mind who knew the streets, the overt and covert actions of human beings, the illegal or subterranean lives of those on the social and sexual outskirts of conventional society. His early life in New Orleans had taught him many things about the distances between appearances and secret facts, about the intricate crossings of bloodlines and cultures, histories and monies. And like any serious student of military history, Lionel knew the opposition in detail. Lionel could analyze white Southerners by class, physical type, and point of European origin, and explain their social evolution. His account would begin with their getting off the boats, move on to the development of an economy based on slave labor and poor white trash, then detail its destruction by the irresistible innovations of the Union Army. He understood the gloomy empire of segregation and violence that rose in the wake of Reconstruction and the importance of Negro colleges in preparing the way for most of the major movers in Negro American political history. "Yes, it was in those lowly little backwater nigger colleges that the intellectual ammunition necessary to take these crackers on was smelted and poured *boiling hot* into those thick woolly skulls."

It was because Lionel knew so much that he was a refreshing answer to simplifications about racial history. "House niggers? What are these fools talking about? I submit that Toussaint L'Ouverture was the greatest house nigger in history! These little fake nigger intellectuals better read. They better sit down with Mr. Frederick Douglass, with Mr. William Faulkner, with a whole lot of goddam books so they can cover their asses with some *facts.* "

In his 1980 novel, *Traveling Light,* Mitchell showed just what his potential was. I still think, as I once wrote, that it, "unlike most contemporary Negro fiction, conceives of black American life as part of a cultural complex that includes many races, religions, and folkways in Southern and Northern situations. Uneven, episodic, and loose-ended, it is nevertheless insightful, eloquent, finely observed, and orchestrated by both an ironic awareness of pretension and an irreverence that do fierce battle with the maudlin (although occasionally succumbing to it)." The book never went anywhere and was soon remaindered, though Lionel lived at the peak of a dream while it was hot off the presses. His boasting led to a confrontation with one of the slew of empty-headed Puerto Rican street boys he paid for their favors, often pretending that he was giving them spiritual and intellectual guidance. The boy, tired of Lionel's patting himself on the back, struck the writer twice over the head with the heavy metal springs of a bull-worker. But Lionel, who had no dog in him, got out his knife and nearly gutted the boy. "All I ever want is the strength to take one with me. I know it's dangerous messing around with these boys. I would have to be a fool not to know it. Right next to my bed I have a knife soaking in garlic juice. If they come for me, all I say is, 'Lord, don't let me die *alone.* ' "

Well, he did die alone, fighting something no knife could stop. I had last seen him about eight weeks ago in the *Voice* office, sitting dejected with his belt all the way over to the last hole and his pants bunched and slipping down beneath the loops. It was then he told me he had had a mild stroke and asked if I could loan him five dollars for some food. I did and walked him out of the office. From what I have been able to gather, Lionel soon got more and more down. Henry LaFarge, a longtime friend from New Orleans, remembers visiting him in the last days. The usually unkempt apartment on 11th and Second Avenue, which had been a clearing house for boy prostitutes, was absolutely filthy. Roaches covered the floor and the walls, cans of cat food were opened and thrown about, the cat box hadn't been emptied for weeks, and all of Lionel's plants were dead. He was soon evicted and began staying with friends, usually leaving because he had lost control of his bodily functions, filthying himself and their homes. At one point, he traveled north near the Connecticut border to try and stay in a monastery. Rejected, he was later arrested for defecating in the park, then sent back to New York, where he finally went to Bellevue. There they pushed tubes down one end and up the other, through his nose, and fixed one for urination. He was incapable of speech when people visited him, sometimes turning in bed until the machines went crazy, which led to his hands being tied. Soon, he was dead.

I don't know if Lionel's story qualifies as a cautionary tale; I don't know if anyone's does. He was much more than the horror of his end, than the obsession with young boys, than the willingness to roar above it all at any time. He was his own man, conflicted, complex, compassionate. I have known few as individual, and I know his like has railed through this life only once.

—Stanley Crouch

Chapter 5 from
TRAVELING LIGHT

WITH a sigh of relief he landed a job. He didn't keep it long but made enough money before he was fired to move out of the couple's apartment into the rooming house where he entered the breathless pace of the city, entered another world of rooming-house New York. Rooming houses had not become the welfare hotels of the present in those days. Still, it was not the end of the world, as he expected. It wasn't Harlem, only the Upper West Side. It was filled up with enough Southern blacks still continuing in the old, recognizable patterns that he didn't feel too isolated. In the evenings the kitchen (one to a floor) exuded homey odors of frying chicken, and in a few weeks, when he was down and out, it wasn't uncommon for people to offer him a home-cooked meal. The old ladies took a special delight in either offering him food or once in a while bringing a plate to his room for him. He had carried phone books for Donnelly as long as he could stand it and saved every penny. Then he noticed, from a polite and reticent distance, as any rural boy would, the young white people, students and forerunners of the hippies, although he took his time before he got in with them. The older blacks did not mix in too much with the young folks, and almost by design or mutual consent they seemed to prefer the lower floors. The students were mostly lodged on the upper ones. Boo's room was at the front of the building on the third floor. In his wing were housed two single men like himself except they went out a lot and worked in the day. For a while a whole family from the Carolinas lived on one side of him, and next to them lived the couple who were always fighting. Except for Joe and his wife, all the other tenants were quiet types living very private lives. Deacon lived down the hall near the stairwell until he moved to another room after their brief friendship busted up. At the other end of the hall, past the stairwell, was a wing occupied by white girls. In this way, people with common backgrounds clustered together. Most of these girls were students deeply involved in psychoanalysis— "the psych ward," it was called. The male students lived on the upper floors along with more artistic types. Foreign students tended to hold one wing of the second floor, and at the other end were the old black ladies who banded together in the storefront on the first floor.

Surprisingly, he found the people in the rooming house to follow rather clean habits, keeping the kitchens clean. The black womenfolk kept curtains at the windows, and the bathrooms (two to a floor) were also kept as clean as possible. It wasn't one of those houses of the hardest transients at all, but everyone seemed fully equipped with fresh bed linen, radios, televisions, phonographs, books—very much at home as though their single rooms were mini-apartments. It wasn't long before he was given an assortment of bed linen and blankets. Old Mother Alice had given him a quilt that she had made for his bed. The hippies, of course, took the beds out and put their mattresses on the floors and made their rooms as cozy as possible with all sorts of murals and symbols on the walls.

But he had almost a bare room, and it took some time before it began to fill up. It was the first time he'd been away from home and a man in his own house, and except for the ideas that Joel's pad had instilled in him back in New Orleans, he had no definite ideas about how he would make this single room "express" himself, as the hippies advised. It took a while of sitting on the bed or lying on his back staring up at the ceiling before he began to give the room the stamp of his "personality," as they said. A girl from the psych ward came into his room and advised him to decorate the room around the water stains on the ceiling and walls.

He had reflected on these images many, many days and nights sitting in his room thinking over the peculiar human plight and seeing the pattern of brown snakes up near the ceiling—is there anything more vile, repulsive, than a watermarked ceiling to look at? It changed with his mood and sometimes he could see, as the girl from the psych ward suggested, its possibilities as a sort of spontaneous art, but he kept thinking how it went along with the first impression he'd had of New York—that of the seeping, creeping, almost alive dirt and soot so like tales that people tell of the incredible growth of jungle vegetation until in the heat one can no longer find the strength to combat it. It was another of those forces of nature that seemed to make a mockery of men and render them lethargic. In a fortnight the dirt that has been scrubbed off the window sill is back again. Only a monomaniac could scrub and clean that much. There would be no time for anything else but a ceaseless cleaning, cleaning. Yet, there is always somebody in the rooming house so determined to beat back the dirt, obsessed with cleanliness as though somehow through cleaning they might efface the depths to which they have fallen that late at night they trudge down to the bathroom to draw mop water, disturbing the whole floor with general cleaning. How futile it all seemed. He could only wonder why they didn't figure out a way to get themselves out of this place instead of always cleaning it up. In the South it had been the bugs—big two-inch roaches that flew about in the dark and landed upon him as he lay hot and naked in one of the rooms of the railroad flat. At least New York roaches were not so open as that, and in the winter they retired and disappeared altogether. Here it was the creeping dirt that bothered him.

He was twenty-seven or thirty weeks in arrears with his rent before he knew it. What was itself a stroke of rare good fortune—the fact that he hadn't been thrown out—completely passed him by. As each week passed he felt a numbness creep over him and spent his days in bed putting it out of his mind. The terror of what to do if he was thrown out on the streets occasionally gnawed at him. His good fortune was due to the downright kindness of a little Russian Jew, Mr. Feingold, who had once served on Trotsky's staff and had traveled on the famous military train with the great revolutionary.

Max Feingold, if that was in fact his real name, was the agent of the building. Some books and writing papers had caught the eye of Max when he had come to collect the rent from Boo. Circumstances cannot break the camaraderie, the recognition, between men of education; Old World people are especially surprised and delighted to meet an American young-ster who appears to be interested in their experiences. Max's sharp eye caught sight of a dog-eared copy of Isaac Deutscher's monumental study *The Prophet Armed: Trotsky: 1879–1921*, a loan from a leftist student from the upper floors. The old man welcomed the chance to unburden himself of the history to which he had been witness. So delighted did he become at finding someone who would listen to him that he soon forgot to ask for the rent and after several weeks only winked when the subject came up. Max provided a transition from Deacon, to Boo's awakening to the rooming house in general.

Europe had thrown away millions of skilled men like Max, who could work with his quick, sharp intellect or with his hands at almost any trade and whose education would be the envy or pride of any "expert" on European twentieth-century history. Max had seen all of the worst and the best days of the holocaust century. He even remembered the 1905 revolution and the czarist prisons and had escaped being transported to Siberia, had walked back on foot to join the great proletarian revolu-tion. Uncle Joe had promptly scheduled him to go back, but the growing alarm and need caused by the Nazi push into Fas-cist Poland had caused him to reconsider and send Max into the tender mercies of the Nazi holocaust. Max had forgotten his family and had no reason to believe that they had survived the combined nightmares of forced collectivization, Wehr-macht followed by the *Einsatzgruppen*.

He escaped the last ride to Auschwitz by being picked out of the line—an SS doctor looked over his record and found him able-bodied and skilled enough to work for the Third Reich as a slave. Max had no papers stating he was a Jew. The SS doctor had no time to make the infamous measurements, and by this time the Jew-baiting Russians were pouring so much hell down on the master race that it didn't matter—the factories of the Reich needed even Jew hands to save their superior asses. They had thought to work little Max to death, but Max was a man who knew how to work and conserve time and energy doing so. His body was still hard and wiry—it seemed to bear the spirit of man itself. It knew nothing under the sun that could master or break it. If there was any truth to the myth of the indestructible

Jew, Max was the Jew of Jews, Jude Seuss down to his very bones! Hitler's system had made him that if nothing else.

After he left the displaced persons camp Max had drifted to Palestine, which became Israel while he was there, but Max couldn't buy Israel either, diehard Bolshevik, atheist revolutionary to the bitter end. He was no "goddamned Jew," he hadn't faced death all those times to spend his life in a theocratic oligarchy, he hadn't prayed in his starvations in the icy steppes, he hadn't prayed at the crossroads to Auschwitz, hadn't given praise to God when the SS doctor in black gloves told him to stand aside, hadn't prayed in the Reich factories as his comrades dropped from starvation and fatigue hourly, daily. The UN mandate creating Israel was to him nothing but a cruel hoax played by the imperialist powers to stave off world revolution by pitting one colonial and subject people against another. He was going to America without any illusions to see for himself the headquarters where they boasted of rolling back the inevitable dialectical interpretation of history.

He had no heroes. When he got down to it, Trotsky was no saint himself. He had accepted the competitive spirit of toughness by which the old Bolsheviks had demanded of the revolution more and more devastating and cruel policies in the earliest days. Lenin, not Stalin, insisted upon the Cheka and the paranoid party elite; Stalin merely used it and drove it over the edge beyond all sanity and humanity. The Bolshevik revolution was always coldly calculated, according to Max; everybody who shaped it was always terrified that it would not prove tough enough to survive itself—it brooked no mystery, no irrationality, but was the result of a perfect scientific or dialectical reasoning. Unlike the so-called Nazi revolution, it was never perverted from its inception but all of its horrors came as a result of its perfect reason being carried out with insane exactitude, and Stalin, not Lenin, was its Robespierre. Hitler was the freak of political nature. It was Stalin's refusal to modify the revolution in the least that produced the horror, and, according to Max, Uncle Joe never violated the orthodox doctrine of Marx, nor did he ever make a doctrinal error.

Max would go on thrashing out the doctrinal fine points while he hammered away with precision at some pipe, patching the unpatchable—never needing much of anything except his tools and his two brown withered hands with the splotches on them. No wire needed to be replaced, just shaved down, reused, or used somewhere else; no fixture gave way to shiny new and expensive ones. Max could make them over when they were beyond repair, or he pirated parts of them before throwing the hulls away. He kept a long shelf with partitions built into it where he had a place for everything under the sun and where he emptied his pockets when he went down there. When once the ancient boiler in the cellar failed to shut itself off and subsequently cracked, Max used cooked oatmeal to seal the crack and the boiler operated for many years afterward—perfectly. It was of a cast-iron type made in 1870 which probably could not be welded by today's methods. Max with his pot of oatmeal repaired it.

There was no way that one could miss the kind of man Max was, for in him one saw the true magnificence of the human spirit, possessed of a toughness that could triumph over the modern calamities. And yet, a black whore, ignorant, tacky, stood in the face of such a man and because he threatened to evict her if she didn't pay up her rent once in a while and because he told her the people on the second floor were complaining about her tricks coming in all night long, didn't she tell such a man that Hitler should've succeeded in making him into a wallet or a bar of soap? And didn't Max sit in the kitchen and sob like a baby, his face screwed up like a prune? Oh, world horror without end; grant us peace. . . .

Once in America Max found out he had a family after all—a brother who had left after the 1905 revolution and who owned a successful factory in the garment district, and he told Boo what a small joy this had turned out to be, because his brother was a completely different man from Max. He was, according to Max, completely Americanized, so much so that he and Max once had a fistfight because after the war Max's wealthy brother wanted to visit the new Europe and above all the new Germany. Max blew up at the idea of this and went off. Max's brother looked down upon Max for not being wealthy. He was planning to go to Europe to put his brother Max down for having wasted his life in political movements and revolutions. Max blew up.

"Didn't they burn us up enough—our mother and our old father—our wives, our sweethearts, our daughters? Isn't this your second or third family? Isn't that enough for you?"

Max's brother had made some cliché remark about burying the past, and Max had gone completely off. Whereupon his brother and his brother's wife and two daughters threatened him with the nursing-home routine—an old man who though approaching eighty could still dare to scrape the fire escape and meticulously repaint it from the top seven stories up, who could hang out on a window ledge to repair a rotted-out frame. Him they would consign, Auschwitz escapee, twice left to starve and freeze to death in the icy steppes, him they would consign to a nursing home where he couldn't take a piss or yank off his withered old cock if he took a mind to without first asking some bitch of a nurse who wouldn't want to be bothered anyway—this is a part of the world horror that is without end. . . .

Finally, Max lost the building to the owner, who reclaimed it. Max had shown too many people too much kindness and therefore he was making almost nothing off of it. Max was to disappear into the suburbs and the small joys of his family with the nursing home hanging over his head and his very alert mind and sharp tongue if he didn't shut up. Or, Boo thought, maybe when he was wandering around Morningside Heights on one of his ceaseless herculean walks, some Harlem jungle bunny out to pull a "geese" on a "whitey"—the first whitey he saw—maybe he'd cut Max's withered old throat for the fuckin' "rebolushin" and the ten dollars Max had begged from his one favorite niece to keep in his pocket on his trip to old haunts in Manhattan. That, Boo thought, would be the crowning irony of the world horror that is without end—Lawd, Lawd, grant us peace and understanding of each other, amen!

It was the whole world, a mini-world all in rooms. The Southern boy was able to hold on there, everybody reached out in some little way, and having lost the Deacon as companion he began to become more venturesome, taking the example of a political youth, Sherman, who more than anyone else came to

Boo's room and taught him how to live totally within the world
of the rooming house. Sherman never left the rooming house
and went from room to room all day. He was a middle-class
youth whose politics did not prevent him from having a
"shrink" like all the rest, and for all of his political readings and
views, he did not exactly set out to proselytize but was full of
curiosity and had an insatiable urge to worm his way in and
drink up each person's viewpoint. He had a winning way due to
a general boyish appearance. He was everybody's baby—especially the girls in the psych ward. And, of course, it was Sherman who told him everybody's story in the rooming house,
there being few into whose rooms he had not penetrated.
"Wow! have you met—you mean you haven't met Alice?
Alice—that's Mother Alice, mind you—is this black lady who
does readings—I mean she has some sort of powers—occult,
y'know. She 'works' for people—makes things that they want
happen!"

Boo knew just what he meant. Once when there had been
some money missing at home, his grandmaw had sent for a
woman of similar talent who moved in with them to work on
the case. This woman had tied a brass key to an old Bible so
that it swung during the seance to point out the guilty culprit,
and though it had cleared him, it never told who the culprit
was. When her oracle proved inconclusive, he remembered
happily that Grandmaw threw her out—another one of those
embarrassing impositions of the weird people Grandmaw was
always putting up in their home.

"You believe in that sort?" Boo asked Sherman, the avowed
Marxist.

"Well," he said with a big grin, "voodoo is as good as paying
a shrink thirty dollars an hour—I mean, isn't psychology sort of
modern voodoo?"

"Thirty dollars an hour! I should think so! But if you feel it's
modern voodoo—I mean, you're supposed to be an atheist,
right?"

"Well—my shrink is sort of—well, I have a weird kind of
relationship with him, and anyway, my parents pay for the
sessions. I had a nervous breakdown when I was fifteen—
rather, I'd say I'm always having a nervous breakdown, maybe

every day is just another more or less subtle nervous break-down."

"Thirty dollars an hour? How long does the session take?"

"Sometimes about an hour—but I don't wanna get into me and my shrink—I missed the last two sessions anyway. Let's go see Alice—er, Mother Alice, that is."

"Thirty dollars an hour—isn't that your exploitation again?"

"What can I tell you, it's a goddamned capitalist system! But I think you'd really dig Alice, Mother Alice—she's real way out—a spaced-out old lady!"

Mother Alice lived on the second floor, on the opposite wing from where the whores lived and worked. When you went down the stairs and out the front door of the building, you always issued out on the street through a cloud and the heavy scent of the incense emanating from Mother Alice's room. She burned acrid as well as sweet scents all day—starting with the pungent-sweet odor of frankincense and myrrh right down to the perfumed floral scents such as jasmine and rose. At other times, she placed kitchen spices such as cinnamon or curry upon a red-hot charcoal and the aroma wafted through the halls. She was an elderly brown queen in lace, with the kind of chiffon-lace curtains you see in the windows of church rectories or Catholic windows. She kept her head covered with an em-broidered cap, trimmed in lace. She had not omitted the lace apron of priests—she was a priestess of a strange cult, the name of which she never uttered. The small shrine in her room told less of her religious affiliation because it was a mixture of flick-ering red lights, white Catholic saints, and ebonywood statu-ettes from Africa. Her shrine had many small jars, decorated with ribbons. She was most certainly what is called a woman of powers. Her face was soft brown, wise and vaguely severe, the look of one who has no enemies; her brown skin in old age was as soft as fine leather. She had an expert's knowledge of natural cosmetics, mixing her own herbal compresses; applying hot wax to her face, allowing it to cool, she stripped it away quickly to relax the skin and to remove grizzled hairs. A woman of light-ning-quick changes of mood, she spoke in a soft cultured voice and could just as suddenly bring forth an incredible intensity and emotional commitment to anything she believed firmly.

She was a devotee and proselytizer of Swiss Kriss and ginseng root. She used "chewing John" and spat the juice about her door or boiled it down and made a tea from it. This made her somewhat wild-looking in a funny way. There was something Indian in her features; she had high cheekbones and her face took on a white, phosphorescent glow in the evening as she sat talking and drinking her teas. Her eyes at such times seemed to bore right through her visitors.

Mother Alice conversed with the spirits. She saw them standing behind people who entered her room. She read their message in the space over people's heads or in their auric emanation. Who knows what she saw, because such people are very secretive about the nature of their vision . . . perhaps faces appeared in the antique mirror of her dresser, a mirror that badly needed resilvering, possessing relatively clear portions and capable of many distortions and weird visual effects. Perhaps it was out of this subliminal distortion that strange figures took shape—especially under the influence of her various teas, which were probably of a highly stimulating tendency, and this fact coupled with years of sheer persistence led to a state in which only heaven knows what weird phantasmagoria boiled up before her mind's eye.

"Boy, you better do somethin' 'bout that problem of yours . . ." And he felt threatened by little things in her tone because he couldn't for the life of him understand what she was actually talking about. She, in turn, spoke to him as though he were knowledgeable of the facts of her mediumship. He wasn't, except in a vague social way, and so her phrase, "must do something," only added to the anxiety he carried daily about his general situation. His superstition, fostered by his so-called liberal arts education, lay in the fact that he could find no rational explanation for the old woman's intimate knowledge of him and his anxieties, but he recognized in her the power to play upon them as one strokes a harp or a lyre. The power of fascination held him fast, just as it had done with the Deacon, and it became an experience that he just could not pass by. At first he had been amused at her reading, smiling to himself as one does when one is lured into a gypsy's storefront.

"As the shadow is to the body, so you look upon yourself,"

she said in a strange voice, like the way they talked in mummy movies; she jerked again and the trance took her over with the suddenness that white sap pops from a broken green stem; a new person rolled up out of her after each violent jerk and from the contortions of her face.

"A stranger to yourself; it drags after you; you care not for it; you drag it through rough terrain—taking yourself for granted—too proud to take any notice of it. Like snot from nostrils and like dried shit across your path, so you wish to be done with yourself and avoid yourself. No wonder your life doesn't work. The young man thinks that he knows . . . a world he sees as through a tube, his vision is as though in a corridor. The wide-open spaces elude his sight, as do the small things. Trouble with women, much trouble with women! A woman is as a mirror who reflects the self you will not see. He who sees not himself will only see others around him as dim shadows. Until you can meet your self, until you can love your self, how can you expect to be loved by others?"

He would remember that strange voice that spoke in a low murmur to him because it was to come from other people in the North. It would account for the strange uneasiness that the words of Malcolm X caused in him, although he scrupulously avoided Harlem in those days when Malcolm was alive. The meaning of those words, "love your self," only became clear to him much, much later—after Malcolm and probably Mother Alice herself were long dead.

Love yourself. They kept saying that in so many ways—everybody, junkies, crazies on the street, Malcolm, militants, blacks and some whites too—as though his deepest misgivings were part of national property. It often exasperated him and ran against the Southerner's grain entirely, for no one who grew up in the South believes that deep private matters can be solved, let alone talked about in public. The Southerner is naturally reticent. His instincts warn him off from any sort of public self-examination. What the hell were they talking about? Anyway, he couldn't see how it applied to him. Love himself, indeed; it seemed like only an invitation to spill out his guts to a perfect stranger, and *that* went against his whole "self." He had grown up forced to keep his private thoughts buried and locked away deep inside. He would never dream of letting them out. His grandmaw had said many times that a man never explains himself to anyone.

More than anything it was the first inkling of that spiritual awareness which was through the course of the sixties to reveal itself to him, very slowly, very patiently. Psychic experiences tend to strike directly at that sense of the individual that is ingrained down to the very street level in each person and that Boo had felt tugging at him from his earliest conscious years. His insides, his private feelings, were something which no one could wrest from him and to which no one but himself had any claim. Now here comes this old brown lady, seeing through him, and like any other American, he soon was filled with a violent resentment about it.

As if life would support only what *they* said and what *they* felt to be true and real. But life was always different when it came down to it—nothing like what they said it would be, or if at any time he thought he caught sight of something that they had said he would, it too was always slightly different from what they said it would be. So he didn't know . . . it only helped confuse him more. "Trouble with women! Trouble with women!" Didn't all men have this trouble with women? Of course, he hadn't had one yet—hadn't had his own woman— but that too would come, and when it did, how could anything this old woman said to him matter? He figured he'd be too caught up in trying to make things work out to even remember Alice's words.

Only thing, he regretted not paying more attention to what the womenfolk had said about this sort of "spirit" thing down home. It was a point in one's favor in the North to be filled up with the legend and folklore of the South, but Louisiana's tradition of voodoo had made not the slightest impression upon him when he was growing up. He had heard plenty of talk about people "fixing" each other and how by a certain method his grandmaw could guarantee that she would dream the number and win a lot of money from the lottery. There was always plenty of guarded talk about "tying up" a man so he couldn't get it up for another woman and such, but when they got to talking about these things he always got bored and excused himself. To him it was old folks' and women's talk. Now up North, it was something that came up as soon as he'd admit being from New Orleans. Even white people up North wanted to hear all about it, and he daydreamed often of being able to spin his weave and seduce whole crowds of broads with his "powers," but that was as far as it went.

Coming out of Alice's room, with Sherman behind him and looking over his shoulder, Boo encountered Deacon, as if for the last time. There along the halls he wearily made his way, supporting himself with one hand against the wall, coughing sporadically and whispering as with his dying breath, "White folks—white folks—white folks."

There they are, he thought fiercely. The two of them together on the same floor! As if Alice wasn't enough with her looking into her "waters" all the time, there was Deacon on the last lap of the trip—the ghostly slave ship that retrieves the souls of black folk, taking them back. At that point he knew he would let Sherman take him around to all the rooms—especially to the girls in the psych ward. Deacon, the phantom slaver, were all fading from his mind; that world was too painful. Anyway, he had come North to escape just those same colorful features and quaint ways of the South, to the North where things were logical and people lived a modern life! For he had mapped out clearly the way he wanted to live up North, eventually—a house with all the walls white, component stereo system and all the albums up on the proper modern racks, a clean, neat life from which all the nagging, all the tensions had vanished. The Northerner's way of life is easily grasped by the Southerner in that it requires strict discipline. The bitter cold itself coming after a brief change of season, the whipping north winds, quietly reminded him of having spent too fat a summer. The icy winds clear up the most romantic of minds soon enough. But not even the cold winds are as cold as the South still living under a hard-ass code. Now here were all these students and bohemians holding forth without working, living a relatively comfortable life—it was only natural that he would want to get out from under that basic Southern code, "All niggers must work!" Cities where "no visible means of support" could get him actually jailed. New Orleans had at the time around forty-nine different forms of vagrancy laws—including "vagrancy by aimless wandering."

All of that—parishes instead of counties, Ti Ton Jemima instead of Aunt Jemima, French law instead of Saxon, salt pork instead of a lean corned-beef sandwich, premature old age and high blood pressure, light strokes at thirty, port wine, poor circulation and heart trouble—had to go! Also, no more "special" white folks who had the power to get one out of jail—his momma's "madame" who had a colored chauffeur and was always listened to when she called downtown from her house in the Garden District. It was like that song they were always playing in their rooms; Bob Dylan's "Like a Rolling Stone." This was freedom, Boo often mused to himself, proud that he had at last had the courage to choose it.

He could think back on that day with his high school class when they had gone to the Cabildo and stood looking at the old slave block—how his ears started to ring and a cold fury welled up in him. He drew away from the thing, backing back to the rear of the crowd of students clustered around—the shackles, the anklets, the old chains now broken. Which was worse, he did not know, the crackers or the icy winds blowing down from Canada. He could think of that hostility that rose up in him when the Northern niggers used to tell him, "Dig yo'self, baby! You're beautiful!" And up North the white girls always wanting to run their fingers through those kinks and later to pluck the lint from the kinks around his balls—this world, like the swirling eddies in the swollen Mississippi that he'd watched from atop the levee a thousand countless days as they sucked in a giant cypress tree, uprooted by the rising river, spinning it lazily around and around at first, and the sucking force of the muddy water might all but stand the tree upright for a last time before finally sucking it under—so this world sucked in a boy forever, imperceptibly and terribly.

Terry McMillan

TERRY MCMILLAN'S novel *Mama* (1987) could simply be another novel about a single Black mother's survival in industrial middle America in the sixties, but the prose and vision of Terry McMillan (1951–) defy the cliché and demand the reader to acknowledge the complexity of her main character, Mildred Peacock. Her story is told in a tenacious and tough voice born out of a marriage to an abusive husband, and of life in an abusive society—a society and time when "most folks had never heard of Malcolm X." Underlying this struggle is McMillan's black humor. Mildred's husband, Crook, can't hold a job but can keep a mistress. At the beginning of the novel she kicks Crook out of the house, or rather gives him to his mistress, Ernestine: "I just want to tell you that you can have the sorry son-of-a-bitch if you want him. He's at the house."

The novel begins as a story of survival for this mother and her five children; freed of one abusive element in their lives they must still face the abuse of poverty and racism. Hardly the romantic woman warrior, Mildred drinks whiskey, lies to bill collectors, mistrusts God (as she says, she doesn't trust His judgment), and finds all the wrong men to love. She tells her daughter:

> . . . niggahs is stupid, that's why. They thank they can get something for nothing and that that God they keep praying to every Sunday is gon' rush down from the sky and save 'em. What it takes is real hard work. Ain't nobody gon' give you nothing in this world unless you work for it. I don't care what they tell you in church. One thang is true, and this is the tricky part. White folks own every damn than 'cause they was here first and took it all. They

don't like to see niggahs getting ahead and when they feel like it, they can stop you and make it just that much harder. But with all you learn in them books at school, least you can do is learn how to get around some shit like that.

Elizabeth Alexander, in the *Village Voice,* describes Mildred's few successes "matched by disappointment; her son becomes addicted to heroin, and Mildred's own habits nearly kill her. McMillan romanticizes nothing, presenting Mildred not as a Black "Mama" monolith but as a complex woman."

In 1989 Terry McMillan published a widely praised second novel, *Disappearing Acts.* In 1990 she edited and published *Breaking Ice: An Anthology of Contemporary African-American Fiction,* which includes the work of fifty-seven writers.

—Shawn Wong

Chapters 1 and 2 from
MAMA

1

MILDRED hid the ax beneath the mattress of the cot in the dining room. She poured lye in a brown paper bag and pushed it behind the pots and pans under the kitchen sink. Then she checked all three butcher knives to make sure they were razor sharp. She knew where she could get her hands on a gun in fifteen minutes, but ever since she'd seen her brother shot for stealing a beer from the pool hall, she'd been afraid of guns. Besides, Mildred didn't want to kill Crook, she just wanted to hurt him.

She hated this raggedy house. Hated this deadbeat town. Hated never having enough of anything. Most of all, she hated Crook. And if it weren't for their five kids, she'd have left him a long time ago.

She sat down at the kitchen table, crossed her thick brown thighs, and rested her chin in her palms. An L&M burned slowly in the plastic ashtray next to her now cold cup of coffee. At twenty-seven, Mildred was as tired as an old workhorse and felt like she'd been through a war. Her face hurt. Her bottom lip was swollen and it would stay that way the rest of her life, so that she'd have to tuck the left corner in whenever she wore lipstick, which was almost always. It would serve as her trademark, a constant reminder that she had quick-firing lips.

Her left foot was swollen, too, from the tire Crook had backed over it last night when she wouldn't move. She had gotten up at five o'clock this morning and soaked it in Epsom salts for a whole hour but that hadn't done much good. Now the combination of this pain and the crisscrossing of her thoughts irritated her like an unreachable itch, so she went

ahead and took the yellow nerve pill Curly Mae had given her
last week. Then she wrapped her foot in an Ace bandage, covered it with a fake-fur house shoe, and pulled another chair in
front of her to prop it up. She took a sip of her coffee.

As Mildred waited for the pill to work, she stared out the
kitchen window at the leafless trees and drew deeply on her
cigarette, one strong puff after another. She twirled her fingers
around her dyed red braids, which hung from the diaper she
had tied on her head. She patted her good foot against the torn
linoleum, something she always did when she was thinking.

The way she figured it, there'd been no sense trying to be too
cute last night and get herself killed thoroughly. Crook had
smacked her so hard outside the Red Shingle that she had
forgotten her name for a minute or two.

He was the jealous type.

Everybody knew it, but Mildred had made the mistake of
carrying on a friendly two-minute conversation with Percy Russell. Crook had always despised Percy because, as rumor had it,
their oldest daughter, Freda, wasn't his, and could've easily
been Percy's. Both men had skin the color of ripe bananas and
soft wavy hair, which Freda had inherited. And both men had
high chiseled cheeks, which, as time passed, emerged on
Freda's face too.

Mildred ignored the rumors and knew that in a town as
small as Point Haven people ran their mouths because they
didn't have anything better to do. Crook never did come right
out and accuse her of cheating because he'd been having an
affair with Ernestine Jackson off and on for the past twelve
years, before Mildred was even showing with Freda. And
before they got settled good into their marriage. He wasn't
whorish, except when he had more than eight ounces of liquor
in him, which was just about every day.

And while Crook ran the streets, it was Percy who nailed
plastic to the windows in the winter, bought Mildred maternity
clothes, fixed the drip in the bathtub, and paid the plumber to
fix the frozen pipes. It was Percy who had shoveled the heavy
blocks of coal from the shack in the back yard and carried them
to the house when Crook was too drunk to stand up, and then
waited for the fire to pop and crackle in the stove. It was Percy

who made sure Mildred was warm, who bought her cigarettes, aspirin and vitamins, lard and potatoes, and even paid her light and gas bills when Crook had done something else with the money, but pleaded amnesia.

The three of them had grown up together, though both men were six years older than Mildred. Percy had always had a crush on her, but he was so shy and stuttered so badly that she didn't have the patience to hear him out when he tried to express his true feelings for her. So Percy was forced to demonstrate his feelings rather than making them audible, which was a lot easier on both of them. And although Mildred always thought of him as kind and mannerly, his slowness and docility annoyed her so much that she never took his intentions seriously, except once.

Last night at the Shingle, Crook had barged in and broken up their conversation, grabbed Mildred by the arm, and pushed her outside through the silver doors. He'd ordered her to get in the car—a pink and gold '59 Mercury—and he jumped in and started gunning the motor. When she didn't budge, he backed the car up so fast that it stalled and ran over her left foot. Drunk and aggravated because his anger was being diverted, Crook leaped from the car and hauled off and slapped Mildred's face until she thought it was in her best interest to go ahead and get in.

She had pushed her platinum wig back in place, pulling on the elastic bands and pushing bobby pins against her skull to make sure it was on tight again. Mildred always wore this wig when she went out. It made her feel like she was going someplace, like she was an elegant, sophisticated woman being taken out on the town by the man of her dreams. She got into the back seat of the car and pushed herself as far as she could into the corner of the soft pink seat because she didn't want to be within smelling distance of Crook. He climbed behind the wheel without saying a word and slammed the door.

"Just take me home, Crook," she'd said, trying hard not to scream or cry, but tears were already streaking her cocoa-colored foundation so that her own lighter skin tone showed through. She rolled her eyes at Crook until the pupils stuck in the corner sockets hard, but Crook couldn't see her or else he'd have hauled off and smacked her again. All she could think of now was how she was going to get him when she got home.

It only took five minutes to drive home from the Shingle, straight down Twenty-fourth and a left on Manual to Twenty-fifth. Mildred's mind was clicking like a stopwatch, trying to remember exactly where she'd situated the cast-iron skillet among the other pots and pans. Was it underneath the boilers? Or in the oven with chicken grease still in it? Didn't matter. She'd find it. She pressed her forehead against the cold wet glass and stared at the clapboard houses, most of which belonged to people she knew, some even family. Crook was barely staying in his lane. Mildred knew he was drunk on Orange Rock, but she didn't dare say anything to him. She'd been on the verge of being tipsy herself, but the lingering sting of Crook's hand on her face had slowly begun to break down her high. Anyway, there were no oncoming cars. Not at this time of night. Not in this hick town.

"I'm taking you home all right, don't worry about that," Crook said, trying to keep his eyes focused on the wiggling white line cutting through the two-lane street. "You think you're grown, don't you? Think you're just so damn grown." He wasn't expecting an answer and Mildred didn't give him one.

"You know you're gon' get your ass tore up, don't you? Gon' get enough of flirting with that simple-ass Percy and all the rest of 'em. You my wife, you understand me? My woman, and I don't want nobody talking to you like you ain't got no man. Especially in front of my face 'cause the next thang you know, I'll be hearing all kinds of mess up and down the streets. You understand me, girl? You listening to me?" He looked at Mildred through the rearview mirror, his eyes dilated so big that it looked like someone had just taken his picture with a flash cube. Mildred simply stared back at him, her tears all dried up now, and kept fumbling with her wig. Her fingers smelled like Evening in Paris, probably because she had sprayed it everywhere—between her legs, under her arms, on the balls of her feet, and beneath the fake skull of her wig. She didn't utter a word, just tried to ignore the pain in her foot and hissed and sucked saliva through her teeth.

Crook pulled into the cement driveway, and the right head-light barely missed the bark on the big oak tree as he cut the wheel and brought the car to an abrupt halt.

Mildred opened the door before they'd come to a complete stop, jumped out, slammed the door, and screamed, "Kiss my black ass!" She limped up the side steps toward the porch, turned, and yelled, "I hate you! I hate you! I hate you!" like a cheerleader.

All the lights were out in the house, but Mildred knew the kids weren't really asleep. She knew that as soon as they'd heard the car pull up the driveway, Freda had sprinted to the TV and flicked it off and ordered the rest of the kids to "hit it." Money, Bootsey, Angel, and Doll would have scattered like mice to their two bedrooms, closed their doors, and dived into bed to hide under the covers and wait to hear the boxing match they knew was sure to come. It was something they always dreaded when their parents came home from the bar. They'd squeeze their eyes tight pretending to be asleep, just in case Mildred or Crook decided to check on them, but they rarely did on nights like this, when Crook forgot he had kids and Mildred was too preoccupied with her own defense.

Mildred flicked on the dining room light and walked toward the bathroom. Her foot was killing her. When she looked in the mirror she saw that the blood from her lip had smudged all over the white mink collar of her blue suede coat. The blood had made the mink come to slick points, like the fur of a wet dog. Mildred felt herself getting mad all over again. She had cleaned a lot of white folks' houses to buy this coat, had kept it on layaway at Winkleman's for almost a year, and she knew that blood never came out, never.

When Mildred looked down, she saw more blood was soaking through the seams of the pockets and staining the white stitching around the buttonholes. The scent of her Evening in Paris permeated the bathroom and started to stink. She wanted to throw up. Instead, she went into the kitchen, grabbed the dishrack, and threw it high into the air so that it crashed and hit the edge of the sink. Everything breakable broke and smashed in the basin. Plates, glasses, cups and saucers, cereal bowls. Some things fell to the floor and shattered into jagged chips.

Mildred gritted her teeth, balled up her right fist, and pounded it on the pile of broken dishes. Her fist bled but she was too mad to notice.

She was just about to look for the skillet when she heard Crook stagger in the side door. Her rage welled up from a hollow cave in her stomach. "Oooooooo! You just irks me so. I'm surprised I ain't had a nervous breakdown by now. Always making a mountain out of a frigging molehill. Thinking thangs is happening when ain't nothing happening. You can't see for looking, you know that? I keep saying to myself, Mildred, leave this pitiful excuse for a man. I keep saying, Mildred, you know in your heart he ain't no good. Rotten, sorry. But how I'ma leave him with five growing kids to clothe and feed?" Her teeth felt like chalk and she scraped them together so hard that they slipped and she bit her tongue.

"Lord, have mercy on my soul," Mildred pleaded. "If somebody could show me the light, clear a path and give me an extra ounce of strength, I'd be out of here so damn fast make your head swim." Mildred was not a religious person, but she made sure her kids went to Shiloh Baptist every Sunday morning, though the only time she ever bothered to go herself was on Easter, Mother's Day, and Christmas. She shook her head back and forth, letting her eyes roll like loose marbles.

"Just keep on running your mouth, girl," Crook said, trying unsuccessfully to kick off his shoes.

Mildred's anger was flowing like hot lava. Pearls of sweat slid down her temples. Her jawbone was tightening as though she were biting down on rock candy.

"If I was trying to flirt with somebody for real, do you think I'd be stupid enough to do it right in front of your frigging face?" She put her hands on her hips and took soldier steps toward Crook. She didn't know where she was getting this courage from and surely it couldn't have been from God because he'd never given her any clue that being a fool would get her anywhere safe. "But you know what? Yeah, I'd love to screw Percy since you and everybody else swear I've been screwing him for years anyway. Who else was I supposed to be flirting with behind your back? Oh yeah, Porky and Joe Porter and Swift! I'd love to fuck all of 'em!"

"Mildred, you better shut your mouth up, girl. You know you're gon' get it. You know I ain't two minutes away from your behind." Crook had managed to get his shoes off, scattering wet red and gold leaves that had stuck to his soles. He slipped and fell backward against the china cabinet and plaster-of-Paris knickknacks tumbled all over the floor. He danced over the glass grapes, wishing wells, and miniature cats as though he were walking on hot sand at the beach.

Mildred didn't care at this point. She knew that whether she kept her mouth shut or open, she was going to get it anyway. His fist would snap against her head, or the back of his hard hand would swipe her face, or he'd hurl her against a wall until her brains rattled. It was always something, so long as it hurt.

Crook stumbled toward the living room and into the bedroom. He found his thick brown leather belt, the one Mildred occasionally used to chastise the kids for their wrongdoings, then he walked back out to the dining room. He pulled his shoulders back high, trying to act sober, and beckoned Mildred with his index finger. "Since you so damn smart, let's see if your ass is as tough as your mouth is, girl. Now get in here. You ain't had a good spanking in a while."

Mildred's courage vanished.

"Crook, please, don't. I'm sorry. I didn't mean what I said, none of it. I was just running my drunk mouth." Mildred was trying to move backward, away from him, but when she found herself in a corner and couldn't move another inch, she knew she was trapped. There was no one she could call to for help. She didn't want to scare the kids any more than they already were, and Mildred knew they were probably leaning against their bedroom doors, shivering like baby birds in a nest. All she could do was hope that he wouldn't take this any further than the belt to the point where he might just kill her this time. A drunk is always sorry later. "Crook, please don't hit me," she begged. "I promise I won't say another word. Please." Mildred was not the type to beg. Had never begged anybody for anything and now it didn't sound or feel right.

"Get on in here, girl. Your tears don't excite me," he said, snatching her by the wrists. "You think you're so cute, don't you?" Crook's face was contorted and had taken on a mon-

strous quality. It looked like every ounce of liquor and Indian
blood in his body had migrated to the veins in his face. He
yanked off her wig and threw it to the floor. Then he made her
drop her coat next to it, then her cream knit dress, and then her
girdle. When all she had on was her brassiere and panties, he
shoved her into the bedroom where she crawled to a corner of
the bed. Crook kicked the door shut and the kids cracked
theirs. Then they heard their mama screaming and their daddy
hollering and the whap of the belt as he struck her.

"Didn't I tell you you was getting too grown?" *Whap.*
"Don't you know your place yet, girl?" *Whap.*

"Yes, yes, Crook." *Whap.*

"Don't you know nothing about respect?" *Whap.* "Girl,
you gon' learn. I'm a man, not no toy." *Whap.* "You understand me?" *Whap.* "Make me look like no fool." *Whap.*

He threw the belt on the floor and collapsed next to Mildred
on the bed. The terror in her voice faded to whimpers and
sniffles. To the kids she sounded like Prince, their German
shepherd, when he had gotten hit by a car last year on Twenty-
fourth Street.

Mildred curled up into a tight knot and tried to find a spot
that would shelter her from Crook. She hoped he would fall
asleep, but he reached over and turned on the TV. Mildred
crept out the end of the bed and put on a slip.

"Where you going?" he asked.

"To the bathroom," she said. She closed the door behind
her and headed straight for the kitchen, tiptoed around the
broken glass, and opened the oven. She yanked the black skillet
out and slung the grease into the sink. Crook heard her and
came into the dining room to see what she was doing. Before he
knew what was happening, Mildred raised the heavy pan into
the air and charged into him, hitting him on the forehead with
a loud *throng*. Blood ran down over his eye and he grabbed her
and pushed her back into the bedroom. The kids heard them
bumping into the wall for what seemed like forever and then
they heard nothing at all.

Freda hushed the girls and made them huddle under a flimsy
flannel blanket on the bottom bunk bed. "Shut up, before they
hear us and we'll be next," she whispered loudly. She tried to

comfort the two youngest, Angel and Doll, by wrapping them inside her skinny arms, but it was no use. They couldn't stop crying. Since Freda was the oldest, she felt it was her place to act like an adult, but soon she started to cry too. None of them understood any of this, but when they heard the mattress squeaking, they knew what was happening.

Money ran from his room into Freda's. They all sat on the cold metal edge of the bed where the mattress didn't touch, sniffling, listening. They waited patiently, hoping that after five or ten minutes all they would hear would be Crook's snoring. They prayed that they could all finally go to sleep. But just when they had settled into the rhythm of silence—the humming of the refrigerator, the cars passing on Twenty-fourth Street, Prince yawning on the back porch—their parents' moans and groans would erupt again and poison the peace.

When Money couldn't stand it any more, he tiptoed back to his room. He flipped over his mattress, because the fighting always made him lose control of his bladder. He would say his prayers extra hard and swear that when he got older and got married he would never beat his wife, he wouldn't care what she did. He would leave first.

The girls slid into their respective bunks and lay there, not moving to scratch or even twitch. They tried to inch into their separate dreams but the sound of creaking grew louder and louder, then faster and faster.

"Why they try to kill each other, then do the nasty?" Bootsey asked Freda.

"Mama don't like doing it," Freda explained. "She only doing it so Daddy won't hit her no more."

"Sound like she like it to me. It's taking forever," said Bootsey. Angel and Doll didn't know what they were talking about.

"Just go to sleep," Freda said. And pretty soon the noises stopped and their eyelids drooped and they fell asleep.

THE kids were already on the sun porch watching Saturday morning cartoons when Mildred emerged from the bedroom. She had a diaper tied around her head and a new layer of pancake makeup on to camouflage the swelling. The kids didn't say anything about the purple patch of skin beneath her eye or her swollen lip. They just stared at her like she was a stranger they were trying to identify.

"What y'all looking at?" she said. "Y'all some of the nosiest kids I've ever seen in my life. Look at this house!" she snapped, trying to divert their attention. "It's a mess. Your daddy was drunk last night. Now I want y'all to brush your teeth and wash those dingy faces 'cause I ain't raising no heathens around here. Freda, make these kids some oatmeal. And I want this house spotless before you sit back down to watch a 'Bugs Bunny' or a 'Roadrunner,' and don't ask me no questions about them dishes. Just pick 'em up and throw that mess away. Cheap dishes anyway. Weren't worth a pot to piss in. Next time I'm buying plastic."

The kids were used to Mildred giving them orders, didn't know any other way of being told what to do, thought everybody's mama talked like theirs. And although they huffed and puffed under their breath and stomped their feet in defiance and made faces at her when her back was turned, they were careful not to get caught. "And I want y'all to get out of this house today. Go on outside somewhere and play. My nerves ain't this"—she snapped her fingers—"long today. And Freda, before you do anything, fix your mama a cup of coffee, girl. Two sugars instead of one, and lots of Pet milk."

Freda had already put water on for the coffee because she knew Mildred was mad. She had picked up the broken dishes, too. She didn't like seeing her mama all patched up like this. As a matter of fact, Freda hoped that by her thirteenth birthday her daddy would be dead or divorced. She had started to hate him, couldn't understand why Mildred didn't just leave him. Then they all could go on welfare like everybody else seemed to be doing in Point Haven. She didn't dare suggest this to her mama. Freda knew Mildred hated advice, so she did what her mama wasn't used to doing: kept her mouth shut.

When Crook finally got up, he smiled at the kids like nothing had happened. And like always on a Saturday morning after a rough night at the Shingle, he had somewhere important he had to go. When Mildred heard the Mercury's engine purring, she felt relieved because she knew she wouldn't have to see him again until late that night when he would most likely be drunk and asking where his dinner was, or tomorrow, when he'd be so hung over that he would walk straight to the bedroom and pass out.

Mildred counted her change and managed to muster up a few dollars. She decided to send the kids to the movies. Told them to sit through the feature twice, which was fine with them.

When they had finally skipped out the door and the house was as clean as an army barracks, Mildred had limped to the back porch and scrounged up the ax.

Her coffee was cold now, so she added some hot water to it and walked slowly into the living room. The house shoe helped cushion her foot against the hard floor, but it still hurt. She collapsed on the orange couch. Good, she thought. No Crook, no kids, and no dog. Mildred looked around the room, scanning its beige walls and the shiny floors she had waxed on her knees yesterday. The windows sparkled because she had cleaned the insides with vinegar and water. She had paid old ugly Deadman five dollars to clean the outsides. The house smelled and looked clean, just the way she liked it.

Her eyes claimed everything she saw. This is *my* house, she thought. I've worked too damn hard for you to be hurting me all these years. And me, like a damn fool, taking it. Like I'm your property. Like you own me or something. I pay all the bills around here, even this house note. I'm the one who scrubbed white folks' floors in St. Clemens and Huronville and way up there on Strawberry Lane to buy it.

Mildred sank back deeper into the couch and propped her good foot on top of the cocktail table. She tucked her lip in and took the diaper off her head. Then she ran her fingers over her thick braids. She began unbraiding them, though she had no intention of doing anything to her hair once it hung loose.

She looked out the window at the weeping willow trees. She remembered when she planted them. And who had had the garden limed? she thought. Paved the driveway and planted all those flowers, frozen under the dirt right now? Me. Who'd cooked hamburgers at Big Boy's and slung coconut cream pies to uppity white folks I couldn't stand to look in the eye 'cause they was sitting at the counter and I was standing behind it? Smothered in grease and smoke and couldn't even catch my breath long enough to go to the bathroom. And who was the one got corns and bunions from carrying plates of ribs and fried chicken back and forth at the Shingle when I was five months pregnant, while you hung off the back of a city garbage truck half drunk, waving at people like you were the president or the head of some parade?

She put her foot back on the floor and lit another cigarette.

Never even made up a decent excuse about what you did with your money. I know about Ernestine. I ain't no fool. Just been waiting for the right time. Me and the kids sitting in here with the lights and gas cut off and you give me two dollars. Say, "Here, buy some pork-n-beans and vanilla wafers for the kids, and if it's some change left get yourself a beer." A beer. Just what I needed, sitting in a cold-ass house in the dark.

Mildred's eyes scanned the faces of her five kids, framed in gold and black around the room.

And you got the nerve to brag about how pretty, how healthy and how smart your kids are. Don't they have your color. Your high cheekbones. Your smile. These ain't your damn kids. They mine. Maybe they got your blood, but they mine.

MILDRED had had Freda when she was seventeen, and the other kids had fallen out every nine or ten months after that, with the exception of one year between Freda and Money. Crook had told her he didn't want any more kids until he got on his feet. Freda was almost three months old when Mildred realized she was pregnant again. She was too scared to tell Crook, so she asked her sister-in-law what she should do. Curly Mae told her to take three five-milligram quinine tablets. When that didn't work, she told her to drink some citrate of magnesia and take a dry mustard bath. A week later she went to the bathroom feeling like she was going to have a bowel movement and had a miscarriage.

Motherhood meant everything to Mildred. When she was first carrying Freda, she didn't believe her stomach would actually grow, but when she felt it stretch like the skin of a drum and it swelled up like a small brown moon, she'd never been so happy. She felt there was more than just a cord connecting her to this boy or girl that was moving inside her belly. There was some special juice and only she could supply it. And sometimes when she turned over at night she could feel the baby turn inside her too, and she knew this was magic.

The morning Freda came, Crook was in a motel room on the North End with Ernestine. Curly Mae drove her to the hospital. From that point on, Mildred watched her first baby grow like a long sunrise. She was so proud of Freda that she let her body blow up and flatten for the next fifty-five months. It made her feel like she had actually done something meaningful with her life, having these babies did. And when she pulled the brush back and up through their thick clods of nappy hair, she smiled because it was her own hair she was brushing. These kids were her future. They made her feel important and gave her a feeling of place, of movement, a sense of having come from somewhere. Having babies was routine to a lot of women, but for Mildred it was unique every time; she didn't have a single regret about having had five kids—except one, and that was who had fathered them.

MILDRED lay down when she felt the heaviness of the pill beginning to work. Bells were ringing in her ears, and it made her think of Christmas, which was only two months away. For the past nine Christmases Mildred had had to hustle to buy Chatty Cathy dolls, Roll-a-Strollers, ice skates, racing car sets, sleds, and bicycles. Crook had helped her sneak them through the side door at midnight. She didn't know how she would manage this year.

She shook her head. Should've never let you come back after you got out the sanitarium, she thought. Should've let you have old sorry, ancient Ernestine, 'cause y'all deserved each other. But I felt bad for you 'cause I thought tuberculosis was gon' kill you. Guess alcohol must be the cure for what you got. You promised me, promised me, that when you got back on your feet you would take care of me and the kids like a husband is

supposed to do. Told me I wouldn't have to worry no more
about everything or work so damn hard. Well, *look* at me. My
nerves is about to pop. Red veins in my eyes like freeways. My
head always throbbing and my skin look like it been embalmed.
I'm twenty-seven years old, and I'm sick and tired of this shit.
And I don't care if I gotta turn tricks or work ten jobs—you
getting out of here this time for good.

Mildred tried to grit her teeth, but the pill wouldn't let her.
She wanted to scream, but the pill wouldn't let her. She felt like
crying too, but the pill wouldn't let her. All it would let her do
was sleep.

2

"KILL him," slurred Curly Mae, as she fell back in the recliner on
Mildred's sunporch. The sun was piercing through the Vene-
tian blinds, leaving yellow stripes across Curly's light brown
legs. "As the World Turns" was on television, but neither of
them was paying much attention to it. Liquor always made
Curly talk crazy.

"And if he put his hands on you again, the sucker deserve it.
I don't care if he is my brother, what give him the right to
disfigure you?" She gulped down the rest of her drink and
carefully set the plastic glass on the floor. It tipped over. "A
skunk is a skunk," Curly said. She lifted her arm up as if it
weighed a hundred pounds and plopped it in her lap.

Mildred was snapping string beans a few feet away from her.
They were landing all over the floor instead of in the bowl. She
was drunk too.

"I don't want to kill him, Curly, damn. I just don't want him
jumping on me when he get back. It's been two days and I ain't
heard nothing from him. I know where he is."

"He down there with that heffa, ain't he?"

"Yeah, I guess so. More power to him," said Mildred.

"Yeah, well, let me put it to you this way. You need something to protect yourself with. A gun'll scare a niggah."

"They scare me, too. You know that, girl."

"Now you tell me, what make more sense? To be waiting in

here scared with these kids, or be holding something to get his
ass on out of here? Remember the last time you called the
police? How long it take 'em to get here? Forty-five minutes,
and you know it take ten minutes from uptown. You could'a
been dead. As long as one niggah is trying to kill another, white
folks could care less."

"You right, chile, you right."

Mildred pushed the plastic bowl aside with her foot and
went to get the rest of the Old Crow. When she came back,
Curly was struggling to get out of the chair.

"Milly," she said, "I'll tell you what. I let you hold my gun
till you get him out of here. Can you lend me twenty dollars?"

"Twenty dollars? That's my gas bill money. Till when,
Curly?"

"Till Saturday morning or Sunday afternoon at the latest."

"Okay. But who's gon' show me how to use the gun?"

"I would, but I got so much to do over in that house today,
and Lord knows some of this liquor gotta wear off first."

There was a knock at the door. It was Deadman. He often
helped Mildred around the house. Of all Lucretia Bennett's
dumb and ugly sons, Deadman was the ugliest and dumbest.
He was in his early twenties and had the reading level of a fifth
grader. But he was reliable and he was as nice as nice could be,
so whenever he stopped by Mildred felt obligated to keep him
busy, even if she didn't have anything for him to do. Trying to
find things that needed to be fixed wasn't hard, because Crook
had never fixed much of anything. After Deadman did whatever Mildred had asked him to, the next problem was getting
him to go home.

Mildred opened the door.

"Hey, good-lookin'," she said. Deadman smiled, showing off
his tiny yellow teeth. His head was shaped like a big almond
from one angle and a small watermelon from another. Deadman knew he was ugly, and for that he was sort of cute. He kind
of grew on Mildred and the kids. He had a contagious sense of
humor. He'd have her and the kids on the floor in stitches when
he'd tell them all the goings on in the neighborhood. He knew
who was screwing who, who'd just been put out, who'd gotten
her behind kicked, whose lights and gas were turned off, and

whose car had been repossessed. He was more like a reporter than a gossiper, because he wasn't malicious. He also knew how to hustle and always had a few dollars in his pockets. Lots of times he lent Mildred money when she was short.

"I was going out to the butcher's and wanted to know if you needed something. Mama say they got a sale on neck bones and pork chops today."

"Why, thank you, Deadman, but I just lent Curly my last. We got enough meat around here to last us for a while, though. Tell me something, you know how to shoot a gun?"

"Yeah, everybody know how to shoot a gun. Pull the damn trigger." He started laughing, and his eyes darted past Mildred. He was looking for Freda. He had a silent crush on her, but he'd never let Mildred know it or else she would've probably changed her mind about him. He always bought Freda potato chips, fruit punch, chewing gum—small things he could give her without seeming obvious. As a matter of fact, that's what brought him over to their house so often. He would rake leaves when there were only a few on the ground. He'd clean out the stoker when it didn't need it; clean Mildred's storm windows; paint the bricks around the base of the house and along the driveway, and do anything else he could find.

"Can you show me how?" Mildred asked.

"Yeah, you got it here?"

"I'll send it over by one of the kids," Curly said, brushing past him. "I'll stick it in my old blue purse."

Mildred slipped her the twenty and Curly inched down the steps and pranced across the street to her house. A few minutes later, her oldest son returned with the purse. After Deadman showed Mildred how to use it, she hid it between her box spring and mattress.

MILDRED knew how to pretend, and that's exactly what she'd been doing since Crook had come home from the hospital. Pretended she didn't know he was still messing around with Ernestine. Pretended not to know that Ernestine's oldest daughter looked just like Crook. She didn't know what he saw in that evil, bug-eyed drunk. Ernestine had never liked Mildred either, from the time they were kids. Mildred was not only better-looking, to put it mildly, but was much smarter and never had trouble attracting boys. Mildred always thought that just because she was poor didn't mean she had to look it.

Ernestine never smiled at anyone because her two front teeth had been knocked out by some man years ago. People said it was Crook who did it, but no one really knew. One thing Mildred did know was that even though Ernestine had had Crook's baby, he had married her, not Ernestine. At the time, she felt like the best woman had won. Hell, any woman can have a baby, Mildred thought, but can't every woman get the man.

When Crook still hadn't come home by evening, Mildred decided she couldn't wait another minute. She put her clothes on, left the kids watching "Million Dollar Movie," and walked down to Ernestine's house. She saw the Mercury parked in the alley. Mildred was furious, not because he had run to Ernestine, but because he wasn't man enough to face her. She contemplated picking up the brick she saw lying next to the car and breaking all the windows. Then she remembered that she was the one who had bought this car. She thought she might throw it through Ernestine's window but finally decided against that, too. Instead, she walked back home in the snow and packed everything Crook owned in cardboard boxes and trash bags. Then she called a cab and rode back to Ernestine's house and plopped them into a huge snowbank.

A week went by and Mildred still hadn't heard anything from Crook. It was snowing again on Sunday night, and she was watching a new group called The Beatles on "The Ed Sullivan Show." Funny-looking little white boys with suits that looked too small, with stingy little collars. There was a noise at the side door, and Mildred thought it was Prince, but she had put him on the back porch. She went to the door and there was Crook, sitting on the steps, snow soaking through the seat of his pants, his teeth hanging out of his mouth, looking like some orphan. She let him in, pushed him toward one of the kids' rooms and cracked open a window because he smelled like he'd been living in a flophouse. Crook passed out.

Mildred put on her snow boots and car coat, went to her

bedroom, slid the gun from under the mattress, and put it in her purse. Then she eased the keys from Crook's pocket and drove down to the Red Shingle, where she knew she would find Ernestine.

THERE was nothing red about the Red Shingle, except for the trim painted around the white windows. And they weren't really windows either, because you couldn't see through them. They were squares cut into the brick wall. The parking lot could only hold twenty or thirty cars—big cars, which is what everybody drove in Point Haven. The bigger the car, the more stature you had, though a lot of the men who drove these cars lived in them, too. Kept their clothes in the trunk, their shaving equipment in the glove compartment, and a quilt in the back seat in case one of their lady friends wouldn't put them up for the night. Most black folks considered their cars evidence of their true worth. That and the gold capped over their teeth. And Lord, they flashed those. Some of them, mainly folks who had migrated from the South to work in the factories near Detroit, tried to out-tooth each other. They started out simple: a gold cap. Then they moved into gold and diamonds, then stars, and last, their initials.

Folks hung out at the Red Shingle because it was the only place blacks were welcome.

Drinking was the single most reliable source of entertainment for a lot of people in Point Haven. Alcohol was a genuine elixir, granting instant relief from the mundane existence that each and every one of them led. It was as though the town had some hold over them, always hinting that one day it would magically provide everything they would ever need, could ever need, and satisfy all their desires. No one was the least bit curious about anything that went on outside Point Haven. Here it was 1964, and most folks had never heard of Malcolm X and only a few had some idea who Martin Luther King was. They lived as if they were sleepwalking or waiting around for something else to happen.

Most of the black men couldn't find jobs, and as a result, they had so much spare time on their hands that when they were stone cold broke, bored with themselves, or pissed off about everything because life turned out to be such a disappointment, their dissatisfaction would burst open and their rage would explode. This was what usually passed for masculinity, and it was often their wives or girlfriends or whores who felt the fallout.

Since the Shingle was in the middle of South Park and everybody lived within walking distance, the majority of these men hung out here. And people came from as far as New Winton and St. Clemens, thirty miles away, to hear an occasional live band.

The Shingle was right across the street from Miss Moore's whorehouse, three doors down from Stinky's Liquor Store. Dove Road, at the mouth of Stinky's driveway, was considered a busy street because it was the artery that led to the intersection at Twenty-fourth. It was also the first side street in the black neighborhood to be paved and get streetlights.

The only time the Red Shingle ever saw a white face swing through its silver doors was when a Canadian came looking for brown thighs and breasts. This had been going on for so long that no one paid much attention to them when they showed up, except for the few women who sat at the bar and called themselves prostitutes. Most of them were just welfare mothers trying to pick up some extra change, or wives whose husbands were out of work or had left them.

Fletcher Armstrong owned the Shingle. He was one of the only black men fortunate enough to have some money in his family. His father, who lived fifty-four miles away in Detroit, was in the numbers business. It was supposed to be a well-kept secret, but everybody knew it and always had. Fletcher lived out on Ross Road in a house he had had built. It was a split—three levels—like the white folks' houses up on Strawberry Lane. Sometimes on their way out to the country, black folks from South Park would drive by Fletcher's house just to ooh and aah. Some were quite jealous, and the most considerate thing they could find to say was nasty. "Niggahs thank they something when they get a little money, don't they? Gotta throw it all up in your face. Look at them pink shingles. Wouldn't you say they was too damn loud to be on your house?

Can't take the country out of a niggah, can you?" But some people were quite proud. "It sure is nice to see colored people moving up in the world, ain't it? Ten years ago, weren't no colored people even living out here. Now look. And look at them pink shingles—they beautiful, ain't they?"

Fletcher had green eyes and peach skin. He didn't associate with the regular black people of Point Haven because he thought he was better than they were. The closest he came was when he opened up the Shingle every afternoon and started heating up the grease in the kitchen for fried chicken and french fries and turned on the grill for the barbecued ribs he was famous for.

In one tight corner of the bar there was a platform barely big enough for a singer and piano player, but on many a night an entire four-piece combo managed to squeeze in and play forty-five-minute sets of jazz, blues, and rhythm-and-blues until the Shingle closed its doors at two o'clock in the morning, when most of the people were fatally drunk and still didn't want to go home. People like Ernestine Jackson.

SURE enough, when Mildred walked in she was sitting at the bar, with her stingy hair plastered down to her head with grease, and lint balls coating the tips of old curls. Ernestine was talking just as loud as always. Mildred sat down next to her and lit an L&M.

"I just want to tell you that you can have the sorry son-of-a-bitch if you want him. He's at the house. I'm divorcing him as soon as the courthouse open up in the morning, or God ain't my witness." Mildred got up from the bar stool, and walked toward the bathroom. She could hear the soles of Ernestine's shoes shuffling on the tile behind her.

Mildred was in front of the mirror when Ernestine barged in. She tucked in her lip and applied more lipstick on top of an already fresh coat.

Ernestine kicked the door shut and put her hands on her hips.

"Look, cunt, you ain't *giving* him to me, 'cause he was about to leave you anyway."

"Is that so," Mildred said, watching Ernestine from the mirror.

"Crook never loved you in the first place, and you know it. You tricked him into marrying you. You was supposed to be so goddamn respectable. Hah! Now look. He done come back to me and his daughter after all this time. Life is a bitch, ain't it, Mildred?"

Mildred wanted to reach inside her purse and blow Ernestine's brains out, but she knew this hussy didn't have any. Besides, she wasn't going to jail for shooting some scag who wanted her trifling husband. She simply looked at Ernestine like she was a bad joke, shook her head back and forth, laughed, and left the bathroom.

So after ten years of sneaking, waiting, and loving the man who had married her rival, Ernestine finally had her chance. And like a fool, Crook went with her. Mildred felt like she'd shed ten layers of dead skin. She knew she'd made the right decision because when she sat down to think about it, the only thing she'd ever appreciated about Crook all these years was the fact that he was a good lover when he was sober and had given her five beautiful and healthy kids. But like most handsome men, she thought, screwing and making babies was about the only thing they did with dedication and consistency, without much thought or consideration, and were so damn proud afterward, that you'd swear they'd won the Kentucky Derby or something.

Sandra Cisneros

SANDRA CISNEROS is one of the most accomplished poets and writers of fiction in Chicano letters. She has published in numerous journals, including *Revista Chicano-Riquena, Spoon River Quarterly, Third Woman,* and *Imagine,* to name but a few. Ms. Cisneros is also the author of *Bad Boys* (Mango Press, 1980), *The House On Mango Street* (Arte Publico, 1984) and *My Wicked Wicked Ways* (Third Woman Press, 1987). Her accolades include honors from the National Endowment for the Humanities, the Illinois Arts Council and the Dobie-Paisano Fellowship.

Cisneros's work always presents a simultaneous reflection between her inner selfhood and the surrounding social world. Her work is thus always personal, sometimes almost painfully so, without falling into a sterile psychoanalysis. Instead, there is a constant, hearty, and perceptive encounter with the local world in which the author lives. The result is a lyrical voice which sings to us about how our own lives are written in and by our relationships with the people and places around us. Whether Sandra Cisneros is writing about a North American barrio or the south of France she allows us to feel how we would know the world if we were all poets.

In her award-winning *The House On Mango Street,* Sandra Cisneros presents scenes from the childhood of a woman named Esperanza. A series of vignettes and reflections allows us to witness a creative spirit come to self-awareness. The first chapters present us with descriptions of the house, Mango Street, and Esperanza and her two friends Lucy and Rachel through the eyes and voice of Esperanza as a child. As Esperanza matures, she develops her voice's range and subtlety, and her life is revealed both through her own action and in the lives of her family and friends. The conclusion to the book is a spiritual rebirth for Esperanza as a writer from Mango Street.

Mango Street is an essential component in Esperanza's story, not simply a mute setting. In the opening story, the family's new house on Mango Street is declared by Esperanza unequal to her expectations. Esperanza's parents had always embodied their hopes for the future in terms of the house they hoped to own. The small, somewhat dreary house on Mango street, while better than previous apartments, is not what her mama had "dreamed up in the stories she told us before we went to bed."

Esperanza shares these dreams. Her hopes for the future are symbolized by a house which she someday hopes to own. Throughout the book, the vision of the house is elaborated. It begins as a physical space, "one I can point to." In the chapter "Bums in the Attic," the house becomes a space for the development of her own values. The final chapter about the house itself reveals it as a place of autonomy: "Not a man's house. Not a daddy's. A house all my own."

In the conclusion, the house of Esperanza's dreams is revealed as a place where she will write story's about her life. "Only a house quiet as snow, a space for myself to go, clean as paper before the poem." The house becomes a place where she goes "back for the ones who could not get out." Thus the house of Cisneros's dreams is not an escapist fantasy. Instead, the house is where Esperanza can incorporate the fact that "she will always be Mango Street" into her sense of self.

This new self-awareness is really a rebirth for Esperanza. Three old sisters (an allusion to witches) tell Esperanza to make a wish and that it will come true. She senses that they know she wants a house of her own, and, for the first time, feels guilty about the selfishness of her wish. Instead of the chiding Esperanza expects, however, the sisters instruct her to always remember Mango Street. "You must remember to come back." they tell Esperanza. "For the ones who cannot leave as easily as you." In the last chapter, Esperanza leaves Mango Street knowing that by writing their stories she will indeed come back "for the ones I left behind. For the ones who cannot get out."

In her work since *Mango Street,* Sandra Cisneros has continued her reflections on life as something lived in an immediate physical and psychic space. *My Wicked Wicked Ways,* a collection of poetry, presents scenes from the many cities and nations where Ms. Cisneros has lived and worked. Houston, Paris, Venice, and other "barrios" become the settings for the poet's encounter with life. The entire collection charts the development of a person over time, from childhood through an adult relationship. The variety of the poems' themes maintains the episodic feel of remembrance struck in *Mango Street.*

All of Cisneros's poems share the same unflinching devotion to capturing the reality of the places and persons in her life. These experiences and memories are presented to us along with the emotions they evoked. The Mango Street that Esperanza left behind is thus carried within Sandra Cisneros as a symbol of responsibility to each of the places about which she writes.

—Rick Olguin

Excerpts from

THE HOUSE ON MANGO STREET

Marin

MARIN'S boyfriend is in Puerto Rico. She shows us his letters and makes us promise not to tell anybody they're getting married when she goes back to P.R. She says he didn't get a job yet, but she is saving the money she gets from selling Avon and taking care of her cousins.

Marin says that if she stays here next year, she is going to get a real job downtown because that's where the best jobs are, since you always get to look beautiful and get to wear nice clothes and can meet someone in the subway who might marry and take you to live in a big house far away.

But next year Louie's parents are going to send her back to her mother with a letter saying she is too much trouble, and that is too bad because I like Marin. She is older and knows lots of things. She is the one who told us how the Baby's sister got pregnant and what cream is best for taking off moustache hair and if you count the white flecks on your fingernails you can know how many boys are thinking of you and lots of other things I can't remember now.

We never see Marin until her aunt comes home from work, and even then she can only stay out in front. She is there every night with the radio. When the light in her aunt's room goes out, Marin lights a cigarette and it doesn't matter if it's cold out or if the radio doesn't work or if we've got nothing to say to each other. What matters, Marin says, is for the boys to see us and for us to see them. And since Marin's skirts are shorter and since her eyes are pretty, and since Marin is already older than us in many ways, the boys that do pass say stupid things like I am in love with those two green apples you call eyes, give them to me why don't you. And Marin just looks at them without even blinking and is not afraid.

Marin, under the streetlight, dancing by herself, is singing the same song somewhere. I know. Is waiting for a car to stop, a star to fall, someone to change her life. Anybody.

Those Who Don't

THOSE who don't know any better come into our neighborhood scared. They think we're dangerous. They think we will attack them with shiny knives. They are stupid people who are lost and got here by mistake.

But we aren't afraid. We know the guy with the crooked eye is Davey the Baby's brother, and the tall one next to him in the straw brim, that's Rosa's Eddie V. and the big one that looks like a dumb grown man, he's Fat Boy, though he's not fat anymore nor a boy.

All brown all around, we are safe. But watch us drive into a neighborhood of another color and our knees go shakity-shake and our car windows get rolled up tight and our eyes look straight. Yeah. That is how it goes and goes.

There Was an Old Woman She Had So Many Children She Didn't Know What to Do

ROSA VARGAS' kids are too many and too much. It's not her fault you know, except she is their mother and only one against so many.

They are bad those Vargas, and how can they help it with only one mother who is tired all the time from buttoning and bottling and babying, and who cries every day for the man who left without even leaving a dollar for bologna or a note explaining how come.

The kids bend trees and bounce between cars and dangle upside down from knees and almost break like fancy museum vases you can't replace. They think it's funny. They are without respect for all things living, including themselves.

But after a while you get tired of being worried about kids who aren't even yours. One day they are playing chicken on Mr. Benny's roof. Mr. Benny says, hey ain't you kids know better than to be swinging up there. Come down, you come down right now, and then they just spit.

See. That's what I mean. No wonder everybody gave up. Just stopped looking out when little Efren chipped his buck tooth on a parking meter and didn't even stop Refugia from getting her head stuck between two slats in the back gate and nobody looked up not once the day Angel Vargas learned to fly and dropped from the sky like a sugar donut, just like a falling star, and exploded down to earth without even an "Oh."

Alicia Who Sees Mice

CLOSE your eyes and they'll go away her father says, or you're just imagining. And anyway, a woman's place is sleeping so she can wake up early with the tortilla star, the one that appears early just in time to rise and catch the hind legs hidden behind the sink, beneath the four-clawed tub, under the swollen floorboards nobody fixes, in the corner of your eyes.

Alicia, whose mama died, is sorry there is no one older to rise and make the lunchbox tortillas. Alicia, who inherited her mama's rolling pin and sleepiness, is young and smart and studies for the first time at the university. Two trains and a bus, because she doesn't want to spend her whole life in a factory or behind a rolling pin. Is a good girl, my friend, studies all night and sees the mice, the ones her father says do not exist. Is afraid of nothing except four-legged fur and fathers.

Geraldo No Last Name

SHE met him at a dance. Pretty too, and young. Said he worked in a restaurant, but she can't remember which one. Geraldo.

That's all. Green pants and Saturday shirt. Geraldo. That's what he told her.

And how was she to know she'd be the last one to see him alive. An accident, don't you know. Hit and run. Marin, she goes to all those dances. Uptown, Logan. Embassy. Palmer. Aragon. Fontana. The Manor. She likes to dance. She knows how to do cumbias and salsas and rancheras even. And he was just someone she danced with. Somebody she met that night. That's right.

That's the story. That's what she said again and again. Once to the hospital people and twice to the police. No address. No name. Nothing in his pockets. Ain't it a shame.

Only Marin can't explain why it mattered, the hours and hours, for somebody she didn't even know. The hospital emergency room. Nobody but an intern working all alone. And maybe if the surgeon would've come, maybe if he hadn't lost so much blood, if the surgeon had only come, they would know who to notify and where.

But what difference does it make? He wasn't anything to her. He wasn't her boyfriend or anything like that. Just another *brazer* who didn't speak English. Just another wetback. You know the kind. The ones who always look ashamed. And what was she doing out at three A.M. anyway? Marin who was sent home with her coat and some aspirin. How does she explain it?

She met him at a dance. Geraldo in his shiny shirt and green pants. Geraldo going to a dance.

What does it matter?

They never saw the kitchenettes. They never knew about the two-room flats and sleeping rooms he rented, the weekly money orders sent home, the currency exchange. How could they?

His name was Geraldo. And his home is in another country. The ones he left behind are far away. They will wonder. Shrug. Remember. Geraldo. He went north . . . we never heard from him again.

No Speak English

MAMACITA is the big mama of the man across the street, third-floor front. Rachel says her name ought to be *Mamasota,* but I think that's mean.

The man saved his money to bring her here. He saved and saved because she was alone with the baby boy in that country. He worked two jobs. He came home late and he left early. Every day.

Then one day Mamacita and the baby boy arrived in a yellow taxi. The taxi door opened like a waiter's arm. Out stepped a tiny pink shoe, a foot soft as a rabbit's ear, then the thick ankle, a fluttering of hips, fuchsia roses and green perfume. The man had to pull her, the taxicab driver had to push. Push, pull. Push, pull. Poof!

All at once she bloomed. Huge, enormous, beautiful to look at, from the salmon-pink feather to the tip of her hat down to the little rosebuds of her toes. I couldn't take my eyes off her tiny shoes.

Up, up, up the stairs she went with the baby boy in a blue blanket, the man carrying her suitcases, her lavender hatboxes, a dozen boxes of satin high heels. Then we didn't see her.

Somebody said because she's too fat, somebody because of the three flights of stairs, but I believe she doesn't come out because she is afraid to speak English, and maybe this is so since she only knows eight words. She knows to say: *He not here* for when the landlord comes, *No speak English* if anybody else comes, and *holy smokes.* I don't know where she learned this, but I heard her say it one time and it surprised me.

My father says when he came to this country he ate ham and eggs for three months. Breakfast, lunch and dinner. Ham and eggs. That was the only words he knew. He doesn't eat ham and eggs anymore.

Whatever her reasons, whether she is fat or can't climb the stairs or is afraid of English, she won't come down. She sits all day by the window and plays the Spanish radio show and sings all the homesick songs about her country in a voice that sounds like a sea gull.

Home. Home. Home is a house in a photograph, a pink house, pink as hollyhocks with lots of startled light. The man paints the walls of the apartment pink, but it's not the same you know. She still sighs for her pink house, and then I think she cried. I would.

Sometimes the man gets disgusted. He starts screaming and you can hear it all the way down the street.

Ay, she says, she is sad.

Oh, he says, not again.

¿Cuándo, cuándo, cuándo? she asks.

Ay, Caray! We *are* home. This *is* home. Here I am and here I stay. Speak English. Speak English. Christ!

Ay! Mamacita, who does not belong, every once in a while lets out a cry, hysterical, high, as if he had torn the only skinny thread that kept her alive, the only road out to that country.

And then to break her heart forever, the baby boy who has begun to talk, starts to sing the Pepsi commercial he heard on T.V.

No speak English, she says to the child who is singing in the language that sounds like tin. No speak English, no speak English, and bubbles into tears. No, no, no as if she can't believe her ears.

Jessica Tarahata Hagedorn

I HAVE known Jessica Hagedorn for nearly twenty years, since I finished the graduate program in creative writing at San Francisco State University. (Jessica herself has never been to college.) Today the literature professor in me labels Jessica Hagedorn's poetry and fiction "surrealistic"—as a good scholar, I opt for the proper definition in order to find a sense of place for Hagedorn's work. I dusted off the literature handbook I've had since high school and looked up surrealism. Instead of the definition there was a picture of Jessica. This is no play on an old Rodney Dangerfield joke; there actually *was* a picture of Jessica. I'd put it there years ago in an irreverent moment, in an attempt to "redefine the mainstream" of American literature. But even "redefining" is too mild—Jessica's words want to "exert control over images," as she stated in an interview in the *San Francisco Examiner.* That's Jessica versus surrealism—one who is the living definition and the other a concept that falls into the school, the form. The school is down for the count when one reads Hagedorn's work.

The setting for her work is America and the Philippines. Jessica Hagedorn's first novel, *Dogeaters* (Pantheon, 1990), was nominated for a National Book Award. Writer Robert Stone called *Dogeaters* "the definitive novel of the encounter between the Philippines and America and their history of mutual illusion, antagonism and ambiguous affection." Hagedorn describes the politics, culture, and identity of her literary Philippines as a colonial sense of self born out of "three hundred years in a Spanish convent and fifty years in Hollywood."

Every Hagedorn word is in active resistance to what the brain holds as conventional literature, conventional normality, our daily life. In her poetry/prose novel *Petfood & Tropical Apparitions* (1981) she writes:

> she fell in love once
> and the wounds never healed
> it was romance
> old as the hills
> predictable in its maze
> what medieval tapestry he wove
> to keep her still
>
> gazelles loped
> past their window
> and veils kept out the sun
> she had her own take on things,
> her perfume-scented version
> of the story
> never mind that
> he always won,
> leaving unfinished poems
> under her bed
> orchestras strung upside-down
> from the ceiling
> traces of blood as souvenirs
> of their exclusive
> combat zone

Hagedorn's literary life as novelist, poet, singer, and performance artist was born not out of a college creative writing class but out of a hip, urban, transpacific and transcontinental, multiracial, multicultural, multilingual mixed-media voice that invades, colonizes, and occupies the reader's mind.

Jessica and I once gave a reading together at Rice University during a celebration of Asian Week in Houston. After a Houston thunderstorm, she told me, "Last night I dreamt you were a yellow snake." I told her, "I dreamt goldfish were melting in the air between us." It may have been the hippest thing I ever said. I had been colonized and occupied. I went home and put her picture next to the definition of surrealism.

—*Shawn Wong*

Excerpts from
PET FOOD AND TROPICAL
APPARITIONS

Pet Food

In the distance I could hear the Four Tops singing
Standing in the shadows of love . . .

"My CANDELABRA ARE MISSING!!!" Auntie Greta's Mario
Lanza shriek pierced the tense silence in the living room of our
tiny, overfurnished apartment.

My mother Consuelo rolled her eyes at the familiar sound of
Auntie Greta's high-pitched voice. "There he goes again," she
muttered to herself, annoyed. She was not speaking to me.

I studied my beautiful mother's face, wanting to touch it.
Even in anger she seemed so vulnerable. I liked to think she was
vulnerable to me, ever since my entomologist father had run off
with the nubile Princess Taratara to the rain forests of Min-
danao. They claimed to be on an expedition hunting for prehis-
toric dragonflies.

We were sitting across from each other in the cluttered
living room: my mother Consuelo on the Empress Josephine
couch, her frail body lost in the busyness around her. A leopard-
skin rug hung on the wall above her head. The rug was one of
her prize possessions—a gift from my father when they were
still together. I was seated on the ornately carved Spanish colonial chair we had brought on the ship with us when we came
from the islands. My mother and I had been sitting like this for
more than an hour, and my ass was killing me. I had been trying
to explain why it was important for me to move out of her
house.

"Dios mio!" she kept moaning. "You'll be the death of me
yet!" Her eyes hardened, and her voice suddenly changed from

weepy martyr to righteous district attorney. "I know who's responsible for this. It's that so-called 'friend' of yours, Boogie. I warned you about him, but of course you never listen. You're always defending those smelly friends of yours."

"Boogie doesn't *smell,*" I retorted. "He wears tangerine oil."

"That boy smells like a fruit, all right," my mother said, smugly. "He's no good—a drug addict with too many crazy ideas. DON'T SMIRK!" she snapped at me. "I wasn't born yesterday, you know. It's all in the eyes, George. I can see the *end* in his eyes. That boy's always hopped up. Pretends he plays the piano. Pretends he plays the guitar. A DISGRACE TO THE RACE, that's what he is. Oh, well," she sighed again, "wasn't he born here anyway?"

"Yeah," I said. "In Stockton. His family covers their couches and lampshades in plastic."

My mother was triumphant. "*I knew it!* That boy's an American-born pinoy with no class. He's going to drag you down with him."

"That's not true," I said. "Boogie's one of the gentlest, most sensitive people I know. He looks out for me."

"Looks out for you??? You think I don't know about your little adventures with that low-life fairy? Always running off to so-called concerts with him, coming home at three in the morning and watching television until seven? He smiles up in my face and says, 'Good evening, Mrs. Sand. Thank you so much for letting George go out with me.' Meanwhile, you come home late and can't sleep at all! *DRUGS!* Drugs and sex—that's all you kids thing about! You were all right before you met him," she whined.

We went around in circles, crying and hurling accusations at each other, until Auntie Greta stormed into the apartment, his Chihuahua Revenge on a rhinestone-studded leash. Revenge was quivering and shaking and yapping at everything in sight.

My mother pressed a carefully manicured hand to her forehead. "GRETA, PLEASE—that dog of yours should be put to sleep. *She stinks.* Everytime you drag her in here I have to get down on my hands and knees and shampoo the rug! And her goddam yelping gives me a headache."

I smiled. "Hello, Auntie Greta," I said, pretending my mother wasn't there. "How's your day been?"

Auntie Greta gave my mother a deadly look. "Thank you, dear—it's been perfectly dreadful. My antique Barcelona candelabra are missing."

"One of your boys must've stolen them," my mother suggested sweetly.

Auntie Greta plopped down on a pink brocade Louis Quinze chair and placed the shivering Chihuahua on his lap. "My boys? My dear, how could you say such a thing!"

Auntie Greta, my dear uncle and aunt all in one, was a distant relative on my mother's side of the family. He had been in America for twenty years and worked in San Francisco as a semi-fashionable hairdresser in a stuffy salon that still believed in pincurls. His clients were a small but loyal group of wealthy matrons who liked their hair set, teased, and dyed silver-blue. When my mother left my father and took me to America, leaving behind all the tropicalismé in our lives, she had no choice but to look up Auntie Greta, the only person she knew in San Francisco. Auntie Greta helped raise me by acting as a handy and enthusiastic chaperone, especially when my mother didn't want to be bothered. I was very fond of Auntie Greta—he loved the movies as much as I did and tried unsuccessfully to sneak me into the gay bars he frequented so I could have my first drink with him, "just like a grown-up." He looked at me with some embarrassment while my mother lit a cigarette and ignored me.

"Greta, dear, you know exactly what I'm talking about," she said coolly. "I'm referring to those boys on the street you pick up and bring home—the ones you feed and clothe, who are always beating you up and burglarizing your apartment."

Martha and The Vandellas "Your Love Is Like a Heat Wave" was churning in my head as I looked away, avoiding Auntie Greta's pained expression. I had to agree—my mother was right. In fact, that was the very reason she had asked Auntie Greta to move out of our apartment—he kept bringing these surly and suspicious youths home, making my mother more paranoid than ever. He finally moved to a studio on the floor directly above us and, except for the times when he was involved in a "hot romance," we saw him everyday at dinner-time.

Auntie Greta's eyes widened in horror. "Oh my god, Consuelo! You don't think that sweet boy Alex could've done it, do you? Not Alex! He's not capable of such an act."

My mother sailed off into the kitchen to make a pot of coffee. "Oh, no?" she called out cheerfully from the kitchen. "Your boy Alex is certainly capable of anything, darling. It's all in his eyes. *I can tell.* Plus he's got a weak chin—that's why he's trying to grow that mangy beard. Who does he think he's kidding? As I was just telling my daughter, George—who never listens to her mother, of course—all these young people are after the same thing these days—drugs and sex, drugs and sex—and they want it all for free."

I sat there quietly, listening to my mother putter around the kitchen and trying not to lose my temper. I turned to Auntie Greta. "I'm leaving."

"Leaving? But you haven't had dinner yet," he said, looking concerned.

I shook my head. "I'm leaving home—and the sooner the better. That's why she's pissed at me."

"I wondered why she was pretending you were invisible," Auntie Greta said, "but then I've always thought Consuelo was into high drama. I never know what to expect when I come downstairs. She's so moody."

"Well, I'm packed and ready to go."

"Do you have any money?" Auntie Greta asked.

I shrugged. "A little bit I saved from the birthday check Dad sent."

He stared at me with some amazement. "But that's not enough! Where are you going to go? You don't even have a job! Where are you going to live? This is all too sudden, even for me—," Auntie Greta said, getting more upset by the minute. "Dear girl, why don't you stay here a while longer, get yourself a job, then move out? That's the sensible way to do things."

I grinned. "Oh, Auntie Greta. I'll be all right. I have friends. They'll look out for me."

"Look out for you? Who's going to look out for you the way

your mother and I look out for you? Consuelo may be tempera-
mental, but she's a tigress who loves you *fiercely.*"
I grimaced, but Auntie Greta ranted on. "It gets in the way
sometimes, but she cares, she really does!"
"I can't take it," I said, "she's too intolerant. And she hates
Boogie so much."
Auntie Greta sighed. "She just doesn't understand the
American way of life. It's too fast for her. Everything's chang-
ing, including you." He paused, studying me carefully. "You're
not in trouble, are you?"
I shook my head, still grinning. I was going to miss Auntie
Greta very much.
"What about drugs?" he asked. "Consuelo informed me
that she found a joint in your bookbag once. I had to give her
some of my Valiums to calm her down. Was that true?"
I nodded, remembering how Consuelo had burst into my
room the morning after she found it, as I was on my way to
school. "Everyone experiments," was all I had said to her,
which sent her further into her rage.
"Dear George," Auntie Greta pleaded, "you must be careful
about the company you keep. Who am I to tell you this, you're
probably thinking . . . but I know. Aren't you going to college?
Don't you have any plans?" Auntie Greta's desperate tone
made me nervous.
"Not really," I replied. "I just want to live on my own for a
while. Maybe write a little bit. See what happens."
"See what happens? My dear, you're much too vague—no
wonder Consuelo's so upset!" Auntie Greta groaned.
I stared off into space.
He got up from the chair and reached into the pocket of his
elegantly tailored gabardine pants. "Here. It isn't much, but it
should help," he said, handing me a roll of bills.
I tried to give it back to him, but he ignored my outstretched
hand. "Take it, for godsake—I know you'll need it," Auntie
Greta said, in a firm tone of voice that was new to me. "Let us
know as soon as you get settled. And please—please be careful."
I felt like a son being sent off to an unpopular war as I stood

uncertainly in the dim foyer, waiting for my mother to come out of the kitchen so I could say goodbye. She never did.

Maybe she heard everything that was said between Auntie Greta and me and, angry as she was, that was enough for her. She often said that walls have ears.

Telling myself over and over again that I had done the right thing, I sang this as I walked down the street:

> Little Richard
> Tutti-Frutti
> Fats Domino
> I'm walkin' . . .
> are you ready for a brand new beat?
> Summer's here
> the time is right
> for dancin' in the street . . .
> Sal Mineo
> James Dean
> Marlon Brando
> Rat-hole
> Rabbit-hole
> and *Goodbye, Feets!*

The sign dangled from the fire escape in front of the shabby building:

STUDIO APT. FOR RENT

I entered the lobby of the dimly lit building, one of those Victorian San Francisco dwellings that must've been grand in the early 1900s. Times had certainly changed—the neighborhood had quietly deteriorated and the building had decayed right along with it. It still had marvelous dark wood panelings and art nouveau, daffodil-shaped lamps along the walls, but the carpets were stained and faded, and you could smell the grease emanating from the apartments. Another faded sign in the lobby read:

STANLEY GENDZEL—MANAGER—APT. 1
COLLECTOR OF ANTIQUES—PARROT MAN
EXTRAORDINAIRE

I hesitated before knocking on his door. Bells tinkled faintly, and someone came toward me down the dark, dank hallway. I put my suitcase down and whirled around to face the young man who stood there, staring at me. Could this be Stanley Gendzel? I wondered.

Barefoot, the young man held a large orange cat in his arms. The cat gazed at me with the same dispassionate curiosity.

The young man and the cat bore a striking similarity—the young man with copper-colored skin, slender and beautiful, with his ominous lion's-mane hair, the color of brown fading into reddish-gold, much like the extraordinary cat's thick fur. After a few moments, the young man put the cat down, and we both watched it scurry away into the darkness.

"I'm looking for the manager," I said.

The young man smiled. "Manager?"

Oh no, I thought, this couldn't be Stanley Gendzel!

"I'm looking for a place to live," I said, as firmly as I could. Looking for an apartment of my own was one of the momentous decisions of my life, and I was determined to act as adult and businesslike as possible.

"Oh," the young man said, still being playful with me. "A place. You need a place."

"I certainly do," I retorted.

"Then you need to see Stanley," he said.

There was a moment of silence, and we looked each other over like two animals sniffing each other out.

Suddenly he said, "Let me show you my guitar."

I shook my head. "No."

"Let me show you my cello."

"No." Where was Stanley Gendzel?

"Let me show you my saxophone."

"No!"

"Let me show you my soprano saxophone."

"Hmmmm. . . ." I was getting curious.

"Let me show you my bass saxophone."

"Oooh. . . ."

He was relentless. "Let me show you my bass clarinet."

"Oh dear," I sighed, slowly wearing down.

"Let me show you my bass."

My favorite instrument. I looked him dead in the eye. "Upright or electric?"

He grinned. "Both."

It had been a long day. I decided I must be falling in love, and to hell with Stanley Gendzel. "Well," I said, "maybe . . ."

His grin widened, and suddenly—like magic—the dank and forbidding hallway seemed less gloomy. "My berimbau? Caxixi? Sansa?"

He was so enthusiastic and strangely radiant, I had to give in. "OKAY!" I responded, smiling back at him and taking his hand.

I followed him up the first flight of stairs, and he pulled out a gleaming gold key and unlocked the door to an apartment. The living room was littered with every kind of musical instrument imaginable, and an orchestra of children was playing. Their faces were painted like ornate African and Balinese masks. Bells hung from the ceiling. We began to dance in slow motion, lost in some kind of trancelike, sensuous waltz.

My first and only lover so far had been Junior Burgess, who could sing as compellingly as Smokey Robinson, seducing me sweetly with his voice while telling me stories of all my favorite Motown groups. But this young man who held me in his arms was different. He *glowed.* He made me so nervous I blurted out "I love you" in the middle of our dance.

His face was devoid of expression, like the cat who sat purring in the room, so sure of its regal beauty. "I know," he said, not unkindly.

"My name is George Sand," I told him shyly.

"I know," the young man said.

"Your name is Rover," I said.

"Exactly," he replied, twirling me around the room. I don't know how much time we spent in that room, the children's orchestra continuously serenading us with their dissonant circus music, the purring orange cat never once taking his amber eyes off our dancing bodies. And I didn't care.

I FLOATED out of Rover's apartment in a daze, starting back down the stairs in my second attempt to locate the mysterious

Stanley Gendzel, manager of this illustrious building. I dragged my battered suitcase behind me, unsure of what had just happened. All I remembered was that late afternoon softly changed into darkness, and the children's orchestra stopped playing, and Rover and I stopped dancing, unwinding slowly like two figures twirling on top of a music box. The big orange cat rubbed against our legs, and Rover picked him up and carried him in his arms, stroking his fur gently. He kissed me on my lips, then once—very tenderly—on each of my eyelids. "I will see you again," was all he said.

A darkly beautiful Sephardic Jewish woman came bounding up the stairs as I was on my way back down to Stanley Gendzel's apartment. She seemed to be in her early twenties, dressed in interesting layers of clothing my friend Boogie would've called "fleamarket glamor." Crocheted doilies had been sewn together into a lacey shirt worn over red satin pyjamas. The pyjamas were stuffed into embroidered Nepalese boots. She was carrying a blender in one hand and a large black portfolio in the other.

"Hey," she called out, in a friendly way. "You new in the building? Silver Daddy's new piece of cheese, perhaps?"

"Uh, no."

She peered at me from under the thick fringe of her black eyelashes. "My name is Momma Magenta," she finally said.

"Hi. I'm George."

She never flinched. "You're very much his type, you know. Are you Indian or something? Mexican? Italian, somewhat?"

"No, not any of those," I said wryly.

"What about Japanese? That's Silver Daddy's new trip. THE JAPANESE . . . he's busy editing an anthology of esoteric Japanese poets. 'O Momma Magenta,' he's always telling me, 'you've got all the right ingredients. Long black hair, black eyes, bit tits, a small waist, and a big ass . . . but you aren't JAPANESE!' I'm always showing him my portfolio, you know," she chattered confidentially. "After all, Silver Daddy's one of America's oldest living legends, with plenty of connections in the art world. But all he ever wants to do around me is talk about pussy."

"Oh. You're an artist?"

Momma Magenta was obviously pleased that I had asked this question. "Yeah, that's right. I do rock n' roll posters. Wanna see my portfolio?"

"No thanks. I don't have time. I'm looking for a place to rent."

"Well, you've come to the right place, sweetie. Silver Daddy owns this building, see. He's what you might call a bonafide *artiste* and slum landlord all rolled into one. He lives on the top floor, in his fashionable ghetto penthouse. You're in luck. Silver Daddy just ordered Stanley Gendzel to kick one of the tenants out. He was a poet from New York named Paolo. Trouble was, he was a smack freak, and broke all the time. HEY—wanna buy a used blender?"

I started down the stairs. "No thanks, really. I think I should go see about renting this apartment," I said, waving goodbye to her.

"Good luck with Stanley," she waved back. "Don't let him chew your ears off. And don't be surprised when Silver Daddy invites you up for one of his famous dinner parties."

SOMETHING that resembled a shrivelled up spider with bushy eyebrows for antennae opened the door. "Whadda you want?" he croaked, looking me up and down.

"I'm interested in renting the apartment," I said. "Are you Mr. Gendzel?"

"Yup. I'm Stanley Gendzel. Come in, come in." He stepped aside to let me through the door. I pretended not to notice that all he had on were faded, yellow boxer shorts. A large green parrot was perched on his shoulder.

He ushered me into his grimy kitchen and pulled out a chair for me. For a long while no one said a word. I watched Stanley scratch the bird's head, cooing softly to the creature. Then he pulled out a box of birdseed and nonchalantly placed some seeds on the top of his tongue. The parrot pecked the food off the old man's outstretched tongue while the old man stared at me suspiciously.

"Are you a college student?" he asked suddenly, when the parrot finished his dinner.

"No, I'm a poet," I blurted out, wondering if I'd said the wrong thing.

Stanley was visibly upset. "A poet! Not another one!"

It had been such a long, grueling day that between my mother and Auntie Greta's hysterics and Momma Magenta's aggressiveness, I decided I just couldn't accept Stanley's disapproval. I had to convince this strange man that I had to have the apartment this very evening. Besides, it was getting late and I was hungry.

"Yes," I said, as calmly and politely as possible. "I'm a very responsible person, in spite of what you might think. How much is the rent?"

"Well," Stanley said, scratching the parrot's head once again, "it's one of the worst studios in the building. That heroin addict never cleaned up after himself. Always sipping grape soda and munching Twinkies! It's a wonder he's still alive. Left behind reams and reams of paper—some with writing on it, some without. I didn't have the heart to destroy his work, even though Silver Daddy didn't think too highly of it. He ordered me to go in there and disinfect everything and burn all the boy's manuscripts. Imagine! I just couldn't do it," Stanley repeated, shaking his head slowly.

"I'm glad you didn't. I'm sure Paolo would appreciate it," I said.

"Humph!" Stanley snorted. "Paolo didn't appreciate anything—that's why he was so self-destructive. Anyway, I haven't cleaned the place at all, so you can have it for eighty dollars a month, no cleaning deposit necessary. The toilet works, and if you wanna paint it, Silver Daddy will insist on raising the rent, so I wouldn't advise it. Just leave well enough alone."

I got up to go. "Thanks very much, Mr. Gendzel."

"What'd you say your name was again?" he asked.

"I didn't. My name is George Sand."

"Interesting name for a young girl. You look very interesting, by the way. You wouldn't happen to be Japanese, would you?"

"No, I'm from the Philippines, actually. My mother brought me here when I was very young," I replied.

He seemed totally disinterested. "Oh. *The Philippines.* All I remember is that big fuss about MacArthur. Well, it doesn't really matter. I'm sure Silver Daddy will invite you to dinner as soon as you move in. It's part of the rituals around here, his own way of getting to know each tenant. The only one he never invited was Paolo. . . ."

"Perhaps I'll show him some of my poems."

Stanley Gendzel arched one of his extravagant eyebrows. "He'd be utterly delighted, *I'm sure*. That's the right attitude to take with that old lecher! He's working on some Japanese translations right now, y'know. Had some Japanese nobility up there helping him out. Flew her all the way from Toyko. Called her Camembert for short. She called him Daddybear."

THE only thing I had when I moved in was a sorry-ass little suitcase crammed with notebooks and journals, a pair of jeans or two, and a memory of my mother Consuelo's face when I went out the door of her house. When I finally telephoned to say I was all right, Auntie Greta picked up the phone and answered in a solemn voice, "Good evening . . . the Sand Residence."

"Hello? Auntie Greta?" My own voice seemed unusually high to me.

"My dear George—are you all right?"

"Yes. I got a place—my own apartment. Is Mom there?"

"Your mother can't come to the phone, dear. She's not feeling well," Auntie Greta said.

"You mean she won't talk to me."

He cleared his throat. "Let's just say your mother is under sedation—high blood pressure, you know. She couldn't handle your leaving us too well."

"Well, tell her I'm all right. I'm living on Webster Street," I said.

"Webster Street??? Webster Street and what???"

"Oh, you know—near the freeway," I replied. I knew what was coming.

"Dios mio! You're living in that part of town?" Even Auntie Greta couldn't bring himself to say it: the ghetto. Bodies bleeding on the front steps of my building, virile young things with guns as erect as their dicks, leaping in and out of Chinese grocery stores. My mother's darkest fears.

I sighed. "Don't worry, Auntie Greta. There's a famous person living in this building. His name is Silver Daddy. He's my landlord."

"I've never heard of him," Auntie Greta said.

"Of course not," I retorted, exasperated. "You don't read the papers, except for the movie listings. Mom doesn't read the papers, either. Well, if you did, you might know about his column in the Sunday arts section. He writes on all the new stuff going on in the art world."

Auntie Greta was obviously offended. "Well, I don't know about that, young lady. I do read the paper from time to time! I know you've always thought yourself above us."

"Oh jesus, there you go sounding like my mother," I said.

"You know what they say—association makes for assimilation. Listen, George, do you have enough locks on your doors and windows?"

"Yes."

"I'll break the news to your mother gently. And please, dear, keep in touch. Are you getting a phone?"

"No. But there's a pay phone in the lobby," I said.

"A *pay* phone! In the *lobby!* OH MY GOD!" Auntie Greta groaned.

I figured it was better if I hung up first.

MY apartment was really a one-room studio, with a dingy closet of a kitchen and a gloomy bathroom where the roaches liked to hide. The best thing about it was the bathtub, a massive boat with lion's paws that had definitely seen better days. I loved filling it with warm water and just sitting in it for hours, thinking. Unhappy with the mattress on the floor I was using to sleep on, I had even considered turning my wonderful bathtub into a bed.

I had left the apartment pretty much in the same state I had found it—the floor littered with papers of every shape and size, including newspapers. Almost all the papers belonged to the poet Paolo, although lately I had gotten in the habit of discarding my poems and stories in the same way—using the sheets of papers as rugs, haphazard decorations on the floor that floated in the air when the wind blew through the apartment.

I had taken to tacking some of my poems, finished and unfinished, on the walls next to or on top of the poems Paolo had glued on like wallpaper. In an eerie way, it made me feel safe and comfortable.

I CALLED Boogie and invited him to see my new home. He seemed highly amused by my surroundings as soon as he walked through the door. I was impressed by his appearance—Boogie had always been very pretty, and his multicultural looks confused a lot of people. He could pass for Latino, Asian, even Native American. His eclectic way of dressing never betrayed the toughness behind the elegance, and I loved the way his beauty drove men and women crazy. Nothing seemed to disturb him, an attribute that could sometimes make me angry. But when I was feeling good about myself, I could think of no one else in the world whose opinion mattered more.

The Milky Way

I COULD almost see my mother swoon when I called her a few days later on the telephone. "Darling," she moaned, "I've been trying to contact you for *days!* It's all over the papers—"

"*What's* all over the papers? What happened?"

"The most horrendous thing. Auntie Greta has been *murdered.*"

I felt sick. "What for? Who'd want to kill him?"

"How should I know? For his antique candelabra, probably," my mother answered. "He was always courting danger, bringing home those boys he picked up on the street. He never listened to me. Maybe he was getting senile, but even after that last burglary, he kept running off to those bars as if nothing had happened."

"My god."

"It's shameful. He was brutally murdered at the age of fifty, and the police have no clues. That could've been ME!"

Dear Auntie Greta, with his crystal goblets and cheap red wine, his dapper suits, his Chihuahuas, and his vacuum cleaners. He was a sweet man, spic and span and deeply religious, confused by his deadly attractoin to young, muscular boys with corrupt hearts and ethereal faces. He went to church for Sunday mass and afternoon novenas. At night, in spite of my mother's persistent nagging, he haunted the bars and the streets.

"I'm having a nervous breakdown," my mother said. "You'd better attend the memorial service. I made all the arrangements—with no help from his family, mind you."

"Aren't they coming?" I asked.

"Hell, no! They're embarrassed by all the scandal and refuse to have anything more to do with him."

"That's very kind of you. Auntie Greta would've appreciated what you're doing," I said, paying my mother a rare compliment.

She acted as if she didn't hear it. "It's just awful," she rattled on. "We aren't going to bury him in the proper way. We're having him cremated. His corpse, if you'll pardon the expression, looked so depressing I just couldn't stand it. What a nightmare!" She took a deep breath. "The memorial service is tomorrow night, and Greta's Father Confessor will officiate. All of Greta's weird friends are going to be there."

"I won't miss it," I promised, fighting back tears.

"Have you heard from your father?"

"Not lately," I said.

"Hmmm. Wonder if he's found any insects lately. Oh, well," my mother sighed, "look your best, dear. Remember, Auntie Greta would've wanted it that way."

I hung up the phone and locked myself in my studio. I refused to answer the door when Stanley knocked, demanding the rent. "Open up! I know you're home," Stanley said. "Wait till I tell Silver Daddy! He'll throw you out in the street!"

I didn't care. Finally Stanley went away, muttering loudly. I sat in the darkness for most of the night, unable to think or write, a numbness creeping over me.

At one point Silver Daddy banged on my door. "My dear, are you all right? Is there a tragedy in your family? Let me in," he begged. "I'll console you. Don't worry about the rent! I understand about the ups and downs in an artist's life. GEORGE! DON'T DO ANYTHING RASH!"

I couldn't take it anymore. Pressing my face against the door, I said as calmly as possible, "I'll be all right, Silver Daddy. *Just leave me alone.*" I was finally left in peace, tears streaming down my face.

The End of the Queen

AUNTIE GRETA'S Father Confessor led the prayers. Hundreds of people were there: hairdressers, waiters, couturiers, dancers, actors, bartenders, mimes in whiteface, aging whores, cab drivers, pharmacists, musicians, successful gigolos, ditchdiggers, poets and novelists, weightlifters, back-up singers in sequined dresses, sixteen-year-old basketball players in sweatpants and sneakers—and, of course, my mother.

The flowers that had been sent by Auntie Greta's numerous well-wishers and grieving cohorts glowed mystically in the semi-darkness of the chapel. The large room was stuffy with burning frankincense mixed with the scent of jasmine oil, tea rose perfume, sandalwood fans, and sweat. "I knew Auntie Greta quite well," Father Confessor began. "Are you aware that he died on the night of the full moon???" He struck a dramatic pose.

I thought it was a rather odd way to begin services for such a famous personality, especially when the entire row of poets and novelists began to snicker.

"Auntie Greta died suddenly and violently by the light of a full moon," Father Confessor continued, ignoring the poets and novelists, "and so his only heir—a ten-year-old Chihuahua named Revenge—inherited all that was left of Greta's belongings: a 9-by-12-foot frayed Persian rug and a set of gold candelabra from Barcelona, recently recovered by the police."

Father Confessor turned his gleaming eyes in my direction. "I believe your mother gave the precious candelabra to Auntie

Greta during one of his frequent and suicidal bouts of depression. . . ."

A murmur went through the crowd. My mother smiled graciously as we both stood up. A spotlight came out of nowhere and beamed down on us, just like the Academy Awards on TV.

"Like mother, like daughter," my mother said, obviously delighted to be the center of attention. "As I'm always telling my daughter, 'Charity Begins at Home.' You know how these homosexuals can get despondent," she said, to my embarrassment.

The young basketball players stopped dribbling long enough to perk up their pretty puppy ears and listen.

"WELL," my mother went on, fluttering her wonderful Minnie Mouse eyelashes, "whenever Auntie Greta got sentimental, he'd always phone me to say goodbye. I'd always say, 'GOODBYE, WHAT?' And the old bag would sniff and snort and moan and announce that he was going to kill himself. I went through this melodrama with him everytime he drank. 'Oh, PUL-LEEZE!' I would sigh. 'STOP FEELING SORRY FOR YOURSELF!' There's nothing quite so loathsome as self-pity, wouldn't you say?"

She directed this question at Father Confessor, who nodded solemnly.

"*Indeed,*" Father Confessor agreed, his alcoholic's face flushed and glistening with sweat, "nothing quite so loathsome."

My mother pursed her bright red lips in satisfaction. "YES, I tried to tell Auntie Greta over and over and over again— *killing yourself won't solve any of your problems!* No one cares. I mean, I care. And Auntie Greta cared. And sometimes my daughter George cares, when she isn't wrapped up with that sleazy friend of hers, Boogie, who's going to come to a bad end too, mind you. BUT no one else cared, and Auntie Greta just wasn't being responsible. His hairdressing career was finished. Sailors mugged him constantly, and he drank too much! His liver was in shreds. In and out of the hospital he went, paying off medical bills with money he borrowed from ME. His only true friend.

"It's like I tell my daughter, 'As you get older, you'll see how lonely life really is!' Even your children turn on you," she said sweetly, giving me and the audience her most effective *Mater Dolorosa* routine.

"My daughter fancies herself an artist—a poet, to be exact. Isn't that wonderful?" my mother said. "I always encouraged her, with no help from her father. He's just an air mail letter and occasional check to her, if you know what I mean. ANYWAY, I've always believed in encouraging people to be themselves. Especially my only child, who's a poet. Or so she says. Although I try to be realistic about the situation. Like I tell her, it's okay to write all that mumbo jumbo stuff, but why not write something that makes money and save all that hocus pocus for the weekend?"

I was cringing in my seat, but I realized my mother was carried away by her own "stuff." She fanned herself grandly with a stiff palm leaf as she went on.

"Times haven't changed *that* much, and I just don't understand why my daughter's so uncooperative with me. She's always getting in and out of strange vehicles, consorting with riffraff, writing strange and confusing curses she refers to as 'poems.' Her so-called friend Boogie encourages these mystifying convolutions. I sometimes think he's also responsible for a large part of them, but I could never say that to her face.

"My daughter certainly has her pride. She wants to be given credit for everything she does. I guess she gets that from me," my mother added, smiling. "I keep warning her over and over again, just like I did Auntie Greta, about her lifestyle and her friends. Boogie's nothing but a lazy drug addict fronting himself off as a piano player. But no, she won't listen to her own mother," she said with disdain.

"*Drugs.* My daughter thinks I don't understand about the nuances of such things. She thinks I'm not *worldly.* But I've said to her often, 'There's nothing new under the sun, and you can't fool your mother!' Blood is thicker than water, and her so-called friends are going to turn on her in the end. Mark my words! I'm always right!"

The crowd held its breath in reverence and awe of her. The heat and the silence in the chapel were oppressive. We all watched in fascination as my mother swayed, her body locked into some kind of marvelous trance.

"What have I done to deserve this convolution as my child?" she asked no one in particular. "Not that I don't love her, mind you! No one knows how to love her like I do! But she doesn't understand *that*, yet. Who are these furry, dark creatures I see her mooning over? They'll never do her any good. They have no breeding! All they know how to do is make noise—and they have the nerve to call themselves *artists!* What's the world coming to, when animals have the arrogance to try to be like human beings, and vice versa???"

She paused, giving the mesmerized audience enough time to catch its breath.

"I don't see the order in it, do you? I'm all for affirmative action and all that sort of thing, but I can't go for these tomcats acting like they're men, sticking it in my daughter and her having kittens for babies. They'd end up drowned in a sack, in some canal on the south side of Chicago! And then what? What are those poems and so-called plays going to get her? Who would've guessed I'd have a POOR-IT for a daughter? Not a poet mind you, but a poor-it?" My mother gazed at me lovingly. "And now, my dear," she said, not missing a beat, "why don't you recite us a poem? Show us how talented you are!"

Another murmur went through the crowd. Suddenly, they all began to clap, politely at first. Then the clapping became louder and more persistent, the crowd rowdier. I was humiliated and terrified by what my mother had asked me to do.

"Tell us a poem!" the basketball players cheered.

"Tell us a poem!" the gigolos whistled.

"Yes, yes! Tell us a poem!" the hairdressers and waiters pleaded.

"Chirp it to us, sister!" the backup singers crooned.

"Tell us a poem! Show us! C'mon. Don't be an ass!" the weightlifters and cab drivers shouted, laughing and making obscene gestures.

"*Whip it to us!*" the poets and novelists demanded, last but not least.

Telephones began ringing as more spotlights beamed down on me. Roses showered from the ceiling, and the crowd's roaring never ceased. My mother kept bowing and blowing kisses to the grateful, bloodthirsty audience.

It was probably the grandest memorial service Auntie Greta could ever have imagined. Hysteria, melodrama, and pandemonium—Father Confessor and my mother Consuelo basking in their glory. They were oblivious to the fact that I hadn't responded to their request and was in fact heading out the door of the chapel, gritting my teeth in helpless rage. Father Confessor growled at me with some compassion, but no one else paid any attention.

"I've had it with your insults and innuendos," I said to my mother. Her eyes were shut, and she was rocking back and forth, totally unaware of my presence. "I'm sorry it had to be this way. GOODBYE."

No one tried to stop me, and I ran out of the chapel without looking back. I packed up my few belongings and took one last look at my little apartment. All in all, I had accomplished a lot of work in that cramped space. But it was time for me to move on.

Kay Boyle

IF you know Kay Boyle (1902–   ) or her work at all, then you know that any biographical notes about her should and must begin with the present. She is living and working in Marin County north of San Francisco. Throughout her long career, she has always been an advocate of human rights and human dignity. Each year the celebration of her birthday is a benefit for Amnesty International.

I was an undergraduate and graduate student of Kay Boyle's at San Francisco State University in the late sixties and early seventies. To simply say she was a mentor to my writing would diminish the real impact she has had and still has on my life. At San Francisco State she placed her body between the students and the police, we planted trees at the old Angel Island immigration detention station for Chinese immigrants, we marched with tens of thousands of others through the streets of San Francisco against the Vietnam War, we held writing classes at her stately three-story Victorian house in San Francisco, where she told us that writing is about belief and commitment. She told us that what we wrote needed to be relevant to what was going on in our lives. She also wrote about the turmoil in our lives at San Francisco State University, the student strike, the struggle for ethnic studies, the Vietnam War—in short, everything that was touching my life in a direct way. My first published words appeared imbedded in the things she wrote about us in *The Long Walk at San Francisco State, Testament For My Students, 1968–1969,* and *The Underground Woman.*

While in graduate school I rented a room from her in that same house. I'm sure that my real education was conducted in her house with her and my other housemates rather than in the classes I attended during the day. Through the doors of that magnificent house came writers, singers, artists, community organizers and activists, and even postcards from Samuel Beckett.

The point in all of this is not to list the things she did for me, but to demonstrate that Kay Boyle is more than an author of over thirty-five books of fiction, poetry, criticism, and memoirs—she is the conscience of our lives. Studs Terkel told Boyle's biographer, Sandra Whipple Spanier, "When I think of Kay Boyle, I think of someone who has borne witness to the most traumatic events of our century: not simply this particular era, but of the whole twentieth century. Starting early. Both as a creative artist as well as being there." Spanier goes on to note, "*There,* indeed she has always been." She was writer in Paris in the twenties, saw the Nazis come to power in the thirties, witnessed the fall of France in 1940 and World War II, and was subjected to investigation by McCarthy and the House Un-American Activities Committee. Spanier goes on to note:

> Throughout the sixties, seventies, and eighties, she has devoted her energies to a wide range of social and political causes, speaking out for the rights of racial and ethnic minorities, traveling to Cambodia on a fact-finding mission with a pacifist group in 1966, demonstrating against the war in Vietnam (and twice going to jail for blocking the entrance to the Oakland Induction Center), supporting the student strike at San Francisco State in 1968, and marching with Cesar Chavez on behalf of California farm workers. . . . "I believed with Camus," she has said, looking back on her life and work, "that the writer, the artist, does not make the choice to fight against oppression. It is his art which does not allow him to remain silent."

In 1929, William Carlos Williams wrote a review of Kay Boyle's first collection of short stories and even then saw in the stories what I saw some forty years later as a student:

> . . . her short stories assault our sleep. They are of a high degree of excellence; for that reason they will not succeed in America, they are lost, damned. Simply, the person who has a comprehensive, if perhaps disturbing view of what takes place in the human understanding at moments of intense living, and puts it down in its

proper shapes and color, is anathema to United Statesers and can have no standing with them. We are asleep.

Kay Boyle once wrote, "Surely no greater reward is offered to a writer than the knowledge that other men are reading the words that he has, by some miracle, retrieved from the depths of his own silence, the knowledge that other men are actually listening for the sound of his voice to call from the page to them, and, above all, the knowledge that they believe the words they hear."

—Shawn Wong

Chapters 4, 5, and 6 from
THE UNDERGROUND WOMAN

4

THE REHABILITATION CENTER spread in a complex of long low barracks across the countryside, with here and there (as far as the women could make out in the blue-white road lights) a tilted, shingled roof or a dark web of ivy around a doorway to give the bleak buildings the look of home. But the avenues lined with cyclone fences and hedged with entanglements of barbed wire said something else entirely. Inside the bowling-alley-like structure of the women's quarters, the demonstrators were locked temporarily inside the steel-meshed cage of the visiting gallery that ran half the length of the entrance hall. In the density of women, the young nun she had not yet spoken with now stood close to Athena, close because she could not do otherwise, withdrawn from them all in her brown wool dress and her shabby moccasins, her eyes lowered, her face small and tight and freckled like a child's under her neat, coffee-colored cap of hair. She could not be said to appear modest or shy, but more that the flesh and its concerns had been, by uninterrupted habit, deliberately effaced. (St. Theresa is said to have willed all worldly emotion within her to perish, thought Athena; but if this descendant of hers could exchange a prayer or a poem or a piece of music with me, then no idle remarks about the strangeness of this place, or the sandwiches the deputy is bringing at this moment to the cage door, would have to be spoken; or if either she or I had Callisto's voice and simply sang, flesh and blood and assurance would be restored to her, and St. Theresa would be visible among us.)

Although the sandwiches had little to do with food (each square thick with a slab of plastic cheese and a slice of baloney) the women ate greedily. Only Callisto, her face sallow under the high, unshaded light bulb, could not eat. She leaned against the wall with a piece of cheese cupped in her palm as mirror as she slapped a flexible slice of bread like a powder puff against her cheeks and chin. The women who were pressed close to her in the crowded cage laughed almost to the point of tears at this, relieved for an instant from their uneasiness for what lay ahead; and Athena looked from one face to another, seeking Calliope. A rumor had begun to dart and flicker among the women as they ate, but where the documentation came from, nobody knew. The story was that rivers of blood had flowed in the streets of Oakland that day, that protesters had fought with bricks and rakes and whatever they could lay their hands on, as they met the ferocious assault of the police. Parked cars were overturned, it was said, and the approaches to the Induction Center blocked, while all day the city wept with tear gas. The emergency rooms of hospitals were swamped, the rumor went, for this had been the day of the guerrilla fighters, the day of the flea, who strikes and leaps away to strike again. The demonstrators of the day before had seen only one act of violence, that moment when the mother of a draftee, with her son in tow, had sought to stampede her way and his across the women and men seated on the Induction Center steps. She had trampled in fury over their legs, over their backs and shoulders as they doubled over, dragging her son behind her in her savage advance.

"In spite of the lot of you, he's going in!" she shouted. "He's going to fight for his country! He could wipe out you bunch of Commies with one hand, do you hear me, with one hand!"

"They've locked the doors from the inside now," the well-known poet had said bleakly from where he lay underfoot, his bowler hat pulled low on his sideburns and his ears. "You may have to take him around the corner to the basement entrance. That's where they're delivering them today." But she did not desist, a big woman titubating on whatever pieces of anatomy happened to be on the steps, continuing to smash her one free fist over and over against the plate glass of the door.

That day of passive resistance, of the lotus position of devotion, of an unfrocked nun who had discarded her earthly flesh, of knitting wool woven in innocence into the glossy braids of a girl's hair—all this was done with and would be forgotten. "In placing our bodies between the draft system and the young conscript," the order of the day had read, "we must seek to persuade others through the non-violent power of reason. In our contact with the police, we must remain courteous and understanding. May our love of justice, and the expression of that love, bring an end to involuntary servitude." Ho, hum, sighed Athena; but as the mythical giver of the olive tree, and the inventor of the flute, she wanted the spirit of that day to prevail. Yet she knew it was the chapters of panting terror and streaming eyes, the tales of men and women clubbed and dragged through the streets, of kicked genitals, and handcuffs locked behind the back, of piercing outcry, that would be remembered in the history of their time. The non-violent, the peacemakers, could not wholly envisage, and thus were not prepared to meet, death in the streets, and on rooftops, death drenching the grass of college campuses, that was to come.

"Did you hear that one cop took off his jacket?" the women would ask one another as they ate, having heard the second or third or maybe fourth-hand account of what had taken place. "They say he laid it down on the curb, and set his helmet on top of it, and said, 'I'm quitting. If this is what I'm asked to do, I've had enough.'"

Through the baloney and the plastic cheese that gummed their mouths, the women, packed cheek by jowl in the visiting cage, talked of this good omen, and of still another that came winging in from the wide night of the California countryside.

"There was a student in a wheelchair, a Vietnam veteran," the story went, "who rolled his wheelchair into the doorway of the Induction Center, and sat there handing out leaflets to the men going in. And the cops refused to arrest him. They took the anti-war leaflets away, but they refused to put him in the paddy wagon, although he wheeled himself right up to where it was."

Aren't these things a sign of something changing, the women were saying to one another in different ways as they swallowed the last of the limp crusts. Maybe even the cops, the fuzz, the pigs, every one of them, will lay jacket and club and medals for bravery down in the thoroughfares of the cities for the people to see that they have finally understood. But none of the women foresaw what lay ahead, what lay, in fact, on the other side of the stained plaster wall that Callisto leaned against. Had there been the place to lie down on the floor, she would have done so, but because of the crowded, standing women there was no room. All her beauty was gone for the moment, and she looked gaunt as a hunger marcher in a country stricken with famine, leaning there incongruously dressed in her tight yellow breeches and her brightly flowered shirt.

"What we need is a little optimism around here, if we're going to make it!" an eager voice cried out from among the women.

"No, no!" said Callisto, shaking her head, the dark curtains of hair falling across her face. "No." Perhaps something of all that was present behind the wall she leaned against had suddenly been communicated to her, and now she held in her trembling hand the words of a terrible message just received. "We are going in there to be with other kinds of prisoners, women whose lives have not been like ours," she said, speaking scarcely aloud. "I don't know if we're ready to go in with them. I think we have to try to believe that our separate lives are really of no importance. For now, anyway, they are of no importance. I think we have to prepare ourselves to accept this—"And Athena thought in sudden panic that if Calliope didn't materialize from wherever she was and get to Callisto in time, Callisto might slide down, unconscious, to the floor. "I don't know if we're going to be able to see these other women's lives, so different from—" she was saying, and Athena wanted to stand beside her, for now Callisto and Melanie had become interchangeable to her, but she could not force a way through the mass of librarians, housewives, teachers, students, packed into the visiting cage. She wanted to stand close to Callisto in acknowledgment of the dilemma of daughters and mothers alive in this time, or in any time, but she could not get through the mass of women to where Callisto stood alone, her eyes closed now, leaning against the wall. "The thing about counting on words is that they may not be the right ones," Callisto said,

speaking scarcely above a whisper. "So we have to go in there
with something else, maybe with our hearts, but anyway without judgment, because words—"

And words, thought Athena, still hearing a voice on a tape
that had never ceased playing, hearing the fearful, delirious
words repeated, repeated, and repeated, until the end. *What
words?* the memory of them demanded of her. *What words? Or
are you afraid to listen to them again or face the meaning of
them?*

(Well, it was like this, she began telling herself as she stood
there silent among the murmuring women; it was one evening
when I dropped in at the commune, if you can picture a parent
dropping in on dropouts, but I was invited for dinner, if you can
believe it, as had happened often enough in the three years
since Melanie joined the order. Whenever I was in that city,
I'd telephone Melanie, and ask her if it was all right if I came
up, and she'd say, "I want to see you, woman." She'd call me
"woman," and she'd ask me to come as quickly as I could, and
I'd sit down before the fire in that cold wintry city, and sometimes brush the grandchildren's hair, or cut their toenails, or
maybe read to them, making sounds like twenty wind instruments, one foghorn, and two ambulance sirens, and the redeemer would be in another part of the commune, in another
of the redeemed houses they had. He would never be there
when I came. And on this one night after the children were put
to bed, Melanie said, "I'll play a tape for you while I'm getting
the mashed potatoes mashed. It will make you laugh." Ha, ha, I
said, ha, ha, has, already delighted, always ready to make the
best of any situation, that's me all over; so I settled back in the
armchair Melanie had salvaged from the Goodwill, handsomely upholstered in mustard velvet by Melanie's own quick,
still childish hands, and the voice began speaking from the tape
recorder, a young girl's voice speaking in strange, bubbling delirium, and even if you only half listened you heard latent in
each separate word a long, far, not quite uttered scream. The
girl was talking with two men, at least it seemed there must be
two, for at times her voice bubbled up out of the morass with
the names Lucky and Pete, and maybe my hearty laughter died
on my lips by that time, because Pete is the redeemer's name.

The little ribbon of tape unwound, unwound, and the girl was telling them some kind of story in which she thought she was a principal character, but neither heads nor tails could be made of what was going on, for whenever her voice began soaring and crying out in ecstacy about being the Hell's Angel in the tale, the two men would titter or snicker on the tape, not laugh outright like honest men, but cackle and laugh up their sleeves, and Pete the Redeemer would say with a quip and a sneer, "You can't be a Hell's Angel, honey; you're a beautiful golden girl"; and then her voice would take flight, would scud, and spiral, and mount the air, and at these moments the lurking scream could almost be heard, and the other man's voice, Lucky's voice, would say with a supercilious twit and jeer, "You're the girl in the story. Don't you remember, you're the girl?" And then the scream would come even closer to being uttered, but not quite, and the girl's voice would cry, "But the girl's burned up! The girl has to die!" So she wanted to be the Hell's Angel instead, and her voice rising higher and higher on the witness stand testified in somebody else's vocabulary, "You see, we was hired by this crazy-looking cat with long yellow hair and long kinda, you know, side-whiskers, and we was to sit on the platform, that was what we was hired to do, we was just to sit on the kinda like the front of the platform while the Rolling Stones and like the other rock groups would be playing, and we was to drink beer all afternoon, that was part of the deal, we'd like sit there on the front of, you know, the platform, and keep people from like climbing up when the groups was playing, and we was to take care of the situation, like that was the order, to sit to the front and see nobody tried climbing up where the bands was playing, and we was being paid with beer, like all the beer you wanted, and we wasn't asking for no trouble with nobody.

("Our bikes was parked around by the side like where the crowd couldn't get to them, but one Angel, you know, he'd parked his bike right there like out front where he could watch it, like to see nothing happened to it, and then the people, there was maybe two thousand of them, they started shoving up close, real close, and they kept pushing a girl up onto the platform, and we had to stop drinking beer and start pushing the girl back down because we was hired for that, to keep anyone like from getting up there, that's what we was doing up on the platform, even between the groups playing we was to keep people from getting up there, and you know if you say you'll do a thing, well, that's a contract, it's like you got to do it, and they kept pushing this girl up. . . ." And then Pete the Redeemer would say on the tape, "You're the girl, honey, you're the beautiful girl," and the girl's voice, drenched with crying, would beg him to let her be the Hell's Angel instead. "Oh, Pete, Pete, don't make me be the girl!" she'd cry out. "The girl has to die!" And even with half an ear you could hear the two men cackling. "This trip, you're the girl. You're the girl," Pete the Redeemer would say to the accompaniment of Lucky the Disciple's snickering and tittering. But maybe her own will wasn't quite gone yet, not quite broken, or maybe it was because the Hell's Angel had moved completely inside her skin and there wasn't room for both of them there, that she could still defy them. Whichever way it was, her voice went stubbornly on with the incessant story.

("They kept pushing this girl up, and almost all her clothes was tore off her," the testimony went in a vocabulary that had nothing to do with whoever she was. "And like a lot of people was pushing her up on the platform, but she was stoned or something and she couldn't stand, and then they, you know, then they started pushing this Angel's bike around, the one that was up to the front, and that was like the end of everything, like we had to save the bike. I tell you, I'm not violent or nothing like that, but you know what, you touch my bike and you've had it. I'll kill you, I'll kill anyone lays a finger on my bike, like my bike's my life, you know, it's my life, and everything on that bike is mine, like my eyes and hands and anything else I was born with is mine. I mean, if you touch my bike, shit, you're a dead man right there, you got to understand that, you're dead because I put my life into that bike, and you touch it and you're like cutting my heart out, and that's what happened. If it was like one Angel knocking that girl back down off the platform, when that was what we was being paid to do, it wouldn't of turned out like it did, any rioting would of been over quick, but it was maybe twenty-fifty people pushing her up right over the bike, and like the Angels pushing her back down, and then what they do is start ripping out the clutch cable, and pulling the fuel lines loose, and then they got knives out, and they was cutting the saddle into strips, and what I mean is, you touch an Angel's bike and you're finished, man. You should of seen what some of these here Angels looked like, they was crying like babies when the bike started burning, because that's what happened, the crowd, they opened up the carburetor valves, and they set fire to it, and when it exploded, that girl had to go with it, she had to go with the bike, like there wasn't no way to stop it. I tell you, lay a finger on an Angel's bike and I don't care who the shit you are, you've had it. The crowd was the ones that done it all. We was just hired to sit up on the platform and drink beer, and we wasn't doing nothing. It had to end like that, because them two thousand people made it end like that. If they hadn't of laid their hands on that bike, or like on that girl they kept pushing up on us, nothing would of happened, and the bike wouldn't of had to go."

(The tape came to an end now, and Melanie, her hair hanging straight and pale to her waist, her cheeks and throat like flower petals, came in from the kitchen with the potato masher in her hand. "So what did you think of it?" she asked. "How did you like it?" And I said, "She seemed to be in an awful lot of trouble, that girl." A look of amazement came into Melanie's wide, green, marvelously fearless eyes. "Trouble?" she said. "That wasn't trouble. She was just finding out who she was. Pete and Lucky were guiding her on a trip. Pete says everyone has to have three trips in a lifetime, that is, if he or she's honest enough to want to know who he or she really is." And I said, "You don't believe that, do you?" And Melanie, as beautiful as Venus riding on the wave, stood there with the potato masher hanging from her hand. "If you haven't studied about drugs, you haven't the right to talk about their effects," she said. "Like I've never studied the Greek myths the way you have, so I wouldn't presume to talk about them. Pete uses these trips like an initiation rite," she went on saying hurriedly, hurriedly, as if knowing already that the time between us was running out. "But he doesn't advise more than three, except in very stubborn cases," she said. "Leary gave his people around two hundred and fifty micrograms of LSD, while Pete gives a thousand, or even twelve hundred. You heard how he keeps it under perfect control." Good God, I wanted to say, this is the Grand Inquisitor's definition of the three powers that alone can conquer the impotent rebels: miracle, mystery, and authority; but I couldn't say anything, I couldn't speak. Melanie went back into the kitchen, and after a little while her voice said, "I've just got to put the steaks on, and then everything will be ready. I'll make them rare." Her voice was less exalted now, and my mind kept on saying, Good God, Good God, and I wanted to get some kind of answer from her, not knowing that once I had been answered, the room would no longer be a room with a lamp lit on the table in one corner of it, and a fire barely burning on the chipped bricks of the hearth, but that it would become in a clap of thunder, a tunnel, a cave, a shapeless, blind, interminable darkness in which I would crawl on my hands and knees, groping to find my way. "That girl on the tape, whatever became of her?" I asked, and Melanie said from the kitchen, "Woman, that girl on the tape was me. Lucky was taping it. That was my second trip." She might have been speaking of a jaunt to Mexico or a weekend on the Cape as she turned the steaks. "I still have one more trip to go," she said.)

5

At fifteen-minute intervals, the women prisoners were taken two by two from the cage and escorted the length of the bare reception hall, and there they passed around a high varnished counter and were lost to view. And as the crowd of women diminished, Calliope, with her modest crown of graying braids on her small head, could finally make her way through the others to where Callisto still leaned against the wall.

"Believe that our separate lives are of no importance?" she said, repeating Callisto's words. "Is anybody ever prepared for that? Isn't that the thing they always forgot to make convincing in church or school or whenever we asked for advice?"

The door of the visiting gallery was being unlocked, and over the heads of the demonstrators the women deputies could be seen, square-shouldered in their navy blue and braid, taking two of the prisoners out, then turning the key in the lock again.

"At this rate, it's going to take five hours to book us all!" cried out one of those who still waited. "I'm an accountant! As I figure it, we'll be here until eleven o'clock tonight, so we have time to plot our future strategy!"

Some of the women laughed at this, and others groaned aloud in mock despair, trapped as they were in the inflexibility of prison time. It was only Callisto who had recognized the dimensions of all that would be asked of them, and who had sought to give it a simple name; and now she slid inch by inch in her foolish yellow breeches down against the wall until she was finally seated limply on the floor. Calliope stood meekly beside her, her lips twitching to speak, to smile, but saying nothing more. There was no need for her to explain that if her daughter had a pain in her gut, and if Callisto's eyes were closed because of that pain, her own eyes, even faded and weary now, could serve for both of them, and her presence serve as custodian for two instead of one.

Near to Athena, St. Theresa waited still, her grave, gray eyes under slightly bulging brows moving with anxious deliberation from the steel wire of the enclosure to the door, and then to the backs of her own hands, wishing neither to see nor be seen. (I had a great-aunt who was a Carmelite, Athena remembered, a poet, born blind; and in my childhood I believed that all nuns were poets, and all born blind, and that all nuns could put their hands through the grating of their impoundment and touch the eyelids and hair of their visitors, as my great-aunt touched mine, and cry out in wonder at the color they sensed in their fingertips; and I believed that all nuns could type, for she typed her poems and the letters to her brother, my grandfather, without making a single error; and I believed that all nuns would say to me, as she said once through the grating, that clothes are a vocabulary that express to others what one is, and that the habit nuns wear can be a language so foreign that others cannot decipher what is being said. "And do you type, dear Sister Theresa," Athena jingled as she waited, "and could you tell in your fingertips the color of my hair?")

Ann moved through the women now to come closer to

Athena, and St. Theresa extinguished herself even further to let Ann pass. Once beside her, Ann slipped her arm through Athena's in desperate haste, and began talking quickly, in a voice so low that no one else could hear the words. She was saying that she was here under false pretenses, that is, here for the wrong reasons, speaking nervously and rapidly, saying she was not like the other prisoners, not like all the rest who had "acted out of purity."

"I have such terrible reasons for being here," she said, holding tightly to Athena's arm, "and I am so ashamed about not having convictions, or anyway not acting on convictions, and I should have got up in the courtroom this morning, the way you did, and told the judge and told everyone, the lawyers, and all the other demonstrators, that I have no principles, because I really came here out of anger, only I have never been angry with anyone, or anyway not let it out—"

But it was Lydia now, her ear trumpet hanging askew on the braided cord around her neck, her white shingled hair pressed as smooth as vaseline on her skull, who took the center of the stage. She was trying to untie the laces of her sneakers, but her fingers were thickened and slowed by arthritis; and when Athena slipped out of Ann's grasp and sat down beside her on the bare boards, Lydia turned her manlike, granite face to her in gratitude. Her mask of intricate wrinkles was white as a clown's as she watched Athena undo the laces and pull the sneakers from her swollen feet.

"They have to take all our things from us. Those are the rules," Lydia said, the echo of deafness in her voice as cavernous as if the words were halloo-ed through cupped hands. "They take away our shoes as well, I've heard, so before we go in, I want to share with everyone here the messages from Tolstoy and Gandhi that I brought in."

She slipped the folded, ruled pages out of the sneakers, where they had served as inner soles for a day and a night and again for this long day, cramping her feet, crowding her hump-backed toes, and now with her heavy, crippled hands she flattened out the papers on the floor, pages not for a moment written by men who were strangers to her, but personal letters the two gentlemen had had delivered to her by special messenger from their graves. She took a pair of steel-rimmed spectacles from her worn leather handbag, and hooked their spindly loops behind her ears.

"Leo Tolstoy wrote this," she said, her unquavering voice strong as a man's as she began reading aloud to the thirty prisoners who were left. " 'I received a letter from a gentleman in Colorado, who asked me to send him a few words or thoughts expressive of my feelings with regard to the noble work of the American nation, and heroism of its soldiers and sailors. This gentleman, together with an overwhelming majority of the American people, feels perfectly confident that the work of the Americans—the killing of several thousands of almost unarmed men (for, in comparison with the equipment of the Americans, the Spaniards are almost without arms)—was beyond doubt a "noble work" . . .' "

Athena was standing again, and Ann had again taken her arm and was clinging to her as if to life itself; and Athena thought, as had happened before from time to time with her girl students, how demeaning both for woman and girl, for teacher and student, to be drawn into this unnatural, this almost shocking, position of dependency. *Oh, be worthy of your looks!* Athena wanted to cry out, thinking how foreign was the cool delicacy of Ann's coloring, and the careful workmanship of her bones, to the chaos and incoherence of her total helplessness. Although the story Ann told in a low, hurried voice at the same time that Lydia read aloud was an uproarious story, it was one that could not be laughed at, for it had taken her from her home, and brought her to this place, and she herself looked on it as tragedy. Ann was saying that she respected her father for all he was, an army officer who controlled them all: her mother, herself, her brother (three years older, and finishing college now), and the dogs they had as well. The dogs sat when her father told them to, ate when he gave them the word to eat.

"He gave us standards," Ann said, speaking quickly and barely aloud. "I know that sounds crazy, but that's the way I really feel about him. I really, really do. You see, I can't discipline myself, I haven't any convictions. I'm just a mess," she said, the tears of self-pity glazing her childlike eyes. It was because of her mother that she had come to the Induction

Center, she was saying, the words, the thoughts behind them, jumbled like the pieces of a jigsaw puzzle that she kept trying, first one way and then the other, to fit together. "It wasn't *for* my mother that I came here, but *against* her, terribly against her," she said, while Lydia's voice read deeply from the tomb Tolstoy's words concerning the men who rule mankind.

" 'On entering this army, you will cease to be men with wills of your own; you will simply do what we require of you. But what we wish, above all else, is to exercise dominion; the means by which we dominate is killing, therefore we will instruct you to kill.' "

And then her mother had suddenly inherited a great deal of money, Ann said; that was two years ago, and at once the money took over, and the authority ceased to be the father's.

"It was like this," Ann said, clinging to Athena. "My father's hair was beginning to get thin on the top, and my mother had it—his hair—transplanted from the back of his neck and put on top. They can do that kind of thing now, you know. Perhaps she had wanted to have that done for a long time, and there were other things: she had his teeth capped, all of them, and then he wasn't able to whistle for the dogs anymore. My mother inherited all this money," she whispered, "and the money took over, it really did, and my father stopped telling us what to do. He allowed—he accepted—the operation on my brother's ears. They stuck out a little from his head, and my mother had them put back flat. She may have been thinking about that too for a long time. We had three Cadillacs, and I was sent away to study in Switzerland for a year," she said, as if confessing to some act of shame. "And my mother, she had—she had her breasts lifted, things like that. And all the time I couldn't stop crying; I cried at least an hour every day, because I could see my father was afraid of the money, and he would do whatever it told him to, and before that I didn't think he could ever be afraid—"

" 'A pacifism which can see only the cruelties of occasional warfare, and is blind to the continuous cruelties of our social system is worthless," Lydia read, offering Gandhi's words steadily, tirelessly, to the silent, weary, slowly diminishing group of women, some of whom had fallen asleep now on the boards of the floor. " 'The idea of accommodating oneself to imprison-ment is a novel thing for us," she read. " 'We will try to assimi-late it . . .' " And she told them that by December 1921, twenty thousand Indians had been jailed for civil disobedience; and the little nun returned from the far place where she had been, perhaps in search of cloister and sanctification, and smiled at the irony of their own small number. In January, ten thousand more were jailed for political offenses, Lydia said in her deep, deaf voice, and by that time whenever Gandhi heard of a friend or colleague who had been arrested, he telegraphed congratula-tions to him. In the courtroom, before being sentenced, Gandhi had stood before the bench, she told them, and called out to men and women throughout the world to overcome their "excessive dread of prisons." He said that "imprisonments are now to be courted because we consider it wrong to be free under a government we hold to be wholly bad . . ."

But there was still one more thing that Ann was trying to tell Athena, if only she could get the words of it out.

"My getting arrested, could it make my father—I don't re-ally know—could it make him the way he was before?" she asked; and Athena, feeling light-headed with fatigue, tried not to visualize the army officer going bald again, and the hair restored to the back of his neck, and his teeth miraculously uncapped, enabling the whistle for the dogs to pierce the air again. "Do you think it could make him strong enough, or angry enough to tell me—you see what a mess I am?—I think strong enough just to tell me I'm wrong," Ann whispered to Athena in something as absurd as hope.

Hour after hour, Lydia read, and when she came to the end of the closely typed pages, she would begin over again. Her voice was little more now than a dark croaking, and her thick, big-knuckled fingers shook, but still she read on until after ten o'clock, when the deputies unlocked the cage door and called hers and Ann's names. Then she folded the typewritten pages over, smoothing them carefully in a gesture of farewell, and put them in the bulging handbag, and removed the steel-rimmed glasses from her nose. She reached for her sneakers and pulled them on, and did not stop to lace them, and Athena took her hands and helped her to her feet. Ann had walked alone to the cage door, and she waited docilely there, her head lifted almost in pride, as if she carried with her now a portion of the message that Lydia's unwavering voice had read aloud. It might have been nothing more than she remembered than Gandhi's gentle chiding to the uncertain that men in the end become what they believe themselves to be.

Even after Lydia was gone, the laces of her sneakers trailing, she and Ann flanked by the deputies, even after they had walked the length of the entrance hall and disappeared from sight, the echo of the old voice could still be heard. The fragments of the letters written personally to her were still captive there within the confines of the visitors' cage, so that when future prisoners were held there they would hear Gandhi saying forever that: "A violent man's activity is most visible while it lasts . . . but it is always transitory . . ."; or hear Tolstoy crying out: "I wish now, this moment, without delay or hesitation, to the very utmost of my strength, neither waiting for anyone nor counting the cost, to do that which alone is clearly demanded by Him who sent me into the world; and on no account, and under no conditions, do I wish to, or can I, act otherwise—for herein lies my only possibility for a rational and unharassed life."

It was half-past ten, and the accountant had been right, for there were only four women left in the cage: Callisto sleeping, a tall, slender, long-haired child, her head in the green velveteen of Calliope's lap; Athena lying with her jacket rolled under her head, as it had been in the forests of other countries so many times before; and St. Theresa sitting with her legs crossed under her, withdrawn in her cassock-like dress in deliberate, considered penance for all that life offered so heedlessly. For a moment it seemed to Athena that the roles of daughter and mother had been abandoned, and that they were four potential lovers waiting there, each waiting for the other to reach out a tender and compassionate hand. But that moment passed, and almost at once Calliope and Callisto were summoned, and the cage door was locked again, and they went, their beauty almost extinguished, down the endlessly long hall.

Half in sleep, Athena wondered what St. Theresa, who was left here with her, would make of Blake's view of God the

Father as symbol of ruthless, relentless tyranny, the highest instrument for the breaking of man's will, and of Christ as the living figure of all that is searching and fallible in man. For Athena did not yet know that they had come to the end of their vocabulary, to the end of all the quotations by which they lived, and that another language must be found, one by means of which the poor could speak to the rich, the rich to the poor, the illiterate to the literate, the fearful to the unafraid. A new and violent place lay at the end of the hall, and she did not know that when she entered it, whatever had been before, whatever had served as experience, would not be able to serve again.

Before the deputies came for the last time, Athena kept herself awake by singing words that Blake had written, telling herself that if Callisto had been there, she would not have dared to sing. She sang the lines of Blake's that Rory had put to music a long time ago (over twenty years now), and sung to Sybil when she was three and four months old in Glenwood Springs, in the cold heart of that Colorado winter and the cold heart of the war. Rory would come down at night from the army ski camp above Leadville, down the long winding road through frozen drifts, past the unending tiers of high moonlit crests and curving valleys, all somberly glowing with snow; down, down, past the black of the forests to the warm lights of the wintry town. And after a drink in the shabby hotel room, while the radiator hissed in anger near the frosted windows, the taste of the cold would be wiped from Rory's mouth, and the blood would move like summer through his veins. He would take Sybil out of the basket where she slept, and hold her, asleep still, over his shoulder in the khaki tunic, his eyes deathless and bright with love. He would pat her on her tiny back, steadily, rhythmically, and when he stopped laughing he would begin to sing. And Athena sang the same words softly now, feeling the weak tears gathering behind her lids.

> *Was Jesus Humble? or did he*
> *Give any proofs of Humility?*
> *Boast of high Things with Humble tone,*
> *And give with Charity a Stone?*

It had become such a part of her life to draw strength (to draw identity even) from words that had been written in other times, music composed in other centuries, that it seemed to Athena the lines of Blake's poem had stirred a response in St. Theresa. Through her blurred lashes, Athena believed she could see the living flesh restored to the little nun's bones, the small cheeks beginning to fill out, as if a painter were shaping them in with oils. For the first time, St. Theresa's lips parted, and her shoulders in the brown wool dress sloped gently and vulnerably. It was only her square hands, the short fingers slightly convexed, as though from long years curved in prayer, that appeared to resist. And Athena sang a little louder now, so that the hands too would change.

> *When but a Child he ran away*
> *And left his Parents in dismay.*
> *When they had wandered three days long*
> *These were the words upon his tongue:*
> *"No Earthly Parents I confess:*
> *I am doing my Father's business."*

When the deputies came down the hall, St. Theresa stood up and smoothed her brown dress with her flattened palms. Then she walked in her scuffed moccasins to where Athena lay, and she held out one open, and unexpectedly palpable hand to her, and helped to pull her to her feet. She stood there, shorter than Athena, not looking at her as Athena picked up the jacket that had served as pillow and put it on, not like a nun at all, but like a student, her brow puzzling over some difficult text. Then she said very quietly, her eyes averted:

"I'm doing my Father's business," and the two of them went with the deputies down the hall.

6

IN each of the two main dormitories of the women's section of the Rehabilitation Center were fifty iron cuts, twenty on one side of each of the two long narrow rooms, the barracks-trim formation of cots divided in mid-center by an archway that gave access to the toilets, sinks, and showers; thirty along the opposite walls, where no archways intervened. The dormitory on the west side of the building ran parallel with the bleak entrance hall and the visiting cage, and thus had no windows. The dormitory on the east side had a row of windows in its outer wall, old-fashioned sash windows, with cracked ancient shades that pulled up and down, pleasant and even homelike to the eye except for the presence of iron bars fixed to the outside sills. By daylight, the demonstrators would be able to see from these windows a ragged stretch of grass bordered by overgrown beds of iris plants, their sabers rusted and split from long neglect. There were also three or four dejected plum trees, and a solid maple that leaned in weariness against the south corner of the fence, its trunk girded with a spiked chastity belt so that it could not serve as avenue of escape. Unpruned rose bushes, their lean arms gesticulating wildly in the breeze, almost reached the tangle of barbed wire that topped the eight-foot barrier standing between the prisoners and the countryside. Above all this soared the wide, ever changing California sky.

But none of it—not the lock-up wards, or the iron-barred massive doors to the solitary cells, or the view of the garden— were the demonstrators able to see that night. By the time the processing and fingerprinting were done, it was close to midnight, and the women groped their separate ways down the aisles between the rows of cots where the regular prisoners lay sleeping in the half dark. Their possessions had again been taken from them, this time their clothing as well, and now they wore the prison-issue nightgowns and sneakers that had been given them after their showers. Over their arms, each carried a towel, a washrag, two sheets, and a gray dress for daytime wear, and each held a cake of soap in her hand. They had been directed to take whatever unoccupied beds they found, designated by a blanket folded over at the foot, and when they had found them they laid their towels and washrags on the night tables that stood between the cots, placed their soap in the night table drawers, and folded the gray dresses for morning across the iron head bars. They spread the coarse, patched sheets over mattresses no thicker than their hands, and, like

obedient children, arranged their sneakers under the night tables, and slipped off the threadbare, prison-issue underpants.
Then each of them lay down in the deeply breathing strangeness of this place, drew the navy or khaki blanket over her, and
sought to sleep.

That was the first night, and before there had been the time
to dream, the lights came on, and a woman's voice spoke
sharply.

"Time to get up, ladies," the woman said, and the prisoners
got silently from their cots. "Stand at the foot of your bed until
count has been taken," said the deputy, neat as a pin in the
dormitory aisle. In her left hand she held a clipboard with the
typed list of their names, black, white, and Chicano, fixed to it,
and the angular fingers of her right hand drummed on the
wood. She was haggared-cheeked and long of jaw, and each
separate name she pronounced might have been a fruit pit she
spat out, the taste of it as bitter as gall. When she was done
with the lot of them, she instructed them to wash and dress.
"Do not line up for breakfast until you have washed and
opened your beds for airing," she said, her eyes sharp on the
watch at her wrist.

Some of the regular prisoners were already making for the
showers, running on bare feet down the dormitory in their
flannel gowns, their towels slung over their shoulders, carrying
with them their sneakers and dresses; black women, and
Chicano women among them, pushing one another aside in
their haste, needing this moment of triumph over others, even
over their own kind, in order to bear the defeats of the day.
They might have been children running eagerly, for the nightgowns, cream-colored and ruffled at the neck and wrists, had an
innocence and charm to them, like the nightgowns of little
girls, and Athena wanted to hold hers fast to her heart. Obedi-
ently and modestly, she dressed beside her cot, pulling the
prison underpants and the shapeless gray dress on under the
gown, and then slipping it off over her head.

"They didn't give us any combs," one of the college girls
called out from two cots away; and another voice warbled from
the far end of the dormitory: "Madame Deputy, what about
toothbrushes?"

In time they were all to learn that this slat-legged, lean, and easily rattled keeper of order feigned an absorption in things of greater moment whenever a question was put to her. She was not deaf, but she could not afford to hear, for a direct response to a question would have unmasked her, an argument shattered her. Thus her single weapon was her ability to convince them that their questions went unanswered because they had not been heard, and not been heard because for her their voices had no sound. Her iron eye advised them that their faces had been rubbed out, their bodies obliterated without trace, her exclusion of them from life permitting them only one reality: that of their names on the typewritten list she held. Any other claim they made to existence was no more than a hallucination of their own disordered minds.

"You have six minutes," she said, her jaw moving up and then down, then up again, as if insecurely wired to her skull.

Corporal Anxiety, Calliope was to name her in one of those hours when any words, whether funny or not, seemed better than no words at all. And now Corporal Anxiety was joined by another deputy, who came in from the eastern dormitory, clipboard in hand, she too having summoned prisoners from their beds. She was statuesque, by which Athena meant she was larger than life-size and handsomely made, almost Grecian in allure despite the navy blue turtleneck sweater worn over the white shirt and the uniform's navy skirt. Her legs in tan nylons were muscular as a dancer's, and drawn in tight at the ankles in unexpected delicacy. She alone in the room seemed without tension as she leaned against the footrail of an empty cot, her hair coiled into a smooth golden bun at the nape of her neck and held in a filet there. Athena hastened past them both toward the washrooms, but in that last instant of quiet she did not reach the doorway before the screams came, rising higher and higher from the showers, and the clatter and crash of flung objects, the slap of flesh on flesh, the shattering of glass, turned them all to stone.

All, that is, except one; for the Grecian deputy at once threw the clipboard she held onto the cot behind her, and sprang forward on her dancer's legs. She crossed the dormitory with such speed that she and the naked black girl collided as, shining with water, gleaming with blood, the girl exploded through the doorway. Behind her came a second girl in pursuit, tall, and handsomely proportioned, with fine, high, blue-nippled breasts, her head turbaned in a towel. Her black flesh was wet and glittering, and there was an animal splendor about her as she let fly the battered and blood-stained metal wastebasket that she swung above her head. But with one hand, the Grecian deputy caught it in midair while with the other she pushed out of the orbit of attack the girl crouched low behind her on the floor, who slipped and toppled now in the slime of her own blood. Then the deputy seized the pursuer by the wrist, but held her only for the instant it took for the soapy flesh to escape her, and the tall girl went dancing off again. The deputy had flung the wastebasket aside, and now she had the girl's slick shoulders in her strong white hands, but the shoulders too writhed, eel-like, from her grasp.

"Get a sheet around Prudence," the Grecian deputy said without turning her head, knowing, although she did not see it taking place, that her long-jawed colleague and the white prisoners would be standing there as if bound hand and foot, handcuffed and manacled by their own uncertainty. It was the black inmates who wrapped their fallen, panting sister in a sheet, and lifted her to a cot, and pressed their towels upon her wounds. "Get the key to the medical supply room," the deputy directed Corporal Anxiety, her voice low, unperturbed, still not turning her head; for now the eyes of the tall black girl and hers had met, and the precise *pas de deux* was engaged, to be danced warily and shrewdly to its end.

"She said she'd get me! She's been waitin' to get me!" Prudence cried from the cot, the words wrung from her in separate, convulsive sobs. She lay shuddering like a night-moth with a pin transfixing its soft, trembling, dying body while the handmaidens stanched her blood. "She came back here to get me!" Prudence screamed out. "She come back with murder in her heart!"

The arms and breasts of the deputy were as firm as stone in her turtleneck sweater as she stood with the sovereignty of a statue before the dancing black girl who spun forward, armed now with a drawer wrenched from a night table, the contents of its scattering as she raised it in blazing fury over her head. The deputy moved serenely in the measure of the dance, reached for the drawer and without apparent effort jerked it from the girl's hands. She did not turn her head as she set it down behind her, as she had the wastebasket with its traceries of bright blood; these awkward weapons she could deal with, but when she sashayed forward to join hands with her partner, the girl slithered away. It was a stylized gavotte that now proceeded, two steps to one side, three to the other, with no music playing, but the breathing of the two women who danced whispering a soft, staccato rhythm on the hushed air. The deputy held the girl's gaze in hers, her arms not yet around her, her eyes alone drawing her closer and closer into the final embrace. If the girl resisted, it was only because the contest was not, had never been, with the deputy, but with Prudence, who lay on the cot beyond. For the third role was neither that of mother nor daughter, and the drama was now between lover and lover, with the deputy usurping a place in the triangle by virtue of her illicit authority.

"That two-timin' bitch, she done me in," the tall girl whispered, dancing still. "Done me in, done me in."

The deputy moved from side to side as the girl moved, seeming to follow but actually leading her in the figure of the waltz; and step by step, breath by breath, she narrowed the distance between them, guiding the girl by nothing more than her unfaltering gaze. Then, without warning, the deputy leaped forward and caught the girl fast in her arms, gripping her just above the high, black, cushioned hips, pinning the girl's arms to her sides. The strong, impervious hands were locked like a steel trap in the small of the girl's back, and in the same instant that she clasped her, the deputy forced one of her dancer's fine muscular legs around the girl's black, gleaming, left leg, and held her rooted there.

"Cool it, baby," the deputy said through her teeth. "Cool it, Marvella," the vise of her hands not breaking, the girl's pear-shaped breasts pressed, soft and giving, against the turtleneck sweater's navy wool.

Even before two more uniformed women moved in battleship formation the length of the dormitory, the girl had surrendered, her rage spent, defeated perhaps by something as unexpected as the deputy's gentle pronouncing of her name. "Marvella," the Grecian deputy had said, and not in admonition, in a place where gentleness was allowed no gesture, authorized no speech. Another of the deputies ripped a blanket from a cot to fling over Marvella's nakedness, and her companion grasped Marvella's upper arm; and Marvella went with them, majestic in the blanket's folds, her turbaned head not lowered, her eyes fixed blankly on the familiar outline of what waited at the end of the long hall.

"Don't let Marvella keep the towel!" the Grecian deputy called after them, cautioning them as she jerked her turtleneck sweater into place, and with the palm of one broad, steady hand smoothed the filet that still held the gold coil of her hair. And then she turned to Prudence on the cot. "Get into chow line," she directed the prisoners quietly. She sat down on the sagging edge of the mattress, and her square-tipped, blunt-nailed fingers set the matted strands of Prudence's hair back from the deepest of the lacerations, scarlet velvet or plush, it seemed to be, hanging over her right eye. She did not so much as glance at Corporal Anxiety, who stood hesitantly there, her long jaw swinging, a bottle of iodine and a tin container of Band-Aids in her uncertain hand. "You'll have to have some stitches, baby," the Grecian deputy said. "It's not going to hurt. They'll freeze it insensible." It did not seem permissible, not acceptable, somehow, that she should hold Prudence like a small child in her arms, but this is what took place. Carefully, carefully, she held and tended Prudence, touching her delicately so as not to harm her in any way, cradling her, wiping the tears from the girl's small, dark, lacerated face, pressing the towel to the jagged slash across her breasts. "You won't feel anything, baby," she was crooning to Prudence, and the girl clung to her and no longer wept. "We'll get you to the hospital right away."

Now that the routine had been disrupted, all was in a state of panic. The day was twelve minutes behind schedule, the prisoners were told, and the hysteria this generated in the figures of authority silenced the speech on every tongue. The pace of activity was so quickened that Athena saw herself and the others as those ludicrous, darting shapes with flailing limbs that flash across the screen when a movie film is accelerated. Breakfast was cut from fifteen minutes to seven, and then the inmates flew to make their beds, were counted again with the swiftness of lightning, and rapidly divided into three work groups. One contingent was dispatched to the laundry, under guard, another began the scraping and waxing of the endless halls, and the third battalion was rushed by deputies to the annex where the sewing and ironing rooms were housed. The walled courtyard that lay between this annex and the women's dormitories was an area that perhaps threatened sexual confrontation, for it was rumored that the men's quarters lay beyond the western wall. It was even said that from the narrow windows, those just over there, the men could look down through the unrelenting bars and covet the women as they crossed the paved yard—the men who were not even voices in the distance, on whom no woman's eye was authorized to rest.

In the sewing and ironing space the demonstrators learned that the long-term prisoners wore blue dresses with smart white collars and cuffs, trim enough for a beauty parlor operator to have selected, while those with shorter sentences must wear the grieving, shapeless garments of steel gray. In this unfamiliar dress that hung almost to her ankles, Athena worked at an ironing board, the sneakers on her feet a size too large and contoured still with the outline of other women's bunions and other women's toes. The ironing board swayed unsteadily as she pressed shirts that reached their denim arms across the scorched padding, empty male arms stretching out for every woman there.

Lydia and Calliope had been assigned a closetful of blankets to sort and fold and stack in two piles. On the left of the closet door were to be placed those which could still be darned or patched and put into service again; on the right, those that were beyond repair. A record of the long durance and endurance of the prisoners was written into the faded khaki or navy wool of these blankets, depositions made in the cacography of dried vomit and the hieroglyphics of blackened blood. But, soiled or not, they were to be spread out on the center sewing table so that the black girls might cut them in half, or even into thirds, working not only heedless of the white faces suddenly there in such profusion, but working as if they, the permanent black prisoners, were contained in a separate world that no one could enter by any of the simple ways that people customarily enter one another's lives. Calliope and Lydia would carry the ailing blankets to them, and four of the black girls would hold the four corners of each blanket, while a fifth girl cut expertly from one side to the other of it with outsized shears. And then Calliope, the bemused half smile on her lips, small-boned and modest in her sad gray dress, would carry the salvaged sections to the women busy at the machines, and they would piece them together, making whole blankets of them again.

Once, when she passed Athena at the ironing board, Calliope paused a moment with the bisected blankets in her arms.

"I've been brought up to believe," she murmured, "that a woman is never happier than when ironing for her loved ones." And another time she stopped long enough to say that Callisto was waxing a dormitory floor. "She's going to be such a help around the house when we get home," she said.

St. Theresa worked at a table apart from the other demonstrators, replacing buttons, repairing pockets, setting neat patches in the seats and the knees of the coarse, white coveralls for men they had never seen and were never to see. Her small, tense, puzzled face with its swollen brows, looked strangely anemic to Athena, actually drained of pigmentation, white as death itself among the black faces and throats and arms of the girls who worked beside her and across from her, and who talked among themselves, but by no word or glance acknowledged her bleached presence there. Perhaps the God to whom St. Theresa had humbly dedicated her life was now beginning to fail her, and so the others were uneasy with her; but however it was, it was only to Calliope that the black prisoners turned, as if she were neither white nor stranger to them. Their Afros were neatly trimmed, and their flesh as smooth as ebony, but their faces were not in any way alike. The white college girls and the white librarians, Athena reflected as she ironed, were scarcely distinguishable one from the other, and this might be because white women were shaped despite themselves and their convictions by the rigid molds of the timeless traditions they upheld. But the look in the black girls' eyes filled Athena with fierce grief. No human being had the right to examine others with such cold, high censure, or with such detached and grudging curiosity; and while Athena raged within herself at all that had brought this about, it was Calliope who won them, for she knew exactly what to do with a sewing machine. She could make it come to humming life, like the sound of a hive of bees, as the needle sprang back and forth, embroidering the names of the girls who pressed around her. In the hours of that first long morning, she began making deeper hems in the trailing gray dresses that the demonstrators wore. And "Love," she stitched quickly inside the man's underpants they had just patched, and "Peace" inside the cuff of a denim shirt. The two deputies at the far end of the room perceived nothing but the diligence of the women at their work, and at that distance they did not hear the voices saying:

"Me, I come here for a rest. I bin in an outta jail so many years, I don't try to count 'em anymore. This time I took the rap for my kid sister, but none of us, we don' go roun' makin' announcements 'bout why we're here. At firs', a long time back, I use go roun' askin' who done what. But after a while it jus' don' interes' nobody, 'cause everybody done jus' 'bout the same. I'm twenty-five, and jail's bin my life since way back. But it ain't bad, not here it ain't. You got a bed with sheets, and no hustlin', and the meals all cooked up fine. I come back, an I know all the deputies, and who'll be like my mama to me, and the other ones who won't. Here is jus' somewhere you come back to rest up in 'fore you go back out and git busted over again."

Or saying to Calliope: "They's two things I knows a lot about. One's dope and one's women. I guess I knows a little about men, too, but when you're in here you get to likin' women, an that's cool. You ever make it with a broad?" Or saying: "You in here for your reasons like I'se in here for mine. We both believes in them jus' as strong. Soon as I git out, I go back, do my thing, an you go back out an do yours. . . ."

It was a woman called Tallulah who first spoke of children, not to Athena and not to Calliope, but to the other black prisoners. Tallulah sat at the head of St. Theresa's table, a woman so large that she might have been two women contrived to look like one, stretched as if at ease in her chair, but she was not at ease, for her shoulders were bowed like an old woman's under the nearly unbearable burden of mountainous flesh they bore. The buttons of her blue and white prison dress (which may have been two dresses stitched together to contain her) were strained to the bursting point across her belly and her ballooning breasts. She had stretched her enormous legs out under the sewing table, and the skin of them above the white socks was burnished to mahogany. Her forearms, heavy as any other woman's thighs, lay idle in her lap, resting from the weariness of merely being alive, and Athena saw that the sleeves of her dress had been slit above the elbows so that they would not throttle her flesh like tourniquets. Her neck was short and as solid as a bull's, and above the three thick layers of her chin swelled the dark stoical face, its placid grief crowned with a multitude of tiny braids that lay close to her skull.

"They keeps me here acause they don' want me doin' for my kids," she was saying. "Tha's the reason for it. Six months ago when I come out, my boyfriend ask me if I wanna go firs' see the kids or firs' have a fix, an I says I take the fix, acause what happen is, sometime you scared to see the kids right off, sometime you gotta kinda collec' yo'self. So now they put the kids in forster homes, all six of 'em, an when I get outta here, I gotta go looking for 'em, like they was los' dogs or cats, mebbe fin' 'em at the SPCA."

"Tallulah," they'd say as her three hundred pounds of dark flesh shook with laughter, "Tallulah, pass the scissors up this way," or "Tallulah, quit integratin' the black an white sewin' cotton you holdin' onto down there," or "Tallulah, you lookin' for a fix, the way you keepin' them needles down there under yo' auspices?" And Tallulah, her rosy-palmed hands lying empty in her lap, would talk about the children again.

"My Auntie, she tol' me when she come out Sunday, the twins is callin' that forster mother 'Mama,' an I told her that ain't right. Tha's what the prison system do, take away yo' kids and make 'em think back on you like you was dead. Tha's what the power structure doin' to me an my life," she said, and for a while she didn't laugh any more.

Russell Banks

RUSSELL BANKS is a novelist and short story writer, has also been an editor and a plumber, and currently teaches in the creative writing program at Princeton University. He is the author of ten books, including the highly acclaimed *Continental Drift*, an epic novel about the pursuit of the American Dream, and *Affliction*, a disturbing and very personal examination of male violence. His novels—whether set in the blue-collar towns of his native New Hampshire or in the cultural and racial conflict of Florida and the Caribbean—are portraits of contemporary American *lives*. Banks avoids intellectual or literary distance from the people he writes about; his narrators intrude and get emotionally involved. Although his style is often fiercely realistic, what concerns him is not just the physical drama (the sex and violence) but the turmoil of vision (the desire and pain), and what matters most is his compassion. He cares about people, their moral dreams and failures, their desire to lead a good life.

Banks writes about "ordinary" working-class people who try their best to live from day to day. They struggle through uncertainty, loneliness, and frustration, not in the mode of rarefied alienation and isolated disenchantment of much modern fiction, but rather as participants in families, in communities, in different cultures, and in a distinctively Western hemisphere. Like many great authors who remain aware of just where they come from, he has an acute sense of place—the knowing of it, the searching for it, the feeling of being stuck, trapped, lost in it, the needing to escape it. The people in his novels are not only trying to find out who they are, but where they stand, where they belong, and how they fit in with other groups of people. Most of all, Banks is interested in survival, how people endure despite failure, discrimination, guilt, and tragedy. He sees "people as part of a community" of the heroic: "We are the planet, fully as much as its water, earth, fire and air are the planet, and if the planet survives, it will only be through heroism. Not occasional heroism, a remarkable instance of it here and there, but constant heroism, systematic heroism, heroism as a governing principle" (from *Continental Drift*).

Russell Banks rejects the patriarchal myth of European culture, of the individualist hero who takes control of his life and those of other people. He unapologetically immerses himself in encounters with other races, classes, and genders—with all the conflict and tension this naturally entails, but without succumbing to well-intentioned condescension. In *The Book of Jamaica*, as a white visitor and tourist in the world of Jamaica's Maroons (descendants of Africans who were brought over as slaves, but escaped to the unsettled woods and mountains, banded together and fought off the British, and survived) he is acutely aware of how their separate racial and cultural identities interact in a New World created out of white European oppression and Black African persistence. It is not an easy or simple task and it involves fear, guilt, and moral outrage. But most of all it requires understanding and compassion. "In denying the humanity of . . . all the nonwhite part of the population, we end up—besides making it impossible to be a good man—making it even harder to be a good white man" (Interview with Sam Anson and Ted Foss in *Scrivener*).

Understanding, like writing fiction, is a creative learning process. Its essence is not in knowing, but in the struggle. Out of it grows respect and admiration. The people in Banks's books encounter and collide with Blacks, and Cubans, and Haitians, and Jamaicans, and women, and white males from the Northeast, who all are striving to lead good lives, who are trying to find the American Dream, who sometimes fail miserably and horribly, who are trying to learn how to live with other people when they are still not quite sure how to live with themselves. The reader, in the case of Russell Banks, shares something with the author: "When you start to deal up close and imaginatively with another person's life, you tend to understand your own life better and the context of your own life better" (Interview, *Scrivener*).

—*Gundars Strads*

Excerpt from Chapter 1,
THE BOOK OF JAMAICA

1

THE first time I visited the country of Jamaica was in mid-December 1975, and I stayed until February 1976. Though I knew little about the island and the people who lived there, I had read two or three travel books on the subject, and I had visited other Caribbean islands in the past—Saba and St. Maarten's in the Dutch Antilles and the several U.S. Virgins. But always as a tourist and never for longer than two fun-filled weeks. In the fall of 1975, however, it became apparent that I was going to be freed of my teaching obligations for an unusually lengthy midwinter break, so I determined to spend that time and regularly forwarded bi-weekly paychecks where I would not have to wage a day-to-day battle against the cold, snow and ice of another New England winter. I would go to some Caribbean island, any Caribbean island, and rent a house on a breezy hill overlooking the sea, staff it with a polite, scrupulously clean, black-skinned housekeeper and cook, smoke cigars I couldn't afford to pay the import duties on, drink frosty rum drinks in the cool of the evening, and maybe take a swim in the pool every morning before I began my regular three or four hours' work on the novel I had been writing for the last three years. I might even be able to rent a terraced flower garden with a fussy but cheerful gardener to tend it.

What I especially liked, however, was the idea of living in a pastel-colored, stucco-walled house up on a hill and away from the tourists, those loud, sunburnt, overweight Americans and Canadians, their whining children, their nervous shopping for souvenirs, their constant computations of the rate of exchange. This time, I told my wife and children, we will not be tourists.

This time we will not even have to *see* any tourists! We will see only the *natives!* They will be black, of course, and mostly slender, smiling, and poor—but when they learn that we are not tourists, they will be honest, and they will like us, because even though we are rich and white, we are honest and we like them.

I phoned an old friend from college, a white man who had been raised in Jamaica and whose parents still lived there. My friend, whose name was Upton West, was a photographer who had recently become a successful producer and director of feature-length documentary films and books with subjects like autoracing, body building, integration in the South. He lived in New York City and New Hampshire, and when he was in New Hampshire I occasionally saw him for dinner, when we would eat fresh vegetables from his garden and thick slices of beef cut from black Angus cattle raised on his own land. Later, over brandy and cigars in the library, we would talk about our days at Chapel Hill, famous people he now knew, the future of the New Left, and sometimes the beauty and mysterious complexity of Jamaica.

Upton loved Jamaica and returned there often to visit his parents and their friends. Two years ago he had taken a whole month away from the production of his film on body builders to travel alone over the entire island, snapping thousands of photographs that he had vague plans for bringing together someday in a large paperback book. You would love Jamaica, he often told me. There's a beauty and a mysterious complexity to the island that are unmatched anywhere in the world.

I was sure that Upton knew what he was talking about, because he had traveled to most of the beautiful and mysteriously complicated places in the world. If you ever decide to go down, he told me, let me know and I'll have my mother find you a house. She dabbles in real estate. She trains the help in her own house. Upton's father was a retired British army captain who dabbled in insurance in Montego Bay. Upton always referred to his father as the Captain. His mother he called Mother. She was an American out of a well-connected family from Cambridge, Massachusetts, and her marriage to the Captain had been celebrated in the society pages on three different continents. Upton thought that was amusing and once had shown me the clippings.

Over the phone I asked him if he thought his mother could find a house for me to rent for two months, a house close enough to the sea and a city like Montego Bay that I would be able to obtain the usual amenities, yet far enough into the country that I would not have to cope with the tourist business. Three bedrooms, a pool, if possible (for the kids, I explained), and a housekeeper who would be able to take care of some of the cooking. It doesn't have to be anything luxurious, I assured him. We're quite willing to accommodate ourselves to a few inconveniences. It was to be a working trip for me and an escape from the New Hampshire winter for my family.

Eager to share his beloved Jamaica with an old friend, Upton immediately contacted his mother and in two weeks I was corresponding with a man named Preston Church, an electrical contractor in Montego Bay who owned two houses in the small town of Anchovy twelve miles outside of Montego Bay. He lived in one house himself; his son and his son's family had lived in the other before their departure for Canada. I did not then understand or attribute any meaning to this departure for Canada, because I did not then understand or attribute any meaning to the flight of capital and capitalists from a country whose government had determined to eliminate, even by gradual and democratic procedures, capital and capitalists. Nor did I understand or attribute meaning to the flight of white people from a black country that had always been black but had only recently come to be governed by people who were black.

The son of Preston Church, I learned from Upton, has been a schoolmate of Upton's and for ten years had helped his father run the contracting business in Montego Bay. They had done exceptionally well during that period, because from 1965 to 1975 there had been a building boom along the north coast of Jamaica, as increasing numbers of Americans and Canadians decided to invest capital in the construction of three- and four-bedroom villas that could be rented to other Americans and Canadians. Now, however, as Upton explained it, there had come a leveling off, and probably young Church could do better for himself in Canada. Therefore, when the elder Mr.

Church wrote and told me that he would be willing to cut the cost of renting his son's house practically in half if I would be willing to pay with a personal check made out to his son and mailed from my American address to his son's Canadian address, I saw nothing wrong or particularly unusual about the arrangement. Naturally, his cutting the rent in half was something of an aid to my not seeing anything wrong or unusual. I merely felt lucky. It's amazing, I thought, how lucky I am.

IT was the wife of Preston Church, Abbie, who met us at the airport in Montego Bay. She was an extremely short woman with a blocky body and the tiniest feet I had ever seen on an adult. She chain-smoked Craven A's and talked rapidly, unsmilingly, and walked ahead of everyone on her tiny feet first to the car rental desk, where I rented a red Toyota sedan, and then to her dark gray Mercedes, where her driver waited.

The house, when we finally saw it, was even more appropriate than I had hoped—four bedrooms, if you counted the maid's quarters, high ceilings and sliding glass doors opening onto patios and terraces that looked down two thousand feet of hillside jungle to the sea. And a pool, too, with lights for night swimming. There were lights and switches all over the house and grounds, and it took an hour for Abbie to show me which switches operated which lights. I could flick a switch over a kitchen counter and flood the side yard with light from a cotton tree; a switch next to the bed in the master bedroom turned scary nighttime into comforting midday all over the grounds; a bank of switches on the patio threw the narrow, winding, private road out into the open for several hundred yards back down the hill toward the main road, halfway to the village center; and hidden in the leaves of the crotons and macca bushes and forty feet up in the breadfruit trees scattered through the terraced gardens in front of the house, blue- and red-lensed floodlights had been secreted, so that a flick of the switch on the living-room wall next to the glass doors would turn the place into something that resembled a cocktail lounge in a Florida suburb. Abbie was naturally quite proud of this system; apparently there was one to match it for the house she and her husband lived in, which, as it turned out, was only two hundred yards away, our only neighbor up here on this hill, for, as it further turned out, the entire hill was owned by Church.

When Abbie had finished showing the place to us and explaining how all its machinery worked and had introduced us to Caroline, the young woman who would be our housekeeper, a small, smiling woman whose starched uniform was so white and whose skin was so black that I did not see her, she wheeled on her tiny feet and trotted her box-shaped body back to her Mercedes where her driver, a man whose face was also so dark that I did not see him, sat reading the *Daily Gleaner.* Then she turned and said with sudden gentleness that my first name was the same as her son's and that my two children, though younger than his, numbered the same as her son's. How old are you? she asked me. I told her my age, thirty-five, and she sighed, then stuck her cigarette into her mouth and jerked herself into the front seat next to the driver. As she closed the door, she spat, It's all that goddamned Michael Manley's fault! Then she drove off, leaving me and my family in our house in the tropics.

ONE Sunday morning about two weeks later, by which time my family and I had more or less accommodated ourselves to our new environment—insofar as that environment went no further than the luxurious and, as I had by then discovered, walled-in compound owned by the Churches—my friend Upton and his father the Captain drove up in a dark blue Land Rover. During a pleasant breakfast on the terrace, while the Captain jovially complimented my wife on the quality of her coffee, Upton told me about the Maroons. It was the first time I had heard the word.

Upton had an interesting and engaging way of speaking: his accent was not quite British, not quite Proper Bostonian, not quite white Jamaican, but a unique amalgam of the three, which he uttered in a nasal monotone that made him sound as if he were reading aloud, an effect heightened by his habit of speaking not only in complete sentences but in whole paragraphs as well. The Maroons, he said, are a beautiful and mysteriously complex people with a noble and violent history. Direct descendants of the Ashanti, who were the most ferocious and independent of the Africans brought over to Jamaica in the sixteenth and seventeenth centuries, they escaped in large numbers into the unsettled and inaccessible bush and quickly banded together. For the next hundred years or so they fought a guerrilla war against the British, until finally the British had to settle with them by granting them relative independence and several large sections of land back in the Cockpit Country here in the west and up in the Blue Mountains in the east. Since then they've lived in relative isolation, with many of the old African ways preserved, in small villages that are governed by self-elected officials. They're not unlike, Upton said as he refilled his cup, certain American Indian tribes.

Remarkable people, the Captain added. The Captain's way of speaking was opposite to his son's: he never spoke in sentences. Expletives, fragments, bits and pieces. Honest too, he said. Not like your typical Jamaican at all. The Ashanti in them. Makes them proud. Quite a remarkable people. Fierce still, even today. Who . . . ? he asked his son. What . . . ? His name, the chief up there in Nyamkopong?

Phelps was his name, I believe, Upton said. Colonel Martin Luther Phelps was what he called himself. Upton had visited Nyamkopong two years ago during his tour of the island, and he had photographed the chief and a man Upton said was his Secretary of State. There was a book I should read, a brief history of the Maroons published and sold by the Sangster Bookstore chain. Then, Upton instructed me, I should drive up to Nyamkopong one day and meet Colonel Phelps. Upton said I should use his name as an introduction. Just tell him you're a friend of mine, he said, getting up to leave.

Quite, the Captain added. Everyone on the island. Upton meets them all. Sooner or later.

Then politely, even graciously, the two men made their way along the crushed stone pathway to their Land Rover. Upton was returning to Manhattan that afternoon; he was scheduled for tomorrow's *Today* show. The Captain had to get back to Montego Bay and start preparing his annual first of January breakfast for a group of black Jamaican men he called "my old boys," veterans of the Great War. Bit of a ritual, the Captain explained. Means quite a lot to the old boys. Biscuits, ham, eggs, lots of coffee. Fewer and fewer of them every year, though, he said, as he climbed into the Rover.

From the driver's seat Upton called out to me. Get up to Nyamkopong on January sixth, if possible, he advised. That's a day of celebration up there, the main Maroon holiday. It ought to be fantastic, from what I've heard. In fact, one of these Januarys I'm coming down precisely for the purpose of photographing that event. Maybe I'll film it with a small crew for television. It's the sort of thing that goes over beautifully on PBS.

I assured him that I'd do exactly as he had advised. I'd buy the little history of the Maroons, and I'd drive up there on January sixth, and I'd certainly look up Colonel Phelps. Give the old boy my regards, Upton said, waving good-bye. I waved back.

THE FIGHTING MAROONS, by a man named Carey Robinson, is a slender, unpretentious, and skillfully written history of the Maroons, popular among foreigners in Jamaica and sold, therefore, at the several stationers and bookstores in Montego Bay and even at some of the fancy hotel shops along Gloucester Avenue near the beach club at Doctor's Cave. It describes, with surprise and admiration, a courageous and intelligent people, slaves who chose the wilderness over slavery and who managed to survive that choice. The book was written, I deduced, by a white Jamaican for an audience of white readers who wished to know more about the beautiful and mysteriously complex land of Jamaica. It was not written for the reader who wished to know more about the ugly and bewildering history of the enslavement of black Africans in the New World. And it surely was not written for the reader who felt morally compelled to attempt to imagine how it was to face the choice the Maroons faced: whether to be a dumb domesticated animal—livestock—or to live the life of a feral pig—livestock gone wild.

For that is where the word *maroon* originated, I learned as I read Mr. Robinson's little book. It derives from the Spanish *cimarrón* which was a term generally used in the New World to refer to feral cattle, but in particular and in Jamaica to pigs that had taken to the woods and gone wild (again). A beast wasn't a cimarrón merely because it had successfully escaped into the swiftly rising hills and wooded, pathless mountains behind the plantations along the coastal plain; it became a cimarrón and, in the case of human beings, a Maroon, only when it had managed to survive there and breed with others like it and provide food and shelter for itself generation after generation.

The morning that Upton West was being interviewed in New York on the *Today* show, I drove down to the village of Anchovy from Church's hill and then down the winding seven-mile-long incline to Montego Bay and purchased there a copy of the book he had recommended. I read it that afternoon and that night determined to take Upton's suggestion that I visit Nyamkopong, the nearest of the four remaining Maroon enclaves in Jamaica. I would go there the following morning, the third of January, alone, and, if it seemed "safe," I would bring my family back with me on the sixth for the festival that Upton had mentioned over breakfast.

My anxiety over the safety of such a venture was not based on anything that I or members of my family had experienced in the several weeks we had been in the island. Rather, it was the result of a hundred conversations I had by then had with white Jamaicans, with Upton West's parents, with the Churches, with Mr. and Mrs. Hilliard Beard, a retired American publisher and his wife who lived on the side of the hill adjacent to the Church property, and with a half dozen or so of the similarly white, retired and semiretired residents and visitors these people had introduced me to. Upton's mother would telephone and invite me to come by their home in Reading for lunch or for drinks that evening, and, because of my friendship with Upton, my idleness and what I thought was my genuine curiosity about this class of human beings, I would accept. When traveling, one condescends to spend a considerable amount of time with people one would find excuses to avoid when at home. Or at least one believes he is condescending. As did I, when I would graciously accept their invitations and later when I would attempt to interest and charm these people and their always white, well-dressed guests—doctors, lawyers, realtors and developers, and, occasionally, because I was known to be somehow "in the arts," clothing designers with boutiques in Montego Bay, Palm Beach, and Fifth Avenue, or a London librettist or the brother of the president of a large midwestern university.

At these gatherings the conversation seemed to turn obsessively to the subject of imminent racial war. A number of newspaper and magazine articles had recently appeared in the United States and England suggesting that racial war was a likely if not a necessary consequence of the Jamaican prime minister's economic policies, and there had in fact been a recent rash of ghetto fires and street shootings in Kingston, events that from the distance of calm, affluent Montego Bay looked clearly political and, therefore, racial. So far, however, no rich or white people had been killed or even shot at. Still, the imagery was there, fire, and wild-eyed, ganja-smoking black people with guns and machetes and raised fists, and a charismatic, self-proclaimed "socialist" leader who was frighteningly popular with the illiterate masses. And the history was there too, three hundred years of relentless racial oppression and economic exploitation. Also, it was a fact that these white people, with their fashion designer gowns and jackets, their cut-crystal cocktail glasses, their parquet floors and real estate holdings, had a lot to lose. Many of them had children in private schools and colleges in New England. Many of them owned lovely, walled-in estates along the coast and in the hills around Montego Bay. Many of them owned several twenty thousand dollar automobiles, jewelry, antiques, boats, Belgian hunting rifles for dove-shooting expeditions in Nicaragua. Most of them had fleets of servants. And all of them, without exception, said that they loved Jamaica.

For these reasons they feared economic collapse and racial war as if the two events were one and the same. If the balance of payments looked bleakly out of balance, they would purchase a second vicious Doberman pinscher to patrol the yard. And if a crazy black man on the street was rude to them one morning on the way to the office, they would smuggle another thousand dollars to Miami that afternoon. Thus racial terror was explained in economic terms, and dissatisfaction with economic policy and conditions was expressed in strictly racist terms, so that it was not shocking, once it had occurred, for me to find myself listening to an elegantly dressed and manicured physician my own age recommend forced sterilization as a solution to the problem of "overpopulation." It was, of course, the poor who were too numerous and whose uncontrolled breeding with each other made them only more numerous. And since with rare exceptions in Jamaica for three centuries the rule had been, simply and purely, as one's skin color darkens so does one's poverty approach inescapability, then the calm, good-looking physician before me was not only recommending forced sterilization, a kind of murder, but the forced sterilization of poor black people, a kind of genocide.

This was madness I had never seen before. And it frightened me. How *could* the island be safe for people like me and my family if people like this man had been running it for hundreds of years? So in that way I began to share in their fear of imminent racial warfare, and I too began to anticipate signs of its coming by how black strangers treated me on the streets of Montego Bay, in the marketplace, in the tavern at Anchovy, even in my own kitchen when I chatted with Caroline, the young woman I had hired as a housekeeper.

THE morning I went to Nyamkopong for the first time I sat out on the patio and ate my breakfast of chilled mango, coffee and boiled eggs and talked with Caroline. She stood in the doorway to the dining room, one hand lightly touching the doorframe, one foot slowly scratching one of her muscular calves, and gave to the content of our conversation barely half her attention, or so it seemed to me, the rest of her attention scrupulously watching out for disaster. Before me a gold-tinted mist drifted up the blue-green, slowly ascending valley to where, a half mile west of the house, a pair of long ridges came together. To the east was the turquoise sea, and looking south I could see the curve of Montego Bay and the tan and white cluster of cubes that made up the city. A pale blue Scandinavian cruise ship had docked at Freeport where, presumably, tourists from Stock-

holm were already lining up to buy duty-free Japanese wrist-
watches and English china. Behind me the hill shouldered a
few hundred feet further up to protect the Churches' other
house, more exposed to the sea and breeze than the one they
had rented to me, their son's home, the house built by the man
my age, with my first name too, who was now in Toronto
depositing the checks I had mailed him from my home in New
Hampshire. I now understood why I had been asked to pay him
in that careful a way, why the rent for this estate had been so
absurdly low, why I felt one kind of guilt for having accepted
the bargain offered by the Churches and a wholly different kind
of guilt for having accepted the bargain offered by Caroline the
housekeeper, whose time and labor cost only fifty cents an
hour. Fifty cents an hour! I had exclaimed to my wife. Imagine
that! Her husband's out of work, and she has five children. How
do they *do* it? I had asked, as if it were a trick performed by a
carnival magician. That has been in the beginning, of course,
for now, after two weeks of consorting with people who were
complaining fearfully of having to get along on a hundred thousand American dollars a year in a country whose rate of exchange worked in their favor, I no longer thought of Caroline's
survival as a magician's trick. I was beginning to see that it had
something to do with character. Insights like this were only
glimpses, however, glimmers that only now and then filtered
through the fog of my greedy ignorance.

I asked Caroline about the Maroons. Had she ever heard of
them?

Oh yes, sir, she had heard of them all right. "Dem ol' Africans," she called them, smiling.

What are they like? Is it all right to drive up there to Nyamkopong and visit them? I asked.

Don't know, she shrugged, slowly scratching her calf with
the toe of her other foot. You planning to go up there? she
asked.

When I told her that I certainly was, and also that I planned
to go up alone, her eyes widened in what looked like amazement and admiration. Then, saying nothing more, she turned
and went back to the kitchen to prepare breakfast for the rest of
my family.

I drained my coffee cup, grabbed my camera from the mahogany sideboard in the living room, and went out to the car. Inside, with the window glass and windshield silvered over by a skin of dew, I suddenly felt cut off, as isolated as a dream in a stranger's sleep. The unreality of the last two weeks and my compulsion to sort out the truth by thinking about it, by reasoning and by applying to other people's terrified descriptions of their world my own understanding of history, had driven me deeper and deeper into my head. Jamaica, which in the beginning may have been for me no more than an image off a travel poster, was now becoming an idea. What made it painful was that it was an idea I did not fully believe corresponded to any reality outside the books I had read, books that were not about Jamaica but were instead about abstractions like history and race and economics.

And the book I had read about the Maroons—what was that really about, I asked myself, but the historical, racial and economic superiority of the people the Maroons had fought against? And if I believed that particular idea was true, then the reason I was driving into the backcountry to see these people for myself was a tourist's reason—merely to wonder at their quaint peculiarities. But if I did not believe that idea was true, in heading off to where no one had invited me, I was going as a social scientist, to collect evidence that would support my own idea about history, race and economics. Is that all I can do with this place, these people? I asked myself. Is it only possible for me to *think* about them? Why can't I simply *see* them, talk to them, engage myself with them the same as I do with my neighbors in New Hampshire? The people I dealt with here were essentially the same as the people I dealt with at home— carpenters, farmers, upholsterers, and now and then a professionally trained person, a doctor or lawyer or schoolteacher, and once in a while a rich man or woman. At home, though, my neighbors were people, concrete people as real as I; here they remained abstractions, and only I was real. It made me feel very lonely. Part of the problem was race, of course. But it was larger, or at least much more complex than anything I'd yet imagined. I believed that I was just as cut off from the white people I had met as I was from the black, just as separated from the middle-class American and Canadian tourists as from the decadent Jamaican neocolonials, just as alien to my old friend Upton West as to the black woman who served me coffee on the patio. It was as if I had slipped into an episode of *Pilgrim's Progress* and everyone I met there and every place I went to had a strictly allegorical function and no real life of its own—except for me, who, alone among the characters, was also the reader of this book.

IT was still early, about eight o'clock, when I left the compound. That was how I referred to it now, the compound, because of the cut stone walls, the elaborate lighting system all over the grounds, and the location of the two houses up here on the hill facing the sea and valley, our well-protected backs to the village and villagers of Anchovy. The Vikings had build compounds like this when they conquered Ireland and Scotland: walls to hold off the peasants behind them, and terraces and towers facing the sea, where the next set of raiders would come from, pillaging seafarers like themselves who would come to displace them, as the British had displaced the Spanish here in Jamaica, and then the British had been displaced by the Americans and Canadians, and now, if you believed the Wests and the Churches and their friends, the North Americans were being displaced by the Cubans or possibly the Russians.

Down the hill I drove, following the steep, narrow lane to the village, goats scattering before my car and scrambling nimbly up the rough limestone hillside to stop and stare back at me with dull irritation, scrawny chickens fluttering for the gutters as I passed the dozen or so small cinderblock houses at the base of the hill where the lane crossed the railroad track and turned onto the main road that connected the interior and the southwest coastal towns of Black River and Savanna-la-Mar to Montego Bay. Strings of children in uniforms—boys in khaki shirts and pants, girls in brightly colored jumpers and white blouses—were walking to school, while cars and huge smoke-belching buses top-heavy with sacks of yams, bread-fruit, and greens whizzed past, horns blasting at the curves and quick bends in the road to force the children into the gutters as the vehicles flashed by. Shopkeepers were opening their shuttered taverns and small, dark grocery stores to the traffic, selling "box milk" and sweets and ten-packs of Craven A's to the kids and people on their way to work, those few in town who had jobs, because at this time in these country towns over half the employable adults were without jobs. And because the public schools were operated after the British model, which meant that parents had to pay for uniforms for their children and for their books, pencils and lunches as well, most of the children were not able to go to school for longer than a few years, when the uniform would get passed down to the next youngest child and the older one would go to sit on a wall in the shade of a breadfruit tree with the other children and talk all day and dream and grow slowly and bleakly and barely literate into adulthood.

Turning left at the main road in Anchovy, I drove south, inland, across the relatively flat grassland plateau to Montpelier, still in the familiar parish of St. James. Sleek red poll and hump-backed white Brahman cattle grazed sleepily in the pale green guinea grass, while behind them, in the shade of cotton wood trees or at the top of a rise facing the meadows, glowered the great houses and barns, one after the other restored in the last thirty or forty years with the energy and cash that depends on a capitalist government's attempts to foster an industry by means of subsidy and tax benefits. These fat cats whine about what they call socialism and creeping communism, I grumped, and the country remains only a little less "socialized" than Canada.

From what I could see, the Prime Minister of Jamaica, in almost any industrialized country of Europe or North America, would have found himself only slightly to the right of the center and probably, instead of calling himself a socialist, would have said he was a Christian Democrat. In the peculiar context of Jamaica, however, Michael Manley, because he was attempting to institute a public education system and a realistically graduated income tax and something like an economy designed to feed, clothe and house the majority of the people who lived in Jamaica, was indeed a socialist. What had happened in modern Jamaica was that the old British colonials had been replaced by a breed of home-grown parasites, neocolonials who, rather than endure the presence of a black entrepreneurial middle class, a class whose existence would had to have been deliberately created by means of decent public education and health care systems, instead had permitted the enterpreneurial functions and rewards to fall into the hands of other groups of people—mainly East Indian and Chinese immigrants, people who had not sufficient identification with the land of Jamaica, people whose history lay elsewhere and who, therefore, were extremely unlikely to need to replace the white Jamaicans who sat at the top of the pyramid. The Indians and the Chinese moved horizontally; the blacks could not be counted on to be satisfied with that. No, if Jamaica in the next decade were indeed to collapse into famine and chaos, as the Wests and Churches kept insisting it would, to be followed, as they assured me, with a "Communist takeover," it would not be because of Manley's policies; it would happen because the country had already died, sucked of its lifeblood for tens of generations until, a generation ago, there was nothing left for it but a series of last agonies.

At Montpelier, little more than an ESSO station, railway shipping station, post office and police station for the farmers and grain producers of the area, I forked to the left, and slowly the land started to lift toward hills shaped like bright green bowlers, strange hills that seemed to have been taken from a child's drawing. Scrawny blond dogs loped alongside the road and ignored my car as I passed. Kids smiled, waved and called, "White head!" and adults gazed blankly after. Bickersteth, Seven Rivers, and alongside the Great River, Cambridge, Bruce Hall, and Catadupa, where I stopped at a roadside shop for a Dragon stout and confirmation that I was on the right road.

Oh yes, man, you're on the road to Maggotty, the barman assured me as he cracked open a warm dark Dragon and set the bottle in front of me. I loved these combination bars and grocery stores the Jamaicans called shops. Usually one side of the room was given over to the sale of tinned food, soaps, boxed milk, and cheese from New Zealand in circular tins the size of paint buckets, rice, flour and sugar weighed out and wrapped in brown paper, and sometimes fresh meat from a pig or goat slaughtered that morning in the back yard, as often as not with the head of the beast grinning from the counter while flies danced joyously in the air around it. On the other side of the room, beyond a screen plastered with cigarette and beer ads, was the bar, a counter ten or twelve feet long, no stools or tables with chairs, nothing to accommodate anyone who did not wish to stand against the counter and drink.

In one corner there was inevitably a juke box that played three songs for a nickel—the ever-present reggae, of course, but also a dozen or more records by people like Al Green, Otis Redding and Aretha Franklin. Jamaican taste in music, and I mean the taste of the average working-class Jamaican in the back country, was perfect taste to me—impeccable and serious, knowledgeable and refined. Sometimes a whole culture has perfect taste, as in New Orleans three-fourths of a century ago or, regarding architecture, in New England two and three centuries ago, so that a wholly ordinary person, even children, can make aesthetic distinctions usually thought to be the exclusive prerogative of only the most elaborately educated members of the society. It seemed to me, regarding music, that Jamaican culture was wise in this way, and for that reason a barely literate or even illiterate workingman, toothless, barefoot, alcoholic, a man who believed that Queens Elizabeth I and II were the same person and thought Jack Kennedy and Jimmy Carter were brothers who had separately employed Martin Luther King on their farms, a bizarre man to someone like me, such a man when it came to music had flawless perfect taste. He could instantly distinguish the phony from the authentic, the derivative from the original, the merely sentimental from the genuinely romantic. And he would be a scholar in this field, would know precisely by what routes and through the work of which musicians calypso had got bebop from black nightclubs in Florida and become ska, how ska got rock and soul from London, Liverpool, New York and Detroit and had become reggae, how reggae, reaching its literary and self-conscious phase, was now reinvestigating African roots while at the same time getting itself electrified in Nashville and Los Angeles. This old cane cutter, scratching the welts on his forearm with the back edge of his machete, would know the effect of poverty on the

sound of reggae, how cheap guitars imitating the tinny thin
sounds of the Beatles on Japanese transistor radios and plastic
stereos from a Woolworth's in the Bronx had stripped sixties
rock of its baroque density of detail to produce a high, thin
clarity not heard in Western popular music since the 1920s.

I left the shop, turned my car onto a one-lane road, headed
southeast into the hills. I was in Cockpit Country now, the
roads unpaved and curling along the edges of ocular pits, huge
pocks, with strangely shaped hills extruding from the earth like
weathered stumps rounded at the tops. The sides of the hills,
almost vertical, were covered by a dense, impenetrable skin of
macca bushes and short, twisted trees, now and then the bone
white ground showing through where a slide, like a gash, had
occurred after heavy rain. Because the cockpits themselves,
deep adjacent craters ridged by their linked edges, were the
result of slow underground erosion of the essentially limestone
surface, a process directly opposite the familiar process of up-
lift, the land forms seemed bizarre and even wrong to me, an
unnatural landscape. Valleys aren't supposed to be created by
the land's dropping; they're created by rivers or when the adjacent land rises. Though topology expresses its own geologic past
and can be read as a text, this text was backward to me. I had
always understood craters as the result of eruption or penetration, valleys as the product of uplifting, of emerging, standing
slabs of earth—all male processes, somehow. Here, though, the
land forms were the expression of female forces. The power of
this geology was the power, by yielding, to create space, not by
coming forward, to penetrate space. It was the difference between tai chi and karate. It was the difference between a
Druidic stone circle and a ziggurat, between Stonehenge and
Summer. And for me to perceive it as "natural" required an
enormous shift in what had seemed natural up to now, natural
and therefore inevitable. The tourist in me took another step
backward, and the traveler came forward one.

On the map where the three parishes of St. James, Trelawny
and St. Elizabeth came together a large area is marked "Cockpit Country." It's an area of about four hundred square miles,
and there are no roads or settlements marked on it. The roads
crawl like vines around the edges, sometimes sending a single

tendril into the area for a few miles before it disappears, as if that blank space on the map had swallowed it. At Mocho, Niagara, and Elderslie, I was traveling along the edge of this Cockpit Country, passing through tiny settlements of a few dozen cabins perched over dark red ground, a patch of yams and an ackee or breadfruit tree in back, the chassis of a wrecked car in front, with five or six small, half-naked children playing by the road, waving and calling out to me as I drove by. "Whitey!" and "White head!" they cried, and sometimes just "White!" I tried always to smile and wave back, but the road was getting rougher with each mile and more twisted as it switchbacked up and then quickly down the sides of the hills and along the rims of the cockpits, and I was forced to hold grimly to the wheel with both hands and keep my gaze fixed in front of me.

From the map, and from Carey Robinson's little book, which had traced the course of the two Maroon wars in admirable detail, with charts and elaborate descriptions of British troop movements and Maroon guerrilla ambushes, I knew that I was now in Maroon country and that many of the people I was seeing were the descendants of those wild Ashanti warriors. According to Carey Robinson and also to my friend Upton West, these people were supposed to look different from the ordinary Jamaica countryman—taller, straighter, more muscular, and with a slight reddish tint to their skin.

Though I wanted it to be true and did attempt to see that difference, I could not see it. In fact, if anything, the people I was passing as they walked along the road with bunches of green bananas on their heads or carted water in cube-shaped tins or simply stood by the road, watching me, seemed stockier than the the people of Montego Bay, and darker. The red was in the soil, rich in bauxite, a deep red soil the color of dried blood that in this dry season made a reddish dust that settled over everything. The huts and cabins, the vegetation, the road, animals and people all seemed to be on the other side of a red-tinted lens, so that only when I looked up at the sharply blue sky could I be sure that the redness over everything was not the expression of my own eye.

This was the region, during the first Maroon war, that

Cudjoe had held for forty years against a half dozen British commanders, one after another falling victim to disease, heat and insects, the tangled unmapped country, these endless cockpits riddled with caves and narrow passageways known only to the Maroons, and the brilliance and courage of Cudjoe and the several separate bands of Maroons he had united under him. From the accounts of the period, British accounts, Cudjoe was not so much brilliant as wily, not so much courageous as stubborn, and not so much a leader as ruthless. But, looking back to the early 1700s and imagining the difficulty of conducting a successful forty-year military campaign against the mighty British army on a tiny island in the Caribbean, with no allies and nothing but three or four rag-tag, quarrelsome groups of ex-slaves who variously spoke versions of several African and at least two European languages, with no weapons except what they made or could steal in raids on the coastal plantations or took from the bodies of the soldiers they killed, and no food except what they could grow in hiding in the cockpits, an army that had no bases and had to move with its women, children and old people or leave them to the British and re-enslavement or worse—imagining that difficulty, one has to believe that a merely wily, stubborn and ruthless man could not have succeeded for six months. If the British hadn't killed him by then, his own people would have.

By now, when I passed a house or a small, hand-cultivated field, the people would stop what they were doing and stare at me with hard faces. Children no longer smiled and waved at me or called out the color of my skin to me; instead they got behind the nearest adult and peeked around pant leg or cotton skirt. Every few hundred yards my Toyota slammed the oil pan or banged the muffler against the craggy limestone road, and I winced, suddenly picturing my isolation if the car broke down here. I could handle a flat tire, but that was about all. The men and women whose country I was passing through did not look friendly or helpful. I didn't dare stop and ask for directions, something, like most men, I was reluctant to do anyhow, anywhere, but here my old barely conscious reasons for driving on regardless of not being sure where I was—fear of losing face (real men are supposed to have a good sense of direction; only sissies get lost), fear of being misled, and a simple unwillingness to delay my forward motion, gambling that as long as I was still moving away from where I had started I was somehow moving closer to my destination—these fears were suddenly given a strange new cast that originated, I knew, in my fear of black people. And even more complex than that, my fear especially of people whose ancestors had fought generations of a just war against my ancestors. Will Americans traveling in Vietnam two hundred years from now feel as I do today? I wondered, as I struggled to separate the several braided strands of my fear, the purely racist strand from the political one, the narrowly economic from the broadly historical. Will a middle-aged American traveler in the twenty-second century, lost in the Montagnard highlands, look at the grim face of a man in a rice paddy next to the road, and suddenly picturing the maddened faces of both their ancestors, drive quickly on, preferring to remain lost a little longer?

My map was out of directions altogether, and when I came to forks in the road I took the one that looked the more traveled—right, then left, then right again. There was no logic to my turns; I had no sense of drawing gradually nearer to a settlement. Now and then I saw a cabin, thatched roof and daub-and-wattle walls, a small shed build from old odd-shaped boards a few yards in back that, I knew from the smoke trickling out the hole in the roof, was a kitchen. Sometimes a woman's sweating face stared expressionless out a window as, taking great care on the rutted track so as not to smash my rented car, I passed slowly by.

At last I began to see small groups of houses, two and three at a time, alongside the road. Behind them, where the ground fell away from the ridge and became the steep side of a cockpit, I saw short, terraced fields tended by men and boys and sometimes women. In the distance, far from any house, more land was similarly cultivated. There was some cane, but mostly I could make out yam plants on poles and corn stalks spaced in what seemed to me erratic relations to one another. No neat rows or files, no geometric patterns—spirals, rather, and splotches, blotches and patches, one crop mixed indiscriminately with another, kalaloo and onions sprawling at the feet of pole beans and yam plants, corn stalks planted like bystanders around a cabbage patch.

Then I was in the village of Nyamkopong itself. Or at least I hoped it was Nyamkopong. Along the curling length of a high ridge that linked a dozen craters were scattered fifty or sixty small houses facing both sides of a central lane, with several narrower, grassy branches off to either side, houses at the end, a small masonry building that was an unfinished church, another, finished, painted white. I passed three or four shops open to the street and, at the far end of town where the ground lifted and flattened into a kind of parade ground, a new masonry school-house and a bare playing field in front of it. Then the cockpits again, with cabins in the distance and the road quickly becoming a footpath.

I turned my car around at the schoolyard and drove slowly back to the center of the village where two shops on either side of the street faced each other. A half dozen people, old people, stood in the shade and watched me. I stopped, and realized that I didn't want to ask if this was Nyamkopong, not because I was afraid that it wasn't but because I was reasonably sure that it was and thus the old woman staring at me with her set face would be able to snarl, Of course this is Nyamkopong, you idiot! So instead I took a chance and politely requested the group to direct me to the head man. With no sign to go on, I was relying not on the evidence of my senses but on a connection between my intuition and my reason to determine where I was now located. I felt as though I had just dived headfirst down a well.

A young man, short and wearing a red, yellow and green knit wool tam and beige sweater, a bearded man and, as I could see from the bulbous shape of his tam, wearing Rastafarian dread-locks, emerged from the mauve darkness of the shop on my left and pointed grandly down the street ahead of me. The Colonel lives there, he informed me in a large voice, and he called me his brother.

The old people, men and women, said nothing and stared darkly after me as, greatly relieved, suddenly exhausted, I drove slowly away. This is not a brave thing to be doing, I thought. Why, then, am I so afraid? I would have liked to have been like

Gauguin in Tahiti, all awash with open-eyed enthusiasm for
the newly revealed alternative to bourgeois France, or Forster
in India, skeptical, shrewdly compassionate, confident that
what one did not know at the moment was really not worth
knowing at the moment, or Dinesen in Africa, tender and secure in the tower of her absent self. But I could be none of
these people, and as a result I saw very little at that time of
where I was and what people I was among.

Oh, certainly I saw the way the light at midday glared off the
palm fronds, baked the dirt yards dry and turned the tin roofs
of the buildings to griddles, and I saw how the people wore
sweaters and caps and complained that it was winter while I
sweltered in my Dacron-and-cotton, short-sleeved shirt. I saw
how the Colonel's pink, four-room, cinderblock house was the
largest and best kept in the village, saw his department store
furniture and dishes, saw the plump, well-fed faces of his children; and when one of those children ran for him in the fields
and brought back to the house a scrawny, rabbit-faced, brown
man wearing tattered clothes and dirt-caked rubber boots, I
saw that the Colonel, despite his office and its emoluments, in a
country that accepted bribery as the sole legitimate access to
those in power, was still a poor man. I heard his mannered
Jamaican English, his careful avoidance of patois, his ingratiat-
ing queries about me. And I heard his sharp, sudden command
to his sour-faced wife in the back room to bring us a bottle of
rum and then his polite request that I sign his guest book and
write my home address next to my signature just below the
name and address of the Canadian professor who had preceded
me by about six weeks.

I saw and heard it all, and yet, throughout, it seemed that I
saw and heard nothing, because at every moment I was aware
of these people being black-skinned. Yes, consciously I could
and did methodically and sensitivy add to that awareness my
new information about them—that they were Maroons, that
they lived on what amounted to a government reservation and
that they owned their land more or less communally, that they
were among the best farmers in Jamaica, that they were proud
of their Maroon past even if only partially aware of it, and that,
however they saw and heard me, they did not see and hear me

the way a black American would. Even so, I could not stop viewing them as if I were seated, not on a stoop in the Jamaican bush, but in Detroit or Roxbury or Watts. And that is why I was afraid, afraid the way only a white American can be afraid and the way Gauguin and Forster and Dinesen were never afraid. They may not have known precisely where they were when they found themselves in Tahiti, India or Africa, but they knew they were not in Paris, Cambridge or Copenhagen. And that, at least, let them see more clearly than I could now where they had traveled to and whom they were moving among. A white American, I was blind, and lost.

Cecil Brown

IN Cecil Brown's work, issues that other American writers are too timid to broach are treated in a manner that is both scholarly and entertaining. His intellectual bravery has brought him into conflict with Black and white members of the American Thought Police.

A film project, based upon his novel *The Lives and Loves of Mr. Jiveass Nigger,* which covered the same territory as the recent *How to Make Love to a Negro,* was scraped after protests from Black members of the Hollywood movie community who objected its subject matter.

A second novel, entitled *King Kong's Revenge,* was actually removed from production after feminists at a major publishing company objected to its misogyny.

In 1989, scenes from his dramatic adaptation of Richard Wright's novel *The Outsider* were censored by a Black theater producer who deemed them obscene.

His brilliant second novel, *Days Without Weather,* an American Book Award winner, was the subject of a vindictive review in the *New York Times Book Review.*

Cecil Brown clearly refuses to be nice by singing from the same song sheet as the Black, white, and feminist segments of the literary establishment, by making the kind of assent to whatever establishment values are in fashion at a given time that can get you the big literary prizes.

Despite his clashes with the ruling cultural cliques, Cecil Brown's enthusiasm for telling the truth as he sees it has not been dampened. He is too prolific to be stopped. Brown has also written plays, essays, poetry, and film scripts. His plays are *Real Nigger* (1968), *African Shades* (1972), *Our Sisters Are Pregnant* (1973), and most recently, *King Kong's Revenge,* which in 1990 enjoyed an eight-week run at Ed Bullin's Emery-ville Theatre in California. His films include *Gila Monster* (1969), *Toy Soldier* (1984), and *Doppenleben* (1986). He was the scriptwriter for *Which Way Is Up?* starring Richard Pryor. Among his awards are the Professor John Burrell Memorial Prize, the Besonders Wertvoll Film Prize, and the Berlin Literary Fellowship. Raised on a farm in North Carolina, Cecil Brown combines the keen savvy of a hunter, the academic hipness of a postmodernist scholar, and the cool and unsparing analysis of a Malcolm X.

—Ishmael Reed

Chapter 10 from
DAYS WITHOUT WEATHER

I DIDN'T feel funny.

I got Cheryl up to drive back to my car parked in front of the Comedy Club. And I said good night to her. I never saw her again.

But there was always a girl from Nebraska who was starting an acting career who had some coke and drove a brand-new Porsche, and always I'd go home with her if I chose, and always would fuck all the rest of the night. This was the life I loved as a comedian.

This was the middle of the trash bin in America.

This was Walt Whitman's "America!"

This was where the dreams and nightmares are indistinguishable!

This was Kafka's *Amerika!*

Oh! Elegant bullshit! Is not Hollywood not your home town! This was the place where thousands of us are driven each year to find a dream that we finally find out never existed at all! We believed in its existence only out of the pain we suffered elsewhere! The pain of the rest of America made us believe that Hollywood existed! It had to exist! If you see your uncle unjustly killed by whites in the South you make Hollywood an El Dorado, a fantasy land where glamour and personal celebrity lift you from the cruel implacable jaws of injustice to the heights of etherized exclusivity. If there was no justice in America, at least pleasure would drive out its pain.

As I inserted my key in the door, a disgusting feeling came over me. I didn't know if it was an abominably dark thought of Lindsey's ignoble death or the stupefied sex with Cheryl or my proud outburst against Thalia or a combination of all three, but

I was suddenly aware of being thrown into a deep pit of depression.

Aunt Lottie was waiting for me. An overprotecting mother, she was too good to me and that made staying with them ever more painful. I closed the door behind me without causing the slightest sound: clowns can be as quiet as a cat walking on fur sometimes.

Using a night-light that illuminated the dark hallway leading to the bedrooms as a guide, I cautiously avoided a noisy collision with the furniture. Reaching the hallway, I tiptoed down it toward my bedroom, but as I passed my uncle and aunt's bedroom I saw that the door was ajar and the bedside lamp was on.

In this brief glance, I read yet another unhappy chapter in the miserable life of this respectable couple. My aunt was reading a book; the place beside her—where Uncle Gadge was supposed to be—was deserted. That empty space meant that Uncle Gadge was out indulging his gambling habits. An image of him sitting at a table with a gram of cocaine at one elbow came to mind, and the cackling laughter of some prostitute at the other elbow.

Just as I was about to turn away she suddenly looked up— she must've heard me come into the hall—and gave me the most pitiful stare I'd ever seen. It really got to me. By the time I got to my room, all I could do was go for the bed. I lay down a few minutes, just thinking what an unlucky asshole I was. "Oh, I'm so miserably depressed!" I wanted to cry out.

I might have felt different about my situation had the women in Hollywood been different, but they were a special breed that doesn't exist anywhere else in the world. Unfeeling and cold-blooded as a dead fish on ice, the woman of Hollywood was beautiful as a silent-screen movie star; and I was attracted to this hollow image because it elevated my emotions coolly out of my own confused identity, giving me a Clark Gable self-image. The woman of Hollywood sees herself—not in the mirror, but on the movie screen. Her color and style of dress, her every minute gesture, the way she flutters her eyelids, the tilt of her head that can run a man crazy with passion, the way she walks in the long skirts with the slits up the side, the way she blows out cigarette smoke—so nonchalantly—the clichés she mouths over oyster shells in fashionable restaurants, the witty interjections after lovemaking, her entire philosophy of politics, poetry, love, economics, blasé manner of painting her face in public places, her soulless lovemaking, the way she worships herself, a base slave to luxury and stupidity and arrogance in various plots—all this she imitates from her celluloid mirror, the movie screen. The movie screen's effect is to decrease one's own reality for the dream world of fantasy, and the woman of Hollywood outstrips everybody else in making this her reality. Consequently, the woman of Hollywood has no reality of her own. She may have come from Harlem or Watts or the coal mines of Pennsylvania, she may have escaped the slums of Chicago or Houston, but when she arrives in Hollywood she dons the external images of the cinematic mirror and social consciousness. It doesn't matter if she's young or old, black or white, Chinese or Irish, tall or short, fat or slim, Jew or gentile, Islamic or Christian—she is beautiful and that's all that matters in her self-image. Sometimes she's an old, wrinkled beldame with a dozen face-lifts, bejeweled and coiffeured in the latest, making one last and desperate grasp at a lost youth; sometimes she's a young girl, barely out of her teens, already an expert at the despicable wiles of whoring, burning with wet desire and lustful ambition to be ranked as the equal of her superiors in vice; but always she's the woman—excuse me—lady of Hollywood.

There are two ways to sleep with the woman of Hollywood, I thought. The first is to be rich. But if you're broke, as I usually was, you'd have to be able to make them laugh. You'd have to be in show business. If you told a really funny joke, then the woman of Hollywood would congratulate herself on having discovered your talent, which would become a promissory note, and so she'd laugh. I just lay there, sinking happily into my misery, my *delectatio morosa*.

I could feel myself slipping into a deep, dark, bottomless well of depression. I needed a cigarette. The thought suddenly sprang into my mind like a solution. I found my package. There was one cigarette left. I looked at it a long time before I lit it up, however.

I hated myself also for not being able to move out for an-

other week and give Uncle Gadge and Aunt Lottie their space.
I felt like an intruder, especially since I knew how unhappy
Lottie was.

I looked around the room again with loathsomeness in my
very soul. Would I ever get away from this disgustingly sick
self-image?

I decided that I'd go down to the liquor cabinet and steal a
bottle of Scotch and get some ice cubes and soda and bring it
all back up to my room and get plastered. That made good
sense to me. Since I was going to get depressed anyway, why
not get depressed and drunk? Depressingly drunk—or drunk
depressingly. The idea appealed to me so much that I thought
for a moment, that maybe I wouldn't get depressed after all.
Perhaps all I needed was a good stiff drink.

But before I go downstairs, I told myself, what I need is
another cigarette. I thought I had an extra pack somewhere in
the room. I went through the things on the top of the bureau
and then pulled out one of the drawers. The only thing in it was
a batch of newspaper clips and an old package of Trojans. Beneath the Trojans was an article on me from the summer I
spent in San Francisco. I started to push the drawer closed but
something made me stare at that article. I was drawn to it, and
yet I knew if I read it, it would make me even more depressed.
The story was about a part of my past which I did not want to
deal with at all, but which I knew, had I the courage to reread
it, would put me on to the road to rebirth, to recovery.

I put on my blue bathrobe and went to the kitchen. The
morning light was rubbing its azure back against the windowpanes, and the kitchen was clean as a monastery. Opening the
liquor cabinet, I saw a bottle of Scotch and two bottles of
bourbon, one half full and one sealed. I took the unopened one.
My uncle was rich, I decided self-righteously, he could afford it.
Anyway, it was cheaper for him to buy me a bottle of bourbon
to kill my depression with than get me a job acting in the studio
where he was so well loved by the whites. Pulling open the
automatic ice dispenser, I grabbed a couple handfuls of those
little ice cubes and threw them into a big bowl I found on the
yellow tiled counter, plucked a glass down from the shelf, and
started out of the kitchen; but just as I was cruising past the bar

I spied a wooden bowl containing packages of potato chips and beer nuts. I swiped those too.

As I was making my way down the hallway again, I heard my aunt moan and call out, "Gadge, is that you?" and I paused before I answered, "No, it's me—Jonah." I wanted to say, "It's me about to get over my depression with alcohol, why don'tcha join me?" but thought better of it, and added: "He'll be home soon, I think?" She didn't even answer me, or anything.

I went on into my room, and put my booty down on the chair in front of my bed. I poured myself a big, stiff drink, and took the first swallow, feeling the liquor anesthetize my lonely pain. It seemed as if everything I'd try to do in my short life had ended in failure. I remembered all the women I'd loved who had eventually scorned me. If I died today the only people who would cry would be my family and the only reason they would cry would be because they were obliged to cry. In my twenty-two years on earth I had made no impression on anybody. I'd traveled the world but I'd not gotten anywhere with the world, or myself. I'd just left the South, just seen my father, and had realized that I could never live there again. Now I was in Los Angeles, the capital of show business, and yet I couldn't do the kind of comedy I wanted to.

Out of the corner of my eye, I caught a glimpse of that newspaper article. I reached over and picked it up. Just looking at it made me laugh—laugh so that I wouldn't cry. I started reading it. When I'm drunk I can read anything—even stuff about myself. The liquor gives me assurance about myself that I do not have without it. Entitled, "COPS DON'T FIND COMIC FUNNY," the article was published in the *Phoenix*, Wednesday, July 8, 1980; the day after I was arrested for obscenity on the U.C. Berkeley campus. At the top of the article is a photo of me in the middle of my stand-up act, with five hundred students laughing in the background. I'm wearing my dashiki—gold and purple—and my natural is big and well kept, and I'm in blue denims and sandals. Also in the picture are two campus cops approaching me from both sides. On the faces of the students—if you look closely—you can see pity, real genuine pity for me. It's not any jive pity—but real human pity—the kind of pity Aristotle talked about. After all, they are not about to get their asses thrown in jail. They knew more than I did what was about to happen to me. So that's my definition of pity: being sorry about something horribly painful happening to somebody else that couldn't possibly happen to you. The caption beneath this picture reads: "Jonah Drinkwater shouting obscenities before being thrown off campus."

I put the newspaper down and took another long drink from the glass of bourbon, my nepenthe, wondering at the mystery of my pain. How had this happened to me, *how?* It seemed only yesterday that I was a child entertaining my father with my mail-order catalogue magic, my boyish ingenuity. What had happened between those innocent boyish desires to entertain my father and the time the police locked me up in the county jail for telling the truth? I still was the same person, the same Jonah.

My glass was empty and I refilled it desperately; the first paragraph of this "eternal bulletin" told the whole story: "Campus police arrested an impromptu comic yesterday shortly after he began a performance in front of the Student Union during his second appearance here in three days."

It was a beautiful summer day, as I remember the incident. Overhead, the blue sky stretched out to eternity. A single cloud floated by. There were no clouds of ambition in this sky; this was not a Hollywood sky yet . . . clouds of chance that grown people chase.

The Berkeley campus was full of students, everywhere pretty girls smiled at you as you passed. I had just arrived in San Francisco to begin my career as a comedian with the campus as my stage. I stopped in front of the Student Union, where a group of street artists were selling their wares of pottery, handmade jewelry, batik and tie-dye shirts, ceramic earrings, leather sandals, and coats with fringe on the sleeves; on the corner a fortune-teller had set up her business. On another corner an impromptu jazz group consisting of a white boy blowing an old saxophone held together with rubber band and glue, a black boy playing a washtub drum, and a white girl playing a child's ukulele amplified by a homemade speaker. As I began my act I noticed my competition approaching: a Hare Krishna group came toward me chanting and beating tambourines. As if they weren't enough, behind them came a religious fanatic, chanting slogans from the Bible. Wearing a checkered too-tight suit, this freckled zealot wandered among the students chanting maxims from the Bible. Behind the zealot came a campus transsexual who had been one of the university's leading psychologists until he flipped out one day and came on campus wearing a dress and long unbecoming earrings and delivering a seriocomic speech about the advantage of hating people overtly as a provable cure for neurosis. Behind him came a group of ROTC cadets. Just as they were about to pass me, I shouted an insult out at them. This is the way I begin my act—usually with an insult. "Hey! Look at those ROTC jerks! There are the fuckers that went to Vietnam! They're ready to go any fucking where and kill people. Look at them!" I broke off and started imitating their stupid walk. A pretty girl started laughing. I had my first audience of the day. I got back up the steps and continued: "We have to realize who the enemy is. Those fuckers will one day be killing people in the Third World so that you and I can live in luxury! They're going to be the army officers who send black marines to Africa, India, Iran, Thailand to exploit other dark people so you can still call yourselves white!"

The young girl laughed again and looked around for approval from the other girl with her; they both giggled.

Just then, the checkered-suit-wearing zealot appeared in my range of sarcasm. "And look at him," I quipped. "This guy's telling us to 'Come unto the Lord,' and I wonder how long it's been since he *came!*"

The girls giggled again and nudged each other—students are really a horny bunch of individuals, quiet as it's kept, and any mention of sex gets their attention.

". . . This guy hasn't had any pussy since pussy had him. . . . Look at him! See? . . . That's what happens to you when you don't fuck! So my message to you students is: Fuck! . . . Fuck as much as you can! Fuck and laugh as much as you can!"

As soon as I said "Fuck" the crowd began to swell with curious, grinning faces. A tall, blond-headed boy turned away and shouted, "Screw you!" and started walking away, giving me a great opportunity to bring in my next subject: fraternities. " . . . Look at Mr. Straight . . . he must be a fraternity boy, huh?

You know who they're going to be when they grow up, right?
They will be our businessmen of tomorrow. And are they dumb
. . . All they do is sit around and drink beer and talk about a
girl's tit and ass. 'Hey, did you see the knockers on Sue-Ann?'
These are jerks who will be telling you what to do in five years.
They will tell the ROTC guys to go kill somebody in another
country so they can sell their businesses . . . and drink some
more beer and tell about some girl's ass!"

The crowd was laughing and applauding me now. Just then
a group of students came by carrying a banner that read: "U.S.
OUT OF EL SALVADOR!" I yelled, "Right on!" and they waved
back, "Right on, brother!" The audience ate that up and
started applauding too. I went into my prop bag and brought
out my pink pig and threw it down on the ground. The pink pig
was the biggest piggybank I could find and I'd put a pair of
movie-star glasses on him, giving him the aura of a celebrity.
Then I took out an American flag and waved it as I addressed
the pig. ". . . Hello, Ronnie, my name is Joe America. Oh,
Ronnie, we really love you, we want to help you cut off food
stamps and job programs so Nancy can redecorate the bathrooms in the White House."

The students went mad with laughter at my satire.

Suddenly the blond-headed fellow came rushing through
the crowd and snatched up my pig. I grabbed him by the shoulder and turned him around and snatched the pig back. "Listen,
motherfucker, you can't do that! This is my act!" I shouted at
him. "This is my fucking pig!"

He turned to me with the reddest face I'd ever seen in my
life. "If you don't like it here in America, why don't you go
back to Africa!" he screamed at me.

"Why don't you go the fuck back to Germany and stop
fucking with my act!"

He pushed me back and I almost fell and that really pissed
me off. I jumped up and reached for him and he socked me
against the jaw. But I caught him by the leg and kicked him.

"Get him! Get him!" I heard somebody shouting and I
didn't know if they meant me or him.

Somebody else said, "Get the police! Get the police!" and
then I heard somebody say, "The police are coming!" and I

grabbed my pig and was putting him in the prop bag when I looked up and saw the police coming in my direction. The crowd had grown larger now that some live action was being enacted in front of them. But I wasn't going to be waiting around to see what would happen when the police got there. I headed off toward the library, hearing the crowd shouting over my shoulder, "He hit him! I saw it!"

When I got to the library, I turned and saw the cop following me at a running gait. I started running faster then. Coming to the corner of the library, I cut it so fast that it must've seemed like I went into the stone wall.

Two days later I was back on campus doing my act when I got arrested. The same blond-headed student appeared with a policeman and accused me of beating him the previous day.

The second paragraph of the article said: "Jonah Drinkwater, 22, of Berkeley, was booked and is being held in Alameda County Jail, charged with unlawfully returning to the campus after being told not to come back here within 72 hours. Drinkwater, who is scheduled to be arraigned this morning, faces a maximum fine of $500 or six months in jail."

What I didn't know at the time of my arrest was that I was being arrested under a law enacted in 1968 during two campus student strikes to ban speakers for three days if they were thought to be likely to interfere with campus activities. In the first place, I was not a "speaker" but a "satirist." "The comic," the article went on to say, "used obscene language and directed it toward the police, a police spokesman said." That was true. Every time the cop put his hands on me to arrest me, I cussed him out. The students went wild with applause for me. They jibed at the cops and threw paper cups at them, but that just made the cops more determined to arrest me.

"Get your stuff," the cop said. The audience of about five hundred kids looked on. They were on my side; they were booing the cops for taking me away.

I reached down to pick up my pig prop. "I'm getting my pig," I shouted out at the audience. "Pig!"

"Right on!" the crowd screamed back.

Somebody else said, "That's bee-yuuuuuu-tiful!"

"I leave with his message from Apostle Paul!" I shouted to

them as the cop led me handcuffed through the crowd. "I speak to you as a fool because the fool is the only person who enjoys the privilege to tell the truth without causing offense!"

A wild shout of support went up from the students as they followed the policemen, who had me in their grip as if I were a common criminal, across the campus.

We passed the check-suited zealot, who was raving at the students like a madman: "Christ is coming—repent!"

"Look at him—he's doing the same thing I'm doing and you're not arresting him!" I screamed at my persecutors, but the cops' only response was to squeeze a pair of handcuffs on my wrist.

But I couldn't stop shouting the truth at them. "He's the one who told me what Apostle Paul said."

One of the cops said, "Yeah, what did Apostle Paul say?" I thought he was serious, so I explained.

"He said, 'I come as a fool because only a fool can speak the truth and not cause offense.' And, officer," I pleaded, hoping he would listen to me, "that's all I was doing—just what you see that old religious fanatic doing."

The cop said: "Well, the difference is that he really is a fool and he ain't offending anybody, but you ain't a fool. You know exactly what you're doing and you're offending a lot of people—including me, 'cause I'm a Catholic. Now get in the fucking car!"

As they were stuffing me into the backseat of the campus police car, I saw a flower vendor looking at me with this incredible scowl on his face. That really hurt me—that scowl—because I'd always pictured flower vendors as my friends, but this guy looked at me and went "YEEUCK!" and then he spat on the ground.

They slammed the door shut but the window was still down.

"What do you mean by 'YEEUCK'?" I asked the flower vendor. "I didn't mean to offend *you*, man."

"I enjoy satire," he said, "but you make me puke! Even Richard Pryor and Mort Sahl know when to stop, you creep!"

As the car was pulling off, I saw the face of a pretty girl.

"It was you! It was you!" she yelled at me, but there was no anger in her voice, there was something else: appreciation, maybe, or wonderment. Her face was so pure and happy that I carried it with me to jail.

They booked me under the 1968 law as they had many student activists—inciting to riot. I was stripped of my street clothes, mugged, given a rubber mat to sleep on, and when I opened my mouth to ask a question, the officer who said he was a Catholic slapped me across the face. Then he looked guilty and I saw the guilt in him and he got mad again, and started hitting me across the head, and when I bent over he kicked me on the back, and I fell to the floor. I decided then and there that Apostle Paul might have been right about fools not causing offense two thousand years ago, but he was sure to get his ass kicked if he came back today.

In the middle of the night they brought a big black man into the cell across from me. He cussed out all the guards for about two hours. Finally he called one of them over to his cell. The officer came over and the big black man threw something in his face. The yellow stuff splattered all over the guard's face. It was only when the guard started wiping it off that I realized that it was shit. The big man roared with laughter, and soon every one of the prisoners was laughing. Even as they took that big black prisoner out to beat him, we were laughing. It was the most exhilarating laughter I've ever heard—pure rebellious laughter of the oppressed.

They let me out the next morning, and when I stepped out into the daylight—you don't know what a wonderful thing daylight is until you've spent the night in the county jail.

I read the article. Most of the time the reporter quoted the flower vendor, who said I was "obscene . . . disgusting . . . sickening . . . abhorrent . . ."

I knew something was wrong with our country then. I saw how easy it was to be treated abusively by the police for speaking the truth, and to go to jail and not be heard of again. I saw how easy it was for students to laugh at the truth of my comedy and then go on to their classes, and never think about me again, except when they needed another laugh. I knew how easy it was for a newspaper to distort my art, my humor, my insight. I saw how easy it was for the white police to take everything I said about religion and television and fraternities and student apathy and turn it against me.

I had gone to Ninevah to preach, and been swallowed by that Leviathan called the experience of the real world, but Uncle Gadge got me out of that whale by purchasing me a ticket to Los Angeles. Now I was swallowed up by this experience, but once out of it, I was going to be a better man. Already I could taste the sand from where this whale would beach me. Already I was anxious to yield to whatever experience living at the Fountain Lanai had waiting for me.

I sat there on the bed and poured the last of my uncle's bourbon into the glass. Just as I looked up I saw a package of cigarettes—the ones I'd been looking for—under my hat on the dresser. I leaped up and opened them and fired up one right away.

As I was lying there I heard Uncle Gadge coming home. I heard him coming into the living room, then down the hallway, and into the bedroom. I heard him undressing and getting into bed, and I heard my aunt's angry voice, asking him where he'd been.

Alma Luz Villanueva

To her first novel, *The Ultraviolet Sky,* Alma Luz Villanueva
brings the poet's divination for image and internal logic, expressed in a series of dream sequences that hauntingly conclude
each section and alter the hard forms of reality like a watercolor
wash applied last. It's a fitting metaphor for her painter protagonist, Rosa, who embodies the modern feminist Chicana
woman's struggle for self-definition in the male-centered Mexican culture as well as in the larger patriarchal picture.

Villanueva is herself well-known for her feminist work. The
five books of poetry that preceded *The Ultraviolet Sky* include
Poems (1977), winner of the Third Chicano Literary Prize,
Bloodroot (1977), *Mother, May I?* (1978), *La Chingada*
(1985), and *Life Span* (1985). Her work has also appeared in
collections such as *Contemporary Women Poets* (1977), *I Sing
a Song to Myself* (1978), and *Hispanics in the United States:
An Anthology of Creative Literature* (1980). Her story "The
Ripening" was included in *Nosotras: Latina Literature Today*
(1986). Her new novel, *Naked Ladies,* will be published by
Bilingual Press in 1991, and she has just finished a collection of
short stories and a new book of poetry.

Like her heroines, Villanueva found that articulating her
experience was not without obstacles, and her voice comes
from a deep reserve of personal power. She dropped out of high
school in the tenth grade to have the first of three children,
later completing college and earning an M.F.A. She currently
is a lecturer on the Literature Board at the University of California, Santa Cruz.

Marta Ester Sánchez, in her invaluable book *Contemporary
Chicana Poetry: A Critical Approach to an Emerging Literature*

(1985), concludes the chapter devoted to Villanueva's poetry on an uneasy note:

> By juxtaposing the two identities of "woman" and "Chicana," Villanueva is at once expressing a hope for their reconciliation and asserting her inability to achieve a synthesis between them. She chooses a mythical community of women because she is thereby permitted to speak to alienated women everywhere, regardless of race. The consequence of her choice is the silence of her poetry on the subject of the Chicana experience. In a curiously paradoxical way, Villanueva shows that the search for a female identity is especially complex when considered in relation to a Chicana self-definition. She challenges her readers to discover how to include a Chicana identity in a female identity.

In *The Ultraviolet Sky*, the Chicana experience *is* extremely complex, and the challenge she poses to her readers is one she grapples with herself directly. Apparently, Villanueva was only awaiting the pace, expanse, and multiplicity of view afforded by the novel form in order to examine issues of Chicana identity.

The Ultraviolet Sky opens bravely in the midst of an argument between people who love each other, Rosa and her Mexican husband, though Rosa would rather sleep in her own backyard than breathe the air of his expectations. The first paragraph states the problem unambiguously: "What didn't go into love and passion went into hate and anger, and there never seemed to be a middle ground, a bridge, to simply stand on and speak, or to cross over in order to touch as friends. Yes, as friends." Rosa and Julio ultimately find peace at a price, but only because Rosa does not compromise the exploration of her identity in the full spectrum of human relationships. She educates her seventeen-year-old son in the responsibilities of love, receives artistic affirmation from her German-born lover and lets him go, and confronts the estrangement between herself and her girlhood friend who tolerates the double standard in her own marriage. Rosa must reject the terms of possession (surrender and exploitation) in order to sustain her hopes for the future she gives her children to. The protagonist has in her mind a painting she cannot finish, a composition of balance and infinite harmonies. Villanueva's ultraviolet sky is overhead for all of us.

—*Kathryn Trueblood*

Excerpt from
THE ULTRAVIOLET SKY

AFTER the enchiladas were made, finally, she sat by the fire. The cheese sandwich had calmed her stomach, and now she sipped a glass of dry cabernet. She sipped it slowly and cautiously, and hoped wine wouldn't have to be given up like coffee. A glass or two of wine at night was a special friend of hers. Rosa loved good wine.

Well, here I am pregnant with enchiladas in the oven—a real prime target for the Mexican Man. First I'll gauge Julio's face, and then, maybe, I'll tell him.

Rosa picked up the drawing pad and closed it, leaving it by the couch. The fire was so warm, her stomach was settled, and the wine was rich and full. Her two paintings waited for her in the bedroom studio. Another painting had begun to form itself in her mind. A painting of Dolores playing the piano, the way she remembered her as a child—before she looked up and saw Rosa standing there. Dolores had looked like she was dreaming.

She woke up to loud knocking at the door and Julio's voice, "Rosa! Rosa! Open up!" Then she remembered the enchiladas. "Oh, shit," Rosa muttered. "Just a second, Julio!" she yelled, running to the oven. Relief flooded her. They were cooked a little dark, but they weren't burnt.

She put them on top of the stove and ran for the door. "Sorry to keep you waiting. I thought I burned the dinner. Fell asleep by the fire."

Julio's overnight bag was on his shoulder and various packages were on the porch. Zack ran past him into the house. "If you hadn't opened up pretty soon I think I'd of frozen to death. Even Zack wanted to come in. You really picked a spot, didn't you?" he said irritably. He looked at Rosa's face which was regarding him coolly. Very coolly, he thought.

"Long drive." Julio reached over and kissed her with his mouth open, and smiled. "Here, let me get the goods." His smell and touch affected her, almost against her will. I love his lips, his full lips, Rosa thought—and he smells like my brother. My lover, my brother, my lover. "Did you get the pan dulce?"

"Dare I even knock on your door without it?" he laughed. "Also, various bottles of wine for madam. Champagne, Sangre de Toro, chardonnay."

"Great. I'll open the Sangre de Toro. Guess what I made for dinner?"

"I can smell it. Enchiladas."

"Are you hungry?"

"Are you kidding? When you said something special, I knew it was enchiladas." He pulled her close to him. "You know I love your enchiladas, Rosita."

They kissed again, gently, and then Rosa pulled away. "Okay, look, they almost burned. Now they're getting cold. Let's eat. Why don't you put all this stuff away and I'll serve. I'm starved." The nausea was creeping up on her. Not like the morning nausea which was almost violent, but subtly like a threat.

"You look good. Rested," Julio said, looking at her. "The solitude agrees with you?" He couldn't keep the hurt out of his voice.

"I don't really know yet, I suppose. But it seems to. I guess I've always wanted to know if I could do it. Be completely alone. Anyway, I've started painting. How're the enchiladas?"

"I want fourths tonight. That's why the Romans threw up, to eat it all over again. Sorry about the symbolism," Julio said, noticing Rosa's wince, "but they're that good."

Rosa took a sip of her wine and dispelled the thought. "It is good, isn't it? Do you want more salad? Help yourself." Rosa caught herself treating Julio as a guest. Well, he is visiting me, isn't he . . . the realization made him seem clearer somehow, as though a heaviness had been shed. An unnecessary skin. Rosa thought of her dream by the river. The beautiful, rainbow, snake skin. Now she knew she would tell him.

They quickly cleared the dishes and went to sit by the fire.

Rosa emptied her glass of cabernet. Julio's had been empty for a while. They stared at the fire for a moment. The dinner had been delicious and Rosa's stomach, the child, was quiet. She leaned into his outstretched arm.

"Do you miss me?" Julio asked.

"I have something to show you," Rosa answered him softly.

"I asked you a question, Rosa." Julio looked at her face and she looked like she was waiting for something. Maybe she wants some more wine, he thought. "Do you want to open another bottle of wine? Which one do you want? You choose."

Rosa could see he was trying to please her. To please her. Yes. She reached for the drawing pad beside her and opened it to the child's face. Luzia's face. She handed it to him.

"What's this? A new drawing? Do you want that wine?" Then the words caught him, 'I'm pregnant.' "

Julio looked at her in disbelief. In utter disbelief. "What is this, Rosa? 'I'm pregnant?' What's going on?"

Rosa looked back at him, straight into his eyes. "That's our child. That's a drawing of our child. I'm pregnant."

Julio was stunned, but he kept staring at the drawing. "Why didn't you tell me? When did it happen? Are you sure? Are you absolutely sure?"

"Yes, I'm absolutely sure. I think I'm close to two months along. I want this child, Julio. Do you?" Rosa stared at him with all her soul. Her soul was exposed, utterly, in her face.

"Rosa, Rosa," Julio murmured, "she's beautiful. Almost as beautiful as you. Are you sure she's a girl?" Julio laughed.

"That's what I dreamt, more than once. I never wanted to tell you. I didn't want to be pregnant, especially not now." Rosa began to laugh, tears streaming down her face.

Julio took her into his arms, stroking her hair and back. Tears stung his eyes and joy grabbed at his throat. "Don't you think this calls for champagne, mi Rosa?"

Julio's lovemaking bordered on violence, and it aroused her in an unexpected way—as though his kisses had to be met, his tongue had to be met, his teeth had to be met. Rosa matched him until he collapsed across her in an attitude of surrender. Whose surrender? It was difficult to tell. They lay silently as though an answer would arrive, the way their orgasms had arrived, the way the child would arrive. From the mystery itself.

Finally, Julio spoke, splintering the silence. "You aren't staying now, are you? You can't stay here now. Pregnant, I mean."

Rosa was silent.

"Rosa, do you mean to tell me that you're pregnant and that you're still going to stay here? That's crazy, Rosa."

"I don't know. Don't ask me now." She paused to look at Julio. His face was tense and angry. "But I've got to be honest, I think I'm staying. I think I've got to stay."

Julio exploded. "How in the hell are you going to pull this one off? Pregnant, here, by yourself? Now you'll really need a man. Me, remember?"

Rosa stiffened at his words and sat up. "Between a part-time job and the money that's left I think I'm fine for a while. Maybe even my grant will come through, but I won't know till December. Anyway, my expenses here are low. I can't, I honestly can't imagine going back right now. I feel like I've got to finish whatever it is I came here to do."

"And what might that be? Tell me! I want to know!" he shouted.

"Julio," Rosa stared straight ahead, "I'm not going to go back because I have to. If I do go back, it'll be because I want to. Do you understand me, once and for all?"

"Then, once and for all, what about this pregnancy? What about that little item?" he said, trying to control himself.

"I wasn't even sure if I was going to tell you," Rosa said evenly.

"And why not?" He raised his voice again.

"Because of the reaction you're having now. Look, I set up an appointment to have an abortion. I'm not saying this to hurt you, I just want you to know. I've decided that I want this baby. It wasn't easy, but I decided with everything in mind."

"Do you love me?" Julio sat facing her, staring at her lips for an answer.

"This is our child. She looks like a relative, doesn't she?"

"Do you love me?"

"Yes, I do."

Julio sighed. "Come and lay in my arms and finish this champagne."

The fierce stars were out, and they hunted without a sound. It would freeze tonight, and they were aware of their bodies stretched out, warm, against the other. The champagne was gone, so Rosa turned to face the sky through the curtainless window.

Julio cupped her belly in his hands. His hand wandered down to her pubic hair and he stroked her gently. "You think it's a girl?" he asked.

"That's what I've dreamt," she answered him sleepily.

"Did you dream that face?"

"No. I just started to sketch it. That's what I think she'll look like." Her voice trailed off.

"Shouldn't you put curtains on these windows?"

"Then I wouldn't be able to see the stars. Good night, Julio."

"Have you considered the view goes both ways?"

"I don't care."

Julio held his breath for a moment. "Good night, Rosa."

Rosa woke to a dazzling sun, and the brief dream came, clearly, to her. They'd slept in. Julio was on his side, breathing softly, covered up to his eyes. She'd go make a fire, immediately.

The dream, she thought. The dream. She'd decided to leave—this had been very clear—she'd decided to go back. And then the tattoo began to melt. To disappear. A great sorrow engulfed her, as though she, herself, would disappear. No, I can't do it, she told herself. I can't leave. I'm staying.

Rosa shut the bedroom door and started some tea water, then the fire. The cabin was freezing. She felt it on the exposed areas of her face. She opened the back door and the sheer whiteness, the cold, assaulted her. How would I shovel myself out nine months along? She shut the door and started breakfast.

"I smelled the coffee," Julio said, coming into the kitchen. "Are you planning to cook something for breakfast? I'll do the dishes." He smiled at her.

"I was thinking of a German pancake stuffed with apples and cinnamon. How's that?"

"I'll do the dishes for that any day. You aren't having coffee?" he asked, noticing the tea bag in her cup.

"It nauseates me."

Julio began to laugh as he drew Rosa into his arms. "I forgot to give you something." He took something small out of his shirt pocket, a small metal heart with a purple ribbon tied through a hole at the top of it. A safety pin was clipped onto the ribbon. "A milagro, for you."

Rosa took it and felt its small strength. She fingered the smooth, purple ribbon. "A miracle. Of course. Could this be your heart, Mr. López?" Rosa smiled at him.

Julio took the heart and pinned it over hers. "Now I don't know whether to pin it over your heart or your womb." His eyes were shining.

"That'll do, Mr. López, for now. Here, the coffee's ready. Let me get breakfast." She kissed him lightly on the lips.

"I'll be sending you two hundred a month to make ends meet until you decide to come back. I want you to come back. Do you hear me, Rosa?"

Rosa fingered the milagro. "I hear you, loud and clear. If I don't eat pretty soon I'm going to be sick."

"THIS is delicious," Julio said, looking at Rosa. "Do you feel all right? You look a little pale."

"It's always like this until the food properly settles." Rosa poured herself some more tea. "I can't believe that the smell of coffee almost turns my stomach." She looked at Julio and said, "I seem to be turning into someone else. That's what it feels like."

"You know, your telling me you're pregnant makes me feel a bit altered; but to actually be pregnant must be like changing into someone else." Julio paused. "Were you really not going to tell me?"

"I was contemplating it."

"Why?"

"Have I ever told you about the Mexican Man?"

Julio laughed. "No, I don't think so. Someone I know?"

"He's the man I never wanted to marry. He's the man I've seen women make the endless piles of tortillas for, as he grows fat and stupid while his brain shrinks to fit his narrow mind that dictates boys are better than girls, boys become men, girls become wives, men have moments of freedom, release, women count the tortillas and the children. Men have affairs, women become whores. Puta. La Puta. You know, that word used to send shivers down my spine. 'Puta.' " Rosa said it deep in her throat, like the sound of coughing up something disgusting she was about to spit out and get rid of. Something so worthless it deserved to lie on the ground, the Earth, and be forgotten. "That's the way they said it. It was like the woman deserved to die. Fuck!" Rosa looked at Julio with a strange desperation on her face.

"Rosa, I may be a little overweight, but my brain's not shrinking. Okay, I guess I've had trouble with your freedom. I was brought up by the women who served me the endless tortillas. But why the Mexican Man? Do you see me as the Mexican Man?"

"Sometimes. It just creeps up on you. I don't think it's something you consciously know that you're doing. But didn't you just say it? You were raised by the women who served you the endless tortillas. Dolores just told me my father was also German. Maybe that makes me la hija de La Gran Puta."

"Rosa, what're you saying? Take it easy. I am not the Mexican Man, for Christ's sake."

"What I'm saying is that in our culture, the culture we were raised in, the puta was the woman who fucked who she wanted to and didn't fuck who she didn't want to, because she liked to fuck. Maybe she loved her body. Maybe she loved being a woman. The Mexican Man was in opposition to all this."

"Do you still have an interest in other men, even now?" Julio asked, suspiciously.

"Watch it, Julio. He's creeping up on you again. I may be pregnant, but I'm not dead. In fact, I feel especially alive."

"Don't women feel motherly when they're pregnant? I mean, isn't that what's happening?"

"I was a mother before. Was I only motherly before? All I know is, my body feels like it's reaching out for the stars and the center of the Earth, simultaneously. I feel like fucking you right now like La Gran Puta." Rosa laughed, reaching for his penis, rubbing it, slightly swollen and soft, under his jeans.

"The Mexican Man surrenders to La Gran Puta, gladly." Julio shivered with excitement, and let her rub him to a full erection. As she took his penis, carefully, out of his pants he threw his head back and moaned loudly as the warmth of her mouth surrounded him. He drew her up and they collapsed on the couch.

"You'd better throw a log on the fire," Rosa mumbled.

"Forget the fire. Take your clothes off."

"Take your clothes off. And throw on a log."

Julio put the log on the fire, and then another one. It would last for a while now. He stripped off his clothing in a few movements. His penis stood out in front of him, proudly. It had no eyes, but it knew where it wanted to go—inside of Rosa. Will I remember this in my old age? The thought flickered and disappeared.

He faced her thrusting out his penis, with his hands, for her scrutiny. For her admiration. And then he saw it. The tattoo on her belly. "Rosa, what's on your belly?" Julio stood there staring at her, holding his penis with one hand.

"What does it look like?"

He sat down on the couch and touched it. "A rose tattoo. Is it real? Not a glue-on?"

"It's the real thing. Do you like it?"

"When did you get it?" He was flabbergasted.

"A couple of months ago. Do you like it?"

"Do I have a choice? Why did you get it?"

Rosa thought of her dream of the melting tattoo and said, "Because I had to."

"Why?" Julio insisted.

"I don't know." Rosa's voice sounded far away and she turned her face toward the fire.

Slowly, Julio bent over her. He kissed her tattoo, and then he licked it, encircling the softness of her ass with his arms. "You taste so good, Rosa."

"Puta," she reminded him.

"Puta," he echoed. His tongue found her again.

"DO you realize I can hear myself think here?" Julio laughed. "And do you know that I love that you're pregnant? The tattoo I'll have to get used to."

"Are you surprised?" Rosa was lying on the crook of his arm staring at the fire.

"I'm still in shock, I think. But I love it. Would you have had the abortion without telling me?" Julio stroked her neck softly.

"I think it's enough that I told you. It's been hard for me. Don't ask."

"Okay. Fair enough. Do you want to take the gun out for a few rounds?"

"Take a look outside. Do you want to shoot a gun in that?"

"I think you should practice with it. What if you have to use it?" Julio's body stiffened.

"Come on, Julio. Let's go for a walk. We could follow the creek. We'll take some brandy."

"On one condition. We make love again." Julio kissed her.

"Save that for tonight, M.M. Let's go."

"Have it your way, La Gran Puta."

They threw pillows at each other for a while and eventually they got dressed.

"Are you really pregnant, Rosita?" Julio held her in his arms and stared, directly, into her eyes.

"It looks like it, M.M.," Rosa laughed.

"Okay, come on. Let's take this walk out in the tundra. I guess I'm ready." Julio looked out from under a ski hat folded down over his ears.

"You look like a pissed-off grizzly," Rosa laughed loudly.

"Listen, I'm from the desert, woman. I am pissed-off. I ain't supposed to be in no snow. Sheeit!" Julio growled at her.

"Do you have your camera, Mr. Bear?"

He growled and nodded yes. Zack was waiting for them on the porch.

"Mush, mush, Zack! Tally ho!" Julio shouted and jumped off the steps.

"You'd better watch it! You're going to fall on your ass!"

Zack ran ahead toward the creek. He was beginning to know which way Rosa would go. This time she decided to walk the opposite way—to cross the creek and follow another trail. The snow was deeper here. The trail led to a meadow covered by the sloping smoothness of fresh snow. Not a single footprint, human or animal, was on it. Then the trail forked and a smaller one followed the creek through the trees again.

"Well, it's beautiful. Look at those peaks in the distance. Nothing but white. And the shadows are incredible, aren't they?" Julio asked, aiming his camera, full of concentration. He hardly heard her answer. He was seeing more than hearing.

"Yes. It's absolutely beautiful here."

They sat on cold, grey stones facing each other. The creek flowed in front of them.

"There's a composition everywhere you look, isn't there?" Julio bent over the water to capture the ice prisms dangling in weird shapes.

"The ice is so still and the water never stops."

"What did you say?" he asked.

"I said, the ice is so still and the water never stops. I like that. They look like water roots. Winter roots."

"I've never seen anything like it. I guess if it gets deeper out here you'll need snowshoes to walk through."

Rosa poured the brandy. "I guess. I'm going to have to equip Zack with a brandy barrel and put it around his neck." Zack ran over at the sound of his name. "How about it, Zack? Do you want to carry the brandy?" Rosa smoothed his ears, and then he was gone, running along the creek.

"He sure likes it here. Doggy's paradise. No fences. I'm glad we stopped here. My feet were beginning to freeze," Julio said.

They sipped the brandy slowly, listening to the swollen creek.

"Do you ever think about making it into the next century? If we're going to survive into the next century? I mean, the whole planet." Rosa stared at the ice prisms as they caught the available light.

Julio looked at her. "Not constantly, but from time to time. You can't help but wonder which missile's pointed on your head. I know in the bay area there're quite a few pointed on it, that's for sure."

"This child of ours is headed for the next century, you know."

"That's right. I hadn't thought of that. Pour me another, would you?"

Rosa poured them both another.

To the Earth and our baby," Julio said, softly, putting his glass out to Rosa's.

"And to transformation." The brandy burned a little, filling her mouth up with its fire.

THAT night as Julio put his arms around her belly, he asked her, "Have you thought of a name for this tattooed baby? If it's a girl, that is."

"I call her a Native Person. She's a mestizo, a mixed-blood. That's what a Mexican really is—a mestizo. We're all mestizos."

Julio laughed. "How's that?"

"She'll be a Native Person of the Earth, that's what. If we're going to survive into the next century, we're all going to have to be Native People. You know?" Rosa stretched against Julio and it was hard to remember tension at that moment.

"But have you thought of a name for this Native Person?"

"I'm going to keep it a secret until I see her. Why don't you think of one, too."

"Are you really going to get big, Rosita?" Julio's voice was thick and sleepy. He waited for an answer and when she remained silent he asked, "You aren't going to stay here by yourself, are you?"

"Yes, I am." Her voice sounded small in the darkness. It was as though they were in a narrow tunnel.

He grabbed hold of her. "I won't let you. You've got to come back with me now. You know that."

"Not now, Julio. Go to sleep. I'm so damned tired."

Rosa fell asleep almost immediately, and Julio struggled, alone, in the dark tunnel until he passed into the brightness of his dreams.

He is following tracks, lion tracks, and then they disappear. They simply disappear. He begins to laugh with joy. He sees that the desert's in bloom. Flowers among cactus needles, fertility within the sand. Spring. Julio cups a handful of sand, and when he opens his hand, the sand is gone.

WHEN Rosa woke, Julio was already up. She could hear him in the kitchen, and the sound of the morning fire. Her dreams, there'd been many small ones, seemed like one continuous thread. Deep, dark and unbroken. Maybe these are the ones that guide me best, the thought came to her, blindly. She smelled bacon and coffee, and the familiar nausea returned with an unusual force.

"Are you up?" Julio asked, looking in.

"Not quite. I feel absolutely lousy." Rosa turned on her side and looked out the window. "Do you mind bringing me some tea and toast? I would sure appreciate it."

"Coming right up. Do you want bacon and eggs?"

"I'll tell you after the tea. Thanks."

They ate breakfast by the fire. Bach played on the stereo. Peace.

"I let Zack out. I fed him, too," Julio said.

"Look at the sun. What a day. Do you want to go for a ride later? We could do some exploring up by Buck's Lake."

"Sounds good to me."

"Also, tonight I was invited to a piano recital—a woman I met at a local restaurant. Her name's Iris. She's also a painter, and a good one. Do you want to go?"

"We don't have much time together. Do you have to go?"

"I want to go."

Julio's face darkened. "Well, then, I guess I'll go with you."

"OKAY, the map says the highway goes out to a deserted Mobil station, and the next left by a school bus shelter. It seems longer than eight miles, doesn't it?"

"Seems like eighty," Julio answered.

"Here it is," Rosa said, turning the car onto a narrow dirt road. "There isn't as much snow down here, at all. Just a powder. I enjoyed our snow fight today."

Julio lit up a joint and smiled. "Me, too. Got you good, didn't I?" he laughed. "Do you want some?"

"Maybe later. I got you good back, though, didn't I?" Rosa teased. "The house is set back, but a banner with a crescent moon will be hung by the fence, it says here."

"Hippieland," Julio muttered.

"What do you mean, hippieland? You're an artist, aren't you?"

"These are white people, right? I mean, it's okay, of course. I have some white friends, but they're just a lot harder to get to know. I mean, I hope we don't have to sit around chanting OM or something."

Rosa laughed. "You can sit around chanting *mierda* for all I care. Anyway, her name's Iris. She's a waitress in town and I like her."

"There it is. Must be that place with the lights on and all the cars." Julio pointed to it.

Forrest opened the door. "Well, it's Ms. Luján! How's the quality wood? Come on in. I'm supposed to welcome everyone. Right, Iris?"

Iris smiled and waved. She was sitting at the piano. A group of people sat on chairs and pillows in a semi-circle, facing her.

"Has she started?" Rosa asked.

"She just started up. Grab a pillow."

"Forrest, this is Julio." Rosa glanced at Julio and he didn't look overjoyed.

They shook hands. "Welcome to the show, Julio. Talk to you in the intermission. I see you brought food and libations. Excellent, I'm starved," Forrest laughed. He went back to his pillow next to Cheryl.

Julio was frowning. "Who in the fuck was that? Golden Boy? I plan to eat some of this myself."

"He's the guy I bought the wood from. Actually, he's going to be my neighbor. Sort of. That's his wife next to him," Rosa added.

Iris looked over at them, briefly, and began to play on a piano as beautiful as Rob's. But, obviously, she was a much better pianist. Her hands took control of the keys, immediately, and the notes rolled fluidly into the small room like a gift. The notes quickly filled the room; every corner seemed filled with its richness. She erased the notes with a silence, and then she began again.

"Go on and sit down." Rosa motioned Julio toward some pillows. "I'll bring some wine. Isn't she good?" Rosa whispered.

"Very. Very good," Julio answered, making his way to the pillows. His largeness dwarfed what seemed to be a roomful of fine-boned people—but he was agile. Agile as a cat.

Rosa handed the wine to Julio and sat down on the floor. A wood stove with a glass door, a square of red warmth, heated the room. On the walls were some watercolors and a large oil. They all had her trademark of delicacy and strength, like the ones in the restaurant.

The oil was bold, though. Striking. A pair of dark horses, very realistic and solid, stood facing each other in a dreamlike plain of light corals. Rosa gazed at this painting while Iris played, glancing occasionally at her face which followed the music that she heard in her head.

"Iris, that was wonderful." Rosa reached over and touched her hand.

"Thank you, Rosa. And thanks for coming." She looked at Julio.

"Iris, this is Julio."

"Very beautiful, Iris," Julio said, smiling.

"I'm glad you enjoyed it. I really am. Have you had some of the food? Help yourself. That is, if you can beat Forrest to it," Iris laughed.

Julio looked at Rosa. "She isn't kidding. Are you hungry?"

"Just a little. These look good. I wonder what they are?" Rosa picked up a cabbage leaf filled with something.

A dark-haired woman answered her. "They're a kind of dolmas filled with brown rice, raisins, chopped vegetables and walnuts." The woman's dark eyes were wide-open and intense. She had high cheek bones and full, sensual lips without lipstick.

"Are these yours?" Rosa asked.

"Yes, they are." She smiled, slowly.

Rosa took a bite. "These are delicious." She put the rest of it in her mouth. "My dish is the tacos." Rosa looked over at her plate and laughed. "Or rather, my dish was the tacos. I'm Rosa," she said looking at the younger woman.

"My dream name is A——. My waking name is Diana." She said this in a low voice, looking at Rosa, closely, to see her true response.

"Are you Indian? A——sounds like an Indian name. I think your dream name is lovely." Rosa looked back at her and the air between them was charged with a restless energy.

Diana's long beaded earrings caught the light and then melted into her thick, dark hair. "My mother's Cree with some Mexican thrown in. Did you just move here? I haven't seen you before, so you must've. Is that your old man?" She indicated Julio.

"Well, first of all, my grandmother was Yaqui Indian, but after my grandfather a good dose of Mexican was thrown in, and my father was English and German. Thought we'd get that straight."

They both laughed.

"And, yes, that's my husband, but I moved here by myself." Now it was Rosa's turn to scrutinize her response. "Do you mind if I call you A——? I love it. What does it mean?"

In a soft, low voice she said, "One who seeks." And then she changed back into her speaking voice which was rather loud. "Well, it appears we have some things to talk about, Rosa. There aren't many Mexican or Indian people up here. Well, there is what's left of the Maidu, the Native People of this area—but they make it a point to keep to themselves. I don't blame them." Diana paused, then asked, "What do you do?"

"I'm a painter and a teacher. I've been painting oils for about ten years. I don't know what I'm going to do here. The college is locked up tight, it seems. Anyway, what do you do up here?"

"For one, I'm a midwife, and I also run the county nutrition and prenatal program on a part-time basis." A little boy around three years old ran up to her and held onto her long, full skirt. "This is Joel. Do you have any of these?" she laughed.

"Mine's eighteen and on his own now. Why don't I give you my number. I live in Lupine Meadows."

"Do you like it out there? I've heard it's Machoville with the ranch there and all. But the lots are pretty nice, and there's only so many of them. Are you renting something back there?"

"Actually, I bought it. Why don't you come by for dinner sometime? Do you live out here?"

"Most of my friends live in Butterfly Valley or Spanish Peak. I live about six miles out toward Spanish Peak. I'll give you my number if you'll lend me your pen."

"Do you live by yourself—with your son, that is?"

"Yeah, but there's a group of us in a small cluster of cabins, so it's kind of supportive. It'll be a little tricky living out in Lupine Meadows all alone, I imagine." Diana kept her eyes on Rosa's face.

Loud voices made Rosa turn around. It was Julio and Forrest.

"Did I ask your opinion, or what?" Julio was enraged.

"Well, I didn't mean anything by it. Take it easy!" Forrest said angrily, but it was clear that he was intimidated.

"You ate all the damn tacos! What's your trip?" He wanted to shout Golden Boy.

Rosa took Julio by the arm. "What's going on? Come on, Julio."

Then Forrest got brave. "It looks like he can't handle his tacos."

Julio rushed toward him and Forrest backed into the food table spilling things. Iris came over and grabbed onto Forrest saying, "You'd better shut up, Forrest."

"All I said was that the tacos were some of the best I'd ever eaten."

"Yeah, well you ate nearly all of them, asshole!" Julio yelled.

"Come on, Julio. It's not worth it. Come on!" Rosa dragged him out the door. "Jesus, calm down!"

"You calm down! I don't have to put up with that shit! First the tacos are good, then you're good, or whatever that asshole said."

Rosa started up the motor and let it warm. Iris came out to

the car. She had a shawl around her shoulders, and a concerned look was on her face. "Rosa, Julio, you don't have to go. You really don't. I'm planning to do another set in about ten minutes."

Rosa glanced at Julio and his face was still angry. "Thanks, Iris, but I don't think we should. But thanks for coming out like this." She didn't know what else to say. It was embarrassing.

"Look, Iris, I'm sorry," Julio said, leaning forward toward the window. "I didn't mean to cause so much trouble back there." His voice sounded strained with effort.

"Don't worry about it. It happens," Iris said, looking at Julio with a trace of impatience. "I'll see you soon, Rosa. Bye, now." She turned and ran toward the house.

They were quiet all the way to town, though it took every effort at silence for Rosa to hold her tongue, and Julio could feel it like a hollowness in his ears, loudly.

"Twenty degrees. It's a bitch tonight. Did you leave the heater on?" he asked in a subdued voice.

"Why did you get in that fight with Forrest?" She asked in a tempered tone because she remembered that Forrest had also pushed her button.

"The tacos are great, and Rosa's not so bad either," Julio mimicked Forrest's voice.

"It seems that the guy can be a pain, but do you think that explosion was worth that measly comment?"

"Yeah, I do! I sure as hell do!"

"Julio, maybe a short, but lethal, comment would've done the trick. I think you overdid it."

"That's your opinion," Julio said in a harsh voice.

"That's right! That was damned embarrassing. I have a feeling if we'd been around people you know, you'd have been a fucking diplomat. If you really didn't want to come, why didn't you stay at the cabin for a few hours?"

"Oh, right. Now that would've been tons of fun." Julio laughed angrily.

"All I know is, there've been plenty of times when I could've really used your back-up, but you left me on my own." Rosa began to cry. "It seems like your possessions were in jeopardy back there, that's all."

"Oh, Christ, not that again. Does it always have to come back to that, Rosa?"

"Apparently, it does. Okay, look, just forget it for now. But why did you apologize to Iris back there?" Rosa shot him an angry look.

Julio started to speak and then he fell silent. Finally, he said, "I guess I thought I owed her an apology. Do you know that I'm leaving tomorrow?"

"Yes, I know."

Julio reached over and touched her hand. "Can't we be friends?"

"That's what I keep trying to do, Julio." She started crying again and pulled her hand away from his.

"Okay, I apologize to you for the scene, but I'm not sorry I did it."

"Great. Then that means, in essence, that you'd do it again."

"I said I apologize, Rosa," Julio said with an edge of anger.

WHEN they got into their sleeping bags Julio reached for her, but she shrugged him off.

"I don't believe this. I'm leaving tomorrow. Will you at least let me hold you in my arms?"

Rosa turned and put her head on his shoulder. Then he tried to kiss her. She turned away.

"I'll lay in your arms, but I just don't feel like making love, at all."

"Great. That's just great." Julio stared out the window. The night was clear and the stars were brilliant with light. An unusual amount of light, he thought. But they were no comfort to him. No comfort at all. He was in the middle of his life with nothing to show for it but a couple of failed marriages, a few bittersweet affairs. The child, he thought. There is the child. And Rosa will probably come back when she starts to get big. At least there's the child . . .

"Good night, Rosa," he murmured, snuggling up close to her, smelling the back of her neck. But she was asleep, as the child was asleep inside of her. Inside of her, he thought with yearning. God, this place is quiet—too damned quiet. She'll come back soon enough. I'll give her two months in this place.

He continued to stare at the stars, and he thought angrily, She ought to put some damned curtains up. Suddenly, he was fourteen camping out for the first time in the desert, and though the night had frightened him, the stars had kept him up with excitement. They'd looked so close. He hadn't killed yet. The next day he would kill his first rabbit. Everything was gone now. The rabbit's flesh, its soft fur, Gonzales, the boy in the night, wrapped by the night; silence instead of screams, a slow burning fire instead of flares, light instead of loneliness.

Now, he opened his hand, and it was true—even the sand was gone. Entirely. No one owns the desert, the words came to him, not even the sand.

JULIO left the next day, and the joy they'd felt when he first arrived, that first night, was equal to the sense of sorrow they felt as he left. Rosa felt drained of any real emotion, and Julio had only one left. Anger. So they parted again, both of them vaguely feeling what would become familiar to them both. Despair.

"I'll send you the two hundred dollars next month. Take care of yourself," Julio said. "Look, I'll take the baby right after it's born. I mean it."

"Oh, sure. I'm just going to give my baby away. Right, Julio."

"It'll be my child, too, you know."

"Goodbye. Have a safe trip." Rosa was anxious for him to go, though she knew an immense wave of loneliness waited for her. She knew it was there waiting for her, as though it were a gate to her solitude.

"I want to come back week after next." He tried to kiss her, but she turned her cheek to him, pulling away from his hold.

"Call me during the week. Bye, Julio." Rosa closed the door as he walked to his car. Pregnant and alone, the walls whispered.

The drawing of the child hung over the fireplace. "Luzia," she said out loud. She could no longer hear Julio's car. Then

Rosa walked into the studio, and her sense of despair included the unfinished paintings. Maybe I am losing my mind, she began. Maybe I am, finally, just seeing things. Who else cares about the fucking lilac sky but me? As Julie said, with my attitude I'm not going to be too popular around here. And then last night. A hermit. And a pregnant hermit at that.

Then she started to laugh, and every time she'd start to calm down, the image of a serious-faced, pregnant hermit made her gasp with laughter all over again. I must be nuts, she thought, laughing by myself.

Rosa took a look out of the front room window. I wonder what old Dale would think of this? Probably call in a posse. This made her laugh even harder. I'm a lost cause, that's what. "A lost cause," she said out loud.

Suddenly she was hungry. Very hungry. She waited for the nausea, but it didn't come. Rosa heated up the leftovers, putting candles on instead of lights. The night's swallowing the forest, she told herself. Let it. Just let it. She felt like laughing again, but, this time, because the food was delicious. Let it.

Toni Cade Bambara

CALLING Toni Cade Bambara! Calling Toni Cade Bambara! Where is your next novel, girl? When I first read *The Salt Eaters* in 1980, I invited you to Smith College to read. You were so generous to that standing-room-only, mostly black audience! They asked for more and more, and you read for two hours instead of for the contracted one—and remember, I had to stop you so you'd have time to autograph copies of your book, which you did for an hour and a half? You talked and laughed with people who wanted to share memories your writing recalled in them. Come on, Toni. Where's the second novel, girl?

When I first met Velma Henry, I saw bits and pieces of me: a Black, middle-class woman, in love with her people and struggling to embrace her past, her ancestry, our ancestry. A Black, middle-class woman who fights her battles over the truth in the world of colleges and universities. A Black, middle-class woman who tries to balance and harmonize the forces of life, much as our ancestors did, as our folklore tells us to, as my momma tells me to. A Black, middle-class woman who encounters the contradictions of individual **versus** community, of diametrical opposition (good vs. evil, white vs. black, up vs. down, male vs. female, rational vs. emotional, etc., etc.), and who tries to make sense anyway despite the awful stereotyping and deadening of spirit and life itself they bring. There are so many of us in Velma, Obie, Minnie Ransom, M'dear Sophie, Doc Serge, and all of them. Come on, Toni, we need more. We need to understand how to identify the best of our traditions, how to merge them with the best of others, how to dispel despair. Will you puleeeze hurry up and write that next novel?

You have so much to say to everyone, and you say it so well.

You told Claudia Tate when she interviewed you that your
determination of your responsibility to yourself and to your
audience was to "start with the recognition that we are at war,"
and

> that war is not simply a hot debate between the capitalist camp
> over which economic/political/social arrangement will have he-
> gemony in the world. It's not just the battle over turf and who has
> the right to utilize resources for whomsoever's benefit. The war is
> also being fought over the truth: what is the truth about human
> nature, about the human potential? My responsibility to myself,
> my neighbors, my family and the human family is to try to tell the
> truth. That ain't easy. There are so few truth-speaking traditions in
> this society in which the myth of "Western civilization" has
> claimed the allegiance of so many. We have rarely been encour-
> aged and equipped to appreciate the fact that the truth works, that
> it releases the Spirit and that it is a joyous thing. We live in a part
> of the world, for example, that equates criticism with assault, that
> equates social responsibility with naive idealism, that defines the
> unrelenting pursuit of knowledge and wisdom as fanaticism.
>   . . . I work to tell the truth about people's live; I work to cele-
> brate struggle, to applaud the tradition of struggle in our commu-
> nity, to bring to center stage all those characters, just ordinary folks
> on the block, who've been waiting in the wings, characters we
> thought we had to ignore because they weren't pimp-flashy or
> hustler-slick or because they didn't fit easily into previously accept-
> able modes or stock types. I want to lift up some usable truths—
> like the fact that the simple act of cornrowing one's hair is radical
> in a society that defines beauty as blonde tresses blowing in the
> wind; that staying centered in the best of one's own cultural tradi-
> tion is hip, is sane, is perfectly fine despite all claims to universality-
> through-Anglo-Saxonizing and other madness. [from Claudia
> Tate, *Black Women Writers at Work*, pp. 17–18]

I tell my students that you, like Gwendolyn Brooks, Ishmael
Reed, Toni Morrison, and Ernest Gaines, write *out of* Black
culture and not simply *about* Black culture. Minnie Ransom
and Sophie Heywood know the old ways as they mixed with the
Bible and Christianity; they know there aren't any quick fixes
to Velma's being healed; that sometimes you're *supposed* to
feel bad; that the snake can bring physical poisoning and death,

and the serpent spiritual poisoning and spiritual death; that salt must never be used in extremes or it ceases to be an antidote or a seasoning, and gives you high blood pressure, or even kills you. Minnie Ransom reminds me of my Aunt Curley, who swore by her folk healing, *assisted by* the physician's knowledge. And M'Dear Sophie is like so many aunt-mothers who would die for their real and "adopted" nieces and nephews. You say so much to all of us, African American, American Indian, Asian American, Euro-American, Latino American, immigrants—so much to all of us—our lives, our consciousness, our days are enmeshed inextricably. The flashbacks, the merging of consciousnesses as Velma goes through her healing, the messages to all of us, men and women, old and young, brown, yellow, red, white, black, that "wholeness ain't no trifling matter"; that the only way one can be healed is for all to be healed; that we all have got to embrace each other, build on the shared best of our traditions, on the old and the new: that we must not "letcha mouf gitcha in what ya backbone caint stand."

Come on Toni, give us more. Velma has all the wonder and energy of the young black girl in "Gorilla, My Love" (1972), and all the intensity of the people in "The Sea Birds Are Still Alive" (1972). Write more short stories like them, if you rather. I don't really care, although I do like the way the novel lets you reflect more deeply and expansively some of the basics of African American folklore and life. You know, how we tell stories to straighten each other out, to teach one another, how our lives are connected in our joys, sorrows, freedoms, and oppressions. You know, how "I am we," and how all that gets mixed up with "I think, therefore, I am" and "rugged individualism."

Anyway, girl, after these readers read this first chapter, you're gonna *have* to give us more. They're gonna want to write you and call you up and tell *you* to stop what ever it is that is distracting *you* and to burst out of *your* cocoon. We know writin' about this stuff ain't no triflin' matter!

Love, Nella.

—*Johnnella E. Butler*

"ARE you sure, sweetheart, that you want to be well?"
Velma Henry turned stiffly on the stool, the gown ties tight
across her back, the knots hard. So taut for so long, she could
not swivel. Neck, back, hip joints dry, stiff. Face frozen. She
could not glower, suck her teeth, roll her eyes, do any of the
Velma-things by way of answering Minnie Ransom, who sat
before her humming lazily up and down the scales, making a
big to-do of draping her silky shawl, handling it as though it
were a cape she'd swirl any minute over Velma's head in a
wipe-out veronica, or as though it were a bath towel she was
drying her back with in the privacy of her bathroom.

Minnie Ransom herself, the fabled healer of the district, her
bright-red flouncy dress drawn in at the waist with two different strips of kenti cloth, up to her elbows in a minor fortune of
gold, brass and silver bangles, the silken fringe of the shawl
shimmying at her armpits. Her head, wrapped in some juicy
hot-pink gelee, was tucked way back into her neck, eyes peering
down her nose at Velma as though old-timey spectacles
perched there were slipping down.

Velma blinked. Was ole Minnie trying to hypnotize her,
mesmerize her? Minnie Ransom, the legendary spinster of
Claybourne, Georgia, spinning out a song, drawing *her* of all
people up. Velma the swift; Velma the elusive; Velma who had
never mastered the kicks, punches and defense blocks, but who
had down cold the art of being not there when the blow came.
Velma caught, caught up, in the weave of the song Minnie was
humming, of the shawl, of the threads, of the silvery tendrils
that extended from the healer's neck and hands and disappeared into the sheen of the sunlight. The glistening bangles,
the metallic threads, the dancing fringe, the humming like

bees. And was the ole swamphag actually sitting there dressed for days, legs crossed, one foot swinging gently against the table where she'd stacked the tapes and records? Sitting there flashing her bridgework and asking some stupid damn question like that, blind to Velma's exasperation, her pain, her humiliation?

Velma could see herself: hair matted and dusty, bandages unraveled and curled at the foot of the stool like a sleeping snake, the hospital gown huge in front, but tied up too tight in back, the breeze from the window billowing out the rough white muslin and widening the opening in the back. She could not focus enough to remember whether she had panties on or not. And Minnie Ransom perched on her stool actually waiting on an answer, drawling out her hummingsong, unconcerned that any minute she might strike the very note that could shatter Velma's bones.

"I like to caution folks, that's all." said Minnie, interrupting her own humming to sigh and say it, the song somehow buzzing right on. "No sense us wasting each other's time, sweetheart." The song running its own course up under the words, up under Velma's hospital gown, notes pressing against her skin and Velma steeling herself against intrusion. "A lot of weight when you're well. Now, you just hold that thought."

Velma didn't know how she was to do that. She could barely manage to hold on to herself, hold on to the stingy stool, be there all of a piece and resist the buzzing bee tune coming at her. Now her whole purpose was surface, to go smooth, be sealed and inviolate.

She tried to withdraw as she'd been doing for weeks and weeks. Withdraw the self to a safe place where husband, lover, teacher, workers, no one could follow, probe. Withdraw he, self and prop up a borderguard to negotiate with would-be intruders. She'd been a borderguard all her childhood, so she knew something about it. She was the one sent to the front door to stand off the landlord, the insurance man, the green-grocer, the fishpeddler, to insure Mama Mae one more bit of peace. And at her godmother's, it was Smitty who sent her to the front door to misdirect the posse. No, no one of that name lived here. No, this was not where the note from the principal should be delivered.

SHE wasn't sure how to move away from Minnie Ransom and from the music, where to throw up the barrier and place the borderguard. She wasn't sure whether she'd been hearing music anyway. Was certain, though, that she didn't know what she was supposed to say or do on that stool. Wasn't even sure whether it was time to breathe in or breathe out. Everything was off, out of whack, the relentless logic she'd lived by sprung. And here she was in Minnie Ransom's hands in the Southwest Community Infirmary. Anything could happen. She could roll off the stool like a ball of wax and melt right through the floor, or sail out of the window, stool and all, and become some new kind of UFO. Anything could happen. And hadn't Ole Minnie been nattering away about just that before the session had begun, before she had wiped down the stools and set them out just so? "In the last quarter, sweetheart, anything can happen. And will," she'd said. Last quarter? Of the moon, of the century, of some damn basketball game? Velma had been, still was, too messed around to figure it out.

"You just hold that thought," Minnie was saying again, leaning forward, the balls of three fingers pressed suddenly, warm and fragrant, against Velma's forehead, the left hand catching her in the back of her head, cupping gently the two stony portions of the temporal bone. And Velma was inhaling in gasps, and exhaling shudderingly. She felt aglow, her eyebrows drawing in toward the touch as if to ward off the invading fingers that were threatening to penetrate her skull. And then the hands went away quickly, and Velma felt she was losing her eyes.

"Hold on now," she heard. It was said the way Mama Mae would say it, leaving her bent in the sink while she went to get a washcloth to wipe the shampoo from her eyes. Velma held on to herself. Her pocketbook on the rungs below, the backless stool in the middle of the room, the hospital gown bunched up now in the back—there was nothing but herself and some dim belief in the reliability of stools to hold on to. But then the old crone had had a few choice words to say about that too, earlier, rearing back on her heels and pressing her knees against the stereo while Velma perched uneasily on the edge of her stool trying to listen, trying to wait patiently for the woman to sit down and get on with it, trying to follow her drift, scrambling to piece together key bits of high school physics, freshman philo, and lessons M'Dear Sophie and Mama Mae had tried to impart. The reliability of stools? Solids, liquids, gases, the dance of atoms, the bounce and race of molecules, ethers, electrical charges. The eyes and habits of illusion. Retinal images, bogus images, traveling to the brain. The pupils trying to tell the truth to the inner eye. The eye of the heart. The eye of the head. The eye of the mind. All seeing differently.

Velma gazed out over the old woman's head and through the window, feeling totally out of it, her eyes cutting easily through panes and panes of glass and other substances, it seemed, until she slammed into the bark of the tree in the Infirmary yard and recoiled, was back on the stool, breathing in and out in almost a regular rhythm, wondering if it was worth it, submitting herself to this ordeal.

It would have been more restful to have simply slept it off; said no when the nurse had wakened her, no she didn't want to see Miz Minnie; no she didn't want to be bothered right now, but could someone call her husband, her sister, her godmother, somebody, anybody to come sign her out in the morning. But what a rough shock it would have been for the family to see her like that. Obie, Palma, M'Dear Sophie or her son Lil James. Rougher still to be seen. She wasn't meant for these scenes, wasn't meant to be sitting up there in the Southwest Community Infirmary with her ass out, in the middle of the day, and strangers cluttering up the treatment room, ogling her in her misery. She wasn't meant for any of it. But then M'Dear Sophie always said, "Find meaning where you're put, Vee." So she exhaled deeply and tried to relax and stick it out and pay attention.

Rumor was these sessions never lasted more than ten or fifteen minutes anyway. It wouldn't kill her to go along with the thing. Wouldn't kill her. She almost laughed. She might have died. *I might have died.* It was an incredible thought now. She sat there holding on to *that* thought, waiting for Minnie Ransom to quit playing to the gallery and get on with it. Sat there, every cell flooded with the light of that idea, with the rhythm of her own breathing, with the sensation of having not died at all at any time, not on the attic stairs, not at the kitchen drawer, not in the ambulance, not on the operating table, not in that other place where the mud mothers were painting the walls of the cave and calling to her, not in the sheets she thrashed out in strangling her legs, her rib cage, fighting off the woman with snakes in her hair, the crowds that moved in and out of each other around the bed trying to tell her about the difference between snakes and serpents, the difference between eating salt as an antidote to snakebite and turning into salt, succumbing to the serpent.

"Folks come in here," Minnie Ransom was saying, "moaning and carrying on and *say* they wanna be well. Don't know what in heaven and hell they want." She had uncrossed her legs, had spread her legs out and was resting on the heels of her T-strap, beige suedes, the black soles up and visible. And she was leaning forward toward Velma, poking yards of dress down between her knees. She looked like a farmer in a Halston, a snuff dipper in a Givenchy.

"Just this morning, fore they rolled you in with your veins open and your face bloated, this great big overgrown woman came in here tearing at her clothes, clawing at her hair, wailing to beat the band, asking for some pills. Wanted a pill cause she was in pain, felt bad, wanted to feel good. You ready?"

Velma studied the woman's posture, the rope veins in the back of her hands, the purple shadows in the folds of her dress spilling over the stool edge, draping down toward the floor. Velma tried not to get lost in the reds and purples. She understood she was being invited to play straight man in a routine she hadn't rehearsed.

"So I say, 'Sweetheart, what's the matter?' And she says 'My mama died and I feel so bad, I can't go on' and dah dah dah. Her mama died, she's *supposed* to feel bad. Expect to feel good when ya mama's gone! Climbed right into my lap," she was nudging Velma to check out the skimp of her lap. "Two hundred pounds of grief and heft if she was one-fifty. Bless her heart, just a babe of the times. Wants to be smiling and feeling good all the time. Smooth sailing as they lower the mama into the ground. Then there's you. What's your story?"

Velma clutched the sides of the stool and wondered what

she was supposed to say at this point. What she wanted to do was go away, be somewhere, anywhere, else. But where was there to go? Far as most folks knew, she was at work or out of town.

"As I said, folks come in here moaning and carrying on and *say* they want to be healed. But like the wisdom warns, 'Doan letcha mouf gitcha in what ya backbone caint stand.' " This the old woman said loud enough for the others to hear.

The Infirmary staff, lounging in the rear of the treatment room, leaned away from the walls to grunt approval, though many privately thought this was one helluva way to conduct a healing. Others, who had witnessed the miracle of Minnie Ransom's laying on the hands over the years, were worried. It wasn't like her to be talking on and on, taking so long a time to get started. But then the whole day's program that Doc Serge had arranged for the visitors had been slapdash and sloppy.

The visiting interns, nurses and technicians stood by in crisp white jackets and listened, some in disbelief, others with amusement. Others scratched around in their starchy pockets skeptical, most shifted from foot to foot embarrassed just to be there. And it looked as though the session would run overtime at the rate things were going. There'd never be enough time to get through the day's itinerary. And the bus wasn't going to wait. The driver had made that quite plain. He would be pulling in at 3:08 from his regular run, taking a dinner break, then pulling out sharply with the charter bus at 5:30. That too had been printed up on the itinerary, but the Infirmary hosts did not seem to be alert to the demands of time.

The staff, asprawl behind the visitors on chairs, carts, table corners, swinging their legs and doing manicures with the edges of matchbooks, seemed to be content to watch the show for hours. But less than fifteen minutes ago they'd actually been on the front steps making bets, actually making cash bets with patients and various passers-by, that the healing session would take no more than five or ten minutes. And here it was already going on 3:00 with what could hardly be called an auspicious beginning. The administrator, Dr. Serge, had strolled out, various and sundry folk had come strolling in. The healer had sat there for the longest time playing with her bottom lip, jangling her bracelets, fiddling with the straps of the patient's gown. And now she was goofing around, deliberately, it seemed, exasperating the patient. There seemed to be, many of the visitors concluded, a blatant lack of discipline at the Southwest Community Infirmary that made suspect the reputation it enjoyed in radical medical circles.

"Just so's you're sure, sweetheart, and ready to be healed, cause wholeness is no trifling matter. A lot of weight when you're well."

"That's the truth," muttered one of the "old-timers," as all old folks around the Infirmary were called. "Don't I know the truth of that?" the little woman continued, pushing up the sleeves of her bulky sweater as if home, as if readying up to haul her mother-in-law from wheelchair to toilet, or grab up the mop or tackle the laundry. She would have had more to say about the burdens of the healthy had she not been silenced by an elbow in her side pocket and noticed folks were cutting their eyes at her. Cora Rider hunched her shoulders sharply and tucked her head deep into the turtleneck by way of begging pardon from those around her, many of whom still held their clinic cards and appointment slips in their hands as if passing through the room merely, with no intention of staying for the whole of it.

"Thank you, Spirit" drifted toward her. She searched the faces of the circle of twelve that ringed the two women in the center of the room, wondering whether God was being thanked for giving Miz Minnie the gift or for shutting Cora up. The twelve, or The Master's Mind as some folks called them, stood with heads bowed and hands clasped. Yellow seemed to predominate, yellow and white. Shirts, dresses, smocks, slacks—yellow and white were as much an announcement that a healing session had been scheduled as the notice on the board. The bobbing roses, pink and yellow chiffon flowerettes on Mrs. Sophie Heywood's hat, seemed to suggest that she was the one who'd praised God. Though the gent humming in long meter, his striped tie looking suspiciously like a remnant from a lemonade-stand awning, could just as well have been the one, Cora Rider thought. Though what Mr. Daniels had to be so grateful for all the time was a mystery to her, what with an alcoholic wife, a fast and loose bunch of daughters, and a bedraggled shoeshine parlor.

Cora Rider shrugged and bowed her head in prayer, or at least in imitation of the circle folks, who seemed, as usual, lost in thought until several members looked up, suddenly aware that one of their number was inching away from the group. Cora looked up too, and like the old-timers and staffers who noticed, was astounded. For surely Sophie Heywood of all people, godmother of Velma Henry, co-convener of The Master's Mind, could not actually be leaving.

Sophie Heywood had been in attendance at every other major event in Velma Henry's life. No one could say for sure if Sophie had been there when Velma had tried to do herself in, that part of the girl's story hadn't been put together yet. But she'd been there at the beginning with her baby-catching hands. There again urging "pretty please" on Velma's behalf while Mama Mae, the blood mother, plaited peach switches to tear up some behind. Calling herself running away to China to seek her fortune like some character she'd read about in a book, young Velma had dug a hole in the landfill, then tunneled her way through a drainpipe that led to the highway connector past the marshes before her sister Palma could catch up with her and bring her back.

All those years Sophie had been turning a warm eye on the child's triumphs, a glass eye on everything else, which was a lot, to hear the old folks tell it, as the girl, breaking her bonds and casting away the cord, was steady making her bed hard. For those old-timers, though, that walked the chalk, why a woman such as Sophie Heywood, chapter president of the Women's Auxiliary of the Sleeping Car Porters for two decades running, would even cross the street for the likes of Velma Henry was a mystery anyway. But there it was, so must it be—the godmother ever ready to turn the lamp down low on the godchild's indiscretions.

The prayer group moved closer to repair the circle, searching Sophie's face for a clue to the break and the odd leavetaking. But the women's eyes were as still as water in the baptismal pit, reminding them that she had been there too the day the congregation had stood by waiting for a moving of the water, had shouted when Velma had come through religion, had cheered when she walked across the stage of Douglass High to get her diploma, had stood up at her first wedding, hasty as you please and in a night club too, and worn white to the railroad station as the rites of good riddance had been performed. And when Velma had swapped that out-of-town-who's-his-people-anyway husband for a good home boy whose goodness could maybe lay her wildness down and urge her through college, there was Sophie in her best threads following the child down the aisle, her needle still working in the hem of the gown.

And here she was now, Sophie Heywood, not only walking away from her godchild, but removing Scorpio from the Mind. Heads turned round as she reached the door and stood there gazing up, they thought, at the ceiling, drawing other heads up too to study the ceiling's luster, the gleam of the fluorescent rods. And study they did, for Sophie was forever reading signs before they were even so.

"Every event is preceded by a sign," she always instructed her students, or anyone else in her orbit who'd listen. "We're all clairvoyant if we'd only know it." The lesson was not lost on Cora Rider, whose bed, kitchen table and porch swing were forever cluttered with *Three Wise Men, Red Devil, Lucky Seven, Black Cat, Three Witches, Aunt Dinah's Dream Book,* and other incense-fragrant softback books that sometimes resulted in a hit. Now, though, like some others, Cora studied the pockmarks in the plaster, the dance of light overhead, searching not so much for a number to box as for a clue to Sophie Heywood's exit.

Buster and Nadeen, the couple from the Teenage Parent Clinic, studied the ceiling too, recalling the counsel of Mrs. Heywood. Close enough to hear each other's breathing, his arm around her, palm resting on the side of her bulging belly, he reviewed the way "sign reading" had been applied by the political theorists at the Academy of the 7 Arts, while she, palms resting on the rise of her stomach, remained attentive to the movement beneath her hands.

What anyone made of the shadows on the ceiling or of the fissures in the plaster overhead was not well telegraphed around the room, though many were visibly intent on decoding the

flickering touch of mind on mind and looking about for someone to head Sophie Heywood off at the pass. What did bounce
around the circle of eleven was the opinion that Sophie should
return and restore the group intact. But what jumped the circle
to pass through bone, white jackets, wood chairs and air for
Sophie to contemplate, did not bounce back. The only answer
was the high-pitch wail of birds overhead like whistling knives
in the sky.

Sophie opened the door without a backward glance at the
group or at the godchild huddled on the stool so mournful and
forlorn. The child Sophie grieved for took another form altogether. So stepping over the threshold into the hall she was
stepping over that sack of work tools by his bedroom door
again, a heavy gray canvas sack spilling out before enemy
eyes—screwdriver, syringe, clockworks, dynamite. She looked
out into the hall of the Southwest Community Infirmary, fresh
white paint dizzying her, temples buzzing, eyes stinging.
Smitty.

Smitty climbing the leg of the statue. The other students
running down the street waving banners made from sheets.
Mrs. Taylor watching from the window, leaning on pillows
she'd made from rally banners. Smitty on the arm of the war
nero chanting "Hell, no, we won't go." Sirens scattering the
marchers. TV cameras and trucks shoving through the crowd.
Mrs. Taylor screaming in the window. A boy face down in the
street, his book bag flattened. The police rushing the statue like
a tank. The package up under Smitty's arm. The other flung
across the hind of the first brass horse. The blow that caught
him in the shins.

Sophie face down in the jailhouse bed springs. Portland Edgers, her neighbor, handed a billy club. The sheriff threatening.

Mrs. Taylor moaning in the window. The boy gagging on his
own blood face down in the street, the cameras on him. Smitty
with a bull horn. A Black TV announcer misnumbering the
crowd, mixmatching the facts, lost to the community. Smitty.
The blow that caught him in the groin.

The blow that caught her in the kidney. Someone howling
in the next cell. A delegation from the church out front talking

reasonably. Sophie face down on the jailhouse bed springs, the rusty metal cutting biscuits out of her cheeks.

Smitty kicking at the clubs, the hands. Smitty jammed between the second brass horse and the flagpole. The package balanced in the crook of the bayonet. The blow that caught him from behind.

Portland Edgers turning on the sheriff and wrestled down on her back and beaten. Sophie mashed into the springs. Portland Edgers screaming into her neck.

Smitty pulled down against the cement pedestal, slammed against the horses' hooves, dragged on his stomach to the van. A boot in his neck. Child. Four knees in his back. Son. The package ripped from his grip. The policeman racing on his own path and none other's. The man, the statue going up Pegasus. Manes, hooves, hinds, the brass head of some dead soldier and a limb of one once-live officer airborne over city hall. A flagpole buckling at the knees.

And a tall building tottering trembling falling down inside her face down in the jailhouse bed springs teeth splintering and soul groaning. Smitty. Edgers. Reverend Michaels in the corridor being reasonable.

Sophie Heywood closed the door of the treatment room. And there was something in the click of it that made many of the old-timers, veterans of the incessant war—Garveyites, Southern Tenant Associates, trade unionists, Party members, Pan-Africanist—remembering night riders and day traitors and the cocking of guns, shudder.

"ARE you sure, sweetheart? I'm just asking is all," Minnie Ransom was saying, playfully pulling at her lower lip till three different shades of purple showed. "Take away the miseries and you take away some folks' reason for living. Their conversation piece anyway."

"I been there," Cora Rider testified, wagging both hands by the wrists overhead. "I know exactly what the good woman means," she assured all around her.

"We all been there, one way or t'other," the old gent with

the lemonade tie said, hummed, chanted and was echoed by his twin from the other side of the circle, singing in common meter just like it was church.

Minnie Ransom's hands went out at last, and the visitors, noting the way several people around them checked their watches, concluded that this was either the official beginning of the healing or the end, it was hard to tell.

"I can feel, sweetheart, that you're not quite ready to dump the shit," Minnie Ransom said, her next few words drowned out by the gasps, the rib nudges against starchy jackets, and shuffling of feet. ". . . got to give it all up, the pain, the hurt, the anger and make room for lovely things to rush in and fill you full. Nature abhors a so-called vacuum, don't you know?" She waited till she got a nod out of Velma. "But you want to stomp around a little more in the mud puddle, I see, like a little kid fore you come into the warm and be done with mud. Nothing wrong with that," she said pleasantly, moving her hands back to her own lap, not that they had made contact with Velma, but stopped some two or three inches away from the patient and moved around as if trying to memorize the contours for a full-length portrait to be done later without the model.

Several old-timers at this point craned their necks round to check with the veteran staff in the rear. It was all very strange, this behavior of Miz Minnie. Maybe she was finally into her dotage. "A hundred, if she's a day," murmured Cora.

"I can wait," Minnie said, as though it were a matter of handing Jake Daniels her shoes and sitting in the booth in stocking feet to flip through a magazine while her lifts were replaced. She crossed her legs again, leaned forward onto the high knee, dropped her chin into that palm, then slapped her other arm and a length of silk around her waist and closed her eyes. She could've been modeling new fashions for the golden age set or waiting for a bus.

"Looking more like a monkey every day," Cora thought she was thinking to herself till someone jostled her elbow from behind and scorched the back of her neck with a frown.

"Far out," one of the visitors was heard to mumble. "Far fucking out. So whadda we supposed to do, stand here for this comedy?"

"Shush."

"Look, lady," tapping on his watch, "We—"

"I said to shush, so shush."

The visitor turned red when the giggles from the rear and side drifted his way. And the woman who had shushed him, a retired schoolteacher from the back district, shifted her position so that she no longer faced the two women but was standing kitty-corner, her arms folded across her chest, keeping one eye on her former student in the gown with her behind out and the other on the redbone who seemed to have more to say but not if she had anything to do with it.

Velma Henry clutched the stool. She felt faint, too faint to ask for a decent chair to sit in. She felt like she was in the back room of some precinct, or in the interrogation room of terrorist kidnappers, or in the walnut-paneled office of Transchemical being asked about an error. She cut that short. She hadn't the strength. She felt her eyes rolling away. Once before she'd had that feeling. The preacher in hip boots spreading his white satin wings as she stepped toward him and was plunged under and everything went white.

She closed her eyes and they rolled back into her head, rolled back to the edge of the table in her kitchen, to the edge of the sheen—to cling there like globules of furniture oil, cling there over the drop, then hiding into the wood, cringing into the grain as the woman who was her moved from sink to stove to countertop turning things on, turning the radio up. Opening drawers, opening things up. Her life line lying for an instant in the cradle of the scissors' X, the radio's song going on and on and no stop-notes as she leaned into the oven. The melody thickening as she was sucked into the carbon walls of the cave, then the song blending with the song of the gas.

"Release, sweetheart. Give it all up. Forgive everyone everything. Free them. Free self."

Velma tried to pry her eyelids up to see if the woman was actually speaking. She was certain Mrs. Ransom had not spoken, just as she was sure she'd heard what she heard. She tried to summon her eyes back, to cut the connection. She was seeing more than she wished to remember in that kitchen. But there she was in a telepathic visit with her former self, who seemed to be still there in the kitchen reenacting the scene like time counted for nothing. She tried to move from that place to this, to see this yellow room, this stool, this white tile, this window where the path to the woods began, this Ransom woman who was calling her back. But the journey back from the kitchen was like the journey in the woods to gather. And gathering is a particular thing where the eyes are concerned, M'Dear Sophie taught. You see nothing but what you're looking for. After sassafras, you see only the reddish-brown barkish things of the woods. Or after searching out eucalyptus, the eyes stay tuned within a given range of blue-green-gray and cancel out the rest of the world. And never mind that it's late, that the basket is full, that you got what you came for, that you are ready to catch the bus back to town, are leisurely walking now on the lookout for flowers or berries or a little holding stone to keep you company. The gathering's demands stay with you, lock you in to particular sights. The eyes will not let you let it go.

All Velma could summon now before her eyes were the things of her kitchen, those things she'd sought while hunting for the end. Leaves, grasses, buds dry but alive and still in jars stuffed with cork, alive but inert on the shelf of oak, alive but arrested over the stove next to the matchbox she'd reached toward out of habit, forgetting she did not want the fire, she only wanted the gas. Leaning against the stove then as the performer leaned now, looking at the glass jars thinking whoknew-what then, her mind taken over, thinking, now, that in the jars was no air, therefore no sound, for sound waves weren't all that self-sufficient, needed a material medium to transmit. But light waves need nothing to carry pictures in, to travel in, can go anywhere in the universe with their independent pictures. So there'd be things to see in the jars, where she in there sealed and unavailable to sounds, voices, cries. So she would be light. Would go back to her beginnings in the stars and be star light, over and done with, but the flame traveling wherever it pleased. And the pictures would follow her, haunt her. Be vivid and sharp in a vacuum. To haunt her. Pictures, sounds and bounce were everywhere, no matter what you did or where you went. Sound broke glass. Light could cut through even steel.

There was no escaping the calling, the caves, the mud mothers, the others. No escape.

She'd been in a stupor, her gaze gliding greasily over the jars on the shelf till she fastened onto the egg timer, a little hourglass affair. To be that sealed—sound, taste, air, nothing seeping in. To be that unavailable at last, sealed in and the noise of the world, the garbage, locked out. To pour herself grain by grain into the top globe and sift silently down to a heap in the bottom one. That was the sight she'd been on the hunt for. To lie coiled on the floor of the thing and then to bunch up with all her strength and push off from the bottom and squeeze through the waistline of the thing and tip time over for one last sandstorm and then be still, finally be still. Her grandmother would be pleased, her godmother Sophie too. "Girl, be still," they'd been telling her for years, meaning different things.

And she'd be still in the globes, in the glass jars, sealed from time and life. All that was so indelible on her retina that the treatment room and all its clutter and mutterings were canceled out. Her kitchen, that woman moving about in obsessive repetition, the things on the shelf, the search, the demand would not let her eyes, let her, come back to the healer's hands that were on her now.

"A grown woman won't mess around in mud puddles too long before she releases. It's warmer inside," she thought she was hearing. "Release, sweetheart. Let it go. Let the healing power flow."

SHE had had on a velour blouse, brown, crocheted. She felt good in it, moving about the booth in it, the cush, the plush soft against her breasts. The kind of blouse that years ago she would have worn to put James Lee Henry, called Obie now, under her spell. She moved about in the booth, the leather sticky under her knees, but the velour comforting against her skin. He no longer thought she was a prize to win. But the blouse was surely doing something to him, she was certain. But certain too that she was, even sitting right there, just a quaint memory for him, like a lucky marble or a coin caught from the Mardi Gras parade. She didn't want to think too much on that.

She was losing the thread of her story. She had been telling him about those Chinese pajamas and the silver buckets but had lost her way.

But it wasn't the blouse feeling good or the memories of their courting days that was distracting her. James Lee had begun moving the dishes aside, disrupting her meal. Her salad bowl no longer up under her right wrist where she could get at it between chunks of steak and mouthfuls of potatoes but shoved up against the wall next to the napkin rack. Her sweet potato pie totally out of reach. And now he moved her teacup toward the hot sauce bottle. He was interrupting her story, breaking right in just as she was about to get to the good part, to tell her to put her fork down and listen. She was seriously considering jabbing his hand with the fork as he reached to grasp her hands, his tie falling into her plate, covering the last two pieces cut from near the bone that she'd been saving to relish after she finished talking.

"Baby, I wish you were as courageous emotionally as you are . . ."

She missed hearing it somehow. Close as his face was to hers, plainly as he was speaking, attentive as she tried to be, she just couldn't hear what the hell he was saying. She couldn't blame it on the waiters. Usually rattling trays and slinging silverware into the washer, most of them were at the busboy table drinking ice tea and murmuring low. No diners were laughing or talking loud, only a few men sat about alone reading the Sunday papers and sipping coffee. The winos who usually parked by the coatrack to bug the diners lining up for the cashier were outside, sitting on the curb. It was quiet. But she still couldn't quite seem to make out what he was jabbering about all up in her face.

"Let me help you, Velma. Whatever it is we . . . wherever we're at now . . . I can help you break that habit . . . learn to let go of past pain . . . like you got me to stop smoking. We could . . ."

She heard some of it. He was making an appeal, a reconciliation of some sort, conditions, limits, an agenda, help. Something about emotional caring or daring or sharing. James Lee could be tiresome in these moods. She pulled her hand away and reached for her bag. If things were going to get heavy, she needed a cigarette. But he caught her hands again. Rising up out of the booth and damn near coming across the table, he pulled her hands away from her lighter and held them, then resumed his seat and went right on talking, talking.

"Dammit, James. Obie. Let go. I haven't finished my—"

"Let me finish. What I want to say . . ." He paused and wagged his head like it was a sorrowful thing he had to tell her. She snorted. There was a shred of spinach clinging between his front teeth like a fang, which made it all ridiculous. "Do you have any idea, Velma, how you look when you launch into one of your anecdotes? It's got to be costing you something to hang on to old pains. Just look at you. Your eyes slit, the cords jump out of your neck, your voice trembles, I expect fire to come blasting out of your nostrils any minute. It takes something out of you, Velma, to keep all them dead moments alive. Why can't you just . . . forget . . . forgive . . . and always it's some situation that was over and done with ten, fifteen years ago. But here you are still all fired up about it, still plotting, up to your jaws in ancient shit."

"Up to my jaws in ancient shit. Nice line."

"Like what you were going on and on about this afternoon. The time your mother wouldn't let you go to the Freeman birthday party because Palma hadn't been invited too. Hell, that was twenty years ago, Vee. And for the hundredth time you got to sink your teeth all in it. The invitation with the little elephant and the party hat and how—"

"So why are you giving me the details of it? We taping this session? If I've gone over it a hundred times, surely I've got it down pat. You seem to. And get your tie out of my plate, James. Obie."

"All I want to know is how long are you going to overload your circuits with—"

"Until I get my pint of blood," she said, shaking one hand free and pulling her plate toward her.

"Mixed metaphor, kiddo."

She stretched her face into a grin that ended in a sneer. If he could only see himself, she thought, the shred of spinach reducing him.

"We're different people, James. Obie. Somebody shit all over you, you forgive and forget. You start talking about how we're all damaged and colonialism and the underdeveloped blah blah. That's why everybody walks all over you."

"You're the only one to ever try to walk over me, Vee."

"That's why I just can't stay with you. I don't respect—"

"That's not why, Vee.

"What?"

"Scared. Anytime you're not in absolute control, you panic."

"Scared?" She chewed with her mouth open, certain the sight would make him shut up or at least turn away. "Shit. Scared of you? Sheeeeet. Obie."

"Intimacy. Love. Taking a chance when the issue of control just isn't—"

She cut him off with a snort when he seemed to be speaking in imitation of her chewing. People trying to be earnest, serious or supercilious with their fly open or a button dangling from their blouse always cracked her up, made her feel sneery and sympathetic at the same time. She wasn't sure which she felt. Mama Mae in the doorway doing her mother act while the safety pin in her bra worked itself loose was usually an object of pity. Or Lil James spreading the peanut butter thick and going on and on about the basketball game and how he'd had to sit it out on the bench when the coach knew full well he could save the day, a bugga hanging from his nose, always triggered a wave of compassion that made her move to hug him, though these days he shied away from her sudden bursts of affection.

She wiped her fingers on the napkin and made her hand available, but her husband did not take it, kept talking, the green leaf waving, mocking. The two hands lay there side by side on the table like a still life. She rubbed his hand and he did not pull it away exactly, just sort of. She rubbed the ridges in his thumbnail and tried to listen to what he was saying now about the atmosphere she set up in the house, what her emotional something or other was doing to the kid, to him, mostly to her. She heard bits of it while floating in and out of the scene, thinking on that first day when she fell in love with his hands or called it love and called it, smirking, falling.

Gerald Vizenor

GERALD VIZENOR (1934–   ) has emerged as one of the leading Native American writers of our time. He has published
three novels, four collections of essays and fiction (the categories sometimes merge in Vizenor's work), and ten books of
poetry. *Griever,* the novel from which our selection is taken,
won the Fiction Collective Prize for 1986.

Vizenor is a mixed-blood Chippewa, or as the Chippewa
prefer to call themselves, Anishinaabe. His family is originally
from the White Earth Reservation in northern Minnesota,
where they were members of the crane clan, the orators of the
tribe, the masters of language.

Vizenor's childhood was marked by loss and violence to
loved ones: his father was murdered when Gerald was two,
possibly over a gambling debt, and his uncle and stepfather
died in bloody accidents. His mother often left him for long
periods of time with his grandmother, or in foster homes. This
would have driven a weaker soul to despair, but thanks to a
loving grandmother and a rich imagination, he not only survived, but emerged triumphant, like his hero, the Anishinaabe
trickster Nanabozho.

At fifteen, Vizenor lied about his age to enter the military,
eventually serving in Japan, where he began writing haiku. The
cryptic poems, with their images drawn from nature, have a
resemblance to traditional Anishinaabe songs. Over the years
Vizenor has published five collections of haiku.

After the Army and attendance at the University of Minnesota, Vizenor worked as a reporter and corrections officer
before becoming a professor. He began at Lake Forest, then
taught at Bemidji State, Minnesota, and the University of Cali-

fornia at Berkeley and Santa Cruz. Currently he is David Burr Chair of Letters at the University of Oklahoma.

Vizenor published some poetry, fiction, and nonfiction in the early seventies, but he did not emerge as a major figure in the Indian Renaissance until 1978, when *Wordarrows* and *Darkness in Saint Luis Bearheart* appeared.

Wordarrows, a novel subtitled *Indians and Whites in the New Fur Trade*, is about Indian-white relationships in the modern urban forests of the Twin Cities.

Bearheart is Vizenor's first trickster novel, the genre for which he is best known today. He has written three trickster novels—*Bearheart, Griever,* and *The Trickster of Liberty*—produced a Trickster film, *Harold of Orange,* and written and lectured on the Trickster as a linguistic phenomenon.

The trickster is a very widespread mythic and literary archetype—Odysseus, Renard the Fox, and Br'er Rabbit are similar figures to Americans. For Native Americans, the trickster has always been the most important culture hero. Tribal tricksters play tricks, and are the victim of tricks. They have enormous appetites for food, sex, and new experiences, and are willing to violate every tribal taboo in order to get what they want. They are drifters, always on the move. They often commit crimes that make them pariahs, but they also save the tribe in its hour of need.

Tribal tricksters come in a variety of shapes. They are often animals, like Coyote, Raven, or Hare, but they may also take the shape of men, like the Kiowa Sendeh, Winnebago Wakd-junkaga, or Anishinaabe Nanabozho.

Scott Momaday and James Welch have characters in their fiction whose footloose, amoral behavior reveals the elements of trickster in their makeup, but Vizenor goes a step further. *Bearheart* is a novel with a trickster narrator who relates a tale of charcters explicitly depicted as tricksters. In *Bearheart* the trickster figure is split between Proude Cedarfair, who represents the trickster in his beneficent role of savior. The trickster in his role as irresponsible, oversexed scoundrel is played by Benito Saint Saint Plumero.

Vizenor's most famous trickster—his alter ego—is Griever de Hocus, hero of the novel excerpted here. Griever, like Vizenor's forebears, hails from the White Earth Reservation. In *Griever: An American Monkey King in China,* Griever is in China teaching English at Zhou Enlai University. Griever has always been a free spirit who challenges authority, and in China he fights to liberate birds in cages, chickens in the marketplace, and political prisoners on their way to execution.

Griever's inspiration in his battles against repressive authority is Monkey, the trickster from the classic Chinese folklore novel *Journey to the West.* Monkey's adventures are also a subject of classic Chinese operas. Griever consciously patterns his behavior after Monkey. When Griever is forced to pose for an identity photo, he paints his face to resemble Monkey as he appears in the operas.

Naturally Griever's defiant acts get him in trouble with Chinese authorities, and he has to flee for his life in a tiny airplane he has shipped in from the reservation. He is last seen flying at treetop level trying to make his way to Macao.

Griever appears as a minor character in Vizenor's last novel, *The Trickster of Liberty,* and will appear again in farflung places (Africa, South America) in works that Vizenor currently has in progress.

—*Alan R. Velie*

Bound Feet

DEAR CHINA: Listen, your foot man is here at last under the silk trees in the land of bare bulbs and no cleavage. This is an enormous reservation with a fifty watter over the main street, but, as Marco Polo said, "I have not told the half of what I saw."

Last night at the train depot two exotic oldies with bound feet hobbled down the stairs in front of me, their elbows out wide for balance. I should have mimicked their miniature moves, by nature, but instead I carried their tattered bundles to the curb. No one, not even you in the best of times, would want lotuses that small, four inches toe to heel.

The new sounds of this place hold me for ransom at some alien border. On one side there are the teachers, the decadent missionaries of this generation, and on the other side, invented traditions, broken rituals, wandering lights, ear readers, and headless ghosts on the dark roads. Here, now, alone on the line, huge beetles maul the rusted screen with their thick brown wings and small mosquitoes wail behind my neck and then bite me on the ears and knuckles, nowhere else.

In the bedroom and near the wide window there are hidden sounds, hollow whispers from the cool concrete. Even the silence bothers me, no whacks from the summer wood, no motors at night, no sirens. Dreams and the urban wither haunt me the most this first hot and humid night.

Thousands of small bats come home to their narrow cracks in the walls around the windows. Their night rolls over to the sparrows, the few that survived the revolution.

Remember that night on the reservation when we were

alone in the woods, on that natural mount, and we heard whispers? Listen, last night was like that time on the mount but the voices came to me in dreams, and then later at the window. We were on the desert silk roads, surrounded by mountains. You buried your toes in the hot blue sand and then the scene turned cool and we were at a glacial stream with luminous animals and birds.

Actually, this dream started much earlier on the plane while I was reading a book about the first explorers on the old silk roads who looted the temples and ruins in the ancient cities on the rim of the Taklamakan, and somehow, over the ocean, the words became a real desert scene. I was there, amused at first, but when I tried to hold the words down, a voice echoed from the page. The plane was transformed into a mansion, then a mountain, and the passengers became bears. The wind howled over the white poplars and the camels shuddered until the woman in the seat next to me asked several personal questions.

"Have you ever seen bound feet?"

"Yes," I said and nodded my head with a smile, certain that she would ask me, with some hesitation, the when and where.

"When?"

"Here, on this very flight."

"Where?"

"There, that woman with the narrow high heels, see how her toes are turned under?" The woman turned her face and then she tucked her feet under the seat. "Notice, however, that few men are aroused by those twisted toes."

China, she wanted to know about you and why you were not with me, and what it would be like to be a teacher here. How the hell was I supposed to know, we were still in the air. She hauled me back from dream scenes with her narrow realities, back at the moment a secret was about to be revealed to me. She held me down to the words, a good tourist.

I finished the book before we landed at Beijing and thought nothing more about it until late last night when I arrived at my new apartment. Time crowds me now, but these words need me here to hold down this place.

Egas Zhang, the director of the foreign affairs bureau, met me at the airport and escorted me back to Zhou Enlai University at Tianjin, which is about two hours by train from Beijing.

Egas chain-smokes and smiles over each word. His cheeks curl, rise and fall, even when he listens, and he punctuates his thin head to the right, the side he favors in conversations, the side he pockets one hand. He never gave his hand, his right hand never appeared last night. House proud translator with a colonial name, but at the same time he seems worried to be seen with a foreigner.

Egas Monitz, he told me, from the side of his mouth as we walked to the train, was a Portuguese doctor who was the father of the lobotomy and who won a Nobel Prize. Later, and in the same tone of voice, he asked me for deer antler, bear paws, and gallbladders from the reservation. Such aphrodisiacs are as rare as hen's teeth here.

Egas carried my two boxes of books to the apartment and then he surprised me with a cash advance. He counted the crisp bills three times, bobbed his head in time, a hesitant kowtow dance, and scurried down the stairs like some rodent. Later, I mocked his sinister sidewinder smile in the high bathroom mirror. Even the sink is too high, the paranoid builders of this guest house must have imagined we were huge barbarians.

So, from bare bulbs, bound feet, colonial names, these high mirrors, this is a stranger place than we ever imagined that night last month back on the reservation.

The desert dreams called me back from this small apartment. I tried to roar in a panic hole, to hold me down like a printed word, but the wind dried my tongue and teeth. Then a luminous man dressed in a white silk coat chased me through the Jade Gate at Dunhuang and over the old cities buried on the silk roads. Below, the deserts turned and boiled, the Gobi, Lop Nor, and Taklamakan, between the Tien Shan mountains in the north and the Kun Lun in the south. There were whole cultures and cities under the fine sand. Deeper, there were columns of poplars, gardens and high mansions; peach, plum, and apricot orchards, all in bloom. The ancient cities of Korla and Aksu opened on the north road, Dandanuilik, and Khadalik, and the Kingdom of Khotan on the south silk road.

China, there were these incredible episodes in the dream that seemed to have something to do with my being here, now, in the present. The first dream drew me close to a bright light which seemed like a star at first. I could feel the heat on my face, but it was a fire on the balcony of the apartment, a fire bear, a shaman. The bear rumbled in the fire and drew me closer to the rail, and then, when my face seemed to burn, a pleasant sensation overwhelmed me. No fear, I reached for the bear, to be the bear, the fire, but when my arms touched her maw, the light withered. There, in the dark, a small terra cotta figure of a humanoid bear stood near the window. I touched the warm figure and mosquitoes swarmed on my knuckles.

The bear appeared once more but this time she led me to the Kingdom of Khotan where she showed me several bear shamans on a mural from the silk cultures. One fire bear wore a black opal ring surrounded with faceted azure-blue stones. She told me that bears mined blue jade and the rare lapis lazuli at secret places and traded the stones on the silk roads. The bear wore a small blue rabbit on a chain around her neck.

The stones burned on the concrete, on the curtains, on a torn map taped to the wall near the balcony door, on the collar of my shirt over a chair, and then flashed on the mirror over the bureau. The luminous stones multiplied, moved in the distance like lanterns on a mountain trail, and then vanished.

The mosquitoes returned to the screen for a minute, no more, and then I was alone on the south silk road. I could feel her heat, smelled wet hair behind me, and then the bear touched me on the shoulders with her paws. Two claws were broken. I tried to stay awake this time, to separate myself from the events in the dream. I focused on the sound of a steam engine in the distance and the mosquitoes on the screen. The sounds seemed real, in the present, but the bed and the room would not return.

The bear led me into another mansion buried on the desert. She was silent when we passed mountain scenes, stone people and wild fires on murals, bears with monkeys on their shoulders, monkeys with bats and lotus flowers embroidered on the backs of their coats, and at the end of the wide murals there was an old man with butterflies on his hands.

China, no shit, he winked at me.

The shaman told me that the mountain bear women saved

the first silk cultures from evil. The old stone man, she told me, lived with a bear woman and their descendants became healers in tribal cultures around the world.

At the end of the murals, behind a wide door, there were baskets filled with bear bones and blue stones, and thousands of manuscripts, histories of the shaman bear cultures from the mountains that surrounded the deserts. She pushed me into the room, closer to the bones, and told me to choose one birchbark manuscript to take with me. Outside, she opened the scroll and held me to the secrets.

China, this is hard to believe, but the figures and marks on the birchbark were the same as those on the tribal medicine scrolls from the reservation. There were shaman bears and humans with lines from their hearts and mouths. The whole scene was unbelievable, tribal visions on birchbark this far from our woodland. The fire bear told me some of the stories on the scroll, the histories of this nation, from the monkey origins to the revolutions, even the persecution of scholars, and the new capitalism, it was all there. But the future stories, what would become of this nation, she told me to read later.

China, a stupid thing happened to me between the desert mansion and this apartment. I hitched a ride with a shrouded woman on a horse-drawn wagon. The slow movement and the sound of the horse lulled me to sleep on a load of fresh vegetables. Believe this or not, I dreamed I was asleep in a dream, and when I woke up in the apartment, I had forgotten the manuscript on the back of the wagon.

The mosquitoes followed me back in memories to the desert, and now, I can even smell the earth, beets, and cabbages, on that wagon, but the birchbark manuscript is lost.

So, strange things are happening to me here, even on the first night. I have no idea what this place looks like in bright light. The last bats return to the concrete. I heard the sound of a cat, then ducks and chickens in the distance. Mosquitoes at the screen are more desperate at the end of the night.

Your feet come to mind,

Griever de Tianjin

Holosexual Clown

WARRIOR clowns imagine the world and pinch their time from those narrow scratch lines dashed between national politics and traditional opera scenes.

This clown, old but seldom stooped, bailed from a faded landscape, unlocks the campus gate at dawn, starts a charcoal fire in a small brazier, and then he totters over the line with two bright butterflies embroidered on the lapels of his blue opera coat.

"Wu Chou, Wu Chou," the children chant from their baskets and spacious sidecars, and some lean out to touch his lapels and the golden butterflies in a natal light. Even a tired peasant, the first to move through the gate that morning, saluted the winsome warrior from his horse cart loaded with platform poles.

China Browne followed the cart from the bus terminal to the campus. She waited outside the gate, a writer at the scratch line, with an invitation to interview a warrior clown about Griever de Hocus, the trickster teacher who liberated hundreds of chickens at a local street market and then vanished last summer on an ultralight airplane built by her brother. Once there, she would continue her research on Alicia Little, past president of the Natural Foot Society.

China folded her arms beneath her breasts and lowered her head to duck a cloud of dust; the street sweepers, two women with white cotton masks, wheeled their brooms down the road as close as they could come to a foreigner.

Wu Chou waited for the dust to pass and then he waved the writer over the line and into the small brick house near the gatepost. China brushed her hair, patted her blouse, and with a tissue, she daubed her teeth, nose, and cheeks.

"China lovers strain at the windows like flies," he said and circled the low backless chairs until she seemed comfortable with his voice and dramatic gestures. "The missionaries and tourists praise the obvious, plastic shoes, steam locomotives, and our ever-black hair, in their clever trinities."

Wu Chou studied China Browne as he circled the chairs: the slant of her shoulders, the round wrinkles on her elbows, the curve of her neck, ears, nose, and her small hands spread like leaves over a miniature tape recorder. She wore white cotton trousers and a pleated blouse with blue sailboats printed in broken rows over her low breasts. Her head seemed to rise with a common pleasance, but her fingernails were trimmed too close, and when she smiled a thin scar creased the right side of her wide brown forehead. He smiled and pinched the humid air near her face, around her dark hair.

China has three unrivaled worries and two obsessions. She is enchanted with the wild energies of smaller men and she is fascinated with pictures of bound feet. As a child she bound her feet and earned her given name; she folded bright blue bandannas around her toes and moved at night on ceremonial lotus feet to exotic places in the world. Once or twice a week, when she is lonesome, she draws silk ribbons between her toes, an unusual method of meditation.

"Most flies bounce on both sides of the pane, but tricksters are different, Griever de Hocus was different." Wu Chou tapped the brazier and watched the scar appear and disappear on her forehead.

China worries about bad blood, small insects near her ears, and those wild moments when she loses connections with time. She is worried that she could be suspended without a season, severed from the moment; these fears have delivered her to the whims of clowns and the vicarious adventures of tricksters. She aimed the microphone at his face and leaned to the side to listen, like an animal at the window.

"Griever was holosexual," said the warrior clown.

"No, not gay."

"Holosexual, not homosexual," he emphasized. "Griever, you see, was the cock of the walk, and he seemed to love the whole wide world, he must have. . . ."

"Well, not the whole world."

"Listen, he was unbelievable, but he freed birds and he never picked flowers, you can write about that." Wu Chou paused to pinch the air around his head. "But the world gave him so much trouble for his time." He pitched his head forward, smiled, and placed a small kettle of water on the brazier. "Griever was a mind monkey."

"Mind monkey?"

"Yes, a holosexual mind monkey," he said and cocked his head to explain. "Griever loved women, heart gossip, stones, trees, and he collected lost shoes and broken wheels."

Wu Chou hunched his shoulders and turned his head to the side, a simian elocution pose from a scene in the comic opera. He raised his hands, wrinkled his nose, and pinched the smoke in the air around her shoulders.

"Holosexual indeed," she said and brushed her sleeves.

"Griever was the first foreign teacher to arrive that summer," he continued, "he endured the air pollution, the water, and the crowds, but not the foreign affairs bureau."

The warrior clown crouched near the brazier to fan the fire. He leaned closer, poured two bowls of black tea, and then he smiled wide and turned his head from side to side until she noticed two miniature butterflies on the loose wrinkled skin below his ears, like those embroidered on the lapels of his opera coat. She watched the insects dance and responded with a polite smile and gentle applause.

The brick house was shrouded under deep sculptured eaves. The room was bare with three backless chairs around the brazier, a polished leather holster, and a metal box on a narrow counter over a window. The wide wooden door had been removed and then burned during the first winter of the revolution. Crickets held the four points of the room and spiders molded the stained corners at the ceiling. Green katydids paused at the threshold in their season but never entered the room.

China watched his hands move in the smoke.

The warrior clown, a master of theatrical gestures, pinched the sun from his summer memories, from his maw and dark crotch, from faded tattoos, and a collection of uncommon names.

"Tianjin is a broken window," he announced with one finger on his ear. "Dreams retreat to the corners like insects, and there we remember our past in lost letters and colonial maps, the remains of foreign concessions.

"Look around at the architecture, the banks and hotels, the old names have disappeared but we bear the same missions in our memories." He laughed and disturbed the butterflies under his ears.

"Your accent is perfect," she said and then pinched her chin too late to hold back the last word. Her hand trembled.

"Colonial excellence," he mocked.

"Forgive me, please." She turned slantwise from one cheek to the other on the narrow wooden chair and brushed the dust from her white shoes.

"We surrendered to the first missionaries," he said and then paused to hail a government official who was chauffeured through the gate in a black limousine. "We were students at the Nankai Middle School with Hua Lian and Zhou Enlai, but now we speak a rather formal and footsore language."

"Premier Zhou Enlai?"

"Indeed, and we practiced new words on the run," he said. "We followed visitors to the parks and picked on their best euphemisms and colonial metaphors, and we even dared to pursue unusual phrases into forbidden restaurants."

Wu Chou supped from the bowl. Steam rose from the hot tea and fogged the small round spectacles high on his nose. "But now, since the revolution, we talk back on hard chairs and wait to translate new verbs from the trick menus."

Wu Chou, which means warrior clown, a name he earned from the classical theater, was an actor before the revolution. He is remembered for his performances as the Monkey King in the opera *Havoc of Heaven.* When he was too old to tumble as an acrobat, he studied the stories of tricksters and shamans in several countries around the world. He returned home to teach, but the communists banished him to a *laogai,* a political prison farm, in the north where he planted trees and attended chickens. The trees were words in poems, he remembers, and the birds became characters he courted in interior operas. A decade later, past retirement and keen on common fowl, his reputation as a scholar and warrior clown was restored, and he accepted a simple sinecure as the overseer of the electronic portal at the main entrance to Zhou Enlai University. He starts the world there now and measures the thin cracks in his memories at dawn.

"Griever came back from the street market that first morning whistling 'The Stars and Stripes Forever' with blood and feathers on his shoes," he said as he pushed the button to open the gate for a wagon loaded with bricks.

"What on earth happened?"

"Griever freed the chickens and a cock spilled the blood," he said and held his mouth open. "He became the master of chicken souls, and that cock, stained with blood, followed him back to the campus."

"Not blood, no more blood, please."

"Griever was a mind monkey, remember that, he was a real holosexual clown in his own parade," said the warrior with a wide smile. His teeth were uneven, stained from black tea.

"But tell me, was he ever evil?"

"Never evil, never, never," he chanted at the rim of the tea bowl. "Cocks never follow devils, cocks chase devils, that cock chased some teachers from the guest house."

China was insecure, she crossed her arms and twisted one foot behind the other. She rocked from side to side on the chair and looked out the wide door toward the gate. The new trees were restrained at the wall, unnatural in the dust and charcoal smoke.

Silence.

Wu Chou reached for the small metal box near the leather holster on the narrow counter over the window. He dusted the box, opened it with care, and then he sorted through the contents, several dozen photographs.

"Look, look at this one here," he said as he moved behind the writer. He leaned over her right shoulder and presented a photograph.

"The same suede saddle shoes, he loved those shoes and those pleated trousers, he wore them on the reservation," she said and pointed at the color print. "He wore those when we first met at King's College Chapel in Cambridge." She held the print closer and studied the trickster. "He found a luminous statue somewhere in the choir stalls there, who could resist that man?"

"Griever was a natural clown," he said. "See, we painted his face white, with red and gold, for a rainbow celebration with the other foreign teachers."

Griever stood on one foot near the gatepost with a bamboo pole raised over his head. He wore a bright lemon raglan coat and loose blue trousers. His face was blurred in each print, but the trees, strangers at the gate, even the old warrior clown, appeared in sharp focus.

"What is this, here, in this print?"

"Horsehair duster."

"No, no, not the duster."

"What then?"

"This, here, he never wore a sporran on the reservation," she said and pointed with her little finger. She wore a beaded bracelet, the same color as the veins on her hands.

"Griever wore a holster," the clown responded as he leaned closer to her shoulder, so close that she could smell garlic and feel his warm breath. His cheek touched her dark hair from behind. He told her stories about the holster and watched the rise of her breasts, warm and brown, over the blue sailboats. When his small rough hand brushed the bare back of her neck she shivered and returned the photographs.

China stopped the recorder and moved to the door where she stood in the frame with her hands behind her neck. Her shadow coasted over the concrete, over the chairs, and folded like a child on the back wall. The clown leaned in the charcoal smoke and pinched a trace of her brown breasts from the floor. When she turned in the frame her shadow broke from his reach.

"Why would he need a holster?"

"To shoot clocks."

"Not the market cock?"

"Clocks, cocks, he loved cocks, he was a cock master, but he hated clocks," he said in a loud clear voice. "He carried a holster to shoot time, time on the clock."

"What was in the holster?"

"Pictures from wild histories," said the clown. He removed the scroll from the holster and turned the rough white paper past scenes with teachers, students, bats, and luminous bodies, and chickens at the street market. The warrior clown turned past scenes with a black opal, a small blue rabbit, a woman with a scar on her cheek, and a blind woman with painted cheeks; past swine on a basketball court, willow trees, small brick houses, blue bones, and ultralight airplanes.

"Wait, the woman with the scar, who is that?"

"Hester Hua Dan," he said and lowered his head. "She is the woman no one wanted him to find." Wu Chou re-wound the scroll and closed the holster.

The old clown pinched the air and whispered to her shadow as she sliced past the window. Two spiders waited near the narrow crack in the pane; fine dust stretched their webs on both sides of the window.

Appendix: Winners of the Before Columbus Foundation's American Book Awards, 1980–1990

1990

Paula Gunn Allen, editor and author, *Spider Woman's Granddaughters: Traditional Tales and Contemporary Writing by Native American Women* (Beacon Press, 1989).

Martin Bernal, *Black Athena, Afroasiatic Roots of Classical Civilization*, Vol. 1, *The Fabrication of Ancient Greece, 1785–1985* (Rutgers University Press, 1987).

Michelle T. Clinton, Sesshu Foster, and Naomi Quiñonez, editors and authors, *Invocation L.A.: Urban Multicultural Poetry* (West End Press, 1989).

Miles Davis with Quincy Troupe, *Miles: The Autobiography* (Simon & Schuster, 1989).

James M. Freeman, *Hearts of Sorrow: Vietnamese-American Lives* (Stanford University Press, 1989).

Daniela Gioseffi, editor/author, *Women on War (Essential Voices for the Nuclear Age)* (Touchstone Books, 1989).

José Emilio Gonzalez, *Vivar a Hostos* (Comité Pro Celebración Sesquicentenario del Natalico de Eugenio Maria de Hostos, 1989).

Barbara Grizzuti Harrison *Italian Days* (Weidenfeld & Nicolson, 1989).

Sergei Kan *Symbolic Immortality: The Tlingit Potlatch of the Nineteenth Century* (Smithsonian Institution Press, 1989).

Adrienne Kennedy, *People Who Led to My Plays* (Alfred A. Knopf, 1987).

Shirley Geok-lin Lim, Mayumi Tsutakawa, and Margarita Donnelly, editors, *The Forbidden Stitch: An Asian American Women's Anthology* (Calyx Books, 1989).

Hualing Nieh, *Mulberry and Peach: Two Women of China* (Beacon Press, 1988).

Itabari Njeri, *Every Goodbye Ain't Gone: Family Portraits and Personal Escapades* (Times Books, 1990).

John Norton, *The Light at the End of the Bog* (Black Star Series, 1989).

Lloyd A. Thompson, *Romans and Blacks* (University of Oklahoma Press, 1989).

John C. Walter, *The Harlem Fox: J. Raymond Jones and Tammany, 1920–1970* (SUNY Press, 1989).

Elizabeth Woody, *Hand into Stone* (Contact II Publications, 1988).

WALTER & LILLIAN LOWENFELS CRITICISM AWARD
Arnold Rampersad, *The Life of Langston Hughes,* Vol. I, *1902–1941: I, Too, Sing America* and Vol. II, *1941–1967: I Dream a World* (Oxford University Press, 1986).

EDUCATOR AWARD
James O. Freedman

EDITOR/PUBLISHER AWARD
John Crawford

LIFETIME ACHIEVEMENT AWARD
Allen Ginsberg
Sonia Sanchez

1989

Isabel Allende, trans. Margaret Sayers Peden, *Eva Luna* (Alfred A. Knopf, 1988).

Frank Chin, *The Chinaman Pacific & Frisco R.R. Co.* (Coffee House Press, 1988).

J. California Cooper, *Homemade Love* (St. Martin's Press, 1986).

Emory Elliott, ed. *Columbia Literary History of the United States,* (Columbia University Press, 1987).

Charles Fanning, *The Exiles of Erin: Nineteenth-Century Irish*

American Fiction, (University of Notre Dame Press, 1987).

Eduardo Galeano, trans. Cedric Belfrage, *Memory of Fire* (trilogy) (Pantheon, 1988).

Henry L. Gates, Jr., *The Signifying Monkey: A Theory of Afro-American Literary Criticism* (Oxford University Press, 1988).

Josephine Gattuso Hendin *The Right Thing to Do* (David R. Godine, 1988).

William Hohri *Repairing America* (Washington State University Press, 1988).

Carolyn Chong Lau, *Wode Shuofa (My Way of Speaking),* (Tooth of Time Books, 1988).

Audre Lorde, *A Burst of Light* (Firebrand Books, 1988).

Leslie Scalapino, *Way* (North Point Press, 1988).

Jennifer Stone, *Stone's Throw,* (North Atlantic Books, 1988).

Shuntaro Tanikawa, trans. William I. Elliott and Kazuo Kawamura (a bilingual edition), *Floating the River in Melancholy* (Prescott Street Press, 1988).

Askia Muhammed Touré, *From the Pyramids to the Projects: Poems of Genocide and Resistance!* (Africa World Press, 1988).

Alma Luz Villanueva, *The Ultraviolet Sky,* (Bilingual Review/Press, 1988).

LIFETIME ACHIEVEMENT AWARD
Amiri Baraka
Ed Dorn